Now the smith appeared, hammer in hand.

That was the danger. Hawley had to deal with Beacher before any villager got involved. Otherwise, he'd be hard-pressed to stop even this band of good-for-nothings taking vengeance on the peasants.

Beacher rolled over, scrambling away on his elbows. "Don't you touch me!" he snarled, blinking away mud from his eyes. His hand found the pommel of his shortsword in the dirt. His fingers curled around the hilt, and his expression changed at once. He clambered to his feet and spat, "You filthy *mongrel*!"

Mongrel. Not one of "the Blood," who could trace their family back through five or more generations of military service. Looking at the state of the men around him, Hawley couldn't take it as much of an insult.

Hawley advanced another step. "Sheathe that sword," he said quietly, almost in a growl. "Sheathe it, or I'll kill you." He held Beacher's gaze, saw the man's eyes falter. Beacher believed him. He was right to.

By Mark A. Latham

KINGDOM OF OAK AND STEEL
The Last Vigilant

THE APOLLONIAN CASEFILES
The Lazarus Gate
The Iscariot Sanction
The Legion Prophecy

Sherlock Holmes: The Red Tower
Sherlock Holmes: A Betrayal in Blood

THE LAST VIGILANT

Kingdom of Oak and Steel: Book 1

MARK A. LATHAM

orbitbooks.net

Copyright © 2025 by Mark A. Latham
Excerpt from *Kingdom of Oak and Steel: Book 2*
copyright © 2025 by Mark A. Latham
Excerpt from *The Outcast Mage* copyright © 2025 by Annabel Campbell

Cover design by Stephanie A. Hess
Cover illustration by Mélanie Delon
Cover copyright © 2025 by Hachette Book Group, Inc.
Map by Tim Paul
Author photograph by Sandi Macleod Photography

Orbit
Hachette Book Group
1290 Avenue of the Americas
New York, NY 10104
orbitbooks.net

First Edition: June 2025
Simultaneously published in Great Britain by Orbit

Orbit is an imprint of Hachette Book Group.
The Orbit name and logo are registered trademarks of Little, Brown Book Group Limited.

The publisher is not responsible for websites (or their content) that are not owned by the publisher.

The Hachette Speakers Bureau provides a wide range of authors for speaking events. To find out more, go to hachettespeakersbureau.com or email HachetteSpeakers@hbgusa.com.

Orbit books may be purchased in bulk for business, educational, or promotional use. For information, please contact your local bookseller or the Hachette Book Group Special Markets Department at special.markets@hbgusa.com.

Library of Congress Cataloging-in-Publication Data
Names: Latham, Mark (Wargamer), author.
Title: The last vigilant / Mark A. Latham.
Description: First edition. | New York, NY : Orbit, 2025. | Series: Kingdom of Oak and Steel
Identifiers: LCCN 2024047376 | ISBN 9780316574457 (trade paperback) | ISBN 9780316574464 (ebook)
Subjects: LCGFT: Science fiction. | Novels.
Classification: LCC PR6112.A86 L38 2025 | DDC 823/.92—dc23/eng/20241018
LC record available at https://lccn.loc.gov/2024047376

ISBNs: 9780316574457 (trade paperback), 9780316574464 (ebook)

Printed in the United States of America

LSC-C

Printing 2, 2025

For Alison, always.

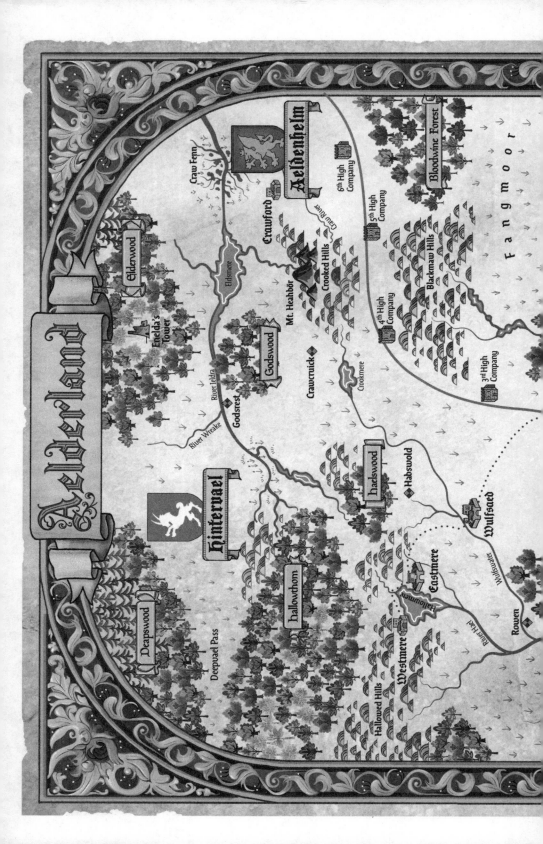

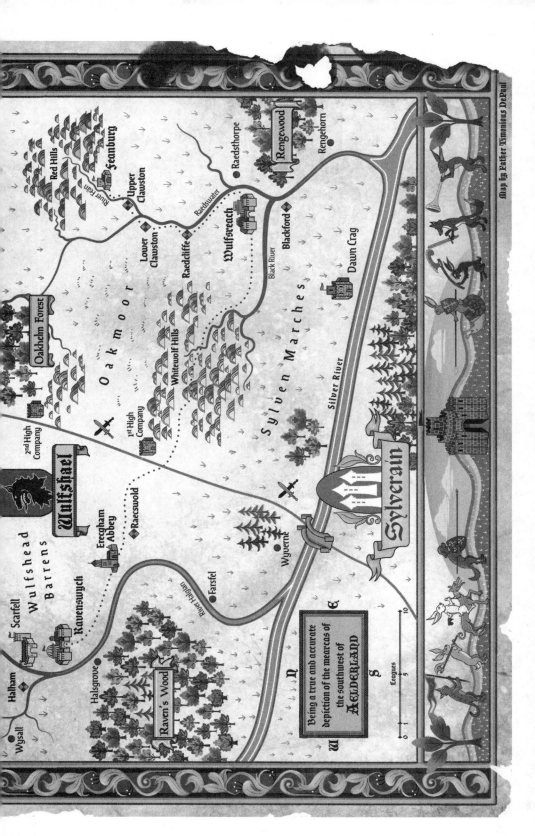

Map by Father Timonious DePaul

Red Hills

River Rätin

Feanburg

Upper Clauston

Lower Clauston

Raedcliffe

Raedsthorpe

Raedswater

Rengewood

Rengehorn

Oakhelm Forest

Oakmoor

Wulfsreach

Whitewolf Hills

Black River

Blackford

Sylven Marches

Dawn Crag

2nd High Company

Wulfshael

1st High Company

Silver River

Raeswold

Eregham Abbey

Scarfell

Wulfshead Barrens

Ravensuuych

Sylverain

Halham

Halsgrove

Farsfel

River Halgain

Wyverne

Raven's Wood

Wysall

Being a true and accurate depiction of the mearcas of AELDERLAND

N

E

W

S

Leagues

0   1   5   10

PART ONE

BEFORE THE DAWN

I am the seeker after the truth.
I am the voice of the meek.
I am the sword of justice.
I am the healer of the cursed.
I am the watcher against the darkness.
I am everywhere and nowhere.
I am everyone and no one.
The gods made me, the gods protect me,
and the gods will one day take me.

—Taken from the Vigilant Oath

CHAPTER 1

Lithadaeg, 23rd Day of Sollomand
187th Year of Redemption

Holt Hawley hunched over the reins, the wagon jolting slowly down the track. Sleet stung his face, settling oily and cold on his dark lashes and patchy beard.

The whistling wind had at least drowned out the grumbling of his men, who sat shivering in the back of the wagon. Their glares still burrowed into the back of his head.

It mattered not that Hawley was their sargent. The men blamed him for all their ills, and by the gods they'd had more than their fair share on this expedition. Twice the wagon had mired in thick mud. On the mountain road, three days' rations had spoiled inexplicably. Now their best horse had thrown a shoe, and limped behind the wagon, slowing their progress to a crawl. They couldn't afford to leave the beast behind, but risked laming it by pressing on. Whatever solution Sargent Hawley came up with was met with complaint. He was damned if he did and damned if he didn't.

Tarbert rode back up the track, cutting a scarecrow silhouette against the deluge. He reined in close to the driver's board, face glum, still mooning over the hobbling horse that was his favourite of the team.

"V-village ahead, Sarge," Tarbert said, buckteeth chattering. "Godsrest, I th-think."

"You see the blacksmith?" Hawley asked.

"Didn't s-see nobody, Sarge."

"Did you ask for him?"

"Not a soul about."

"What about a tavern?" That was Nedley. It was only just dawn and already he was thinking of drink.

"No tavern, neither."

"Shit on it!" Nedley grumbled.

"That's enough," Hawley warned. He pulled the reins to slow the horses as the wagon began to descend a steeper slope.

"Typical," Beacher complained.

Hawley turned on the three men in the back. Beacher was glaring right at Hawley, face red from the cold, beady eyes full of reproach.

"What is?" Hawley said.

"Three days with neither hide nor hair of a living soul, then we find a deserted village. Typical of our luck, isn't it, *Sargent*?"

Ianto sniggered. He was an odd fish, the new recruit. A stringy man, barely out of youth, yet his gristly arms were covered in faded tattoos, symbols of his faith. His hair showed signs of once being tonsured like that of a monk, the top and rear of his scalp stubbled, fringe snipped straight just above the brow. He'd proved able enough on the training ground, but would speak little of his past, save that he'd once served as a militiaman in Maserfelth, poorest of the seven *mearcas* of Aelderland. He'd bear watching; as would they all.

Hawley turned back to the road, lest he say something he would regret.

"*Awearg*," someone muttered.

Hawley felt his colour rise at the familiar slight. Again he held his tongue.

The men mistrusted Hawley. Hated him, even. Bad enough he was not one of "the Blood" like most of them, but even Ianto was treated better than Hawley, and he was a raw recruit. For Hawley, the resentment went deeper than blood lineage. For his great "transgression" a year ago, most men of the Third agreed it would've been better if Hawley had died that day. They rarely passed up an opportunity to remind him of it.

These four ne'er-do-wells would call themselves soldiers should any common man be present, but to Hawley they were the scrapings from the swill bucket. Hawley's days of fighting in the elite battalions were over. Now his assignments were the most trivial, menial, and demeaning, like most men not of the Blood. Beacher, Nedley, and Tarbert served under Hawley in the reserves only temporarily—it was akin to punishment duty for their many failings as soldiers, but their family names ensured they'd be restored to the roll of honour once they'd paid their dues. For those three, this was the worst they could expect. For Hawley and Ianto, it was the best they could hope for. Command of these dregs was another in a long list of insults heaped on Hawley of late. But command them he would, if for no other reason than a promise made to an old man.

The words of old Commander Morgard sprang into Hawley's mind, as though they'd blown down from the distant mountains.

What you must do, Hawley, is set an example; show those men how to behave. Show them what duty truly means. But most of all, show them what compassion *means. When I'm gone, I need you to lead. Not as an officer, but as a man of principle. Can you do that?*

Hawley had not thought of Morgard for some time. He reminded himself that the old man had rarely said a word in anger to the soldiers under his command. He had trusted Hawley to continue that tradition when he'd passed.

He'd expected too much.

From the corner of his eye, Hawley saw Tarbert cast an idiotic grin towards Beacher. Then Tarbert spurred his horse and trotted off down the slope.

The dull glow of lamps pierced the grey deluge ahead. Not deserted, then.

They'd travelled two weeks on their fool's errand, as Beacher liked to call it. And at last they'd found the village they searched for.

Godsrest.

*   *   *

"Godsrest" sounded like a name to conjure with, but in reality was a cheerless hamlet of eight humble dwellings, a few tumble-down huts, and one large barn that lay down a sloping path towards a grey river. The houses balanced unsteadily on their cobbled tofts, ill protected by poorly repaired thatch.

Two women summoned their children to them and hurried indoors. That much was normal at least. As Hawley knew from bitter experience on both sides of the shield, soldiers brought trouble to rural communities more often than not. There was no one else to be seen, but though the sun had barely found its way to the village square, it was still morning, and most of the men would be out in the fields. There was no planting to be done at this time of year, especially not in this weather. But it was good country for sheep and goats, for those hardy enough to traipse the hilly trails after the flock. In many ways, Hawley thought soldiering offered an easier life than toiling in the fields. A serf's lot was not a comfortable one, not out here. Here, they would work, or they would starve.

Hawley cracked the thin layer of ice from a water trough so the horses might drink. Tarbert unhitched the hobbling gelding from the back of the wagon and led it to the trough first.

Beacher spat over the side of the wagon. "I can smell a brew-house." He looked to Nedley, hopefully, who only snored.

The yeasty scent of fermenting grain carried on the wind. A late batch of ale, using the last of the barley, Hawley guessed. It'd be sure to pique Nedley's interest if the man woke up long enough to smell it.

"We're not here to drink," Hawley said.

"Why *are* we here? There's nothing worth piss in this wretched land. You know as well as I there's no Vigilant in those woods. Not the kind we need."

"If they've got his ring, stands to reason he exists."

"Pah! Dead and gone, long before any of us were born. More likely the merchant found an old ring and was planning to sell it, but when he lost his consignment, he invented this fairy story to save his neck. Face it, he had no business being this far north. The only people who use the old roads are outlaws and smugglers. Mark my words, we're chasing shadows. There's no True Vigilant anywhere."

Hawley had been ready for this since they'd left the fort, but it made him no less angry.

"So what if there isn't?" Hawley snarled. "You reckon that frees you from your duty?"

"My *duty* is to protect the good people of Aelderland, not travel half the country looking for faeries."

Ianto leaned against the wagon, watching the argument grow. Nedley stirred at last, peering at them from the back of the wagon through half-closed eyes.

Maybe Beacher had a point, but this wasn't the time to admit it. Hawley took a confident stride forward, summoning his blackest look. Beacher shuffled away from his advance.

"If there's a True Vigilant, he'll be able to find them bairns. It's them you should be thinking about."

"There's only one child Lord Scarsdale cares about—that Sylven whelp—and only then because his bitch mother wants to start a war over him. That's what you get, putting a woman in charge of an army."

Hawley waved the protest away tiredly. He'd heard it all before.

"Besides," Beacher went on, growing into his tirade, "even you can't believe they still live."

Even you. Beacher's lack of respect was astounding. He'd barely known Hawley at the time of the sargent's great transgression. His animosity was secondhand, but seething nonetheless. Men like Beacher needed something to hate, and in times of peace, that something might as well be one of their own. Sargent Holt Hawley, the Butcher of Herigsburg, bringer of misfortune: "awearg."

"Then we'll find the bodies, and take 'em home," Hawley snapped. "If you can't follow orders, Beacher, you're no use to me. Leave if you like. Explain to Commander Hobb why you abandoned your mission."

Beacher looked like he might explode. His face turned a shade of crimson to match his uniform. His hand tensed, hovering over the pommel of his regulation shortsword.

Do it, you bastard, Hawley thought. The sargent had taken plenty of abuse this last year, maybe too much. Some of the men mistook his tolerance for cowardice instead of what it really was: penance. It made them think he would shy from a fight. It made them overreach themselves.

"They say a True Vigilant can commune with the gods." The voice was Ianto's, and it was so unexpected, the tone so bright, that it robbed the moment of tension.

Hawley and Beacher both turned to look at the recruit, who still leaned nonchalantly against the wagon, arms folded across his chest.

"Commune with the dead, too. And read minds, they say. That's how they know if you're guilty of a crime as soon as they look at you. Such a man is a rarity in these times. Such a man would be...valuable."

"Speak plain," Beacher spat.

Ianto pushed himself from the wagon. His fingers rubbed at a little carved bone reliquary that hung about his neck, some trapping of his former calling. "Just that the archduke sent us, as the sargent said. The Archduke Leoric, Lord Scarsdale, High Lord of Wulfshael. Man with that many titles has plenty of money. Plenty of trouble, too—we all know it. The Sylvens could cross the river any time now, right into the Marches. Might even attack the First, then it's war for sure."

"The First can handle a bunch of Sylvens," Beacher said.

"Maybe." Ianto smiled. "But maybe there's a handsome reward waiting for the men who find the True Vigilant and avert such a war. I don't know about you, brother, but I think it would be not unpleasant to have a noble lord in my debt."

"And what say you, *Sargent*?"

Hawley almost did not want to persuade Beacher to his cause at all. Part of him thought it would be better to throw the rotten apple from the barrel now, and be done with it. There was a saying among the soldiers "of the Blood"—something about cutting a diseased limb from a tree. But for all his faults, Beacher was liked by the others. Hawley was not. That would make harsh discipline difficult to enforce.

"I say if by some miracle we turn up a true, honest-to-gods Vigilant after all this time," Hawley said at last, "they'll be singing our names in every tavern from here to bloody Helmspire. But if you don't follow your orders, we'll never know, *will we?*" Hawley added the last part with menace.

"And if...*when*...we don't find the Vigilant?" Beacher narrowed his eyes.

"Then we return to the fort, and be thankful we've missed a week of Hobb's drills." Hawley held Beacher's contemptuous glare again.

In the silence, there came the ringing of steel on steel, drifting up the hill from the barn.

Hawley and Beacher looked at Tarbert as one.

"No blacksmith?" Hawley said.

Tarbert laughed nervously.

"There you go," Ianto said. He came to Beacher's side and patted the big man on the shoulder. "Our luck's changing already."

Beacher finally allowed himself to be led away, still grumbling.

The sargent stretched out his knotted back, feeling muscles pop and joints crack as he straightened fully. Only Tarbert matched Hawley for height, but he was an arid strip of land who barely filled his uniform, with a jaw so slack he was like to catch flies in his mouth while riding vanguard. By contrast, Hawley was six feet of sinewy muscle, forged by hard labour and tempered in battle. He shook rain from his dark hair, and only then did he remember he was not alone.

Nedley was still on the wagon, watching. For once, he didn't look drunk. Indeed, there was something unnerving in the look he gave Hawley.

Hawley shouldered his knapsack, and hefted up Godspeaker— a large, impractical Felder bastard sword. Non-regulation: an affectation, a prize—a symbol of authority. The men hated that about him, but Hawley could barely care to add it to the tally.

"Make yourself useful, Nedley," Hawley said, strapping the sword to his back. "Find some supplies. And bloody *pay* for them. Show the locals that we mean well."

Hawley snatched the reins from Tarbert, who still looked forlorn. He cared more for the gelding than for most people. Baelsine, named for the blaze of silver grey that zigzagged up its black muzzle. He talked to it like a brother soldier.

"Help Nedley. I'll go see the smith."

* * *

A small forge blazed orange. A stocky, soot-faced man with a great beard and thick arms tapped away at a glowing axe-head.

"A moment, stranger," the man said, without looking up from his work.

Hawley basked in the welcome warmth of the bloomery, indifferent to the acidic tang of molten iron on the thick air.

The smith gave the axe-head a few more raps, before plunging it into a water trough, creating a plume of steam with a satisfying hiss. Only then did he look up at his visitor. Only then did he see the crimson uniform. "My apologies. I...I didn't know."

Hawley waved away the apology. "We need your services."

The smith squinted past Hawley. "How many soldiers?" he asked, suspicion edging into his voice.

"Five."

"Expectin' trouble?"

"No more than the ordinary." It had become standard wisdom that five men of the High Companies were worth more than twenty militia, and no outlaw of the forests would dare confront them. Fewer than five, and there'd be insufficient men to perform sentry and scouting duties. More importantly, there would not be enough to adopt the fighting formation favoured by the companies. The wall of steel. In full armour, every High Companies soldier clad their left arm in pauldron, gardbrace, and vambrace of strong Felder steel, adorned with an ingenious system of five interlocking crescent-shaped plates. When the arm was locked, a spring-loaded mechanism within the soldier's gauntlet would push the plates outwards, forming a rough circle of steel petals, almost like a shield; but when the arm was straightened, the plates retracted, leaving the arm free of any burden. Some men of the High Companies even had the skill and speed to trap an enemy's blade within the plates, snapping it in twain with a deft movement. In the press of battle, the soldiers would stand with their armoured left arm facing the foe, right hand wielding the short, thrusting blade, attacking in pairs with one man free to protect the rear and pick off the stragglers. That man was usually Hawley, whose heavy Felder sword needed room to do its grim work.

"This horse threw a shoe a few miles back." Hawley pointed to Baelsine, tethered near the barn.

The smith squeezed past his anvil to the horse. He lifted the hoof, and sucked at his teeth.

"Won't be fit for ridin' today. I'll shoe him. He can go in the paddock with my dray."

"Our own drays need feed and water."

"Ye planning on staying long?"

"Not if we can help it." Hawley didn't need consent to bunk in the village, but didn't like to flaunt his authority. "Perhaps we can be on our way today...with your help."

"I'm no miracle-worker, sir. That horse'll go lame if—"

"We can travel on foot from here. But I need you to point the way."

The smith's expression grew guarded. Hawley wondered if the man had cause to be suspicious of soldiers, or whether it was the custom of such isolated folk to be wary of strangers.

"Don't know what help I can be," the man said, wiping his hands on a rag. "Nor anyone else here, neither. We're simple folk. We keep to our own."

"Three weeks ago, perhaps more, an ore merchant passed through Godsrest. He'd been set upon. Beaten, nearly killed. You remember?"

"Aye, I remember."

"Men from this village helped him fetch his belongings. And among those belongings was a silver ring. You remember that?"

"Something of the like."

"Someone saved that merchant's life. We think it was the same man who owned the ring. We need to find him."

"Don't know nothing about that. Some o' the lads brung him to the village. I mended his wagon, he stayed a couple o' days while he recovered his strength, then he left."

"Fair enough." Hawley took out his map and unfolded it. "You can show me where he was found?"

The smith squinted at the map. "Old map," he said. "Them roads aren't there any more. Forest claimed 'em, and nobody in their right mind would travel 'em. Exceptin' your merchant, o'course."

"Show me, as best as you can."

The smith pointed at a spot in the woods, near to a road that supposedly was no longer there.

Hawley circled the spot with his charcoal, and frowned.

"How did you know?" he asked.

"How'd you mean, sir?" Was that nervousness? A quaver of the voice; a twist of the lip?

"You said you brought him here. But how'd you know to look for him?" Hawley studied the map. "No shepherd of any sense would graze his flock north of the river, let alone enter that forest. Unless he's particularly fond of wolves—or bandits."

"Had a bad season. Some o' the younger lads were out hunting the game trails. Heard the commotion. When they got there, they found an injured man and an empty wagon."

"Poaching in your lord's woods?" Hawley said.

"Nobody lays claim to the Elderwood, sir. Not our lord, not nobody else. Them woods is cursed, they say. Them woods is... *haunted*."

"But your hunters aren't afraid of ghosts?"

"They've the good sense not to stray too far." The smith eyed Hawley carefully. "You're not a soldier born," he said at last.

Hawley glowered.

"I mean no disrespect. All us folk of Godsrest abide by the king's law, and serve the king's men when required. It's just that... well... you try to speak proper, sir, is what I mean. But your roots are clear. It's like working a bloom that don't contain enough iron, if you take my meaning."

"I'm a sargent of the Third Company, that's all that matters."

Footsteps squelched loudly along the muddy path. Ianto appeared, that thin smirk upon his lips. He looked at the smith with keen eyes—*mean eyes*, Hawley thought.

"I told you to stay with the wagon," Hawley said sharply.

"I thought you'd want to know there's some . . . trouble."

There was something almost lascivious about Ianto's manner, and it sent a cold, warning creep up Hawley's spine.

"What kind of trouble?"

"The kind that gives soldiers a bad name."

* * *

Hawley followed the sounds of shrieking, pleading. The odd obscenity. The pained bleating of some animal. Hawley rounded the cob wall of a cottage to see three women of middle age remonstrating with Nedley. The soldier was stood near the largest hut, foot resting on a keg, sloshing ale down his throat from a flagon. Two more kegs lay on the track nearby. One had cracked open, dark ale foaming into the dirt. Behind Nedley, Beacher played tug-of-war with a red-headed boy, over the rope around the neck of a nanny-goat swollen with kid. The beast bleated pitifully as the noose tightened about its neck. Tarbert stood near, clapping his hands in joy at the unfolding chaos.

The woman doing most of the shouting rushed to Nedley, shrugging aside the half-hearted attempts of the others to hold her back. She pounded her fists against Nedley's chest. The soldier belched in her face, and shoved her away roughly. She spun into the arms of her companions as Nedley drained his flagon.

"Nedley!"

At Hawley's shout, Nedley narrowed his eyes in an insolent glare, the likes of which Hawley had never seen from the man. He wiped ale foam from his beard, but he did not answer.

As Hawley drew near, Nedley's hand moved just an inch towards the pommel of his sword.

That was everything Hawley needed to know. He lowered his head like an angered bull, and didn't so much as check his stride. Nedley thought better of drawing steel. Hawley shoved Nedley away from the hut. The drunkard shot Hawley another glare, but did nothing.

The boy cried out. The three women wailed and cursed.

The boy was in the mud now, holding his face, sobbing. Beacher had slapped him to the ground. But the boy cried not from pain but from sorrow. The goat was dead, blood spilling onto dirty straw from an ugly wound in its throat. Beacher had his sword in his hand, a grin on his blood-flecked face. Tarbert laughed like an imbecile. His laughter died on his lips when he saw Hawley.

Hawley kicked open the gate of the animal pen.

Beacher hadn't even noticed Hawley. At the interruption he said only, "Nedley, I told you—"

Hawley grabbed Beacher by the ear, twisted hard, and pulled him away from the goat with all his strength. Beacher squealed like a stuck pig as Hawley dragged him to the gate. Hawley spun the man around, and gave him a kick up the arse that sent him face-first into the dirt, his shortsword skittering from his hand.

Tarbert had taken a step forward, slack-jawed face more agawp than usual. Hawley slapped him hard across the side of the head for his trouble. Tarbert cowered like a kicked dog.

Hawley took one look back at the weeping boy and the dead goat. The animal was worth far more alive than dead to these people. The family's meagre fortunes may well have depended upon the creature. And now they would struggle, for the simple greed of a soldier. Hawley stepped onto the track, Beacher in his sights.

Nedley had picked up his flagon again, more concerned with saving the last undamaged ale keg than helping his brother soldier. The villagers could scarce spare the ale either, Hawley thought. But one thing at a time.

One of the women pushed past Hawley to see to the boy. The

other two, realising Nedley was no longer standing in their way, came to scream at Beacher.

Ianto reappeared. He stood over by the cottage, leaning against the wall, watching. Grinning.

Now the smith appeared, hammer in hand. That was the danger. Hawley had to deal with Beacher before any villager got involved. Otherwise, he'd be hard-pressed to stop even this band of good-for-nothings taking vengeance on the peasants.

Beacher rolled over, scrambling away on his elbows. "Don't you touch me!" he snarled, blinking away mud from his eyes. His hand found the pommel of his shortsword in the dirt. His fingers curled around the hilt, and his expression changed at once. He clambered to his feet and spat, "You filthy *mongrel*!"

Mongrel. Not one of "the Blood," who could trace their family back through five or more generations of military service. Looking at the state of the men around him, Hawley couldn't take it as much of an insult.

Hawley advanced another step. "Sheathe that sword," he said quietly, almost in a growl. "Sheathe it, or I'll kill you." He held Beacher's gaze, saw the man's eyes falter. Beacher believed him. He was right to.

Beacher pleaded with his brother soldiers left and right for support. Hawley heard Tarbert behind him, but the dullard was of little concern. Nedley... now there was an unknown quantity. Up until now, Hawley hadn't taken the drunkard seriously. That could have been a mistake. Nedley was staring at Hawley with utter detachment, like a butcher appraising which cut of meat to take next. But he didn't make a move. When Beacher looked to Ianto, the recruit gave only the merest shrug of his shoulders, as if to say, "This is not my fight." He may not have been a friend to Hawley, but nor was he one of the Blood. He'd wait and see which way the wind blew before committing himself.

Beacher stood alone, and he knew it. He took a moment to weigh up his chances against Hawley, and found them lacking. He sheathed the blade and spread his palms.

Hawley marched to Beacher, loomed over him, pressed his

forehead into the bridge of the man's nose. Beacher averted his eyes, like a wild dog that had just lost a pack challenge. Hawley reached to Beacher's belt and took the man's sword away with no resistance.

Other villagers arrived now. Seven or eight men and youths tramped up the hill, pointing, chattering. Their approach was cautious. There weren't enough men in this village to cause the soldiers real problems, but enough that they might try. And die.

Any sense of decorum was lost. Any chance Hawley's reserves had of looking like proper soldiers was gone.

"Ianto, Nedley. Get him away," Hawley said. "To the bridge. Wait for me there."

Neither man moved. Nedley gazed at the flagon, weighing up the order.

"I said get him away. *Now*."

Ianto exchanged looks with Nedley and shrugged again. Nedley finished his dregs, tossed the flagon aside, and weighed in. Together they led Beacher away from the gathering villagers, down towards the river.

Tarbert staggered from the pen at last, nursing his sore ear. Hawley jerked his head in the direction of the others. Without a word, Tarbert followed.

Rightly or wrongly, Hawley had done the men an insult—one that might yet come back to bite him on the arse. As king's men, they had the right to claim whatever they wanted from a serf, and by denying them their perceived due, Hawley had only deepened their loathing of him. He might even face more punishment back at the barracks, once Beacher had made his inevitable complaint. Hawley was past caring. What he needed to do right now was make amends with the villagers.

"Master Smith—" Hawley ventured.

"Godsrest is a peaceful place," the smith interrupted. "Apt named, for we honour the gods here and invite no trouble. You've brought trouble to our door."

The other men drew nearer. Hawley weighed up his chances of regaining the smith's trust before they took exception to his presence.

"They're soldiers...not good ones, I admit. But you'll have no more trouble."

"No?"

"No. Look, Master Smith—"

"Gereth. My name is Gereth. And that boy over there is my son."

Hawley turned to see the dishevelled lad on his feet at last, being comforted by a woman. From the mane of red hair that tumbled from her bonnet, Hawley guessed she was his mother—Gereth's wife. She held her son close, and glared accusingly at Hawley, who cursed Beacher's name under his breath.

"Gereth, then. You know the law. You know the power of the High Companies. I would choose not to exercise that power. Let's come to an arrangement instead. See to our horses as agreed, and I'll pay you fairly."

"That much I'll do, sir, as duty to manor and king dictates."

"You don't have to call me 'sir.' My name's Hawley. Holt Hawley. You were right before, I am a common man, from a place much like this. I chose this life 'cause I was tired of seeing common folk—people like us—downtrodden and uncared for."

"Then you chose poorly, Holt Hawley."

"Maybe. But there's no leaving the companies once your bunk is made, unless it be on a pyre, an enemy's blade, or the end of a noose. So I do what I can, and I'll at least talk straight with you."

The others gathered around. Hawley didn't know how much they'd overheard, and it didn't matter. As a craftsman, Gereth was of a higher station than they. Gereth was the one he needed to convince.

"You had little reason to trust me before," Hawley went on, "and even less now. But I'll tell you why we're here. This past year, six bairns have been taken from their homes. Six—that we know of. One of them is a lad of wealth, a foreigner. You've no reason to care for such a boy, why would you? But the others... they're from villages like this, poorer than this. Boys and girls of Aelderland. Boys younger than your own. They're lost, and nobody can find them. Not the high lords, not the companies,

18   Mark A. Latham

and certainly not the bloody Vigilants. But it's said that there's somebody in these parts who could help. A *True* Vigilant, of the old order. If it's true, then maybe he can find those children, where others have failed."

Gereth shook his head. "Fairy stories, Holt Hawley. There's nobody alive who's ever seen such a man. Not many who've even heard of one, neither."

"That merchant," Hawley persisted, "said he was helped by a mysterious stranger. Didn't get a good look at him, but he did find his ring. A Vigilant's ring."

Gereth waved a dismissive hand. "As I've said, there's nowt in them woods but trouble. If you want to go chasing shadows, that's your affair. All we can offer you is food and water for yer horses and a dry place for yer wagon."

Hawley sighed. He reached to his scrip and took out a few silver pieces. "For your trouble."

"Keep it."

"Come on...you've lost livestock, supplies. Let me compensate you."

Gereth looked Hawley square in the eye. "Keep it, and go in peace."

The villagers stared at Hawley. Women had come out of their homes to scowl at him. Hawley put the money back in his scrip and nodded ruefully.

He went to the wagon and retrieved two packs, heaving them one on each shoulder. "I'll come back for the rest," he said.

"No, we'll bring 'em," Gereth replied. He didn't want the soldiers in the village a moment longer than necessary, and Hawley couldn't blame him.

Hawley walked past the assembled villagers, down the hill to the bridge where his men idled, doubtless cursing his name still.

Gereth followed, a couple of young lads in tow, with the rest of the packs. They weathered the sullen glares of the reserves just as well as Hawley. Hawley was impressed, but then he'd always thought the northerners were a tough breed.

As the villagers piled the supplies at Hawley's feet, Gereth leaned in.

"Just don't stray far from the trails," he said. "The Elderwood has no end, and it's easy to get turned around. You're like to get lost...or worse. Cross the bridge, then head north. You'll pass a trapper's shack after a few hours, so you'll know you're on the right path. It's near enough a day's walk to the old trade road."

"You really don't know any more?" Hawley tried once more to plead with the man. He still felt like the smith knew more than he was letting on.

"All I know is, you're more likely to find a witch in them woods than a Vigilant."

With that, Gereth and the youths returned up the hill, leaving Hawley to weather the glares of his men, and their whispered accusations of giving up the secrets of their mission to a commoner.

CHAPTER 2

The great, dark Elderwood was the largest expanse of virgin woodland in the north. It felt like a foreign place to Hawley. Back home, most of the forests had been stripped to flush out outlaws. Those patches of woodland that remained were now skeletal and sparse, their foliage not yet replenished from the ravages of winter. Here, the trees were tall and evergreen, towering firs, canopies conical and black, full of scurrying animals and the screeching of unfamiliar birds.

With aching limbs and sweat-soaked uniforms, the soldiers had finally found a break in the trees, where at last the Third Company reserves could breathe free air and catch a glimpse of the moon and stars above. Tarbert took point, carrying his torch ahead.

They'd found the old trade road sure enough. Once providing passage east to west, skirting the mountainous border with Reikenfeld, it had long since been left to ruin.

A wagon lay wrecked on a rough, wide dirt road lined irregularly with crumbled stone long broken by twisted roots. Its front axle was split, and two wheels were splintered. Why a merchant would venture on this ill-used road in the first place was a mystery—presumably someone had questioned the man on the matter, but the details hadn't been conveyed to Hawley. Most likely Beacher was right. Maybe the merchant had been skimming off the profits, taking excess ore from the mines to sell to the Felders. Whoever had attacked him had taken his consignment with them.

"It's this way," Tarbert called.

Hawley realised he'd been caught in his thoughts. The others were already gathered around Tarbert. Beacher wore an expression of impatience.

"Signs of a fight, Sarge," Tarbert explained as Hawley joined them. "And something got carted off this way." He pointed east.

"How many men?" Hawley asked.

"Tracks is too old, Sarge. An overloaded wagon and at least four horses, but everything else has been washed away. Road's overgrown down there. You can see how it's been trampled."

Hawley just nodded. Tarbert was an idiot, true enough—it was repeated incompetence and forgetfulness that led to his stint in the reserves—but he was a good tracker. It was the one thing Hawley trusted the man for.

"No sign of any rings, Tarbert?" Beacher asked, voice dripping with sarcasm.

"Rings? Like, jewellery? No, not seen any rings."

"No? How about staffs, or grey robes, or medallions emblazoned with the Eye of Litha? No?" Beacher smirked as Tarbert shook his head. "Well, there's a fine thing, Sarge. Not so much as a note showing us where this hundred-year-old Vigilant vanished to. What are we to do?"

Hawley tried his best not to react. He repeated Morgard's words in his head like a mantra.

"The only lead we have is these bandits, or whoever they were," Hawley said. "If the merchant really was rescued by a Vigilant, then maybe the bandits saw where he went. If we track 'em down, then…"

"For pity's sake!" Beacher snapped. His anger was real, but the snarl on his face was immediately checked by fear—the memory of his earlier beating, perhaps. He lowered his tone just a shade, but not enough for Hawley's liking. "Whoever they were—bandits, raiders, rival merchants—they're long gone. They could be over the mountains to Reikenfeld by now."

"You knew what you were signing up for," Hawley said. "Finding the wagon was only the start. From here, we have to work out where this bloody Vigilant might have gone."

"Come on, Sargent," Beacher said, for once using Hawley's rank, though not respectfully. "It's a tall tale from a desperate man. The Vigilant never existed."

"Oh, I wouldn't go that far," Ianto chimed. "Who knows the ways of the old Vigilants? Maybe he can appear and disappear at will. Like a ghost."

"Don't say that!" Tarbert said. "Don't say...*ghost*." He'd been on edge ever since he'd heard the village whispers about ghosts and witches.

"Look," Beacher said, trying and failing to sound reasonable, "nobody really expects us to find him. And as you say, we don't have any leads other than some old tracks and a couple of empty carts. If you were hoping for some miracle to point the way, it hasn't come. Let's just make camp, rest up, then go back. Maybe we take a few extra days, to make it look good, y'know?"

Everyone looked at Hawley hopefully. Except maybe Ianto, whose thin, knowing smirk was one lip-twitch away from baiting Hawley's temper again. Hawley puffed out his cheeks.

"Meet you halfway," he said. "We make camp, and in the morning we follow that trail for one day, and one day only. If nothing turns up, we can leave."

"Waste of time..." Beacher grumbled.

"One day, Beacher," Hawley said more firmly. "At least we can make a show of doing our duty."

Hawley pushed past Beacher and walked a few yards along the road. He was acutely aware of Nedley staring at him, silently, as he had back at Godsrest. He shook his head in frustration.

"Spread out," he called back. "Check the area, make sure nobody can get the drop on—"

Hawley almost tripped as his boot hit a half-buried stone in the dark. A pitted and moss-covered marker, of a kind he had seen many times on the mining tracks of Hintervael as a youth. It pointed northeast.

Hawley stopped, and rubbed his scrappy beard thoughtfully, staring into the dark woods.

It was Ianto who was first to approach.

"What is it, Sargent?" he asked. Although Hawley had little time for the man, it was the first thing anyone had said to him all day that wasn't laced with either disrespect or outright malice.

"I think...there's another trail, down there." Hawley nodded into the shadows.

Ianto squinted. The others approached, Tarbert stepping forward with his torch, cautiously scanning the ground in the direction Hawley was looking.

"What now?" Beacher said, coming to join them.

They were interrupted by a sudden "oof" from Tarbert, and the jerk of his torchlight in the dark.

"I'm all right!" Tarbert called. "Nearly went down a ditch. There's a sunken trail here. A holloway."

Hawley went to look. Sure enough, a narrow road, even more ancient than the trade road, wound off to the northeast, right where the marker was pointing.

"That's not a road," Beacher said. "A beast trail, at best. You can't surely be thinking..."

Hawley nodded to Tarbert, who clambered down the bank, lighting the way for the others to see. It was a road all right, now a deep, V-shaped trench in the earth, concealed by arching branches that gave it the appearance of a tunnel. Called *holl wægs* in the old tongue, holloways were well-worn paths, some said to be a thousand years old, sunken by the constant tread of long-ago traffic, and now forgotten. But it wasn't merely the holloway that had piqued Hawley's interest.

"That stone marker," Hawley said. "It's not a waymarker like the others. It's a sanctuary marker, from long before the last war. They point to the next safe haven in the wilds. A watchtower, a keep, a fortified inn..."

"An inn?" Beacher scoffed. "If only that were true, Nedley could blaze us a trail in no time."

"I've seen its like many times," Hawley said. "Those abandoned outposts are often used as shelter by outlaws. Or...desperate folk. If the marker's here, the haven can't be far, and it'd be a good place for our quarry to hole up." Something in Hawley's memories almost made his throat dry up and his voice crack just a little, but he fought to keep his composure. He was right about this; he knew it in his gut.

"The tracks lead east... *Sargent*." There was the barb Hawley had come to expect from Beacher.

"Aye. But our path leads north."

Beacher flapped his arms in exasperation.

"Make camp," Hawley said. "Tarbert, scout the area. Nedley, you're on first watch. We head out at dawn."

*   *   *

Feorndaeg, 24th Day of Sollomand

The men had been quiet since breaking their fast, and in Hawley's experience that usually spelled trouble. They laboured through uneven terrain, into a part of the Elderwood that seemed impossibly ancient. There was a chill in the air. Drizzle pattered on dark leaves. Otherwise, there was silence but for the breaths of the soldiers and the snapping of twigs beneath their mail-shod boots.

It came as some relief when they saw light ahead, where the holloway broadened and the forest opened up into a clearing. The relief was short-lived.

Here, the character of the woods seemed to change. The air felt colder still, the light weaker, somehow grey, as though the colour was drained from the world. Dead, skeletal trees leaned in overhead, trailing off alongside the clearing to create a broad, shadowed avenue. And at the end of that avenue, just as Hawley had predicted, was a tower.

Ancient structures such as this lay scattered across the land, a reminder of long-ago days when the seven mearcas of Aelderland were each kingdoms in their own right, who warred with each other relentlessly. So much so that they were too weak individually to fight the much larger kingdoms of Reikenfeld to the north, Sylverain to the south, and Tördengard beyond the western mountains. Centuries of war laid waste to palaces and bartons, cities and monuments, which some elders claimed were finer than any standing today.

Hawley did not think the tower before him could ever have been very fine. The upper portion was mostly fallen away. If ever it had maintained battlements, they were long gone. Ivy clung to its south face, as though holding together the weak stonework. The tower was probably older than the forest itself, built at a time when the north was said to be home to vile creatures, and the men who lived here were held in thrall to witchcraft. It seemed unthinkable that anyone could live here, so far removed from fellowship. But someone did: Wispy smoke drifted idly from the open roof.

He took half a dozen steps before he realised the men were not following. He turned to see them staring at the tower warily. Tarbert in particular had the look of a spooked horse about him, his wide eyes and long face compensating for the absence of a steed. Their arrival at the tower should have vindicated Hawley's decision to march this trail, but it seemed only to unsettle the motley reserves. Hawley pulled his roughspun cloak more tightly about his shoulders, and beckoned the soldiers on.

"I don't like the look of this place," Beacher grumbled.

Hawley found himself in agreement with Beacher for the first time on the journey. "For good or ill, this is the end of it. If the Vigilant isn't here, I don't know where else to look."

As if in reply, a black cloud passed overhead, enveloping the clearing almost entirely in darkness. Tarbert whimpered softly.

"Tarbert, light a torch," Hawley said, as much to give the simpleton something to do as to provide some light. Tarbert pulled off his leather gauntlets and fumbled in his knapsack for a tinder. Hawley noticed the man had cut himself, his left hand bound clumsily. Another mishap to blame on Hawley, no doubt.

With the torchlight making the minutest improvement to the forest's oppressive atmosphere, Hawley led the way to the tower's ironbound door. Hawley weighed up the risks, considering carefully that the tower was more likely occupied by outlaws than by a True Vigilant. Gereth could well have sent them into a trap, which was as much as this band of miscreants deserved.

Hawley felt the restless shifting of the men at his back. So, decisively, he pounded thrice upon the door. The raps echoed within the tower. Hawley shuffled away from the door, possessed abruptly by a strong sense that his presence here was unwanted. Forbidden.

At first there was a deathly silence over the clearing. Then came the drawing of a metal bolt, rasping and squealing. Then the turning of a key in a large, old lock. The door inched open with a creak, revealing dancing shadows and the reddish hues of flickering firelight within the tower.

From the darkness beyond the door, a face emerged. Not the face of a powerful man who could read thoughts and commune with gods. Not the face of a man at all.

An old woman squinted at Hawley through eyes framed with wrinkles. All Hawley could see of her was that she was slight, and wore a grey bonnet, from beneath which snow-white locks of hair protruded. Small, gnarled fingers wrapped around the door, preventing it opening further. Her eyes, narrow slits in a well-worn face, darted from man to man, each appraisal increasing the suspicion in the elder's features.

"I..." Hawley began, his apprehension replaced by the slow drip of disappointment. "I'm Sargent Hawley of the Third. Is your master home?"

There was an awkward silence. Finally, the woman replied, "Third what?"

"What? I...The Third Company." Silence. "Of...the High Companies. What else?"

"Very grand, I'm sure."

Hawley glanced over his shoulder at the men. Tarbert smiled like a fool; Nedley was expressionless as ever; Beacher glowered, both at Hawley and the woman. Ianto offered his familiar shrug. With a sigh, Hawley turned back to the woman.

"Is your master home?" he tried again.

"Master?" The woman gave a small chuckle. "There's been no master here for many a long year."

"Mistress then," he ventured.

"This is *my* home," she said again. Then scowled at the soldiers. "You're not here to throw me out, are you?"

"Throw you out? Why would we?"

"They always said, 'That place be too grand for you, Nell. Get ideas above your station, you will. King Ealwarth will throw you out on your ear if he finds you.'"

"Ealwarth?"

Hawley heard one of the men behind him snort with laughter. King Ealwarth had died before Hawley was born. He had been the Usurper, who overthrew his cousin, Athelwyn, during the War of Silver and Gold, and was widely credited with ushering in the Age of Peace. His great-grandson, Eadred, the Boy King, now sat on the throne. Hardly a boy, in truth, but barely in manhood either.

Hawley looked at the woman's blank expression. All of this history of kings would doubtless come as news to her. He thought hard; his frustration was making it difficult to keep a clear head.

"Do you live here alone?"

"Eh?" she said loudly.

Deaf as well as daft, Hawley thought. "I said: Do you live alone?"

"Alone? No, I got Bartholomew for company."

"Ah." Hawley almost laughed with relief. "And where is Bartholomew now?"

"In 'ere." She turned her head into the gloom and called out, "Tell 'im, Barty. You tell 'im."

There came an avian squawk, followed by a screeching utterance.

"Tell 'im! Tell 'im! Barty-Barty-Barty!"

Hawley pinched at his furrowed brow and took a deep breath. "And besides... 'Barty'... does anyone else live here? Or nearby?"

"Oo... no. I ain't seen a living soul since... What day is it?"

"Feorndaeg," Hawley answered, although he was not entirely sure himself.

The woman counted on her bony fingers, then replied, "No, I forget when."

"Some Vigilant…" Beacher scoffed.

The woman's eyes fixed on Beacher, then one by one examined the soldiers again.

"You're bleeding," she said, looking at Tarbert.

Tarbert winced as if noticing for the first time. The binding around his hand was stained with fresh blood. He hid his hand behind his back and looked shiftily at Hawley.

"I can give you a poultice," the woman said. "Many herbs and remedies here. The forest provides for Old Nell."

Hawley felt Beacher draw close to his ear, the man's breath on his skin. "She's a bloody witch," he whispered.

"Witch?" the woman said, her hearing apparently much keener than they'd thought. "I'm a respec'ble woman! I knows my way around a forest, an' I know what'll kill or cure, but I'm no witch."

An idea occurred to Hawley. "Your remedies…you peddle them at Godsrest?"

"I stay away from people as much as possible. Nowt but trouble, they are. But Old Nell makes herself useful when she can. Like to see you young 'uns do as well when you get to my age."

Hawley could not conceive of any soldier reaching this woman's venerable age. Even Commander Morgard had succumbed before his sixty-first winter, and he had looked not so old as her.

"Do you remember a merchant wagon passing through the forest some weeks ago?" Hawley persisted. "An ore merchant, attacked on the old forest road."

"We don't see many strangers, Barty and me…Remember him, I does. Saw 'im, we did, but he didn't see Old Nell, oh no."

"You saw who ambushed him?"

"Who? Or *what*? Long way from home, he was. Brung trouble on himself. There's things that dwell hereabouts. Dark things. You must've heard 'em, or seen 'em. Or…felt 'em?"

Hawley suppressed a shudder.

"What are you saying, woman?" Ianto interrupted. "We've seen no 'dark things.'" He sounded stern, but rubbed the reliquary about his neck nervously.

The old woman fixed Ianto with a steely glare. "Seen a lot of things in my time here," she said. "But I never seen a monk dressed like a soldier."

"He's no monk," Beacher scoffed. "He's from Maserfelth. Touched in the head he is."

Ianto's smirk dissipated for the first time since Hawley had known him. He shot Beacher a look of annoyance, then said, "Careful, woman. This here is the Butcher of Herigsburg. Maybe he *will* throw you out of this tower and reclaim it in the name of the king."

Hawley gave Ianto a look that could turn back a mountain stream.

"You know what that merchant was carrying?" the woman asked. If Ianto's callous threat was meant to frighten her, it appeared not to have succeeded.

"Iron ore," Hawley replied, though now he felt less certain.

"Ha! Iron ain't worth fightin' over. No. Whoever set on him was after blackrock."

Almost in unison, the soldiers stepped away from the door, as though the woman had put a curse on them all. Ianto touched his upright forefinger to his brow—the sign of the Saint's Sword, to ward off evil. Nedley spat into the dirt.

"Blackrock," Hawley muttered. A rare ore, of immense value. Its only use, as far as anyone knew, was in sorcery, long outlawed in Aelderland. It was mined in small quantities and sold to other kingdoms—its dark properties did not deter the king from profiting from its sale. And the old woman's implication was clear. Everyone knew dark forces were drawn to the blackrock.

"You're saying those men were attacked by...by..." Beacher stuttered, "*Riftborn?*"

Hawley resisted the urge to clout Beacher around the ear. The Riftborn—what some men called demons—were creatures of myth and legend. Veterans of the War of Silver and Gold claimed to have fought against them, during great battles where immortals and men allied against evil. But these were nothing more than the fancies of old soldiers who had suffered much. And yet those stories held great sway in the High Companies, where tradition—and superstition—were valued more highly than common sense.

The old woman chuckled. "Maybe. Weren't no bodies left behind, were there? Maybe they got spirited off to the pits of Uffærn."

Hawley thought he could hear Tarbert's knees knocking at the naming of the hellish underworld. He wanted nothing more than to be away from the old woman himself, but she was the only soul they'd encountered in the woods, and if she knew a single thing of use, he had to coax it out of her.

"There was something else found nearby. A ring."

"A ring, sir?"

"Yes. A silver ring. One that once belonged to a Vigilant."

"A *vig'lant*? Well, I never!" the woman gasped. "And you have it, do you, this ring?"

"No, it's in the possession of Lord Scarsdale."

"Who?"

Hawley sighed. "Never mind. No, I haven't got the ring."

"But you seen it?"

"No, I—"

"Well then!" the woman said resolutely. "Seein' is believin', ain't it?"

"She has a point, Sargent," Ianto said quietly. "Think about it. What if the ring was just a trick by . . . *them*?"

"Clever one, he is," the woman said. "Aye, the Riftborn know all the tricks. Maybe they sent the ring so's you soldiers would come runnin'. If I were you, I'd wonder why they wanted you here, in these dark woods, so far from home."

"It's not us they bloody want," Beacher snarled.

"Awearg . . ." Tarbert whispered, taking another step back. Hawley turned crossly. Tarbert gave him the most fearful look.

"Pull yourselves together!" Hawley snapped. He addressed the woman one more time. "If you don't know about the Vigilant, maybe you know where the local outlaws make camp? You're out here all alone—it'd be safer for you if we brought them to justice."

Nell shrugged. "If I were you, good sirs, I'd worry more about yourselves. Dark forces are at work here. *Very* dark." She widened her eyes to emphasise her point. They were of a deep sea green, lively as cresting waves—Hawley found them unsettlingly youthful-looking in one so old.

"I don't believe in Riftborn, or curses..." Hawley said.

Beacher grumbled something unintelligible. Hawley could guess what it was.

"But there's no point staying here longer than we have to," he finished.

The woman seemed to be looking past Hawley, scrutinising the other men quite keenly. Then she nodded, and said simply, "Good day, sirs."

She closed the door before Hawley could utter another word. And that, he supposed, was that.

CHAPTER 3

Enough!" Hawley snapped.

He'd put up with their grumbling for too long. Now, as they neared the camp, Hawley wanted nothing more than a moment's peace before beginning the long journey home beneath the shadow of failure. Hawley could almost hear Commander Hobb's sneering reprimand now.

Someone sniggered.

Hawley rounded on the men sharply. Ianto was the only one smiling, but that meant nothing—it was his customary expression, like he was mocking everyone and everything; as though he was somehow above them all.

"Pack up the tents. We'll head back to Godsrest...and I'll have no bloody trouble." Hawley punctuated this order with a glower at Beacher.

Beacher gave a huff and marched past Hawley, barging his shoulder as he passed. The others followed, each man in turn touching a hand to his forehead in a lazy salute.

Hawley stood alone. His mind wandered again to Fort Fangmoor, when he had served as steward to Commander Morgard. He remembered the old man's advice to him before he'd finally been forced to "retire" by Hobb—forced to leave the fort and die elsewhere. Morgard, Commander of the Third, the Silver Lion. Frail and dying.

"I have taught you all I can in the time we've had," he'd said. "But it is not enough. Not enough to name you my successor."

Hawley remembered how surprised he had been, how he'd stood there half in disbelief, half in panic.

"Fear not, Hawley—I know you wouldn't want the post even if it were offered. It will go to Hobb, in good time. Oh, I know, you've disliked Hobb from the moment you set eyes on him, and perhaps your instincts guide you well. However, Hobb has been prepared for this duty his whole life, and it's one tradition even I am not ready to dishonour. Listen to me—I'm on my way out, but I'm not done yet. I'll see to it you're afforded every privilege when I'm gone, if you will swear to uphold my legacy."

"How?" Hawley had asked. "I'm not of the Blood. I can't be promoted further, even if you willed it."

"The prerogative of the outgoing commander is a powerful thing. You would know that, if you had spent a lifetime steeped in our traditions. And that's precisely why you're important—you and your kind. Because as fine as these soldiers are, as feared as they are, they have become too obsessed with tradition. Too concerned with the purity of their bloodlines and the proud history of more illustrious forebears. I've heard them whispering that I've diluted the blood. Poppycock! I've made this company stronger. I've brought in honest, hardy, dedicated soldiers that have made this company rival almost the First in strength. Blood be damned! I could have done more to widen the net of recruitment, perhaps. *Should* have done. But I was afraid."

"You, afraid?"

"Always! To command is to fear. A leader who never fears making a mistake is an arrogant one. Or worse: a complacent one. The truth is, I wasn't brave enough. I didn't want to throw away tradition entirely, for fear of unbalancing the company. I didn't want to stir up resentment between the old soldiers and the new."

"Too late for that." Hawley had regretted the remark immediately.

But Morgard had only laughed, which had brought on a coughing fit. "Ruffled a few feathers, haven't you? Good. That's how you know it's working. Now listen to me: Like it or not, you're a leader now. And the men you lead know everything there is about soldiering, and nothing whatsoever about what makes a *good* soldier. Oh, I don't mean they won't follow orders—they do that very well, too. But they forget why we're here. Unlike you, Hawley. You volunteered, and I know damn well you remember why."

That memory caused Hawley to wince even now.

"The men of the Third fight because their fathers fought, and their fathers before them. But they haven't known *real* war—the kind that threatens to consume the world. I'm the last man of the Third who remembers what that's like, and it's not an honour I cherish. In the barracks they say they're champing at the bit to fight a 'proper war,' but by the gods, I pray it never comes. These days, the Third is tasked with upholding the law, and we must do it fairly and justly."

The commander had gripped Hawley's hand firmly and spoken the words that had haunted Hawley ever since:

When I'm gone, I need you to lead. Not as an officer, but as a man of principle.

Now Hawley stared back into the dark woods and allowed himself a heavy sigh. How much longer could he endure the resentment of the men? Maybe this business with Tarasq was a blessing. Maybe Aelderland really did need a war—something to unite the High Companies against a common foe; make them remember their purpose.

"I'm sorry, old man," Hawley whispered to the night.

"Not as sorry as we are," someone said behind him.

Something struck Hawley on the temple, cold and unforgiving. Pain shot through his body. Hawley's vision blurred, pinpricks of light dazzled him. He couldn't feel his legs, but knew he was staggering backwards. The shadows gathered before him.

Hawley fell. A dark grey sky and crow-black trees loomed over him. It seemed an age before he hit the ground, and dull pain spread across his back.

"Why'd you say that, Ianto?" a voice hissed. "You bloody warned him."

"Seemed...poetic, I suppose." Ianto's voice, sing-song in its mocking quality. Always on the verge of breaking into laughter.

"Shit on your poetry." That was Beacher.

Hawley's vision began to clear. He willed his arms and legs to move, but they didn't respond quickly enough. He tried to speak, but no words came. Why was his mouth so dry? A man leaned over him, just a silhouette, broad of shoulder, lean, hair long and lank.

"Hold still, Sargent," Nedley said. "I'll make it quick."

Hawley's arm finally moved. His hand reached up, outstretched. "Don't..." he managed.

Light glinted from an object in Nedley's hand. A blade. The sight of it brought Hawley's senses rushing back to him.

Nedley pushed a firm hand down on Hawley's chest. His dark, ringed eyes searched for the join in Hawley's armour, looking for the best place to stick his blade.

Out of instinct, out of sheer bloody-mindedness, Hawley pulled Nedley towards him, setting him off-balance. He felt the knife slice his side. He gritted his teeth; ignored it, prayed it hadn't bitten deep enough to kill him. Then he drove his forehead into Nedley's nose. It crunched satisfyingly.

Hawley scrambled away on his elbows as Nedley tried to right himself.

Pain exploded in his ribs. Not the wound. A kick. Beacher. Hawley rolled away as another kick swung at him and missed.

"Tarbert, you useless cretin!" Beacher squealed. "Get him!"

Hawley was half up. Blood rushed to his head, red rage washing over him.

Footsteps crunched to his right. Hawley swung a punch. The blow only brushed the cheek of the onrushing Nedley, but Hawley followed it with a big right hand that squelched against the drunkard's broken nose. To his credit, Nedley did not cry out. He grunted, and hit the ground.

Beacher advanced, but checked his stride as Hawley wheeled to face him. Tarbert circled around Hawley, but he was the least of the sargent's worries. They all held small knives. Why knives? Why not swords?

As Beacher hesitated, Hawley fumbled for the straps of the sword on his back. His fingers curled around the hilt of his bastard sword, and that lent him strength. He shook the sword free with a flourish and staggered into a fighting stance. His head spun. Blood trickled down the side of his face. Hawley looked Beacher in the eye.

"Bastard," he growled. He looked at Beacher's knife, then to his own sword, then back to the man's now-quivering face. "Wrong tool for the job."

"You can say that again." Ianto, leaning against a tree, too far away to be a threat, but his tone mocking.

Groggy, Hawley didn't take Ianto's meaning. Nedley barged into him, blindsiding him. The wind left Hawley's lungs. He swung wildly. The sword hit a tree and fell from his grasp. Nedley was already back to his feet. The sword, so deadly in open battle, had betrayed Hawley at such close quarters.

"Tarbert!" Nedley roared. "Hold him down."

Tarbert scrambled through the dirt. He grabbed Hawley's hands.

Nedley jerked his head at Beacher, who rushed forward, too, grasping for Hawley's legs even as the sargent kicked and flailed, struggling with all his might.

Nedley threw his small blade aside and drew his shortsword.

"No!" Beacher shrieked. "We must do it properly. It must be the knives."

"Shit on the knives," Nedley said, spitting blood into the dirt. "You can stab him after I'm done." He came forward on unsteady legs, features grim.

Hawley had no idea what they were talking about, nor where the strange daggers had come from, but he could worry about that later.

"Ianto!" Hawley shouted. "You're not part of this. What are you doing?"

"Sorry, Sargent," Ianto's voice rang out. "Hobb's orders. The gods forbid me from shedding your blood, but I cannot raise a hand against my sworn brothers when they are conducting their solemn duty. You know how it is."

"Duty...?" At the thought of Hobb ordering his murder, Hawley's rage grew, his struggle intensified.

"Shh, shh!" Nedley hushed, as though quieting a distressed horse. "Nothing personal. Consider it a noble sacrifice."

Nedley pushed his hand down on Hawley's chest as before, this time holding his sword, ready to deliver the practised, piercing thrust so often used by the companies to dispatch their enemies.

Hawley tried one last time to free himself, but Beacher pinned his legs firm, and though Tarbert was not a strong man, he virtually lay across Hawley's outstretched arms. Hawley knew he was about to die at the hands of the men he had sworn to lead.

The dull squelch made Hawley's stomach lurch. The sound of flesh tearing, bone cracking like a chicken leg being torn from the carcass. Warm blood spattered his face.

Not his blood.

Tarbert screamed like a child.

Hawley realised he had closed his eyes. He opened them as Nedley's body fell to the ground, blood spraying from the stump where his head should have been.

A roar echoed through the forest, loud enough to shake Hawley's bones. A bestial, animal roar, throaty and wet and full of rage. It was close.

Weight lifted from Hawley's legs. Heavy footsteps pounded earth. Beacher was running.

Hawley wrenched his hands away from the screaming Tarbert, staggered to his feet. He looked about, disorientated. The already weak sunlight had faded further. Shadows hung about the trees, thick as years-old cobwebs. Hawley felt about for his sword, found it, put his back against the nearest tree. Hawley's eyes scanned the forest for any sign of movement. He glanced down at Nedley's decapitated body. He looked to Tarbert, lying in a foetal curl near the dead man, gibbering in terror.

"*Psst!*" Ianto's pale face popped around the trunk of a pine. "Over here."

Hawley saw no sign of Nedley's killer. He heard nothing but his own heartbeat drumming in his ears, and Tarbert's sobs.

Ianto beckoned.

Hawley took a breath. He stepped away from the tree, and was about to hurry to Ianto, but he paused. Morgard's words sprang unbidden into his mind once again.

Show them what compassion means.

"Damn you, old man," Hawley muttered.

He hoisted Tarbert to his feet and dragged him along by the arm. Tarbert's legs worked automatically, but his expression suggested he had no idea where he was or what was happening. A lifetime of military training, all that "good breeding" the Third boasted of, snapped like a twig in the face of an unknown enemy.

They reached Ianto's position and ducked down behind the tree.

"What was it?" Hawley whispered. "Did you see it?"

Ianto shook his head. "The sky went dark. *Something* came from the trees, over there. Something big. Next I knew, Nedley was dead and Tarbert was screaming like a girl."

"A bear?"

"Has to be," Ianto said. "Unless..."

"Don't bloody say it," Hawley snapped. "That old woman has driven you all mad."

"It...it's you..." Tarbert whimpered. He pulled away from Hawley's grasp, eyes wide, suddenly lucid. He stepped away, staggering backwards, arm outstretched, pointing accusingly at Hawley. "She said...they'd be drawn to you! *Awearg.* Awearg!"

A chill wind whispered through the forest. The trees bent and creaked.

Tarbert stepped backwards into darkness, shadows enveloping him.

Then came the roar. A hulking, black mass whisked Tarbert away into the shadows. One moment he'd been standing there, pointing; the next, he was gone.

Hawley gaped into the darkness. Then came a distant scream. It was unmistakably Tarbert, but it seemed so far away.

"We need to get out of these woods," Ianto said.

Hawley wanted more than anything to agree. But something

stirred within him, some memory of a dark time in a town square, where innocents had died, and Hawley had left his men to meet a grisly fate. Before he had thought it through, he found himself saying, "Not without Tarbert."

"He tried to kill you. You forgotten already?"

"No, I haven't." Hawley shoved Ianto hard into the tree and looked him in the eyes. "Beacher and Nedley can rot. I'd've killed 'em myself given half a chance. Tarbert's a simpleton—he's only in the bloody army because his father was, and *his* father before him. He's not beyond saving. And you, Ianto...you stood by and watched. You're shit on my shoe. But I'm your sargent, and that means you're in my charge, just like Tarbert."

"He's dead," Ianto hissed. "If we stay, we'll be dead, too." Ianto wasn't smiling now, but there was something immensely unsettling about his expression. Like he knew something Hawley didn't.

"What's out there is a beast. It's no match for men of the Third."

"I haven't even been two months in the Third. I owe them even less than you, and I owe Tarbert less than that."

Another scream. Whatever had taken Tarbert wasn't rushing into the kill this time. Hawley couldn't shake the notion that it was using the man as bait. But what kind of bear could think like that?

"I'm giving you an order." Hawley pushed Ianto into the dark clearing. "It came from over there. You go first."

The smirk returned to Ianto's thin lips. He drew his dagger, turned, and ran into the shadows.

Hawley followed, struggling at first, clutching his wound. He gritted his teeth and picked up the pace.

Soon the two soldiers were racing through the forest, branches whipping at their faces, mud sucking at their feet, ragged breaths misting on cold air.

Streaks of weak grey sunlight filtered into a small clearing ahead, giving the woods the aspect of a sombre temple.

"They can't have gone much farther," Ianto panted.

Hawley doubled over with a stitch.

A fat raindrop sploshed upon Hawley's brow. Another rainstorm? That was all they needed. He wiped it away, and another came. Then another. A tangy iron scent reached his nostrils. Hawley held his hand to the light, and saw dark stains on his leather gauntlet.

"Ianto…" Hawley looked up into the trees.

Ianto followed Hawley's gaze.

Tarbert was in the tree, some twenty feet up. A sharp branch protruded from his chest, glistening with blood, which dripped to the ground in scattered droplets. Hawley wiped his face again, realising dumbly he was smearing Tarbert's blood on himself.

"Now can we get out of here?" Ianto was already backing away.

Hawley nodded. He couldn't take his eyes from Tarbert's body. What could have done that to a man? And why?

A guttural roar tore through the silent woods with the violence of claws through flesh. The pounding feet of some great beast shook the earth. Branches cracked and dirt flew. The creature circled them, swiftly, keeping beyond the tree line, beyond the light.

Ianto cursed. He held out a strange, iron dagger meekly.

"Where's your sword?" Hawley hissed.

"Lost it, didn't I?"

"Here." Hawley drew his shortsword, held it out hilt first. Ianto gave an appreciative nod and reached out for the sword.

The roar was deafening. A great mass swept Ianto from his feet and barrelled Hawley to the ground with the force of an avalanche. Ianto cursed at the top of his lungs, his dagger glinted in the half-light, rising and falling. The beast shook him violently from side to side.

Hawley was on his feet now, staggering towards the vast black shape, sword hoisted high. He swept it in a vast arc. It hit flesh, bit deep. The creature's roar became a howl, throaty and high. Ianto fell to the ground. A huge black paw struck Hawley in the chest. He felt the ground vanish, the air whistle past his ears.

Only when he hit the ground did he feel the pain in his chest. Agony. A broken rib, maybe a few.

"Help!" Ianto's voice was thin and shrill.

Hawley pushed through the pain. He couldn't see much, and what he could see was double. He stumbled in the direction of the cries, sword digging a furrow in soft loam as he dragged it along, every step sending shooting pains through his body. He saw Ianto through blurred vision, struggling against the beast. It was almost formless in the unnatural dark, like a thing of shadow. It had to be a bear. Hawley kept telling himself that, muttering it under his breath. He would accept no other explanation, or he may as well turn tail and flee right now.

He drew near. He could have sworn Ianto had ceased his struggles and was speaking to the creature in a low voice. It sounded like, "Why? This was not..."

With one almighty roar, the great shadow lifted Ianto high. His legs kicked air like a hanged man's jig.

Ianto's eyes met Hawley's. "Sargent..." he said. His dagger dropped. His eyes went glassy.

The beast tore Ianto in half. Blood cascaded to the ground.

Hawley wanted to run, but his legs betrayed him. The creature turned and sprang.

A great weight pressed down upon him. Hawley's sword-arm was pinned. Dank, wet fur smothered his face.

Fur! It *was* a beast. It breathed, it lived. It could die.

Rancid breath blasted Hawley's face. The gleam of yellow eyes flashed from indiscernible features. Thick drool matted Hawley's beard.

He turned his face away, teeth gritted, disgusted more by his failing strength than by the vile beast. And there in the mud lay Ianto's dagger. The blade was dulled with dirt and blood, but the hilt was traced with strange patterns, sigils, picked out in white, and these shone faintly in the weak light.

Sharp claws pricked at Hawley's cheek. The beast was toying with him, savouring the final kill.

Hawley's fingers touched the dagger. They curled around the

hilt, gripped it tightly. He thrust the blade upwards as hard as he could. It punched through tough hide and into soft tissue. He withdrew the dagger as the creature's ear-piercing roar filled the air, then stabbed again, and again. He was roaring, too. The weight lifted from him. Hawley leapt to his feet, his blood pumping, giving alacrity to limbs that had been weak and leaden moments ago. He lashed out in wild, sweeping arcs, dagger in one hand, heavy sword in the other. He felt the sword point tear into something, heard another roar. He paused, strength almost expended. The beast had retreated a few yards and now crouched into a great blackness.

Hawley sensed its muscles twitch and tense. As soon as he broke, it would give chase. Hawley knew it could catch him and kill him, like it had killed the others. He also knew he had no choice.

Hawley turned and ran.

The ground shook behind him as he leapt through the undergrowth. The grunts of the beast and the noise of its thunderous feet pounding the dirt spurred Hawley on like a devil was at his back.

A true devil. *Riftborn.*

No. He couldn't think about that, about anything. Hawley poured all his energy into his flight. He ran until his legs burned and his breaths came in sharp gasps. Thorns tore at his clothes, like the forest itself was trying to hold him back. Several times he almost tumbled down hidden defiles, and scrambled up the other side as foul breath plumed against his neck. He did not—could not—look back. To hesitate was to die.

He ducked beneath a low branch, heard a growl. The pounding footfalls receded for just a moment, then it was on him again, rancid breath upon the back of his neck. Something clipped his heels. Hawley tumbled, rolled, dived aside as a black shadow almost enveloped him entirely. He felt matted fur brush his face, smelled the odour of dead leaves and stale piss.

The ground disappeared from under him. The forest spun as Hawley tumbled down a steep bank. He grabbed at roots and bushes to slow the fall. He tried to dig his heels into the dirt, but it was nothing but mud, sliding down the hillside like melting wax. Hawley fell.

He hit solid ground with a jolt. There was daylight in the distance. Beneath Hawley's feet a path wound away towards the light—another holloway, deeper and older than the last. And it led to the edge of the forest.

Above him, a pair of yellow eyes gleamed from thick, black shadows. Hawley looked along the path—the way out—then back at the creature. Its eyes darted to the light and back to Hawley. It moved swiftly along the ridge, knocking branches and rocks down the hillside as it went. It was trying to cut him off.

Hawley urged himself on. He stumbled towards the light. His breaths tore their way in and out of his lungs. Now he saw past the hazy light ahead, to distant hills and rain-filled sky, to a world beyond the Elderwood. So close now. He didn't know why the thought of an open road gave him any comfort. The beast could just as easily tear off his head out there as in here. But it would not venture into the light. Somehow, he knew it. He *felt* it.

The trees thinned, the shadows lifted like a widow's veil, fresh air caressed Hawley's face.

Then the creature barrelled into Hawley, carrying him off his feet. He crunched against a tree. His head swam. He still had the knife. He gripped it as tight as he could, out of sheer desperation. The creature was on him now. Drool dripped onto Hawley's face. The stench of putrid breath brought bile to his throat. Darkness clouded Hawley's mind. He felt consciousness fade. Perhaps not such a bad way to go. Perhaps he wouldn't feel a thing.

And then light. Such searing, white light that Hawley felt it rattle his every nerve. The creature roared, and that roar became a howl, then a fearful screech. The shadow was no more; there was only the light.

Only the light.

CHAPTER 4

Hawley blinked his vision clear. He lay staring up at a cracked ceiling, across which shadows danced by orange firelight. He watched the shapes chase each other, dumbly, until the memories crept into his head. Memories of dark woods. Of slaughtered soldiers and yellow-eyed monsters.

He jolted upwards, and pain flared across his ribs. Hawley gritted his teeth so as not to call out, and fell back down. Onto a bed. A straw-filled mattress cushioned his back. Fire warmed his skin. His ribs were bound tight; wet poultices bulged beneath neat linen dressings.

Slowly, a circular room came into focus. It was full of clutter: shelves, tables, barrels, cupboards, jars and bowls, stacks of books and rolls of parchment. The room smelled strongly of herbs, masking an underlying odour of soot. Somewhere behind him, fire logs crackled.

At last Hawley battled through the pain and turned his head to where a fire blazed within a great stone hearth. A cauldron hung over the flames, bubbling and steaming. And sitting beside it, stirring the pot, was a woman. Old Nell.

His heart beat faster. The men had called her a witch, hadn't they? Gods, and now they were dead. What was it she'd said? *Dark forces are at work here.* Very *dark*.

Hawley's eyes darted left and right, alighting at last on the bastard sword, leaning against the wall just out of reach. He pushed himself up on his elbows, every movement causing him to wince again.

"Hawley-Hawley-Hawley!"

The screech was so loud Hawley forgot his injuries and rolled out of bed, clattering to the floor in a heap. He spat a curse.

A raven peered down at him from a perch near the bedhead.

"Awake, are you?" the old woman said. "Good."

Her voice was stronger than before, though it still retained the grit of age. Almost entirely gone was the local accent, replaced with something almost cultured, like one from the cities of the east.

Hawley pushed through the pain and crawled to the sword. He grabbed the hilt, leather creaking reassuringly in his grip. He turned as quickly as he could, resting his back against the wall for support, and pushed himself to his feet on shaky legs.

Old Nell stood before him, watching with a bemused frown. In her hand she held only a ladle.

"Water?" she asked.

"What?" Hawley said. The dusty croak of his voice made him realise just how thirsty he was.

"Have no fret, Sargent," she said. "Back to bed with you, before you aggravate those injuries."

A hundred questions rattled around Hawley's head. He took a step forward and grunted as pain shot through his ribs again. His legs buckled. Before he could speak, the old woman was by his side. Somehow, with her on one side and the sword on the other, he hobbled to the bed and sat, all resistance drained from him.

"How did I get here?" Hawley asked.

The woman brought a ladle of water to Hawley's lips. "With difficulty," she said.

Hawley gulped the water down. "Were you...out there? In the woods?" he asked.

"I found you, if that's what you mean."

Hawley tensed. "Did you see...*it*?"

The woman turned her back on him and shuffled to the fireside. She was different somehow, less frail than Hawley recalled. But she was still slight, and very old. She surely couldn't have carried him back to the tower.

"What do you think I should have seen?"

"Dunno. I think...a bear?" Hawley tried to remember clearly what had happened, but the memories came in brief glimpses, then were snatched away like remnants of a dream.

"There are many strange beasts in the Elderwood," the woman said. "Beasts forgotten by the men of the south, perhaps. But beasts nonetheless."

"But you said—"

"That there are Riftborn in the Elderwood?" She sat, facing Hawley, and sighed. "I suppose I did. It was no lie—the Riftborn, after all, are everywhere, and yet nowhere. But they do not haunt the Elderwood. Not unless they are invited." She held up an object to the firelight, and fixed Hawley with a singular stare. "Did you invite them, Sargent Hawley?"

It was Ianto's dagger.

"What?" Hawley didn't know how else to respond.

"This is a *wunscæd*. A blade of covenant. Yours?"

"I...I don't..." Hawley's head hurt. "It belonged to Ianto." He grimaced as a vision of Ianto being torn in twain flashed into his mind's eye.

"The monk?"

"Once, I s'pose."

"And he was killed by the beast?"

Hawley nodded.

"Was he taken first or last?"

Hawley frowned. "Last. That is...I should've been last."

"Should you indeed?" She pursed her wrinkled lips thoughtfully. "Blades such as this are rare. It is old. At one time, during the war, they were used to bind powerful spirits to the mortal world."

"What...kind of spirits?"

"*Powerful* ones," she repeated.

The woman set the knife down, and Hawley looked at it warily.

"But as I say," she continued, her tone brightening all at once, "the blade is very old. And these are just stories told to frighten common folk...like yourself."

"You said the Riftborn attacked the merchant. That's why there were no bodies with the wagons."

"I suggested it as a possibility. You don't have to take everything so literally, Sargent. *Tsk.* What a life to lead, without imagination. No: The truth is, there were never any bandits. Your merchant was betrayed by his own men, and I imagine the blow to the head he received made his recollection somewhat hazy. Mercenaries, you see. Loyal to a fault...until they get a better offer."

Hawley rubbed at his aching head. "They double-crossed him, for the blackrock?"

"Worth a fortune, if you know the right buyer. If you think about it, it's a strange coincidence. You're the second person to come here of late, betrayed by his own people."

"How did you—?"

"Ah! The broth is ready." The old woman stood again, gave the pot one last stir, then cast about for some bowls.

Hawley's stomach grumbled loudly. He hadn't realised he was so hungry. Then he noticed something. His bruises had darkened and yellowed. Most of his cuts and scrapes were scabbed over.

"Wait a minute...How long have I been here?" he asked.

"Two days."

"Two days!" Hawley parroted. He tried to jump up, too quickly, immediately doubled over clutching his ribs, and sat down abruptly on the straw-filled mattress.

The raven squawked.

"Do not work yourself into a state, Sargent," the woman said. "You are on the mend, but only if you rest. Here: Eat."

She passed Hawley a bowl and spoon. The broth smelled good, but he stirred it suspiciously all the same.

"Parsnips, carrots, mushrooms...a few special ingredients to get you on the mend. I'm not trying to poison you."

Hawley took a mouthful. It was a little bland, but when he swallowed he felt warmth spread out from his stomach, across his chest, into his aching legs and arms. It felt good. He nodded thanks.

"There's somethin' different about you," he said between mouthfuls. "Nell, isn't it?"

"That's what the good folk of Godsrest call me—those who know of me. Old Nell."

"You're the Vigilant."

"What makes you say that?"

"When I were here last—when I mentioned the Vigilant's ring—you were very interested in it. I thought nothing of it at the time. But there's an impression on your finger, from a ring." He pointed to Nell's left hand, to the indentation on her forefinger. "You must've worn it a long time."

Slowly, the woman's wizened features softened, and then she smiled. "I take it back. You are no common soldier."

"So you did lie to us."

"Lying is an unbecoming habit," the woman snapped. "My name is Enelda Drake—'Old Nell' to some. I was a Vigilant once, but I have not trod that path for a long time."

"That's not what I've heard."

Enelda shrugged. "The oaths we swore were to the gods, and they were unbreakable. When the order was dissolved by King Ealwarth, the Vigilants chose exile, on pain of death. We went our separate ways, but few indeed could set aside the teachings of the elders...or the dangers brought by those teachings. And so I live out here, out of sight and out of mind."

"I thought Vigilants were supposed to help people in need. Isn't that part of your oath?"

"I suppose it is."

"You weren't so quick to help me," Hawley said sullenly.

"You're alive, aren't you?"

"I meant when you turned us away."

"If you recall, you and your men became so frightened by fairy tales that you never told me why you came. I determined that, if it was truly important, you would have persisted."

Hawley tried to remember exactly what had been said when he'd called at Enelda's door, but remembering hurt his head. He decided to forgo thinking, and instead slurped his broth. He considered what an opportunity he had missed earlier, and what misfortune he had brought upon himself by giving up too easily.

"Are you going to sulk all day, Sargent? Or are you going to tell me why you came here?"

"It's important, m'lady," Hawley said at last, adopting as deferential a tone as he could. "I should've tried harder, I know. But the journey had been...hard. And the men...How did you know they betrayed me?"

"I observed all I needed when you came to my door. They took the blood pact." She must have noted Hawley's surprise. "You are surprised I know of the High Companies' little rituals, yes? You've heard of it, but you know not what it means, because you are not of the Blood. Let me tell you what I saw: three men of the Blood, at least one with a cut on his left hand, drawn by the ritual daggers they carried sheathed at their sides, but which apparently you hadn't noticed. They had made a ritual promise to 'cut the diseased bough from the tree.' A polite way of saying assassinate one of their own. It had to be you—they called you 'awearg,' and obviously held great animosity toward you.

"The monkish one was the complicating factor. From the way he exchanged looks with the others, he was clearly complicit, but he wore no gauntlets, so I could see his hand was not cut. The way he rubbed that reliquary of his made me think his soul was promised to a higher power. If he had taken holy orders, he would not be permitted to swear a blood oath, even if the others allowed it."

"Bloody hell," Hawley muttered under his breath. Then, quickly, "Sorry." He slurped the last of his stew and wiped his mouth with the back of his hand. Enelda took his bowl and shuffled off to refill it.

"I was sent lookin' for a Vigilant, because a child's gone missing," Hawley said. "Nobody can find him."

"Children go missing all the time," Enelda said without turning around.

"Not ones like this. He's Anton Tarasq, the son of General Tarasq of Sylverain, a hostage at the castle of Lord Scarsdale."

"Ah." Enelda came back to Hawley's bedside and handed him a fresh bowl of stew and a hunk of bread. "They still exchange hostages, after all this time?"

"It's the only way to secure peace."

"Is it working?"

Hawley shrugged. "It was. More or less."

"How did it happen? The child, I mean. How was he taken?"

"Nobody knows," Hawley said, dipping up his broth. "It was in the dead of night. His bed was found empty one morning."

"Did he run away? Back home?"

"They don't think so, m'lady. The boy is barely ten years old, he couldn't have gone far. There were no horses missing, and the castle is well guarded."

"Which castle?"

"Scarfell."

"A veritable fortress," Enelda muttered.

"You know it?"

"I was there once, a long time ago. It was home to Lady Aenya, the Warrior Maid."

"I've heard of her," Hawley said. "I don't think they call her that any more. Not since women were forbidden from fighting, by order of the king."

"Ah," Enelda said again. There was something rather disapproving in her look; whether it was for the king or his decree, Hawley couldn't tell. "It must have been a skilled intruder indeed who could steal into that castle and kidnap a child without raising a hue and cry."

"That's why we were sent here...to find a legendary Vigilant. You."

"Do not flatter me, young man, I have no time for it. And that is *not* why you were sent."

"Beg pardon, m'lady?"

"You were sent to keep up appearances. How long did it take you to find me? Ten days? Twelve? And during that time, we must presume Archduke Leoric has been searching for the boy? He cannot expect to find him, or he would not have settled on such an unorthodox course of action. Yet he must be seen to be doing *something*, because if the boy is not found, this Tarasq fellow might very well provoke a war, isn't that right?"

"*War!*" Barty shrieked.

"Tarasq is a woman," Hawley said.

"Really?" Enelda arched an eyebrow. "I wonder how your king reconciles that fact with his little decrees?"

"I...um..." Hawley faltered. Disrespecting the king was punishable by ten lashes. A punishment Hawley himself had administered, under orders. And yet here stood this old woman, fearless. Or ignorant of the king's reputation.

"Lord Scarsdale is trying to buy time, though for what end who can tell?" Enelda said. "After all, he cannot honestly expect to find a Vigilant."

"But...we have. Found a Vigilant, I mean."

Enelda smiled. "Yes, I suppose you have. But it is no good."

"Eh?"

"I cannot go with you, and even if I did, there would be little point. Most likely the abductor is a member of Lord Scarsdale's own household. That's usually the way of it."

"Impossible," Hawley said, glancing around as though the archduke himself might materialise from the very stones of the tower and seize them both for treason.

"It is logic," Enelda snapped. "If Lord Scarsdale cannot or will not do what is required, then he shall have to suffer the consequences. He doesn't need me to tell him that."

"Why not come with me and see for yourself?"

"Because I prefer to stay well clear of politics, and even further clear of children. This little mystery of yours seems to include a good deal of both."

"My lady, I'm afraid you misunderstand. Now that I've found you...you must come with me to Fangmoor. You have no choice."

Enelda stood abruptly, her expression darkening like the arrival of a sudden storm at sea. Hawley leaned back as far as he could, at once reminded of the reputation of the old Vigilants.

"I live as far from ordinary folk as I can for a reason," she said. "Your men believed you cursed. 'Awearg,' they called you. An old word. A powerful word. But in your case somewhat misplaced, I think. If you were burdened with my knowledge, Sargent Hawley, you would know what it means to be cursed. It is safer if I remain here."

"Safer? Who for? You? Not for them missin' children!" Hawley felt his colour rise. His anger gave him strength and courage. It always had. It was how he'd stayed alive this long. It was also the root cause of his misfortunes.

The storm passed. And was replaced by something else. A deep, aching sadness behind Enelda's sharp old eyes.

"At last, the truth," she said, shaking her head slowly. "*Children*. Not one child, but several. You did not say that before. Why not?"

"Because...my orders start and end with Anton Tarasq. That's my duty."

"*Fie!* Let me tell you one thing very clearly, Sargent. In the unlikely event that I spend any longer in your company than absolutely necessary, I require two things: facts, and truth. Without those things, I cannot help you. Without those things, I am just an old woman. But, armed with facts and truth, I am the most powerful woman you will ever meet. Armed with facts and truth, I can slay dragons, topple kingdoms, and return missing children to the loving embrace of their warmongering parents."

"*Dragons?*" Hawley whispered.

Enelda rolled her eyes. "Now, start again. You were sent here because of Tarasq's son. Because such a child might be considered more important than other children."

"That's why I was sent, but it's not why I'm here, if you take my meaning."

"You will have to spell it out for an old woman."

Hawley sighed. "You said yourself—children go missing all the time. If them bairns are serfs, nobody bats an eyelid, 'cept for the parents. And nobody listens to them. But for the past few years, somethin' strange has been afoot in Wulfshael. All the villages of the south have seen more than their fair share of bairns go astray. And it's getting worse. Just days before the Sylven lad vanished, a girl was taken from the village of Rowen. What's worse, the local Vigilant was in the village at the time."

"The new Vigilants," Enelda said disapprovingly. "Yes, I've heard of those."

"He investigated, but when no trace of the girl was found, he decided the culprits lay closer to home. Said the girl must've been taken for a dark purpose. He accused the villagers of witchcraft."

"Of course he did. And what happened?"

Hawley winced at the memory. "He arrested the girl's aunt. And...had her drowned in the river."

Enelda spun about and began to pace the room. She muttered something under her breath. Her hands twitched, her thumb tapping each of her fingers in turn, as though counting.

At last she stopped. "How many other children have gone missing under similar circumstances?"

"This year? Five that I know of."

"This year has barely begun."

"Like I said...it's getting worse."

"And last year?"

"Eight...Nine? I don't hear as much as I'd like, but I listen out for what I can."

"And why do you hear of it at all? How does a soldier of the High Companies remain so well-informed of the crimes outside his fort? And why, for that matter, were you sent instead of Lord Scarsdale's men?"

"The Third Company has sworn for the Vigilants. The, eh, *new* Vigilants, that is," he added quickly. "We help them keep the peace, time to time. Hobb is the first High Companies commander to recognise the Vigilants as wielding the absolute sanctity of the king's law."

Enelda arched a silver eyebrow. "Is he? What's in it for him?"

"M'lady?"

"Men do not give up even an ounce of power unless they are playing for a greater prize."

Hawley shrugged. He only knew Morgard had never trusted the new Vigilants. Hawley had simply assumed Hobb was dismantling the old man's legacy out of spite. Hawley was part of that legacy.

"And why *you*?" Enelda pressed. "Your men took a solemn oath to slay you, which means they were following orders. Commander Hobb's orders, most like. So why would he send you on such an important mission?"

"How do you—?" Hawley began.

"Answer the question."

Hawley hung his head. He stared into his stew, but found no answers there. At last he said, "Because you're right. Nobody at Fangmoor believed we'd succeed. But so far from home, in these woods, I s'pose a man might meet with all kinds of accidents. I thought it was a fool's errand...just another insult in a long line. Turns out it was something more."

"What was it Ianto called you? The 'Butcher of Herigsburg'?"

"Don't—!" Hawley quickly checked his temper. He felt Enelda's cool eyes scrutinising him intently. A piercing, inquisitorial gaze that he somehow knew would detect any whiff of a lie. "I... Look, it's just another insult. I don't like talkin' about it."

"You see, I knew what kind of men they were as soon as I set eyes on them. The only thing I could not tell is what kind of man *you* are, Sargent Hawley. And I am still not entirely sure."

"There's nothin' complicated about me."

"*Pish!* A low-born man, fighting in an elite regiment, for a commander who despises him. A man of honour and duty, and one who cares more for the lives of peasant girls than he does for his fellow soldiers. Your ordeal in the woods has troubled you, as it would trouble anyone. But the pain in your eyes when you spoke of that girl from Rowen...that was real. And yet, despite your rough talk and rougher appearance...despite the many scars you bear, and the marks of past floggings upon your back"—at this Hawley fidgeted uncomfortably—"you still talk like an officer. You still put faith in the regulations and customs of a regiment that will never accept you, because you are not of the Blood. How many times have you scratched your beard since you woke up? I'll tell you: seventeen times. That tells me you are unaccustomed to it. You grow it while on campaign, as is tradition, but now you are already thinking about returning to barracks and shaving it off. You would still return to barracks knowing that your comrades—and your commander—would see you dead."

Hawley had been about to scratch his beard and paused mid-motion. "I...I've nowhere else to go. Maybe I can explain things to Commander Hobb. He'll blame me for the deaths of my men..." Hawley paused. He'd been about to say "again," but realised that really did make him sound cursed.

"You talked a lot in your feverishness," Enelda said. "You mentioned Hobb more than once. And another name...Jon Gale. Who is he? Another soldier?"

Every muscle in Hawley's body tensed. Memories began to surface, memories of death and destruction. Of broken promises and decisions that had cast a long shadow over Hawley's life. Guilt knotted his stomach.

All he said was, "Nobody. Just someone I used to know."

"Nobody indeed. Yet the name haunts you in your darkest moments."

"Anyway," Hawley said hastily, "maybe Hobb will change his opinion of me when he sees you. Maybe he'll see the truth of it."

"Me? Oh no, I am not going to Fort Fangmoor."

"But...you said..."

"I intimated I could help, and mayhap I can. But there's little point in travelling all the way to see this Hobb character, and thence to Scarfell, where courtly men will bow and scrape and attempt to deceive me. Remember, they do not really want me there. They don't truly believe I exist. If they did, they would not have sent four motley assassins and a cursed sargent. No offence intended."

"None taken."

Enelda took Hawley's bowl away once more. "Getting cold," she said. She ladled in some more broth from the cauldron and thrust the bowl back into Hawley's hands. "Where is Rowen?" she asked.

"It lies beside the Wulfswater, a half-day's ride north of Scarfell. Six days on foot from here." Hawley looked the diminutive old woman up and down, cleared his throat, and corrected, "Nine days."

"We won't be on foot. I presume you left your wagon at Godsrest."

"How did you—? Never mind. We aren't going to Rowen, m'lady."

"There is no better place to start."

"But...without Hobb's sanction, I have no authority."

"*Pish!* Your commander wants you dead, and the word of an old woman will not change his mind. Your best hope is to have me accepted in Lord Scarsdale's court, that I might reclaim my ring and prove I was once a Vigilant. Without that, I very much doubt you will survive a day in Fort Fangmoor once it is discovered your men are dead."

Hawley looked at her in dismay. He felt very much like a fish on a hook.

"You shall escort me to Rowen," Enelda declared, "or leave here alone."

"My lady..." Hawley wanted to protest, but he did not have the words.

"I shall make it easier for you, Sargent," Enelda said. "Your company has sworn for the Vigilants. You swore to find me. So it is your duty to assist me in what way you can, correct?"

"I...Yes, I s'pose." He was on uncertain ground. The woman was ignoring the small matter of him disobeying Hobb's orders.

"And if I were in any way endangered, you would be honour bound to protect me, correct?"

"Aye, of course." This he was surer of.

"Then upon your honour, Sargent Hawley, swear an oath to me. An oath in sight of the gods, to protect me wherever I should go, until such time as I am returned safely home."

"I..." Hawley didn't know what to say. She made it sound

simple, and yet to Hawley an oath was a solemn thing. Swearing it would bring him further into conflict with Hobb. Not swearing it would likely mean the woman would refuse to help him, and he'd fail in his mission.

"Swear it," she said more forcefully.

Hawley relented, and struggled to take a knee.

"Don't kneel," Enelda interjected. "You'll do yourself a mischief. Just say the words."

Hawley rubbed at his face. "My lady, upon my honour, I swear to protect you."

"Wherever I may go?"

"Wherever you may go."

"Swear it by the gods."

"I swear."

"Swear it by the Three."

"All right, all right...I swear! My sword is yours."

"Very well. But not today." She turned her back on him and waved her hand dismissively.

"What?"

"You need to rest. Now finish your stew and get some sleep. I've never known a soldier talk so much."

CHAPTER 5

As travelling companions went, Hawley had suffered worse, though none stranger.

Enelda Drake was a mine of information, and as the wagon rumbled along dirt lanes and drove ways for hour after hour, the old woman would announce facts about every tree and shrub, every bird and insect, the formations of the clouds, the ancient names of landmarks from the time before Redemption. She knew precisely how much rain had fallen that day by the amount the wagon's wheels sank in the mud. When they passed the tracks of horses, Enelda would proclaim how many hands high the beasts must have been, how recently they had passed, and how far they'd travelled, not to mention the probable weight and skill of the riders. At night she would point to the stars and name the constellations. She would know the next day's weather from the smell of the wind and the shape of the clouds. Her knowledge of herbalism, history, and theology was astounding, though for Hawley much of what she said on these scholarly topics went in one ear and out the other. Sometimes she spoke with an almost childlike passion; other times she would simply recite facts dully, as though she had committed to memory entire passages of a book.

In the back of the wagon, Barty travelled mostly in his cage, though sometimes Enelda allowed him to fly free. He always came back. Behind the wagon, Baelsine plodded dutifully on a tether. Gereth had kept his promise, and now Tarbert's horse was in rude health. Better than Hawley, at any rate.

When they made camp, Hawley would go hunting, and was not always successful. He'd never been the best marksman in his troop, but now—even though Enelda's remedies had worked wonders on his injuries—just pulling back the bowstring was a labour. When he returned to camp empty-handed, he would find Enelda already cooking up a stew with her hoarded vegetables, complemented with freshly foraged mushrooms, horse-parsley, nettle, and sorrel.

For the most part he worried only when Enelda fell quiet, whereupon she would spend hours at a time staring at nothing, muttering to herself. Her fingers would twitch, tapping upon her thumbs as they had back at the tower, counting out a rhythm the purpose of which only she knew. In the rare event that they encountered a fellow traveller on the road, Enelda would fall quiet as the grave, refusing to so much as greet the stranger, yet all the while watching, observing.

Enelda Drake was nothing at all like the Vigilants Hawley had pictured in his mind.

On the afternoon of the fifth day they finally emerged from wooded terrain and were greeted by the sight of long, sloping strips of waterlogged farmland. Atop the slopes, a huddled collection of hovels stood like crooked teeth against a dun sky, smoke drifting idly from uneven chimneys.

"Finally," Hawley said with some relief. "If I'm right, we're almost at the Halgian Valley."

"Your bearings are right," Enelda said. There was an odd look in her eyes, but she had proven such a strange woman that Hawley shrugged it off.

"We'll be in Eastmere before dark. I'll secure beds for the night, then tomorrow we'll go on to Rowen—"

"No."

"No?"

"We shan't stay in Eastmere. We will take the less-travelled path around the lakes."

Hawley was tired, wet, aching all over, and thoroughly sick of the old woman's broth. He wanted fresh bread in his belly, some salted meat—of any kind but squirrel, which he could not abide—and a good night's rest in a warm, dry bed. He'd even entertained thoughts of a bath.

"Eastmere is where the ore merchant was found," Hawley said. "I thought you'd find that interesting."

"I do," she said. "Insofar as he told me he was travelling directly to Helmspire, and this town lies far from his route. That he lied about his destination proves only that his dealings were not legitimate, but it has nothing to do with why we're here."

"No?" Hawley said again, starting to feel quite stupid as Enelda adopted a patient tone.

"You are thinking of the ring. But both the merchant and the people who acquired the ring from him are surely long gone. What's important is that Lord Scarsdale now has it, and I imagine we will see him in good time."

"And the blackrock?"

"In the old days I might have pursued this wayward merchant across the country to find out where he was taking his contraband, but I left my home to find missing children, not a peddler in prohibited ore. Tell me, is there a garrison at Eastmere?"

"A militia... Sometimes the Fourth Company patrols there."

"And what if we were to encounter the Fourth?"

"I'd tell 'em to mind their business," Hawley said, though he couldn't keep the uncertainty from his voice.

"Let me tell you how precarious your situation is. If we go into town and start asking questions, we will attract the attention of the authorities. They will want to know what we are doing and why. They will discover who I am... or rather, was... and a chain of events will unfold that neither of us can control. Eventually you will have to reveal what happened to your men. Word will be sent to Fort Fangmoor, and your fate will rest in the hands of Commander Hobb. I will be whisked away to Scarfell without ever seeing the village of Rowen. An opportunity to see things for myself, without hindrance or interference from these new Vigilants, will be lost. But all of that pales in comparison, Sargent, to the true danger posed by Eastmere."

"What danger?" Hawley grew agitated, mainly because the woman was right, and he could feel the promise of a comfortable bed slipping away. But he failed to see how anything could be worse than what she had just described.

"Stop the wagon," Enelda commanded. "This instant!"

Hawley reined in the horses.

Enelda was shaking. "Do you really want to know the dangers I face? Are you ready to know?"

"Aye. I want to know if I'm like to meet some dark fate due to your...powers."

"Powers? You mean the power to read men's thoughts and commune with the dead? You mean...*necromancy*?"

Hawley spluttered.

"*Pish!*" Enelda scoffed. "Vigilants do not practise the dark arts. Let the Sylvens and Felders chase those secrets to the grave. Our skills are more mundane. Deliberately so. We watch, we listen. We *observe*. And from our observations, we glean details others would overlook. And we do this not merely because we are trained to do so, but because we must. We must be ever watchful if we are to survive. We must...be...*vigilant*."

Hawley felt immensely uncomfortable under the woman's unflinching gaze, but still his curiosity got the better of him. "What d'you mean, 'must'?"

"Through ritual and mental discipline, a Vigilant learns not only to see more keenly, and intuit truth from the merest trifle, but also to truly *see*. See beyond the mortal realm and into the realm beyond."

Hawley frowned. "You mean...ghosts?"

"Sometimes. And other things, too. You know of what I speak."

Hawley shuddered. He managed to nod understanding.

"The problem with seeing *them*, Hawley, is that they have an annoying tendency to see you right back. And when they see you...well, that's when you are in real danger. An unprepared mind is like an open castle gate, and the Riftborn a besieging enemy. The Riftborn use mortals for all manner of reasons, none of them good. And if they were to take possession of a Vigilant, with all of our 'powers,' can you imagine what horrors they would visit upon the world?"

"Thought you said you had no powers."

"I said no such thing, and your rather dim capacity for recalling details means you would make a poor Vigilant indeed. Be thankful. The Riftborn rarely trouble the unimaginative."

"And so...what? You spend all day staring at the walls? I don't understand." Enelda's insult had not been lost on Hawley, and his temper raised its ugly head once again.

"No," Enelda said firmly but patiently. "The Riftborn are drawn to people, and to conflict, but often they are powerless to break through the veil into our world. A Vigilant might provide the means for them to succeed, but only when there are weaker minds around to sate their appetites and act like stepping stones to one such as me. When I am alone, I can know peace. Otherwise, I must focus all my efforts on filling my mind with details, the less interesting the better. A full mind allows no space for the demon to inhabit. An empty mind is a vessel into which darkness may be poured. Do you understand?"

"I think so," Hawley said.

"If we go to Eastmere, simple-minded fools and petty councilmen will come to gawp at the silly old woman calling herself 'Vigilant.' And when they do, the Riftborn will see me. They will see Enelda Drake, out of hiding at last. And through the feeble-minded mob, they will attempt to corrupt me. That is the danger I must face, and I must face it alone."

Enelda seemed so earnest that Hawley checked himself.

"With all due respect, when you agreed to help me, you knew it would involve meeting other people." Hawley could not hide his frustration. "Village, castle, town...sooner or later you will have to face them. Might as well get it over with."

"No!" Enelda's reply was so sharp, so angry, that Hawley was taken aback. She turned from him. "I...I am not ready!"

For a split second she had betrayed her emotions, and Hawley had recognised that look in her eyes. She was afraid.

He thought of the thing that had killed his men. What if it hadn't been a bear? What if it was something more ancient, more evil? Was that what the old woman feared?

Enelda gazed up at the row of shacks absently. She trembled. She looked frail and old again, like when they had first met, and it dawned on Hawley just what was happening. Enelda claimed she carried a great burden. Likely that was true. She'd locked herself away so long from the world that she was fearful of everything. On the journey, she'd chattered on about the trees and birds and weather because it made her feel better about being outdoors. It gave her a feeling of control. Hawley could understand that. How many times had he tried to rationalise the actions of the men who loathed him so he could work out how to rise above them? When the whole world seems against you, even the sound of your own voice could be a balm against fear. If you didn't take control, you'd go...mad.

He looked at the woman's shaky hands. Her fingers began tapping against her thumbs in sequence.

She's mad. Just a little. Maybe a lot...

"Very well," Hawley said at last. He kept his concerns to himself, though he was not yet convinced she couldn't actually read his thoughts. "But can we at least go up to them farms? The horses need fresh feed, and I'd give anything for a bit of meat and bread. Dead soldiers' rations and a barrel of parsnips can only go so far."

Enelda's fingers stopped twitching. In a more confident manner she said, "I will wait here. I...I will be ready by the time we reach Rowen."

You'd better be, Hawley thought. *If I present a madwoman to the archduke and call her a Vigilant, he'll be more likely to hang me than Commander Hobb.*

He said none of this. Instead, Hawley alighted from the wagon, grabbed an empty sack, and started up the slope.

"Sargent Hawley," Enelda called. She sounded suddenly cheery, like all was forgotten.

"Yes?"

"Ask if they have any eggs. I like eggs."

* * *

Hallowmere
Feorndaeg, 1st Day of Nystamand

A chill wind blew in over the vast, black expanse of the lake. They were exposed to the elements here, but relatively safe. No outlaws would come so close to town, and no militiaman would challenge them once they saw Hawley's uniform. Yet still Hawley could not rest.

He oiled and cleaned his armour, keeping the mechanism of his sprung shield in perfect condition. Its manufacture was a secret long lost to company smiths, its value best not dwelt on. He sharpened his sword, not that the Felder steel needed much maintenance—it was the finest steel in all the ancient nations of Erevale, and held an edge like no other. But he conducted the tasks anyway, to busy his mind.

Because whenever he closed his eyes, a hulking black shadow bore down upon him. Yellow eyes, sharp fangs. He saw his men torn apart by massive claws. He saw Ianto hoisted high into a tree. He heard Ianto speak to the creature.

"*This was not…*" he'd said.

Not *what*?

In the dreams, sometimes he heard, "*This was not the promise made.*"

Hawley muttered those words as he stared into the campfire. "This was not the promise made."

"What promise?"

Hawley started. His hand was on the hilt of his sword before he saw Enelda shuffle into the firelight.

"My lady," he said, embarrassed.

"Please stop calling me that." She smoothed a blanket across a small boulder and lowered herself upon it. Her knees cracked.

"You couldn't sleep either?"

"I cannot decide if you are incredibly alert or incredibly nervous. Does something trouble you?"

Always answering a question with another question. Hawley

sighed. He knew she was fearful of the morrow, when they'd reach Rowen at last, and she'd have to face ordinary folk. But naturally, she avoided the matter.

"I was thinking about Ianto," he said. "The monk. I think they were his last words."

"You think?"

"It comes to me in...in dreams." He felt very foolish.

"We should pay more attention to dreams. Dreams are not sent from without. Not usually. They come from memory. Not always reliable, true, but sometimes. What happens next? In the dream?"

Hawley shuddered. "Ianto dies," he said. But that was not quite the truth. In the dream, if he listened very carefully, straining his ears beyond the sound of his own heart thumping within his chest, Hawley always swore he heard the shadow reply. He didn't know—nor did he want to know—what it said.

Enelda stared at Hawley as if she knew he was withholding something.

"We've been lucky not to meet any bandits on our travels," Hawley said, grasping for something to say so as not to speak further of nightmares. "I keep watch so's our luck might hold."

"And if I were a bandit, only two paces from you, would you be able to draw that heavy blade and hew me down before I knifed you in the back?"

Hawley rolled his shoulders indignantly. "You'd be surprised."

"I most certainly would. Sargent Hawley, I said I would not ask about your past, but I have made one observation..."

"Oh?"

"That ridiculous sword is the weapon of a Felder foot knight. A knight of the inner circle, no less. The runes on the blade read 'Godspeaker's Oath' in Old Felder."

"Godspeaker, aye. That's the sword's name. It sends foes to meet their gods."

"Not quite." Enelda smiled. "A Godspeaker is a type of priest in the old Felder tradition, who officiates over trials by combat. Upon a Godspeaker's oath are combatants said to be fairly matched. And it is the Godspeaker who advocates for the soul of the defeated duellist before the gods, if they fought bravely. That sword is intended to be drawn only against worthy opponents."

Hawley squirmed awkwardly, remembering the number of decidedly unworthy foes he'd hacked down with the sword. One in particular, long ago—not duelled, but executed. A deed that had cursed him. A deed that haunted him still.

"What I find interesting," Enelda went on, "is the number of inner-circle knights to fall in battle in the last century can be counted on the fingers of one hand. Despite your size and strength, I don't believe even you could best one if it came to it. Besides, Aelderland has not seen war with Reikenfeld since before you were born, so you could not have acquired it in battle. The sword's value is more than a sargent could earn in a tenyear, and as you were raised up from commoners, you could have no fortune with which to buy it. So . . . either it was given to you or you stole it. Probability dictates the latter."

"I'm no thief!" Hawley's temper flared. He had done well to keep it in check these past days, but gods knew, Enelda Drake could be trying.

"A gift, then?" the woman persisted.

Hawley nodded. "From a great man. Commander Morgard."

"I know that name," Enelda said. "When I . . . made my home in the Elderwood . . . the war against Reikenfeld had recently ended. I heard stories of a certain Lucas Morgard, who earned promotion at the Battle of Aeflund Field."

Hawley nodded. Enelda's reticence wasn't lost on him. When had she gone to that tower? The war against the Felders had ended four decades ago. Where had she been in the interim, between the two wars, with her order disbanded? He said only, "That's him. You spoke of size and strength—Morgard weren't as big as me, yet he slew two Felder foot knights, and turned the tide that day. They say he fought like a Majestic."

"Oh, I doubt that. He was a great warrior, I am sure, but Majestics are something entirely different."

Hawley gaped in disbelief. "You're saying Majestics are... real?"

"Are you saying you believe in devils but not in angels? What a strange man you are."

"You've *seen* them? The Majestics?"

"No one has seen them; leastways not in this world. Majestics do not so much appear as... *inhabit* people. They come to the world on invisible wings, and find hosts worthy of the gods' blessings. And with a Majestic at the reins, men can do great things. Glorious things. Dangerous things."

"But you've never *seen* one?" Hawley asked again, incredulous.

"If you see one—*really* see one, in its true form—it is said you will be driven quite mad. Do I look mad to you?" When Hawley didn't answer, she said, "You were telling me about Morgard."

Everyone had heard tales about how Majestics—angelic emissaries of the gods—had fought alongside men during the War of Silver and Gold, more than sixty years ago. But they were only stories... weren't they? Hawley swallowed, and went on with his story.

"After the war, the father of one of the knights Morgard killed presented him with this sword, as a mark of honour for a true warrior. It became part of the Third's rituals—a symbol of our code. But Morgard's dead now, and the code doesn't mean as much as it did." Hawley stared bitterly across the black water. "He named me sword-bearer. Thought he was doin' me a favour, but it's caused more bloody trouble than enough."

"And this is why Hobb wants you dead?"

"That's part of it, maybe. Morgard was the last of us to see open war—the last to be a hero. Seeing me with this sword must seem like an insult to Hobb. To all the men of the Blood. There's hardly a man in Fangmoor who wouldn't like to knife me in my sleep and take it from me."

"So why have they not?" Enelda asked.

"Same reason Nedley and Beacher waited to attack me in the Elderwood. Hobb ordered me dead, but they still had to perform their bloody ritual before they could act. Morgard made sure to name me sword-bearer in his last decree. The code o' the companies makes the last decree of a commander sacrosanct. Maybe they don't truly believe the code any more, but it's still written, and it's still followed. Rules are rules."

Enelda nodded. "From what I hear, the men of the High Companies do not always follow rules."

Hawley looked at her warily. "Oh?"

"Do they not take what they want from the serfs they encounter? Forcibly, should it please them."

"Not under my watch, they don't."

"You are particular about such things? But other sargents are not."

"I s'pose."

"Hardly the work of honourable men."

"Not honourable, no. But it's common law."

"Ah."

Hawley rubbed his hand over his face. He needed sleep, but in its absence he would have to suffer Enelda's questioning. "Look: When I was nothing but an orphaned bastard, I was little more than property. I knew this, I accepted it. All my folk did. Our lives were subject to the lord o' the manor...that was just the way it was. Way it'd always been. When I joined the militia, I was elevated to a higher station. Not a freeman, but no serf, neither. When Morgard started recruiting outsiders to the Third Company, I took the king's shilling and joined up. I was elevated again to king's man, above the lowliest freeman, and above the law of any one manor. This is the way of things. If a soldier o' the High Companies wants to take his pleasure at the expense of a serf, then as long as reparations are made to that serf's lord, there's no crime to be answered."

There was a momentary silence, which Hawley took to mean that his explanation had been accepted. He stood and fetched another log, and threw it onto the fire. Sparks swirled upwards, carried by the wind.

"But you personally do not allow it?" Enelda said abruptly.

Hawley tried not to groan. He sat back on his rock and shook his head.

"Therefore you think it wrong. So would you say that if the law allows things to happen that are inherently *wrong*, the law itself is wrong?"

Hawley hoped she spoke in jest. Unfortunately, Enelda seemed deadly serious.

"No, m'lady," he said, eyes darting left and right lest anyone be listening, "I wouldn't say that, 'cause that'd be treason."

"Of course. How silly of me." She smiled sweetly.

Hawley felt momentary relief.

"But then, would you not say," Enelda pressed, to Hawley's dismay, "that any law designed to prevent criticism of the law is merely tyranny in disguise?"

Hawley coughed loudly. For the first time that day he felt the pain in his ribs stab sharply beneath the linen wraps.

"No, m'lady," Hawley said. "I wouldn't say that, neither, 'cause I like my head right here on my shoulders, where it belongs."

"Excellent!" Enelda said, clapping her hands together and beaming broadly.

"It is?" Hawley asked.

"Yes. Now I know exactly what I'm dealing with."

"And ... what exactly is that?"

"Try not to pry, Hawley. It's an unbecoming habit." The woman stood, still smiling. "Now get some sleep."

"Can't. Have to keep watch."

Enelda waved a dismissive hand from beneath her bundled blanket as she shuffled towards the tent. "Have no fret, Sargent. There's nothing to worry about out here. Not tonight."

CHAPTER 6

Scarfell

"Gods be with you, my lady," Jens whispered. The old poacher's voice was weak upon the cold night wind.

"And with you," said Iveta. Jens was troubled, that much was clear, but there was no time to question him.

Iveta hurried away. When she crested the hill, she turned back to wave one last time to Jens, then began the walk to the castle. The moon peeked between black clouds, insufficient to light her way along the hidden trail. At least the interminable rain had relented for her journey. A blessing indeed.

By night, Iveta always thought Scarfell was as beautiful as it was sinister. The rocky foundations were gnarled, like the roots of ancient trees, growing upwards until they became one with the ancient, ochre stones that the Sylvens had used to first build a stronghold on this site. Above them, brutish and less organic, the Aelders had used hard, square, grey blocks to create their own functional castle from the ruins. It was ugly, really. But from here the braziers and guard-fires looked like distant stars. The many tenements that huddled around the castle like waifs in the rain were dark now, their occupants all abed, which was precisely where Iveta should be. She had tarried too long tonight. The good folk of Halham were in a poorer state than she had expected. Last month's medicine had not lasted. Sickness was rife, for nothing more than want of a better diet. So many now fell to ague that the very old and very young would do well to see the spring. Worse, Lestyn had paid the villagers a visit, arresting two of the colliers for non-payment of taxes, and putting a serf to death for killing one of the archduke's deer.

Uncle Leoric's deer, she thought, bitterly. A deer that fed two families for a month and had now cost a man his life, so that his wife and children would be thrown from their homes. No one in Halham could afford to feed extra mouths. The only fate awaiting that poor family was begging in the streets of nearby Ravenswyck, blowing to the slums of that sprawling city like leaf litter on an autumn breeze.

Iveta sniffed back a tear. She pulled her hood lower, as if to conceal her weakness from the eyes of the gods. She offered a silent prayer to Litha. She did not think it would do much good, and not just because the dark of the moon approached, and with it the waning of Litha's influence. It was Iveta's lack of faith that had driven her to direct action. She told herself it was what her mother would have done. In truth, she could not possibly know, but it made her feel better regardless.

She was nearing the castle walls, skirting the lower track that wound between the workshops and the forest, when the ground beneath her feet began to rumble. It was four hours until sunrise, on the least-travelled path for miles around, but horses approached.

The rumbling intensified, the drumming of hooves piercing the night air. Iveta felt panic rise; she could not be seen. If the riders brought some news that might rouse the household, her uncle would discover that she was not in her bed. Questions would be asked. The punishment would likely be severe.

Iveta looked around desperately and plumped for the forest. She hopped across the ditch that ran alongside the road, landing half in sludge and scrambling up the opposite bank. She dashed into the sparse woodland—barely a forest at all, but a managed and cultured approximation of one, planted by her great-uncle as a private hunting ground. It provided scant cover; most of the leaves had migrated from the spindly birches and young oaks.

Iveta moved as quickly as she could in the darkness, her feet remembering the way from her many previous forays.

The sound drew nearer still, the pace of the horses not slowing. Iveta could not outrun them, and at the last moment she crouched low, shielded from the track by tangles of blackthorn, and she watched as the horses thundered past. Six riders, cloaked and determined. The horses were large, of the type used to carry armoured men. It was too dark to make out much more, but as the last rider's cloak flapped outwards in the wind, Iveta saw a flash of blue tunic, and a glint of heraldry woven in cloth of silver.

Men of Sylverain had come.

When they were out of sight, Iveta ran as fast as her legs would carry her.

CHAPTER 7

Rowen sat in a sheltered hollow, nestled in the embrace of a broad ridge that curved around the eastern side of the settlement. Atop that ridge was an ill-maintained road, along which Hawley steered the wagon with care.

"Now remember, Sargent," Enelda said. "When we get there, I'll have no more of this 'my lady' business."

"M'lady?" Hawley replied instinctively. He flushed. "Sorry."

"I have suffered your courtesy six days too many. I have not been a Vigilant for many years—I am not a lady. In front of commoners, you shall address me as Madam Drake, or Mistress, or simply Enelda."

Hawley clipped the reins. The wagon bumped down an uneven slope, which broadened ahead into a meagre square. A few youngsters toiled with water pails and bundles of linen, but otherwise the village was strangely quiet. Across the square, another track led up to a large barn. And outside the barn, a banner fluttered on the cold wind. A black banner, bearing the Eye of Litha. Hawley cursed.

Vigilants. The new sort. Once sheriffs, now granted the title of an old order in a bid to make them more respectable. More feared.

"Have no fret, Sargent," Enelda said. "I grant you, the timing is inconvenient, but that is all. I would find this girl's parents before speaking with one of these 'Vigilants.'" She enounced the word with disdain.

Hawley drew them to a halt. "Let's see what we can find," he said. "I expect most folk will be at the court."

Vigilants were charged with holding courts in the villages under their watch every few months, dispensing justice, collecting taxes, and hearing the grievances of the locals. They were less formal than the "hundred courts," which often saw large gatherings of officials from across the entire hundred at towns like Eastmere, but they were still the only way for the king's justice to reach these far-flung communities. Rowen was barely due another visit, but the Vigilant of this hundred was Lestyn, and once the scent of fear was in his nostrils, he was wont to make his presence felt more keenly. Besides, for all its misfortunes of late, Rowen was prosperous—its large proportion of freemen generated strong income for the tax chests, and Lestyn would never pass an opportunity to squeeze hard-working craftsmen and pocket some coin. Hawley could only be thankful that, as a company soldier, he was beyond the reach of that particular corruption.

Hawley reached over the driving board for his sword.

"Leave it," Enelda said. "We aren't here to fight."

Enelda clambered awkwardly from the wagon, bundled so much against the cold she looked twice her usual size. She pulled the hood of her woollen cloak over her head. Hawley tried to push aside the thought that she resembled a witch. Given the proximity of the puritanical Vigilant Lestyn, such comparisons could only tempt fate. Hawley hitched the horses as Enelda waddled to the nearest lean-to for shelter. The rain started again almost immediately. She had a sixth sense for such things.

While Enelda wasn't looking, Hawley took up his regulation shortsword and strapped it to his waist. He guessed Enelda still wouldn't approve, but he was buggered if he'd go unarmed. He could smell trouble on the wind, and he was rarely wrong.

A young girl dashed across the square, feet slapping on the wet ground. Enelda called to her, and she approached, but thought twice when she saw Hawley's uniform.

"Don't be afraid, lass," Hawley said, though his reassurance seemed to have little effect. He found it difficult to put people at ease, with his imposing stature, weather-beaten features, and nose bent out of shape from one too many breaks. He wasn't fooling himself: It was the uniform that common folk mistrusted most, and often with good reason.

"We seek Master Rolfe and his wife. Which toft is theirs?"

The girl, perhaps no more than twelve, but already with sharp eyes and pinched features hardened by toil, considered how best to answer, then looked a little afraid, as though expecting a cuff round the ear for her non-compliance. Enelda pulled down her hood and smiled. At this gesture, the girl pointed across the square.

"Behind that one. There's a white goat outside, you'll see it... sir." She added the honorific hastily.

"Tell no one you saw us," Hawley said gruffly. "Understand?"

The girl nodded nervously, then ran off as fast as she could.

"Soldiers..." Enelda tutted.

Hawley shrugged, and led the way. He squeezed his frame between houses built too close together, picked his way through mud and pig muck, and rounded a wicker fence where a white goat stood tethered to a post outside a stone-built hovel with a sagging roof.

Like most of its neighbours, the Rolfe house slouched in on itself, the dark holes of its windows like lifeless eyes. A breeze sighed heavily through the reeds of the roof. Hawley could feel the sadness emanating from the house. He felt like a mourner at a grave. He rapped at the door, which rattled gamely in its frame at the merest touch. When at last it opened, it was only a crack, and the face that appeared was a fearful one. A woman, visibly trembling.

"Please, sir, we've done nothing wrong, and we have naught to give. Nothing more. Please..."

Just the sight of Hawley was enough to frighten the woman half to death. Hawley looked to his feet, ashamed on behalf of all his kind.

"Mistress Rolfe?" he managed.

"I beg you, sir, tell the Vigilant..." She began to cry.

Enelda pushed past Hawley before the woman could say more. "Forgive this 'un," Enelda said, and in that moment she was again Old Nell, with the rough accent of the northern folk and the bemused expression of a woman without all her wits. "He's a rough sort, but 'e means well. 'E's wi' me. We've come to help."

"Help? What do you mean?" The woman looked again at Hawley with great suspicion.

"My name's Enelda Drake, but you can call me Nell. I've come to talk about your wee one. The sargent here thinks not enough's been done to find her."

"Find her...? My Mildrith? You think she...she's alive?" This came out in a great sob.

"We don't know, child," Enelda said, with all the warmth and kindness of a wise old matriarch. "But why not let us in, eh? For nothing more than your time and hospitality, we'll do what we can."

Mistress Rolfe sniffed again, wiped away a tear, and opened the door. She stood straight, smoothed her apron out with chapped hands. "I can't offer much, but what I 'ave is yours."

*   *   *

As Enelda and the woman talked, Hawley lifted the flap of hide from the small window and peered out towards the square. Perhaps on a bright day Rowen would have a pleasing aspect, but in this weather it was as grim as the scene inside. The atmosphere in the Rolfe home was not just sad, but stifling.

Mistress Rolfe had not accepted the loss of her daughter— Hawley saw the evidence all around them, from the child's dolls on the mantelpiece to the shrine by the window—candles lit, keepsakes strewn around it. It had been weeks now. Hawley knew that, nine times out of ten, if a child didn't return after a few days, they never came back at all.

"How old was Mildrith?" Enelda asked, as their hostess poured them a tea of blackberry and dandelion.

"You mean...'How old *is* she?'"

"Of course, dear. When she was taken, I meant. Be precise."

"She's a winter bairn," the woman said with a half-smile. "Only just in her tenyear by a month."

"Mildrith was born during the Winnowing?" Hawley asked.

The mother nodded, wincing at the memory.

"Winnowing?" said Enelda.

"The great sickness," Hawley said. "You must've heard of it."

"There are a great many things I did not hear while I...was away."

"Oh...sorry," Hawley said. It was true that the Winnowing had been a problem peculiar to Wulfshael, but still, Hawley had never met anyone who'd not heard of it. "It's said one in five of Wulfshael's people died—mostly the very young and the very old."

"You should say it like it is, sir," Mistress Rolfe said bitterly. "The very poor, more like. There was more serfs than not taken by the Winnowing. My Mildrith almost died—she had the sleeping sickness almost as soon as she were born."

"Sleeping sickness?" Enelda asked.

Hawley explained. The Winnowing had brought horrible afflictions to the people of the mearca. Stigmata: long, black welts, like infected claw-marks all over the body. They preceded madness or death. The old died quickly. The young fell into a deep sleep, their life ebbing away, until they wasted to nothing. Strangest of all, the plague had been heralded by an ominous sign—fire in the sky. It could be seen far across the mearca, and holy men had thought the end times had come.

Enelda knitted her brow. "And the girl was cured?"

"She weren't cured, madam," the woman said. "Not with medicine, at any rate. She woke up with all the others. The *Awakening*. And we thank the gods for the miracle. The gods, and St. Baerloc, blessed be His name."

Enelda looked to Hawley, with exasperation now. She was unused to not knowing everything.

"Nobody knows for sure how the Awakening came about," Hawley said. "It's said the power of St. Baerloc ended the

Winnowing. They say he died in a forest fire when the sickness began, but rose again from the blackened woods to end it. He walked abroad for a full day and night, then fell into a pile of burnt-up bones. The Flaescines gathered his remains and installed 'em at an abbey ruin, not far from here."

"It were the act of consecration that finally ended the great sickness," Mistress Rolfe added, reverentially. "It's written in the *Canticle o' Baerloc*. Ten moons of sufferin', to the very day, from the fire in the sky to the consecration."

Enelda looked as incredulous as Hawley felt. The Flaescine order had not thrived in other parts of Aelderland as they had in Wulfshael. Their doctrine supported the belief that men could be suffused with the power of the gods, and become themselves divine. While other orders regarded the saints merely as holy men, or angels in disguise, the Flaescines elevated them alongside the very gods. For the Flaescines, there wasn't just the Three, or the Six Elders, but a whole pantheon of blessed saints. This belief was regarded by some to be heretical, and had led to hostility between the monastic orders in the past, particularly the Trysglerites and the warlike Sygellites.

"The Flaescine abbot has a seat on the archduke's council in recognition of the deed." Hawley shrugged. "So who am I to say it weren't so?"

"If you please, sir, I will not have doubt cast on the gods or saints in my house," Mistress Rolfe said. "Especially not St. Baerloc."

Hawley bowed respectfully.

"Describe her to me, dear," Enelda said, changing the subject. "Mildrith."

"A strong girl," the woman said. "Not pretty, you might say, but fine of feature, and skilled with her hands. Gets that from 'er father. Her hair is the colour of acorn flour, her eyes bright hazel. She loves being outside, in all weather, which is why 'er cheeks are always so rosy..." She dabbed at her eyes, unable to go on.

"You're sure she was taken? She did not simply wander off?"

"She's a good girl. She went to bed like normal. When I came to wake her in the morning, she were gone."

"Her bed had been slept in?"

"Aye."

"None of her belongings were missing? No clothes or toys?"

"No, madam. Not even...not even her little shoes."

"Nothing else was amiss in the house? Nothing stolen? Whether it be possessions or food?"

The woman shook her head. Enelda frowned.

"The door has a sliding bolt of oak. Your husband's work? Was it bolted on the night Mildrith disappeared?"

"No, madam. My husband, he...It was after that he made the bolt. No reason for us to lock our doors before. But after what happened to Agatha..."

"His sister?"

The woman nodded.

"And you testify Agatha was no witch?"

"She was a good woman!" Mistress Rolfe gasped. She looked about awkwardly, and lowered her voice. "I mean to say...if the Vigilant decided she be evil, then far be it from me to say otherwise."

"What did she do to arouse his suspicions?"

"Nothing. She were a midwife. Oh aye, she helped nearly every woman in this village one way or another. But they all lined up and accused her. One woman almost lost her son in childbirth, and if it weren't for Agatha the lad would've died for sure. All twisted about he was, and blue in the face. Poor lad were never quite right, sort of sickly. And Vigilant Lestyn, he said Agatha saved the boy's life only to watch him live accursed. Said he was *awearg.*" The woman spat into the hearth when she said this. "That poor lad has barely left his toft since, for fear of the other boys throwing stones at 'im, and them 'is friends an' all!"

Hawley turned away and looked out of the window again, half desirous to storm over to the barn and knock out some of Lestyn's teeth, for all the good it would do. That boy would have to live not only with his affliction, but also with the deep suspicion that old word brought, and that was Lestyn's doing.

"I should speak with your husband," Enelda said.

"He is...unwell."

"I may be able to help."

The woman squinted at Enelda as though seeing her for the first time. "Who *are* you? I mean, who are you really?"

"Oh, nobody. Not any more. But once, a long time ago, I helped people like you, and even people like him." She jerked her head towards Hawley. "I healed folk, I brought bairns into the world. I found people who were lost. I did all the things your poor sister-in-law did and more. Some might call *me* a witch, but if they tried to do anything about it, it would be the worse for them. Because in the old days, I spoke with the voice of the king himself." She leaned forward, a look in her old eyes so utterly convincing it made Hawley shudder. A gleam of authority that so few who wielded power truly possessed, but that Enelda could summon effortlessly.

Mistress Rolfe leaned away. "You sound like one of the old Vigilants from Mildrith's fairy stories," she said. "And by the gods I wish you was, but they're all gone. And what we have in their place are just men. Cruel men."

"Let me see your husband, Mistress Rolfe," Enelda said.

The woman led the way into the other room, where a bearded man slept on a low bed, breathing fitfully. He was heavily bruised, one eye swollen badly.

His wife would not name the cause, but it was clear Master Rolfe had suffered a beating, and his injuries had led to illness. It was likely the tithing men who had administered the punishment—it was Rolfe's sister who had been drowned by Lestyn on a charge of witchcraft. Blamed for making a pact with the Riftborn to spirit Mildrith away. Association with that kind of evil was bad enough, but if Rolfe had objected in any way to his sister's treatment, the average tithing man would need little excuse to execute their duty with wanton exuberance. Now Rolfe could not work. That would make life harder for them.

Enelda looked over the man's injuries, and her quick eyes scanned every detail of the squalid room. Satisfied, she nodded assent to Mistress Rolfe and led the way back into the other room.

"Make your husband a strong tea each day," Enelda said when the door was closed. "Steep one bunch of comfrey and two bunches of ice leaf in hot water. It will work wonders on his muscles and bones. Crush the rest of the comfrey into a salve of beeswax and rub it on the bruises. You'll soon have him right."

"I...Thank you, madam."

"Now, back to the matter of your daughter. There are no other rooms in the house?"

"No, madam, we are not wealthy folk."

"And Mildrith was sleeping in here, or in there?"

"In here, but the door was open so we could feel the warmth from the hearth."

"So whoever took the girl would have been stealthy indeed."

"I don't know what more to say, madam. I'm a poor woman, poorer still with my daughter gone and my husband laid low. What more is there for you or anyone to do but pick clean the bones of my life's carcass?"

"You know Mildrith is not the only one?" Enelda said matter-of-factly.

Mistress Rolfe looked wary. "You speak of that boy from the castle. Aye, there's not a man, woman, or child who has not heard. And worse, they say Sylvens are abroad again, like as in the old days."

"Sylvens? Here?" Hawley interjected. The thought of the old enemy setting foot in Wulfshael sent a chill through him. It was but a short step away from war.

"Not in Rowen, but we hear tales. And Lord Scarsdale does nothing. That Sylven boy is all he cares about. No one batted an eyelid when my girl went." A tear formed in her eye. She was trembling, full of anger and grief that finally began to spill out.

"They rarely do," Enelda said gently. "But we are here to find the truth. And it is not just the boy. There are others, too, from villages like this one."

"Others...?"

Hawley stepped forward. "Anton Tarasq is the Sylven lad the Vigilants are searching for. Before him was Mildrith. But before her, children were taken from Halsgrove, Ravensgirr, and Fars-fel. And they're just the ones I know of."

Mistress Rolfe shook. "Why hasn't anything been done? If we'd known, my Mildrith might never have been taken. And Agatha…"

"We're doing something now," Hawley said. The woman needed hope. "If them bairns are to be found, we'll find them."

Enelda shot Hawley a dagger-sharp look at that.

Mistress Rolfe, on the other hand, softened at once and wiped more tears from her red-ringed eyes.

Enelda changed the subject. "How much time passed between finding Mildrith's bed empty and raising the hue and cry?" There was an annoyance to her tone, and Hawley knew it was for him.

"An hour perhaps? We looked all around the village, spoke to her friends…then we knew she were gone."

"And the tithing men were called?"

Mistress Rolfe looked angry. "Yes, for all the good it did. We have three. They went across the fields calling Mildrith's name. When she'd not returned by dusk, they sent word to Wulfsaed."

Wulfsaed was not the largest town in the vicinity, but it was the seat of the hundred court. It was where Lestyn would usually be found when he wasn't courting the High Vigilant's favour at Scarfell.

"When this kind of business occurs," Enelda said, "strangers to a village are normally questioned. Were there any such fellows abroad?"

"We have folk passing the road up on the ridge there regular like."

"What kind of folk?"

"Pilgrims, mainly. But some merchants and market men favour this road to the highway, especially if they seek shelter or have goods to trade."

Enelda looked to Hawley accusingly. "You never told me the thoroughfare was so busy, Sargent."

Hawley shrugged. "It's common knowledge."

"Not to me."

"The Pilgrims' Road," Hawley sighed. "Supposedly a man can reach the doors of three high temples, five abbeys, and a sacred shrine, without ever leaving it."

"There's no suppos'dly about it," Mistress Rolfe said with some pride. " 'Tis the reason Rowen exists at all. And that is why we can be sure there's no witchcraft here. Pilgrims settled this village. Why, Agatha's grandfather was among the first settlers, and he himself a preacher."

"So that is why the village lies unguarded from the road," Enelda said. "Nothing to fear from holy men, I suppose. The tithing men searched for strangers, however? Even if they were only passing through?"

"Ha! They did nothing but wait for help from Wulfsaed, and by then it was too late. If any visitor had stolen my girl away on a wagon, they would have been long gone. No, when the Vigilant arrived, they were quick to look to their own."

That was certainly Hawley's experience. Tithing men performed their duty to keep the peace, but often their enthusiasm was as limited as their imaginations.

"Who is your chief tithe?"

"Fyrne. And may the gods strike me down if I don't call him a wicked pig of a man!"

"I imagine he knows a thing or two about how your husband came by his injuries?"

Mistress Rolfe bunched her small hands into fists. This confirmed Hawley's suspicions about the tithing men. He'd seen it often—local men given an ounce of power, filled with suspicion and superstition and a goodly quantity of ale. Such men would turn from upholders of the peace to bullies at the drop of a hat. If Rowen had only three of them, the eligible serfs fit for tithing must be in short supply. Those that took the tithe often resented freemen like Rolfe, and would jump at the chance to knock him down a peg or two.

The sound of voices came from outside. Idle chatter, voices growing in number. Hawley peered again through the window. The square was only partly visible between the nearby houses, but men and women were passing by, away from the barn, going back to their work.

"The court must have finished early," Mistress Rolfe said. "No hangings or drownings today. Fyrne will be disappointed."

"No sign of the Vigilant," Hawley said.

"He'll be up at the barn awhile yet, counting up the taxes and what have you. We won't see him again this month unless there be trouble. You see, we know all about your little Sylven boy here. Since Agatha met her end, all eyes are on Rowen. Vigilant Lestyn would burn this village to the ground if he had his way. A village of witches, he'd say."

"I am sure he would," Enelda muttered.

"What are you doing here...really?" Mistress Rolfe asked.

"My duty, some might say," Enelda said with a smile. "Though it has been a long time coming."

"Madam Drake..." Hawley warned. She'd said too much for Hawley's comfort already. "We should take our leave. Time is against us."

Enelda moved to the door at Hawley's gesture. "You still have friends in this village, I presume?" Enelda asked the woman.

"Aye, madam, of course. It is a good village, for the most part. The people are afraid, for sure, but bonds of kinship are not easily cut."

"Good. I would ask you to go to them. Surround yourself with friends and family. Tell them...there is hope."

The woman looked puzzled. "What do you intend to do, madam?"

"I intend to present myself to the Vigilant."

Hawley looked as confused as Mistress Rolfe at that.

"Come along, Sargent," Enelda said. "We have business at the barn."

They stepped outside into the drizzle.

"Wait," Mistress Rolfe said. She ducked inside, then out again before Drake and Hawley could take their leave. "Sargent," she said. "For you."

She held out an amulet. A small corn dolly upon a leather

thong, with wooden beads and a single white goose-feather dangling from it.

"Mildrith used to make these," she said. "She was wearing one...that day. Never took it off. Said it were for luck. You promised to bring her back, so please take it. Mebee it'll bring you some luck, too."

Hawley hesitated, but took the trinket. He nodded thanks.

When he turned back, Enelda was already trudging up the slope towards the barn, and Hawley followed.

CHAPTER 8

"This is a bad idea," Hawley whispered.

He peered over Enelda's shoulder into the barn. Within, four men stood around a long table, counting coins into bags. Two were commoners, one with a head like a ham hock—Fyrne, Hawley guessed. The third was a Vigilant Guard, marked out by his smart, clean armour of black boiled leather. The fourth was dressed in a plain robe of pale grey. He was slight of stature, with a long face that looked as though it had been kneaded into shape by a baker's knuckles. His close-cropped hair thinned patchily as it met a bulbous forehead, which shadowed a pair of large, deep-set eyes. Hawley recognised him at once.

"Shit...He's still here."

"Vigilant Lestyn, I presume? You know him?"

"Aye. He's one of the worst."

Perhaps it was just the way the gods had made him, but Lestyn always looked angry. Hawley had the feeling he was about to look angrier still.

Drake and Hawley watched as purses of copper and silver coins were placed into a strongbox. One purse was given to Fyrne, another to the guard. With a sly grin, Lestyn pocketed another.

A prickle at the back of Hawley's neck caused him to look over his shoulder, sensing he was being watched. "My la— Enelda," he warned.

A few locals had gathered, curious about the strangers. More curious still that Drake and Hawley were skulking around outside the barn, spying on the official business of a Vigilant.

"That woman was no fool," Hawley hissed. "She guessed what you are."

Without reply, Enelda pulled open the door and stepped inside the barn.

"Bugger..." Hawley groaned, and followed.

"Court is closed," Lestyn barked, without bothering to look up. "If you have a grievance, come to the hundred court in twelve days. If you have unpaid taxes, leave them with my man."

Lestyn had finished with the coin and was now picking through a table of offerings. Bottles of mead, loaves of bread, eggs, meat and fish, finely woven baskets filled with mushrooms, beets, and cabbages. All more than the people of Rowen could afford. Hawley imagined their tribute would have been considerably less before the drowning of Agatha in the River Halgian.

"I owe no taxes to this hundred," Enelda said, her voice disguised like the croak of some old crone. "And I have no grievance, save for the poor state of justice in this land."

With a frown, Lestyn looked up. His large eyes surveyed the impertinent old woman before him, dressed in her bundle of rags. Then they alighted on Hawley, and the expression of callous disregard changed to one of mild vexation. His lips pursed. He straightened himself imperiously.

"What is *your* business here, soldier?" he asked.

"*Sargent.* I'm with her," Hawley said.

"Sargent, eh? Where are your men?"

"North." That much, at least, was no lie.

Lestyn's frown deepened so much his whole face crumpled. "What is your company?" His voice rose in pitch.

Hawley recalled how easily Lestyn grew frustrated with uncooperative subjects. Good. "The Third," he said simply.

"Then you should know better than to intrude on a Vigilant's business," Lestyn snapped.

"And what business is that?" Enelda said, shuffling up to the end of the long table, idly inspecting the offerings upon it. "Is it the business of drowning innocent women in the river, or the business of stealing from the king's coffers?"

Hawley could have died on the spot. Lestyn's eyes bulged from his head. His cheeks turned a deep crimson.

"Do you know to whom you speak, crone?" he snarled. "Guard: Throw this woman out on her ear, and do not be gentle about it."

The guard moved around the table and managed three strides before Hawley intercepted him. Hawley said nothing, only shook his head slowly. The guard stopped. He looked to his master, who was too exasperated to respond.

"I shall try a simpler question," Enelda said, breaking an awkward silence, but still not looking up. "The woman, Agatha—on what grounds did you accuse her of witchcraft?"

Lestyn threw a daggered look at Hawley. Hawley only shrugged.

"Agatha Becker," Lestyn said haughtily, "claimed to possess the powers of healing. She tended children, men, women, and even beasts, claiming cure-alls, though she was no physician. She more than once performed bloodletting upon a sick man, though she was no surgeon. She bewitched a newborn babe so that the boy would evermore be sickly and crippled. I received testimony that the woman kept a familiar and would walk abroad in the dead of night, praying to the Other. Rowen is better off without her kind."

"Pity," Enelda said. "She could well have attended her brother's injuries, for it seems no one else has the wherewithal to do so."

"Her brother?"

"Yes. Master Rolfe, the carpenter. You may recall his daughter was the one abducted. The one you claim was taken by Agatha Becker." As she spoke, Enelda unclasped her woollen cloak, folded it neatly, and placed it on the table beside a basket of vegetables.

She took another step along the row of produce and began to inspect a bundle of linens as if it contained the answer to some great mystery.

Lestyn looked as though he might combust. "The girl is dead.

Most like spirited away by the dark servants of Agatha Becker. Justice has been served."

"But has not Anton Tarasq been abducted in similar circumstances? Strikingly similar, I have heard. If the culprit were proved the same in both cases, would that not mean Agatha Becker was innocent of the charge?"

"How do you know—?"

"Answer her," Hawley said, still staring down the guard, who looked increasingly like he might challenge Hawley given half a chance. A hard man, a fighting man. Ex-militia, most like. Well paid and loyal to his master. Hawley took one quick glance at Lestyn's enraged expression, and added, "If you please, my Lord Vigilant."

Lestyn gave a surreptitious look to the two tithing men, who loitered at the far end of the table. They didn't seem overkeen to dirty their hands, but they shifted and stretched, ready to answer the command should it come.

"Most likely unrelated," Lestyn said with extreme annoyance. "Coincidence."

"Not likely at all," Enelda corrected. "Your presence here alone suggests that. I imagine Archduke Leoric has ordered all Vigilants in the mearca to search for Anton Tarasq, and yet here you are, in Rowen."

"If they were taken by the same culprit," Lestyn spluttered, "it would only prove that Rowen is at the heart of the mystery. Where there is one witch, there are likely others. A coven, best put to the sword."

"But what of the other children?" Enelda said. She unwrapped her bulky shawl, folded it, and placed that on the table, then took another step along the row, another step closer to Lestyn. As she did, she stood a little straighter, a little taller. "Four others this year, more last year, and all within three leagues of Scarfell. Curious, would you not say?"

"All the more reason to increase our presence in these godsforsaken villages. To bring justice; to shine the light of Litha upon the wicked."

"Justice?" Finally, Enelda raised her eyes to meet Lestyn's. "More like lining your own pockets." She glanced at the table, then back to Lestyn.

Lestyn's colour deepened to a shade of purple. Failing to find words to counter the impertinent woman before him, he instead pounded a fist upon the table. "How *dare* you!" he shrieked.

Enelda casually unfastened the laces of her bulky grey smock and smiled sweetly. "I dare," she said, "because those who terrorise the people they are charged to protect are beneath contempt. And those who defame the once-sacred office of the Vigilants are deserving of the most severe punishment under law."

"Who *are* you?" Lestyn spluttered.

"I am the seeker after the truth. I am the voice of the meek. I am the sword of justice. I am the healer of the cursed. I am the watcher against the darkness. I am everywhere and nowhere. I am everyone and no one. The gods made me, the gods protect me, and the gods will one day take me." Enelda's voice rang strong, like a priest delivering a sermon.

Hawley didn't know what the words meant, but the hairs on his arms stood on end. Lestyn's bottom lip wobbled. His purpled cheeks now drained to lily white. Hawley had always taken the man for a coward who hid behind the mantle of authority, but he never thought he'd witness Lestyn truly quail.

"Impossible..." Lestyn said, voice thin and querulous. He stepped back, clenched his fists. Finally, he seemed to recover his wits. Lestyn nodded to the two tithing men, who put hands to their cudgels and sidled closer to Hawley. The Vigilant Guard reached to his sword.

Enelda loosed the smock at last, and threw it aside, then the bonnet. Even Hawley had to blink twice to check his own eyes. The doddering old crone was no more. The elderly woman who stood before them seemed taller, stronger, pale green eyes conveying a powerful, commanding presence. She was dressed in a simple grey robe, much like Lestyn's. Her snow-white hair shimmered in the weak light of the barn. In her hand she held a carved wooden amulet—a disk, bearing the Eye of Litha. The symbol of the Vigilants. Enelda placed this slowly and deliberately around her neck.

Lestyn's mouth worked soundlessly.

With the thinnest of smiles, Enelda swept the offerings from the table.

"Crone! Witch!" Lestyn spat, amidst the sound of breaking glass and clattering plates. "This is a mummer's farce. You are not who you claim to be—it is impossible. And you will suffer for your insolence!"

One of the tithing men had already backed away. Enelda had looked at the man with an expression of supreme confidence, and the dullard averted his eyes as though Litha Herself had materialised before him. Only Fyrne and the guard remained.

"Imbecile!" Lestyn cried at the tithing man. Then he turned his ire to the remaining two men. "You two—arrest that woman."

The guard and Fyrne looked at each other, seemed to come to some silent agreement, and advanced.

Hawley stepped between Enelda and the men. Something stirred in Hawley's breast. He felt liberated from the shackles of solemn duty. The look in Enelda's eyes chased any doubt from his mind. He felt... righteous. And it was the first time he had felt anything of the sort in a long while. He reached for his sword, but felt a hand on his at once.

"No, Sargent," Enelda said softly. "Do not kill them."

Hawley groaned inwardly. The Vigilant's black-armoured guard was one pace away, reaching for his own sword. Hawley had no time to think. From the corner of his eye he spied a solitary bottle of mead still rocking back and forth on the table. In one fluid motion, Hawley snatched it up and smashed it gleefully over the guard's head.

The guard's helmet absorbed most of the blow, but he still reeled away sideways, showered in mead, slouching into a wooden post, gasping.

Fyrne swung a wooden cudgel wildly. Hawley batted aside the blow on his vambrace. He punched an armoured fist into Fyrne's face. The tithing man careened backwards, landing unceremoniously in a pile of splintered wood and scattered libations.

Enelda had slipped past them already. She trod slowly towards Lestyn, one hand raised. She spoke loudly, her tone commanding, her words indistinguishable. The old tongue, Hawley guessed, used now only by the priests of the high temples. Whatever she said made Lestyn edge away from her.

The guard recovered his wits. He dashed at Enelda.

Hawley stuck out a foot. The guardsman tripped, sprawling to the dirt.

Enraged at the thought of a trained soldier assaulting the diminutive Enelda Drake, and more than a little insulted that he'd tried to do so while ignoring the very real threat of a company soldier, Hawley strode to the prostrate man, slammed a foot onto his back, pinning him to the ground.

"Never turn your back on a fight, lad," he snarled.

"Good advice." Something struck Hawley's temple hard, sharp. Stars danced before his eyes. He staggered sideways.

Out of the corner of Hawley's eye, a black shape moved.

A shadow. A creature with yellow eyes.

The memory was an unwelcome distraction, a dangerous one. This was no monster.

Fyrne advanced again. The cudgel struck Hawley's back. When Hawley didn't fall, Fyrne pulled back his arm for another blow.

Hawley swung his left arm back, the arm-shield's edge connecting with Fyrne's doughy face with a metallic ring. Hawley staggered, holding his head. Fyrne was on the floor again, already crawling away.

A sword scraped from a scabbard. Hawley sighed. The Vigilant Guard was up again.

"Draw your sword," the guard growled.

"Don't need a sword 'gainst the likes of you."

The guard looked Hawley up and down, saw the fighting stance, the ready bend of the knee, the look of malice in Hawley's eyes. Years of training. It was the guard's turn to falter.

Good.

Hawley lurched forward. The guard thrust the sword. With a flick of his wrist, Hawley formed the thick steel plates across his arm into a shield. The blade scraped across it, deflected. Hawley stepped close and smashed his forehead into the guard's nose. He grabbed the man's sword-arm and bashed it mercilessly into the pillar. The sword fell from the man's hand.

He prepared to deliver a solid punch to the man's teeth, but Fyrne grabbed Hawley's arm. He used all his weight to pull Hawley away.

The Vigilant Guard launched a kick to Hawley's bound ribs. Pain ripped through Hawley's body like wildfire. Hawley dropped to his knees, grunting through gritted teeth.

Through his rage Hawley almost didn't feel the fists and feet pounding at him. He pushed and pulled with all his might. He could see nothing, feel nothing; he heard only his own roar of defiance and anger.

Then soft light met his eyes. The assault stopped. The barn filled with voices, the sounds of a struggle.

Hawley stood. His hand went to his sword. To hell with Enelda's order. He wanted blood.

"Gods preserve you, sir!" A man's voice, thickly accented with a local burr.

A stranger nodded to Hawley and tentatively reached out, smoothing sand from Hawley's shoulders.

There were a dozen villagers in the barn. Men remonstrated with the guard, who eventually sat on the sandy floor, defeated. The tithing men fled under a barrage of insults and pelted muck. One by one the villagers turned in awe—not of Hawley, but of Enelda.

Lestyn, the firebrand Vigilant, knelt prostrate before Enelda. She was speaking softly. Finally, she finished whatever oath or prayer she had been reciting, and bowed her head serenely. As she did, a reverent hush fell over the villagers.

"I told ye," a woman said at last. Mistress Rolfe stepped to the front. "A True Vigilant. Here, in Rowen. Come to seek justice for my girl. For my sister-in-law. For my husband."

"Justice for all," Enelda said.

Mistress Rolfe gave an awkward curtsey.

Enelda looked each man and woman over. Some avoided her gaze, as if in the presence of a saint. "Too long have villages like Rowen existed in fear," Enelda said. "Fear of sickness and death and financial ruin. Fear of what might happen if the crops fail or the taxes cannot be paid. Fear of the tyranny of harsh masters. And worst of all, fear of justiciars who would persecute the innocent rather than punish the wicked. Aye, I was a Vigilant of the old order. I make no promises, but if the children are to be found, then I'll do what I can to find them. Not just Mildrith Rolfe, but all those taken. But do not take this for more than it is. I am not here to restore the old order— that is beyond my power. When my work is done, I will leave."

"You will leave now!" Lestyn shrieked.

He sprang to his feet and swung his staff, striking Enelda across the arm. She stumbled, pain contorting her face. She dropped to her knees before the astonished crowd.

Before Hawley could reach Lestyn, the villagers surged forward in a wave of righteous fury. They seized Lestyn roughly and tore the staff from his hands.

When Lestyn finally stopped struggling, the point of Hawley's shortsword was at his throat.

"Kill me and your life is forfeit," Lestyn snarled. He raised his voice so all could hear. "All your lives will be forfeit! This crone can't protect you. I am the authority here. This is rebellion! And the sentence for rebellion is death."

Hawley had heard that before. He'd heard it on the day of his "transgression." A man of authority had spat those very words, and Hawley had been the one who'd carried out the sentence. Hawley had killed the wrong man that day. Now he spied a chance to set things right.

"You're a disgrace to your profession," Hawley said. "You don't deserve to live."

Lestyn's eyes widened as he realised Hawley's threat was not an idle one. Here stood his executioner.

Hawley took a deep breath to still the doubts in his mind. There would be no turning back after this.

"Leave him!" Enelda's voice was strong enough to stay Hawley's hand. "Stand down, Sargent Hawley."

Hawley spat on the ground contemptuously and sheathed his sword. Lestyn hung his head in relief.

"This man has transgressed against the code of his office. But it is not I who will punish him, nor any of you. Nay, not even the good sargent here. It is Litha: she whose light shows only truth. This man has become corrupted, and it is Litha who will chase the shadow from his heart. Release him!"

At this, the villagers bowed their heads and relinquished their hold on Lestyn. Mistress Rolfe picked up the man's staff—a tall, pale rod of yew, its tip a ball of twisted branches trained upon the living tree. It was the one remnant of the old order that the new Vigilants carried still. The woman brought the staff to Enelda and held it out as an offering.

Enelda reached out hesitantly. Her hand trembled just a little. Finally, she took it. "Thank you, dear," she said. She leaned on the staff, and a wistful smile spread across her careworn face.

"The archduke shall hear of this," Lestyn quavered. He stuck out his weak chin like a petulant child.

"It was Archduke Leoric who sent for me, young man," Enelda said, though Lestyn was not so very young. "Presumably because he is less than impressed with your efforts. Perhaps it is not your fault. Without the proper training, your mind is open to the influence of . . . malign forces."

"Y-you dare suggest . . ." Lestyn spluttered. Then he lowered his voice to a fearful whisper. ". . . that *I* am in league with Riftborn?"

"In league? No. Only that where corruption is seen, the taint of the Rift can be found. They leave a mark on a soul, like dye dripped into water. Perhaps they have left such a mark on you. A mark only Litha will see, when the time comes to be judged."

There was a palpable change in the air. The villagers muttered, shuffled, glared. One man said, "Then it's 'im. He's the witch!"

Another man called out "Aye!"

"Was it you all along?" Mistress Rolfe wailed. "Did you steal my little girl away?"

Panic flooded Lestyn's eyes.

A man seized him by the arm. "Mistress 'Nelda . . . say the

word and we will have his confession! We'll drown it out of 'im, like 'e drowned Agatha."

"No, no," Enelda said, raising her arms. "Be calm."

But the villagers would not be calm. Hawley stepped a little closer to Enelda as the cries grew louder. Long-suppressed anger trickled from the little assembly. Soon it would become a flood of rage. Hawley had seen it before, and the deaths that had followed were a bloody stain on his record. Even these few villagers, should they become an angry mob, would be sufficient to overcome Hawley and tear Lestyn apart.

As the villagers pulled Lestyn this way and that, a figure leapt forth. The guard, loyal to the end, barged aside two villagers, sword in hand. Lestyn lurched into the guard's embrace.

The guard looked to Hawley. His eyes were full of challenge. And fear. He wasn't seeking battle, he was seeking permission.

Hawley granted it with a nod. The guard pushed Lestyn towards the rear door of the barn. Lestyn ran as fast as his legs would carry him, out into the cold. The villagers advanced towards the guard, wary, angry.

Hawley felt a tug at his sleeve.

"Hawley," Enelda said weakly. She rubbed at her arm where Lestyn had struck it. Her eyes were squeezed shut. "Get their attention."

The last thing Hawley needed was another brawl—he already felt like he'd been kicked by a mule. Instead, he went for the scattered offerings and took up a weighty bag of coins. Lestyn's taxes—or extortion money. Hawley took a large handful and threw them over the heads of the crowd. The men stopped at once when pieces of gleaming silver landed at their feet.

"If you won't listen even to a True Vigilant," Hawley bellowed, "maybe you'll listen to this."

Everyone turned to Hawley as he held the bag aloft. "If you harm this man, Lord Scarsdale will punish you for it. All of you. Stop now, take back your money, and let Vigilant Drake worry about seeking justice."

There was some grumbling. A few dissented. Most agreed.

The guardsman quietly made his way to the door and slipped away.

"Sargent Hawley is right," Enelda said, gathering herself. "Lestyn has taken more from you than is fair, but that may be his only crime."

"What about Agatha?" Mistress Rolfe cried.

Enelda raised her hand, palm outward, and the crowd hushed. "I will see that justice is done. Take back your offerings and return to your homes."

"Will you not take an offering, Madam Vigilant?" a bearded man asked. "A gift."

"I would ask no more than food and water for our journey, but only if you can spare it. Beyond that, we have need of little."

Speak for yourself, Hawley thought, stomach grumbling and bones aching. He took a rueful sideways look at the offerings, half of which were strewn on the floor.

It was too late to protest, and it would have seemed churlish to do so. Enelda was already ushering the villagers forth to take back their bread and beer, fruit and vegetables, linens and trinkets, and handfuls of silver and copper coins. This act of perceived benevolence only cemented the villagers' love of Enelda, and it took an uncomfortably long time for Hawley to wrest her away from the fawning gathering. It wouldn't do to tarry too long—who knew how many men Lestyn had nearby? That it may have proven expedient to simply kill him played on Hawley's mind.

At last they trudged back to the wagon, followed by their entourage, who thankfully for Hawley insisted on packing more food than they needed. Enelda bound Hawley's aching ribs again with fresh linen wraps. Then at last they were away, the villagers waving them off cheerfully as they circled up to the ridge of the Pilgrims' Road.

CHAPTER 9

They'd travelled some little way along the road when Enelda said, "You should have told me about the Winnowing."

"Thought you knew. Even in Godsrest they—"

"I am not a villager of Godsrest," she snapped. "A few years ago I was barely known to them, and I do not engage in idle chatter. You know why."

Hawley grunted as the wagon jolted over a rock, sending a dull pain flashing through his tender ribs. He felt another pain he hadn't noticed before. He touched a hand to his jaw, fished in his mouth with two fingers, and took out a bloody tooth. "Gods..." he muttered.

"They gave you some trouble back there," Enelda said. "I thought a High Companies man would handle those thugs more easily."

"I'm not at my best." Hawley threw the tooth over the side of the wagon and spat a trail of blood after it. "I'd have spilled their guts, but you asked me not to."

"Then I thank you."

Enelda had not thanked him once on their journey so far. Not for carrying her things, or hunting, or standing watch all night long at camp, or driving the wagon in pouring rain while Enelda had rested in the back under covers. He almost could not believe his ears.

"Just doing my duty," Hawley said.

"You are a curious fellow. I saw the look in your eyes. You

wanted to kill Lestyn—and not out of sheer bloodthirstiness. You wanted justice. For a man who puts so much stock in rules, you seem quick to break them when it suits you."

Hawley shifted uncomfortably. "We shouldn't have let him go. We'd better have a good story when we meet the archduke or we'll both end up dead. They're rules even you can understand."

"Do not judge Lestyn too harshly. Men of mean spirit and weak mind are easily swayed by the Riftborn. He may have succumbed to their will without even realising it, such is their subtle influence."

"I've seen plenty who don't need demons to blame for their evil ways. Maybe if you'd left your tower a bit more you'd have seen 'em, too."

"That's precisely *why* I did not leave my tower. Look at what has happened already. Understand this—the Riftborn scratch at the veil between the worlds always. Poking and prodding, looking for ingress. And when the veil thins, they corrupt everything. Men are oftentimes too weak to resist the influence of the Rift. When you understand this, you'll stop spoiling for a fight and start looking for the truth."

"What truth?"

"The truth of a man's nature. The truth of what he has done and why. And we find that truth through careful observation."

"Pah!" Hawley spat over the side of the wagon. There was less blood in it this time. "And what'd you 'observe' in Rolfe's house?"

"Nothing."

"Nothing?"

"Mildrith was the same age as Anton Tarasq, but that could mean anything. This 'Winnowing' that so piqued your interest is likely insignificant—it would make a pleasing story if the answer could be found in curses and miracles, but the lure of fancy is one to be avoided. Facts and evidence are what I need, not wishful thinking. What I found more interesting was you, Sargent Hawley."

"Oh?"

"I learned that you are incredibly rash."

"Me?" Hawley blinked incredulously. "I'm not the one who cast aside the element of surprise. I'm not the one who made an enemy of a Vigilant."

"No. You did worse than that. That trinket around your neck... You should not have made such a promise to the woman."

Hawley squeezed the charm in his hand. "She needed... something. Hope."

"False hope."

"Not if the girl's alive," Hawley muttered.

"There is no promise so hollow as one that cannot be kept," Enelda chided. "We must never allow ourselves to become personally involved."

"Who's this 'we'?" Hawley said, flicking the reins in annoyance. The horses quickened their pace. "You mean you and me? Or the old Vigilants?"

"I..." Enelda faltered. "Let us just say we all have our reasons for what we do. But when a Vigilant learns life's lessons, the consequences can be... severe."

Hawley recognised something in that look that spoke of painful memories. It was something all too familiar to him. But he was tired and sore. All he could say was, "So I took a beating for nowt? You learned nothing?"

"Oh, don't be such a baby, Hawley," Enelda said. "I'll have you right as rain in no time."

"With more parsnip stew? Where next anyhow? I s'pose you'll want to visit every village in Wulfshael before we visit the castle."

"Circumstances are about to change."

"How so?"

She pointed along the road.

Enelda's senses again proved keener than Hawley's. He saw the spear tips first, black pennants fluttering. Four riders crested the rise ahead, armoured and grim.

Hawley stretched out his aching muscles, heard his joints crack and groan. He reached into the back of the wagon for his sword.

The man who led the riders was no ordinary soldier. He rode alongside three of the Vigilant Guard, but he wasn't one of them.

He wore a quartered tunic of green and black, a pair of golden wolves emblazoned upon his breast. This was a man of Scarfell.

Hawley laid Godspeaker across the driver's board as surreptitiously as he could.

"Easy, Hawley," Enelda said quietly. "This may be a time for diplomacy."

"Diplomacy is easier when you've got strength on your side."

"Then it's unfortunate we do not."

There was no time to argue. Two soldiers stopped dead in the road, forcing Hawley to come to a halt. Another trotted by under Hawley's watchful eye, inspecting the wagon and its two unlikely occupants.

The leader of the riders approached cautiously. He wore no helmet. Fair hair swept across his youthful brow. His eyes shone keenly over a long, thin nose.

"Identify yourselves," he said. His words were crisp, vowels overstated. Not from Wulfshael. From one of the cities of Aeldenhelm perhaps. A long way from the king's court.

With a last rueful glance at Enelda, Hawley sighed. "I'm Sargent Hawley of the Third." He glowered at a soldier beside him, who had come alongside the wagon like a warship preparing a boarding action. The man stared at Hawley with suspicion from beneath the prow of his domed helmet, eyes full of challenge.

"A sorry excuse for a man of the High Companies," the fair-haired man said.

"But High Companies I am," Hawley replied. He swept up his heavy sword and hopped down from the wagon, trying not to wince at the pain in his ribs upon landing. The soldier beside him made a poor show of stopping Hawley, and instead struggled to keep his horse in check as it shied away.

"Stay where you are," the fair-haired man snapped.

Hawley spat into the dirt and took a few steps clear of the wagon. His sword remained bound, held loosely in his hand. He needed room to swing it, if necessary.

Hawley drew himself up to his full height. Even that was enough to tweak his ribs. But still he fixed the stranger with his most commanding stare. "Why should I take orders from you, lad," he said. Closer now, Hawley realised the man was barely his junior, though he certainly looked it. A comfortable life could have that effect.

"I am Sir Redbaer, Captain of Lord Scarsdale's guard. You do not have to obey me, but you would be wise to. I'm told you accosted one of the king's Vigilants, going about his lawful duty. What say you?"

"Aye, I 'accosted' him." Hawley heard gauntleted hands creak around spear shafts. "But his duty was far from lawful. If he hadn't run, I'd have kicked his arse from here to Helmspire."

"Bold words; bawdy words." Redbaer remained expressionless, his eyes still fixed on Hawley. An odd fish, and a cold one. "Who is your commander? Hobb, isn't it? He has sworn for the Vigilants, and yet here you are, doling out your own form of justice. Is this to be the way of it now? Is the Third Company above the law?"

Now there were nerves on show. Hawley saw it in the man's youthful eyes. The Vigilant Guards were agitated, too. What Redbaer was suggesting was that Hobb might be making a play for power, dethroning the Vigilants and becoming justiciar himself. Wasn't that what Enelda had implied? Redbaer's seriousness all but confirmed it. Damn, but the old woman was sharp.

"Not my intent," Hawley said simply. "Didn't even know Lestyn was here. I hesitate to call him 'Vigilant' in present company." He jerked his head to the wagon.

Redbaer allowed his cool eyes to take in Enelda as if for the first time. If he had not before noticed her pale robe, and the sigil of Litha about her neck, he did now.

"Arrest him!" the soldier behind Hawley said, wheeling the horse so close Hawley felt its tail swish across his back. "He'll be hanged for assaulting the Vigilant. Commander Hobb can't deny the rule of law."

"Hold your tongue, Swire," Sir Redbaer snapped. "Sargent Hawley, explain yourself. What are you doing here? Who is this woman?"

"I'm serving the archduke, same as you. And this *lady*," he stressed, "is Enelda Drake. Formerly Vigilant Drake. I travelled a long way to find her, and now I escort her to Scarfell."

"Vigilant..." Sir Redbaer muttered. "You surely don't mean a *True* Vigilant?"

"Of the old order," Hawley confirmed. "And her first encounter with her successors was a craven coward who takes a cut of the king's taxes for his own pocket."

"Liar!" the guardsman, Swire, spluttered. The horse nudged into Hawley. The soldier lowered his spear. "I'll have your tongue."

Hawley spun about, grabbed the spear, and gave it a hard shove. The man had braced himself to be pulled, not pushed, and the surprise almost unseated him. The horse turned away with a whinny, and the spear clattered to the road.

The other two soldiers lowered their own spears in Hawley's direction.

"Enough!" Redbaer shouted. "You men, stand down or I'll have you flogged."

"But he—" Swire stuttered.

Hawley grinned, showing his teeth wolfishly.

"I said enough." Now Redbaer's tone was calm, cold as ice. Far more menacing than his shout. Hawley approved. "Sargent: Return to your wagon and follow me."

"To where?"

"Scarfell."

"I must protest..." Swire spluttered.

"Protest all you like, Sargent Swire. But if this man speaks the truth, it is not for you, nor I, and certainly not Vigilant Lestyn, to impede him. He will go before the archduke, and if there is a charge to answer, he shall answer it. I take full responsibility."

Swire didn't even bother to retrieve his spear. He spurred his horse away with an angry *"Har!"* The other black-garbed soldiers turned and followed in his wake.

When they'd gone, and Hawley was back on the driver's board, Redbaer turned his own horse, and led the way.

"Well handled, Hawley," Enelda whispered.

Hawley felt that praise indeed.

* * *

They travelled south, escorted by Redbaer's men. Hawley was thankful no Vigilant Guards had come along—time enough later to settle those scores. Instead, they flew under the pennants of Scarfell.

Redbaer brought his horse alongside the wagon. "We should reach the castle by nightfall," he said. "I fear you have arrived too late to be of much service now."

"How so?" Hawley asked.

"A child's body was found yesterday, washed up on the banks of the Silver River. A Sylven child."

"Tarasq?"

"Gods, no! But of a similar age, and in circumstances most strange. Lord Scarsdale believes the Sylvens themselves are responsible for the disappearance of the Tarasq boy."

"They took him back to his mother?"

"Worse than that. We think the boy has been murdered."

"Tell me, dear," Enelda said, her tone throwing Redbaer immediately off guard. "Why would the Sylvens wish ill upon their own children?"

"That's just it, my lady. This body found yesterday...it had upon it strange marks. The High Vigilant says it is the curse of the blackrock. None but the Sylvens are mad enough to meddle with such powers."

"I would advise caution before accusing the Sylvens of anything."

"I agree," Redbaer said, "but it may be too late. A Sylven diplomat named Sauveur is already at Scarfell. He heard about the body in the river—nothing escapes that one. Some say he was in the Inquisition, back in the day."

"Then I doubly advise caution," Enelda said gravely.

Hawley looked askance at Enelda, wondering what a snake-pit he was taking her into. Even here in Aelderland, where the borders were tightly controlled and foreign influence was scant, the Sylverain Inquisition was held in awe and dread.

Redbaer nodded. "If Sauveur is here, General Tarasq must have petitioned King Alberic for aid. She can't come herself without breaching the Accords, but under the guise of diplomacy, Sauveur can extend his reach far."

"How did you find out about the boy?" Enelda asked. "Before the Sylvens, I mean. Who found him?"

"The Border Companies."

"Then who knows how long he lay there?" Hawley scoffed.

"Do not speak ill of the Borderers in my presence, Sargent," Sir Redbaer said. "I spent three years commanding an outpost on the Marches, and I can tell you we saw a damn sight more trouble than a few outlaws plaguing the Gold Road."

Hawley grunted a response halfway between an apology and a rebuttal. Redbaer's aggrandising of the Borderers was precisely why the High Companies and the Border Companies were such fierce rivals. Those who protected Aelderland's interior saw action more regularly, though usually against bandits, agitators, and petty bands of raiders. The men of the borders guarded the Marches, spits of harsh land contiguous with Aelderland's neighbours. As far as Hawley could tell, Redbaer's "trouble" was little more than the odd squabble, not real fighting.

"The sargent does raise one good point," Enelda said. "Did the High Vigilant ascertain when the boy died? Or how long his body had lain in the water?"

Redbaer looked puzzled. "Ascertain it how?"

"By examining the body."

"Such a thing would be unseemly. Some might call it... necromancy."

"You know of my order and our ways?"

"A little."

"Then perhaps you should be careful what you say of my methods."

Redbaer paled. Hawley did his best not to smirk.

"I trust the cadaver is still untouched?" Enelda asked.

"Yes, but only until it can be sent back to Sylverain. They can tend to the corpse in whatever heathen ways they see fit."

"Good. Then I shall have a chance to practise my...what do you call it? 'Necromancy.'"

Redbaer coughed, bowed curtly, and spurred his horse. As he rode off to join the van, Enelda smiled deviously at Hawley.

"A pleasant enough fellow," she said. "But I do so like my peace and quiet. I have enough company with you and the bird."

As night fell, they skirted the archduke's private woodlands. Once, it had been a vast tract of virgin oak forest, but it had been stripped almost bare to build warships and siege engines in preparation for the War of Silver and Gold. The archduke's father had ordered it replanted so he might have somewhere to hunt in peacetime, though he had died before he could enjoy his opulent work. It was a folly. Already it was plagued by poachers, who risked a sentence of mutilation or even death in order to feed their families. In another tenyear, it would become home once more to outlaws, "wolfsheads," as in days of old, and it would fall to men like Hawley to round them up, as it always had.

They passed rows of gibbets, themselves planted like trees on either side of the road, wasted corpses in their iron cages. Perhaps the work had already begun.

Enelda's cold fingers curled around Hawley's. She was trembling. Scarfell had swung into view, and her eyes were fixed on the great black edifice of the castle. Torches danced across jagged battlements, carried by soldiers now alert to the presence of strangers in the middle of the night. Voices rang out ahead and behind them in the darkness. The gates opened.

Enelda closed her eyes and squeezed Hawley's hand tighter. Hawley realised this was her fear. All these people, and likely— or so she believed—a den of corruption and subterfuge. Weak minds and wicked wills, representing danger at every turn.

"My lady...Enelda," he ventured. Then, "Nell."

She opened her eyes. There was no powerful Vigilant beside Hawley now. Just a little old lady who had lived too long in a tumbledown tower in the woods.

"I'm with you," Hawley said.

They passed through the massive gates and under the portcullis. The cartwheels clattered on a cobbled track, and the wagon began the winding ascent to the keep. They passed by a guardhouse, a tavern, a temple, an empty marketplace. Soldiers waved them on through the next gatehouse at the inner walls. Dozens of servants and guards awaited them, and more filed from the castle to line the courtyard of the inner ward.

Enelda drew herself up, took a deep breath, and pulled her hand away. "I can't do this alone, Hawley." She sounded like a frightened child. "Not alone. What if they send you back to Fangmoor?"

"Call me your servant. I'll tell 'em I swore an oath. They'll have to let me stay."

"Are you sure?"

Hawley didn't answer directly, for fear of being caught in a lie. "I'll protect you," he said.

"And who will protect you?" she whispered.

*   *   *

Iveta peered around her bedroom door as another pair of servants ran breathlessly along the corridor. She'd heard her uncle bellowing orders just minutes earlier, and was sure he'd gone downstairs already. She wondered whether she dared steal across to the minstrels' gallery to see what was afoot.

"Lady Iveta, please!"

Iveta started at the intrusion on her thoughts. She hadn't even noticed Everett following behind the other servants, and the castle's steward looked at her now with a sort of resigned exasperation that she'd become quite accustomed to.

"What's happening?" she asked.

"Nothing to concern you, my lady. Your uncle would not be pleased to see you up."

"Everett," she said sternly.

The steward sighed. He straightened his green cap, considering whether to allow Iveta into his confidence. He always did, in the end.

"We have a visitor. And if the auspices are good, it's someone we've been waiting for...nay, praying for."

"Is it *him*?" Iveta gasped.

"My lady, please go back to bed. I'm needed downstairs, and your uncle would not approve of us even having this conversation."

"My uncle approves of nothing I do," Iveta scoffed.

"He has much on his mind."

"It's more than that, I think. And you have noticed his ailments?"

"I..." Everett stopped himself from saying more, but his look of sadness said it all. "The archduke is in fine health, and when this is over, all shall return to normal. You'll see."

"Ah, yes, 'normal,'" Iveta said bitterly. "He can go back to ignoring my existence instead of being openly hostile."

Everett shifted nervously and glanced along the corridor. "I must go. Lady Iveta, I implore you, go back to bed. We can speak another time."

She nodded sadly and pushed the door closed. Everett rushed off down the corridor to catch up with the others.

Iveta waited until the clamour had died down, and the family corridor was silent once more. She smiled.

Yes, she thought, *I think I shall visit the gallery tonight after all.*

CHAPTER 10

The Great Hall was draughty and cold. Fires had been lit at either end, but it would take an age to warm the vast chamber. Enelda had been seated at a long table, and Hawley stood behind her. He struggled not to sway with tiredness. Guards flanked the door, casting suspicious glances at Hawley and warier ones at Enelda, when she wasn't looking.

They had seen no one else since the castle steward showed them into the hall. Now they waited for their audience with the archduke.

Enelda pushed a plate of barely touched bread and butter away, and rapped her fingers on the table impatiently. Hawley's stomach groaned at the sight of wasted food.

"We are being watched," Enelda said very quietly.

"Eh?"

"Up there." With the minutest move of her head, Enelda indicated a dark gallery above them.

Hawley, too tired for circumspection, squinted into the shadows. A sharp movement drew his attention. For the merest moment, he saw a slender figure, a smooth, pale face. A young woman, or a girl. Then she was gone.

"Clumsy," Enelda chided.

Voices echoed somewhere beyond the hall, growing steadily louder. The guards swung open the doors, and the clamour that followed was a rude interruption to the deathly quiet that had preceded it.

The steward rushed ahead before he was trampled. Four men followed, arguing loudly, surrounded by attendants.

"But it changes nothing..."

"Be careful, my lord..."

"Spies!"

"A criminal act, my lord, against a King's Vigilant..."

"Redbaer had no right..."

"A Sylven ploy..."

"Silence!" The man at the centre of the commotion came to a sudden stop, the servants at the rear almost tumbling over each other in his wake. He held up a hand, and everyone obeyed. The man's cool eyes fell fixedly on Enelda Drake.

"Archduke Leoric, Lord Scarsdale, Marshal of the Borders, High Lord of Wulfshael!" the steward proclaimed, belatedly.

Hawley instinctively smoothed his tabard. He was acutely aware he didn't look fit to be seen in the presence of nobility. He'd barely had time to change, and his spare tunic and cloak were creased and crumpled after weeks folded in his trunk. Still, better than the alternative of greeting an archduke covered in shit.

Enelda rose slowly, infirmly. Hawley stepped forward and offered her an arm, but he took one look at her and knew it was an act. Hawley congratulated himself on becoming wise to Enelda's ways—she would conceal her true strength until it suited her otherwise. He made a show of helping her, then stepped back into position.

The steward waved a hand in Enelda's direction. "May I present Enelda Drake," he said. "The... Vigilant." This last part was added with an air of uncertainty.

There was a moment of silence again. The robed men behind the archduke gaped at Enelda. The archduke's lips curled into a smile, and he strode forward.

"It is an honour, my lady. Never had I thought my hold would be graced by the presence of a True Vigilant. And yet, here you stand."

"The honour is mine, my lord," Enelda said. "But if I might not... 'stand'? I mean, my knees are not what they once were."

"Ha! Of course, my lady, sit. Sit."

"My lord, I must advise caution," one of the other men said. He was a stout fellow, with a round belly too big for his otherwise modest frame, and a flabby second chin that clung to his face like a baby on a teat. Even had he not been wearing his pale grey robe and tall, domed hat, Hawley would have recognised the High Vigilant of Wulfshael anywhere.

"Caution?" Lord Scarsdale gave a shrug to Enelda and said, "Forgive High Vigilant Clemence. He is not known for his trusting nature—I am sure you of all people understand."

"It is not a matter of trust," Clemence said, shuffling hurriedly to the archduke's side. "It is a point of law. This...this woman... impeded Vigilant Lestyn in his administrative duties. Look—she bears Lestyn's staff even now."

"It is not his staff," Enelda said, with the sullen air of a cantankerous old woman. "It's older than he is. *Much* older." She held Clemence's glare defiantly, and it was he who looked away.

"I heard Lestyn assaulted our guest, with this very staff," the archduke interjected. "Is that right, my lady?"

Enelda rubbed at her arm sorrowfully. Hawley suspected another act—she hadn't mentioned her injury once since leaving Rowen. "It's...nothing, Lord Scarsdale."

"You are gracious for saying so," the archduke replied. He shot a withering glare at Clemence, whose chins shook like a hen's wattle.

"How was he to know?" Clemence asked. "Indeed, we have nothing but her word to say who she is."

"And the word of Sargent...Hawley, was it?" Lord Scarsdale said. Then to Clemence, "A sargent of the Third Company, who you yourself insisted on sending north."

"But a mere sargent nonetheless, my lord!" Clemence spluttered, then added to Hawley, "No offence, of course."

Hawley only shrugged.

"Perhaps if we send for Commander Hobb," Clemence said, "this matter can be proven beyond doubt. One way or another."

"Forgive me, my lady." Another man approached the table—balding, in the winter of his life, his severe tonsure and dark brown robes marking him out as a monk of Erecgham. The famous Flaescine abbot, Hawley supposed. "Did I hear correctly? Your name is Drake?"

"Aye," Enelda said. "I doubt you will have heard of me."

The monk bowed. "On the contrary. You will recall where you were on the day of the Vigilant Dissolution?"

"I could hardly forget it," Enelda said. "It was the third day of Weodermand. I was at the High Temple at Shaelcrest when the message came."

"Investigating the mysterious incident of the Vanishing Martyr, if I recall rightly." The old monk beamed, and his eyes took on a sparkle. "A matter quite dear to the hearts of my order."

"Forgive me...Master Abbot?" Enelda seemed unsure of herself, and Hawley sensed this was not an act. The monk had wrong-footed her with his knowledge.

"Abbot Meriet," the monk said, still smiling.

"As you might expect, I have quite a memory for detail, and I do not recall you present at the temple."

"And why would you? I was but a page then, an orphan taken in by the temple. And yet I was somewhat distracted that day, by the presence of a master Vigilant and his young apprentice."

Hawley sensed Enelda's discomfort. Something about the memory unsettled her.

Meriet turned to Lord Scarsdale and the others. "I have no reason to doubt Madam Drake," he said. "But if it is proof you need—more proof, even, than her ability to cow the inimitable Vigilant Lestyn—then it is a simple matter. Madam Drake does not remember me, but I remember her. More so, I remember her master, the famous Cerwyn Thawn. On that day, he received a message from King Ealwarth, gods rest him, commanding him to abandon all services to the Order of Vigilants, and return to Helmspire immediately. He read the message, and proclaimed simply, 'My duty is not to the throne, but only to the truth'..." He paused, expectantly.

Enelda stood, leaning heavily on the staff. " 'And ere my duty is done, I shall answer no summons but the call against the dark.' "

Silence once more descended. All eyes were on Enelda now.

It was Meriet who spoke first. "There you have it!" He clapped his hands together.

"This proves nothing," snapped Clemence.

"On the contrary, Lord Clemence. The conversation Madam Drake recalls occurred sixty years ago. Everyone else present at that time is long dead. Only Madam Drake and myself survive to tell the tale. The years have taken their toll on us both, but I would testify that she is the apprentice of Cerwyn Thawn."

"An apprentice is not what we require," Clemence persisted, still agitated. "If she was not fully trained when the order was dissolved, how are we to know if she can help us now?"

"*She* is growing quite tired of being talked about like she is not here," Enelda snapped. Hawley was relieved to hear some of the strength return to her voice. "Yes, I was the apprentice of Cerwyn Thawn, and he did indeed defy the Dissolution. I travelled with him a few years more, beyond these shores. I completed my training in Sil-Maqash, across the sea in far Cravania, where...where my master breathed his last. But that land is dangerous for the likes of us, and so I returned in secret...in exile...for no other reason than to breathe familiar air, and feel the earth of my homeland beneath my feet. If I was to live out my days alone, I at least wanted it to be...home."

Clemence had no response this time.

"Might I inquire how the famous Cerwyn Thawn met his end?" Meriet asked.

"It is not important," Enelda said, too hurriedly. "Suffice to say there was no glory in it."

Meriet smiled benignly and bowed once again.

Enelda took her seat, looking still as though she might fall down at any moment. Hawley could not fathom her ebbing and flowing of strength. And there was something in her reaction to any mention of her old master that clearly caused her pain.

The doors swung open. The steward entered first, looking even more flustered than before. A man garbed in midnight blue strode past him as he blurted out, "His Excellence Phillippe Sauveur of Allaincouer."

The man was tall and slender, with neat hair the colour of old lead swept back from a flawless, tanned brow, barely touched by age. A small moustache sat beneath a long, narrow nose. His eyes were dark and full of suspicion. He walked confidently to the table, almost feline in motion, then stopped and bowed.

"My lord Scarsdale," he said, his Sylven accent making every word a purr, "your servants must have forgotten to wake me. Luckily, I am a light sleeper, or I may have missed the arrival of your guest."

The archduke forced a smile, though his eyes betrayed his annoyance. "On the contrary, you are just in time." He stretched out his neck, again appearing in some discomfort. "We have been verifying the credentials of this good lady," Lord Scarsdale said. "Abbot Meriet is satisfied that she is Vigilant Drake, of the old order. And if Abbot Meriet is satisfied, then so am I." He leaned across the table and offered a silver ring, inlaid with a motif of dark blue agate and pearlescent moonstone. A motif of the Eye of Litha, set within a V.

Enelda took it gratefully and slipped it onto the forefinger of her left hand.

"For the record," Clemence chimed, "the Vigilants are *not* fully satisfied. We have never heard of Enelda Drake."

"But I have," Sauveur said. He bowed low, both tone and posture more respectful than it had been to his host. "Madame Drake, it is a rare honour."

Enelda nodded graciously.

"But... but... a *woman* no less," Clemence spluttered. "The king would never agree to this. I must protest—"

"Is not General Tarasq, greatest strategist in the army of Sylverain, also a woman?" Sauveur said.

Clemence spluttered something indistinct, and the archduke raised a hand to silence him.

"It can only be to our fortune," Leoric said. "Perhaps General Tarasq might look more favourably on Vigilant Drake. And yet, my lady, I fear your journey south has been made somewhat in vain."

"In what way?" Enelda asked.

"Surely Sir Redbaer informed you that the mystery is solved."

"Sir Redbaer informed me that a Sylven boy was found on the riverbank some way south of here."

"Again, Lord Scarsdale," Sauveur said, "with the utmost respect I remind you of our conversation earlier. There is no evidence the boy is from my country, and without evidence we have only baseless accusations."

The archduke waved his hand tiredly. "So you say, Sauveur. But the boy was found on the border, and the marks speak for themselves. Perhaps General Tarasq should look to her own province for answers."

"Forgive an old woman, my lord," Enelda said, "but are you saying that the missing peasant children of *this* mearca were also taken by foreigners?"

"I..." The archduke faltered. He looked to his councillors. None of them replied. "I suppose they might have been."

"Preposterous!" Sauveur snapped. Hawley could scarce believe the tone the Sylven took with the High Lord of Wulfshael. In Aelderland, only the king's own family outranked Lord Scarsdale, and the gibbets outside the castle were testament to the man's reputation.

"There is one way to settle the matter," Enelda said, as though nothing at all was amiss. "As I told Sir Redbaer, I could simply examine the boy's body. With your permission, of course."

"To what end?" The archduke looked at her suspiciously.

"That it might reveal its secrets to me."

"Superstitious nonsense!" Clemence cried. "I have seen the corpse, and the foul marks upon it bear the telltale signs of Sylven witchcraft."

"Nevertheless, if I am to be of any assistance, I must be allowed to employ my own methods." Enelda was calm.

The archduke became anything but. A thunderous look crossed his dark features. He rubbed at his neck agitatedly, then paced up and down, before spinning on his heels to confront Enelda.

"I cannot have you casting doubt upon my trusted advisors," he said flatly.

"My lord," Enelda said, in her sweetest way, "you sent for me. Indeed, I was brought here against my better judgement. You must let me help you now that I'm here, in my own way, or I might as well go home."

"She has a point, my lord," Meriet said. "None of us here know the methods of the old Vigilants, save what the history books and bards' tales record. But we do know they were successful."

"Successful in ridding Aelderland of the Riftborn's servants," Lord Scarsdale said. "But there are no Riftborn any more."

"If there ever were..." Clemence muttered.

"Who can say, my lord?" Meriet replied, ignoring Clemence. "Dark work is clearly afoot, and I can see no other way of appeasing General Tarasq."

The archduke rubbed at his face. Hawley couldn't fathom why the man was so agitated—he had what he wanted, after all. He did, however, look very tired. Those deep-set eyes were ringed with purpled bags that spoke of sleepless nights. What pressures must rest upon the shoulders of a man like Leoric, who alone was responsible for defending the south.

"I grant permission to inspect the corpse," Lord Scarsdale said. "But High Vigilant Clemence shall be present."

"And me," Sauveur said, courting a daggered glare from the archduke. "I would put the matter of the boy's identity to rest. Then I shall return to Fort L'trinité and make my report." There was something unnerving about Sauveur's dark eyes. He put Hawley in mind of a torturer, rather than a diplomat.

Archduke Leoric sighed. "You can wait until the morrow, I presume?"

Enelda smiled. "Of course. And...I will need something more."

"What else?"

"Permission to question all within the castle. Servants, nobles, guards...family. All."

"Outrageous!" Clemence said.

"Why would you need to question anyone?" Lord Scarsdale said, ignoring the High Vigilant once again.

"In the event that the examination of the body proves inconclusive, then I will need to go back to the beginning. I would explore every possibility, leave no stone unturned."

"Even if Lord Clemence and his men have already questioned everyone in the castle?"

"Even then, my lord."

"Chamberlain Tymon, you've been damnably quiet. What say you?" The archduke now addressed the last of his council—a black-robed man of middle age, who had so far remained silent.

The fellow bobbed his head up and down, much like Enelda's raven often did. Indeed, the chamberlain's manner was entirely too avian for Hawley's liking; his head jutted awkwardly from the furred trim of his heavy robes. The silver chains of office about his neck looked far too heavy for his frame.

"I can see no harm in it," Tymon said at last. "Now she's here, she might as well...well...yes." He grew quieter as he realised everyone was listening to him, until finally he trailed off altogether.

"Very well," the archduke assented. "Though the hour is late, I call to session an emergency meeting of my council. Sit—eat, drink. We have much to discuss."

The steward began to usher the servants from the Great Hall. Even the guards marched out. The steward looked to Hawley in expectation. Hawley resolutely ignored him.

"Thank you, Sargent Hawley, for bringing Vigilant Drake to my hall," said Lord Scarsdale. "We are all indebted to you. You are dismissed."

Hawley looked to Enelda. She didn't meet his gaze, nor did she speak.

"That is *all*, Sargent," Lord Scarsdale said sternly. "You may return to Fort Fangmoor on the morrow, after you have rested."

"I would ask that Sargent Hawley be granted the same freedoms as I," Enelda said. It had taken her a moment to speak up, and she didn't sound convincing.

"Why?" The archduke raised his brows.

"He is...my servant. For the time being."

"Servant? A king's man?"

"M'lord," Hawley said, becoming painfully aware of his provincial accent, "if I might speak."

"We await the explanation with bated breath," Lord Scarsdale said.

"I swore an oath to safeguard Vigilant Drake, until such time that I might return her safely north. It was part of her condition for coming. I'm...honour bound to see it through." Hawley hoped it sounded convincing.

The archduke barely credited Hawley with acknowledgement, but instead looked directly to Enelda. "You have no need of a soldier. You are in no danger here."

"Perhaps, but then neither was Anton Tarasq." Enelda had grown visibly more confident when Hawley had spoken up. Now she appeared unruffled by the black look that crossed the archduke's features. "If someone were to try to spirit me away, what then? Would you leave an old woman defenceless?"

Vigilant Clemence, standing off to the side and pretending thus far not to listen, coughed and spluttered abruptly.

The archduke glowered, but said finally, "No, my lady. Of course not. Sargent Hawley has the freedom of the castle. *Provided*," he added forcefully, "that you are with him while outside the common areas."

Enelda bowed. "Thank you, Lord Scarsdale."

"But he is not needed now. We have sensitive business to discuss that I would not even entrust to my own castle guard. My steward shall make the sargent comfortable—I promise you shall survive the night so that the sargent might uphold his oath tomorrow. Agreeable?"

Enelda nodded.

The steward cleared his throat and glared sharply at Hawley.

Hawley knew he had little choice. He didn't want to leave Enelda, lest she have one of her episodes, but reluctantly he followed the steward as the council was seated. As he left, he could not fail to notice the daggers glared at him by Clemence. There would yet be a price for the assault on Lestyn, but Hawley was too tired to worry about that.

As the steward pulled the doors shut behind them, Hawley chanced one last look back to the gallery. And there again, just for a second before the great doors closed fully, he thought he spied a pale face, lit only weakly by the candlelight from below, and now, he saw, framed by raven-black hair.

She could have been the castle ghost for all he knew. He had seen only the merest glimpse, the suggestion of face and form. And yet he thought her beautiful.

CHAPTER 11

Did you see him?" Ermina hissed.

Iveta pushed the bedroom door quietly closed, and tiptoed across the room to the little girl's bed. Ermina's eyes were full of anticipation.

"Not *him*," Iveta said. "*Her*. Her name is Enelda Drake."

Ermina gasped in wonderment. "A lady Vigilant...Is she very old?"

"Very. Older than Abbot Meriet, even."

Ermina wrinkled her nose. "I thought Abbot Meriet was the oldest person alive!"

Iveta laughed, and drew the girl close. "Not quite, little one... and don't let him hear you say it!"

"Do you think she knew Lady Aenya?"

"I don't know. I suppose she might have."

"Do you...do you think she'll find Anton?" Ermina's delight quickly turned to sadness. Anton was like a brother to them both. Each time the girl remembered the unoccupied bedchamber next door, the feeling of emptiness returned. The boy who had so often shared these moments was gone.

"Maybe she's mentioned in the book," Iveta said, conjuring what levity she could. "Such a pity it's too late to read it tonight." Iveta paused for effect, waited until Ermina jutted out her bottom lip, then gave the girl a wink.

Ermina clapped her hands together with glee. Iveta envied Ermina's capacity to forget the loss, even for a moment.

Iveta slipped across the room, fumbled about beneath the wardrobe, and slid out a heavy book from its hiding place. She heaved it into her arms and returned to the bed, presenting the tome theatrically to Ermina by candlelight.

Ermina took a moment to study the title, *The Deeds of Aenya the Protectress, Volume Four*, then stood on the bed and jumped up and down, until Iveta finally managed to shush her.

"Be quiet, Ermina," Iveta reminded her young cousin. "Remember I shall get into awful trouble if anyone finds out. If you promise to keep our secret, I will read to you."

The girl nodded enthusiastically. "I promise!" she hissed.

Iveta hopped onto the bed, and the girl cuddled close. "Good," she whispered, kissing Ermina's flaxen hair. She pulled the candle nearer and opened the book.

Ermina gasped at the sight of the frontis, an exquisite rendering of a heroic figure, sword held aloft, summoning the Majestics from the heavens to bring victory on the field of battle. No detail was overlooked: the hero's uniform of green and gold, the shield emblazoned with the Aelderland dragon, the sword painted in silver so that the candlelight gleamed from it. Magical flames of yellow and orange danced around the blade. The Sygellite who had painted the scene had been skilled indeed. But none of that was what thrilled the girl. No, it was the subject matter that led Ermina to fix upon the image, to trace over it with her fingertips, a gleeful look on her face, her blue eyes open wide. For the hero in the painting was a woman, and images of women at war had been outlawed from display since the reign of Eadred had begun.

This book, Iveta guessed, had survived only because the text within was one of the few written records of Lady Aenya's history, and as such was a valued family heirloom, exempted from the law so long as it was kept under lock and key. But Iveta had never been one for obeying the rules, and the cofferer was careless with his keys.

Finally, Ermina took her hand away, allowing Iveta to turn the page.

No bedtime story had ever enraptured the girl quite like

this one, although Iveta had a job on her hands to transform a dry history book into a tale of adventure suitable for a young lady. But whether or not Iveta was successful, her cousin hung on every word. Iveta recited the history of Lady Aenya from the earliest days, when her father—Archduke Leoric's great-great-grandfather, Albertus—was slain by rampaging Northmen, forcing his wife, Aela, to take control of the manor. Driven by a desire for revenge, Aenya, no older than Ermina at that time, ran away to join the Sisters of Oak, who resided in a fortress long since ruined. There she swore oaths that prevented her mother from reclaiming her, and learned the arts of war from the fierce warrior women of the order. At age seventeen she joined the march north to Jotungärd, where she campaigned for eight months, returning home a hero, with her father's killer in a cage. When she had distinguished herself in three campaigns, at the age of twenty-three she earned the right to purchase a release from her oaths, which she did only because her ailing mother needed her at Scarfell. For ten years, Aenya ruled the manor of Scarsdale, marrying only after securing the king's consent that she be allowed to retain control of her manor and not relinquish it to her husband. The marriage was not the happiest, but it produced two sons nonetheless, both of whom Lady Aenya would outlive. However, the call to war was never far away in those days. Such was Aenya's fame and notoriety that when the War of Silver and Gold erupted, every freeman within thirty leagues marched to Scarfell to pledge allegiance to her, and she rode to Sylverain with an army to rival a king.

Ermina had never stayed awake so long for a story, and Iveta found her own eyelids growing heavy. Her lack of sleep of late was catching up with her. She knew she would have to be careful if her forays into Halham were to remain unnoticed.

Iveta was about to close the book and persuade Ermina to go to sleep, when the sound of heavy footsteps echoed from the passage outside. A deep voice followed, muffled but commanding.

"Father!" Ermina cried. She leapt from the bed and rushed to the door before Iveta could stop her.

"No!" Iveta hissed. She quickly pushed the book under the bedclothes.

Ermina threw open the door. "Father, Father! Did you meet the Vigilant? What's she like?"

Leoric was speaking with Redbaer and now wheeled around to face his daughter.

Iveta at once recognised the look on her uncle's face, and jumped out of bed herself to save her young cousin from the archduke's wrath.

"*She?* Who has been telling you...Why are you awake? Back to bed!" Leoric's anger was sudden, unwarranted. "Back to bed this instant!"

Ermina stopped in her tracks, looking up at this dark-eyed man who could so easily change from loving father to iron-fisted tyrant, as he did more frequently since Anton's disappearance. Over Uncle Leoric's shoulder, Redbaer wore a sympathetic look, but there was nothing he could do.

Leoric put a hand on Ermina's shoulder and shoved her hard back into the room, causing the girl to cry out. Iveta was there in a trice, catching her, pulling her into the sanctuary of the bedchamber.

"You!" the archduke growled at Iveta. "Why are you not in your own room? Stories again, I suppose? Filling my daughter's head full of nonsense."

Iveta struggled to find some response. Uncle Leoric could not know exactly what kind of "nonsense" she had been reading to Ermina tonight, but the guilt she felt left her tongue-tied.

"Put those candles out; get to sleep!" With that, he slammed the door closed.

Ermina began to sob in Iveta's arms.

The archduke could still be heard beyond the door, and was now turning his ire to Redbaer. "Why are there no guards outside this room?"

"The guard is doubled, my lord," Redbaer replied. "They're patrolling—"

"I will not have my daughter stolen away as well. Am I understood?"

"Yes, my lord."

More guards. Iveta would have to be extra careful. She might have to put a stop to her missions of mercy altogether...but what then for the people she had come to care for?

"I'm going to my chapel," the archduke said, "and am not to be disturbed."

Lord Scarsdale's footsteps boomed again and faded down the hall.

Iveta led her cousin back to bed. She tucked Ermina in and retrieved the book. "No more stories tonight," she said.

Ermina sniffed. "Will you stay, though?"

"Of course." Iveta climbed into the bed.

"I wish I was as strong as Aenya," Ermina said. She looked to the other door, the one that joined her room to Anton's empty chamber. "Then I could have saved Anton."

"Anton will be saved," Iveta said.

"Do you really think so?"

"I do. Vigilant Drake will find him, I'm sure. Now go to sleep, little one. It's very late."

The girl squeezed Iveta tight and closed her eyes. Iveta waited until her breathing grew deep and her head heavy against her, before snuffing out the candle.

She well knew of the powers of the old Vigilants, but Iveta did not truly believe Anton would be found. Unlike others in the castle, Iveta knew of the world beyond the walls, of the villages gripped by fear. She had heard many times of children snatched in the night by silent intruders.

And they never came back.

*   *   *

Wealsdaeg, 5th Day of Nystamand

Despite his fatigue the previous night, Hawley was up with the birds. A soldier's habits died hard. He treated his many bruises with the foul-smelling unguents from Enelda, then strapped up his ribs before donning his spare uniform, woefully creased from his travels.

Hawley poked his head from his room into a shadowed corridor, where the waxy orange light of dawn filtered weakly from high, barred windows. He'd been instructed to remain in the servants' quarters until he was sent for, and so he left the cell-like room he'd been allocated and, guided only by his rumbling stomach, strolled as far as the kitchens, where servants came and went busily, ignoring him completely.

Eventually, a large, matronly woman waddled into the vast kitchen, heralding her arrival by cuffing a lollygagging lad around the ear and ordering him to "get that parcel to the groomsman or there'll be 'ell to pay." She fixed her formidable gaze on Hawley.

"Wot'choo doing in my kitchen?" she said.

"Cook?" Hawley asked.

"Who else?"

Hawley shrugged. "Was hopin' I'd find some food." Everyone knew the authority of a cook in her kitchen was like to a captain on a ship. But Hawley would not be bullied by the serving staff, even in the castle of a High Lord.

The woman squinted at him. "Well sit thee down, then! Big lump like you'll only get in the way of my girls."

Hawley sat on a hard bench at a long wooden table. It reminded him of the refectory back at Fort Fangmoor. He would often break bread alone there, too—better that than suffer the whispers and jibes of his so-called brothers in arms. Oh, he had friends at the fort, true enough. He'd wished many times the likes of Sherrat, Nasbeth, or Ernaeld had been with him in the Elderwood. He doubted they'd have conspired against him, but even they were the fair-weather kind, who'd stand by him only as long as their own reputations were not tarnished by association.

"You're 'ere to find the boy, then?" the cook called over, interrupting Hawley's woolgathering.

"Aye."

"And you brung a Vigilant, they say."

"How did you—?"

"Word travels fast, 'specially down 'ere. Folk have had enough o' Vigilants these past few years, mind. Since Lord Clemence came, at any rate."

"I know," Hawley said. The Third had been called many times to help Lord Clemence's justiciars enforce the king's law. Lestyn was not alone in his predilection for harsh penalties for the most trifling infringements.

"He was in 'ere all the time, you know," the cook said, as she carved into a dark-crusted loaf.

"Lord Clemence?"

"Don't talk daft. The boy. Anton. Right little scamp he were. I'd catch him 'ere late at night sometimes. Or see him running about the corridors, quiet as a temple mouse."

"What was he doing?"

"Looking for cake, most like. Proper little lord he were, didn't care none if he was caught. And he had free run o' the castle, I hear. But he were all right, I s'pose. He weren't wicked." She turned to squint at Hawley. "Like boys can be."

"You said 'were' ... 'was,'" Hawley said, dodging the cook's scrutiny. "You think the boy's dead?"

"What else?" She looked back to her work with a sniff. She'd been fond of the boy—a Sylven boy, no less. That said a lot. "Been weeks now. Children don't just—"

"Beggin' your pardon, sir," a timid voice interrupted them.

It was a young maid, barely in her teenage years yet already accustomed to hard work. In her chapped, red hands she held a bundle of neatly folded clothes, topped by a pair of battered boots. Hawley's belongings. "I brushed these best I could," she said. "My apologies, sir, that they weren't ready when you rose. I came lookin' but—"

"Quiet, Agnead," the cook snapped. "He don't need your life story."

Agnead's cheeks reddened like she'd been slapped. Her eyes flicked down to the stone floor.

"It's all right, lass," Hawley said. He tried to adopt a gentle tone, though even to his own ears his voice always sounded anything but. "Just put them here." He patted the bench beside him.

The girl approached tentatively, deposited the clothes, and curtseyed as though Hawley were a lord. The status of the High Companies was not something a man like Hawley could ever become accustomed to. Once, he'd been a low-born, like this girl. Perhaps lower—an orphan of uncertain parentage, lucky to have ever seen the outside of a mine, let alone don the uniform of the companies.

Hawley remembered to say "Thank you," which only made Agnead blush even deeper before she scurried away, like one of those temple mice Cook had mentioned.

Hawley started at a loud clatter on the tabletop. A plate of food appeared before him, and Cook loomed over him, fixing him with a disapproving stare. He remembered other things soldiers were known for, and felt more than a little shame on their behalf.

However, the sight of bread and salted butter, hard biscuits, smoked sprats, sweet dates, and two hard-boiled eggs before him gave Hawley the mental fortitude to shrug aside Cook's misplaced suspicions. The food was nothing more than leftovers from Lord Scarsdale's table, but after weeks on the campaign trail it looked like a feast indeed. He shoved a handful of dates into his mouth eagerly, the juice spilling messily down his chin. He closed his eyes, not remembering when he had last had the luxury of time to himself and a plate of food that was more than mere nourishment. And then his momentary peace was rudely interrupted.

"There you are, Hawley." Enelda Drake's voice was unmistakable, as was the sombre silence that followed.

Hawley opened his eyes to see a dozen or more servants, the cook included, frozen like statues, gawping at the door. He wiped his scrappy beard with his sleeve, forgetting that he was wearing his clean tunic, and slid around to see Enelda standing before him.

If the servants had heard of Hawley's arrival, they had most certainly heard of Enelda's, and they could not have imagined that she would be standing in the kitchen, in the heart of their little domain. She was dressed in her white robe, though she had a grey woollen shawl about her shoulders for warmth. The carved wooden seal of Litha hung about her neck, and she carried a pale leather knapsack, which bulged heavily. The only real change in her—and it was a stark one—was her hair. No longer was it fastened up, but now hung loose, brushed long and straight past her shoulders, lustrous and white as driven snow. Were she a younger woman, this in itself would have caused a scandal. With this simple act, Enelda marked herself as someone quite different from the other denizens of the castle.

Enelda sat beside Hawley. Hawley glowered at the cook, who in turn clapped her hands together and barked orders at her kitchen staff and delivery boys, spurring them all back to their duties with sharp words and sharper slaps.

"Your meeting with the council was productive?" Hawley asked in a hushed voice.

"Oh, yes. They made a show of telling me nothing whatsoever, but I learned a great deal."

"Such as?"

"You first."

"Me?"

"Yes," said Enelda. "You've proved yourself singularly observant, for a soldier, and your instincts about people seem...surprisingly sound. I'd like to know what you thought of the noble lords."

"I'd rather not..." Hawley looked around circumspectly.

"Always so coy! Come now: Lord Clemence. What do you make of him?"

Hawley squirmed in his seat and loosened his collar as though hot, even though the kitchen was still chilly.

"Never met him before," Hawley said, only with great reluctance. "By reputation he's a hard man, and a clever one—he was a physician before he came here, by all accounts. But I'll be honest, he was a lot more...irritable...than I expected. Thought he'd be a bit steadier, if you take my meaning. You...you sure you really care for my opinion?"

"Would I have asked otherwise? Go on."

Hawley sighed. "Right. Well, he's more of a politician than a physician, if you take my meaning. Not sure I'd trust a word he said."

"Not bad. Now the chamberlain."

Hawley looked around again. Cook was out of sight and hopefully out of earshot. "Didn't get much of a look at him. Seemed a bit on edge, like a dog expecting someone to steal his dinner at any moment. I'd say he had a guilty conscience, but I doubt he's got the stomach for kidnap or murder. Doubt he's got the stomach for much at all."

"Lord Scarsdale."

Hawley flinched. "I'm saying nowt. Not here. You're as like to get me flogged."

"You betray your feelings about him with your silence, but no matter. Very well: Abbot Meriet."

"Too pious for his own good. Never met a holy man who didn't have some secrets squirrelled away up his cassock."

Enelda tutted loudly. "Two out of three. As I said, you have good instincts. But you must learn to use reason. Investigations rely on observable facts and hard evidence."

"I suppose you know better?"

"Naturally. Here's what I learned. The High Vigilant is a skilled apothecary, and his irritability comes not only from a naturally mean disposition, but from partaking too much of his own remedies. A tincture of star root and Sylven rue would be my guess. The former would explain the discolouration of his fingernails and the slight redness of his nostrils, and the latter would account for his nervous tic—when he tells a half-truth, his left eyelid twitches every thirteenth syllable. Most curious. Contrary to your belief, he is not a physician of any note, or he would have done more to salve the archduke's physical ailments. I suspect Lord Scarsdale would benefit greatly from the application of snail paste, but that is neither here nor there.

"The chamberlain has a deep mistrust of everyone, it seems, and he is particularly concerned with balancing the castle's accounts. A man after my own heart, truth be told, for he says little and sees much. I expect he knows better than anyone the comings and goings of Scarfell, and their motivations. As he is not naturally a brave man, this knowledge frays his nerves. One slip of the tongue and I'm sure he could seal the fate of someone or other, if not himself.

"And as for the abbot…that's where you are wrong, I'm afraid. Your assertion is made for once not on instinct but on assumption, which is even worse. Meriet is a fine fellow, though I find it queer that a man of his advanced years would choose not to rest here at the castle. We did not conclude our business until the small hours, and even then, the abbot insisted on returning to his abbey."

"Why?"

"I suppose he is of a singularly dutiful nature."

"You seemed surprised last night, if you don't mind me saying. That the abbot knew your master, I mean."

The flicker of Enelda's eyes betrayed her uncertainty, or perhaps annoyance. "More surprised that he remembered me."

"Was he a great Vigilant, your master? Thawn, wasn't it?"

"You mean you have never heard of him? And why would you? He was a humble man, who sought neither fame nor glory. He required no reward but the diminishing of the darkness."

"You said you'd travelled far with him. I thought you'd lived in that tower forever—a bit like a monk yourself."

"I have travelled farther than any could know. And monks have often lived a life, too. Even Meriet, the holiest of men."

"What do you mean?"

"He was once married, to start with."

"He said so?"

"Don't be foolish, Hawley. I observed a pair of small scars on his ring finger. His wedding band must have become too small to remove, possibly due to the swelling of his knuckles with age; and so the ring was cut away by a smith. He must have been old before taking his holy orders, and he must have been free to do so, which means his wife had already passed over."

"Never would've imagined it."

"You must always look closer. The twists and turns of a life lived are written on men and women like script on parchment. In scars, in bearing, in the lines on the brow, the look in the eyes. You're testament to that."

Hawley fidgeted in his seat.

"I almost forgot about the castle's foreign guest," Enelda said. "How did you find Sauveur?"

Hawley shrugged. "All Sylvens are slippery. He's no exception."

"Assumptions, Hawley..."

"Go on then. Enlighten me."

"Phillippe Sauveur knows far more than he ought to about the comings and goings in this castle. No one else seemed to notice, but I would venture he has a spy here."

Hawley glanced furtively over his shoulder at the cook, who was now engaged in conversation with a scullery maid.

"Do you know who?"

"Suspicions, nothing more. But be doubly careful—the walls have ears, my lad." Her expression warmed, and she said more loudly, "Walk with me, Hawley."

"Can I finish breakfast first?"

"No time."

More servants hurried in and out now, bustling and buzzing like bees making honey. Sensing there would be no more privacy here, Hawley stood and tucked his clothes under one arm and offered the other to Enelda.

She swiped a boiled egg from his plate, and bit it before taking Hawley's arm.

"I do like eggs," she said.

Hawley sighed. "What are we going to do first?"

Enelda smiled devilishly and said, "Necromancy."

CHAPTER 12

T his is most irregular," Clemence said, not for the first time.
"If it was regular, you would not need me," Enelda
replied.

The look Clemence gave her over his shoulder suggested he
didn't think she was needed at all.

Hawley noticed now the slight redness around Clemence's
eyes and nose, a twitchiness about his general manner. Maybe he
really was taking a little too much of his own tinctures, as Enelda
had surmised.

Clemence saw Hawley observing him, and gave a snort of
superiority, before clicking a heavy iron key in the lock.

Beside them, Sauveur stood in silence. Hawley thought the
Sylven looked like a necromancer himself, with a wide-brimmed
black hat casting his stern face into shadow.

Soon, the unlikely group descended a long slope into a darkened cellar. A servant led the way, lantern in hand, a roll of leather
tucked under the other arm. Hawley wondered what it was for.
The slope flattened out, and the passage broadened. The servant
went ahead and lit torches, throwing light onto a large storeroom.

"You keep your dead in here?" Enelda asked.

"We *burn* the bodies of the dead," Clemence replied. "But this
is the only place in the castle cool enough to store the boy until
we send him back to Sylverain."

"You keep saying 'back' to Sylverain," Sauveur said. It was the
first time he'd spoken since they'd left the keep.

"Quite so," Enelda agreed. "Until we are certain of this boy's origins, any such action will only serve to provoke General Tarasq. For the time being, it will not do to store the body here. What if the food—"

"Pah!" the High Vigilant scoffed. "Farther back there is the ice chamber, kept cold most of the year round by the underground stream that feeds the moat. Everyone knows ice can destroy any foul humour."

"Then it seems I was correct in my assumption," Enelda said.

"What assumption?"

"That you are no physician."

Enelda marched past the High Vigilant, leaving his mouth working soundlessly, the sack-like jowls beneath his chin contracting like a salted slug. Sauveur followed her. Hawley would have laughed were his position not so precarious. Enelda antagonised the High Vigilant in front of a foreigner—a potential enemy. It was a dangerous game.

They entered a vaulted cavern. Ice was packed around the far wall, growing almost organically from the stones. Small, milky stalactites hung in clusters from the arched ceiling, droplets of water echoing in the gloomy chamber, feeding slippery, half-frozen moss beneath their feet. Near the ice was a table. And on the table was a lumpen form beneath a shroud of stained linen. A small corpse.

"Bring light," Enelda said.

The servant did not move.

"Come," she encouraged him. "Bring light, there's a good fellow. Lay those tools down, then you may go."

The servant swallowed, then did as he'd been asked, before backing from the chamber. He flinched at Clemence's disapproving scowl as he went.

Hawley looked only at the wrapped bundle. "Tools." It was no wonder the High Vigilant looked so grave.

Enelda unrolled the bundle, revealing a number of large knives, curved blades, a saw, pincers, and tongs.

"From the butcher," Clemence said with some distaste.

"They will suffice." Enelda opened the sack next, and took out a leather apron, splattered with dubious stains. This she put on over her robes. She tied back her hair. "There is another here, Hawley. For you."

Hawley looked down at his clean uniform, sighed, and took the apron from the sack.

Finally, Enelda rummaged in her bag and produced a set of eyeglasses unlike any Hawley had ever seen, adorned as they were with three sets of lenses. She pinched them onto the bridge of her nose, and hooked their thin metal arms behind her ears. She flipped the lenses up and down one by one until satisfied that she could see clearly. When she looked up at Hawley and Clemence, her eyes appeared enormous.

"I shall...observe," the High Vigilant said.

Enelda simply waved a hand towards him dismissively.

Hawley stared at the shroud. The cloth sank in around the eyes and lips, giving the corpse the appearance of a ghost. This boy, it was said, was the victim of witchcraft. Even if Hawley had been standing beside a roaring fire rather than a mound of ice, he would have felt just as cold. "I'd rather not meddle with the dead," he whispered. "Bad luck."

"Be firm, Hawley. You've made enough corpses in your time, I'll wager. It is rather hypocritical to fear them after the fact."

Enelda threw back the sheet, revealing the naked torso of a young lad. The boy was gaunt and pale, with long, dark hair plastered against a smooth brow. The eyes were set in sunken pits, disturbingly reminiscent of Vigilant Lestyn's skeletal sockets.

Hawley sucked air through his teeth and stepped away.

"What?" Enelda asked.

Hawley stared at the marks on the body. Black welts the size of hen's eggs, trailing in three rows from left shoulder to navel, each surrounded by purplish bruises, and dozens of tiny branches of thin, dark veins. Purpling buboes clustered around the boy's throat and under his armpits.

"The Winnowing," Hawley said. The words escaped his throat in a wheeze.

"These marks are the same?"

"Near as I can remember."

"Impossible," Clemence intoned. "There have been no reports of the Great Sickness for a tenyear."

"Still think the Winnowing's insignificant?" Hawley whispered.

Enelda turned to the High Vigilant. "You have experience of the Winnowing?"

"I...That is...From my studies, yes."

"Studies from books?"

The High Vigilant nodded sheepishly.

"You have never seen the stigmata for yourself?"

"A *practical* study would have been desirable, of course. But the bodies of the afflicted were customarily burned. What I *have* seen, however, are the stigmata brought about by the misuse of the blackrock. And that, Madam Drake, is what we have here."

Clemence's left lower eyelid twitched at the words "desirable" and "customarily." *Well, I'll be...* Hawley thought.

"What say you, Viscount Sauveur?" Enelda asked.

The hawkish Sylven stroked his moustache. "Possible," he purred. "But the implication that only my people would dabble with the blackrock is insulting."

Enelda turned back to the table without another word and handed Hawley a pair of elbow-length leather gloves from the sack. "Just in case," she said.

"To prevent contagion?"

"If there is contagion here, it is likely already spread. If not to us, then to others who handled this corpse. It is possible that any disease is borne only in the fluids of the body...That is all we can protect ourselves against now."

Hawley balked. Had he survived the Winnowing, battle, and attempted assassination, only to be killed by a dead boy?

"Courage, Hawley," Enelda said, as though reading his mind. "The Winnowing did not affect those in good health. As I am almost at the end of my days, I have more to fear than you. But I fear it not. Now turn him—I must see his back."

Hawley set hands on the corpse gingerly and lifted it from the slab. The boy was cold and stiff; his joints creaked like rusted hinges.

"More marks...and something else," Enelda mused. "This boy has been flogged, more than once. How long ago I cannot tell—the wounds were well healed when he died. All right, Hawley, put him back."

With that, Enelda flipped down the other lenses of her strange eyeglasses, making her eyes appear three times larger than usual, and bent over the corpse. "More light," she commanded.

Hawley held the lantern close.

Enelda opened one of the boy's eyes and stared deep into it through her lenses.

"His eyes are blue," she said. "An uncommon colour amongst Sylvens. Not yet clouded, which tells us a little about when he died." She peeled back the boy's upper lip. She looked closely at his teeth and gums, and then forced open the mouth with a loud click. She ran a finger around inside the mouth, withdrew it, and inspected the residue on her glove. She wiped this on her apron before clicking the boy's mouth closed.

Hawley shuddered—the boy's one open eye stared up at him accusingly.

Enelda asked, "Lord Clemence, the bruising on the boy's neck...what make you of that?"

"I...That is..."

"Overlooked, perhaps, due to the prominence of the welts?"

Clemence said nothing. Enelda took up a cloth, dampened it on a nearby mound of ice, and rubbed at the boy's neck gently. Sure enough, when the grime was removed, raw marks were evident on the boy's neck, obscured by welts.

Sauveur leaned in slightly now.

"Strangled," he said.

"Indeed," Enelda replied.

"Impossible..." Clemence muttered.

"With a knotted cord," Enelda went on. "A cincture perhaps."

"Cincture?" Hawley said. "From a monk's habit?"

"Monk, nun...some priests. Funny things, cinctures. The

number of knots, and the colour and width of the cord, is unique to every monastic order."

"You can tell how many knots there were?"

"From the impressions in the skin, at least four. Unfortunately, that only rules out one order: the Trysglerites. They only use three knots, as you might expect. The thickness of the cord is perhaps five *linies*... That may help us narrow down the search."

Hawley's thoughts turned to the monks he'd seen around the castle, and the abbot in particular. Flaescines were hardly uncommon in Wulfshael, but hardly murderers either.

Enelda now scrutinised the boy's fingernails, one by one, and uttered a quiet "Hmm" through pursed lips. Then she moved to the other end of the table and lifted the sheet. She looked at the soles of the feet and the painfully thin ankles. Finally, she returned to the top of the table, reached to the boy's head, and took up a handful of long, matted hair. She gave it a gentle tug, and a substantial clump came away in her hand. She held the hair to the lantern and peered at the roots.

"As I thought," she muttered, raising her eyeglasses.

"What is it?" Clemence asked.

"The boy was malnourished. I doubt he had eaten a good meal in some time. The pale gums, the bloodshot eyes, the loss of hair... He would have been incredibly weak. If he escaped his captors, I doubt he would have been able to run far."

"Captors? So you agree he was held prisoner?"

"Almost certainly. The feet are calloused from standing on stone for prolonged periods, barefoot. And his skin is unnaturally pale. He could not have seen the sun for many months. His fingernails are cracked and worn, his fingertips aggravated from scratching, possibly at the door of his cell, although the river has washed away the evidence. But there is something beneath those fingernails that ought not be there."

"Oh?"

"Flesh, Lord Clemence. Someone else's flesh. An attacker's, or a captor's. The boy scratched someone, and those jagged, damaged fingernails would have made quite a mark. The target's flesh is wedged deep under the nails—deep enough that even the river did not wash it away."

Clemence cleared his throat. He looked decidedly uncomfortable.

"There is something more," Enelda went on. "The decomposition was hindered by the water, but from the condition of the body, I do not believe he could have been in the river for more than a day, and probably less than that."

"You can tell all that from..." Clemence began, then cleared his throat and said, "How does any of this help us?"

"It could be of more help than you know," Enelda said. "But I can only be sure after I have looked inside."

"If you cut open that boy," the High Vigilant said, "you insult the gods."

At this, Enelda wheeled about and fixed Clemence with her most penetrating glare. "The gods care little for the follies of men. But I care, for without exposing such folly, superstition and prejudice make a mockery of justice. Let the gods judge me all they will; let me be the judge of other mortals."

The High Vigilant's mouth dropped open. That anyone would speak to him thus must have come as a shock. That it would be a diminutive old woman was almost too much for him to bear. By the time he managed to close his mouth, his expression told that he had dismissed Enelda's words out of sheer disbelief. To his credit, he said nothing more.

"Light, Hawley," Enelda said.

Hawley had let the lantern droop, and now raised it again.

Enelda took up a thin knife, which gleamed in the yellow light. Without hesitation or the merest tremor of her hand, she pushed the tip of the blade into the boy's throat and sliced a neat line all the way to his navel. Slimy, pale fluid bubbled forth from beneath the skin, followed by thin tendrils of dark, purplish blood. With the blood came the odour of decay, almost nauseatingly sweet.

Hawley tried not to breathe, mindful of Enelda's warning of contagion. He already had visions of waking on the morrow covered in black welts. He tried to push such morbidity aside. As for the stench, he told himself it was no worse than a wounded soldier's gangrenous limb, and that Enelda's grim work was no different from a routine amputation.

Enelda made two more incisions, outwards from the first, then peeled back the boy's flesh like the rind of a fruit.

Clemence made a sound like air escaping bellows.

Enelda set down the knife and picked up a heavy butchering axe with a crescent-shaped blade.

"Hawley," she whispered. "You must help me. I...I lack the strength."

Through gritted teeth Hawley asked, "What must I do?"

Enelda handed him the axe and took the lantern from him. "Split the breastbone lengthways," she said.

Hawley nodded grimly.

"Then prise apart the ribcage so I can see inside," she finished.

"Prise apart the..." Hawley cleared his throat three times, the distaste lodged in his craw.

"Barbaric," Clemence snapped.

Hawley looked to the heavens momentarily—or, rather, to the arched ceiling of the damp cellar—asked forgiveness from the gods, then struck. The bone crunched. The frailty of the body—a child's body, Hawley reminded himself—was just as surprising as it ever was on the field of battle. One blow was all it took. Hawley set down the axe and pulled the ribs apart, exposing the boy's organs. The stench was almost enough to topple him. Hawley willed himself not to retch. The boy's one open eye stared at him throughout.

What are you doing to me? How can I know peace, so defiled?

Hawley held the lantern aloft once more and looked away, more in shame than disgust.

"Now, that is curious," Enelda said.

Hawley squinted at the gruesome sight. Something was amiss.

"Is it...s'posed to look like that?"

"No, it is not."

The lungs and heart were black, cracked and scaled like charcoal.

"My god..." Sauveur said. It was the first time he'd reacted at all.

"It's like he was...burned," Hawley said. "From the inside."

"You see!" Clemence exclaimed. "More evidence of the misuse of blackrock. What else but sorcery could have done such a thing?"

"For once, you may be right," Enelda muttered. Then she took up a wickedly curved blade, and Hawley could look upon the scene no longer.

From the squelching sounds that followed, he knew Enelda was rummaging around in the boy's innards. He heard the scrape of the knife, and a stench like fish guts assailed his nostrils. Clemence, though farthest from the body, vomited. Hawley kept the contents of his own stomach in place, thanking an iron constitution developed slowly and steadily over a life of unpleasant necessities.

After what seemed an eternity, Enelda threw the sheet back over the body. She peeled off her gloves and set them down on the shroud.

"Sir Redbaer said the Border Companies found the body," she said to Clemence sternly.

"What of it?"

"How close was he to the water's edge?"

"I know not," the High Vigilant said with a shrug. "He was found face down in the mud of the riverbank, pale as a fish. He drowned."

"That is the problem, Lord Clemence," Enelda said. "The boy did not drown. He was strangled *before* he was placed in the water."

"How could you know that?"

"We need only look to the amount of water in the lungs. The trauma of his passing ruptured the opening to the lungs, preventing the river water from entering. Furthermore, he has an undigested meal in his belly—scraps of thin gruel that an orphan might eat. Or a prisoner. From those scraps I calculate he was killed just hours after eating, and carried thence to the water's edge. What we have here is a prisoner, fed and watered, murdered shortly afterwards, and then left in a river where he could be discovered. I must know the exact location of the discovery. Was it on a straight? A bend? In a ford?"

"Why does it matter?"

"Because it will skew the probability of the boy drifting idly until he snagged on a rock or branch or reached shallows. Or it will tell us he was most likely placed somewhere quite deliberately, where he would be discovered."

"Who would do that?"

"Who indeed...? He was found by a Border Companies patrol, was he not?"

"Yes." Clemence mopped his brow.

"How far from the patrol route was he? Do you know that?"

"Sir Redbaer will know for sure, but I believe he said the body was seen from the road."

Enelda pursed her wrinkled lips. Her eyes narrowed, giving her a strangely feline appearance. "If, in the unlikely occurrence the boy drifted continuously until he washed up on the riverbank, he could have been placed in the water ten leagues upriver, even more... You should send word to the Border Companies to search that stretch for signs of miscreants."

"Ten or more leagues!" Clemence spluttered. "Do you know how long that would take?"

"Yes," Enelda answered flatly.

"But you said it was unlikely."

"But *possible*, and thus we cannot rule out pure chance."

"What's the more likely prospect?" Hawley ventured, tiring of the sparring between Vigilants old and new.

Enelda smiled at him kindly. Approvingly or patronisingly, Hawley couldn't tell.

"That he was taken to the river and placed near a patrol route," she said. "It would be folly for the Sylvens to do such a thing, as it shifts blame upon them. Besides, as I said, the boy was in the water less than a day. He could not have been dead more than a day over that. And so?"

Hawley frowned as he puzzled it out. "If he was only moved after he was killed, the men who put him there must've been a day's ride from the river—two at most."

"Very good, Hawley. Pray tell me: How far are we from the river now?"

"A day's ride," Hawley said. "Two at most."

"Now, listen here," Clemence said. "What you are suggesting is quite impossible. I will not hear it."

"You must hear it!" Enelda said. "Look there. The boy on that table was kept prisoner for weeks, or months, then killed. He was *kept* somewhere. And if we are to think for one moment the same people who imprisoned and killed this boy also took Anton Tarasq, then it changes *everything*."

"Changes what? Why?" Clemence was certainly annoyed, but he also sounded very unsure of himself.

"Because, Lord Clemence, I came here expecting Anton Tarasq to be dead. Now I believe he could still be alive."

CHAPTER 13

Whan they left the claustrophobic cellar, even the weak, greyish light outside caused Hawley to squint. He took a sniff of fresh air into his nostrils—the smoky, dung-spattered courtyard smelled sweet compared to the stifling scent of decay.

"Your conclusion, Vigilant Drake?" Sauveur asked.

"I am satisfied the boy is not Sylven, and it is unlikely he was killed on your side of the river. Beyond that, I would speculate no further."

"I must speak with the archduke before I leave," Sauveur said.

"Leave?" Clemence said. "Our talks are not concluded. The boy—"

"The boy is no longer my concern. In order to keep the peace between our peoples, I am prepared to discount the discovery of the body entirely, and omit it from my report. But if it is ever again suggested that the people of Sylverain would murder one of our own, the repercussions will be severe."

Clemence purpled. "Do not threaten us! You stand now in Aelderland, and long have we been free of Sylverain's influence."

"It is no threat, Lord Clemence. General Tarasq, she is...not as understanding as me. No, I will speak with the archduke, then return to Fort L'trinité at once. Now that I know we have a True Vigilant, and one who is unafraid of the truth—wherever it may lead—I can perhaps reassure the general that her boy will be found."

"And if she is not...reassured?"

Sauveur shrugged. "I will send word as soon as I can."

The Sylven removed his hat and bowed to Enelda with a flourish. "Vigilant Drake, it has been my great honour to meet you. Never had I thought to see one of the old order with my own eyes. I am glad it has happened during a time of peace, however fleeting."

With that, Sauveur replaced his hat and strode purposefully to the keep.

"'However fleeting'!" Clemence sneered, when Sauveur was well out of earshot. "What do you suppose he meant by that?"

"Be thankful the body in the ice house is no Sylven," Enelda said. "Or I fear you'd soon find out."

Clemence grumbled. "What to do with the body..."

"It may yet be of use as evidence," Enelda said. "A horrific crime has taken place, but we know not who perpetrated it, or why."

"Looks to me like someone was trying to start a fight," Hawley said.

"That is the second astute thing you have said today, Sargent Hawley," Enelda said. "You truly are full of surprises."

They set off across the courtyard. Hawley stretched out his neck. It felt good to be out in the open again. Still, the thought of the cellar led to a thought of the boy, and that one open eye staring up at Hawley. He shuddered, and looked back over his shoulder, half expecting to see a ghost gliding after them.

Instead, he saw movement against the stone steps of the curtain wall. A slender figure had been stooped behind a pile of sacks, and now, discovered, moved swiftly up the steps to the battlements. A pale young woman with long black hair, in a dress of cornflower blue, a dark woollen cloak flowing out behind her. Had she been spying?

"That girl," Hawley said. "Who is she?"

Clemence turned and followed Hawley's gaze, just as the girl slipped through the tower door and out of sight.

"Lady Iveta Snowsill," Clemence said with a huff of haughty

disapproval. "Hardly a lady, truth be told, but she is Lord Scarsdale's niece and ward, and therefore commands the respect that her late mother barely deserved."

"Lord Scarsdale's ward?" Enelda interrupted.

"Yes."

"Does she spend much time with the archduke's daughter?"

"Sadly, yes. Young Ermina idolises Iveta, and according to her nurse the girl's studies are the poorer for it."

"I see. And did Lady Iveta exert a similar influence on Anton Tarasq?"

Clemence stopped walking. "More so, as it happens. Lady Iveta has a habit of sneaking around the castle, ending up in places she should not be, and the Tarasq boy was wont to follow suit. And let me tell you, as much as that boy was treated as the archduke's own family, there were some in the castle who did not appreciate a Sylven having free run of the place."

"And Lord Scarsdale did nothing to curb these habits?"

"Lord Scarsdale has more important things on his mind than the escapades of children."

"Lady Iveta seems hardly a child."

"Then she should start to act her age," Clemence snapped. "Now, will that be all?"

"No, not yet." The look of annoyance on Clemence's flaccid face was almost comical. Enelda continued unperturbed: "It is well you mention the children. I need to see Anton Tarasq's room."

"I have already made a search of the boy's chamber."

"But I have not. And I should speak to the nurse whilst I'm about it."

"She saw nothing."

"She can speak for herself," Enelda said firmly.

"I am afraid it is out of the question. At this time of the day, the chambers are likely to be occupied by Lord Scarsdale's family."

"Good. What use would it be otherwise?"

"You would take this...soldier...into the family's private chambers?"

"As I told Lord Scarsdale, where I go, Hawley goes."

"Then I shall accompany you," Clemence sighed. "Both of you."

*   *   *

Enelda walked slowly around the bedchamber, hands folded behind her back, squinting at every surface and trinket.

It was grander than Hawley had expected. Some lords would have put a troublesome hostage up in a chamber no different from a high-status servant's, but it seemed the archduke was considerably more charitable. The room was large, the furnishings luxurious. Anton Tarasq was a boy of ten, but he had slept in a four-poster bed and played with toys made by master craftsmen from across the land.

Absently, Hawley pushed the head of an exquisitely carved wooden horse, which rocked back and forth on curved runners, clacking softly against the hard floor.

"Do be careful, Sargent," Clemence said from his position by the door. "These toys would cost your life's pay to replace."

It didn't dignify a response. But nonetheless Hawley held out a hand to steady the horse.

Enelda shuffled past them. "These doors"—she gestured left and right—"where do they go?"

Clemence pointed to the left-hand door, through which muffled voices could be heard. "That is Lady Ermina's room. The other is the nurse's room."

"They are kept locked?"

"It never used to be necessary, but since the boy's disappearance, they have been locked at all times."

"All times?"

"Yes, under my orders."

"So now the only person who enters this room is the nurse?"

"Yes."

"And who else has a key?"

"Myself, the archduke, and Sir Redbaer."

Enelda fixed Clemence with an unblinking stare, which at

first made him frown at her impudence, but slowly his expression changed to one of discomfort. Hawley knew she was studying the man, compartmentalising every detail of his manner and response for later use.

It was only when Clemence could bear it no longer and looked away that Enelda asked her next question. "I suppose Anton Tarasq and Lady Ermina often played together?"

The sudden change in questioning visibly wrong-footed Clemence. Hawley wondered if it was a deliberate tactic on Enelda's part to keep her subject guessing, or whether they were all just racing to keep up with the unfathomable workings of her keen mind.

"The nurse says the two were nigh inseparable," Clemence said. "Forever going to each other at all hours, whispering secrets in that way children do."

"But not on the night in question."

"Evidently." His tone dripped sarcasm.

"I can hear Lady Ermina and her nurse engaged in their lessons next door. They are not speaking loudly, and yet they can be heard. But no one heard the boy that night."

"They did not."

"And the guards? I note they patrol the corridor outside, but what of that night?"

"The patrols are more frequent now, certainly, but they have always done their rounds each night."

"At the same time each night?"

Clemence sniffed. "Take that up with Sir Redbaer."

Clemence made a pretence of superiority, but he was careful not to lock eyes with Enelda, and Hawley didn't blame him. He'd suffered that piercing stare himself, and didn't care for it one jot.

Enelda merely smiled innocently. "So there is no question that someone within the castle could have committed the crime? Someone with knowledge of the guards' movements, perhaps."

"Madam Drake, I—"

"*Vigilant* Drake," Hawley said.

"*Vigilant* Drake," Clemence corrected, with some annoyance. "Might I remind you—"

"I will see the nurse now," Enelda said, cutting him short. She went to the door and knocked before Clemence could respond.

When the door creaked open, the woman who stood before Enelda looked at first annoyed at the interruption, then at once flustered. She curtseyed awkwardly.

"Begging your pardon, m'lady," she said. "I was in the middle of Lady Ermina's lessons."

There was something entirely characterless about the woman's features, mousy hair, and deferential demeanour; she looked as though she might disappear into the background at any moment.

"We shan't keep you long," Enelda said. "What is the lesson?"

"Beg pardon?"

"Lady Ermina's lesson."

"We're studying the Sylven language."

"Wonderful. *Comen esla progrèe?*"

The woman blinked confusedly. "I don't speak the foreign tongue so well, m'lady," the nurse said, reddening. "I just sit with her while she reads."

Enelda simply smiled at her.

"Madam Drake wishes to ask you some questions," Clemence said.

"*Vigilant* Drake," Hawley corrected again. The barely restrained gnashing of the High Vigilant's teeth was of great satisfaction.

"I've already told Lord Clemence everything I remember," the nurse said.

"Humour an old woman," Enelda said. "Might we?" She entered the chamber without waiting for permission.

Now Hawley saw the inequality in their treatment—he had thought the Tarasq boy's chamber unusually lavish, but Ermina's was even more opulent. The four-poster bed, with its gilded frame, was covered in the finest foreign silks and plump, tasselled cushions. Every shelf was lined with dolls and trinkets. The window was inset with coloured glass, through which dappled light streamed. Where Anton Tarasq had played with a wooden rocking horse, Lady Ermina had a tiny golden carriage to ride within, pulled by a whole team of button-eyed stallions.

Beside the carriage, sitting atop a pile of cushions, with books and parchments strewn all about her, was Ermina. She offered Hawley a dazzling smile, and had an even broader one for Enelda.

"You're the Vigilant!" she squealed.

Enelda nodded.

"The lady Vigilant."

"My dear," Enelda said, "in my day there were no lady Vigilants, nor lord Vigilants. There were only Vigilants."

Clemence coughed. Enelda was dangerously close to breaching the king's own decree, filling the girl's head with ambition for a life she could never pursue. Hawley thought of the Vigilants and the many legends told of their deeds. He had always imagined them all as men—an assumption that had almost seen him leave the Elderwood empty-handed, or not at all. It seemed to him that the lot of women had worsened considerably in the pursuit of the long peace.

Enelda looked to the nurse. "I need you to think back to the night young Anton was taken."

"My lady, please," the nurse implored. She jerked her head to Ermina.

"I don't mind," Ermina said. "Vigilants have to ask difficult questions. Only then can they find the truth."

Everyone looked at the girl in surprise.

"Clever girl," Enelda said. "She'll go far. Now, think back. I trust that each night there is a routine when the children retire abed?"

"Yes, of course," said the nurse. "I always read to the children together for a short while..."

"Though not in Sylven," Enelda said.

"Indeed not," said the nurse. "Thankfully, little Anton's Aeldritch was almost as good as his Sylven."

"Was?"

"Why...I...I'm sorry, m'lady. That was thoughtless of me." She glanced to the little girl, who appeared too absorbed in studying Enelda to notice the implication.

"Where was Lady Iveta, on the night in question?" Enelda prompted.

"I'm sure I don't know," the nurse said haughtily. "I called in to see if she'd like a glass of warm milk, but she wasn't in her chamber. It's not uncommon—she's oft found in the library, reading into the small hours. Other times she's taking food from the kitchen and bringing it up here. Anyone'd think she weren't never fed! Not fit behaviour for a young lady, if you ask me, but his lordship don't seem to mind none."

"Don't be impertinent," Clemence said.

"And then?" Enelda asked. "You fetched milk for the children?"

"Even after a story, I always have a devil of a time settlin' the children. Forever hopping in an' out of each other's beds—I don't know where they get their energy from, I'm sure. So I sometimes give 'em a cup of warm milk to calm them, and finally they'll nod off to sleep. I'm off straight after; run me ragged, they do."

"And you always prepare the milk yourself?"

"Madam?" The nurse's voice wavered.

"There is no other who might prepare food and drink for the children at such a late hour?"

"N-no. Why do you ask?"

"Because with his best friend on one side, his nurse on the other, and perhaps even guards in the corridor, a shout or cry from Anton Tarasq would have alerted someone. And so we must assume the boy did not cry out. If he was carried off in the night and did not cry out, it stands to reason either he trusted his kidnapper implicitly, or..." Enelda looked to Hawley.

Hawley fumbled quickly for an answer to pass this latest test. "He was drugged?" he ventured.

Enelda broadened her smile and nodded.

"There was nothing in his milk, I can tell you!" the nurse said, utterly flustered. Hawley could almost feel the heat from her reddening cheeks.

"It was you who raised the alarm?" Enelda said.

"Of course, m'lady."

"When?"

"Daybreak."

"A little early to raise the children?"

"I was getting ready for the day's work and thought to leave my chamber by the children's rooms, to make sure they were safe and in their own beds. I am apt to do so, from time to time."

"But not all the time?"

"No, not all the time, I suppose."

"Did you not search for the boy before raising the alarm?"

"I...I looked in Lady Ermina's room. He was nowhere to be seen."

"I hear the boy was wont to wander about the castle," Enelda said. "Why then would it seem unusual to find him *not* in his bed?"

"I...That is to say...He was fast asleep when I saw him last, and when he was snoring like that, he was not like to wake until morning."

"You are sure?"

"Of course I am!" The nurse grew more agitated. "I think I know my own charges well enough."

Hawley felt a tug at his arm. Ermina had approached silently, and now looked up at him with her large eyes.

"You're frightfully tall," she whispered.

Hawley, ever awkward in the presence of children, practised a smile, nodded, and looked away.

The tug came again. "I bet you've killed lots of men. You look like you have."

Hawley coughed.

"Good idea, Hawley," Enelda said. "Why don't you take Lady Ermina to the other room while I continue here? Some things are not for the ears of children."

Clemence glowered at Hawley. The nurse's eyes threw daggers. And as the attention of the pair of them was upon Hawley, Enelda quickly stooped and peered under Ermina's wardrobe. A distraction, then. But for what?

The little girl smiled toothily and took Hawley's hand.

Hawley reluctantly allowed himself to be led away, looking back pleadingly to Enelda, who only shooed him out.

* * *

"Do you like him? His name's Bandit." Ermina stroked the mane of Anton's wooden horse.

Hawley made a grunt of approval, straining his ears to listen to what was being said in the other room.

"Oh, don't worry," Ermina said. "You won't miss much. Nurse doesn't know *anything*."

That got Hawley's attention. "And what *should* she know?"

Ermina stroked the horse once more and giggled. "She should know how to speak Sylven. Then she'd know lots more things. Then she'd know Anton's secrets."

The girl was playing games; that was plain enough. Hawley knew he had to tread carefully—an opportunity had perhaps presented itself, but he could not very well interrogate the girl or shake the truth out of her. This was uncertain ground.

"Does Anton keep a lot of secrets?" Hawley said, as nonchalantly as he could.

"Anton is very clever. Much cleverer than Nurse. He can get into all sorts of places around the castle."

"Like Iveta?" Hawley had a sudden insight. He wanted to test the girl.

Ermina looked shocked—perhaps the gambit had worked. "You know Iveta?"

"I know she likes to explore the castle, too."

That giggle again. "She's even better at it. Anton tried to follow her lots of times, but she always gets away...He said he saw her once getting a book for me. If it wasn't for Iveta, I'd go exploring with Anton all the time, but she won't let me. She made me promise."

"And you're a good girl, so you stay here."

She nodded, but looked a little sad. "But Iveta brings things back to show me. She reads to me sometimes—stories about soldiers and heroes, like Lady Aenya. But the best ones are about monsters. Have you ever seen a monster?"

Hawley tensed.

Yellow eyes. Black shadow. Just a bear...just a bear...

"There's no such thing as monsters."

"That's what Anton said, but I think one took him away. Maybe he went exploring and got eaten."

The girl stroked the horse a little more slowly, and her eyes grew moist. She sniffed.

"So where did Anton like exploring the most?" Hawley needed to take her mind off thoughts of her friend being devoured, but he couldn't risk changing the subject entirely.

"That would be telling, and I promised I wouldn't tell. But he found out all sorts of things."

"Like what?" Hawley's patience wore thin.

She giggled. "Anton only ever told his secrets to me and Bandit. Like this."

Ermina began whispering something very softly into the ear of the wooden horse. From the form of the words it sounded like Sylven.

"...*Doo-say...Des-ear doo-cor-on*..."

Hawley didn't understand a word of it. There was more, but at that moment the nurse marched angrily into the room and took the girl firmly by the arm.

"Lady Ermina! You are not to talk to strangers!" Her dull face contorted, now pinched and sharp, her eyes ablaze. "Lord Clemence, it is not right for common soldiers to speak so familiarly with my charge."

Hawley stood, and bowed respectfully—more so than he had need to. "Not a *common* soldier." He tried not to sound churlish, but he'd had quite enough of castle servants treating him like a villein.

"Even so, Sargent Hawley," Clemence said, "I am inclined to agree that rough men with rough ways are perhaps not suitable company for children."

Hawley wanted to point out that the nurse hadn't looked after Anton Tarasq terribly well, but held his tongue. Enelda was of no help—she was staring back into Ermina's room, seemingly oblivious to Hawley's situation.

"I like Sargent Hawley!" Ermina said, stamping her foot.

"Now, now, my lady," the nurse said. "You must mind your manners before Lord Clemence."

"Sorry." Ermina stuck out her bottom lip.

"Vigilant Drake," Clemence said, "if your business here is con-cluded, you may remove your man from the family chambers."

"Hmm?" Enelda said, finally turning about. She looked to the nurse, the child, Hawley, and then Clemence. "Oh, quite finished, yes. Shall we go? Come along, Hawley, there's still plenty to do."

Ermina seemed sorry to see Hawley leave; he made sure to nod goodbye to her, and the acknowledgement made the girl brighten a little. Hawley followed Enelda from the room with Clemence behind, his disapproval of Hawley hanging over him like a rain cloud.

"Now, if your intrusion into the family privacy is quite fin-ished..." Clemence had been talking for a moment already as they walked the corridor, but his voice had become such a tire-some drone Hawley barely listened. "My work is very important, and I cannot spend the day chaperoning the two of you."

"*Our* work is the same, is it not?" Enelda asked.

Clemence gave a great harrumph. His manners had dimin-ished with his patience. "The answer to our mystery lies not within these walls, but out *there*. Someone knows something—they always do—and I shall find them, even if I must flog every beggar on every street from here to Helmspire. Thankfully, I sus-pect the culprit shall be found closer to home. Even now, my Vig-ilants ride out to the benighted settlements hereabouts. Rowen, Halham, Raecswold...grubby dens of iniquity all, harbouring outlaws, poachers, and worse. We'll give them a good shake, see what falls out."

Again, Enelda only smiled innocently, but Hawley saw the bit-terness behind it. He felt it, too.

Another sound came from behind them. A latch rising and falling; hinges creaking slowly, softly. Hawley looked over his shoulder, along a second corridor that trailed off from this one, darker still. A great door closed, but not before a face had peered out at Hawley for just a second.

"Something the matter, Sargent?" Clemence tapped his foot impatiently.

"No. Nothing."

"Actually, Lord Clemence," Enelda said. "You speak much of the importance of your work, and I confess I feel guilty for keeping you from it. I hope you will forgive an old woman her strange ways—I have not been in company for some time. For that reason, I wonder if I might accompany you."

"Accompany me...?" Now the High Vigilant really did look wary.

"It has been long since I have set foot in the Chamber of Vigilance. Would that I might do so again, to pay my respects to those who have gone before, and pray for those justiciars who even now serve the king in the name of our order."

Clemence looked taken aback by the sudden show of respect, and though his eyes told a different story, he agreed to Enelda's request.

"Thank you, Lord Clemence, you have made an old woman very happy. Now, would you take my arm? I find these steps a struggle. My hips, you see. Oh...Hawley, I almost forgot. Take the servants' stair, there's a good fellow. I shall send for you later. The Chamber of Vigilance is no place for a soldier, isn't that right, Lord Clemence?"

Enelda's eyes darted along the corridor, towards the door, and then to Hawley.

Hawley bowed, and said goodbye. As soon as Clemence and Enelda were out of sight, Hawley doubled back along the dark corridor, to find his ghost.

CHAPTER 14

As Hawley pushed open the heavy door, he felt uncommonly reticent. Not fearful of consequence, but entirely out of place, like a harlot in a temple.

He entered a large library. Bookshelves lined every wall, towering over him, the upper shelves accessible only by ladders. Hundreds of thick tomes, bound in leather and cloth, titles gleaming in silver and gold by the soft daylight filtering in through two tall, thin windows. A small fire crackled in the grate against the far wall. Standing by that fire, an open book in her hands, was the girl.

She turned a page idly. She looked up, as if noticing Hawley for the first time.

"Oh, I didn't see you there. Are you lost, Sargent?"

"I..." The impression Hawley had received from the few brief glimpses had been proven correct. Raven-black hair, eyes like pale sapphires. She was pretty. So much so that Hawley almost forgot why he'd come to the library in the first place. "You know who I am?" he fumbled.

"Everyone knows who you are. There's not a maid in this castle who hasn't been gossiping about the brilliant Vigilant Drake and her handsome bodyguard. Although I think they exaggerate: You are rather scruffy for a High Companies soldier."

Hawley searched for a response, but in the end settled for remembering to close his mouth. He approached awkwardly.

She watched Hawley with affected aloofness, then closed her

book. "I expect you wish to question me," she said. "At least, I rather hope so. It would be terribly unfair for Ermina to have all the fun."

"There's nothing 'fun' about it, Lady...Iveta?"

As Hawley came within a stride of her, she whisked herself away, passing one of the great windows, tracing her fingers across the polished top of a library table as she went.

"I saw you this morning, at the ice house. Clemence would never have allowed me to see Vigilant Drake work her magic on that poor Sylven boy, more's the pity."

"It wasn't a sight for ladies," Hawley said, in equal measure entranced by this graceful young woman and vexed by her face-tiousness. "And he wasn't Sylven." He cursed himself under his breath. The words had slipped out; when had he become so easily flustered?

"And how did Vigilant Drake ascertain that, I wonder?" She fixed Hawley with a devilish look that stopped him in his tracks. "Did she do it? Tell me she did!"

"Do what?"

She came two quick steps closer, and Hawley withdrew, as propriety dictated, though not before drawing in a breath of her perfume that made his heart quicken.

Stop it, you idiot. She's too young, too pretty, too clever, and a good deal too rich...

"Did she enter the Eternal Night? Did she...commune with the dead?"

"What?" Hawley didn't know what she was talking about, but the way she said it made him shudder.

"The Eternal Night...the other place...Don't be coy, Sargent. Everyone knows the old Vigilants possessed such powers. The power to enter the spirit world and see the secrets of the past revealed. How else could they know so much?"

This, Hawley gathered, was what Enelda had spoken of when they'd first met. "If Vigilant Drake has such a power, I've seen nothing of it. Sounds like fairy stories, nothing more."

"And what if I had proof? Of sorts..."

"Eh?"

Iveta drew closer, her breath on Hawley's cheek as she whispered. "The Book of Vigils, written nearly a century ago by the leaders of the Vigilant Order."

"I thought they were burned after the Great War."

"We have fragments in the archive, nothing more—but proof nonetheless."

"You'd have to ask Vigilant Drake about that," Hawley said.

"I will be sure to. A True Vigilant, here in the castle. And a woman! We are starved of excitement, Sargent, and of opportunity. To think, my great-grand-aunt was a warrior maiden, who rode to battle bathed in an aura of holy light, the strength of her sword-arm blessed by the angels. But I am not supposed to even speak of these things, let alone read them. Such stories are kept under lock and key, where young ladies cannot find them."

"Sounds like you found 'em."

"Do I shock you?"

Hawley shrugged. "It's not me who has anything to fear from such talk."

"Of course not. You are not a woman."

"You sound like Enelda Drake—you'd get along famously."

"Oh, I'd like to think so. You're certain she did nothing... strange?" Iveta pressed. "With the corpse, I mean. No laying on of hands? No entering a trance? No speaking in tongues?"

"No, m'lady; just gruesome work, not for the faint of heart."

Iveta looked disappointed. "Fine, keep your secrets, but they won't stay secret for long. Not in Scarfell. Here, the walls have ears." She skipped away again.

Hawley followed. "Anton had secrets. Some he shared with your cousin, some he didn't."

Iveta stopped. She looked grave for the first time. She looked her age for once. "And what, pray, did Cousin Ermina tell you?"

"It's what she didn't tell that interests me most." He knew he couldn't reveal too much—he'd have to prise information from this one. "I think Anton knew something he shouldn't, and that made him a target."

"A target for whom?"

"No one's above suspicion. Especially not those who are wont to wander the castle at all hours. Even on the night a crime is committed."

"You think *I* might have carried Anton off?"

"Where were you that night?"

"Fine manners! If you must know, I was here, where I often am when sleep eludes me."

"That's not what I've heard, beggin' your pardon. And this isn't the kind of library where rare books are found...books forbidden to young ladies."

Iveta's eyes flashed with such bright anger that Hawley was quite taken aback. There was strength in the girl. "You've been talking to Nurse," she said.

Hawley shrugged.

"And did she tell you where *she* was that night?"

"In bed, asleep."

"I think not. She was away from her chamber, as she often is. I have not yet worked out where she goes, but I hear things."

"What kind of things?" Hawley asked, impatiently.

"She meets a man," Iveta purred.

"What man? Where?"

"I care not. As long as she's occupied elsewhere, I have my freedom."

"Why didn't you tell Clemence, or your uncle?"

"Nurse is entitled to her fun. Gods know, the women of this castle see little enough of that."

"Fair enough. But how'd you learn of her...tryst?"

"Tryst?" She laughed. "From Ermina, if you must know—but she would say no more."

"Ermina told me she keeps Anton's secrets..." Hawley said, now deep in thought.

"You're not seriously suggesting Anton was kidnapped because he was witness to his nursemaid's romantic liaisons? His position at this house is a condition of peace between two great nations—no one would be so stupid."

"Somebody was. Maybe the nurse knows more than she admits."

"You possess a quick mind for such a scruffy soldier. Or is it merely low cunning? You guess one thing correctly—Anton explored the castle because he was copying me. Quite the little sneak he is, too. Maybe he did see where Nurse went, though he wouldn't tell me. He likes knowing things. We both do." She flashed a mischievous smile.

"You don't seem very upset about his disappearance, my lady."

Her cheeks reddened, her eyes narrowed. "I love Anton like a brother, and I would do anything to see him returned safe and well. You really think me callous because I dare make jest at the absurdity of it all? Let me tell you something else about this castle: It is a house of sadness. I do what I can to lift spirits, to bring a little joy into people's lives, and for what? So soldiers can walk into our library and accuse me of not caring? Is that what you think of me? Do you think I'm a poor little rich girl who gives not a fig for the misfortunes of others?"

"I...No, I mean..."

"Let me tell you what I *do* care about. While you're in here, taking up my time with your impertinent questions, Vigilant Lestyn and his guards are out there." She waved a hand towards the window. "They're putting the terror into every settlement in the mearca. Making false accusations, arrests...executions. But then, I suppose it's the kind of work you're used to, now that the Third has sworn for the Vigilants."

Hawley's mind involuntarily leapt to Herigsburg, and the memory made him choke on his response. His hesitation damned him. Lady Iveta was as keen-eyed as any Vigilant, and she surely saw the guilty look in his eyes.

"Well, Sargent Hawley, *your* mind is made up, and now so is mine." Her eyes darted to a door behind Hawley briefly, and she smiled thinly. "But...you're here with a True Vigilant, and that must count for something. I shall say only this: I am here because I like books, as you have already heard. I think Anton was rather fascinated by the *wrong* type of books, too. Perhaps it was in looking for those that he discovered his little secret."

"What do you—?"

Footsteps resonated from somewhere behind Hawley. He looked over his shoulder at a little door squeezed between fireplace and shelves. When he turned back, Iveta had slipped through the opposite door, her tread light on the stairs.

The small door swung open. A guard entered, took one look at Hawley, and jerked his head to the corridor. Hawley took his leave under escort.

As he went, Hawley rubbed at the patchy beard that clung to his angular chin like lichen to a rock. Out of all Lady Iveta had said, only one word stuck in his mind.

Scruffy.

*　*　*

"You possess some skill as an apothecary, do you not?" Enelda said. She swung her aching legs down the last of the stairs, trying not to grimace at the thought of ascending them when her business with Clemence was done.

"More than a little," Clemence said, as if annoyed by the suggestion he was anything other than a fine physician. "I studied medicine under the great Johan of Ottona."

Enelda had no idea who that was, but presumed he must be important. From what she knew, the art of medicine had dwindled considerably since the Dissolution, and Aelderland had ceased to trade knowledge freely with the lands of far Cravania. She'd seen for herself the miraculous surgeries performed by the *chirugaie* of those lands; life-saving procedures Clemence would doubtless denounce as witchcraft.

Clemence led the way along another corridor, this one of bluish stone and ornate archways. Light rippled from the dimpled slabs like reflections on water. This part of the castle was old indeed, wrought with the skill of the old Sylven Empire, using stone-craft long forgotten.

"You think it possible the children were drugged?" Enelda

asked, trying to keep pace with Clemence and catch her breath at the same time.

"Both of them? Why? If any were drugged, then it was only the boy. The nurse would surely have noticed otherwise, even dull-witted as she is."

"A draught, indeed," Enelda said. "And other than yourself, would anyone else in the castle know how to prepare such a potion?"

Mercifully, Clemence stopped, and wheeled about to face Enelda. "Madam, for a moment it sounded as though you were suggesting *I*—the High Vigilant of Wulfshael—might be implicated in this ghastly affair."

Just plain "Madam," now, is it? Enelda wondered if the platitudes had ceased because he was angry, or because Hawley was not present. No matter.

"Lord Clemence, I merely wish to ascertain whether such a concoction—or its ingredients—might be acquired in the castle. And if so, who would have the skill to brew it."

"A sleeping draught is child's play, as I am sure you well know. The ingredients, however, are not so easy to come by—not in Wulfshael, at any rate. I do keep some in stock, as it happens, but they are locked away securely in the counting house, and that is the domain of Chamberlain Tymon. A more fastidious man you could never meet—every phial is recorded in his ledgers. Even I am forced to endure the watchful eye of the cofferer whenever I use my own stores. No, madam, I am afraid you must look elsewhere. If a drug was used—an unlikely prospect—the intruder must have brought it along with him."

"Or her," Enelda corrected. "We should never make assumptions until the facts are revealed."

The High Vigilant sniffed. "Come along, the Chamber of Vigilance is just here."

While Clemence had talked, Enelda had counted, her fingers tapping lightly against her thumb. There again had been the subtle tick in the High Vigilant's lower left eyelid at every thirteenth intonation.

They rounded a corner into a large hallway, into which narrow shafts of light streaked hazily from small windows high above. Before them was a great door, as tall as two men, inlaid with semi-precious stones. Moonstones, sacred to Litha.

Clemence checked his stride, allowing the place to impress itself upon Enelda. He need not have bothered. She'd been here once before, in the days when the castle was alive with the light of a thousand lanterns, when the halls had rung with the ballads of the ancestors on the eve of war.

She squinted through the striated light, and the impression of past glory faded. An echo, nothing more. The archway around the door was carved into a frieze, once chased with silver, now worn away. Deliberately: The messages encoded into the carvings had been chiselled smooth in places, so that the many doctrines of successive kings might not be usurped by the teachings of a defunct order.

Clemence pushed open the doors. They glided inwards, silent and graceful, the craftsmanship in their devising as perfect as it had been a hundred years ago. And beyond those doors, framing Clemence in podgy silhouette, was a golden glow, warm and glorious.

That's new.

Enelda followed Clemence into the large chamber, with its thirteen sides and improbably high ceiling. A gigantic, orbed chandelier hung overhead from a thick chain, a hundred candles burning within its gilded frame. The stone tables, once piled high with books and scrolls studied by novitiates, were now covered in ceremonial trappings of gold and silver. In all her years, Enelda had seen such opulence only in the palaces and households of the very wealthy, or in the high temples of the vulture-headed gods of the east. Here, in the Chamber of Vigilance, they were singularly out of place, and brought to Enelda's mind the shameless profiteering of Vigilant Lestyn. She trembled, this time with anger, but she said nothing.

"This chamber is very old," Clemence said. "It is one of only three such chambers in the kingdom, and we are lucky to have it.

Your friend Meriet covets it for his order. I see it in his eyes. But this place shall become a cloister over my dead body."

It was always akin to a cloister, Enelda thought. *Now it looks like a sultan's pleasure palace.*

A dozen adjutants scurried about the shadows. They were monklike in appearance, true enough, but that was where the similarities ended. They carried strongboxes, parchments, and ledgers to and fro, stopping only to scratch lines upon their scrolls. Worker ants, counting coin, polishing silver, making records not just of laws, but of the wealth of their office.

"Why would Abbot Meriet want the Chamber of Vigilance?" Enelda asked.

"Probably so he can inveigle his way fully into palace affairs. The seat on the Privy Council was the first step, mark my words; he will not stop there. Men like him never do."

"And what sort of man is he?"

"The pious sort. What could be worse?" Clemence beckoned an adjutant to him, a callow youth in russet robes, and began to check over the lad's scrolls, muttering something about the local knights being behind on their tributes.

Enelda's eye was drawn to the statues in each of the thirteen niches between the walls. Each represented the face of Litha during the cycle of the moon; all but one, the large statue opposite the main doors, of Litha resplendent. And at the sight of Her, Enelda's stomach rolled over. The statue had been altered, clumsily, without wit or wisdom. Enelda gritted her teeth. Again, she said nothing.

Clemence, oblivious to Enelda's feelings, took the adjutant's quill, wrote something on the parchment, then thrust both back into the lad's hands. The adjutant hurried backwards, bowing and scraping all the way, until he had melted away into the shadows, his presence diminishing like his confidence.

"And are these your novitiates?" Enelda asked.

"Gods, no," Clemence scoffed. "Scribes and clerks, nothing more. We do not train Vigilants in the old way. A lifetime of study and meditation to face an intangible foe? No, no. You are testament to the inefficiency of that method."

"And so how are your ranks grown? How are new Vigilants found?"

"The best of them were sheriffs, until it was deemed that our offices were duplicating too much work. Then the sheriffs were dissolved, and the Vigilants took their place. Now all the justiciars and tax collectors of the land ultimately answer to the Crown, instead of serving the interests of their own mearca."

"Justiciars and tax collectors. Is that all the Vigilants are now?"

"That is all they ever were. Do not pretend otherwise, not here. All of this loose talk of devils and angels was quashed when the war ended. It is tantamount to heresy! All we need to root out is the wickedness of men, not some malign presence from beyond the veil. And there are none so good at rooting out wickedness as my men, I promise you that."

Clemence strode around the chamber, taking stock of the work produced by his industrious adjutants. He puffed out his chest like a peacock. This was his domain, and he had not one thought in his head for those great men and women who trod these stones before him. Or perhaps he simply thought himself above them.

Enelda's mind raced. She saw the shadows move by candlelight, and fancied something else was amidst them, lurking on the periphery of her vision. Her heart beat faster. She swore she heard the picking, scratching, tearing at the veil. The rasping breaths of creatures long banished from the world, drawn to corruption. And where better than here? What would the Riftborn desire more than the defilement of a place once tended by their arch-enemies?

The room began to swim around her. The shadows thrown by candlelight flickered faster, and the thirteen facets of the room began to merge into one undulating mass, a carousel of flaming orange and darkest black, spinning around her. The veil—the fabric of reality—was more fragile than the likes of Clemence could know.

Enelda's fingernails bit into her palms painfully. She realised Clemence was still prattling on about the rightful position of the new Vigilants, and the respect that must now be earned through toil and diligence rather than superstition and fear.

Calm, Enelda. Calm. Face as of stone. Heart as of oak...

"It must be an uneasy relationship you have here," Enelda chanced. The sound of her own voice chased away the demons. Clemence stopped speaking. The room stopped spinning. "With Lord Scarsdale, I mean."

"Why so?"

"Your office answers to the king. You remain here under Leoric's roof; you sit on his council...but your authority outweighs his own, does it not?"

"Only in...certain matters."

"Matters of law, yes. But your Vigilants collect taxes on the archduke's behalf—a task other lords undertake for themselves. Indeed, is it not writ into law as part of his duty of maintenance over his workers?"

"We *are* the law here. I have the men, and so I relieve the archduke of a burden. He does not seem to mind having one less administrative duty to fulfil. Besides, Lord Scarsdale maintains this magnificent chamber, lodging for my men, and a levy of guards to protect them as they execute their duties. All this he does without interference into the business of the order."

"Forgive me, Lord Clemence, but Lord Scarsdale does not seem to have extricated himself entirely from your affairs. Indeed, he appears to take a keen interest in the duties of the Vigilants these days."

"Given the circumstances, can one blame him?" Clemence's blubbery lips wobbled with annoyance. "The threat of war is a great weight upon his shoulders, so I forgive him his outbursts."

"Your Vigilants are sanctioned by the king himself, but the new order does not have the autonomy of the old one. You rely on Lord Scarsdale's patronage, do you not? He decides how much of his gold to apportion your order...how much control to permit the Vigilants in his mearca." Enelda noted Clemence's face purpling. "I imagine Lord Scarsdale could be a thorn in your side should he be...dissatisfied...with the work of your men."

"Lord Scarsdale has barely given a thought to my order. Not since he found a new faith at the altar of St. Baerloc. Barely a week ago, he was inducted into the 'mysteries' of the saint. Mysteries! Pah! Superstitious nonsense."

"He was at Erecgham?"

"When he's not at the abbey, he's locked away in his chapel. He may as well not be present at all. Were it not for me, Wulfshael would be a place of lawlessness and heresy. And yet now... now the archduke has personally been affected by the corruption he has so long ignored, he rages against the Vigilants. He needs someone to blame, and my men, ever contrite and diligent in their duties, present an easy target for a man consumed by anger and worry."

"And so they redouble their efforts, out there in the hamlets and thorps, to shift the blame elsewhere. Your men, Lord Clemence, seek witches where there are none. They offer scapegoats rather than culprits."

"*Witches...*" Clemence hissed.

He spun away from Enelda, unable to look her in the eye. Even in his vexation, he lied about his relationship with the archduke. Enelda could tell by the quiver in the voice, the carefully chosen words. A pretence at outrage, but a genuine annoyance all the same. Not at the undermining of his order, but of scrutiny finally being turned upon his affairs. "The corruption so long ignored" lay not out there in the towns and villages of Wulfshael, but here, in this very chamber.

She bunched her small hands into fists, digging stubby fingernails into her palms again, hard enough to quiet the internal voices that clamoured for her attention.

Old memories give the lie to old feelings. Feelings open the door to the Riftborn.

Clemence rounded on her.

"I put it to you, *Madam* Drake, that the world has changed a great deal since you took yourself away from it. There is evil in those hamlets and thorps you care so much for, festering like sores. It is the duty of my order to seek out that evil and cut out the infection before it spreads. These witches...they dabble in superstitious claptrap, which they use as an excuse to commit heinous crimes. They possess no real power, but are an affront to our gods and our king. Their practices are outlawed as surely as the use of the blackrock within the borders of Aelderland, and since they were outlawed we have had no need for the old order. Your kind blamed demons for all the ills of the world, for the war—strange, then, the long peace came when the Vigilants were disbanded. You should have concentrated your efforts on the immutable rule of law, not conversing with the dead in your... *blasphemous* rites."

The novitiates nearby turned their eyes down to their ledgers. An ungainly youth who was carrying a heavy bundle across the room almost tripped over his own feet.

There was no point reasoning with Clemence. The Vigilants had helped end the War of Silver and Gold. While great heroes had fought on battlefields, imbued with the power of Majestics, Enelda's master and his kind had waged their own war, in secret, sending demons back to the Rift and saving the souls of the meek. An invisible war, a thankless one. In the years that followed, history had been rewritten to exclude the old Vigilants. Men like Clemence had been appointed to enforce the new "truth" and, worst of all, had come to believe it themselves.

Enelda set her lips into a half-smile, as innocuous and innocent as she could manage.

"I see the archduke is not the only one under great strain," she said. "I would advise a tincture for your humour, but I'm sure you have the skill to mend thyself."

"I shall have one of my novitiates escort you out," Clemence said, almost in a snarl.

"That won't be necessary. I know the way." As she turned to leave, she said, "That statue." She pointed to the statue of Litha that had so vexed her.

"What of it?"

"Litha has never been depicted with an owl upon her shoulder, as far as I recall."

"Stories of the goddess and the wise bird are well known, and you will find such images throughout the land."

"The 'wise bird' is a raven," Enelda said.

"Like that creature you brought with you? The idea of such an ill-omened bird adorning statues of a beloved goddess much disturbed the late King Ealgad; it was he who ordered them altered. But owl, raven, what does it matter?"

Enelda focused all her energy on remaining calm. This was a deity, and the raven a part of her divine aspect. She had thought Aelderland to have descended into ignorance; now she saw it as more than that. It was arrogance. Did the upper echelons of Aelder society really think themselves above the gods? Rather, did they even really believe in the gods at all if they could disrespect them so?

All this sped through Enelda's mind, but none of it passed her lips. Instead, she said only, "It matters, Lord Clemence, because the raven is a carrion bird, and teaches us something the owl cannot."

"Oh?"

She marched away towards the great doors, reclaimed staff tapping on the polished stone floor, and said, "That the dead can tell us just as much as the living."

CHAPTER 15

There were too many prying eyes and pricked-up ears within Scarfell for Hawley's liking; he had Iveta to thank for the warning. Eyes were upon them always: guards, servants, Vigilant novitiates, the blasted steward—even the Flaescine monks seemed always on hand to stare at the visitors from beneath shadowed cowls. Worse, news had reached Hawley's ears that Lestyn had come to Scarfell, and he was out for vengeance.

It had been Hawley's idea to instead meet Enelda on the walls at dusk. If it was a good enough hiding place for Iveta, then it'd suit him just as well. At least up here they had solid stone and whistling wind to shield them from spies. A sound idea, but now he felt guilty as Enelda shivered in the cold. The crackling brazier—a luxury for a soldier on watch—proved insufficient ward against the elements for an old woman.

"Did you find your ghost?" Enelda asked.

Hawley prodded at the coals of the brazier circumspectly. It was an innocent enough question, he supposed, but he was not entirely sure yet how he felt about his encounter with Iveta; how she had made him feel.

"Lady Iveta wasn't . . . what I expected," he said.

"Then we have both had surprising days." Enelda pulled her shawl tighter about her shoulders, and gazed across the courtyard.

Hawley rubbed his hands together over the small flames. There was something troubling Enelda, but he knew better than to ask. If she wanted to tell him, she would do so. He followed

Enelda's gaze, but saw nothing other than distant watch-fires in the gloaming.

"You shaved the beard," Enelda said. "Surely not on account of Lady Iveta?"

Hawley touched his cheek awkwardly, which was sore and spotted from his clumsy efforts with a razor.

"She's trouble, that one." He changed the subject quickly. "Sneaks about where she shouldn't; eavesdrops; reads forbidden books—"

"Wonderful! Which ones?"

"Something about her aunt? No, great-grand-aunt, Lady Aenya. She said books about her were kept under lock and key, away from young ladies."

"Interesting. I wonder if Lord Tymon keeps them. He seems to be in charge of restricted items in Scarfell."

"There was another. Something called the Book of Vigils. Mean anything to you?"

Enelda's eyes blazed. "Where? Where is this book?"

"I think she said the archive. Is it important?"

"Perhaps...If her uncle knew she had read such a text, she could be in trouble. But I suppose you found her carefree and rebellious?"

"I s'pose. She said she was reading in the library when the boy was taken, but I'm sure she was lying."

"It is good to see you were not entirely bewitched by a pretty face. That puts you one step ahead of most soldiers I've met." Enelda nodded thoughtfully. "There was a book in Ermina's room. Large, gilt-covered...It was hidden beneath her wardrobe. Not the kind of book a little girl her age would read alone. I wonder if Iveta took it from the archive?"

"Most likely," Hawley agreed. "Or the boy. He liked roaming about the castle at night as well. Looks like he saw something he shouldn't have."

"The nurse," Enelda said matter-of-factly.

"How did you—? Never mind. Yes."

"Good. It was clear she was hiding something. What did you discover?"

"She's got a lover. Don't know who. She sneaks off to meet him."

"Why so secretive?"

Hawley shrugged. "A child's nursemaid is tied to the family … lives in their quarters. If she took a husband, she'd lose her post."

"So a secret tryst would suggest … ?"

"That her lover is poor and hasn't the means to offer her a home. A soldier? One of the night patrol—that'd explain why neither she nor the guards saw anything."

"A fine deduction. But you do not sound confident—did you learn something else from Lady Iveta to give you pause?"

"Not from Iveta … from Ermina."

"Oh?"

"She told me the boy liked to keep secrets. But he let slip some morsel. Something he overheard about the nurse and her lover. But it made no sense."

"How do you mean?"

"I mean it was gibberish. And she only whispered it before Clemence barged in."

"Let me be the judge. What did she say?"

"I … can't remember."

Enelda sighed. "Every detail matters, Hawley. Now, I want you to think very carefully. Close your eyes."

"What?"

"Close them!" she snapped.

Hawley did as he was bid.

"Forget where you are now. You feel nothing of the cold wind. You cannot hear the crackling fire. You see what I tell you to see; you hear what I tell you to hear. It is midday. You are in Anton Tarasq's room. Do you picture it?"

Hawley squinted his eyes tight and tried to remember as best he could. Stone walls, tapestries, that wooden horse. He nodded. "I see it."

"I am in the next room, with Clemence and the nurse. Perhaps you can hear us talking. But you are with Lady Ermina. What are you doing?"

"I...I'm crouched by the wooden horse. Ermina's telling me about Anton."

"Now think hard, Hawley. Force your memories into the correct order. Imagine all your memories are a flotilla of ships on a stormy sea. And one of those ships is the memory of that conversation with Ermina. Send all the other ships away, until there is only that one. Think of nothing else. Relive it from the very beginning, so that you hear every word she said. Don't say anything, just think. And when you have it clearly in your mind, isolated from all other memories, repeat those nonsense words to me, precisely as you heard them."

Hawley felt foolish. "She didn't say it to *me*. She said it to the horse. Bandit. The horse's name is Bandit. Anton would whisper his secrets to the horse, and Ermina would overhear, and this time he said...he said...'Doo-say...Des-ear doo-cor-on.' That's all I can remember."

Hawley opened his eyes. He blinked profusely. For the most fleeting moment, he really had felt like he was back in that bed-chamber. Now he saw only Enelda's grinning face. He shuffled his feet. "Told you it was nonsense."

"I am not making fun of you," Enelda said. "What you heard was not a child's fancy, but the Sylven language."

"So it was Sylven. And I spoke it!"

"No, you butchered it, but that's all one can expect from a soldier. Are you sure what you heard was not *Dou'se, l'desír du coron*?"

Hawley's eyes widened. "That's it!"

"*Dou'se* means 'sweet.' *L'desír du coron* means 'heart's desire.' There is a book—a very famous Sylven poem—which uses those very words at the end of every verse. It is called *L'chansse d'Eyundes et Ocienna*. I wonder if a copy exists in this castle, and to whom it belongs."

"But the nurse doesn't speak Sylven, or so she said."

"I believe her, as it happens," Enelda said. "But Sylven is the language of love to the well-educated, and a woman like the nurse might be easily impressed by a little romantic poetry. This discovery suggests the nurse's tryst was not with a soldier of the watch, but a learned man."

"Or a Sylven spy," Hawley said.

"Quite. Sauveur was not here at the time, but he has a source, I am certain."

"Maybe that's why Lestyn's here."

"You've seen him?"

"No," Hawley said. "Servants told me. We'd best tread careful. The Vigilant Guard aren't pleased with me. The castle watch are all courteous enough, but whenever I see a man in black, it feels like a challenge is coming."

"You insulted their sargent. What was his name? Squire?"

"Swire," Hawley said, grinning at the memory of embarrassing the oaf. He swallowed that self-satisfaction quickly, realising the deed may yet land them in a world of trouble. "I can look after myself."

"I'm sure, but you would do well to remember that you are one man, protected by a reputation that is…precarious. There may yet be something I can do to help you, Hawley. I just need time to think."

"Well, don't trouble yourself putting in a good word for me. I think you've made more enemies than friends since we arrived."

Enelda's stern expression now cracked into a real smile. "Well then," she said, "at least we have something in common."

* * *

Hawley saw Enelda off to the keep, then made his way down several winding servants' stairs to the kitchen quarters. Yawning wearily, he walked the narrow corridor to his tiny bedchamber by silver moonlight. He stopped at the door, teeth gritted, muscles tense.

A single word had been painted across the door, spilling onto the pale stone wall.

AWEARG.

Hawley looked left and right. Seeing no one, he dipped a gloved finger into the lettering and gave it a sniff. The iron tang of blood was unmistakable.

It wasn't the first time something like this had happened. But it was the first time he'd experienced such tricks outside Fangmoor.

Who here even knew his fell reputation? The Vigilant Guard were the obvious suspects, but what if it was more sinister than that? What if someone was sending a message? A warning?

He thought of Enelda.

Hawley dashed down the corridor, burst into the kitchen. A bearded guard sat at the long table, and in surprise tried to stand. He reached for his sword.

Hawley grabbed the man's arm before he could draw steel, and dragged him to his feet.

"Do you know who I am?" Hawley growled.

The guard nodded, too surprised to form words.

"Then you know what happens when you pull a sword on me. This way. Now!"

He yanked the guard through the door, along the corridor, and pointed at the painted words.

"Who did this?" Hawley demanded.

"I...dunno. Wasn't there when I last came by."

"No? And you saw no one else?"

"At this hour? No."

"That's blood," Hawley said. "That's a threat, and it happened on your watch. If you're lying to me—"

"No. Erm...no, *sir*."

"Right. Vigilant Drake may be in danger. Do you know where she sleeps?"

The man nodded.

"Show me."

"I can't, sir...my patrol..."

"Hang your whoring patrol," Hawley snarled. "If anyone hurts that woman, I'll tear this place apart, and you'll be first. Understand?"

Whether from the moonlight or fear, the guard looked ghost white. He swallowed hard and led the way.

* * *

Enelda had had quite enough of stairs for one day. Indeed, she'd had enough of stairs to last a lifetime. Today, by her careful count, she'd trod three hundred and seventy-three. She was unused to it. The stairs in her beloved tower were shattered remnants, and what remained were used only as bookshelves.

She hobbled along the cold, dark corridor, musty carpet beneath her feet, vaulted arches and cobwebbed statues and suits of armour on either side. She'd asked for a room as far from other people as possible, as she liked it, and the archduke had obliged. She had not reckoned with such a lengthy walk to and from her chamber.

And she had not expected company on that walk.

Enelda kept her pace steady and deliberate. The shadow slipped between the arches to her right. By the glimpses she'd caught that morning, there was a maze of passages and stairways, and a long gallery hung with grimy portraits, overlooking a large bower. This wing would once have been the domain of the lady of the house, the archduke's late wife, but it lay now disused.

The figure in the gallery moved silently, gracefully. Enelda caught the impression of a long robe or cloak, hooded and dark.

An assassin? If so, the obvious place to strike would be Enelda's chamber, where there would be no risk of discovery until long after the murderer had escaped. That suited Enelda. In her room, she had the means to see off an attacker. Or worse.

It had been a long time since she had felt threatened. As she walked the long corridor to the endmost room, she became more painfully aware than ever of the frailty of her body, the toll of years. She felt small, weary. This part of the castle was particularly cold, and it bit at her. She felt it in her knees and hips and knobbled knuckles.

The shadow dashed again. The figure in the dark no longer matched her pace, but gained on her. Perhaps there would be no opportunity to reach her room. Or, more importantly, her bag of tricks.

Enelda's heart beat just a little faster. Litha's light, she was afraid. She couldn't help it. As a young woman she'd have stepped into the dark and put the fiercest marauder to flight. But now...

Abandoning caution, she quickened her step. Her staff thudded on the carpet as she went. Her breaths became ragged. Her master would be shaking his head in disappointment if he could see her now. But he was dead, and she wasn't ready to follow him. Not yet.

She reached the door, touching her fingers to the cold metal handle. She knew she had no time to take out the key. Instead, Enelda took a deep breath, clutched her staff firmly, and spun around.

A figure cloaked in black slipped from an archway, facing her.

Enelda whispered a prayer to Litha.

Heavy footsteps echoed along the corridor. Two men. Mail-shod boots. The jangling of chain mail.

"You! Stop!" Hawley's voice, full of menace.

The figure dashed through another archway, vanishing into blackness.

As dancing lamplight approached, gleaming from Hawley's sword, Enelda breathed a sigh of relief.

"Get after him!" Hawley commanded.

The soldier ran through the arch, footsteps soon receding on yet more infernal stairs.

Hawley bent double, one hand at his ribs, puffing and blowing.

"You all right?" he managed.

"Better than you, it would seem. What alerted you?"

"Someone..." he wheezed, "defaced my chamber door... Thought you might have trouble."

Enelda pursed her lips. Who would put Hawley on alert at the same time as plotting to kill her? It was highly illogical.

"Who d'you think it was?" Hawley grunted.

"I was about to find out when you blundered in," Enelda replied.

"I...What?"

"Never mind, Hawley. Go and put the ointment on those ribs. We've a big day tomorrow."

Hawley looked thoroughly confused. "But..."

"I'll be quite all right."

"I'll have a guard posted."

"If you must. Good night, Hawley."

Hawley managed one more exasperated "What?" before Enelda closed the door of her chamber behind her and locked it.

* * *

Enelda now doubted very much that the figure in black was an assassin, but that didn't quell her jangling nerves. What if it *had* been? Would she have been able to defend herself? Hawley may well have inadvertently foiled the attempt of an informant to pass on vital information to her, but she could not be angry with him.

She waited awhile, listening intently, until she was sure Hawley had gone. Then she struggled with a chest of drawers, pulling it across the door. Better safe than sorry.

Barty cawed softly.

Puffing and blowing from exertion, Enelda waddled over to the perch and stroked the bird's gleaming feathers.

"Enemies move against us," she muttered.

She'd hoped for a day's grace, but should have known better. No one she had met at the castle so far was above suspicion. They had threatened Hawley now. Removing him was the most sensible tactic. And if they got to him, what then for Enelda Drake? Could she survive Scarfell alone? Hawley could be a brute, true enough, but for now that was precisely what she needed.

The thing that troubled her most was the boy in the ice house. She'd told Clemence he was of no more use, but that had been a lie. The internal organs had been blackened, charred.

"That's not blackrock," she said, partly to Barty, partly to herself. "I've heard of it before, I'm certain. But where?"

Barty cocked his head.

"I know, I know. But you know the risks. Better than anyone, you know."

"*Barty!*"

Enelda sighed.

With great reticence, she cleared a space on the rug beside her bed. She lit as many candles as she could lay her hands on, and arranged them on the floor in a circle. Then she knelt in the centre of that circle, knees resisting every inch of the way. She closed her eyes and took a deep breath.

All was darkness. Then came the sound of crashing waves. She drifted towards them, weightless, until from utter black there came a flotilla of ships, bobbing upon turbulent waters. Lantern-light swung from their bows, inviting. Enelda focused as hard as she could. She swept over the ships until she could hear their sails fluttering, and she chose one, a memory of a time long past.

As she reached the deck, the wind howled. Fiercely, it battered against her. She had no form here, no body, but she felt it, raw and cold and carrying salt spray. Fear welled up within her, like she hadn't felt for a long time. A voice raked upon the wind, disembodied; lipless and lungless and dreadful.

Draaaakkkke... It hasss been... too long.

Enelda lay on the rug, shaking, heart pounding. She blinked away her confusion, pushed herself up from the floor.

The room was dark. All the candles had gone out, still smoking, as if extinguished by a sudden wind.

Barty scraped his beak on his perch. The rhythmic sound was somehow soothing.

Enelda relit the candles.

Cursing herself for a fool, she fetched her knapsack, and knelt once more within the circle. With a trembling hand, she fumbled around inside, and at last pulled out a small box. And within the box was a strange powder, so black it absorbed even the candle-light. The mere proximity of the substance made Enelda's head swim.

She reached forefinger and thumb towards it. Just a pinch. That's all it would take. And the blackrock would see her through.

"*Dark!*" Barty screeched. Enelda almost dropped the box in fright. Barty flapped his wings loudly, his claws clattering on the perch as he danced left and right. "*Dark—Dark—Dark!*"

Enelda snapped the box shut and aimed a sullen glare at the bird.

"You don't know how hard this is!" she snapped.

"*Barty!*"

"Oh...perhaps you do. You sense it, don't you? The thinning of the veil." She returned the box to the bag and pushed it away, out of reach. "Not yet," she said.

Again she closed her eyes. She concentrated harder on her breathing. She drifted on currents of memory, until again the ships appeared with their dancing lanterns. The wind battered her once more. The parchment-whisper of a threat blew raggedly past her ears, but she ignored it. She was not in the Eternal Night. Not yet. The Other could not reach her here, no matter how hard it tried. Not as long as she followed her training.

She strode across the deck of a ship, to the door of the captain's cabin, as the waves crashed over the rails and the ship tossed about like a child's toy. It was not real.

Enelda flung open the door and stepped inside her tower room.

Now she had a form, or the illusion of one. She could almost feel the heat from the crackling fire and smell the stew in her cooking pot. Every stone in the crumbling old walls was perfectly in its place. Every nook was filled with her trinkets, every shelf stuffed with books. The holes and worn threads of her rugs were right where she remembered them. Her heart ached for this place. She looked longingly at Barty's perch, empty. Even he couldn't be in two places at once. Such an incongruity would shatter the memory and pull her from the rigid structures she had made within her carefully ordered mind.

The room warped slightly, as though viewed through aged glass. Another memory came unbidden into Enelda's mind, bleeding into the simulacrum of the old tower. A painful memory that might yet be her undoing. The death of her master in a far-off land.

Quickly, she pushed it deep down into her subconscious mind, locked it away in a box. A box she now held in her hands. It was small, well-worn—a keepsake of patterned brass.

Enelda conjured another box in front of her, a larger one bedecked with many locks. This was a fabricated memory, created so perfectly that an intruder into her thoughts would not know what was real. She locked the small box inside the larger, as she had been trained to do. She locked the truth within the lie, as only a Vigilant could.

Enelda pushed the boxes aside, and her emotions with them. The tower became solid once more.

She crossed the floor to a cupboard, opening it to reveal a stack of her most precious books, wrapped in linens. Something about the boy in the ice house had reminded her of this. A fragment in a book.

She pulled them out, each in turn. Five of the seven volumes of Vigilant Staede's *Books of the Underworld*, and two of the three volumes written by her master. Cerwyn Thawn's *Books of the Majestic*. To the common man, these tomes would appear wildly different: one concerning demons, the other angels. To the Vigilant, such entities were merely two sides of a coin. Their goals were worlds apart, but the means by which they reached those goals transcended any mortal concept of good and evil. Only the Vigilants had understood this, Staede and Thawn foremost amongst the scholars of the divine and demonic.

She flicked through the worn and age-spotted pages, memories of their contents flooding back. Every word, every image, imprinted upon her memory in vivid detail, squirrelled away until needed, as was the way of the Vigilants. It was fire for which she searched. What demon or even angel would burn a child from the inside, and for what purpose? She knew she had seen it, but where?

The *Books of the Underworld* were of little use. The ways of the Riftborn were too disordered, too anarchic. A Majestic, then? But what angel would torture a poor boy so?

Page after page she skimmed, through the great List of Names and Sacred Numbers, and the descriptions of all the known Majestics and their myriad powers. Those who could read the thoughts of men or inveigle their way into dreams. Those who commanded the creatures of the oceans, or summoned storms, or bade crops to grow, or made trees wither and die. Page after page, hundreds of Majestics. And as the pages turned, Enelda's vision blurred. The words became indistinct, the letters jumbled.

The heat in the tower room became almost unbearable, the illusory air thick with smoke.

"Impossible," she croaked, throat drying in the acrid air.

This was her memory, her sanctuary. She had built it here in her mind, away from all danger. She could alter it to her will, should she choose, weave memories from nothing. But now some external force pitted itself against her. Something powerful and dark. Something *frightened* her.

As a papery voice reached her ears, Enelda Drake felt very much out of practice.

Something pounded against the door. Dust cascaded from the badly patched ceiling. The noise came again.

The tower vibrated. Potion bottles rattled on shelves. The cauldron spilled its contents over the fire, making the coals hiss. There came a low hum, increasing steadily in pitch and volume.

"This can't be..." Enelda whispered.

A stone block tumbled from the wall. Beyond it was a void of blackness.

Enelda squinted into the dark. A dim light came into view. An arterial strand of pulsating red light, faint, distant.

The Eternal Night. The place beyond the veil. It could be reached only through extreme concentration. And for the novitiate, the unpractised, it was possible to slip into that twilight realm by accident. The consequences of doing so were severe indeed, as Enelda Drake of all people knew too well.

Another stone came loose and flew back into the void. Then another, and another, until one half of the tower was gone, and Enelda stood upon a precipice overlooking the vastness of an endless abyss.

Drake, a voice whispered—scraped—within her mind. *It hasss been too long...*

Lights danced in the darkness. A pair of red orbs, growing larger. Closer. Surrounded by a shadow so black it made the void look bright.

Sssooo long have we waited...to sssavour your flesssh and... sssnip-crack your bonessss...

Enelda held her staff before her, desperately reciting the incantations of protection against the Other.

A fierce wind whipped around her, buffeting her backwards. She shielded her eyes.

The shadow was upon her. She felt herself go weightless. Talons scraped across skin. A large hand—hot, gnarled—squeezed her throat. She closed her eyes. She had failed.

Then came the light.

Enelda opened her eyes again. She was on the floor of the tower, as books and pots and debris spun around her in a torrent. A black shadow, formless like smoke, pummelled into a figure of white light. For a moment, the figure looked like a man, who even now thrust out a hand towards Enelda.

"Master..." she murmured.

"Go!" a voice boomed.

And Enelda felt herself pulled from her memory, from the tower, and the dark. Pulled back into consciousness, violently.

"*Go—Go—Go!*" Barty screeched, again and again.

Groggily, Enelda pushed herself up from the floor of her bedchamber. Her head throbbed, her bones ached. Drops of blood pattered from her nose onto the dusty carpet.

The candles had long since burned out. Dawn broke, reluctantly.

The raven shook out his feathers.

"Out of practice," Enelda murmured, still shaking. "Very much out of practice."

CHAPTER 16

Enelda looked frail. She spoke seldomly, and eyed every passer-by with deep suspicion. If anyone came too close, she flinched away and trembled.

"You all right?" Hawley said.

She didn't reply.

"We going to talk about last night?"

"No," she said.

Hawley had been cross with Enelda the previous night, but now he wondered if her brusqueness had merely been bravado. Her brush with an unknown assailant had left her more shaken than she would ever admit. And who was that assailant? He'd found no one, but the old wing was a rat warren where an intruder could easily hide. The guard had suggested it was the castle ghost—a woman in black, he'd said, often seen on cold, dark nights. It had been all Hawley could do not to cuff him around the ear.

And so, rather than face their problems, Drake and Hawley spent much of the day traipsing around the castle interviewing servants, watchmen, courtiers, and anyone else who might have been present when Anton was kidnapped. This task represented, Enelda said, the most important part of a Vigilant's work. Hawley decided if that were true, it was no surprise so many men preferred to settle their quarrels on the battlefield.

Enelda had requested an audience with the archduke, and had been told curtly he'd been summoned away on urgent business.

"What business could be more urgent?" Enelda had asked.

No satisfactory answer was forthcoming.

Lord Scarsdale was gone, Meriet too, and Clemence's patience had worn thin. There was only one member of the council left to interview. And so, watched hawkishly by guards at every turn, Drake and Hawley set out across the ward, to the twin towers of the inner gatehouse. To the counting house—the domain of Chamberlain Tymon.

They were led to Tymon's chambers by the cofferer, Malbuth—a grumbling, lank-haired man, most aggrieved at having to leave his clerks unsupervised for even a moment. He announced the guests to his master and returned to his duties as quickly as he could.

Almost the entire upper floor of a counting-house tower was given over to the chamberlain's quarters, and the office took up at least two-thirds of that space. Tymon ushered Drake and Hawley towards chairs, and lit more candles. Little light entered through windows that had once been arrow slits, and the room was gloomy, entirely panelled in dark wood. Large, austere furniture gave a cramped feel to what should have been a spacious chamber. There were few surfaces not covered in books and papers. The fire smoked unpleasantly, the chimney badly in need of sweeping. This was not the room of the fastidious, ordered man Hawley had expected.

Despite being one of the most senior figures in the castle, Lord Tymon appeared distracted, fumbling, and nervous. He constantly wiped his palms on his black robe, and looked about surreptitiously before answering even the most innocuous questions. He tried his best to distract his guests, taking any opportunity to offer wine, or water, or cake, to gaze out of the little windows and muse on the comings and goings through the gatehouse. In the end, Enelda opted for directness.

"In the archduke's absence," Enelda said, "perhaps you can tell me about General Tarasq. What precisely has been her reaction to the loss of her son?"

The question set Tymon fidgeting in his seat. "I'm sure that has no bearing on the...ah, the...kidnapping."

Enelda smiled sweetly. "Why don't you let me be the judge?"

"She was...angry. Understandable, in the circumstances. She is one of seven Sylven lords to volunteer a hostage, and likewise seven Aelder lords. The tradition has been maintained since the war ended, and there has never been an incident like this."

"But Lord Scarsdale does not have one of his own children in Sylverain?"

"No. By terms of the treaty, a host cannot also volunteer—a straightforward exchange might lead to...ah, recriminations... should anything ever go amiss."

"Anything like this?" Enelda was still smiling.

"Ah...yes...well, precisely."

"You said she was angry. What did she say?"

"Say? Oh no, she has only sent word so far through her intermediary. General Tarasq is of the military caste. Should she set foot on Aelder soil, it is war."

"And by intermediary, you mean Phillippe Sauveur?"

"Yes. Twice now has he been to Scarfell."

"Twice? When was the first occasion?"

The chamberlain looked especially nervous. His eyes swivelled about as though scanning the hall for eavesdroppers. Strange behaviour, Hawley thought. The chamberlain was being asked nothing that wasn't common knowledge. "Two weeks ago," he said at last. "The twenty-second day of Sollomand, if I recall correctly."

"And through Sauveur, General Tarasq threatened war, I gather."

Tymon turned even greyer of aspect than usual. "Indeed. She offered respite until the moon next began to wane."

Enelda nodded thoughtfully. "The Sylvens still respect the old ways. A fortuitous circumstance that the body of a young boy was found by the Silver River just a day before that respite was up."

"Ah...yes...most fortuitous. And, indeed, it seems your arrival may have changed things further. Sauveur, you see...I believe he personally persuaded General Tarasq to stay her hand,

on condition that a True Vigilant take up the case. And now...
here you are."

"Strange, then, that I am not permitted freedom to conduct
the investigation as I see fit."

"Not true, Vigilant Drake. I assure you..."

"Don't take me for a fool," Enelda said.

Now it was Hawley's turn to fidget awkwardly. Enelda was like
to get them both thrown out of the castle sooner than expected.

Colour came to Tymon's cheeks. Not anger, but embarrassment. "Appearances, you see...Ah, that is to say...Lord Clemence is the king's justiciar. Your position is more...ceremonial."

"Ceremonial?"

Tymon coughed nervously. "Your very presence buys us time."

"Time for what? From what I have seen, Clemence's Vigilants
do nothing but drown innocent peasants as witches."

Tymon looked around nervously. "My lady, *please*," he hissed.

Enelda's fingers twitched, each tapping her thumb in turn as
she thought. "Sauveur," she said at last. "I doubt he would advo-
cate on behalf of the council if he knew about my *ceremonial*
position."

Tymon spread his palms. "That, Vigilant Drake, is politics.
We had hoped the matter would be resolved quickly when that
poor boy washed up in the river. But that avenue now appears
closed to us. What Lord Scarsdale plans next...it is not for me
to say."

"I see. Then I should put these questions to Lord Scarsdale
himself, upon his return."

Tymon nodded, the lines of his face smoothing in relief. Then
he realised Enelda was staring at him pointedly, and his relief
turned to anxiety.

"Apologies, Lord Tymon, but I must ask as a matter of routine. Where were you on the night Anton Tarasq disappeared?"

He reddened again. "I-in my chambers, naturally. Asleep."

A stammer? Hawley caught himself frowning suspiciously at
the chamberlain, and Tymon caught it, too, which flustered him
even more.

"Did you join the search parties?"

"To my shame, no. I slept through the whole affair. I had been feeling unwell. I took a…sleeping draught. By the time the cofferer came to rouse me, it was too late for me to do anything. I only wish I could have played my part."

He looked towards the door, as though desperate for some urgent business to arise that might save him from Enelda's inscrutable gaze.

"These things are sent to try us. Thank you, Lord Chamberlain, you have been most helpful."

Enelda stood as though to leave. Tymon looked delighted.

"Lord Tymon, might I ask a favour?" Enelda said, her tone much brighter.

Tymon hesitated. "If it is within my power, my lady," he offered, tactically.

"I would very much like to peruse your archive."

"The…archive? I see. I mean…I would be delighted to escort you. Ah…tomorrow perhaps?"

"Time is against us. Perhaps now?"

Tymon heaved himself up to his feet, accompanied by loud popping sounds as both knees clicked into position. His head bobbed up and down in a curiously avian manner.

"I…that is to say…I could rearrange some appointments, I suppose."

"You could give me the key," Enelda said.

"Oh, dear lady…" Tymon looked almost amused at the idea of handing the key to his archive over to a woman, then immediately thought better of whatever he was going to say. "Not necessary," he said instead. "Now is as good a time as any."

* * *

They passed through a small antechamber, crammed with books in various states of repair. Beyond, the chamber opened up into a much larger space, rising high into the counting-house tower, containing storeys-high bookshelves accessible only by tall ladders. Row after row vanished into darkness.

Hawley's breath misted in front of his face. Tymon had brought with him numerous shawls and scarves, and had bundled himself up in them so he looked like an egg. He handed a shawl to Enelda.

"No money for fires," he explained. "And I don't like the smoke around the books anyhow. You know that we have a Book of Vigils here? Some of it, at any rate."

"I heard it rumoured, and it would give me great pleasure to see it."

"I was minded to consult it just yesterday, and sure enough there you were, listed in the Great Roster . . . as a novitiate, but the book is very old." He looked wary, as though he may have caused some offence.

Enelda waved away his concern. "I was very young when the roster was last drawn," she said. "And sadly it was never again updated. All the prospective novitiates were dismissed, but I had nowhere else to go, and so I remained in my master's service until . . . until his end. To the best of my knowledge, I am the last."

Hawley felt a sense of wonder. He'd known that Enelda was the last of the old order, but had simply assumed it was because she was very old, and the others had all passed away. The thought that she was the last to be recruited was somehow very sad. That the other novitiates—children—had been dismissed save for Enelda . . . Had she nowhere to go? Was she an orphan, like him? And if so, had her master become a father to her on their long travels?

"Cerwyn Thawn," said Tymon, reverentially. "I confess a pang of jealousy when Abbot Meriet said he'd laid eyes on the man himself. He is in the Great Roster, and more besides. There is a psalm by his hand in our copy of the book, and his mighty deeds are recorded in the *History of the Aelders*, volume . . . thirty-three, I think . . ."

"By his hand?" Enelda gasped. "You have one of Vigilant Thawn's psalms?"

"Indeed!" Tymon rubbed his hands together with glee. "There is treasure here, for those who—as you say—value knowledge. I think you'll be pleasantly surprised."

Tymon led on through the shadowy archive, on stick-like legs that dangled from his swaddled body, his movements like a marionette's, his long, slippered feet barely seeming to touch the floor at all. As he went, the chamberlain lit a row of lamps that hung from stone buttresses. The yellow glow from each gave strength to those before them, until the true size of the archive was revealed by their light. It was not merely a chamber in a tower, but a long gallery within the very walls of the castle, with staircases of iron spiralling down into cellars, and rickety wooden ladders vanishing into the gloom overhead, where musty old tomes huddled together like roosting bats.

"I imagine it takes a good many archivists to maintain a collection as large as this," Enelda said, eyeing the stacks with reverence.

"Ah, if only. The records of all Wulfshael wend their way here, copied out meticulously by scribes across the mearca, and collated by my clerks. But there has not been an archivist here since before Archduke Leoric inherited his title. Master Thayall, the old chief archivist, was a fine fellow—very fine. But his lordship would not permit him an apprentice after the king's decree regarding...certain texts. When Master Thayall passed, there was no one to look after the place."

"You surely don't tend it alone?"

"There is little to be done. The new ledgers arrive and are categorised. The old find their place in the stacks. I just ensure they... ahem...that is...remain safe."

"A little knowledge is a dangerous thing these days."

Tymon bit his lip. His eyes brimmed sadly. Then he seemed to decide he could confide in Enelda. "Actually, when Master Thayall died, I had some help from the monks of Erecgham. That was when the Sygellites ran the abbey. But the Flaescines would think most of the texts here heretical. And so yes, I tend them alone."

"Heretical?" Enelda said. "Have the Flaescines grown so dogmatic in their beliefs since my day?"

"Two-thirds of the documents in the archive at least are devoted to theological matters, my lady. And few of them support the Flaescine belief that the saints are truly the gods in mortal form." He chortled to himself. Hawley didn't see the jest.

"By that reckoning, I imagine every priest in Aelderland would find something blasphemous here," Enelda said.

"Ah, well...I fear the day when his lordship comes asking questions. It is a matter of time now he's found a new faith."

"The worship of St. Baerloc?"

The chamberlain nodded. "A true saviour, the saint. True saviour. But is he a god? Well, wiser men than I would debate that until Haelstor's Reckoning, and still have no answer." He coughed, somewhat nervously.

"Then I am glad that is not my purpose here, for I do not have such time to spare."

Tymon smiled. It was the first time Hawley had seen him do so, and there was something about him in that aspect. He had a twinkle in his eye, and his avian features became somehow stronger. A clever old bird, Hawley thought, but not a wicked one.

"Of course," Tymon said, bobbing through the stacks in a manner not unlike a heron wading across a ford, "things were different in Thayall's day. We used to see monks in here of every order. The Trysglerites...they're an especially studious lot. But alas, they visit no more. Now only the Flaescines are permitted entry to the castle, but they care more for trade than book learning."

"The Trysglerites have their own peculiarities," Enelda said.

"*Ahem*, well, yes! Worship of the Trinity, but denial of the lower gods. Including Litha, yes?"

"Including Litha," Enelda agreed, disapprovingly.

"But at least they were open to ideas. Even if a man only worships the Blessed Three, there's common ground. The abbot's beliefs are more in common with the Sylvens, if you ask m—" He broke into a cough, and looked circumspectly over his shoulder, as though expecting the abbot to be standing behind him. It appeared his love of knowledge loosened his tongue beyond propriety.

"Please, speak your mind," Enelda said. "I owe no allegiance to any order. Not any more. Tell me, do you suggest Abbot Meriet places the saints *above* the gods?"

Tymon shuffled to a halt. "Saints? No, not all the blessed saints, but one. When I say he puts me in mind of the Sylvens, I mean because of their curious belief in only one god. Meriet worships one saint alone, and that is Baerloc, the Living Saint, who came to the world to end the Winnowing, and whose bones reside still in Erecgham."

Hawley frowned. "He worships Baerloc to the exclusion of all others, gods and saints alike?" Hawley wasn't a godly man by any stretch, but he felt a shiver just saying such a thing. Ignoring the gods was one thing; courting their disfavour was quite another.

"That is my understanding. And do we not call the Sylvens heathens for such ways? But alas, there are few wise men left who would be so bold as to continue that debate."

"Why is he called the Living Saint?" Enelda asked. "No one has yet explained this to me."

"*Aha!* Fewer still of the wise would dare speak of the miracle, save in whispers. It is all legend now, of course. No one knows for sure, except perhaps the abbot. But they say during the height of the Winnowing, when fully half the children of Wulfshael had been taken, a comet was seen in the sky. It crashed into the woods not far from Erecgham and set the forest ablaze. From the flames came a man, skin like ash falling from his bones. But though he was surely dead, he walked abroad, and any who approached were blessed. They received rapturous visions, and their ailments were cured. After a time, he collapsed in a pile of blackened bones. When the Flaescines learned of this, they said the man was St. Baerloc, returned in our darkest hour. They took his remains to the abbey and sanctified the ground in his name. Sure enough, thereafter the sick began to recover. The sleeping awoke, and the Winnowing was over."

"Just like that?" Enelda asked.

"Just like that. Or so it's said. No one recorded it, and only the abbot himself bore witness. But this is what they believe. Baerloc the Saviour, whose power resides in his very bones still. Ah, here we are!"

Finally, they stopped. Tymon, appearing less lordly by the second, put light to a lantern, revealing a narrow aisle ahead, lined with huge, tattered books, each chained to the bookshelves as though in fear it might escape. At the end of the row, gleaming in lamplight, was a glass-fronted cabinet, a piece of furniture more valuable than Hawley's worldly goods combined. Inside was a book. Or, rather, a pile of tattered parchments, sandwiched between two leather-bound boards that had long ceased being a binding. It was only Enelda's soft intake of breath that confirmed to Hawley what it was. The Book of Vigils.

"I shall bring it out to you," he said. "Such treasures are my responsibility alone, which I take not lightly."

"Treasure indeed," Enelda whispered. "All of them burned..."

"Ah, yes!" Tymon said, overhearing. "You are too young to remember, Sargent. All these books were thrown on pyres. Not out of malice, nor even disrespect, but in celebration, strange as that might sound."

"King Ealwarth proclaimed the Vigilant Order surplus to requirements," Enelda said, eyes moistening at the memory. "He believed the order wielded too much power owed to superstition. He said the time had come for men to take charge of their own destinies. Once the Vigilants were exiled—or executed—the trappings of the order were declared 'shackles,' binding common folk through superstition and fear. They should be locked away or destroyed, lest future generations think the Aelders backward in their beliefs. And so the people streamed into the Chambers of Vigils and stripped them bare. Thousands of scrolls of lore were taken, thrown onto the bonfires that signalled the end of the war. In that one night, our knowledge of physic, of herbology, astronomy, and a dozen other disciplines was consumed by flames. A century of demon lore was lost. Should the Riftborn return, there are few who understand how to fight them."

Tymon squeezed past Hawley and Enelda, and placed the tattered book reverently on a leather-topped table. "This copy is incomplete," he said. "I have gathered pages from all over the land. Five scraps even came to me on a merchant wagon from Tördengard, if you can believe it. I have pieced them together as much as my knowledge permits. Three hundred and thirteen pages of the original nine hundred and ninety-nine. I am only sorry it is not more. Perhaps one day I will see it restored further."

Enelda traced her fingers lightly over the book's cover. "You said there were psalms in here, by the hand of Cerwyn Thawn."

"Aye. Including one of the most radical, most secret texts in the whole of my collection!" He tapped the end of his aquiline nose. "A prayer to protect travellers into the Eternal Night."

"The Eternal Night..." Hawley repeated. "That's twice I've heard it mentioned."

Tymon and Enelda turned to Hawley as one.

"Where else?" Enelda demanded.

"I...erm..." Hawley was unsure whether to say in present company, but decided Lord Tymon was now in Enelda's confidence. "Lady Iveta," he said.

Enelda raised a silvery eyebrow. "You did not think to mention this earlier?"

"It slipped my mind."

"Which is precisely why I should not have let you speak to the girl alone."

The chamberlain looked on amused as Hawley shuffled his feet awkwardly.

"What is it?" Hawley said at last. "The Eternal Night, I mean? Lady Iveta said it was how you commune with the dead, but that can't be true...can it?"

"Heh! Indeed it is," the chamberlain interrupted, to Enelda's obvious annoyance. "Why, Vigilant Thawn himself advises great caution when 'walking between worlds.' He calls it the Shadow Realm, where the twilight is everlasting, and ghosts flee from the presence of the Riftb—"

He stopped suddenly, noticing Enelda's thunderous demeanour.

"As I said earlier, a little knowledge can be a dangerous thing," Enelda said quietly.

Hawley weighed up Enelda's behaviour carefully. What Iveta had told him had been disconcerting, true enough, but he had not believed it. Not really. Now, Enelda's guardedness made him doubt. What if she did possess some strange power? Was it as dangerous as black magic?

"You know the whole contents of your archive?" Enelda asked of Tymon.

"Better than anyone alive, but there are too many manuscripts for one man to remember."

Hawley saw a look of doubt cross Enelda's face, and he fully believed she could memorise the archive's contents, given time.

"But you have records?" Enelda pressed.

"Of course."

"And should a book leave this archive, you would know of it?"

"I would," he replied. He stiffened, perhaps sensing some accusation coming. "I make note of every manuscript to enter or leave this collection."

"And every visitor?"

"Beg pardon, Vigilant Drake?"

"You note every visitor who comes and goes?"

"No... but as I said before, I don't get many."

"What of the High Vigilant? Does he browse your collection?"

"Lord Clemence is... shall we say... not one for history," Tymon said. "Time was, the Vigilants would bring their records here for me to file away, but those days are gone. When Lord Clemence took the position—some three years ago—he brought his own people to manage the order's affairs."

To hide their embezzlement of the archduke's taxes, Hawley thought, but held his tongue.

"So you have no records of crimes here at all?" Enelda asked.

"Our records are primarily for accounting," Tymon said. "We have all the transcripts of the hundred courts from before Lord Clemence's time. But I expect the High Vigilant has already looked over those for information about the other missing children."

"What others? You mean the girl from Rowen?"

"I don't know anything about that. As I said, it's been three years since we kept the Vigilants' books down here. But children have been vanishing for many a year in this mearca, never to be found."

Enelda looked at Hawley. Hawley shrugged—he'd heard nothing of disappearances beyond what he'd already told Enelda.

"Over what period did these disappearances occur?" Enelda asked.

"A tenyear at least, maybe more. And from the scant rumours I hear, they never stopped."

"And how many children were taken?"

Tymon scratched his head. "It began with one or two, from the villages to the south. It caused a frightful stir at the time. Then each year it seemed more and more followed, 'til it became commonplace—just one of the things that befall the poor folk, I suppose."

Enelda's fingers tapped on her palms, counting out the rhythm of her thoughts. Her eyes were half-closed. Finally, she turned to Hawley and said, "You knew nothing of this?"

"How could I? Local crimes are not the business of the High Companies. Not until last year..."

"Ah yes, you're from the Third, aren't you?" Tymon said. "Commander Hobb has sworn for the Vigilants, because Lord Clemence needs more soldiers. He wants to find these kidnappers more than anyone!"

Enelda looked to Tymon, then to Hawley, and back again. "Can no one simply present to me the facts?" she cried. "You mean to say the High Vigilant enlisted the favour of Commander Hobb *specifically* to aid with this business of missing children? *Before* Anton Tarasq was taken."

Tymon swallowed hard. "I...*think* so," he ventured, in an inflection more a question than a statement. "I cannot think what other matter would prove so important."

Enelda began to pace, thumb and fingers tapping rhythmically, her face like thunder.

She stopped. "If the Sylvens were involved in the abductions, as we have so recently been assured, you would have heard *something*, Hawley. What lord would permit foreigners to prey upon his serfs so frequently and for so long without raising the militia? It is a nonsense. It smacks of obfuscation."

"Obfuscation?"

"A conspiracy, Hawley. Someone does not wish the wider world to know about these missing children."

"Who? Who would conceal these crimes?"

"The same someone who would rather Aelderland and Sylverain go to war than have their crimes exposed. But the important question right now is not 'who?' but 'why?' That is the question we should be asking. When we know the answer to that question, we shall know what the culprit has to gain, and then we shall have the key to unlock this mystery."

Hawley jerked his head towards Tymon, who Enelda had seemingly forgotten about. The chamberlain was standing very still, looking very much like the odd one out, even in his own domain.

Enelda squinted at Tymon now, perhaps debating internally whether or not he could be trusted. "Could you show me the old records?"

Tymon nodded, and led the way in silence to a long row of bookcases, stuffed with ledgers.

Enelda walked along the row, fingers tapping the spines. When she reached the end, she spun around, vexation writ large across her wizened features.

"There are several volumes missing. A rather sizeable gap in your record-keeping, my lord."

Tymon shifted on his feet. He cleared his throat. A lord chamberlain, now looking like a youth admonished by a superior. "I can only assume Lord Clemence took them after all..."

"You said you knew the whereabouts of all the books entering and leaving the archive."

He coughed again. "Lord Clemence," he said more confidently. "I'm certain."

"I shall need to find out for sure..." Enelda muttered. She said something more, but it was garbled and low, and Hawley wasn't convinced it was in any familiar language. When finally she stopped, she said, "Lord Chamberlain, do you have maps here?"

"Of course."

"I need a map of the Silver River."

Tymon went off at once, vanishing into the shadows of the archive, perhaps grateful to be spared further scrutiny.

"In the morning," Enelda said quietly, "I would have you find Sir Redbaer."

"Me? Why?"

"Speak to him as one soldier to another. Find out what you can about his guards' movements on the night of the disappearance, and who else might know of those movements in advance. Take the map. I need the precise position of where that boy's corpse was found, and the routes of the Border Company patrols."

"I don't think Redbaer will give me the time o' day," Hawley said. "And what if he's part of your...conspiracy?"

"If he were to betray his part in this sordid affair, that would be equally useful to us. But Redbaer struck me as an honest man, and such a man is hard to find these days. I know of only one other in Scarfell."

"Who?" Hawley asked, then felt his cheeks grow hot at Enelda's kindly expression.

"You will need to set aside your rivalries with the Borders, Hawley. Go to Redbaer as a brother in arms. Show some humility, and I am certain you shall reap the rewards. Now in a moment, Lord Tymon will return, and I need you to keep him busy."

"Why?"

"Because in his chamber he had a book, open on his desk, its pages marked in several places. *L'chansse d'Eyundes et Ocienna*."

Before Hawley could reply, Tymon returned with a large map, beautifully drawn, which he proudly flashed around to his guests before folding it neatly. He handed it hesitantly to Hawley, eyeing the soldier's rough hands warily.

"You will look after it, won't you, Sargent?"

"Like it was my own," Hawley said.

"Very good," Enelda said. "Now, if you wouldn't mind giving me a little peace, I have much to study. I'll call you if I need you."

She shuffled to a table, opened the Book of Vigils, and began to read. She shushed Hawley's questions away, and so all he could do was accompany Tymon back to the antechamber, where he partook of some wine with a lord for the first time in his life, while the chamberlain prattled on about the seven great monastic orders and their peculiarities of doctrine for what seemed an eternity.

CHAPTER 17

Lithadaeg, 7th Day of Nystamand

Hawley washed and dressed before the first servant set foot in the narrow corridor outside his room. Today he would not simply be following Enelda Drake around the castle. Today he had a mission.

He regarded his armour thoughtfully. There was danger in the castle. But what statement would it make if he insisted on wandering about Scarfell ready for battle? He left the armour in his trunk. He hung Morgard's sword on a hook over the bed, touching two fingers reverently to the scabbard. Then he took up his dagger. He could conceal it in his boot, but something about arming himself only secretly did not sit well. As he put the dagger in the trunk, he glimpsed a folded scrap of oilcloth poking out beneath his helmet. He didn't know why, but he felt compelled to unroll it and look once more upon the wretched thing within. Ianto's knife.

Enelda had called it a "blade of covenant." But a covenant with whom? Not his brother soldiers, that was certain. When those bastards had sworn their oath to kill Hawley, it had not been with this thing. He squinted at the swirling sigils on the hilt, the dinks and blemishes of its rough-hewn blade of iron. It felt like dark magic in his hands. It felt wrong.

Wrapping it quickly, he tossed it back into the chest.

Walking back his earlier decision, Hawley strapped his High

Companies shortsword to his side. Old habits died hard. Finally, he threw his newly brushed black cloak over his shoulders and fastened it with the bronze pin, proudly displaying his rank. He had only a tiny shaving mirror to check his appearance, and decided he would do. It might not be enough to impress Sir Redbaer, but it was all he had.

"Bloody Borderers..." he muttered.

Striding from the room, Hawley collided with a young girl, blinded by the enormous stack of linens in her arms. Half of them spilled to the floor.

"Gods!" She stared at her feet, cheeks turning crimson. "I'm sorry, sir. Terrible sorry!"

"Don't fret, girl," Hawley said.

He retrieved a blanket from the floor, and the girl snatched it away, hurrying to pick up the rest, mumbling indecipherably.

"It's Agnead, isn't it?" Hawley asked.

She nodded, and adjusted the bundle without once looking up. "Beggin' your pardon, sir, but if you're off out, might I make up your chamber?"

"If you like, but you don't have to do it every day. It suits me well enough."

"Yes, sir. Sorry, sir. It's just that...I been told, sir."

"Told?"

"Cook says we're to treat you like a lord, sir."

"A lord?" Hawley laughed. What small impression he'd made on the cook must have been more favourable than he'd thought.

The girl looked more flustered then.

"She...she says it's not every day we get such a guest down here, sir, with the likes of us."

Hawley smiled and shook his head. "Girl, I *am* the likes of you."

He reached out to offer Agnead's shoulder a reassuring pat. She shrank away. The mirth gone from the moment, Hawley withdrew his hand at once, nodded, and went on his way before he frightened the mouse further.

The sun had barely risen as Hawley descended the steep, cobbled road into Scarfell's small town. Rain threatened from a slate-grey sky, but this was not enough to deter the traders from setting out their stalls, nor the entertainers from staking pitches before the morning crowds arrived. Already, the square reeked of horse manure, forge smoke, and night soil. Gods knew how it would smell come summer.

Hawley passed two hooded, silent monks, arms folded into their sleeves. He eyed them suspiciously as they made their way up towards the castle. They seemed altogether too at home at Scarfell, and Hawley's unease returned.

Reaching the bottom of the hill, Hawley turned onto a narrow lane, where washerwomen wrestled the castle's laundry into great tubs, and burly men hoisted sacks of grain onto the backs of mule-carts. Suspicious eyes alighted on him. The common folk were used to soldiers, but not so much those from the High Companies. If Hawley himself was not the talk of the town, his strange companion still was.

Black-uniformed Vigilant Guards lollygagged about outside a baker's shop. One of the men gave Hawley a mean squint.

Hawley held his head high and strode on. As he rounded the corner, he found himself eye to eye with a familiar face: bulb-featured, wide-mouthed, eyes too far apart to be trustworthy. Swire. Two other guards stood at his shoulders.

Like spooked horses scenting trouble on the air, gawping peasants drew away from the unfolding quarrel.

A boot scuffed behind him. Shadows gathered as the men came closer. Someone growled, "Awearg."

It was them. It was the Vigilant Guard who'd painted blood on his door. Hawley clenched his fists. Twice now at Scarfell he'd been subjected to the old insult. But who knew of it? Those who used it were far away at Fort Fangmoor. Or dead.

"Stand aside," Hawley growled.

Swire grinned. "And if I don't?"

Hawley leaned forward. "Then I'll put you on your arse, in front of your men."

"We serve the Vigilants. The Third Company works for the High Vigilant now. We *own* you."

"Stand aside. I won't ask again."

He stared into Swire's toad-like eyes. The other man didn't yield.

"What's this?" A man in Aelderland green came from the direction of the nearby barracks, his boyish figure belied by an authoritative drill-yard swagger.

Hawley had not expected to be glad of the sight of Sir Red-baer, but he was.

Swire stepped immediately away, eyes fixed on the newcomer. "Nothing to trouble yourself with, Redbaer."

"But I am troubled, Sargent Swire." Redbaer stepped within reach of the man. "Troubled at discourtesy shown to an honoured guest outside my barracks."

"I—"

"Troubled also"—Redbaer raised his voice—"that you forget your place when addressing me."

Swire glared at his men, who now as one shuffled their feet like chastised children.

"Forgive me... *Sir* Redbaer." Swire nearly choked on the words.

"There, is that not better?" Redbaer said brightly. "Now, apologise, and be on your way. I am sure your master will have need of you up the hill."

Swire reddened. "I... I apologise, Sir Redbaer."

Redbaer cocked his head. "Not to *me*, Swire."

Swire ground his teeth. He turned to Hawley, who grinned despite himself. That grin almost set Swire off, though he thought better of it. "I... apologise, Sargent Hawley. For delaying you. We should continue our talk later."

"Look forward to it," Hawley said. And added as an after-thought, "That'll be all."

Looking fit to combust, Swire barged through his men, who followed in his wake.

"Back to work," Redbaer commanded the onlookers. He offered a hand to Hawley, who shook it firmly. "What brings you down here?"

"Business. With you."

"Me? Well, I shall count my blessings your necromancer is elsewhere. Tell me, have you broken your fast?"

"Not yet."

"Then I know just the place we can talk, and eat while we're about it."

*   *   *

The tavern hadn't yet opened for business, but it seemed the doors were always open for Redbaer.

The barkeep set a board upon the table: pea-meal bread, butter, cheese, apples, and a pot of salted fish in brine. The man brushed down his apron, took a coin for his trouble from Sir Redbaer, and shuffled off.

Hawley took handfuls of food to his plate, stuffing fish and bread into his mouth, savouring every bite. He took a swig of foamy goat's milk and wiped the juice from his chin with his sleeve.

"They feed you not well in the servants' quarters?" Redbaer asked in amusement.

"Well enough, but only just," Hawley said, holding in a belch.

"But kitchen scraps are for sustenance, not for the pleasure of the eating."

Hawley nodded agreement. "I find myself nibbling on rations from my pack of an evening," he said.

Redbaer laughed. "Black biscuits, with a few weevils for extra flavour, eh?"

"You know it."

Redbaer broke bread over his own plate. "Aye. I know you think me a fop playing soldier, but I've seen battle. I have marched the trails. They may call it the 'long peace,' but just because we aren't crossing swords with Felders doesn't mean there's no fight to be had."

"So, what brought you to Scarfell?" Hawley asked. "There are few safer positions in the kingdom."

"It is one of the great ironies that fighting men who live long earn advancement. It takes us far from what we're good at, and chains us to a life of politics. Every bit as dangerous, but immeasurably more tedious... I imagine I'll spend my old age pining for past glories in the field."

Hawley thought of Morgard, and nodded.

"I do what I can to not turn soft," Redbaer went on. "I run the castle garrison tight... train my men well. If only all here were subject to my regime."

Hawley stopped chewing and looked at Redbaer more warily.

"Ha! Not you, Sargent. It is an honour to have you. No, I mean the Vigilant Guards. Some once served under me, but on the whole they are a motley lot. Grown fat and lazy on the not-inconsiderable scraps from their new masters' table. You know what an idle soldier makes, Hawley?"

"Trouble." He'd seen it himself. The rot had already taken hold in some quarters of Fort Fangmoor. Beacher had been a prime example before he'd met his end. And if it was so for the Third, it would be so for every other company.

Redbaer nodded. "Indeed. Nature as black as their uniforms. Oh, they salute me when I pass, but even at this early hour they'll be looking for some slophouse in which to carouse and curse my name. That man Swire—he's an oaf, but a dangerous one, and he has Lestyn well on side. You should take care."

"So I'm told." Hawley drained his tankard and poured more milk from the pitcher. "On the subject of your soldiers, that's why I am here."

"You want to know the movements of my men the night the Tarasq boy was taken. Vigilant Drake was overheard discussing as much yesterday."

"The walls truly do have ears in this castle," Hawley grumbled.

"Aye, but not here. The innkeeper protects my privacy while I'm in his establishment."

"On pain of death? Or death of payment?" Hawley glanced through the gloom towards the bar, where the bald-headed innkeeper busied himself quietly.

"I once saved his son's life."

Hawley nodded. That kind of loyalty was hard to find. It was the best kind, the reliable kind.

"So, your guards...?" he said.

Redbaer smiled thinly. "To business, it seems." He took a folded wad of parchment from a pouch, flattened it on the table, and scrawled some rough shapes on it with charcoal. "The castle is really two domains—the townstead, where we are now, and the keep. Most of my garrison naturally lies out here, ready to defend the castle. I have thirty men on watch at any given time on the outer curtain, and only twelve on the inner. They patrol in pairs, crossing each other's paths at regular intervals. Inside the keep are another ten men, each assigned to a section of the castle. One man walks the family wing, crossing the path of his partner on the servants' landing."

It seemed standard practice. The distance a soldier could cover slowly and carefully in a fixed period determined how large an area he could watch. On a castle wall, this was sizeable. Indoors, with corridors and stairs to traverse, and nooks and crannies to search, much less so.

"I rotate the watch every three days. No man knows precisely where he will be assigned. They know the patrol routes by heart, so may be given the task at a moment's notice."

"And you know where every man was that night?"

"I do."

"And the men patrolling the family wing that night?"

"Armsman Hamlyn, an experienced man. Known him three years."

"The second man?"

"He does not enter the family corridor."

"But he would know when Hamlyn had left the corridor, and how long he would take before returning."

"You have a suspicious mind," Redbaer said with some caution.

"Maybe I've been around the Vigilant too long," Hawley said. "Or the wrong kind of soldier."

Redbaer swigged his milk. "Wickswill. The other man's name is Wickswill. A little green, but a good lad."

"How green?" Hawley was now in mind of another green soldier—Ianto, who had been recruited only recently to the Third and was not all he'd seemed.

"At the time, four or five months. You know how it is in places like this. We've few veterans, and recruits come and go."

"You questioned both men, naturally?"

Redbaer's eyes narrowed. "Naturally."

"They reported nothing out of order?"

"Of course not. Neither was delayed on their patrol. They met on the landing, exchanged brief words, and met again ten minutes later."

"Can anyone vouch for that?"

"How could they? Everyone was asleep at that hour, even the servants."

Possibilities raced through Hawley's mind. What if the soldiers had lollygagged, knowing no one would check on them? A spy could have seen them dragging their heels and snuck into the boy's chamber unchallenged. What if one or both had been bought off?

"You said you change the guard every three nights. How many nights had these two been rostered?"

"This was the third." Redbaer's tone darkened.

"Is it common knowledge how often you change the guard?"

"It's no great secret. I know what you're thinking. I'd be a liar if I said I hadn't thought it, too, but I questioned those soldiers most forcefully, as did the Vigilants, and I'm satisfied with their answers. The fact is that there are some rooms in the family wing off-limits to the guards unless they are summoned. The kidnapper was likely lying in wait in one of those rooms, waited for the guard to go past, and took his chance."

"The library," Hawley said. He thought of Lady Iveta's swift escape the day before yesterday.

"Why do you say that?"

"I...entered there by mistake. Got turned around. There are two exits, and from the main door you can see the family corridor. An intruder would see a sentry pass by."

"It *is* the most likely hiding place, and if the timing was right, it would also provide a means to escape—although gods know how they would have avoided the second pair of guards on the ground floor, whilst carrying the boy."

"Seems unlikely," Hawley agreed.

"That's why it's a mystery, Sargent. That's why your necromancer is here."

"But you trust your men?"

"Obviously."

"So someone from the household is involved?"

Redbaer studied Hawley carefully. "Lower your voice. There are some secrets that might not be safe even in here." He glanced about circumspectly. "If not someone from the household, some visitor intimately familiar with the castle. And probably more than one culprit—one to evade the guard upstairs, who would have handed the child over to another downstairs."

Hawley's thoughts solidified on the chamberlain. If he had the book, was he a spy? What if General Tarasq had grown tired of her boy being a political hostage? What if she wished to engineer a war, and had instructed an agent to instigate it? But the man's arthritic knees hardly qualified him for carrying a boy down several flights of stairs. And who then was the accomplice? The monks? How many of the Flaescines had Hawley seen skulking about the place? And Meriet didn't strike Hawley as trustworthy, no matter what Enelda thought. But why would monks aid a Sylven spy?

"You have an idea, don't you?"

"Maybe." Hawley was annoyed his thoughts were so transparent.

"Care to share it?"

"I've been here three days. Don't want to jump to conclusions."

"I hope you don't suspect me."

"Enelda would say everyone's under suspicion...But no, I don't."

"You admire this Vigilant. Is she really all they say?"

"Dunno what they say," Hawley said. "I haven't known her long enough to find out. And—"

"You don't want to jump to conclusions." Redbaer smiled. "I think you'd make a good Vigilant yourself."

"So, let's say somebody got past the guards on the lower floor...How would he escape? I've seen the sentries on the walls. I've seen the watch-fires in the courtyard. A lot of eyes to avoid, 'specially carrying a hostage."

"There was a storm that night. Fierce wind, heavy rain. The guards could barely see a few yards from their fires."

"But the gatehouses...?"

"Two in the inner walls and three in the outer. The North Gate is the most heavily fortified, but the others are well enough protected. As I said, I run a tight ship."

"So how'd they escape?"

"You know the whole of Scarfell was built atop a ruin of the Sylven Empire? Half the inner keep is Sylven still, and there have long been rumours of secret ways in and out of the castle. More than rumours, really—similar passages are well known in the castles of Sylverain. If anyone knows for sure, it is perhaps Lord Scarsdale himself, though he claimed ignorance when questioned by Lord Clemence."

"Claimed? You think the archduke might lie?"

"No, of course not. I know not if any search has ever been conducted to find these passages, but the Sylven masons were the most cunning in history, it's said. If there's a trick to it, it is a trick that eludes our architects."

But not a Sylven spy. Hawley drained his tankard again, wishing it were ale despite the hour.

"I hope you don't gamble, Hawley," Redbaer said. "Your face betrays your suspicions."

"It's why I prefer to keep quiet," Hawley said. "When the lad was discovered missing, who conducted the search?"

"I did. I organised the parties...my men, volunteers from town, the most able servants. We searched through the night. We sent messengers to every farmstead and hamlet within a half-day's ride. We had rangers scouring for tracks, and dispatched hounds out on the boy's scent, but the rain made it impossible.

We continued for three days, fruitlessly. At the end of the third day Clemence sent word to Fangmoor that a diplomatic incident was brewing. After that, we had no choice but to send word to General Tarasq and inform her that her son was gone."

"Who delivered that message?"

"I took it to the Border Companies. They carried it onwards."

"The search continued in your absence?"

"It carried on further afield. Your friend Lestyn was in charge. He was most zealous in the execution of his duties."

"Execution being the right word," Hawley growled.

"Be bloody careful with that one, Hawley. I've heard whispers...He will not let the insult you paid him rest. Now, I must ask, is there anything else you need? I have other duties."

Hawley had taken a mouthful of bread and cheese, and held up a hand to motion pause while he finished chewing. "There is, as it happens." He wiped his hands on his breeches and produced the map.

"The border," Redbaer said. "So your Vigilant does think the boy has crossed to Sylverain?"

"No. At least, I don't think so. This is about the other boy. That lad in the ice house."

Redbaer's brows knitted. "The Sylven? What of him?"

"Not Sylven. We think he's one of ours, dragged from some backwater, held captive, then murdered. Here."

The milk in Redbaer's tankard sloshed as his hand shook. He put the mug down on the table, forcefully. "Murdered?"

"Aye. Someone dumped the lad's body where it might be found."

"How could you know this?"

"Vigilant Drake. She...found clues. On his body. Inside...in his organs."

"What? That makes no sense."

Hawley shrugged. "I know, but that's what happened. Clemence seemed convinced enough. Some power of the old ways the likes of us can only guess at, I s'pose."

Redbaer pulled his cloak more tightly about his shoulders. "Or perhaps she truly is a necromancer."

"I saw no magic in it. But that's not important. You're familiar with the Borderer river patrols?"

Redbaer nodded.

"Good. I need you to mark on this map where the boy was found, and how close to the patrol route it was."

"Yes, yes of course." Redbaer cleared his throat. There was something decidedly anxious about his manner. Maybe it was talk of dark magic that'd spooked the knight.

Redbaer took up his charcoal, fumbled it, cleared his throat, and placed a small X on the map, beside a river straight, less than half a mile from a series of jagged islets. He then drew a narrow oval, starting and terminating at Dawn Crag, a Borderer fort on the north bank.

"The patrol," he said.

Hawley looked where the lines were drawn, at the roads they followed, and how close they were to Redbaer's X.

"They were right on top of him."

"A lucky find. Or perhaps an unlucky one."

"Oh?"

"We all hoped he was from south of the river. We hoped the Sylvens were the culprits. If it's proven otherwise, it weakens our position. Still...I suppose the boy could have nothing to do with any of this."

"I hope he doesn't," Hawley said earnestly.

"Does the threat of war trouble you that much?"

"It's not the war. It's the manner of the lad's death. He'd been caged. And there were"—Hawley looked about, and lowered his voice to a whisper—"marks on him. Dark marks, the likes of which I haven't seen since the Winnowing."

Redbaer visibly paled. "Be damned sure you know what you're saying, Sargent."

"I wish I could say different."

"Does...does anyone else know of this?"

"Vigilant Drake, Sauveur, Clemence, me, and you. Far as I know."

Redbaer straightened. "That's too many for my liking. If a

word of this gets out, there'll be widespread panic. Lestyn's gallows will groan under the weight of so-called witches. Do you see?"

"Aye, I see."

"Good." He held Hawley's gaze a moment too long. Fear? No...something else, but Hawley couldn't fathom it.

Hawley pointed at a tiny dot beside Redbaer's charcoal line. "This village is near where he was found. Were the villagers questioned?"

"Aye, but none of them knew anything. And it's not a village, it's little more than a thorp—Wyverne, it's called. A pimple on the arse of nowhere. Popular as a resting place for weary Borderers, though gods know why."

"There's nothing else you can think of that might help?" said Hawley, keen to give Redbaer the opportunity to explain his guarded behaviour.

"I've told you all I know. If there is more to discover, that's for your necromancer...gods willing." He pulled on his gloves and made to stand. "I must ask that you excuse me. Stay—finish the meal. It's paid for."

Hawley nodded. He watched Redbaer leave, waited a few minutes deep in his thoughts, then rolled up his map and left the inn. He'd quite lost his appetite.

*　*　*

Iveta regretted not wearing her hooded cloak by way of disguise. A few of the market traders and local workers recognised her, doffing caps and tugging forelocks as she passed. A flower seller delayed her, insisting that she take a posy of late winter roses.

It embarrassed her. She didn't feel at all like a lady of the household, and when people treated her as such, she felt like a fraud. She always wondered if the deference was given out of fear of her uncle, rather than genuine respect.

As a result of that deference, she had lost sight of Hawley through the market crowd. She felt sure he was going to the barracks to meet Sir Redbaer.

She quickened her pace, taking the quieter path behind the stalls.

"My lady Iveta, what a pleasant surprise."

Iveta cursed inwardly as she almost collided with Lestyn. The Vigilant blocked her path through the market. One of his guards stood behind him, and he stared at Iveta impudently.

"Vigilant Lestyn! I...I'd heard you were...away."

He leaned forward, impertinently close, and took a smell of the roses that she clutched to her breast. "Your interest in my whereabouts flatters me, my lady." The man's attempts at smiling gave his pallid, doughy face a quite appalling cast. "Indeed, I was away, but urgent business called me back all too soon. You know how it pains me to interrupt my vital work beyond these walls."

"And what work is that?"

"The discovery of sin, and its eradication, my lady. I was rather hoping to begin with Halham, but alas."

That smirk; that chuckle. He knew something about Iveta's connection to Halham. She thought quickly, trying not to betray how her heart thudded and her hands shook.

"I'm sure the innocents of Halham share your pain, Vigilant Lestyn. They must look to your...protection...in these dark times."

Lestyn's beady eyes lit up. "Innocents? Oh, they are few and far between, especially in Halham. Those wretches have been afforded far too much leniency of late. The archduke is too kindhearted for his own good."

Iveta struggled not to laugh in Lestyn's face.

"But still," the Vigilant went on, "it seems there is plenty of sin to be found right here in Scarfell. Speaking of which, was that Sargent Hawley I saw in town just now? I do hope you aren't here on his account."

"What business is it of yours?" Iveta snapped, too readily. He'd drawn a rise from her, and she could see in his mean, dark eyes that he enjoyed it.

"Oh, the sargent is very much the business of the Vigilants, my lady. I am not at liberty to disclose why...not yet, leastways."

Lestyn glanced down at his bag, which contained several rolls of parchment. Iveta couldn't make out the seals. What had Lestyn discovered? "He is a blackguard, my lady, though he hides it well. Suffice it to say that you would do well to stay away from him and his ilk."

"Thank you, Vigilant Lestyn. Your advice is…always appreciated."

He bowed, as discourteously as it was possible to bow. "Of course," he said, "I offer this advice only as a friend, my lady. Your uncle, however, might be more…vigorous…in this matter. In fact, I believe he is to meet with the Drake woman this very morning, probably to inform her of his decision."

"Decision?"

"To send Hawley away before the oaf brings his name into disrepute. Though if what I hear is true, I don't think the Third will be very pleased to have him back. At least he will no longer be a thorn in our sides."

She knew from Lestyn's expression that she'd given away her concern. He seemed delighted. He perhaps thought it was Hawley she was worried about, but that wasn't the case, not truly. No: She remembered Enelda Drake's plea to Uncle Leoric, about not being left alone and undefended in the castle. It was obvious that forces were already moving against Vigilant Drake, and whatever dark deeds besmirched Hawley's record, he was the old Vigilant's best defence.

"My uncle knows best, I'm sure," she managed.

"Might I have my man escort you to your destination, my lady? Where is it you're going, exactly?"

"That won't be necessary," Iveta said hurriedly. "I…I forgot my cloak, and the morning is chillier than I thought. I shall return to my chambers. Good day, Vigilant Lestyn."

"Your servant, Lady Iveta."

As Iveta hurried back to the castle, she could feel Lestyn's eyes at her back. She would have to be doubly careful now.

CHAPTER 18

Censer smoke drifted so thick it stung Enelda's eyes. The air was oppressive with it. She stood patiently, bemused at the show. The archduke had summoned her to the gloomy little chapel, but seemed intent on finishing his prayers before even acknowledging her presence.

The chapel's walls were painted blood-red. Dappled light in a dozen colours filtered weakly into the centre of the room through a narrow stained-glass window depicting a scene from an old Sylven legend of one of their seafaring prophets' many miracles.

Beneath the window was a statue carved of ebony, in the form of a thin man clothed only in rags. The skin of the figure was cracked and pitted. Part of the face was carved crudely away, revealing a polished silver skull beneath. Similarly, silver ribs gleamed through holes in a dark wooden chest. A bronze sword protruded from the figure's right hand, while a pair of scales hung from its left. At its sandaled feet were five smaller figures carved from soapstone—piteous serfs, bowing and scraping at the feet of their saviour. The Living Saint, risen from the ashes.

It would not have concerned Enelda one jot; after all, what was it to her if Lord Scarsdale chose to worship the saint who had, by all accounts, saved his mearca from a great catastrophe? No, what concerned her was the treatment given to the other idols in the gloomy chapel. The patron gods of Aelderland, all present in statue form, all covered by tapestries, hung deliberately to conceal them from view.

Or to conceal the dealings of mortals from the eyes of the gods, Enelda thought.

Never in her days had Enelda heard of a lord—of any manor—encouraging such disrespect for the gods in his own hall. Not that she had seen many halls of Aelderland for a long time. Perhaps things were done differently these days.

After what seemed like an age, Lord Scarsdale stood from the altar beneath the idol of Baerloc and stretched out his limbs. He had prayed in silence, kneeling prostrate before his patron saint, as the Flaescines did. His cold eyes regarded Enelda as though for the first time, taking her measure as she took his. His black hair was freshly trimmed, his fringe poker-straight across his deep-lined forehead, framing a pale face furnished with thick black eyebrows and affectatious waxed beard. He was dressed all in black, too, from his high, stiff collar to his shiny boots; the only slash of colour on his person was the heraldry of his mearca, the twin devices of wolf and boar, embroidered over his heart in Aelderland green. He wore his black gloves still, which Enelda had never seen him without. A stark figure, immaculately presented. Indeed, too immaculate for simple prayer and a meeting with an old woman. He had dressed to cut the most imposing figure possible. If he had done so for Enelda's benefit, either to impress or to intimidate, he would have done as well not to bother. Something in the pursing of his lips and the flicker of his powder-blue eyes suggested he now realised this, a little too late. Perhaps he would feel silly. Enelda hoped not. There was naught so tiresome—or, sometimes, as dangerous—as a man who felt belittled by a woman.

"Thank you for coming," he said. "I thought it time we spoke privately."

"I would have liked to meet with you yesterday, but I understand you had business with the monks of Erecgham."

The archduke raised a bushy eyebrow.

"I should have liked to accompany you," Enelda continued. "Abbot Meriet and I have much in common."

Was that relief on the archduke's face?

"The abbot will grace us with his presence soon enough, I'm sure," he said. "The council has much to discuss—it seems we can go no more than a day or two without some new vexation. Here; it arrived this morning."

The archduke took a rolled note from a table and passed it to Enelda.

She strained to read it in the gloom.

"General Tarasq offers us more time," she said.

"No, she offers *you* more time. It appears you made quite the impression on Sauveur."

"I did what I could."

"You have until the new moon to do more. Seven days..." he scoffed. "General Tarasq's generosity knows no bounds."

"Forgive me, my lord," Enelda said, "but if you wish me to do more, I require certain freedoms that have not, perhaps, been yet forthcoming."

"Freedoms? From what I hear, liberties were already taken when my back was turned."

"Liberties, my lord?"

"You questioned my daughter."

"In the presence of both her nurse and Lord Clemence. Was this remiss of me?"

"I...would rather you had waited for my return before questioning my family."

Enelda knew she must tread carefully. Her usual strategies would only anger a man like Leoric, so used to being the highest authority in the land. So unused to the likes of Enelda.

"Forgive me," she said. "I have been away so long, I have perhaps forgotten my manners. If I need to speak with Ermina again, I shall come to you first."

"Perhaps it is not you I'm worried about."

"You mean Sargent Hawley?"

"Sargent Hawley, indeed."

"I am not sure he had terribly good manners to begin with. I shall endeavour to teach him the error of his ways."

"Sargent Hawley has put some noses out of joint in Scarfell. In time he will have to answer for assaulting the Vigilant Guard, and there will be nothing I can do about that. And there's more. I have heard loose talk regarding the sargent. 'Awearg,' they call him."

"Who?" Enelda asked, more sharply than she'd intended. "Who calls him such?"

"As I said, loose talk. But it reflects poorly on the man. We have ill omen enough in these halls, without taking in such a black talisman as he. It hardly bears saying that he should not be running around unaccompanied in the family wing. He was seen questioning my niece, alone."

"He told me he got lost while running an errand. A chance meeting, I expect."

"I would rather such things were not left to chance," Lord Scarsdale said with a glower.

"I shall speak with him."

"Be sure to. I need little enough excuse to dismiss him—he has other duties to attend to, I presume?"

"He assures me that my protection is his primary duty. He swore an oath...you know what these High Company fellows are like with their oaths."

"When it suits them, yes. But Hawley is not of the Blood. I advise you to keep your dog on a tight leash. If I hear more complaints, he will be sent back to Fort Fangmoor, oath or no."

"I should like to speak to her, though. Formally," Enelda ventured.

"Who?"

"Your niece."

"I'm sure she cannot be of any assistance. She swears she saw or heard nothing the night the boy was taken."

"I do not doubt it. You know, of course, that she's prone to wandering the castle of a night? I do not wish to make trouble for the girl, but it has come to my notice that she has a...rebellious streak?"

"I am aware of Iveta's proclivities. I do not encourage her, but...some young women have a mind to grow restless in such confines, grand as they may be."

"Such traits often run in the family."

"What?"

"Rebelliousness. Wanderlust. From her mother, perhaps?" Enelda held the archduke's gaze. His eyes narrowed a fraction and cooled further.

"Her mother was a fragile soul. Too fragile for this world, some might say."

"Your sister, then?"

"Sister-in-law. Iveta's mother was Lady Brithwen of Cyneshold. My fool of a brother got himself killed fighting the Northmen while his wife was heavy with child. Brithwen was never the same after that. She had the chance to remarry, and twice refused. When finally the end came, she left the child without an estate."

"Forgive me, but could not the same happen here? You have not remarried, and thus you can produce no male heir. What then of Ermina?"

The archduke stretched out his neck, wincing as much in agitation as discomfort. "I did not call you here so that I might be interrogated."

Enelda smiled her sweetest smile. "I would not insult my host so. If this was an interrogation, you would know it."

"Are we not on the cusp of war? Now is not the time for talk of marriage."

"Of course. A pity, though...In my day, as in Lady Aenya's, girls could still inherit when they came of age."

"That was a long time ago, too long ago to have helped my niece, even if she'd had the maturity to rule. Numerous petty lords petitioned the king for control of Cyneshold. One even attempted to claim Iveta's hand—still only a child. The others would have cast her out, even as the Winnowing raged beyond their walls."

"The Winnowing? That is when Iveta came to your custody?"

"Aye. Imagine if she had been sent out to live as a pauper, a girl of only nine years. It would have been a death sentence. Thankfully, her mother had had some wherewithal before her last days. She wrote to me, requesting I take the girl in and raise her as my own. Thanks to that letter, Iveta became my ward."

"Fortuitous." Enelda nodded. "And kind of you to allow her these freedoms."

"I...owed a debt to her mother."

"And you have not found her a suitor? I imagine she is becoming a burden by now." Enelda studied the archduke closely.

"I think the girl may be too headstrong for the foppish ninnies who pass for noblemen these days." His voice was filled with whimsy. Admiration for the girl? Something else? Whatever it was, it was laced with bitter regret. "When I was young, this mearca was strong, and proud. Wulfshael was full of young lords with iron wills and strength of arms, who would have leapt at the challenge of proving their worth to a fair maiden. Now, one harsh word from the girl and they shy away like kicked puppies. Truly, the long peace has allowed weeds to flourish amidst the roses."

"Be careful what you wish for. War, after all, knocks ever more loudly at your door."

"Would that be so terrible?" He strode away, beckoning Enelda to him.

The archduke stepped behind his shrine, to a black curtain that hung ceiling to floor. When Leoric pulled the curtain aside, Enelda expected to see another idol. Instead, the archduke stood before a tall cabinet, glass-fronted, even more finely crafted than those in the archive. Inside were artefacts almost as venerable. Enelda's sharp eyes took in a tarnished breastplate inscribed with sun motifs and inlaid with gold; a tattered habit of green with a coif and veil strengthened by strips of studded leather, a knotted cincture about the waist. Beside the garments hung the broken fragments of a sword, too long and too thin for a soldier of Aelderland, but just the weapon a warrior maid would have used. Its blade was inscribed with sigils—the Majestic script, used in olden times as blessings. Fragmented as they were, Enelda committed what she could to memory.

"Lady Aenya's," Enelda said.

The archduke looked vaguely surprised. "Aye. I suppose you're going to tell me you knew her?"

"I saw her, once. I was a novitiate, visiting Scarfell with my master. She was turning grey with years then, but still strong. A pious woman. Some would call her a saint."

Leoric's eyes narrowed. "No. Formidable, undeniably, but no saint."

"Touched by a Majestic, some say. That sword burned with righteous fire in her hands, smiting the wicked in their droves."

"A fairy story—and not one I would expect to hear repeated by a Vigilant. But then, I suppose the old order was known for its superstitious ways. When you saw her...this was following the war? Only a year before I was born. She was not long for this world then, and I do not believe a blessed saint would meet such an ignominious end as she."

"I never heard how she died."

"We do not speak of it."

"Nor do you speak of how she lived."

Lord Scarsdale hung his head. "It is forbidden. The great irony is that her reputation made Scarfell truly great. She was the first Warden of the March, a title I now carry—a title created so a woman might rule Scarfell. And yet I can never speak of how she came to be granted such a boon. You know that I am the only man in Aelderland permitted to wear a hat in the presence of the king?"

"I did not."

"I wouldn't, of course. I do not favour hats. But it is a courtesy earned by my great-grandmother, the only holy sister ever to rule a manor, and thus unable to remove her coif in the king's presence. As she had just personally slain twelve Sylven men-at-arms, captured a duke, and led her army to victory, the king decreed she could do as she damn well pleased. Yet she died an embarrassment to our hold. Her body was not returned—my father had her buried near where she fell, in a pauper's grave marked only by a rough-hewn slab of silver alabaster. It is untended and forgotten by all but me. A relic of the past. Out of respect for the king's law, I can never tell my daughter. We are all of us ordered to forget. Everything that came before the war might as well not

222 Mark A. Latham

have happened. Instead, a new history has been written, and we must all accept it as truth. And when we are dead, there will be nothing left but stories."

Enelda tried not to smile. She recalled Iveta's visits to the archive. She recalled the book in Ermina's bedchamber. The girls of Scarfell would not readily forget.

"I would not see Iveta suffer the same fate as Lady Aenya," the archduke went on. "I fear my great-grandmother's influence lingers still. There is too much of her in Iveta, and it causes me worry."

"One might say bravery and even stubbornness are no great failings."

"Failings." He laughed, ruefully. "Let us just say Lady Aenya casts a long shadow—a shadow felt most keenly here in Scarfell. It is a curse. I pray to Baerloc every day that it might soon be lifted."

"And Ermina? You think she shares this curse?"

The archduke rubbed again at his neck. "Must you ask so many damned questions?"

"What else is there? We are born with questions. We meet our end with questions. We strive for certainty our whole uncertain lives, and so we... question. I myself not only pursue that elusive certainty, but have sworn to provide it for others, like you. And so I must ask twice as many questions, to be doubly sure. You think it impertinent?"

"No...I..." He paused, and stretched out his neck a little. "Not impertinent, but tiresome. This talk of Ermina...I could not countenance anything happening to her."

"And I should hope nothing will," Enelda replied. "But she and the Tarasq boy were close. I wonder if she may know more than she realises."

"What do you mean? What could she know?"

"Did you know Anton Tarasq tried to copy Iveta? He too crept about the castle at night. Who knows what he might have seen, and who he might have told."

"Told? Told what? Are you implying Anton was taken because

he saw something he should not? That someone in my household may be responsible?"

"I never rule out a possibility until I have evidence to the contrary. It is a theory, for now."

"This is why you spoke ill of the nurse...If she is at fault, I shall dismiss her at once!"

"No need for that, Lord Scarsdale. At least not until I have had the chance to question her more thoroughly. With your permission, of course."

The archduke looked uncertain, as if mulling over whether or not Enelda had just tricked him. In the end he only nodded.

"If I may be so bold, my lord, I would advise a close watch be kept on Ermina. Even if she knows nothing, someone might *think* she does, and that is enough to put her in danger."

"If any man harms my daughter, I'll tear them to pieces!" In the red light, his face took on a murderous grimace.

"She will be safe, so long as she does not stray. She does not share her cousin's spirit of adventure, I take it?"

"Thankfully not. Ermina is a girl of sweet temperament, much like her dear mother. She was born only three months after Iveta came to us, at the cost of her mother's life. The physicians did not blame the Winnowing, but what else could it have been? My dear Athilda had been the picture of health, and then she was taken."

"So when St. Baerloc ended the Winnowing, you were doubly in his debt," Enelda mused.

"Debt?" The archduke looked guarded. "St. Baerloc is a blessing to this mearca. A god in mortal form. We owe him everything."

"The same used to be said for the gods of the Aelders, and the Blessed Three above them, but I see their praise is not sung in your halls."

"The suffering of mortals is milk and honey to the old gods. They hope we shall turn to them in our darkest hour. But when that hour came, and the Winnowing ravaged Wulfshael, it was a new god who healed the sick. St. Baerloc came to us from the heavens, a burnt and broken man, who lived in eternal pain so that we would not have to."

"Is that what he does?" Enelda asked. "He takes on mortal suffering for himself?"

"We believe it so. And his continued blessing is worth the sacrifice."

"Sacrifice?"

Leoric gazed reverently at the idol. His gloved hand reached out, trembling, almost touching the blackened face of the saint. "I have given everything to him. There is not much more left to give."

"And your reward?" Something about the idol gnawed at Enelda. She felt the back of her neck tingle. Despite herself, she looked over her shoulder, expecting someone to be there, watching. There was nothing but darkness and a thin haze of smoke.

"I ask for nothing in this life. Not for myself."

"You pray here often?"

"Daily."

"You were here when the boy was taken?"

That brought the archduke to his senses. His dark glower returned. He withdrew his hand from the presence of the idol. "I was. And before you ask, yes, I can prove it. Abbot Meriet was with me."

"I had not heard so."

"Well, that's why I was here. The night was bitter, and the abbot had stayed too late. Rather than send him back to Erecgham, I offered him my hospitality. It is not his custom to stay away from his abbey, but on this occasion he agreed, on condition he might use the chapel for his evening communion. I asked if I might join him, and he was good enough to guide me in prayer. I am afraid we became quite lost in our meditation."

"You saw or heard nothing out of the ordinary?"

"I did not. It was only in the small hours when the castle was awoken that I learned what had transpired. It shook the abbot greatly. He has not stayed another night in this castle since. I do not question him on spiritual matters, but I suspect he believes his absence from the blessed shrine that night might have led to the misfortune."

Enelda glanced at the window. The sun had moved upwards through several panes of coloured glass, and now illuminated the spiked crest of a sea serpent, which looked down upon the deck of the prophet's ship, beholding the Sylven holy man with a curious expression of awe and wonder. The morning was almost done. Hawley would have met Redbaer by now.

"Was there anything else you needed, my lord?"

"I...No. Vigilant Drake, I invited you to Scarfell, and I'll see you are able to do your duty, within reason. But know you have given me great cause for concern. You must swear to protect my daughter."

"I will do all I can."

"Swear."

"Those of my order swear but one oath, to the goddess Litha. We are forbidden from swearing others."

"Why?"

"Because there is no promise so hollow as one that cannot be kept. I will do what I can. Often, that is enough."

The archduke nodded, though he looked suddenly crestfallen. His moods seemed erratic, and writ large on his face. He again rubbed at his neck.

"Lord Scarsdale, I might recommend a tincture of rue steeped in vinegar and warm water. Some say an ointment made of the fat of a heron can ease the ache and *euel* of the joints—"

"I am quite well!" he snapped.

"As you will. Then, with your permission, I shall return to my investigation."

He nodded assent.

Enelda stepped into the long corridor, closing the door behind her. She breathed air free of incense with relief. But there was something else. The faintest scent of woodruff oil lingered in the air. Pleasant, sweet, earthy. A shadow moved at the end of the corridor, accompanied by the soft shuffle of a slippered foot. Then it was gone.

Enelda managed a smile. Perhaps there was hope yet for the future of this cursed hold.

CHAPTER 19

Iveta's heart raced. She'd been careless, but the thrill of almost being caught was exhilarating. Yet she felt guilt, also: How could she continue her work if she was discovered? Other lives depended on her discretion. But still ... even ladies deserved a little fun.

She took a circuitous route, past the bedchambers, slipping through the dressing room to the little servants' stair behind, along a narrow corridor lit only by arrow slits, up another short flight of steps, into the library corridor. It was how she'd escaped Hawley when he'd encountered her in the library—how she always slipped away when her uncle came looking for her.

She swung open the narrow door to the library. The curtains were half closed as always, to protect the old books from the sunlight, and she smiled to herself as she entered the gloomy chamber and closed the door quietly behind her.

"Good day, Lady Iveta."

Iveta spun around in surprise. Her heart thudded so hard she thought it might leap out of her mouth.

There, in the half-light, sitting at the reading table, was Enelda Drake, sea-green eyes fixed on Iveta, like a cat hunting at twilight.

Iveta curtseyed. She didn't know why—as a lady in her own home, she outranked every member of the fair sex to enter Scarfell. Foolish as she felt for the error, she did not think it an entirely unfitting courtesy to pay one so venerable, of a station so renowned. "How did you ... ?"

"Know where to find you? By paying attention, my dear."

The Vigilant stood, and shuffled closer. As she came into the light of the tall window, Iveta saw her as little more than an old woman—but she knew it was an act. It had to be. She had read the old books about the Vigilants' ploys. What was it now? *Be one who goes unnoticed, but upon whom nothing is lost.* Part of the Vigilant creed that Iveta had herself tried to adopt.

"Let me have a look at you, my dear," the old woman said. There it was again, the kindly smile, the weak voice...almost grandmotherly. But she reached out and took Iveta's hands with a grip strong as a soldier's. "Barely out of breath, not a hair out of place. You are surprisingly athletic for your size, particularly as ladies are forbidden physical exertion. Strong hands...calloused hands. And is that dirt beneath the fingernails? *Tsk*...I wonder what it is that you get up to, Lady Iveta."

Iveta pulled her hands away. "Do you accuse me of something?"

Enelda smiled. "No. I'm advising you to be more careful doing...whatever it is you do. You draw too much attention to yourself. Even the nurse has commented on your voracious appetite, and the woman is as dull-witted as they come. She'll surely wonder why a girl who eats so much remains so slender."

"It's not all for m—!" Iveta started indignantly, then bit her lip. She turned away and walked slowly to the nearest bookcase. She had allowed herself to become flustered in Enelda Drake's presence. Wasn't that just what the Vigilants wanted? Wasn't it how they drew so many confessions from the guilty? These days, Lord Clemence's men simply used torture—far more expedient.

"Ah, missions of mercy, is it?" Vigilant Drake said. "Is that where you were that night? During the storm?"

Iveta sniffed. "I'm sure I don't know what you mean." Her mind raced, formulating excuses to get out of the library, away from the old woman's inscrutable gaze. She'd wanted nothing more than an audience with Enelda Drake, but this was not how she'd imagined it.

"I suppose it is natural to seek adventure. It must be hard for you, my lady, being so alone. I see no friends your own age. No suitor. Your uncle says you were a rebellious child—always a solitary girl, were you?"

She wants me to make a mistake, Iveta told herself.

"No," she answered at last. "Not always. I used to play with the castle servants as a girl. Uncle Leoric put a stop to such... 'unseemly conduct.' It seems all I do is unseemly in his eyes."

"And yet some things do not change, my lady. Still you have the run of the place. Still you rebel. The book hidden in Ermina's room—your doing, I take it?"

"Will you tell my uncle?"

"My dear, if reading books were a crime, I should be burned at the stake by now."

Iveta looked up now at the old woman, held her gaze for just a moment, and laughed. Enelda Drake laughed, too—more a chuckle, but at least it made her less intimidating.

"It's a book about Lady Aenya. I...heard you once met her."

"Heard? Or overheard?"

Iveta stared at her feet.

"What's so important about the book, that you would risk so much to take it?"

"I thought Ermina should know the truth about the Lady Aenya, before the archives are emptied and the books destroyed. It's only a matter of time—it is only Lord Tymon who keeps the archive alive."

"And what is the truth?"

Iveta frowned. "What?"

"The truth about Lady Aenya that you so desperately want Ermina to learn."

"That she was powerful, and clever. That kings came to her for aid, and her enemies feared her. That there was a time when the women of this land could make their own choices, and even rule their own people. Lady Aenya didn't stay shut up in her castle. She rode out, clearing forests of dangerous beasts, bringing alms to her subjects, defending them from raiders, tending the sick. She was a fair and just lord. The people could do with a little more of that these days."

Iveta shook as the words tumbled from her. Pride in her illustrious ancestor had given way to something else: anger. Anger at her own lot in life, and Ermina's.

"Your uncle is not a fair and just lord, I take it?" the old woman asked.

"No. I mean... Yes. He was... At least, I think he was. These days I'm not so sure. The Vigilant Guard are the law in Wulfshael now, and like all soldiers they do as they are bid, even if it makes them tyrants. The people live in fear."

The Vigilant nodded. "All soldiers? Am I not here with a soldier? Do you think I would ally myself with such a man?"

"I... don't know. The soldiers of the castle speak of him with disdain. Vigilant Lestyn implied Hawley has a chequered past. I think he means him ill."

"And you put stock in what Lestyn says?"

"He's a cruel little man who needs his comeuppance. But I think he has something. Incriminating evidence, perhaps. He implied Hawley has some dark secret... Do you have any idea what he meant?"

"If I knew that, it wouldn't be a secret. Besides, I take folk as I find them—the past makes us what we are, but it does not define *who* we are or what we might become."

"I confess there is something different about Hawley. I've heard what they call him, and I... I know a little something about being treated as an outcast."

"It seems you know a great many things, Lady Iveta." The Vigilant smiled more broadly. "But you do need to be more careful, especially with the likes of our friend Lestyn sniffing about. I hazard that you've kept the book longer than usual, for instance. If someone else does not find it, Lord Tymon will notice its absence eventually."

"I know. Things have been difficult. Nurse Parnella watches us like a hawk now. The guards have doubled their patrols. And my uncle... He has become so strict. He flies into the most frightful rages. It is all he seems to do of late. I know he's just worried, since Anton... but sometimes I feel like... like—"

"A prisoner in your own home?"

Iveta nodded.

"But you still manage to find your way about the castle," Enelda said. "Two nights ago, for instance. Tell me, what was so important that you had to follow me to my chamber in the dead of night, and frighten an old woman half to death?"

"How did you—?" Iveta stopped herself when she saw Enelda's devious smile. "You didn't know it was me, did you?"

"I do now. You let Hawley scare you off?"

"No. There was a castle guard with him. If he'd seen me, my uncle would hear of it, and what then? Because what I wanted to tell you is…It's very serious, and I don't know who I can trust."

Enelda Drake shuffled to the servants' door, peered outside, and closed it. Iveta closed the other door likewise.

"Tell me, dear," Vigilant Drake said. She took a seat and bade Iveta sit beside her.

Iveta lowered her voice. "The day before you arrived, Phillippe Sauveur came to the castle. It was the second time he'd come here in as many weeks."

"The first being to deliver General Tarasq's ultimatum?"

"Yes. And this time because he'd heard of the boy found at the border. Nothing escapes him. They say he's a spymaster."

"I imagine that's not far from the truth. Go on."

"That night, my uncle held a dinner for the Sylven delegation. All the council and courtiers were present, except Abbot Meriet. He was still at Erecgham. Ermina and I are excluded from political affairs, and we took supper in my chamber."

"You did not stay there, naturally."

"No. I may have…overheard a few things."

"Naturally. From the old minstrels' gallery?"

"It's not used for anything else these days. Uncle Leoric sent all the entertainers away when he found his faith." Iveta flushed, and forced a smile. "It was all frightfully dull. Whatever had been discussed that day was kept away from the dinner table. I'd about decided to retire when I saw something suspicious. A serving boy passed behind Sauveur and pressed something into his hand. A note, I think. I tried to see where the boy went, but he left the hall immediately, and there was no way I'd have been able to catch up with him."

"Presumably another of the party passed the note to the boy," Enelda said.

"If so, I didn't see it. Anyway, shortly afterwards, my uncle called for more wine, but Sauveur refused. He and his party retired, and many of the other guests took this as an opportunity to excuse themselves. I'm afraid my uncle's company of late has not been agreeable. And so Uncle Leoric remained with a few favoured courtiers too polite to leave him, and Lord Clemence, who's never one to turn down wine. Everyone else drifted away. As soon as it was safe to move unseen, I went to find Sauveur."

"And had he retired?"

"He'd gone to his room, but left less than half an hour afterwards—when the passages had quietened and the guards had passed by on their patrol—then, he stole away, out across the ramparts of the inner ward, and into the Blacktree Tower. There's no way a stranger to Scarfell could know which path to take, or how to avoid the guards, without some assistance. That the Blacktree Tower door was unlocked was of equal concern. It's home to the dovecote, from where messages are sent to all corners of the kingdom. The guards always lock it on their patrols."

The old woman tapped her fingers in sequence against her thumb, as though counting. "You followed him across the ramparts?"

"I had to. I'm only glad I was wearing shoes."

"And inside the tower?"

"The Blacktree Tower isn't the most hospitable place. The stairs up to the dovecote can be treacherous, and below are some old storerooms. I saw lantern-light above, so I crept up as far as I dared. There were two men talking."

"You're certain both were men?"

"Yes. I'd not expected Sauveur to meet anyone. I thought he was just using the carrier pigeons to send a note to his masters. They were both speaking quietly, in Sylven. I'm afraid I could not recognise the voices, or catch everything that was said. Cousin Ermina speaks much better Sylven than me."

"I've heard."

"Sauveur was saying something like 'You'd better be sure.' Then the other man said, 'Evidence has come to light,' or something to that effect."

"Could the other man not also have been Sylven? One of Sauveur's servants, perhaps?"

"I don't think so. His accent was very different from Sauveur's. I think he was an Aelder."

Enelda closed her eyes, deep in thought. "And you have no idea who the other man was? This supposed traitor?"

"I couldn't get close enough to see, and when they were finished I barely had time to escape. I'm sorry..."

Enelda Drake opened her eyes and dismissed the concern with a wave of her hand. "What else did they say?"

"Sauveur said, 'So Anton was not the first?' And the reply was, 'And he will not be the last.' There was something more, before I heard Sauveur say, 'You must find them. Lives may depend on it.' He went on to say something about a message hidden in a book. I couldn't catch it. But the other man whispered, 'How will I know it?' I couldn't work out Sauveur's reply, save one thing. The name of a book I recognised."

"*L'chansse d'Eyundes et Ocienna*," Enelda said.

Iveta gasped. "How did you guess?"

"I never guess, dear. Is there a copy here in the library?"

"There was... It was over there, with the Sylven books Nurse uses so Ermina might practise her words." She pointed to the shelves. "But I haven't seen it since that night. Someone has taken it."

"Indeed." Enelda looked deep in thought.

"They are true, aren't they? The stories about Lady Aenya, I mean." The thought had come suddenly—that perhaps she wouldn't get another chance to ask. There couldn't be another alive in the whole world who had actually stood in Aenya's presence.

Enelda came out of her reverie. She reached out and smoothed Iveta's hair behind her ear. An almost motherly gesture, of the sort Iveta barely remembered. Enelda smiled sweetly, but her eyes, of pale sea green, seemed to stare straight into Iveta's soul. The old woman studied Iveta carefully for a moment longer before withdrawing. Without a word, she stood, and shuffled towards the door. Just as Iveta wondered if she'd somehow offended the Vigilant, Enelda looked back.

"When I saw Lady Aenya," the old woman said, "I was left in no doubt that the stories were true. My master certainly believed them. And do you know, my dear...I think—in another time, perhaps—you would have been just like her. The kind of woman who could set a sword aflame...and change the world."

Iveta couldn't muster a reply. And she didn't realise she had a tear in her eye until Enelda Drake had gone.

CHAPTER 20

Hawley was glad of the archive's chill. He'd worked up a sweat wandering the castle in search of Enelda. He should have known she'd be here.

"*Barty!*"

The raven's squawk nearly made Hawley jump out of his skin. Barty had been quiet, and nigh invisible against a benighted archway. Now the bird shook itself, hues of oily purple and blue gleaming from preened feathers.

Enelda craned her head over a pile of books that had entirely obscured her from view. She was wearing her ridiculous eyeglasses, which reflected the light from a single candle so that they looked like a pair of round lanterns.

"Barty does not much care for torchlight," Enelda said. "And my old eyes do not care for candlelight."

Hawley pulled a chair out from the table with a deep woody scrape and sat down heavily.

"You took your time," Enelda said.

"Didn't know where you were, did I?"

"You ate well while you were looking," she said. "That oil stain on your doublet is fresh. And you still have breadcrumbs upon your breast. Such manners."

Hawley smirked. "Thought you couldn't see in this light."

"But Barty can."

Hawley didn't know how to interpret that, so he said only, "I'm surprised they let you bring him in here."

"*They*, whoever *they* are, have no say in the matter. He was lonely in my chamber. He's homesick, I suppose."

"Aren't we all?"

"No, not all of us," Enelda said gently. "Not you."

Hawley flushed. "Still reading the Book of Vigils?"

"No. I have found something more pertinent to our cause. It seems not every ledger of import is missing from the castle records. Look here." She pushed the huge book she'd been studying towards Hawley and spun it around for him. "Births, deaths, and marriages of every inhabitant of Wulfshael, going back to before the Winnowing. Look here, do you see?"

Hawley squinted in the candlelight. "Mildrith of Rowen," he muttered.

"Thirteen pages earlier, her birth was recorded. Here, it is her death."

"We can't be sure she's dead!" Hawley snapped, despite himself.

"Quite. You see this mark next to the name?" Enelda tapped a bony finger next to a strange sigil—a stick figure beside a crescent. "The goddess Nysta, having taken a daughter unto her. They use this symbol here in Wulfshael to signify a body as missing, presumed dead. We may not have all the court records pertaining to missing children, but here is a list of every child in the mearca given to the keeping of Nysta. I've been working out which ones were born around the time of the Winnowing."

"Why?"

"Because the Winnowing has come up rather too many times to be irrelevant, in my opinion."

"And...how many are there?"

"Seven out of ten."

Hawley blinked in surprise. "Out of ten? How many missing bairns we talking about?"

"In total, over the last ten years? A hundred and three."

Hawley rubbed at his face. "Life's hard here. I...I don't know if that's unusual."

"A hundred and three missing children from a single mearca, in ten years. Yes, you could be forgiven for thinking it commonplace. Do you know how many such incidents were recorded in the tenyear before that?"

Hawley shook his head.

"Twenty-four. And in the tenyear before that? Eighteen. Now do you find it significant?"

"Aye." Hawley clenched his fists tight. "And nothing has been said. No hue and cry for those bairns. I s'pose nobody cares for poor folk."

"Ah, but fifteen of these children were not poor. They were the sons and daughters of freemen. One a dignitary from Scarsdale, no less."

"Impossible... There'd be uproar!"

"There should have been, I concur. But knowledge only spreads if powerful men allow it, and I fear what we have here is a conspiracy to suppress that knowledge."

"Clemence has the court records—if they contain evidence, we must seize them. We could go right now. I'll break down his door if—"

"Your pragmatism is admirable, but we still must be cautious. If Clemence even has the records, we have no idea whether his intentions are honourable. If not, the evidence is likely already destroyed, and all we'll do is hasten our journey to a gibbet. Thankfully, we can find some evidence of our own, right here."

"How?"

"Only those court proceedings that directly brought accusations of kidnapping or disappearances are gone. But what of related crimes? What of strange incidents that might yield further clues? We have the dates—all we need do is look." Enelda turned her eyes to a pile of parchments and books to her left, stacked almost as tall as Hawley. "Luckily you are here to help."

He slumped down wearily into a chair. "Where do we start?"

"No time for sitting around," Enelda said. "These ledgers barely scratch the surface. I need you over there in the stacks. When I call out a date, you find every record for it and bring it here. Whether it be from the manorial courts, the reports of tithing men, or a merchant consignment. It may all be important."

"All...?" Hawley groaned. "But that could take all night!"

"Do you suppose the work of a Vigilant is all adventure and excitement? It is not. Most of it entails precisely this. Gathering evidence. Finding connections. Now step to it, there's a good fellow, or we'll be here for days."

* * *

Hawley didn't know whether it was day or night. He was of little use to Enelda. He knew it; she must have known it. All he could do was scour the pages before him for anything...unusual. But what?

He failed to see how bills of lading and monastic books of days could illuminate this dark mystery. All he knew was that he was tired, and impatient. Had Enelda not said herself the boy was out there, possibly alive? That time was of the essence? By the gods, Hawley would feel better if he could ride out on a horse and start looking for the lad outside these accursed walls. And not really the lad, he reminded himself. Mildrith, and every other son and daughter of peasants who had been so mistreated, whose pleas for their children had been so ignored.

Hawley touched his hand to the amulet beneath his jerkin. It represented a foolish promise, he knew, but a promise nonetheless.

He rubbed his eyes. The book before Hawley was a hefty tome, penned by a scribe in some remote Eriestene monastery, detailing the "passing of the seasons in Wulfshael." It was the fifth volume in a series, apparently, and Hawley could only wonder if the scribes had gone blind while copying these passages onto thousands of pages, illuminating some chapters in glorious blocks of red, gold, and green, while leaving others bereft of ornament. Page after page of small, neat writing blurred before Hawley's eyes, such that soon he began to lose all concentration, and his eyelids grew heavy.

And then, at the foot of a page, he saw something that dragged him into wakefulness. A drawing of two figures, one woman and one man, tied to a stake, with flames licking around their feet.

And beside the figures, leaping from the page as though it were the only word in the accompanying passage: "awearg."

"Something the matter?"

Hawley blinked away his tiredness. He slid the book across to Enelda.

"Something about burning witches," he said. "But they don't usually burn witches in Wulfshael. They hang 'em, or drown 'em." He thought of Agatha of Rowen, bitterly.

"Burning is an old punishment," Enelda said. "Reserved for..." She didn't finish. Instead, she read the passage that Hawley had shown her. "This was only last year... The first day of Blotisstede."

That made Hawley shudder. Blotisstede, or the "festival of blood," was the month spanning the dark of winter, when livestock were sent to slaughter. Many of the more backward manors still practised the tradition of sacrificing livestock to see the people through the winter. It was a month of ill omen.

"The Witches of Wyverne..." Enelda went on. "It says here they were husband and wife—by the name of Thrussel—only six months in Wulfshael, having travelled north from Wyverne, 'that place well known of divers strange customs and superstitions.' I've never heard of it."

"I have," Hawley said. "Just today."

Hawley pulled out the map, now creased and battered and scribbled upon—the chamberlain would be cross. "This was where the dead boy was found, by the river. Redbaer told me the nearest settlement is a backwater called Wyverne, where the Borderers sometimes stop to rest on their patrols."

Enelda pursed her lips thoughtfully and returned to the book. "It says, 'Content not with the sacrifice of Blotisstede Day, the witches did reputedly slay the young daughter of Master and Goodwyffe Mostyn, whose corse has never been recovered. Three witnesses did speake of this great evil, testifying before the Vigilant that Goodwyffe Thrussel did once pricke her finger to squeeze blood into her bread, and once by the light of the Mother Moon did take the form of a hare and race across the fields.' Yes, well," Enelda muttered, "people will say all kinds of things when the likes of Lestyn are threatening them for false testimony."

"Lestyn was the prosecutor?"

"He's named here. The witches came from Wyverne to Raecswold...Lestyn's jurisdiction."

"The manor of Earl Wynchell," Hawley said. He pointed the village out on the map. "Less than a day's ride, again...Close to Erecgham. I think Raecswold serves the abbey, or rather, the monks serve Raecswold. It's a poor manor."

"It says here the Thrussels were untrustworthy," Enelda said. "Something about Wyverne being a place of ill repute. It calls them 'awearg.'"

Hawley shifted uncomfortably in his seat.

Enelda turned the page. Hawley's blood ran cold.

At the top of the page was another drawing. Beside it was written, "The blade recovered from the Thrussels was evidence enough of their crimes. The poor children of Raecswold had surely been sacrificed in the black rites of these witches. After much questioning did they finally confess, and for these heinous acts were the Thrussels put to the torch under the watch of the Vigilant."

"What does this mean?" Hawley asked.

"Fetch it, Hawley," Enelda said. "Go now."

Hawley pushed his chair away from the table with a loud scrape. He marched from the room, leaving Enelda to study the picture of the cursed blade.

The blade identical to the one in Hawley's pack. Ianto's blade.

* * *

It was an hour after nightfall, when every Lithadaeg Iveta would stand upon the battlements looking west, to see if Jens would signal. She did not expect him to. The old woodsman rarely did unless circumstances in his village were dire, but she had promised.

She pulled her fur-lined hood around her ears to protect from the chill. Clouds drove over the face of the sky, blanketing out the moon and stars. Her duty would be somewhat easier come spring, she told herself.

From this vantage point, Iveta could see over the outer wall and across to her uncle's forest. Skeletal black trees stretched out as far as the hills, but Iveta knew well where the forest split in twain for the passage of the ill-used Halham trail. It was there she focused her attention, for that was where the wily poacher would be.

She waited a quarter of an hour, perhaps more, and was about to leave the wall, her duty fulfilled, when she saw it. A soft, golden light, steady at first, then three blinking flashes. Then it was gone. Three flashes meant Jens was going down to their meeting-place.

Iveta had to hurry.

CHAPTER 21

Hawley pounded on the door for the third time. At last there came sounds of movement from within. A key turned. Bolts were withdrawn.

"What is the meaning of thi—" Chamberlain Tymon began. When he saw Drake and Hawley before him, his eyes swivelled about, first in annoyance, then confusion, before finally settling on weariness. "What now?"

"May we come in?" Enelda said innocently.

"It...it really isn't a good time. I am very tired."

"This won't take long," she said.

Enelda breezed past Lord Tymon, who flapped after her in a bluster. He wore a long gown and carpet slippers, which at least made him look less like a stork than his usual garb. He shepherded Enelda to a chair beside the hearth, though the fire was already dying.

"What's all this about?" Tymon asked. "It's really very late."

"I wanted to ask you about the Witches of Wyverne," said Enelda.

Tymon coughed nervously. "W-witches?"

"Quite. But first, perhaps we should discuss why you are spying on behalf of Phillipe Sauveur."

Hawley did his best not to choke. He hadn't expected Enelda to be so direct. But as the blood drained from Tymon's face, Hawley saw her deductions were again correct.

A bumping sound came from behind a door at the other end of the room.

"What was that?" Hawley asked.

"What? Nothing," replied the chamberlain.

Hawley looked suspiciously to the door. Tymon had someone in his bedchamber—he hadn't seemed the type, truth be told. Given his embarrassment, it was most likely a harlot from the town, or some fancy youth.

"The cat…yes. That is, she's always knocking things over. Good mouser though. One needs a good mouser in a place like this."

"Lord Tymon," Enelda said sharply, "don't take me for a fool. Hawley…" Enelda jerked her head to the door.

Tymon, abandoned by any semblance of lordliness, objected weakly as Hawley strode across the room and flung open the door of the bedchamber.

Nurse tumbled out of the room, spilling half-naked into Hawley's arms. Her face reddened. She covered her modesty with a blanket, and made some indistinct pleas for forgiveness, though Hawley had no idea what she needed forgiveness for.

"Get your things, my girl, and leave us," Enelda said. "We have business with Lord Tymon not for your ears. Though mark my words, I'll be speaking with you again soon enough."

At this prospect, the meek nurse looked truly terrified. She gathered up her things as fast as possible, and hurried out without bothering to dress. Her eyes met Tymon's as she left the chamberlain's rooms, perhaps imploring her lover for support. He only looked away, shamefaced.

*　*　*

"It isn't how it looks, not really," Tymon said. He'd thrown a log on the smoky fire, which was taking its time about catching. The chamberlain drew a shawl around his shoulders. "I am no spy."

"Yet you have been spying," Enelda said.

"I've been trying to prevent a war! Everything I've done has been for this mearca."

Enelda fixed her pale green eyes on Tymon, almost unblinking, which made the chamberlain squirm uncomfortably in his seat. "You passed information to Sauveur that proves the disappearances of children are somehow linked to Anton Tarasq's kidnapping."

Tymon nodded.

"Clemence doesn't have the court accounts," Enelda pressed. "You gave them to Sauveur as evidence. And I imagine he has agreed to keep them to himself until such time as war threatens and they are needed to cast doubt on the rulers of Wulfshael."

"Yes."

"Why not send them to the king?"

"If the king knew the extent of the misfortunes to befall this mearca, Lord Scarsdale would be ruined. I... owe this family too much to let that happen."

"So you believe Lord Scarsdale complicit?"

Tymon shook his head. "No... no! But Leoric—Lord Scarsdale— has not been himself for some time. I heard troubling things about his state of mind, even before the boy was taken."

"Heard? From the rather indiscreet nurse, I presume?"

Tymon nodded again, now looking ashamed indeed.

"The problem, Lord Tymon, is that you didn't really side with Sauveur out of love for the mearca, or Lord Scarsdale. You did it to salve a guilty conscience."

Tymon trembled. He tried to protest, but only a croak came from his dry throat. He looked away, unable to stand Enelda's inquisitorial gaze a moment longer.

"You made a *dwale* using ingredients from Clemence's stores. This is a potent sleeping draught, which you gave to the nurse that she might put the children into a sounder sleep when she slipped away to meet with you. Am I right?"

Again Tymon nodded, but now he buried his sallow face in his hands. By the firelight, he looked every one of his years. He took a deep breath to compose himself.

"I have eyes and ears everywhere in this castle," he said. "Parnella—the nurse—she... she acted only under my instruction, you understand. And you're right, I do feel guilt, and shame."

"If you hadn't used the dwale, the children would have woken

that night. Someone would have heard. What you overlook, Lord
Tymon, is that the person or persons who abducted Anton Tarasq
probably knew about the sleeping draught, and timed their dark
business accordingly. Someone else has eyes everywhere—even
on you."

"You mean...you don't think I took the boy?"

"I know you didn't."

Tymon slumped back in his chair and muttered some praise
to the Three. When he composed himself, he said, "What shall
become of me?"

"I do not know," Enelda said. "The law—nay, my own
strictures—dictate you should be handed to Clemence."

"Wait! I told you I have eyes and ears everywhere, and I meant
it. I can be of great service to you—"

Enelda held up her hand, and Tymon closed his mouth
abruptly. "Funny you should say that, my lord. Because I was
thinking much the same. Why don't you come with us to the
archive and help us piece together the rest of this mystery? I offer
you a rare chance at redemption—help us find the boy, and avoid
sending your beloved mearca into the front line of a war."

"Yes. Yes!"

"And if you prove unhelpful..." Enelda said with a glare, making Tymon shrink back, "Hawley here will drag you to Clemence
himself. Now, shall we go?"

*   *   *

Hawley unrolled the dagger. He could not bring himself to
touch either hilt or blade, and so he held the artefact gingerly in
its wrapping, and carefully placed it on a table beside the open
book, so the chamberlain could inspect the artefact next to the
drawing. The similarities were uncanny.

Tymon's breath escaped as a whistle through gritted teeth.
Enelda said nothing.

"A demon-blade," the chamberlain said at last. "Here, in the
castle."

"No," Enelda said firmly. "The scribe who wrote this account was doubtless ignorant of this knife's origins, and so he merely took Lestyn's word. And Lestyn, as I'm sure Hawley will attest, is a sadistic charlatan who would swear up was down as long as it meant he could exact his blood price. No, my lord, this is old knowledge. Old magic."

"The same knife from the picture?" Hawley asked.

"No," said Enelda. "It is a rarity, but not unique. Blades like these were created long ago by holy orders. Orders such as the Sisters of Oak."

"Ah, now I see," Tymon said. "I do not know how this knife came into Sargent Hawley's possession—I'm not sure I want to know—but I do know a thing or two about Wyverne. And the Sisters of Oak, come to mention it. Wyverne stands on the site of their old convent. After the order was dissolved, the entire thing was torn down and removed, stone by stone, so there's no trace of it at all these days. Now there are all kinds of rumours, about how the loss of the sisters let the devils in, and how the folk of Wyverne are...odd. Taken up with a strange religion. Speculation and hearsay, of course."

Enelda frowned.

Tymon, receiving no prompt one way or another, cleared his throat. "Well, when a child of Raecswold disappeared, the villagers suspected the Thrussels right away, but there was no evidence. Not at first. Then Vigilant Lestyn found the blade, and that changed everything, because then it seemed as though the child had not just been abducted, but *sacrificed*." He widened his eyes to emphasise the horror of his tale.

"I doubt it," Enelda said. "This is a wunscæd, a blade of covenant, also called a blade of *unbinding*. It is old magic, as I said, but not dark magic. Oh, I know the king's men would have it that all magic is dark, but that's because superstition has replaced enlightenment in this country. These sigils are Majestic script, passed down from the angels themselves, it is said. Such a blade is used not in battle, but in ritual, both to bind and cut the earthly tethers between Riftborn and host, and send the demon back whence it came."

"Why would the Witches of Wyverne have possessed such a thing?" Tymon asked.

"It must have something to do with the Sisters of Oak. And, of course, their most illustrious sister, Lady Aenya."

"You didn't want to ask about the witches at all, did you?" Tymon said with a papery smile. "You wish to know about the Warrior Maid."

"Most astute, my lord."

"I sit on the archduke's council...for now. Discerning a questor's true purpose from their guarded words is nine-tenths of my duty. You know, of course, we are all forbidden from speaking of her?"

"I do. Were it not for the decrees of a fearful and narrow-minded king, there would be a statue of Aenya twenty feet tall out there in the courtyard, and that would not be enough to mark the debt this mearca owes her."

"True enough, which is why I shall indulge you. You asked of Wyverne...You must know that's where Lady Aenya died?"

"What?" Enelda said, too hurriedly.

Tymon looked wary at first, but his pride at knowing something a True Vigilant did not shone through. Soon he was regaling his guests with the story of Lady Aenya, his tale taking a circuitous path through her famed exploits in the War of Silver and Gold, through to the first turbulent years of peace, when Aenya ruled Scarfell as the only female High Lord in all of Aelderland.

"But there came a darker chapter in Aenya's tale," he said. "Many feared Aenya had gone mad, so quick to anger was she, so eaten up inside with enmity for the Sylvens, and so full of yearning for past glories. Twice, over minor infractions of the treaty, she led the army of Scarfell to the Marches, almost rekindling the war—which in those days was a wound barely healed. Such was Aenya's fame that even the king could not openly move against her, so he commanded the Sisters of Oak to intervene, hoping Aenya would listen to them if not to him. The last of the sisterhood came to Scarfell and spent three days and nights in private prayer with Lady Aenya. When they left, they seemed to have taken something of Aenya's spirit with them, for she was never the same again. It's said she looked her age, at last, and more. It catches up with us all, some sooner than others."

Enelda seemed somewhat affected by this statement. Hawley caught her looking at her hands, which trembled slightly. He realised the tale must have resonated with her: a powerful woman, stripped of that power in middle age and left to her regrets. Enelda must have been of a similar age when she entered the Elderwood. How heavily must the years weigh on one so isolated?

Tymon, naturally, had carried on his tale, oblivious.

"No sooner had Aenya apparently been tamed," he said, "than the king himself came to Scarfell. In a greatly unpopular move, he dissolved the Sisters of Oak, declaring such an order of 'warrior women' heretical under the new laws. The sisters were an ancient order—it is said that their earliest acolytes brought the Royal Oak to Helmspire as an acorn, and in planting the tree they founded many of Aelderland's traditions. Can you imagine how news of their dissolution was received?'"

He saw that Enelda plainly knew all this and was uniquely placed to understand the tragedy of a dissolution. He cleared his throat nervously and got on with his story.

"Most went quietly into exile," he said, "but the Sister Superior resisted and was put to death. Notably, Lady Aenya said not one word in protest. After that, King Ealwarth sent Lady Aenya on a diplomatic mission to Sylverain, to make amends for her warmongering. Despite the order being seen as a punishment, Aenya did as she was bid and travelled south to the Marches. There, on the outskirts of Wyverne, she was ambushed by brigands. Legend has it she cried out to the angels for her old strength, to light the sword aflame once more, as in older days. But there was no fire, no magic. Indeed, the sword shattered with its very next stroke. They say she lost heart, as though the gods themselves had abandoned her. And with that, she lost her life. The greatest warrior Aelderland had seen for nigh a hundred years, slain by common outlaws."

"Which angels?" Enelda asked. "To whom did she call?"

Tymon shook his head, sorrowfully. "The records say not. Is it important?"

"Perhaps. And her body...Lord Scarsdale said she wasn't returned home, but instead was buried near where she fell."

"Did he?" the chamberlain said, eyes widening in surprise. "I don't believe he has ever spoken of her with anyone outside his council before. It is true: Under pressure from the king, Aenya's grandson, Wulfsige—Leoric's father—could not give her a hero's funeral, and so he buried her near Wyverne. It was a poorly kept secret—many poor folks made pilgrimage to see her grave. Some even stayed on and made a temple in her honour. Some thought she was a saint in all but name. The Flaescines almost canonised her, but I suppose the king put a stop to that."

"Was this before the convent was torn down?" Enelda asked.

"I believe that's what prompted it. I don't know why exactly Wulfsige gave the order, but I suppose grief does funny things to a fellow." Tymon laughed nervously. "No one talks about Lady Aenya, and they haven't for a goodly long time. All the books about her were moved here, out of reach of Lady Ermina, and his lordship forbids mention of her name. A shame, really."

"Presumably it is not just Aenya's martial reputation that is kept secret," Enelda said, "but rather the fact she ruled a hold in her own name."

"Ah, yes...quite. The law was never officially repealed, you know, but the archduke would not have Ermina's head filled with ambition she can never realise. Imagine the outcry if she laid claim to the hold!"

"Indeed. Lady Aenya seems much on the archduke's mind," said Enelda. "He sees some of her wilful spirit in Lady Iveta."

"Forgive me, but that is quite impossible. Lady Iveta is not related to Lady Aenya by blood, and they certainly never met."

Enelda frowned. "But the baron's brother was her father— there was no love lost between them by the way he spoke, but still."

"Sir Anselm was not of the line of Albertus," Tymon corrected. "No indeed, he was the baron's stepbrother, from the second wife of the last archduke. I think I have the book of the peerage some-where here..."

"Do not trouble yourself, I take your word for it." Enelda turned to Hawley. "The map," she said.

Hawley produced the map of the river, unfolding it gingerly atop the pile of books, noting the look of abject horror on the face of the chamberlain at its condition.

"The map shows the Sylven Marches in their entirety," Enelda said. "This is why I was confused. In the days of the Empire, where now stands Wyverne was only a camp formed by Syl-ven labourers. Here, you see?" She tapped on the map, at a site roughly in the vicinity of Wyverne. "The *Collines Pierrelune*. Or, as we would say, the 'Moonstone Hills.' A misnomer, for it was not moonstone quarried there at all, but silver alabaster."

"I have heard such," Tymon said. "But it has not been quar-ried there for decades."

"Indeed not. It is expensive to dig, and there are few masons in Aelderland with the skill to carve it."

Hawley yawned, and rubbed at his eyes. "What's this got to do with anything?"

"Just something I heard earlier," Enelda replied. "I half expect we shall have to visit Wyverne before too long."

"Why?"

"It's at the heart of the matter. It is where Lady Aenya is bur-ied. It is where the supposed perpetrators of a related crime came from. It is where the boy in the ice house was found. It is where your blade was likely forged."

"*Ianto's* blade," Hawley corrected.

"Who?" the chamberlain asked. Both Enelda and Hawley shot him warning looks, and he bit his tongue, remembering his predicament.

"Why did Ianto have the bloody thing anyway?" Hawley asked.

"A fine question. I believe it was not by chance he joined your company, nor was it chance he was sent north with you, when all others in your troop were of the Blood. Someone sent him. Some-one with influence."

"You said Ianto was a monk…Meriet! I knew—"

Enelda raised a hand to silence Hawley. She shook her head. "Don't jump to conclusions. It's true, I suspected he was a Flaescine from the reliquary he carried. But how could Meriet have sent him? The abbot has no influence over Commander Hobb."

"Seems more likely than the alternatives," Hawley said. "Clemence? He's got no power over the monks. Lord Scarsdale…? He's got men of his own. Spies, even."

Enelda shrugged. "I was told Lord Scarsdale was recently inducted into the mysteries of Baerloc." She looked at Tymon for confirmation.

"He was indeed," Tymon said, relieved to have permission to speak. "Very few receive the honour, for it involves standing in the presence of Baerloc's blessed remains. If…one holds with such things."

"So the archduke holds considerable influence at Erecgham," Enelda said. "Could not he have persuaded Hobb to recruit a man of his choosing? A man of his own faith?"

Hawley stroked his chin. "Aye. Hobb would probably listen to a High Lord—he's a preening peacock. But Meriet must've known."

"Who says either of them are involved? Have you thought perhaps someone might wish to implicate the abbot for reasons of their own?"

"No, I haven't," Hawley snapped, tiredness and frustration finally besting him. "I've seen his monks skulking about all over the place. They travel freely on monastery business, from here to Eastmere. Aye, and Rowen, too. Everywhere I look I see them bloody monks. Even Raecswold lies so close to the abbey it'd be less than an hour's work to snatch a bairn and escape unseen. Why do you *not* suspect Meriet?"

Enelda stood abruptly. "Because he is a good man!" She raised her voice, and the strength of her words was sufficient to silence even Hawley.

Tymon cowered now. But Hawley and Enelda looked to each other, then to him, realising that here was a man who might use any morsel of intelligence to his advantage.

"Lord Tymon," Enelda said, "though the sargent has a suspicious mind that would rival even a Vigilant, he has given me cause to remember something. A book—the *Canticle of St. Baerloc*. Do you know it?"

"Of course. Shall I...fetch it for you?"

"If you'd be so kind. And would you do me the service of fetching the Book of Vigils? It is a heavy tome for an old woman."

Tymon agreed readily and shuffled away, fumbling nervously for his keys.

"Not a word, Hawley," Enelda warned, with a hard stare that made Hawley think twice about questioning her.

When the chamberlain returned with the books, Enelda said, "I think we have taken up too much of Lord Tymon's time. Perhaps we should continue our studies alone."

"Have I been...helpful?" Tymon ventured.

Enelda weighed up the question, perhaps considering how much more fear to instill in the chamberlain. "You've given me much to consider," she said.

"Well...I am very tired..." Tymon said.

Enelda fixed him with a searing glare. "I would speak with you again tomorrow. Our business is not concluded."

"Of course, my lady. I am at your disposal." Tymon bowed, already backing away.

When Tymon's ungainly footsteps had faded from the long gallery, Enelda beckoned Hawley over. She opened the Book of Vigils, turning the fragile pages carefully, some mouldering and half-destroyed, others burned away. She paused at a swirling symbol that filled a page: a triskelion, surrounded by gaily painted runes.

"Let me tell you a thing about good and evil," she said. "Men and women have long been treated as pawns in a great game. It began with the Trysglerimon, the Gods Three, who created us in their image. As we conquered this world and grew in number, the Three tired of us, and looked elsewhere for their amusement. New gods rose, born of man's limitless capacity for belief and hope. But the gods, like men, have dark in them as well as light. And it is this darkness that attracted the Riftborn to our world. They scratch behind the veil, waiting, longing, to feast upon our souls. Sometimes they break through, manipulating the weak-willed to their designs, spreading messages of hate and intolerance. Sometimes, some rare few times, they gain a foothold in this world so firmly that they get what they desire: chaos. And so it was when King Hratha of Tördengard cast the first stone in what would become the War of Silver and Gold, dragging Aelderland into a conflict that would weaken us for generations to come."

"I doubt the Riftborn were to blame for Hratha's madness. Besides, we won."

"At what price? The Sylverain Empire fell, and we were at last liberated. But in the years that followed, has life been better or worse than before, would you say? What am I thinking? You weren't even born...Let me tell you, I don't recognise this country now. And I love Aelderland, in spite of everything. But when I was a girl, I had every opportunity to make something of my life. A girl now—even one of noble birth like Lady Ermina—has nothing before her but duty to her house. She can never study in the great universities of Aeldenhelm, or fight in the armies of Wulfshael like her great-great-grandmother. If she's lucky she will marry a kind man, rather than a brute, and will die of old age rather than in the blood-soaked sheets of her birthing bed, because physicians are no longer commonplace, and midwives fear accusations of witchcraft for practising their arts. This is the world you know, the world you accept, but it is a world shaped and moulded by dark forces. Can you really say that King Hratha's actions were not driven by the Riftborn? Is this not precisely what demons would want for us?"

Enelda turned the page. Row after row of bizarre script surrounded an image of something black and gangrel—some long-limbed, wet-jawed creature, sketched in frantic strokes as if by a man possessed. A maw painted in red. Eyes in yellow triangles. And it made Hawley cold to his bones.

Just a bear...

"Are you all right?"

Hawley realised he'd been staring at the page, as though mesmerised. "Why wouldn't I be?" he said gruffly.

"We won the war, Hawley," Enelda went on, turning the page quickly. "We defeated Sylverain at the Battle of Four Crowns, and then in turn defeated King Hratha when his ambitions fell upon our western border. Finally, we turned back the Northmen who had so long raided our lands and pillaged our coasts. And do you know how we managed such a feat? How this little country triumphed over all the odds?"

Hawley did not, beyond what he'd been taught at Fort Fangmoor of superior Aelder strategy—that, and the madness of King Hratha, who had unexpectedly pitched against both sides in an ill-advised grab for territory. But Hawley knew what Enelda believed, and so he ventured, "Majestics?"

"*Jestics!*" Barty squawked, so suddenly that Hawley jumped.

"It seemed the gods were on our side, for they sent from the heavens the angels themselves to fight for Aelderland. They worked their miracles through mortal vessels, many of whom are now saints."

"Careful," Hawley said bitterly. "Your friend Meriet would call that blasphemy."

"Perhaps. But Meriet was not there for the final battle. He did not see the chosen few turn the tide in our favour, with the golden light surrounding them."

"You…you were *there*?" Hawley found it hard to imagine this small woman as ever being young, let alone fighting.

"I had hoped never to see such horrors again, but time is against us."

"You think war will come?"

"General Tarasq has given us seven days to find her son. If we don't, she will break the Accords, and war will be inevitable."

"Gods…" Hawley muttered.

Enelda turned a page to show a faded painting. A horde of Sylvens in blue and black, and their half-naked mercenaries, clashed with a handful of grim-helmed warriors clad in pale grey.

"The *Baeldorn*," she said. "The old Vigilant Guard. They were not the petty militia we know today, but soldiers, hearthguards, and heralds combined—freemen who fortified mind, body, and soul against the forces of darkness, and swore to accompany the Vigilants into the very pits of the underworld if need be. At the Battle of Four Crowns, my master commanded thirty Baeldorn, as I stood by his side. We would struggle to find a handful of such men these days—aye, and women, too."

"The High Companies are—"

"Skilled warriors, yes. But do you know why they say each High Companies man is worth five lesser soldiers? Do you know where the saying really comes from? Your armour, Hawley. The cost of that armour is worth the lives of five men. The knowledge of its construction is lost to time, and so it can only be maintained. Men have fought and died to retrieve it from the fallen."

Hawley shifted uncomfortably. He'd heard it said before, but only as conjecture. The High Companies preferred to write their legend the other way.

"Oh, have no fret, Hawley. I don't mean to disparage you. The High Companies are implacable warriors indeed, but we have not seen the like of the Baeldorn since the Dissolution. Perhaps we never shall again."

"What's your point?" Hawley regretted his petulance. But he was tired, angry at Enelda's refusal to investigate Meriet, and agitated at being compared unfavourably to long-dead Baeldorn.

"It means the Majestics and the Riftborn—perhaps the gods themselves—have plans for us yet. And it is not for mortals to understand them. *Most* mortals, at any rate." She looked at Hawley down the brim of her nose. "Abbot Meriet is a devout man. I believe that. If he did send Ianto north, as you suggest, could it not have been for some righteous purpose?"

Hawley frowned. "The knife..."

"What if he was trying to banish evil, not conjure it?"

"Ianto betrayed me, at the end. He betrayed the company."

"So did you."

"It's not the same," he muttered. In truth, Hawley knew his disobedience would be the end of his career in the High

Companies, and in the eyes of Hobb would be tantamount to treason. "Sometimes evil men appear good," he said. "And sometimes good men do evil things. Who knows what Meriet's up to, out there in his monastery? Who knows what reason he might have for his actions? All I know is, I've never met a 'good man' without sin. But I've known some bad 'uns who never feared justice, because they were protected by power and position."

Enelda closed the book with a sigh. "It is too late to discuss such matters. I would suggest you retire. You look dead on your feet, and your manner is disagreeable."

"I'm perfectly—" Hawley protested.

"There you are, you see? Disagreeable. Go and rest—I have more to do here, and I need you fresh tomorrow. And take that with you." Enelda nodded at the dagger.

Hawley wrapped it gingerly, being careful not to touch it with his bare hands. He tucked it into his breast pocket, dismayed not to be rid of the wretched thing.

"You shouldn't stay here alone," he said.

"I'm not alone. I have Barty."

"Barty—Barty!"

Hawley flapped his arms in frustration, almost resembling the raven himself. He was tired, it was true. But each day they seemed to make more enemies, and Enelda was wholly too unconcerned about them for his liking. "Look, if you insist on staying, just be careful."

Enelda turned her back on Hawley and fetched down another book from a shelf. "I bid you good night," she said.

CHAPTER 22

For the first time in a long time, Iveta craved her bed and a good night's sleep. Leaden limbs carried her to the top of the cramped, dark stairway. Her little expeditions had taken their toll. Yet her troubles paled into insignificance compared to the plight of the ailing folk of Halham. Gods only knew how she would help them this time. She'd given Jens assurances that weighed heavily upon her. She would have to speak with her uncle, or at least try. She had to find a way to stop Lestyn heaping further misery upon those poor souls.

Iveta placed her candlestick in the small niche beside the door, and extinguished the flame, plunging her into total darkness. Iveta didn't fear the dark. Indeed, she had grown accustomed to it. What was there to fear in the benighted passages behind her, save some long-dead Sylven lords? She feared the living, not the dead.

She listened at the narrow doorway, determined not to allow fatigue to make her careless. Iveta knew of three secret entrances to the catacombs: one in the Green Tower and two in the keep. As a simple precaution she never returned the same way she left. Tonight she had chosen the entrance closest to the comfort of her own bed.

At last satisfied that no guards trod the corridor outside, Iveta clicked open the door. She slipped from the panel in the tall oak wainscot, squeezing past a life-size statue of Lady Huneald, wife of the first Lord Scarsdale. Iveta closed the secret panel shut behind her, ran her hand across the join to ensure it was once more invisible to prying eyes, and gave a customary bow to Lady Huneald. There was something about the knowing expression of the statue... Iveta fancied the infamous firebrand of a woman would have approved.

The north corridor was illuminated by faint moonlight from the tall windows, which fell in angular shapes upon the floor. She hurried noiselessly along the corridor, up the twisting stair to the library, and into the family corridor, where portraits of her uncle's forebears looked down with cold eyes. Distant aunts, uncles, and cousins many times removed, their storied deeds reduced to little more than footnotes in history.

There she paused, gazing along the corridor towards the door that lay at the very end, always locked. Her candlelight barely kissed the shadows that lingered ever outside the door of Leoric's chapel. Her uncle was probably there now. Rarely did he sleep in his own chamber these days. She wondered if he slept at all.

Iveta was torn between action and inaction, until at last she summoned her courage. She strode to the end of the corridor. Uncle Leoric may be doubly angry at seeing Iveta up at this hour; he may even notice her outdoor attire, splattered with mud. But crucially, he would be alone. With no attendants, no councillors, no abbot, and certainly no Vigilants to set themselves against her, perhaps she could persuade him to help his people.

Soft light flickered under the crack in the chapel door. Iveta listened, but heard nothing. She raised her hand to rap on the door, but didn't do it. Her hand hovered, trembling. She cursed herself for a coward.

Iveta started at a shrill, muffled cry somewhere behind her. A child's protestation, followed by an adult's rebuke.

Iveta abandoned her mission and rushed to Ermina's door. She tried the handle in vain. She called out to her cousin and heard only a wail.

"Wicked girl!" came a woman's voice. "What lies you tell. What *lies*!"

Iveta ran to her own room, through it, to the adjoining door.

Beneath a rug by the door she kept a purloined key, and now she fumbled with it, finally unlocking the door as Ermina's cries grew louder. Iveta threw open the door.

Ermina was bent over Nurse's knee, screaming as the nurse brought her hand down sharply on her behind with an almighty crack.

Iveta hesitated only from sheer shock. A spanking was not entirely unheard of, though Ermina had rarely warranted it her entire life. But the force of it was unmeasured, and the nurse's wrath so great she seemed neither to notice nor care about Iveta's arrival as she raised her hand for another strike.

Iveta was across the room in two strides. She snatched Nurse's wrist and hauled her to her feet. Ermina tumbled to the floor, a tousle of golden hair, her shift stained with tears. Nurse stopped, face contorted now in shock. She tried to slap Iveta, but Iveta blocked the clumsy blow and pushed Nurse so hard the woman flew across the room, dropping to the floor in a startled heap.

Iveta gathered up Ermina in her arms and glared at the nurse. "What is the meaning of this?" she snarled.

Tears streaked the nurse's face. "I'll not be spoken to like that! I will not tolerate such...*lies*!"

"I didn't lie," Ermina sobbed. "Nurse c-came back late and w-woke me, and I said I knew where she'd been. It was a secret... Anton's secret. But I only said it to Bandit. And Nurse heard me and she...and she..." The tears flowed again, Ermina's great sobs causing her to struggle for breaths.

Nurse slowly rose to her feet. "Wicked!" she said. "Both of you wicked. And I see you, my girl. Wet from rain, mud on your dress. I know where you've been, and I know how you got there. You have no more secrets from me. I'll see you ruined, my girl."

Iveta glanced down at the muddy hem of her dress. She narrowed her eyes at the nurse, whose face was no longer dull, but pinched and red, eyes gleaming in triumph.

"Tell me," Iveta whispered into Ermina's ear. "It's time to tell me the secret."

Ermina sniffed, and blinked away tears. At last, through

broken sobs, she said, "Nurse meets a man at night. Anton saw them. The man told her things... private things. '*Dou'se, l'desír du coron,*' he said."

"You little—" the nurse snapped, lunging forward.

Iveta placed herself between her cousin and the nurse. In an instant, her dagger was in her hand, and Nurse stopped in terror as the point almost met her throat. Iveta never left the castle without protection. The Sylven poniard had been a gift from Sir Redbaer on her eighteenth birthday, and she carried it as surety against beast and bandit alike. She knew how to use it.

Nurse saw in Iveta's eyes that the threat was not hollow. She backed away.

"Tell me," Iveta whispered to Ermina, not once taking her eyes off the nurse. "Who was the man?"

"It was... L-Lord Tymon."

No sooner had Ermina uttered the words than the nurse howled, and sank to her knees.

"An affair with a member of the council is one thing..." Iveta said. Her mind raced. What would Enelda Drake deduce from this situation? "You've been meeting Lord Tymon, whispering to him secrets about the family, that he might vie for higher position? Or is it more than that? His fluency in Sylven... in poetry... I wonder what else the chamberlain gets up to with the knowledge you give him. Are you a spy, Nurse Parnella? Are you our enemy?"

"No... no! Mercy, my lady," the woman cried.

"Are you complicit in Anton's disappearance? Do you know where he is? Speak!" Iveta's anger grew as she pieced together the extent of the woman's treachery.

Nurse stood again. "I never harmed a hair on that boy's head. But if you accuse me to his lordship, I'll see you ruined. I seen your secret ways out the castle. I seen the things you steal. I know it, and now my master knows it. You'll have no more freedom if I have my way, my girl!"

Iveta left Ermina, strode towards the nurse with the dagger held out. Nurse shrieked.

"Give me your keys. Now!"

Nurse fumbled at her belt and untied her ring of keys. She threw them at Iveta's feet, wincing at the proximity of the slender blade.

"Go to your chamber. By all the gods, you'll be lucky if my uncle only has you flogged when he hears of this. If you come near Ermina again this night, I'll have you thrown from Scarfell with naught but the clothes on your back. Do you understand?"

There was some protest, more threats, and much weeping, but at last the nurse fled from the room. Iveta locked the door between Ermina's and Anton's chambers, then the outer doors.

Ermina sobbed, more quietly now. Iveta held her close.

"Sleep with me tonight, love," she said. "Nurse won't lay another finger on you, I swear."

Iveta considered running to her uncle, but she knew not what state he'd be in. She could find a guard, but Nurse's threats gave her pause. How much did she really know?

She thought also of Lord Tymon. Was he indeed the spy she'd heard talking to Sauveur? All the evidence suggested so.

Iveta double-checked the doors, dressed for bed, and let Ermina curl up beside her. She would wait until morning, and find Enelda Drake. She'd know what to do. Until then, she would try her best to stay awake and keep watch.

She kept a candle burning and her dagger close.

*　　*　　*

Feorndaeg, 8th Day of Nystamand

Hawley slept with difficulty, and when slumber had taken him, it was fitful. The nightmares had changed of late. They started as they had always done, but now, when Hawley looked down at the stricken corpse of Jon Gale, his greatest regret, the dead man opened his eyes. And those eyes were yellow, and gleaming. That was when the nightmare took a very different turn. Hawley was no longer in Herigsburg but in a dark forest. His every step was hounded by the sounds of guttural grunts and growls and the wet snapping of enormous jaws. He ran deeper and deeper into the twisting woodland, where the bough of every tree was carved with swirling sigils. Old magic—good or bad, Hawley could not tell, but it filled him with dread. And when finally he thought he'd lost the monsters that hunted him, he saw his men hoisted high into the trees by formless things of shadow and smoke. Nedley, Tarbert, Beacher, Ianto. One by one they went, torn limb from limb, their terrible screams all Hawley could hear. Ianto's was the worst of all, so shrill and high it jolted Hawley from the nightmare's embrace and into wakefulness.

The scream did not stop.

Hawley half leapt, half fell from his cot. Daylight stung his eyes. He was face to face with the maid, Agnead, whose screams were enough to wake the dead.

He'd not retired immediately last night, choosing instead a goodly amount of wine, and that decision now added to his confusion.

Hawley grabbed the maid by the arms. "Quiet, girl!" he said. "What the devil's wrong with you?"

Mercifully, she stopped screaming, but still trembled in fear. Her eyes darted to Hawley, and then away, to the chest beside his bed.

Hawley followed her gaze. Atop the chest was an open leather roll, upon which lay the wunscæd. He'd been so tired when he'd turned in, he'd forgotten to stow it.

"The blade?" Hawley asked. His voice sounded rough even to his own ears. His head felt full of straw.

The girl did not reply. Hawley had rarely seen such fear.

"Look at me, girl. That blade—you've seen one before?"

"Please...d-don't hurt me, sir."

"Why would I—?"

The door swung open before Hawley could finish his question. The formidable figure of the cook stood in the doorway, clenched fists resting on copious hips, her face wearing an expression that could curdle milk. She surveyed the scene, looking Hawley up and down in disapproval.

Hawley now realised how it looked. He was standing in his bedroom, hands on a young maid, wearing nothing but his *braies*. He let go of the girl at once.

"What's all this?" Cook growled. She looked as cross with the maid as with Hawley.

Agnead tried to speak, but immediately broke down into fitful sobs. Hawley spread his palms in despair and looked to the cook for help. To his surprise, she pursed her lips, nodded at him, and entered the room. She put an arm around the girl and patted her on the shoulder. Her eyes then alighted on the knife.

"*Hmmph.*" She shook her head sadly. "Thought we'd left this wicked business behind. A bad state o' affairs, and no mistake."

"Will someone explain to me what's going on?" Hawley said. "What do you know of that knife?"

With utter distaste, the cook reached out a hand towards the knife and flicked the wrapping over it, concealing it from view as though the very sight of the thing was a curse. And sure enough, as soon as its swirling sigils were covered, Agnead's sobs dwindled to a sniffle.

"Aye," Cook said. "I don't think you're a wicked man, Sargent. Not like some o' the others I've met, leastways. But then again…if'n I'm wrong 'bout you, I'm as like to wake up tomorrow with me throat slit."

She indicated for Hawley to sit on his cot, and then pulled up a stool for Agnead. Hawley pulled on his britches and sat. Cook closed the door softly.

"Last time we had a soldier stayin' here was—oo, lemme see—about six week ago. I remember it well—me brother works the farm out past Briars Brook, and he'd just finished rebuilding after an awful bad frost. An' it were only a few days before poor Master Anton went missin', gods save him. But the castle were full to brimmin', for the master was playin' host to half of the abbey, and them monks were takin' up every spare room we had."

"From Erecgham?"

"Where else? Since the master found faith in Baerloc—gods praise him—we've 'ad no other holy brothers in this castle."

"You said a soldier stayed here. What'd he have to do with the monks?"

"I were gettin' to that," Cook snapped. "This soldier *were* a monk, you see, or rather, he started out as one, though we din't know it at the time. Stayed in this very room, he did, which was unusual, as they normally bunk up together. Don't need no comforts when ye've got religion, I s'pose. Anyways, one night young Agnead here comes in, and as all the other monks were out fer evenin' prayers, she thought there'd be no one here. But there was—the monk were still in his chambers, only he weren't dressed as a monk no more. He were dressed in uniform, like a soldier."

Hawley's stomach knotted. "What kind of uniform?" he asked, his words a croak from his dry throat.

The Cook looked to Agnead, and jerked her head impatiently. "Well, tell 'im, girl. You got a tongue in your 'ead still, I take it."

Agnead's bottom lip jutted out, making her look even younger. That made the haunted look in her eyes all the more disturbing. She pointed a trembling finger at the pegs on the wall, where Hawley's belt, tunic, and cloak hung. "Like that one," she said.

Hawley rubbed his hands across his face. "Exactly like that one?" he asked, gently. "A High Companies uniform?"

"Oh aye," Cook interjected, cutting Agnead short a little too eagerly. "He came here a monk and left one of your lot. A queer business that. And that ain't all. Tell 'im what else, girl."

The girl's eyes moistened again. She clamped her mouth shut and shook her head.

Cook sighed theatrically. She leaned forward, such that Hawley had to avert his eyes from the woman's ample bosom, and said in a low voice, "Then he threatened poor Agnead. He had a dagger—like that one, from what she told me. Leastways, when she were able to talk again, which weren't 'til long after that scrawny bugger had left the castle. And he holds the dagger up to Agnead's eye, an' he tells her it's old magic, an' if she breathes a word o' what she seen, all the power o' the angels will cast her from the Garden of the Aelders and curse her to 'ternity in the Rift. Now, have you ever heard the like for a monk to go sayin'? An' then, when he got her good an' frightened, he..." She looked to Agnead, who had turned deathly pale, and had drawn her knees up onto the stool, hugging her legs close to her body. Cook closed her eyes and seemed at last to realise the effect she was having on the girl.

Cook drew the girl in close, and when Agnead's back was to Hawley, Cook pulled the girl's smock down over her shoulder.

Scars. Sigils, like the ones on the dagger, carved into the girl's flesh, over the shoulder blade.

"Said now the mark o' the devils was on her. Said 'e'd be able ter see Agnead any time, and know if she were tellin' tales on 'im. And if'n she did..." Cook drew her finger across her throat, then quickly checked to make sure Agnead still wasn't looking.

Hawley felt sick. He stood gingerly, walked around the cot, and poured himself some water. He was going to take a drink, but then decided the girl's need was greater, and so passed it over to Cook to give to her.

"And you say he did this before Anton Tarasq was taken?" Hawley asked. He could scarce believe it. How much of what had happened these past weeks had been accident, and how much design? And whose design? Hawley fancied he knew very well, and maybe now he could persuade Enelda of the truth of it.

"Aye, I told ye. A few days before."

"You are *certain*?"

"Sure as eggs is eggs."

"His name," Hawley said. The words grumbled from his mouth so savagely they caused Cook to recoil. Hawley bit his tongue, lest his rage frighten Agnead even more. But by all the gods, rage was what he felt. This man, this traitor, this defiler... Hawley was sure enough he was dead, and perhaps that meant justice was served, but it barely made up for what he'd done in the name of the Third. "His name," Hawley said again.

"A queer name," Cook said. "Though I hear it's a common one over the fens. I s'pose that's where he came from. Yan, was it? Ewan?"

"Ianto," Agnead said timidly. "His name was Ianto."

And a voice whispered in the back of Hawley's mind, from a nightmare never forgotten:

This was not the promise made.

                    *   *   *

Enelda had woken at first light, as was her custom. She'd barely dressed when Barty alerted her to an approaching visitor, and sure enough there came a rap at the door.

"Never a minute's peace..."

Enelda shuffled to the door, bones creaking.

Outside her door stood a monk, silent beneath his brown robes. In his outstretched hand was a neatly folded note, which Enelda took and held up to the light.

> *Vigilant Drake,*
>
> *I would seek an audience in strictest confidence. If convenient, please allow my blessed brother to escort you.*
>
> *Galdwin Meriet,*
> *Abbot of Erecgham, Chief Advisor to*
> *Lord Scarsdale*

"Interesting..." Enelda said. "You'd better lead on, young man. Wouldn't want to keep the abbot waiting."

CHAPTER 23

A gnead made a small squeak. Hawley put his arm across her path instinctively.

The kitchen was full of monks, helping themselves from Cook's pantry. One of them beheld Hawley impassively, then turned his back, leaning nonchalantly on the kitchen table in a manner so familiar he might have been a lord rather than a pauper in holy orders.

Cook drew up alongside Hawley, like a warship with ballistas bristling. She patted Agnead on the shoulder.

"Make yourself scarce, girl," she said.

Agnead scurried off down the narrow corridor, not once looking in the direction of the monks.

Hawley balled his large hands into fists. He stepped forward, the scabbard at his side slapping his hip reassuringly. But he was stopped by a podgy hand.

"I'll have no trouble, Sargent," Cook whispered. "I'm the 'thority down 'ere."

"All right," Hawley growled. "But I need to see Vigilant Drake."

Cook nodded. A young page squeezed through the crowded kitchen, gawping in surprise at the sudden appearance of the silent brotherhood. Cook beckoned him over. "You, take Sargent Hawley up to Lady Enelda's chamber."

"Before breakfast?"

"You'll do as you're told, and do it sharp, less'n you want a clip 'round the ear!"

"Only...I don't think she's there. The Vig'lant, like."

"How would you know where she is an' where she ain't?"

"Because I saw her not an hour ago, Miss, with..." The boy glanced around nervously.

"Spit it out, lad."

"With one o' the holy brothers."

"Where were they going?"

"The Great Hall, I think."

Hawley was already walking away.

"You ain't s'posed to be roaming about unescorted," Cook called out. But Hawley simply waved her away.

*   *   *

The nurse was gone, and half her belongings with her.

Iveta had questioned the maid, the first guard patrol, and even the steward. None had seen Nurse Parnella. And so she'd marched directly to Vigilant Drake's chamber, but had been surprised to find it already vacated. The only reply had been the squawk of her raven—if the old woman had been abed, the bird would have woken her sure enough. It would have woken the dead.

In better circumstances she would have gone to her uncle, but now she worried Nurse might have beaten her to it. And if so, what punishment awaited?

Iveta stood thoughtfully, staring out of a narrow window across the inner ward. Where had Enelda Drake gone?

She had almost decided to seek Hawley in the servants' quarters, when she saw shadowy figures glide across the courtyard like ghosts. Flaescine monks, hoods concealing their faces. When they came in such numbers, and unannounced, it meant Abbot Meriet was here.

*   *   *

The monk showed Enelda into an antechamber beside the Great Hall, where a fire crackled merrily in the grate. He left the room and closed the door behind him. Enelda noted his footsteps did not recede along the echoey corridor.

Another door creaked open, a narrow arch more befitting a temple than a castle.

Abbot Meriet ducked as he entered, then spread his arms in greeting, smiling broadly.

"My dear lady," he said. "Please forgive me. I should have managed an audience much sooner, but affairs at the abbey have demanded all my attention."

"And the clandestine nature of this meeting is because...?" Enelda asked.

Meriet looked momentarily confused, then laughed. "Oh, forgive me, Vigilant Drake, I see now how it looks. No, there is nothing clandestine about it. It has always been my custom to avoid pomp and ceremony where possible. I am a...creature of habit."

"A pun—a man of wit, too, I see. But you do wish privacy, I presume? The brother you sent for me is still outside the door, suggesting he has been asked to prevent interruptions."

"Sharp as a Sylven's poniard!" the monk said. He bowed. "My dear lady, it is gratifying to see the years have not dulled your famous talents one jot. It gives hope to us all. Yes, of course, this is one of the more private chambers in the castle, and I had hoped we could speak candidly before the rest of the council hear of my visit and hunt me down. If you recall, I offered assistance before, and I am here to help."

"Ah, that would suggest you think I need help, Lord Abbot. You have heard something?"

"Whispers, nothing more."

"Whispers carried to you on the wind? Or on the lips of those holy brothers who frequent the castle grounds?"

"I see you are suspicious of me."

"Not at all. Sargent Hawley, however, is."

Meriet frowned. "Why?"

"Perhaps he...has little faith."

"As it happens, Sargent Hawley is one of the reasons I'm here."

"I'd rather hoped a High Companies escort would help keep undue attention away."

"On the contrary, the two of you have made enemies in your short time here. They would not dare strike against you, but Hawley, on the other hand...Some say he is your attack dog, and his teeth need to be pulled."

"Who?" Enelda snapped, despite herself. "Who says so?"

"My lady, I am a loyal servant of this mearca, and I come to you in confidence, as a friend. What I am about to tell you should remain between us, unless there is no other recourse."

Enelda nodded. That was careless. She could not betray her weakness so easily. Not in a place like Scarfell.

"The Vigilants are threatened by your very presence. Clemence feels undermined. His man, Lestyn, bears you no small animosity after you exposed his...excesses. The archduke turns a blind eye for now, but should word of the humiliation you inflicted upon Lestyn reach the king's ears, it would put into jeopardy the position of the Vigilant Order."

"They are not Vigilants," Enelda said firmly.

"Oh, I agree. There are few old enough to remember how it came to pass, but you and I both know the truth. Clemence is nothing more than a sheriff, with an inflated sense of self-worth to match his grand title. And his men...well, you've seen how they conduct themselves when out of sight of their master."

Enelda nodded. "If Hawley is my attack dog, then Lestyn is his, and Lord Clemence would do well to shorten that particular leash."

"Be careful, my lady. You would surely not wish to see open conflict between the old order and the new?"

"There is no old order. When this business is done, I will go home and never return. But until then, I have greater concerns than Clemence's bruised feelings, and no concern at all for Lestyn's."

"But you and Sargent Hawley are of great concern to *them*. That's why I came to warn you. The Vigilants have already sent word to Commander Hobb of the Third Company. I do not know the nature of the exchange, but Lestyn seems to know something about Sargent Hawley that could well be used against him. Something…serious. And you must be careful—if Hawley has a chequered history, I would urge you to distance yourself from him. Clemence will undoubtedly seek to discredit you by association."

"You would leave an old woman with neither servant nor protector?" Enelda shook unsteadily as she leaned on her staff. Now she would make a show of weakness. Great age had its advantages at times.

Meriet looked her up and down, a sympathetic expression on his careworn face. "I would not wish that at all, and instead I come to offer greater assistance."

"And what assistance might that be?"

"I have already vouched for you with Lord Scarsdale, but I fear there may be those present in this castle who would dare plot against you anyway. But my brothers have the freedom of Scarfell. They can watch over you and, should things become…dangerous…transport you away from here, to Erecgham Abbey."

"You think the abbey safe from men who could steal into this castle and kidnap a member of the noble household?"

"I know it, my lady. Erecgham was built by Sygellites in more troubled times, and it is a veritable fortress. The devoted of St. Baerloc have swelled in number this past tenyear—we may not be warriors, but one must never underestimate the strength of faith."

"Lord Scarsdale is one of your faithful, is he not? Why then is Scarfell such a place of danger and subterfuge?"

"Because, sadly, Lord Scarsdale is but one man. A candlelight in a storm."

"Indeed. Some might say the opposite. Some might even dare suggest his people suffer while he locks himself away, that he fails in his very duty of maintenance over the subjects of the mearca and abrogates responsibility to the somewhat suspect integrity of Clemence's men."

"They say that, do they? Brave they must be, these confidants of yours." Meriet raised a flinty eyebrow. There was a wry smile on his lips, though it lingered only a short time. "In seriousness, I would ask you to judge not Lord Scarsdale by his present situation. Recent events have placed a great burden upon him. I fear even his faith might not be enough. Should he falter, those men of ambition who clamour about him shall pounce like a cat upon a mouse. They would have a slice of the second richest mearca of Aelderland."

"Lord Scarsdale is no inexperienced boy. Why now does his resolve fail him?"

"Because it brings back black memories. You know about Lady Ermina?"

"What of her?"

"Ah, you see? *This* is how I can help you. When Ermina was a babe in arms, and Lord Scarsdale was racked with grief at the death of his dear lady wife, Athilda, a terrible event befell the girl. Her wet nurse, some simpleton from Farsfel, convinced herself she was the girl's natural mother, and stole Ermina away in the dead of night."

"How could no one have mentioned this before?" Enelda snapped, louder than she had intended. "This is a detail of singular importance!"

"Lord Scarsdale forbade anyone to speak of the matter, and in this place, the baron's word is law . . . but in the sight of a True Vigilant, I cannot be bound by a command rashly given."

"What happened?" Enelda felt as though only now was some great truth being revealed.

"They were found not far from Erecgham, in the woods north of Raecswold. The girl was malnourished and sick—we feared she had fallen prey to the Winnowing—but she was brought to the abbey, and by the grace of St. Baerloc she was nursed back to health."

"And the wet nurse?"

"She was burned at the stake."

"Burned?"

"An unusual punishment befitting an unusual crime, or so Lord Clemence insisted."

"Of course he did . . . Lord Abbot, how long was Ermina missing before she was found?"

"Three days."

"A 'simpleton' from Farsfel evaded the law for three days, and made it all the way to Raecswold? And this with a newborn in her arms, while a great sickness plagued the land?"

"A miracle, some said. Lord Scarsdale certainly believed so, for it was soon after that he was initiated into the faith."

"And thence you into his council?"

Meriet smiled and bowed. "A great honour, but I like to think I have repaid his trust many times over."

"Why refuse to speak of it? It was not his fault Ermina was taken."

"No, but he blamed himself anyway. He had just lost the love of his life. It is not for nothing he has never remarried—he carries a torch for Lady Athilda still. He believed it his solemn duty to watch over Ermina, and in that duty he had failed. He was driven to despair. In those dark moments he even blamed poor Lady Iveta. She had been here just a few weeks, her dear mother having passed away. One can only imagine how the loss of his sister-in-law, then wife, then daughter, could take a terrible toll on a man."

"Iveta would have been ten years old..." Enelda muttered to herself. "The same age as Anton Tarasq. Ten years... Why is this span so significant?"

"My lady?"

Enelda chided herself inwardly. Such musings should be reserved for private moments.

"Why blame Iveta?" Enelda said more firmly.

"Perhaps he felt the responsibility was too much. He had spent so much time making Iveta feel welcome that he had neglected his newborn daughter. And such misfortune had befallen him so soon after her arrival, that he thought she bore some... curse. I am afraid almost to say it. He thought her..." Meriet faltered, embarrassed.

"Awearg," Enelda finished.

Meriet nodded. "His disposition towards Iveta became so dark, I feared for her well-being. I offered to take her in, perhaps deliver her to a convent where she might take holy orders herself, but Leoric would not hear of it."

"What changed?" Enelda asked. "He seems fond enough of Iveta now."

"I suppose he is, in a way, because she reminds him so much of those he loved and lost. She is wild and carefree, and Leoric offers her neither guidance nor discipline. But Lady Ermina loves her, and perhaps that is why Leoric tolerates her presence."

"He closets himself away in his chapel," Enelda said. "If his rivals really do circle him like crows over carrion, his absence only emboldens them."

"Let them grow bold," Meriet said dismissively. "If Leoric trusts in St. Baerloc, he shall yet triumph. This land was built on faith. Some say we won the war because of it—but you know perhaps better than I that faith always comes second to politics. Kings and barons and privy councillors—they all invoke the names of the gods when it suits them, but only until loss of influence and power stares them in the face. Then they will do all manner of things that the gods would judge unfavourably— voting to dissolve the Vigilant Order, for example."

Enelda nodded bitterly. "If only we had foreseen the consequences of that decree. My master may not have met such an ignominious end."

"I'm sorry to hear that, my lady. I...had not heard how Cerwyn Thawn passed."

"It was a long time ago, in a baking-hot land far from here. How I wish he'd seen home once more...Such was the sorrow wrought on my order, I often wonder if the king's decision was not influenced by outside forces."

"You speak of the Oldest Foe. I have wondered it myself, many times. When one eschews the material and embraces the spiritual, as my brothers and I have done, it is hard to accept the Rift-born have truly gone from the world. We do not shelter behind the walls of our monastery, my lady. We go out into the world, and we see injustice...evil...at every turn. We pray the light of St. Baerloc can hold it at bay."

"As it held at bay the Winnowing?"

Meriet touched a straightened forefinger to his brow in the sign of the Saint's Sword. "Aye. And protected Lady Ermina from certain death. Too long has it been since the Living Saint walked among us. We pray he may one day rise again, that he might usher in a more enlightened age."

Satisfied with the answer, though not—she felt sure—in a way that would please Meriet, Enelda replied, "In the absence of a saint, we mere mortals must battle the darkness ourselves. There is wickedness here in this castle, and I will shine light upon it."

"I have held a lifelong respect for the old order, but I fear the world is too much changed. You are not immune from the machinations of ambitious men. Should you ruffle the wrong feathers, you will find yourself a feast for the crows."

"So what would you have me do?"

"Come with me, this very day, to Erecgham Abbey. Let me show you our work there. Let me help you." The old monk grew animated. This clearly was the purpose of his visit. "It would be an honour undreamt of to welcome a vanquisher of the Riftborn into the fold. Especially if...well..."

"If war comes?"

Meriet nodded. He acted coy about the prospect of war, but there was something in his manner...as though he was resigned to the eventuality.

"I am no vanquisher," Enelda said. "War is for soldiers, not scholars. Soldiers like Sargent Hawley—what becomes of him if I leave with you?"

"If he has charges to answer, he must answer them at Fangmoor. He is surely of no concern to a True Vigilant."

Again, Meriet suggested she and Hawley must part ways. Perhaps it would even be in Hawley's interest if they did. But not yet. Not yet...

"And the Tarasq boy?" She changed the subject before she betrayed her feelings. *Face as of stone. Heart as of oak...*

Meriet shook his head solemnly. "A good lad, make no mistake, but mayhap he is lost forever. Even if not, he is long gone from here." Meriet gestured vaguely towards the door. "There's a whole world out there, and I have the resources to help you search it. If he lives, we'll find him together."

Enelda wondered now at Meriet's persistence, dressed as eagerness to share in the exploits of the old order. She locked away these doubts, betraying nothing of her innermost thoughts.

"It is indeed a kind offer," she said, "and I am touched by your concern for my welfare. But—"

There came a knock at the door, and whoever it was did not wait for an invitation before opening it.

* * *

Hawley was in a black mood, the kind that made him rash despite his best intentions. He'd shoved the monk aside. The cowled man had almost gone on his arse, and to his credit had kept his vow of silence.

Hawley flung open the door before the Flaescine could recover. He'd half expected to find Enelda assaulted, or dead. Instead, Enelda and Meriet both beheld Hawley with identical expressions of serene bemusement. He'd come to grin and bear it from Enelda, but felt his colour rise at even the hint of mockery from the abbot. They locked eyes.

"I would have words with Vigilant Drake," Hawley demanded.

"Go ahead, Hawley."

"In private."

"Abbot Meriet is here as a friend. You may speak freely before him."

"Not on this matter."

Meriet clapped his hands together and laughed.

Laughed. Hawley wanted to throttle the old man with his own cincture.

"It rather sounds like the sargent has some quarrel with me," Meriet said. "Have I wronged you in some way, Sargent Hawley?"

"Not yet," Hawley growled.

"That's enough, Hawley," Enelda said. "If you cannot behave calmly, take yourself away until you can."

"But—"

"Do I make myself clear?"

"Aye," Hawley said, still glaring daggers at Meriet.

At last Hawley tore his eyes away and made for the door, only to collide with a new arrival.

Iveta bustled into Hawley, breathless, flustered. The sight of her quelled a portion of Hawley's rage. Iveta stepped away, averting her eyes embarrassedly at their near embrace.

"You should...mind where you're going," she managed.

"Mind yourself, m'lady," Hawley said.

Iveta only then looked about and, seeing Enelda and Meriet standing behind Hawley, flapped and reddened.

The monk appeared at the threshold. Meriet said, "That will be all, Brother Collen," and waved him away.

"Forgive the intrusion, my Lord Abbot," Iveta said. "I had not expected to see you here so early."

"No?" Meriet cocked his head innocently. "Who were you expecting? Presumably you came dashing in with some great purpose."

"I...came to find Vigilant Drake," she said. "I wouldn't ordinarily interrupt, but it is a matter of grave import, and I am afraid it cannot wait."

"Speak, dear girl," Meriet said.

Iveta eyed the old monk warily.

Hawley watched with interest—it appeared he was not the only one who mistrusted Meriet. Not that he usually trusted anyone.

Meriet shook his bald head. "What did I do to earn such suspicion?" he said with a heavy sigh. "I've known you half your life, dear lady."

Iveta bit her lip. She looked over her shoulder at the open door.

Hawley closed the door and stood against it, arms folded. There would be no more intrusions. Enelda didn't repeat her request for him to leave.

"This is a delicate matter," Iveta said. "I didn't know where to turn for the best. I...wouldn't add to my uncle's worries unnecessarily."

"Speak, dear," Enelda said kindly. "I shall judge whether it is important or not."

"It's Nurse Parnella. I think...I think she's..."

"A spy?" Enelda finished.

"Yes!" Iveta stood taller, as though a weight had been lifted from her. "You know about her affair? You know who—"

"I know." Enelda gave a knowing look. A look that said, *Don't give everything away. Not yet.*

"The thing is, last night I caught the nurse in a frightful state. She was...not herself. She was arguing with Ermina."

"Lady Ermina is but a child," Meriet interrupted. "What was the nature of this argument?"

"Ermina knew of the affair. I doubt she grasps the sordid details, but she must have taunted Nurse with this knowledge. In response, Nurse...laid hands on Cousin Ermina. Had I not entered when I did, I fear she would have caused Ermina harm."

"You are to be commended," Meriet said, "and the nurse is to be dismissed at once!"

"I'm sure she would be...but she's gone. Stole away in the night."

"Ah," Enelda said. "And now you have pieced together fragments of a puzzle. Here is a woman ruled by her passions, with a secret that would lead to her dismissal by the archduke, and shame amongst her fellow servants. There was already some suspicion upon her—after all, how did she not hear anything the night Anton was removed from his chamber? And now she has not only proven capable of harming a mere child, but has herself disappeared without a trace. Given these facts, it seems a logical assumption that she was involved in the kidnapping, yes?"

"Yes."

"No," Enelda said.

Meriet and Iveta looked at Enelda in puzzlement. Hawley smirked. It was good to see Enelda perform her tricks with someone other than him for a change.

Enelda smiled. "She had a part to play, certainly, but she's no kidnapper, or murderer."

"What more proof do you need?" Iveta asked.

"I will explain everything—perhaps we should visit the nurse's chamber?"

"Of course..." Iveta glanced furtively at Meriet.

"Abbot Meriet, I would value your opinion. Would you accompany us?"

"I would be delighted to see a True Vigilant at work again after so long."

"Good." Enelda beamed. "Hawley, get the door. Lady Iveta, after you."

* * *

Hawley stood by the door that adjoined Ermina's room. The girl had expressed her dissatisfaction at being shut out. She wanted to know where Nurse had gone, when she'd be back, if there would be lessons today. She'd asked if it was another of the nurse's *l'desír du corons*.

Enelda had immediately seen something of interest. A silver pendant, hanging on a wood-framed mirror.

"The woman has not gone far," Enelda had said.

When Hawley had queried this assertion, it was Meriet who explained, in a tone almost like a Vigilant himself. "She would not have left without this. Solid silver. The engraving is an old Garder symbol for the spirits of hearth and family. Not a lover's trinket but an heirloom of some kind. It must be the most valuable thing she owned."

Enelda had gifted Meriet a broad smile at his cleverness, which made Hawley loathe the old man all the more.

Moments later, Enelda noticed a loose flagstone beneath one of the bed legs, and soon Hawley had dragged the bed away from the wall and prised up the slab. Within a cavity under the stone was a wooden lockbox. A further search of the room yielded no key, and so Hawley had broken it open.

Now they stood and watched Enelda rummage through the box. There was a purse, which Enelda emptied into the box, revealing two dozen silver coins, a bundle of letters written in a florid hand, an array of bottles and pouches filled with herbs and unguents.

"A fair sum, for a nurse," Meriet said.

"Too much to leave behind," Hawley added. He felt sure she'd met with some dark fate, or else had fled into the night in a hurry to avoid such. Had the chamberlain threatened her—or even killed her—to keep his secret safe from the archduke? Hawley looked askance at Meriet: It seemed too convenient that the abbot and his monks had arrived as soon as the nurse had gone missing.

Enelda untied the string around the letters, and held one of them up to the light, giving the contents only a cursory inspection. She sniffed the paper, smiled to herself, and handed it to Meriet.

"A love letter," he said after a moment. "Unsigned."

"These are of greater interest," Enelda said. She picked up several of the small bottles in turn. "Moonflower root, dried bryony flowers, a phial of sow's bile, powdered henbane..."

"Henbane?" Meriet said. "A rare herb. What would a nurse be doing with these things? You don't think she was...a witch?" He made the sign of the Saint's Sword.

Enelda chuckled. "Witches are rarer than you'd think, despite what the likes of Lord Clemence might have us believe. Henbane is scarce in Wulfshael, but I am sure it can be found here in this very castle. In Lord Clemence's own stores, for instance. But it confirms my theory."

"Which is?"

"That the nurse drugged Anton and Ermina, to prevent them following her when she stole away to meet her lover. These ingredients are used to make a dwale. It would take but a few drops to send a small child into a slumber. Too many and they may not wake at all."

"Then we have our solution," Meriet said.

"Go on."

"The nurse administered this...dwale...to the children, and went about her tryst. Upon her return, she realised she had made a fatal miscalculation in the dosage—Anton Tarasq was dead. She went immediately for help, doubtless to her lover. Between them, they conspired to dispose of the body, blaming some thief in the night for the disappearance. And, dear lady, though you attempt to keep his identity a secret, I know the man in question is Lord Tymon."

"Really?" Enelda arched an eyebrow.

"He has not been as careful as he thinks over the years, and Nurse Parnella is not his first...indiscretion."

"Are you so quick to accuse your fellow councillor?"

Meriet hung his head. "It pains me. Nay, it shames me. But sometimes the simplest explanation is the truest. You said these ingredients might be found in Lord Clemence's stores? The stores are in the cellars of the counting house, and Lord Tymon surely has the key, or governs those that do. What is it that your order used to say? A guilty man must have means, motive, and opportunity. In Lord Tymon, I fear we have all three."

"No, Lord Abbot. I've spoken with Tymon already. His motive is not as it appears."

"As you say, but there's no escaping the remaining facts. The archduke must be informed. Tymon must be questioned."

"He has already been questioned," a voice boomed. "By the *proper* authority."

None had heard the approach of Lord Clemence, but now he entered the room with a swagger. There was a gleam in his eye— of superiority. Of triumph.

Enelda glared at the man. "So. The nurse came to you, did she?"

"At least someone in this castle remembers their duty," Clemence sneered.

"And what good did it do her?"

"It secured my . . . leniency. I was just on my way to inform Lord Scarsdale that the mystery is at last solved. We have our spy, and doubtless we shall soon discover what he did with Anton Tarasq."

"And where is Lord Tymon now?" Meriet demanded.

"In his chambers." Clemence smiled slyly. "As befits his station, I did him that one final courtesy. Better than dragging him through the ward in chains."

Hawley locked eyes with Enelda, and knew what she was thinking.

He knew what Clemence had done.

PART TWO

BETWEEN TWO FIRES

We place our faith in the power of the Majestics, and call them angels. We reserve our deepest fears for the creatures of the Rift, whom we call devils. Both come from places beyond mortal imagining, and desire that which we possess. Both, as I have proven many times over, will stop at nothing to achieve their goals.

Can we really know that one is fair, and one is foul?

—From the *Second Book of the Majestic*, by Vigilant
Cerwyn Thawn, 125th Year of Redemption

CHAPTER 24

Tymon was dead, to begin with.

He lay slumped over his desk, blue veins bulging at his temples, spittle foaming from his lips. A bottle of brownish liquid lay on its side near his outstretched fingertips.

Malbuth had admitted them to the office; sheepish, head bowed in mourning. Hawley wondered if the cofferer would be well treated when a new chamberlain was appointed, or if he would be thrown out on his ear, as so many loyal servants were when their masters departed, especially in such an ignominious manner. Hawley remembered also the chamberlain's fears that there were some who would see his precious archive diminished: books burned, heretical texts locked away to protect ignorant minds from the burden of knowledge. The vultures would circle soon enough.

Hawley stood aside as some of those vultures filed into the chamberlain's office. Clemence, Meriet, the archduke himself, a pale shadow of the man Hawley had met just a few nights ago. He was attended by the castle steward, Everett, who seemed particularly anxious at his master's infirmity. The Vigilant Guard stood outside, not even permitting the forlorn cofferer access.

The office was untidier than Hawley remembered. Papers spilled onto the floor from every surface. Candles, almost burned away, guttered in their sconces.

"I had not taken the chamberlain to be a man of such messy habits," the archduke muttered.

"Carelessness often betrays anxiety," Clemence said. "Or guilt."

Enelda walked slowly around the room. Hawley observed her fingers twitching, tapping the measure of her thoughts as was her custom. She circled the desk.

"Lord Tymon wrote something before he died," she said. "Whatever it was is not here."

"How can you know that?" Clemence asked.

"A pot of ink has spilled across the desk, but this patch here, where the page lay, is clean. His quill is here on the floor. There are fingermarks all over."

"His suicide note—or his confession."

"Where then is the note?"

Clemence was about to reply, but thought better of it.

Enelda shuffled to the fireplace. Taking up a poker, she prodded at the coals and then, deciding that they weren't hot enough to burn her, reached towards the grate. She pulled out a scrap of parchment—just a corner of a page, with black, flaky ends—and held it to the weak light of the window.

"What is that?" the archduke asked. Gone was his commanding tone, replaced with a meek croak.

"There is nothing to be read upon this little scrap, but it was not long for the fire. I would surmise the chamberlain wrote no confession, but rather named another guilty party with his final act. The evidence is, alas, destroyed." She added this last sentence rather pointedly, looking down her nose in the direction of the archduke, or perhaps the High Vigilant. Hawley wasn't sure which.

"E-evidence of what?" Lord Scarsdale faltered.

Enelda continued her way clockwise around the room, peering intently at the spine of every book. She stopped at a reading table.

"Lord Tymon was not entirely forthcoming with me when last we spoke," she said. "I see now that he kept some secrets to the very end. What I do know is that he had been doing some investigating of his own. He had found a series of court records detailing the disappearances of children from across this mearca, under suspicious circumstances, dating back ten years. Children of a similar age to Anton Tarasq, and whose abductors were never brought to justice."

"These are dark times, Vigilant Drake," Meriet interjected. "Children wander off all too frequently, especially out on the moors and crofts. Much as the High Companies have done to clear this mearca of bandits and wild beasts, there is only so much they can do."

"I do not think bandits and wild beasts are to blame, my Lord Abbot. No indeed, I believe something darker is at work. The machinations, perhaps, of the Oldest Foe."

"And where are these court records now?" Clemence asked. "Where is this proof of dark deeds and darker foes?"

"Taken."

"By whom?"

"That remains to be seen."

Hawley felt a wave of relief. If Enelda had revealed Sauveur had the records, and neither she nor Hawley had come forward with this information, they'd likely both be for the gallows.

Clemence scoffed. "It is as I thought, my lord, there is not one jot of evidence for anything this woman has said."

"There is something else," Enelda said distractedly. "This book should not be here. I had this particular book last night, in the archive. And yet now here it sits—either Lord Tymon fetched it himself in the early hours of the morning, or someone else placed it here, though for what purpose, who could say?"

Hawley recognised the book at once. The one containing the account of the Witches of Wyverne. He'd last seen it in Enelda's possession.

Clemence marched over to Enelda, and without looking her in the eye wrested away the book. Hawley bristled, but Enelda had already thrown him a warning glance and the most minute shake of the head. He stayed his hand.

Clemence leafed through the pages, then carried the book over to the archduke. "I think I know what is really going on, though it pains me greatly to say it."

"Do enlighten us," Enelda said.

Clemence drew himself up to his full height, his sack-like chins swaying as he turned his nose up at Enelda. "If the books ever existed at all, Tymon took them not to *find* the evidence, but to *conceal* it! I have investigated similar records, as has Vigilant Lestyn, and we found no link between the misfortunes of these peasant children and the abduction of our noble ward, Anton Tarasq."

"I doubt very much the children were all peasants," Enelda said.

"Then it only furthers my point," Clemence snapped. "The books were stolen to hide Lord Tymon's part in a most heinous crime."

"So why even tell me of their existence?" Enelda asked, her disbelief at Clemence's dull-wittedness barely concealed. "Why not destroy them immediately, rather than leave them around for a visitor to see."

Clemence ignored her, and instead turned to the archduke. "Look here, my lord." He handed the tome over to the archduke, open at a familiar page. "Sigils of witchcraft. The very evil that Enelda Drake has warned us of, but which has been amongst us the whole time. It is clear that Lord Tymon was embroiled in some dark conspiracy to steal away innocent children."

"Why would he do that?" Lord Scarsdale asked.

"To sell them into slavery? To conduct forbidden rituals? Who knows? But we will find out! He was a wealthy man who could come and go as he pleased. We now know he was involved in some sordid affair with the nurse—your children's nurse, my lord—doubtless seducing her that she might do his bidding without question. She took Anton Tarasq at the chamberlain's behest, but finally the guilt overcame her. Knowing she had likely given away his secret, Tymon killed himself before the truth could come out."

There was silence in the chamber. Clemence afforded himself a self-satisfied smile.

"Nurse Parnella..." Leoric croaked. "She has confessed?"

"She will, my lord. Be sure of it."

The archduke slammed the book shut and pushed it into Clemence's arms. He staggered away, pulling at his stiff collar like he was being strangled.

"I...cannot believe it," Lord Scarsdale said.

"Nor I," Meriet agreed. "But still..."

"A fanciful tale, nothing more," Enelda said.

Clemence rounded on her, his face turning crimson. "How dare you!"

"How dare I speak the truth? Someone has to. You'd have us believe Lord Tymon was a practitioner of the dark arts?" Enelda dismissed the notion with a wave of her hand.

"I know he met you last night, here in this very chamber. And I know witchcraft was discussed." Clemence's voice grew louder, more shrill. "Who here knows more about the dark arts than you? Who else would bring a black-winged *familiar* into Scarfell? Perhaps Lord Tymon found a kindred spirit in you and sought your allegiance. Perhaps he had heard of your blatant disregard for the law, or the callous way you hacked into the body of a dead child, and thought he had found an ally. Perhaps you are something worse than a witch...a *Fallen Vigilant*."

Behind him, Meriet gasped and made the sign of the Saint's Sword.

Hawley didn't understand precisely what was meant, but his hand was at his sword all the same. He glanced over his shoulder, counting three guards at the door. He'd take those odds.

Enelda's smile, intended to humour Clemence's ravings, evaporated. Her eyes shone with cold anger. "Be very careful what you say." Her words were like ice. "If a True Vigilant I am, you would do well enough not to anger me. If a *Fallen* Vigilant I am...Well, you could not truly believe it so, or you would fear to utter the words. And you would be right to."

Clemence looked around nervously for support. "Y-you see," he quavered. "She is party to the misfortune that has befallen this hold. How could she not be? Why appear now, after all this time? Hidden for decades, and yet her ring is found at just such a time that she is needed, prompting us to send out a search party. It is too much of a coincidence."

"Lord Clemence, please," Meriet interjected, his palms spread in a gesture of peace. "We have lost a fellow privy councillor, and if he was involved in some horrific crime, we will discover the truth in due course. But for now, tempers run hot, and we should consider our words carefully."

"Where is he?"

Everyone turned to see who had spoken, because it did not sound at all like Lord Scarsdale. But it was he, trembling, eyes downcast, voice broken. "Where is Anton?"

Clemence pointed at Enelda. "We should ask *her*, my lord. If she cannot rustle up the answer from the ghost of Lord Tymon, then it is as like she had a hand in the boy's disappearance herself."

Meriet's head sank into his hands. Hawley lurched across the room, reaching for Clemence's throat as the steward struggled to hold him back. Enelda was calling for calm, but Hawley barely heard her. All he could see were Clemence's flapping jowls as the High Vigilant shrank away, tripping over his own robes in his haste. Then there were guards in the room, Hawley was surrounded, and everyone was shouting at once.

"And what is your part, Sargent?" Clemence shrieked. "How fortunate that you were the one sent to find Vigilant Drake. You! A man with a questionable reputation for following orders. A man of dubious loyalty to his company."

"I am a High Companies sargent," Hawley snarled.

They were words that usually served to cow any opposition. But a devilish gleam appeared in Clemence's eyes. His blubbery lips upturned into a crooked smile. "For how much longer?"

Hawley's fists clenched tight. "Maybe Tymon learned something about *you*. Maybe you burned that letter to save your own arse. Why else are you so keen to hang every peasant from here to Westmere? To point the finger at a True Vigilant? Something to hide?"

Clemence shook like a towering jelly at a feast table. When he spoke, his voice was high and phlegmy. "By my word as High Vigilant, I shall see the truth. Guards, arrest them both!"

The black-uniformed Vigilant Guards stepped forward. Had it really come to this?

Hawley couldn't bring himself to look at Enelda—he knew what she'd think. But the time for talking was over. He'd get them out of Clemence's trap his own way.

Hawley threw a punch at the nearest guard. He felt the man's face yield beneath his knuckles like kneaded dough. The other guard stopped as Hawley rounded on him with a wolfish grin. The third guard pushed into the room.

Clemence was shrieking incoherently. Hawley caught the vaguest impression of the archduke over by the door, doubled over, holding his head, Meriet at his side.

Swords scraped in scabbards. Steel flashed. Hawley's short-sword shot upwards, knocking aside the Vigilant Guard's blade. He kicked the man back, and the guard staggered into Clemence, who was so surprised he ceased his mewling. Hawley spun about, aware of danger from all sides.

Enelda caught his wrist. She held Hawley's gaze with surprising calmness. And more: There was sadness in her eyes. Or perhaps disappointment. She shook her head.

Meriet pushed past Clemence. He threw himself between the guards and Hawley, hands held high. "Stay your hands!" he shouted.

Enelda gestured for Hawley to lower his weapon. He'd had no intention of yielding, but Enelda's serene demeanour sapped the fight from his limbs. No one tried to disarm him, and so he sheathed his sword. He took some small satisfaction from the sigh of relief from the guards. The fearsome reputation of the High Companies still counted for something.

"Take him away! Take both of them!" Clemence's spittle soaked his unfortunate guard.

"You cannot arrest Vigilant Drake," Meriet said. "Lord Scarsdale...Leoric, my lord. Please!"

The archduke said nothing. He looked very pale, and very weak, and at the shake of Leoric's head, Clemence grinned.

The High Vigilant snapped his fingers, and the guards stepped forward to usher Drake and Hawley from the room.

"Easy, Hawley," Enelda whispered.

They descended the tower steps, passed by the counting house, where clerks gawped in wonderment, and out into the drizzly courtyard, where they were met by two more Vigilant Guards. Meriet led the archduke timidly behind them.

"Halt!" A familiar voice interrupted the procession.

Sir Redbaer strode through the ward gate. He was armoured. At his back were eight watchmen, halberds readied. At Redbaer's command, they lined up in a rank, stamping their feet as one.

"Where are you taking these two, Clemence?"

"Not that it's any of your business," Clemence said, "but the jail seems their rightful place."

"A True Vigilant and a High Companies sargent, arrested by guardsmen? I think not."

"Stay out of this, Redbaer. I warn you."

Redbaer marched forward. Clemence's guards blocked his way. At their movement, Redbaer's men hurried forward, halberds lowered. Something palpably changed; the balance of power shifted.

"You men," Clemence shouted to the castle watch, "stand down this instant!"

Redbaer glowered. "I command the guard of Scarfell, Lord Clemence, not you. Your men are given leave to execute their duties at my sufferance, and their heavy-handed attempt at subduing our *guests*—without evidence or just cause, in my opinion—has led to this disgraceful incident, in the presence of my lord, the archduke, no less."

"I speak with the voice of the king himself!" Clemence cried. He turned to the archduke, who looked as though he was about to faint. "Lord Scarsdale, what say you? Surely these rabble-rousers cannot be permitted to walk free. They are likely in league with dark forces! They could be behind the abduction of poor Master Tarasq. To delay their interrogation is to risk never finding the boy."

"Can't you see Lord Scarsdale is ill?" Meriet snapped, with uncharacteristic forcefulness.

The archduke muttered something softly to the abbot.

Meriet nodded. "Until hard evidence can be produced as to their guilt or innocence, perhaps it is best that Vigilant Drake and Sargent Hawley do not have free roam. I for one vote that they are *not* held in the jail. Incarceration may be interpreted as presumption of guilt, and hardly befits their status."

"What then do you suggest?" Clemence said, face still contorted in rage.

"There's space in the barracks," Redbaer said. "I can prepare a room for Vigilant Drake. Hawley can bunk with the men. There's no more secure place in all Scarfell."

"It seems a fine compromise," Meriet said, nodding. "But they will be your responsibility, Sir Redbaer. If there is a repeat of today's incident, you will be accountable."

"I understand."

"Well *I* do not!" Clemence snapped. "I have been insulted. My men have been attacked by this... this brute! And not for the first time."

"Insults are not themselves against the king's law," Meriet said, "unless they be against the king himself. You speak with his voice, Lord Clemence, but you are assuredly not the king. As for your men... I am afraid a High Companies sargent outranks them quite significantly."

"Not for long!"

Again, Clemence implied Hawley's rank was in jeopardy. What did he know?

"But for now," Redbaer replied. "And that means any injury done to your men by Sargent Hawley is unfortunate, but not unlawful."

"It is unlawful when they are prevented from executing *my* orders," Clemence said, his beady eyes wild, nostrils flaring like a snout in a trough.

"Nevertheless, we have now decreed Sargent Hawley and Vigilant Drake are not to be apprehended after all. The archduke's law is beyond reproach within these walls, without a writ from the king. Unless you disagree, Lord Clemence?"

Clemence snorted and gnashed his teeth. Then his shoulders sank. He shook his head like a sullen child.

The archduke pulled himself fully upright, again tugging at his collar. He muttered something unintelligible, then with a twirl of his cloak marched away towards the keep. All eyes followed him confusedly.

"Lord Scarsdale is not himself," Meriet said. "This business with Lord Tymon...I am afraid it is all too much right now."

"He requires a physician?" Clemence offered.

"His needs are more of the spiritual kind," Meriet said firmly. "I shall attend him, with prayer." Meriet came to Enelda and took her hand. He said quietly, "If your liberty is threatened, my lady, come to the abbey. You'll be safe there."

Enelda gave no reply.

Redbaer led them away down the hill, leaving Clemence seething impotently in their wake.

When Hawley chanced a look back, his eyes were drawn over the heads of the Vigilant Guard, up to the walls, where Lady Iveta stood watching. She gave a nod, and Hawley knew who he had to thank for Redbaer's timely intervention.

CHAPTER 25

Iveta chanced a look over the gallery railing, almost not daring to breathe lest she be discovered. Meriet and Clemence stood below. Lestyn had joined them, his black-uniformed guards standing by each exit, permitting not even the castle servants to enter.

Iveta had entered just as Clemence was cursing Redbaer's name. She steadied herself to listen more closely.

"Come now, Lord Clemence," Meriet said. "I doubt Redbaer has been anything but loyal. The archduke has always spoken highly of him."

"My Lord Abbot, Sir Redbaer would once have been above suspicion, but his intervention on the witch's behalf puts his character in doubt. We have uncovered one foreign agent in this castle... Why not another?"

"I would humbly suggest that Sir Redbaer was following orders, in his own way. Did not the archduke command every courtesy be extended to our guests? Irrespective of circumstances, those orders have not yet been rescinded."

Iveta hadn't expected the abbot to speak up for Redbaer, but was heartened he did.

"They shall be, I assure you! And we certainly will not have to suffer Hawley's presence much longer. From the moment he arrived, he made the guardsmen ill at ease—you know how soldiers talk. I heard the rumours... and, I'm afraid to say, those rumours are not unfounded."

"Rumours?"

Clemence clicked his fingers, and Lestyn hurried obediently to the High Vigilant's side, dark eyes gleaming. He handed Clemence a rolled parchment.

"This is a letter from Commander Hobb of the Third High Company," Clemence explained. "You know him, of course. A good man, Hobb. I suspected certain...irregularities...about Sargent Hawley's story, and finally I have them confirmed. A full written account—see for yourself."

Meriet took the scroll and began to read.

"Sargent Hawley has played us all for fools," Clemence said, too eager in his condemnation of the man to allow Meriet time to finish reading. "Shamed a year ago at Slaughter Hill, where his bloodthirsty and brutish nature led to gross insurrection. In the subsequent violence, Hawley showed his true colours: His cowardice and insubordination led to the loss of his entire troop, and ultimately the death of Herigsburg's ruling lord. He avoided the gallows and received a flogging, but for some reason was not discharged."

Meriet looked up from the letter, sorrow writ across his age-lined face. "Sargent Hawley is...the Butcher of Herigsburg? I can scarce believe it."

Iveta almost choked on the lump in her throat. It couldn't be. Her hands shook.

"Believe it, Lord Abbot! Sent north to find our so-called Vigilant, Madam Drake, with strict orders to return to Fort Fangmoor with or without her. But what did he do? He brought her straight here, on the pretence he'd sworn an oath to the woman. And where are the men he led north? They have not returned to the fort, and they are not here. He has not even mentioned them. What dark fate might have befallen yet another troop under Sargent Hawley's command?"

Meriet's head sank into his shoulders, echoing the sorrow that Iveta now felt. Slaughter Hill was the greatest atrocity inflicted upon the common folk in a generation. If Hawley was responsible—if that was his dark secret—then he had taken Iveta for a fool.

"When Lord Scarsdale is out of his chapel," Clemence went on, taking back the letter from Meriet, "I shall persuade him that Sargent Hawley *must* be arrested, and the Drake woman expelled. We cannot tolerate their interference and *sedition* any longer. I intend to have this wayward sargent delivered to Commander Hobb before the week is out, Redbaer be damned. I trust I have your support?"

"In light of the evidence," Meriet said, "I see no other choice. But what then? Without the Vigilant, what chance is there of avoiding conflict?"

"*I* am the Vigilant!" Clemence snapped. His confidence grew with his anger. He took the two steps up the raised dais from where Iveta's uncle conducted castle business. Now, peering down at Meriet—himself a lord, and the most trusted advisor of the archduke—Clemence sneered, "Everyone would do well to remember it. *Everyone.*"

Meriet bowed his head. "As you say, Lord Clemence." Iveta could hardly believe her eyes or ears. Clemence swaggered upon the dais like an archduke himself, and Meriet submitted.

"As I have said since this whole sorry affair began, the boy was taken to one of the villages hereabouts." Clemence had said no such thing—he'd been quick to blame the Sylvens right from the start. Still, he went on, "What was it Drake said? Within a day's ride of the castle? That's where we shall start. The old woman's pretence at cleverness is wearing, but perhaps on that occasion she inadvertently hit upon something. I'll have every hovel torn apart if I must. I shall give these blackguards no quarter, leave them no sanctuary. The serfs will soon turn on the guilty party to save their own worthless skins. They always do—isn't that right, Vigilant Lestyn?"

"Always, my lord," Lestyn said. He licked his lips in anticipation, like a hungry hound waiting for leave to seize a deer.

"All I will say," Meriet said, "is that perhaps now is not the best time to seek an audience with the archduke. I doubt you will find him in the most agreeable mood."

"The archduke's moods are no concern of mine. His permission is not necessary."

"Your powers are not in doubt, Lord Clemence, but remember you speak of the High Lord of the mearca."

"Do I? The title of archduke is gods-given, but the position of High Lord is bestowed by the king. If the incumbent proves unfit for duty—perhaps not being of sound mind—then the position can be taken away. Temporarily...or permanently."

"I have never heard of such a thing," Meriet said.

"It is the law, my Lord Abbot. It is for me to know."

"And who might replace the ancestral lord of Scarfell?" Meriet's challenge was half-hearted. He looked and sounded defeated.

"Who else has the will and the authority to guide this mearca in these dark times?" Clemence scoffed, glaring down his nose at the abbot. "This hold is the first line of defence against Sylven invasion. Wulfshael needs a man of principle, a man of commitment."

"The archduke won't give up his hold without a fight, Lord Clemence." If it was meant as a threat, it was a hollow one.

Clemence sneered. "I am the archduke's physician—I know his frame of mind. He has no fight in him. But maybe *you* do..."

"Me? You mistake me for a politician, Lord Clemence."

"Do I? Ha! For too long has Leoric been under the influence of your order. When he speaks, it is with your voice. But you have been outmaneuvered this time, my Lord Abbot. Accept it with magnanimity."

"I am a servant of the Blessed Saint. My aspirations are humble."

"Of course, of course. But you will doubtless go hence to the archduke? To whisper into his ear once more?"

"Nay, Lord Clemence, my business with the archduke can wait. What transpires next is between you, him, and the king. Lord Scarsdale needs time to reflect, and to pray—as do I, truth be told. I will return to my brothers and reflect on your words."

Before Meriet's back was even turned, Clemence waved his hand to shoo the old monk away. *Shoo* him, like a servant. Meriet, like Iveta, must have sensed the balance of power shifting in the castle.

Meriet shuffled from the hall. True to his word, he left by the outer door rather than head for Leoric's chambers. Once he was out of earshot, Clemence and Lestyn exchanged hushed words. Iveta strained to listen.

"What of the message?" Lestyn asked.

Clemence replied with what sounded like, "Proof of Tymon's crimes...Sylven code...a book of poetry..."

"A cipher? Clever." Then Lestyn said something Iveta couldn't make out.

"Go to the chamberlain's quarters," Clemence commanded. "Find every book of Sylven poetry and bring them to me. Handle it yourself."

A few more whispers were exchanged, before Clemence left in the direction of the Hall of Vigilance. Lestyn hurried the same way Meriet had gone, his guards in tow.

Finally, Iveta dared move, her limbs almost asleep. As she stood, she saw movement from the corner of her eye, and her stomach lurched as she realised she'd been discovered.

Everett stepped from the shadowed doorway, a finger to his lips urging Iveta to be quiet. He beckoned her to follow and slipped into the old servants' corridor beyond.

"I don't need a lecture," Iveta said when at last they stopped. "I suppose you plan to tell my uncle what I've been up to?"

The steward sighed heavily. "I would have hoped, my lady, that after all these years you would trust me, just a little. I am your uncle's servant, but have I not always seen to your welfare? And that of Lady Ermina? Believe me, if I wanted to make trouble for you, I'd have done so before now."

"What do you mean by that?"

"You aren't as careful as you like to think. I know you spy on council meetings. I know you steal from Clemence's supplies and forge his signature in the ledgers. I know you signal someone out in the north forest, and go to meet them sometimes, as you did the night Anton was taken."

"Are you accusing m—"

Everett held up his palms. "No, my lady. In fact, I lied to Redbaer and Clemence to protect you. I lied to Lady Drake."

"Why?"

"You...you've been treated unfairly your whole life, my lady. Whatever it is you do, there's no doubt in my mind it's for the right reasons. It is my duty to keep the confidences of this family...and that includes you. Right now, however, it's for the welfare of the family that I come to you for help."

"Help? How?"

"You aren't the only one taking an interest in Lord Clemence's schemes. I didn't catch much, but I'd wager Clemence seeks to overthrow your uncle, and believe me, he won't stop there."

"How do you know? *What* do you know?"

"He plans to write to the king. He believes my lord Scarsdale has had enough time, and now Clemence seeks to take matters into his own hands. That means more powers for him, more soldiers here at the castle, and more misery for everyone."

"You must speak to my uncle. He'll listen to you!"

Everett shook his head sadly. "No, not these days. But he might listen to you."

Iveta laughed bitterly. "When has he ever listened to me?"

"He speaks of you sometimes. I think...that you remind him of the way things were, before all this trouble. He has a deep regret for the way he treated you in the past. I think he wishes he could make amends."

"Then he should do so—and do it himself. It's not your place to speak for him."

Everett leaned back against the cold wall, head hung low. "I may not have a place much longer, the way things are going."

Iveta had never seen the steward look so pitiable. She thought about Clemence...It was quite possible that the king would deem Uncle Leoric negligent in his manorial duties, too weak to defend his mearca. If that were the case, Clemence would be the obvious choice to take charge, at least temporarily. Once he sat on the throne of Wulfshael, there was no way a man like Clemence would relinquish that power.

"Where is my uncle?" she said at last.

"His chapel, of course."

"You'll make sure we aren't interrupted?"

"It's the least I can do." He looked even more sorrowful. "Thank you, my lady."

"Don't thank me yet," Iveta said, and strode away to the stairs. She couldn't think a moment longer; couldn't even look back, lest her resolve falter.

*   *   *

More than once, Iveta had stood here, outside the great iron-bound door at the end of the family corridor. More than once, she had hesitated, as though some powerful force repelled her, sapping her of courage, driving her away. She didn't truly believe that. Somehow, as the years had rolled on, and she had become more estranged from her guardian, Iveta had created in her mind a bugbear of an uncle, one she barely dared approach. It wasn't even Leoric's temper she feared—she'd grown quite inured to that. She realised now that she feared facing the truth about what her uncle had become. What if he really was weak? Mad? A driving disappointment to more illustrious ancestors? What would it mean for Iveta, and the poor people of the mearca, if the storied Archduke Leoric was a wreck of a man, and a pious tyrant to boot? There was a finality to learning that particular truth that Iveta wasn't sure she was ready to face. Unfortunately, she had no more time to prepare herself.

She rapped loudly on the door and did not wait for an answer before entering.

Iveta had set foot inside the chapel only once, when she had first come to Scarfell and had been desperate to see the artefacts belonging to Lady Aenya. That had perhaps been the last time her uncle had humoured her as a child.

The chapel was very different now.

Iveta squinted into the chamber's wine-red gloom, waving censer smoke from in front of her eyes. She could make out only the statue of St. Baerloc above the altar, looking all too real in the half-light.

"Everett? Is that you?"

Iveta turned in the direction of a voice so strained, she hardly recognised it as her uncle's. He sat huddled on a wooden bench in the shadowy corner of the chamber, a dark figure outlined only by the dim orange flickering of candlelight.

She approached cautiously. There was something in her uncle's manner wholly disconcerting.

"No, uncle," she said.

The dark silhouette moved. She saw her uncle's eyes reflected in the candlelight.

"Iveta..." There was far less reproach in his voice than she'd expected. He sounded tired; weak. "Why are you here?"

Iveta was so surprised her uncle had not instantly rebuked her, she fumbled her response.

"I...came to...to see how you are. I heard you were unwell."

The shadowed figure rose unsteadily, leaning heavily on the bench. Now Leoric's face was illuminated, and he looked ghastly pale, eyes ringed and dark.

"Heard?" he said. "From who?"

"Well, Everett said...Not in as many words, but..." Why was she so fearful? Now she'd gotten Everett into trouble.

"No. You didn't come out of concern for my health. That is not our way, is it?"

"My lord?"

Leoric let go of the bench and came to Iveta.

"As a youth, I was much like you. It surprises you, I'm sure, that I was ever young, let alone wild and carefree. But I had responsibilities to tame me. Obligation, duty...a legacy to uphold. And what a legacy! Links of a chain forged for centuries, and quite unbreakable. You carry not these burdens, but you feel them all the same. They are a weight around the necks of this family. They are an invisible wall between me and thee. It is a terrible thing, to have your spirit broken. A more terrible thing to break the spirit of those dear to you."

"Uncle..." Iveta had no idea what he was talking about. This was already the longest conversation she'd had with her uncle for some months.

He waved her away and limped across the chapel, making the sign of the Saint's Sword as he passed the idol of Baerloc. He paused to stretch out his neck and pull at his high collar, then continued on to the cabinet in which Aenya's relics were kept. He threw aside the curtain and beckoned Iveta over.

She went cautiously, keeping her distance. Something felt very wrong with her uncle.

"As a boy I dreamt of Lady Aenya," he said. "I believed one day I would reforge the sword and set right all the ills of the world. Until lately, I had forgotten that dream. I put aside such fancies long ago, and closed my heart to faith in false prophets. I thought I had rid this castle of her influence once and for all, but no. When the people invoke the name of Scarfell, they see not me, nor my illustrious father, but *her*. My deeds are measured against words in a storybook. How can any man break free of such a legacy?"

"That's why I came to see you," Iveta said.

"Ah. The truth at last."

"The people do look to you, uncle. But soon, I fear they will see only Vigilant Clemence."

"Explain."

"Clemence seeks to seize power. He aspires to become High Lord."

"Nonsense."

"It's true, uncle. He believes you unfit for the trials to come."

"Clemence and I have found ourselves in opposition of late, not least over the appointment of Lady Drake. Soon he will find our cause more...aligned, and this foolish talk can stop. Or perhaps..." he said distantly. "Perhaps it is a blessing in disguise."

"Uncle...?"

"Let the weight of expectation fall to someone else. What does it matter?"

Iveta frowned in confusion. "But...he seeks to undo all that Vigilant Drake has done. He wants to send his troops across the mearca, to force confessions from the innocent."

"The innocent?" Leoric turned from the relics and fixed his

niece with a world-weary stare. "If they be innocent, surely they have nothing to fear. If Clemence thinks Anton is out there, then let him look."

"Please, uncle. His soldiers go soon to Halham. He'll inflict misery on the people—*your* people. Isn't this why they look up to Lady Aenya's legend? Was it not always said she was fair and just, and protected her subjects?"

"Exactly!" He stepped forward, a sudden strength in his eyes. Iveta recoiled instinctively. "And look where it got them. They became weak and soft—ripe for conquest, prone to disease, heads filled with aspirations beyond their station, and thoughts of sedition. Aenya is nothing to aspire to. She did more damage to this mearca than any before her."

"You can't mean that!"

"You don't understand, girl. It's as though the Warrior Maid looks down upon her descendants through the veil of time, and curses us. We are trapped in a prison of her making, unable to meet the weight of expectation, unable to appease a weak and greedy populace."

"But...you have faith in St. Baerloc. Did not he deliver the meek from harm? Did not he sacrifice himself for them?"

"You misunderstand the teachings of Baerloc. He has no time for the weak of will, or worse, the weak of faith. While Aenya inspired the masses to depend upon her, to fawn over her, Baerloc inspires them to find their inner strength. Their own strength— the only thing on which a man can depend. The Winnowing was not a curse from which He delivered us. It was a *test*, sent by Him, to separate the strong from the weak. It took me a long time to understand, but now it is clear. Another such test is needed to bring salvation from this darkness, mark my words. And it is coming."

"You'll do nothing about Clemence?" Iveta sniffed.

"He is the High Vigilant. Let him carry out the king's justice. Lord Clemence will scour the villages for accomplices in Tymon's dark arts, and the whole mearca will take a step towards godliness."

A tear moistened Iveta's cheek. She saw her uncle now for what he really was. A zealot. A tyrant.

"Godliness?" she said, her anger getting the better of her. "St. Baerloc is not a god. It is the Elders who receive our prayers, and they would have the anointed High Lord stand up for his people."

Iveta didn't know where her courage had come from, but the pure rage that flashed behind her uncle's eyes made her regret finding it.

He grabbed her arm sharply, his grip painfully strong considering the state he'd been in just minutes ago. Now he stormed towards the door, Iveta in tow, ignoring her cries.

"It seems Abbot Meriet was right..." Leoric said, flinging open the chapel door. "We have been remiss in the spiritual education of you and Ermina. I'm told you have a penchant for forbidden books—the influence of that damned fool Tymon, no doubt. The abbot has suggested his brother monks take over the archive, and purge it of heretical texts. That should put a stop to it. They shall take over Ermina's education, too. She shall be raised in a more devout fashion henceforth, and you had better step into line, my girl, or you'll be sent to a convent."

"No, uncle, please..."

"You may have no responsibilities to tame your wild ways, but I'll make sure you have faith. For those without faith will very soon be damned."

He released her, throwing her into the corridor. Iveta spun around immediately, so angry now that she still had fight in her.

But it was too late. The chapel door slammed shut.

She had failed.

CHAPTER 26

I t's cold," Hawley said. "I'll light a fire."
Redbaer looked embarrassed at the austere surroundings
of his quarters. "I seldom have guests. I'm sorry it is not the
most comfortable arrangement..."

Enelda had merely seemed relieved to take the weight off her
feet, sitting unbidden in a chair next to Sir Redbaer's desk. "Do
not go to any trouble on my account. My needs are simple."

That was true. Hawley had found her living in a leaky ruin,
and in their travels since, she'd never once complained at having to
sleep outdoors or ride for miles in the rain. Still, just because she'd
learned to endure didn't mean she should suffer hardship at her age.

Hawley set about sweeping out the grate. He needed to do
something...anything. After that brush with violence, he could
still feel the blood rushing hot through his veins.

"You were rash to accuse Lord Clemence of complicity," Redbaer said over Hawley's shoulder.

"But not necessarily incorrect," Enelda intervened.

Hawley turned around, surprised. "You think Clemence *is*
involved?"

Enelda shrugged. "Someone of high station certainly is. If
today has revealed anything, it is that the conspiracy is very much
real."

Redbaer coughed, and went over to the window. His fingers
rapped agitatedly on the ledge. "Nonetheless, you've made an
enemy of Clemence."

"He was already an enemy," Enelda said. "He just lacked the courage to reveal it sooner."

Hawley sparked his flint and tinder thrice, the kindling catching at last. He stood, dusting off his hands. "In truth, I spoke in anger. I know who's behind the kidnapping, and it's not Clemence."

Enelda cocked her head inquisitively but said nothing. Redbaer looked like someone had just walked over his grave.

When Hawley didn't immediately continue, Enelda prompted, "Spit it out, Hawley. No one likes a show-off."

"I'm not...It's just..." He jerked his head in Redbaer's direction.

"What do you mean by that?" Redbaer snapped.

"I'm not inclined to trust anyone in this gods-forsaken hold. Why invite us to stay here anyway? For our safety? Or so you can keep a close eye on us?"

"Is this the thanks I get?" Redbaer huffed. "I'll say only that I have little time for Clemence, but I did have plenty of time for Lord Tymon. The chamberlain was always straight as an arrow in his dealings with me, and I respected him a great deal. With my master in such a...disturbed state, someone had to do *something*, otherwise Clemence would have hanged you this very day."

"We appreciate the intervention," Enelda said. "Hawley, I believe you can trust Sir Redbaer. Now do stop being so tryingly circumspect, and spit it out."

Hawley sighed. "It's Meriet," he said.

"This again!" Enelda groaned.

"Ianto was here, in the castle, when the boy was taken."

Enelda tutted. "Well why didn't you say so earlier?"

"I've been trying to tell you all day!" Hawley spluttered. "You were...indisposed. I reckon Ianto took the lad, and it must've been under orders. Meriet is the obvious choice." He felt eyes boring into him.

"Who in the blazes is Ianto?" Redbaer asked.

Hawley shifted uncomfortably on his feet. He had no desire to go into detail about his missing cohort. "One of my men. Least,

I thought he was. Turns out he was an imposter. A monk from
Erecgham."

"And how do you know this monk is the guilty party?" Redbaer asked.

"A dagger, first off." Hawley knew that wouldn't make much
sense. He noted Enelda's amusement as he tried to straighten it
all out in his head. "Ianto had a ritual dagger. Almost identical to
one described in some records we found in the archive."

"What are you wittering about, man?"

Hawley gave a frustrated huff. "The drawing of the dagger
we found in the book was from a witch trial overseen by Lestyn,
in Wyverne." As soon as he said the name of the village, he saw
Redbaer pale. The captain's hand trembled. Hawley narrowed
his eyes; he was on to something, and it put the scent of the hunt
in his nostrils. "Wyverne isn't far from where the other boy was
found—the boy in the ice house. Pretty big coincidence, don't
you think?"

Redbaer said nothing.

"You were acting twitchy in the tavern yesterday," Hawley
said. "What aren't you telling us?"

"I think I know," Enelda said. "I think you're right about
Ianto, Hawley, at least partly. And you were also right about Sir
Redbaer having an ulterior motive for inviting us here. Isn't that
right, Captain?"

Redbaer stared at his feet, shoulders sagging. He nodded.

"I don't follow..." Hawley said.

"Of course you don't. What did I tell you before? You have
good instincts, but you rely too heavily on them. You've hit upon
several facts of the matter, quite by chance, and have arranged
them in such a way as to prove your theory. It is a technique worthy of the new Vigilants, but not the old. It is a technique that
leads to hasty accusations, and innocent women being drowned
in rivers."

It took a moment to sink in, and when it did, Hawley felt
too ashamed to be angry. He was certain he was right—and if
Ianto took the boy, then who else but Meriet could be behind

the scheme? Yet Enelda's disapproval weighed heavily on his shoulders.

She went on, "I wonder if Sir Redbaer, loyal to the end, is protecting his master. A man of great power, now one of the inner circle of Erecgham. Does Lord Scarsdale have the blood of two boys on his hands?"

Redbaer turned to the window, head hung low, hands gripping the sill so tight he might have crumbled the stonework.

"Two...?" Hawley muttered.

"Come, Sir Redbaer," Enelda said, "let's put Hawley out of his misery, shall we?"

At last Redbaer spoke, but very quietly. "In executing my duties I...I have done something terrible. And only now are the consequences of those actions becoming clear."

Hawley could only stare at Redbaer in stunned silence.

Enelda's bones clicked into place as she rose from her seat. "Seems there's a weight on your mind," she said. "Talking's the best medicine in these situations, I always say. Hawley, get that pot on the fire and boil some water. Let's find some tea, Sir Redbaer, and you can tell us all about it."

Soon they were sitting around the fire as the daylight waned, hugging cups of barley tea sweetened with honey. A marked improvement on Enelda's usual nettle brew.

"I want you to know that everything I have done, I have done out of loyalty. And more than that, I did what I believed was for the greater good. I am not a weak-willed man, and I am not a power-hungry man. I understand that following orders blindly, without question, is no defence when those orders are wrong. Not in the eyes of the gods." Redbaer stared into his cup. "I...I think I was wrong. That's the long and short of it. For a while now, I've feared for the archduke's state of mind. Can you understand the horror of that realisation? The thought that Lord Scarsdale, my master of many years, the man who knighted me, might have taken leave of his senses? Or at least that he be suffering from some sickness that has diminished his reason, and his judgement? If those things are true, then the orders he has given me these past months cannot be proven as the commands of a rational man. And therefore, in carrying out those orders, I have committed a sin...a crime."

"What did you do?" Enelda asked, gently.

"In the weeks before you arrived, the archduke had become increasingly uneven of temper. When the Vigilants failed to find Anton's kidnappers, my lord feared the culprits may have headed for the border. It was probably too late, but even so, I was sent south to warn the Border Companies personally. I was gone for three days. I learned later the archduke had spent much of that time at Erecgham, where at last he had been fully inducted into the mysteries of St. Baerloc. When I returned, his absence was the topic of all gossip in Scarfell. I did my best to quash any malicious rumours in the town, and Tymon did likewise in the castle, but it wasn't easy."

"What kind of rumours?"

"Some said the archduke was going mad. Some even suggested he had...murdered the boy himself, in a fit of rage."

"Why would they suggest such a thing?" Hawley asked.

"I believe the rumours began with some of the older servants, who remember an unfortunate incident some years ago involving Lady Ermina."

"She was kidnapped," Enelda said. "By her nurse."

Hawley stared at Enelda dumbfounded. "Eh?"

"Indeed," Redbaer echoed. "When did you learn of this?"

"It matters not."

"Bit of a coincidence," Hawley said, "given what's happened with the current nurse."

"I don't believe in coincidences," Enelda said. "But that does not mean the nurse is responsible."

"I don't understand."

"Of course you don't. Now, are you going to let Sir Redbaer finish his story, or are you intent on dredging up old history?"

Hawley spluttered in exasperation, drained his mug, and gestured to Redbaer to continue.

"Vigilant Drake is quite right," Redbaer said. "When Ermina

was a baby, she was snatched away by a madwoman. Lord Scarsdale had barely recovered from the loss of the girl's mother, and his behaviour at that time raised more than a few eyebrows. The girl was found safe and sound, of course, but some stains are hard to remove. It didn't help that Lord Scarsdale seemed to blame Lady Iveta for his ills, and pushed her further and further from him. All who observed this came to the conclusion that the archduke was a bad father, and that in his grief he might perhaps have wished away his children. I didn't believe it then, and I don't believe it now. He lets Iveta do as she wishes, true enough, but Ermina...he is fiercely protective of that girl. He has barely allowed her out of the castle in her ten years alive, and even then not without him. My faith in Lord Scarsdale led me to defend him twice as hard against those who doubted him. And it led me to accept, almost without question, the order he gave to me that would change everything.

"As I said, the archduke was absent when I returned to Scarfell. But a day later he returned, in the dead of night, during a driving storm. He sat where you sit now, soaked to the skin, and told me he had uncovered a great evil that threatened to consume Wulfshael, and possibly all of Aelderland.

"Earlier that day, at Erecgham, the monks had found the body of a boy. A body bearing stigmata, like unto the symptoms of the Winnowing. But it was something else."

"Blackrock," Enelda said.

Redbaer nodded. "Aye. Dark magic, the like not seen for decades. The archduke feared Lord Clemence was right—witchcraft was on the rise across the land. Anton Tarasq had been taken by a coven, perhaps as a sacrifice to the old enemy. He said if word got out, we would face panic within, and war without. His position would be untenable, and who knew what General Tarasq would do? He was so sincere that when he asked a great favour of me, I could not refuse.

"He told me he had left the body in the woods, watched by the monks. He bade me ride out immediately, in the storm, and retrieve the boy's corpse. Thence I would go directly south, and throw the body into the Silver River, near to one of the Border Company patrol routes, where it might easily be discovered."

"And you know those routes as well as any man," Hawley said.

"I do. I'd been with them just a day earlier. I knew precisely where the patrols would be. It was a simple task for a lone rider, under cover of darkness, in foul weather. The Border Patrol would find the body and raise the hue and cry. The identity of the boy was unknown—he passed for a Sylven well enough. The idea was that word would be sent to the Sylven fort across the bridge, notifying them that evidence of their witchcraft had been found on our side of the river, in contravention of the treaty. If we could sow the seeds of doubt that the Sylvens themselves were responsible for the sacrifice of a child, then we might be able to blame them for the kidnapping of Anton, too—if he wasn't found, of course.

"Before I left my lord, he said something to me most peculiar. It didn't make sense until later, but I remember it now as clear as day. He placed a hand on my shoulder, stared right into my eyes, and said, 'Redbaer, I place my faith in you, that you might be our salvation. You must complete this mission for the good of Aelderland, whatever the price. This is the darkness that confronts us. Even if it means you fear for your very soul, do not shrink from your duty, for St. Baerloc watches over us in this, our darkest hour, and he demands sacrifices of us all.' I swore I would not fail. I was not happy about the task—who would be?—but I did as I was bid, expecting no trouble. As it transpired, there was a complication..."

"Go on," Enelda said softly.

"I had the boy wrapped up tight in sackcloth, tied to the back of a horse the whole way to the border. When I reached the riverbank, I dragged him into the mud, and I cut open the bindings. But he...he..." Redbaer's voice stuck in his throat. His face was a ghastly shade of grey.

"He was not dead," Enelda finished for him.

Redbaer nodded, then stood. He paced away to the window

again. "I swear," he said, "I thought he was already dead. I would never have gone had I thought otherwise."

"Say you didn't murder him," Hawley groaned.

Redbaer wheeled around. The room was growing darker by the minute, and firelight glinted from his moistening eyes. "Do you not see? Lord Scarsdale's parting words suddenly made sense. He *knew.* And he had sent me anyway, knowing that once there, with no one else to do this terrible thing, I would have no choice. Or, rather...I would be less inclined to take the more difficult choice and disobey my orders, in front of my men. Yes, Hawley, I did it. I strangled him."

"And so implicated, you said nothing until now," Enelda said.

Redbaer nodded.

"How could you?" Hawley said. He felt numb; the fire no longer warmed him. He remembered that one dead eye, staring up at him accusingly.

"I did it to protect my master, but by the gods it did not feel right."

"That's because it wasn't!" Hawley leapt to his feet and threw his cup across the room. "Think of that lad's family. They'll never know what became of him."

"No one can ever know. Even if this thing is resolved, if the truth ever came out that we'd murdered a child and deliberately tried to blame the Sylvens, it'd be war just as surely as if that child was Anton Tarasq. We needed someone—anyone—to blame. Lord Clemence took the same tack. While the Sylvens scrabbled about their own lands looking for a fictional coven of child-murderers, Clemence had Lestyn scouring the countryside looking for witches. Keep the serfs terrified, and eventually they'll testify against the culprit, even their own father, mother, sister, or child. Anything to save their own skins. Fear does strange things to men, Hawley. Fear of death, sickness, war...of failure."

"One thing does not sit well with me," Enelda interrupted.

"Only one thing?" Hawley cried.

Enelda pretended she hadn't heard and said, "You said the boy showed signs of stigmata, believed to be from blackrock. Why?

Where did the blackrock come from? If the boy was a victim of witchcraft, where were these witches?"

"They were never found," said Redbaer. "But it's well you ask. You remember of course the blackrock merchant who unearthed your ring near the Elderwood?"

Enelda nodded warily.

"I heard he'd left Eastmere, counting his blessings for a narrow escape. Only, I made some enquiries. That merchant was never seen in Eastmere. Not a soul would vouch that a blackrock consignment ever came so far south—why would it?"

"Perhaps the buyer was in Sylverain," Enelda mused.

"No one would dare sell blackrock to the Sylvens. We turn a blind eye to shipments headed north, but it's a death sentence to be caught smuggling it to Sylverain."

"Maybe the buyer was closer to home," Hawley said.

Redbaer stared at him. "I have thought the same, and I curse myself for it. For all his faults, I cannot believe Lord Scarsdale would be part of such dark work."

"Now will you believe me?" Hawley demanded of Enelda.

"Believe what? Speak plain, Hawley."

"When have I not spoken plain? That those bloody monks are behind it all. They said they found him. Held him hostage, more like, for who knows what purpose."

"No, Hawley. Again you let your dislike of the Flaescines cloud your judgement. Before this is done, we may yet need Abbot Meriet."

"The monk you spoke of…Ianto?" Redbaer interjected. "I suppose it makes sense—the Flaescines have free run of the castle when the abbot is in attendance, as he was that night. I still don't see how he could have got past my men. But if you're so certain he's the kidnapper, why aren't you out looking for him?"

"Because he's dead!" Hawley blurted angrily. He took a breath and held it—he hadn't intended to get into that particular matter; not here, and not with Redbaer.

"Did you not say he was one of your men?"

Hawley rubbed at his face. "Yes."

"How did it happen?"

Hawley considered very carefully what he should say. He knew he was quite likely to be arrested at some point; the less Redbaer knew, the less he could say in evidence at a trial. Not that Hawley truly expected a fair hearing. A knife in the ribs on a backwoods road would be more to Hobb's liking.

"We were attacked in the Elderwood. Ianto didn't make it."

"Attacked by whom?"

"Never saw them," Hawley lied, trying to block out the images that still plagued his dreams. "Ambush."

Redbaer nodded, but suspicion was etched in every line of his thin face. "And the others? Is that why you brought Vigilant Drake here alone? You were the only one left?"

"Aye."

Redbaer puffed out his cheeks. "Well, Hawley, perhaps your reputation is not undeserved."

"What's that supposed to mean?"

"You know damned well. Word travels fast, particularly amongst soldiers. I was going to have you bunk down with the men, but I don't imagine they'd like that. You've got them spooked. They think if you sleep amongst us, the Riftborn will come for them."

"And what do you think?"

"I think soldiers are a superstitious lot. But I know someone else who was once maligned in much the same way as you. 'Awearg,' they called her, as they call you. She did not deserve it, and I swore never to succumb to such petty nonsense. Besides... if my men knew what I'd done; if they'd seen that boy... Let's just say they would worry more about me than about you."

"You have committed a great sin." Enelda spoke quietly. "I think you had noble intentions, Sir Redbaer, and I wish I had it in my power to forgive you, but I do not. The gods will judge you, when the time comes. I hope when weighed against the good you have done—the good you may yet do—you will be found worthy to enter the Garden of the Aelders."

"You believe that?" Redbaer took his seat again and stared

imploringly at Enelda for some comfort. "You believe a man might balance such a dark deed, and remove the stain on his soul?"

"I have to believe it. No one should spend eternity paying for one mistake, no matter how grave. If they did, I..." She trembled. "As I said, I have to believe it."

"I thought the old Vigilants were beyond reproach," Redbaer said.

Enelda did not reply.

"What did Clemence mean earlier?" Hawley asked her. "About 'Fallen Vigilants'? It seemed to offend you."

Enelda turned away abruptly and stared into the flames. "More than offend!" she said. "Sir Redbaer talks of the severity of certain sins. Well, there is no greater sin than for a Vigilant to renounce the order, and act in the service of evil. Few know of such things, but it has happened—twice in my lifetime, as far as I know."

"Is this what you meant when you spoke of not letting the Riftborn in? What might happen if they were to take control of you?"

"Partly. It is more complicated than that. You see, the Riftborn are the embodiment of destruction and anarchy. They can be cunning, yes, and oftentimes go undiscovered amongst the teeming populace of cities. But ultimately they give themselves away, and the Vigilants can send them back beyond the veil, whence they came. But sometimes, a Vigilant might fail. They might see too far into the abyss and become overwhelmed at the enormity of the evil arrayed before them. In that moment, they are tempted; they make a pact with otherworldly powers that might lend them the strength to defeat the ravening hordes that couch at our door."

"I...don't understand," Hawley said with a shudder. He stooped to throw another log on the fire.

"Nor I," Redbaer intoned. "They use demons to fight demons?"

"Not demons," said Enelda. "Angels. Majestics."

"Majestics?" said Hawley. "How can that be a bad thing? You said they lent power to the saints, and helped us win the war."

"They did. But what happened afterwards demonstrated their capricious nature. We are but mortals—how can we truly understand the machinations of divine beings? The Book of Vigils attempts to explain it thus: The Majestics came to us in answer to our prayers. They are creatures of light, from a realm beyond our own. They each serve one of the gods, their patron, and share many qualities with that patron, but they are not gods themselves. They exist in a sort of half-life, undying, untroubled by mortal woes, never needing anything, never feeling anything. As men became aware of these divine messengers, the Majestics grew in power. They fed on belief itself, appearing in this realm as ghostly beings of light. They became themselves worshipped, and then they began to feel something. They felt *needed*. They felt pride. And soon after, desire...and jealousy."

"Jealousy?" Redbaer asked, bemused. "Gods who are jealous of men?"

"Not gods," Enelda said. "Scions of the gods. Servants. It is a very important distinction. When these creatures saw mankind, warts and all, they became fascinated. They wanted to know how it was to feel...anything. Love, loss, pleasure, pain... hate, and rage. And soon, as the belief of men grew, so too did the Majestics' power. As war threatened, men prayed harder for assistance—until at last they invited the Majestics in.

"No one knows who was the first, but we have seen it many times over the centuries. Men and women wielded the power of Majestics—angel and mortal combined as one. One body, one mind, acting to overcome some great trial, or win a seemingly unwinnable battle. The problem was, some Majestics learned too well how it felt to be mortal, and began to feel longing and ambition. They found a lust for life, and wanted nothing more than to eschew their own realm, forsake their patron god, and live among men. Adored. Loved...Feared. My order was duty-bound to 'persuade' these misguided angels to return to their own realm, though it was difficult indeed.

"To answer your question, a Fallen Vigilant is one who is so terrified of failing in their duty to battle the Riftborn that they accept the help of a Majestic. They listen to the honeyed words of the angels and allow them ingress. A Vigilant's mind coupled with the power of a Majestic is a terrible thing to behold, and a dangerous thing. The Vigilant affords the Majestic cunning and guile, so it might evade detection. In exchange for long life and sorcerous power, the Vigilant slowly but surely sacrifices their humanity. What begins as a pact for mutual benefit soon becomes one-sided. The Majestic's personality always consumes the host's. There can be no compromise for long. And so the Fallen Vigilant turns his back on the order, and uses his power for a darker purpose."

"Darker?" Redbaer said. "But these are angels..."

"These creatures were never meant to walk among us, only bestow their blessings from afar. The one truth about Majestics is that they cannot escape their nature. Each of them derives their purpose from their patron god—they are a shard, a facet, of that god. Feorngyr is god of the hunt, of forest and heath, yes? One of his Majestics might embody the true aim of the greatest archer—a fine and great power to bestow on a mortal. Another might devote all of their energy towards protecting a sacred grove from any who dare wander into it—man, woman, or child. One might hunt relentlessly with packs of hounds—stalking even innocents—for nothing more than the thrill of the chase. Yet others would embody the cunning of the wiliest prey, to make better sport for the hunter. You see, when there are no Riftborn to fight, the Majestics are compelled to do the only thing they know, and their host is *impelled* to dance to their tune. A Fallen Vigilant, however, believes to the very end that they control their Majestic, not the other way around. As one, they become twisted and corrupt, locked in an eternal tussle for control, spiralling ever further into madness. A Fallen Vigilant is the most dangerous being imaginable. To falsely accuse a Vigilant of becoming such a thing is the most terrible insult. Once upon a time, I'd have had Clemence's head for it."

Hawley and Redbaer exchanged worried glances. Hawley tried not to dwell on the part about Fallen Vigilants attaining "long life and sorcerous power." There was quiet for a spell, then Hawley asked, "You said the order rooted out the Majestics, but if they're so powerful, how do you fight them?"

"When a Majestic is discovered, it will go to any lengths to protect itself. You might kill the host, if you're lucky, but without the proper methods of banishment, the Majestic will remain in the mortal realm, looking for a new host. To even stand a chance against the Majestic, you need two things: years of training, and its name."

"Its name?"

"Its true name. Armed with its name, one might weaken or even temporarily control the Majestic, and command it to return whence it came. It cannot refuse an order given to it using its true name. But the name is hard to find. There are nine hundred and ninety-six Majestics…that we know of. Each has their own unique methods and tricks, which can be used to identify them, but it's not easy. If you get the name wrong when confronting a Majestic, it's the end for you, my lad. Even the most benign angel will fight tooth and nail to remain in this realm.

"Recording the names of the Majestics was my master's life work. His early tracts on the subject were so thorough that the order's inner circle incorporated his work into the Book of Vigils. The Scarfell copy is badly damaged, and much of Cerwyn Thawn's labours are perhaps lost forever. I tell you, it is my one regret that such a book must remain here even after we leave. That such knowledge must be left in the hands of Lord Clemence and his ignorant followers…"

Hawley threw two logs on the fire and pulled his cloak tighter around his shoulders. Rain began to patter on the window casements.

"I've never known it rain so much," Hawley said, just to hear himself say something mundane, comforting. "Feels like spring will never come."

"It will come, when our work is done."

"Speaking of work," Redbaer said, "what do we do next? This talk of angels and demons is well and good, but it is not within my expertise. Give me a tangible foe any day."

Enelda nodded. "I understand. As it happens, I think our business at Scarfell is almost concluded."

"Clemence won't let you leave," Redbaer said.

"Well then, we'll need help, won't we?" Enelda smiled.

"Vigilant Drake, I—"

Enelda raised a hand to silence Redbaer, then pointed to the door and whispered, "The walls have ears."

Hawley and Redbaer both leapt to their feet, reaching for their swords.

There came a knock at the door, quiet, repeating urgently.

Redbaer marched to the door and flung it open. In the dark passage outside was a slight figure, cloaked and hooded.

Small, gloved hands withdrew the hood.

"Lady Iveta!" Redbaer said. "Why are you here? How long have you been standing there?"

She didn't reply. Instead, she rushed to Enelda, pale face burdened with worry. Rain dripped from her cloak, leaving a damp trail behind her.

"My lady," she said breathlessly, "I came to warn you. You're in great danger." She gave Hawley the strangest look of sorrow and suspicion, and added, "Both of you."

CHAPTER 27

S o it's come to this." Redbaer paced the room. "This is rebellion. I'll fight him. I have the men."

Iveta sniffed. "Lord Clemence has been preparing for this. I fear he is set to secure power by any means necessary. But he won't dare make a move until everything is in place. He will petition the king to grant him power over Scarfell, and I doubt my uncle will resist. You'll have no choice but to obey then."

"We'll see about that!" Redbaer snapped.

"The fool will lead us into a war," Enelda said with unusual vitriol.

"He counts on it," Iveta said. "I think he intercepted a message from Fort L'trinité. It was coded in Sylven, but Lord Clemence has already worked out that the cipher lies in a book of poetry in the chamberlain's room."

Enelda sucked at her teeth. "Perhaps he's not quite as dull-witted as I thought."

"He's clever enough to know who his most dangerous enemies are," Iveta said. "His first duty will be to arrest you and Sargent Hawley."

"I s'pose it's the gallows for me," Hawley said. He'd sat quietly as Iveta told her story, with more on his mind than merely Clemence's latest machinations.

"Very likely," Iveta said. Hawley didn't think he deserved such a lack of sympathy. "Especially as Vigilant Lestyn had a message from Fort Fangmoor."

Hawley's blood ran cold. This was it, then.

"Your commander...Hobb? He writes that you were not given leave to be here, that your cohort has not been heard of. He says... you're a traitor, and should be returned to Fangmoor immediately."

So it would be the gallows, Hawley thought, but by a circuitous route.

"Are you going to say nothing?" Redbaer snapped. "Why does Hobb call you 'traitor'? A week's absence is hardly befitting the death penalty. What black mark does he hold against your name?"

"Hobb hates me, and I him," Hawley said. "Ever since...a misunderstanding."

"Hardly a misunderstanding!" Iveta snapped. Her anger took Hawley entirely by surprise. "Tell Sir Redbaer what you did at Herigsburg a year ago."

"Herigsburg?" Redbaer said. "Surely you weren't at Slaughter Hill?"

Hawley only nodded. He supposed it had only been a matter of time before it all came out, but it still filled him with remorse and shame.

"They say the High Companies men were wiped out. All save one..."

Hawley couldn't even look at Redbaer.

"All except the Butcher of Slaughter Hill," Iveta said.

"You...?" Redbaer sucked air through his teeth. "Gods, Hawley; talk about ill-omened...Every Borderer knows about Slaughter Hill. It's the biggest failure the High Companies have known since...forever."

"Aye, and your lot like to remind us of it," Hawley growled. "But they don't know the half of it."

"Then perhaps you should explain it. Because hundreds died in the riots that day—men, women, children—even the noble Baron Rolston. All because the Third were heavy-handed and bungled the operation. Or, rather, because one man panicked and went on a murderous rampage that led to chaos."

Hawley stood so suddenly that his stool toppled over, and both Redbaer and Iveta took a step back. "No," Hawley growled. "That's what the guildmasters said, and that's the story that stuck.

And the Third never challenged it, because I was the only survivor, and even they didn't believe my version of events. Because I'm not one o' the Blood. I'm a bastard, an orphan. I was recruited by Commander Morgard against the judgement of the other officers, 'cause he thought the companies needed fresh blood. But the others...they called it Bad Blood. They disliked me to start with. When I made sargent, that dislike turned to hate. And after Slaughter Hill, well... they'd have preferred it if I hadn't come back at all."

"So it's not true?" Iveta asked coldly. "That's what you're saying?"

"Aye, that's what I'm saying. The guildmasters drummed up a few witnesses to pin the blame on the Third, and the Third were quick to make me their scapegoat."

"But we only have your word for it."

"Unless you can speak with the dead like Old Nell here, my word is all you've got."

Silence. Redbaer weighed Hawley's words carefully, though Hawley couldn't care less whether the knight believed him or not. Iveta, on the other hand...He felt her glare boring into him. He knew she wasn't convinced, and it hurt him more than any battle wound or flogging ever had.

He glanced in Enelda's direction, hoping for some semblance of solidarity, but the old woman only stared into the fire. Hawley righted his stool and sat down again, sullen and deflated.

"When will Clemence make his move?" Redbaer asked, clumsily trying to change the subject.

"Without a writ from the king, he'll have to speak with my uncle first," Iveta said. "Everett will try to delay him, but I would expect Clemence here at first light."

"It seems we need a plan," Enelda said. It was the first time she had spoken in a while, and all eyes turned to her. "I'm afraid I must ask your help one last time, Sir Redbaer. It could bring you a great deal of trouble, but Hawley and I must leave Scarfell before dawn."

Redbaer sank into a chair and rubbed at his brow. "Hawley, Vigilant Drake is asking me to risk everything by helping you. If it transpires that you're a traitor and a killer of your own...so help me, I'll hang you myself."

"Get in line," Hawley said.

"You don't have to trust Hawley," Enelda said, "but I hope you trust me. This is how you make amends. Can I count on you, Sir Redbaer?"

Redbaer looked around at the expectant group. He sighed heavily and nodded assent.

"Good," Enelda said. "We need a wagon and horses—the ones we brought with us would be ideal, so that theft cannot be added to the charges against us. And we need our belongings, and provisions for at least three days. Oh, I do wish we could take the Book of Vigils...just in case we don't return."

Hawley thought this last part was added overdramatically, given everything else that had transpired, but he had learned not to underestimate Enelda's love of books.

"Where are you going?" Redbaer asked.

"Yes," Hawley said. He shot a questioning glare at Enelda. "Where *are* we going?"

Enelda held up a hand to quell further questions. "The less you know, the better. Sir Redbaer, if pressed you should recount my desire to return home to the Elderwood. With any luck, scouts will be sent on all the northward trails. But we shall not be there."

"I'll do what I can," Redbaer said. "As long as my men don't get wind of Hawley's past, they'll turn a blind eye if I tell them. Anything to get one over on the Vigilant Guard."

"What shall I do?" Iveta asked.

"Stay here, and look after your cousin. Both she and your uncle will have a trying time if Clemence gets his way."

Iveta looked crestfallen. "There's nothing else? Have I not proven myself an asset to your investigation?"

"You have, dear, in more ways than you know." Enelda smiled, and the warmth of it seemed to lift Iveta's spirits. "You'll need to be careful now. Who knows what secrets the nurse has given to Clemence? Perhaps, even, she knows about your Sylven tunnels."

Now all eyes were on Iveta, who turned a bright shade of red.

"You...know?"

"I know on the night Anton Tarasq was kidnapped, you were

outside the castle walls, delivering alms to the people of Halham. You returned during the storm, using one of the secret tunnels to reach the family wing. Much was made of the kidnapper knowing the guard patrol routes intimately, but I don't think he did: *You* knew the patrols, Lady Iveta, so all the kidnapper had to do was hide until you returned, and then he'd know the path was clear for his escape. You know this, and for all this time you have carried the guilt that without you, Anton's kidnapper would likely have been caught in the act."

Redbaer and Iveta stared at Enelda open-mouthed. Hawley became aware that his own mouth hung open, too, and quickly shut it.

"How long have you known?" Iveta said.

"About you? I had my suspicions since the first time we met. I suppose you have long been using your knowledge of the castle to steal medicine from Clemence's stores—how did you evade the cofferer's attentions? Did you forge Clemence's handwriting?"

Iveta nodded.

"Clever girl. And you stole food from the kitchen. And all this you took to the people of Halham, long neglected by their lord. A regular little Puck the Wayfarer, like the stories of old; taking from the rich and giving to the poor, is that it?"

"You really are as brilliant as the stories say!" Iveta seemed as thrilled as she was nervous. But her half-smile quickly faded. "So you know how the kidnapper did it. But... you don't know where Anton is?"

"The kidnapper is dead, we think. What I don't yet know is where the boy was taken, for what reason, and on whose orders."

"It's my fault..." Iveta whispered.

"No, dear. You were doing good out there, I understand. You could not have known."

"I wish I had never found those cursed passages."

"The day may come when you find them a blessing in disguise. Especially if open war reaches Scarfell. If Hawley and I fail, that may yet be the consequence."

"So now... I go back to my room like a good little lady and pretend nothing is amiss? I wait for Clemence to take control of our home?"

"I'm afraid that is the lot of young ladies in this new world," Enelda said. "You just try to keep your cousin's spirits up. Perhaps find an interesting book and read to her. A *very* interesting book."

Iveta paused, half smiled as something occurred to her, and stood. "I shan't delay you any longer. I came here to warn you, and now my duty is done. I wish you luck on your journey."

Enelda smiled. "I never rely on luck, dear. If I did, I'd hardly travel with Hawley."

Hawley flapped his arms. Iveta managed a smile, clearly not yet ready to forgive him, or to trust him.

Redbaer said his goodbyes and showed Iveta the door. This time they all waited until her footsteps receded before continuing.

"So we have the ghost of a plan," Redbaer said.

"There is one more thing…" Enelda said. "Something not for Lady Iveta's ears. Something you may find difficult."

"More difficult than smuggling you two out of the strongest fortress in Wulfshael?"

"In a sense. You see, there's the matter of a dead body in the ice house. At least, I hope it's still there. The boy…"

Redbaer paled, the memory shaming him. "What of him?"

"Walk with me a moment, and I shall explain…"

*   *   *

Iveta regretted not thinking her plan through more thoroughly. She'd hurried to the counting house as soon as she left the barracks. Ordinarily, the archive key was hard to purloin so early in the day, but the cofferer was in deep mourning for his poor master, and Iveta had—to her shame—used that distraction to secure the book. A few hours later she'd made for her late aunt's bower, only to find Clemence's men standing guard. They knew about the tunnels, but had not yet found the way in.

It seemed that everyone had now guessed Iveta's secret. Once this ghastly affair was done, she knew everything would change—there'd be no more slipping out of the castle at all hours, missions of mercy or otherwise.

But they didn't know all her secrets. Not yet.

And so Iveta raced to the Green Tower, to another tunnel, less well marked but quicker for someone as practised at traversing it as she.

The passage was narrow. A full-grown man would think twice before trying to squeeze through, but Iveta went with relative ease until she found the narrow stair that led down to the catacombs. She had lined the steps with candles, and usually lit them so as better to find her way upon her return, but she would take no such precaution now. She lit just one to light her way. A sack bulged nearby—supplies for her missions. She quickly exchanged her shoes for a pair of old boots, and threw on a hooded travel cloak. She placed the book in the sack, with her emergency rations, lantern, and tinderbox. Then she hoisted the sack over her shoulder and pressed on.

The stairs wrapped around on themselves, terminating eventually at a stone corridor far below the ward courtyard. Passages branched off in several directions: One led to the catacombs—the last resting place of Leoric's ancestors—a route designed to be used in desperate times to weather out a siege; one terminated in a foul-smelling drain that ran from the tower drops to a culvert above the moat; yet another connected with a second tunnel that led to the inner ward. But Iveta had only one path in mind. She raced ahead to the secret exit beneath the castle's postern gate, where she hoped a wagon would be waiting to take Drake and Hawley far away from Scarfell.

It was then that Iveta faltered.

Why had she dressed for travel? Why had she brought the rations? She'd been so caught up in her quest that she hadn't stopped to think it all through. She hadn't even admitted to herself what she was really doing, up until this moment.

She was leaving.

Enelda and Hawley would probably try to stop her. Redbaer certainly would. But Enelda Drake had awakened something within Iveta. Not curiosity, or thirst for adventure—she already had those in droves. No. Enelda had made Iveta believe in herself—that she could have the power to change the world like Lady Aenya had. But she'd also made Iveta realise just what a prison her life would become in the very near future—what the lot of all young ladies was in this miserable, backwards world that the current line of kings had made. Yes, Enelda Drake had awakened something in Iveta all right.

Anger.

She tried to tell herself that there was nothing for her at Scarfell, but that was a lie. Ermina was here. Iveta's escape—if such a thing was even possible—would only condemn Ermina to the very life they both dreamed of avoiding.

Iveta only wished she'd said goodbye.

She told herself at least Ermina would be safe. Uncle Leoric might have forsaken Iveta, but he'd never turn his back on his only daughter. Unlike Iveta, Ermina had family. Real family. Unlike Iveta, Ermina belonged here.

Iveta hardened her heart, and ran.

*   *   *

Redbaer had made some room for Enelda in an upper chamber of the barracks, where she prepared herself, alone. They'd kept up appearances that they'd be staying with Redbaer, but darkness fell now. The hour was almost nigh.

Enelda's heart pounded. "I know, I know. I never should have brought us here. Curse these old fingers. No flesh for the ring to cling to. That's what did it."

Barty cocked his head sympathetically.

"Tymon is dead because of me. Litha's light! I misjudged the nurse, and the chamberlain paid for my mistake."

Enelda spoke quickly, breathlessly. She felt overwhelmed. Her head spun. She could see the shadows all around her chamber warping. She grew dizzy.

"This is how it begins," she said. "Darkness has come to my door, and it wants to get in. And if it gets in, everything is lost. Everything!"

She walked in circles, round and round as the floorboards creaked and the raven squawked.

"It's all a jumble. I've been carried along on the tide, and the enemy knows it. The more I fight them, the more careless I become. Concentrate, Enelda. Details, details. Fill your mind with details. Keep the Riftborn at bay."

She tried her best to order her thoughts, focus on the clues that had presented themselves so she might find the ones that remained stubbornly hidden. Her head swam, her eyesight blurred. The round room spun all about her. The shadows made leering faces on the wall. She could almost hear it, the snip-snickering of mandibles and the scraping of claws of the things that lurked beyond the veil. She had to concentrate. More details.

But her failures haunted her. Most recently, Lord Tymon. A young Enelda Drake would never have let the nurse do such damage. A young Enelda Drake would never have let harm come to the undeserving.

A lie you tell yourself, said a voice inside her mind. *Men's lives are but a means to an end in the eyes of a Vigilant...*

"Rational. I must be rational, Barty."

"Barty-Barty-Barty..."

Round and round she went, faster and faster, until she stumbled from dizziness. She took up the staff of twisted ash. She leaned on it to steady herself. Then she took a deep breath and held out the staff, before striking its base firmly on the floor, rapping once, then twice, then thrice. At the third blow, the shadows retreated, her heartbeat slowed, and Enelda saw more clearly.

She filled her mind with another memory entirely. A memory of her master, Cerwyn Thawn, breathing his last in a far-off land. Pain. That was all she had left to make anything real. After so many years in cages of her own making, that memory was all Enelda Drake could truly call her own.

She looked at Bartholomew. The bird cocked its head.

"Do not play the fool," Enelda chided. "You know what I'm thinking."

"Barty!"

"I can always depend on you. Perhaps I've depended on you too long."

She hobbled to the bird's perch and stroked his feathers with a trembling hand.

"Barty!"

"I know. This place is wicked. It's killing you, I see that now. It's killing me, too, I think..."

The raven looked at Enelda with an unblinking eye.

She shuffled to the small, arched window and opened it out to the cold, damp air.

"Come on, Barty, stop lollygagging, or I'll change my mind."

The raven craned his neck and gave his lustrous black wings an experimental flap. He was a fine-looking creature, despite his unusually old age. Now, with a flutter, he hopped from his perch onto the windowsill, and sat there, looking first out across the bustling courtyard below, and then back to Enelda.

"You'll know the way—you always do."

"Barty!"

"Have no fret; I'll be all right."

"Barty-Barty-Barty!"

"It is not up for debate. Be off now. I...I do appreciate you, you know."

Barty rubbed his long black beak on Enelda's sleeve. He looked her in the eye, with a keen intelligence. Then finally he hopped about to face the wind, and took flight.

She watched him circle high, barely flapping his wings as he soared up and over the outer walls. Soon he had joined other birds on the distant horizon, nothing more than black specks tumbling before silver-grey clouds, like charred scraps thrown up by a bonfire. Then he was gone.

Enelda wiped her eye with a knobbly knuckle as Barty vanished from sight completely. The presence of tears surprised her. "Silly old fool," she muttered to herself. She closed the window.

There came a knock at the door.

"Yes?" Enelda caught her voice cracking with emotion. She cleared her throat. "Yes?" she called again.

Hawley entered.

"Everything all right?" he asked. "We heard some banging..."

Enelda smiled. "Everything is fine...now."

He closed the door behind him. "You going to tell me where we're going yet?"

"Not yet."

Silence.

"I've been keeping you in the dark, Hawley, on a good many things. For your own protection, and mine. But I've failed us both on that score. If this plan doesn't work, we are finished."

"So we've ruffled some feathers. Hardly the first time. That's how you know it's working. A wise man once told me that."

"Wise indeed."

"I've been thinking about him a lot. I made him a promise on his sickbed. I think...I'm going to break that promise." He touched the breast of his tunic; feeling for the charm given him by Mildreth's mother.

They stood in silence, staring out of the window.

"The bird?" Hawley said at last.

"We take a different path. Lady Iveta reminded me how being caged in this castle is anathema to the untamed spirit." She turned to look at Hawley, as kindly as she could. "You two are more alike than either of you know. Both trying to make a difference, both falling short. And both stubborn as mules."

"I picked the wrong occupation if I wanted to make a difference."

"Took you long enough to realise it."

Hawley hung his head. "No. I realised it a long time ago... Just didn't think I had any choice. You once asked me about a man named Jon Gale, remember?"

Enelda nodded.

"He was the closest thing I ever had to family, and I did wrong by him. They say I was cursed that day, and it might as well be true. I betrayed Gale, and I did it for the Third, but it wasn't enough. Nothing I can do is ever enough for that bastard..."

"You mean Commander Hobb?"

"Aye. And now I find out he's part of it...He's a bloody part of it! Ianto was no trained soldier. Hobb took him into the Third, and I don't know why, but it wasn't because he was a good soldier. Most likely for coin, or the favour of somebody powerful. The whole company's corrupt. Root and bloody branch."

Enelda nodded. "You aren't going back to Fangmoor, are you?"

"No."

The very act of this confession seemed to somehow lift a weight from Hawley's shoulders. He stood a little taller.

"What will you do?"

He shrugged. "Dunno. I've never done much else. Never been any good at anything else. If it hadn't been for Morgard, I..." He stopped before emotion took him. He hadn't the words. "I'll finish what I started, then I'll take you home, like I promised. After that, I'll have to go far away. Reikenfeld, maybe. Tördengard if there's no other option."

"Not Sylverain?"

"No. The men are dishonest and the women are dangerous. And, as I've learned, they talk funny."

"And if they come for you before our work is done? What then?"

"Maybe Hobb will respect the oath I swore to you, and give me time."

"You know he won't."

Hawley nodded. "So I suppose I'll have to run, like a thief in the night."

"You'll have to...leave me..."

"I don't want to. I want to see justice done—and not just for that Tarasq lad, but for Mildrith, and the others like her. But if Hobb takes me back to Fangmoor, I'm a dead man."

"I told you never to make promises you could not keep, Hawley. You promised that girl's mother you'd avenge her daughter. You promised to stay with me."

"You'd rather see me hang?"

"No."

"Maybe you can go to Meriet for protection, if it comes to it." The look on his face told Enelda what truly he thought of that idea.

"Not yet, Hawley. Not yet." She looked out of the window at the horizon. The moon was rising. Fading into its last quarter—Litha the Mother in her twilight days, becoming Litha the Crone. An auspicious time for secrecy and subterfuge; auspicious, Enelda hoped, for her, and not her enemies. "Come," she said at last. "It's almost time."

CHAPTER 28

N ow will you tell me where we're going?" Hawley grumbled.

"South," Enelda said.

"I gathered that. Not Erecgham, surely?"

"Not yet. Just stay clear of the main roads."

The sky was turning a pale yellow on the eastern horizon. They'd travelled all night, hoping to put plenty of distance between themselves and Scarfell before Clemence sent out the search parties. They'd need every second of their head start if horsemen came after them. In truth, Hawley was just glad of an open road and fresh air. Scarfell's oppressive atmosphere had weighed on him almost as heavily as on Enelda. If anyone came after them, he'd rather fight them in open combat than bandy more words with the vipers of the castle.

The road ahead forked, and Hawley turned the wagon onto a narrow track, keeping the rising sun on his left, heading deeper south, away from the Gold Road. Away from Hobb.

He stole another glance at Enelda, who gave nothing away. She was staring into the middle distance as though daydreaming. Hawley knew better by now; Enelda's thumb tapped a rhythm on her fingers, one by one. She was deep in thought, calculating some variable. Or, Hawley considered, repeating mantras to keep the Riftborn at bay.

Hawley didn't know why that thought had popped into his head, but he wished it would pop away again as quickly, because it brought with it a vision of gleaming yellow eyes and fangs.

"Once we have passed Raecswold," Enelda said, "it should be safe to follow the river. It's no more than a day at this pace."

"So we're going to Wyverne?"

"Concentrate on driving the cart, would you? Leave the thinking to me."

He shot her a look out of the corner of his eye, and saw she was smirking.

As if to validate Enelda's words of caution, the cart's front wheel crested a large rock, jolting them both in their seats.

There came a piercing scream from the back of the wagon.

Hawley swore, loudly and colourfully. He pulled hard on the reins. The wagon came to a sudden stop, horses braying. Enelda didn't move a muscle—didn't so much as blink—as Hawley reached over and threw back the canvas.

Iveta screamed again, jumped up like a bird for a berry, and threw her arms tight around Hawley, who was too surprised to react.

Hawley looked about in confusion—at the panic-stricken Iveta, at Enelda, who was trying all too hard to play the innocent, and then at the contents of the wagon. He saw immediately the source of Iveta's shock. The girl flinched as a pale, dead hand lolled from beneath a shroud, brushing against her ankle.

Hawley swept Iveta up into his arms and hopped down from the driver's board. Mud slopped around his boots. Growing increasingly embarrassed that he was now carrying a young noblewoman in a way unbecoming of a common soldier, he looked around urgently for somewhere to set her down that wouldn't leave her ankle-deep in mud. Finally, he took two broad strides to the side of the road, where the grass grew in thick round tussocks, and deposited Iveta gently down.

Her cheeks turned beetroot red; Hawley's heart skipped a beat.

"Don't gawp at the lady, Hawley," Enelda said.

Hawley rolled his eyes and spun around in the mud. "You knew she was there!"

"Of course I did. I'm not an idiot. Why do people keep mistaking me for an idiot?"

"And I am, I s'pose? Don't answer that. Why didn't you tell me?"

Enelda shrugged. "I knew. Thought you did, too."

"How would I know?" Hawley spluttered. "If I knew, I'd hardly leave her in the back of the bloody wagon." Now it was his turn to redden. He looked over his shoulder at Iveta. "Pardon my language, m'lady. And...I don't mean to speak of you indirectly."

Iveta, having now composed herself, drew herself up straight. She raised her chin slightly and looked at Hawley down her nose. "Never mind, Sargent Hawley," she said haughtily. "Do carry on."

Hawley puffed out his cheeks. He looked to Iveta, then to Enelda. He threw up an arm in the direction of the wagon. "And I s'pose you knew about *that*."

"Whatever do you mean?" Enelda asked. "You're behaving most erratically."

"I'm..." Hawley stopped himself. He heard Iveta smother a snort of laughter. He took a deep breath. "The corpse. The boy from the ice house, yes?"

"We need him," Enelda said.

"For what?"

"Evidence."

They exchanged pointed looks.

"I brought the book, like you wanted," Iveta interrupted.

"Good girl," Enelda said, beaming. She reached over the backboard and dug around in a bundle beside the dead boy's shroud. The worn gold of the Book of Vigils' spine gleamed momentarily in the weak light.

Now Hawley realised why Enelda had gone on so about the blasted book in front of Iveta. *Women*, he thought. They could say more with a knowing look than with a hundred words.

"I thought you didn't want to be taken for thieves," Hawley chided.

"It's not stolen, is it?" Enelda said, covering the book once more. "Lady Iveta's here. She's practically its owner."

"Then she can take it back to the castle," Hawley said firmly. "Lady Iveta can't come with us."

"I'll do as I please!" Iveta said. She marched forward gamely, sinking into the mud, almost falling over as the ground sucked at her shoe. Hawley held out an arm to steady her, which robbed her of some of the bravado she was attempting, at least for a second. She blew a loose strand of hair away from her mouth, gave Hawley a hard stare, and said, "I am a lady of Scarfell, and I am instructing you to take me with you."

"That's not how it works," Hawley said. "Out here, a soldier of the High Companies has authority, 'specially when pertaining to a lady's safety."

"*Barely* a soldier of the High Companies," Iveta said. She tried to affect a commanding tone, but was clearly unused to it, sounding instead pettish. "You're a fugitive from justice now. An outlaw! We all are."

Hawley let out another exasperated huff. He glared at Enelda. "Tell her," he said. "If she stays with us, we'll be accused of kidnap on top of everything else."

"Can't hang us twice," Enelda mused.

Her little wink to Iveta did not escape Hawley's notice.

*   *   *

They were already losing light by the time they reached the gentle curve of the River Halgian. Hawley found the most sheltered spot he could, stopping near a copse of scrawny birches sprouting in the shelter of a tall outcrop. He unhitched the horses and gave them some feed, and set about gathering kindling.

"We can't stop for long," Enelda said. "Don't get too comfortable."

"We need to eat," Hawley said.

"I know. Your stomach's been grumbling for two hours. Loud enough to wake the dead."

Hawley twitched at the remark. He glanced towards the back of the wagon.

Iveta came up and took hold of the bundle of sticks in Hawley's arms. "Let me help," she said.

"M'lady..."

"I'm perfectly capable of starting a fire," she said with a sniff.

Hawley bowed awkwardly. "Of course. Sorry." He realised he was still holding on to the kindling, and his hands brushed Iveta's as he released them and pulled away. He scratched his head nervously and said, "I'll go bag something for the pot."

"With your aim?" Enelda called out. "We'll as like starve to death."

Hawley had already unhooked his bow from the wagon and was marching through the trees. He offered a dismissive wave as he went.

She was right, of course. Almost an hour passed, and Hawley's snares were still empty. He'd seen a hart, but had frightened it off before he could loose his arrow. Knowing time was against him, and he had to put something in his growling stomach, he made his way shamefacedly to camp, bracing himself for a weak vegetable broth cooked up from their lacklustre supplies.

As he drew nearer the camp, Hawley heard singing. Humming, really, in a tone as lovely and welcome as a cool stream on a summer's day. Not wanting to startle Iveta to silence, he slowed his step, listening to the melody, both uplifting and strangely sad at the same time, like the folk songs sung by peasants as they toiled in the fields. When at last he reached the edge of the camp, where the faint glow of firelight held back the encroaching shadows, he stopped completely, his curiosity changed to surprise.

As Iveta sang, she turned a spit over the campfire, on which two skinned rabbits browned. The flames crackled and danced from dripping fat. Beside the rabbits was a boiling pot, into which Iveta now cast a handful of salt and another of fresh sorrel.

"Are you going to join us or not?"

So confused was he for a second, Hawley hadn't noticed Enelda. She was sitting beneath the rocky outcrop, sheltered from the drizzle that had settled over Hawley's cloak, and which had turned Iveta's normally glossy black hair into unkempt tousles. Enelda remained engrossed in the pages of the Book of Vigils.

"How?" Hawley asked, stupidly. His stomach rumbled as

the smell of roasting meat filled his nostrils. He rubbed his belly apologetically.

"I learned to hunt almost before I could read," Iveta said. "And not just on horseback or with falcons, like my uncle. Real hunting, with snare and sling, bow and spear."

"Who teaches young ladies to do that?"

Iveta unskewered the rabbits. "Not my uncle, if that's what you mean. I was taught all I know by an old man named Jens."

"How long have you known him?"

"We met when I was small. I used to run away from the castle to play in the woods, and my uncle did not care a jot as long as I was out of his sight. But one day I met Jens, dragging away a deer he'd just shot. I remember being very confused that he looked so terrified of me. Later, of course, I realised why: He thought he'd been discovered poaching in the archduke's protected woods. At the very least he'd lose a hand for the crime...maybe his life. But instead of reporting him to my uncle, I befriended him. He taught me about the land and its creatures. He taught me how to move silently, like a ghost. He taught me how to hunt, but only out of necessity, never for pleasure. I've never known anyone with a greater respect for life than Jens, or a gentler soul."

She turned around, holding a bowl half filled with meat, and a hunk of thick-crusted bread, both of which she handed to Hawley. Then she ladled some of the broth from the pot over the rabbit. "Eat," she said, and immediately began preparing the next bowl.

Hawley nodded thanks and stuffed his mouth with broth-soaked bread. "It's good," he mumbled, forgetting his manners. "So all this sneaking about at night...It's to see this Jens?"

"The reason Jens hunts in my uncle's woods is because the forests around his village were hacked down years ago, by soldiers like you, to rid the land of outlaws. It also rid the people of their livelihoods. Game and lumber were all they had, and these days the people of Halham can barely pay their taxes and still feed themselves. And so, fearing retribution from the Vigilants, who in Wulfshael serve as tax collectors and justiciars both, they choose to go hungry, even die. Excuse me."

Iveta took a bowl of food over to Enelda, exchanged a few words with the old woman, then came back to prepare her own meal.

"Hunger leads to sickness," Hawley said. "Sickness that medicine from Clemence's stores can cure."

"I do what I can," Iveta replied.

"When we first met," Hawley said reticently, "I...misjudged you. I meant no offence. You've proven me wrong, and I'm not too proud to say so."

"I'm glad you think so, Sargent."

"Hawley. Just call me Hawley. Not sure I can lay claim to rank any more."

"Hawley, then. And do you have a first name?"

Somehow the question reminded Hawley of the very few people who'd ever called him Holt, and how they were all in their graves. And so he said, "Just Hawley will do, m'lady."

"All right. Just Hawley it is. And as it happens, I judged you on first appearances, too. Whether I was wrong remains to be seen, given...everything. But you're certainly unlike other High Companies men I've encountered."

"Because I'm not of the Blood?" Hawley said. "There's maybe one in thirty of the Third Company drafted from the peasantry—the most of any company. Commoners, like me. They're usually so grateful for the chance to be somebody, to be raised up from serf to king's man, they let the power go to their heads. They turn a blind eye to corruption and cruelty for so long that they themselves become corrupt and cruel. I've seen it many a time."

"But you weren't corrupted?"

"I've done many things I'm not proud of in the name of king and country."

"And more besides, if Lord Clemence is to be believed. Killer, traitor even...'Awearg,' they call you. They say ill luck and dark fates follow in your shadow."

"Does that scare you?"

"It fascinates me. But how much of it is true?"

"Some."

"You don't like to talk about it? Even if people think you're a monster?"

"That can come in handy, on occasion."

"And what of Herigsburg? Will you speak of Slaughter Hill?"

Hawley froze at the words. She hadn't forgotten, or forgiven. He stared into the flames, unsure of what he could say that hadn't already been said.

"Well," Iveta said, answering Hawley's continued silence, "if I am to ever trust you, I'm afraid you must explain yourself. You know my feelings about the common folk...about the injustice they suffer daily. There was no greater injustice than what transpired at Slaughter Hill."

"I told you, m'lady," Hawley said sullenly, "it weren't like they say."

"But you did get your men killed? At Herigsburg, and in the Elderwood. If we travel together, will the same fate befall me?"

"No! I'd never—" Hawley stopped himself. He felt anger stir in his breast, and sorrow, too. More quietly, he added, "No harm'll come to you while you're in my company. On my oath, m'lady, you're safe with us."

"So tell me what happened, Hawley, that I might sleep easier in your company."

Hawley coughed embarrassedly at that image. "Gods, I have never known the like!" He drank down the last of his broth and put the bowl aside. Hawley bade Iveta sit down on the rock beside him.

"All right," he said.

"All right what?"

"I...I'll tell you. I've never told anybody the whole sorry story. But I can see you already think ill of me, so it can't do any harm, I s'pose."

Hawley took a swig of tea, set things straight in his head, and began.

"A year ago, I was part of a cohort sent to Hintervael. To the town of Herigsburg—everybody knows the story. Big crowd in the town square, protesting against Baron Rolston, saying he'd failed in his duty of maintenance towards 'em. The High Companies men got heavy-handed, sparked a riot, and every one of 'em was killed. Well, all except me. Herigsburg is built around a steep hill, and the town square's been called 'Slaughter Hill' ever since. That's the story you know, right?"

"It is," Iveta said.

"Aye. But it weren't quite like that. See, Rolston was guilty on all charges. Proper bastard he was—took over the manor after his uncle got too old and frail. Rolston the elder wasn't the fairest lord, but he were soft compared to his nephew. All the new baron cared about was putting coin in the pockets of the guildmasters. To do that, he had to increase productivity in every mine, on every farm. He worked the peasants to death. Them who got too sick to work and pay rent were evicted. So it went on, until one day a man stood up and said no. Made a speech in the middle of the square, and got people proper worked up. He was arrested as an agitator, and flogged that same day. That flogging changed everything.

"The man's name was Jon Gale. I knew him. We were raised in the same orphanage, and back then we were like brothers. We *were* brothers, pretty much. But we'd had a falling out, see. He'd never been fond of the law, and 'specially not of soldiers. When I joined the town militia, we'd come to blows. When I joined the High Companies…well, we didn't speak again. Not until I turned up in town, a full sargent by decree of Commander Morgard. It was Morgard who sent me, on account of my connection with Hintervael. The officer in charge was Captain Carrow, and he had a reputation for being a bit too bloodthirsty…a bit too eager to use force against civilians. Morgard entrusted me to find a peaceful solution—uphold the honour of the Third. Although what he thought I could do is anybody's guess. Carrow never liked me. Didn't like to march with anybody not of the Blood. So imagine my surprise when I got him to listen.

"I told him I knew Jon Gale…that I could talk to him, get him to calm the workers down, maybe call off the protest. Carrow agreed to let me try, and so off I went, alone. Found him and his 'outlaws' sheltering in an old watchtower where we used to play as nippers—same kind o' tower where I found Old Nell over there, as it happens. It was no pleasant reunion, I can tell you. Jon was different. A zealot. He'd found a cause to fight for—it was like finding religion for him. And the workers…They worshipped him like a saint. When he spoke, they came from miles around to listen. They thought he was Puck the Wayfarer reborn, come to rescue them from tyranny. And he didn't do much to shatter their illusions.

"We had a set-to, me and him. But in the end, I made a peace of sorts. I convinced him to stay away from town on the day of the protest, and to persuade his followers to go unarmed. But he told me if the soldiery got rough, he had people ready to light the town's warning beacon, and it'd summon outlaws from the forests. And thanks to Rolston's evictions, there were plenty of outlaws in Hintervael.

"Anyways, the day comes, and it looked like Jon kept his side of the bargain. But we didn't. Rolston was scared. He didn't think his militia could be trusted to tackle their own kin, so he hired mercenaries from across the border. Garders, and worse. When you've got men like that, plus Carrow, you've got a recipe for trouble. Hundreds packed into that square, old and young; men, women, and children. 'Course, soon as they see Rolston up on the balcony of the Merchants' Hall, they start shouting and jeering. Somebody threw some rotten fruit at him. And Rolston goes and gives the order. There were four roads into the square, all of 'em blocked by soldiers. And the soldiers advanced.

"I was guarding one of the roads, and I ordered my men to stand down and let people through. But there were so many people, they all got turned about and trapped, then the panic started. Then the fighting. A few people funnelled out past us, but more mercenaries came up the hill behind and started laying into the people as they fled; claimed they were looking for Gale's men. So now I'm trying not to get swept up by the crowd, and I'm scrapping with these bloody mercenaries, and it's chaos. The riot starts. Then in the thick of it all, I saw Jon at the Merchants'

Hall, and the militiamen on guard patted him on the back and let him through, like he was one of their own.

"By the time I got through the crowd, Jon was already upstairs, and there was the devil of a commotion. Jon was bearing down on Rolston like a man possessed. And…I stopped him. We fought, I wounded him bad. The baron came and spat on him. Said the sentence for rebellion was death, but it wouldn't be an easy one. Said he was going to draw and quarter Jon in the square, and leave his carcass on a spike outside the walls."

"I know a thing or two about that," Iveta said quietly. "It's how my uncle handles wolfsheads."

"Aye. Believe me, it doesn't always work as intended. Anger and revenge are more powerful than common sense. That's something *I* know a thing or two about.

"Anyway, Jon looks up at me and says this was his plan. He knew he wasn't getting out of the Merchants' Hall alive…that his death would rally the people to the cause, and be the end of tyrants in Hintervael. He said somebody would light the beacon and bring the power of the people down on the oppressors. I still wonder if he was mad. Never can tell with fanatics.

"Then…he pulled out a dagger…lurched for the baron. He didn't have the strength to kill the bastard, but Rolston didn't know that. Squealed like a bairn, he did. And I took the chance. I couldn't let Jon go out in torture like Rolston had promised. I used that last gasp o' defiance as an excuse to bring down Godspeaker once more. And Jon died. Just like that."

Hawley stood, and wiped a hand over his face. He took a deep breath. It was never easy to think about Jon's final moments. He turned his back on Iveta while he composed himself. She waited patiently until Hawley was ready to sit down again and continue.

"Rolston was spitting mad," Hawley said. "He wouldn't get his public execution after all. And you know what? Jon wouldn't have wanted saving either. He'd wanted a martyr's death. I denied them both their due.

"So Rolston strides out to the balcony and gives a signal. I followed him outside and saw Carrow in the square. At Rolston's command, Carrow ordered his cavalry to charge the crowd—I've never seen anything like it, and I hope to the gods I never do again. And Rolston laughed. He'd wanted an example made of the dissenters. He'd wanted a slaughter that would make sure the survivors never rose up again. He told me he'd planned the whole thing with Carrow. *I'd* gone to Jon under a flag of parley. *I'd* persuaded the townsfolk to march unarmed. *I'd* led them there like lambs to slaughter. They were the closest thing I had to kin, and they were being murdered. Later, that was used against me. That's what they used to pin the whole bloody thing on me.

"I don't remember much about what happened next. I found my way outside. People saw my uniform and tried to get away from me, terrified. I just wanted to get out of the square. I had to fight my way out. I followed a trail of bodies all the way to the north gatehouse, with the sounds of screaming ringing in my ears. I didn't really know where I was going 'til I got there. I climbed up to the signal beacon, tipped oil over the kindling, and lit the fire. Then I sat there, on the battlements, the flames growing hotter at my back, smoke stinging my eyes. I sat there and I waited.

"I watched the outlaws arrive and rush up the hill. I watched the rioters fight back all the harder at the sight of their arrival. I watched some of the militia flee, and others turn on their own kind. I watched the foreign mercenaries ride out of town, abandoning the baron to the mob. Half the militia surrendered. Some threw in their lot with the outlaws. I sat there, couldn't think straight, couldn't hardly move. I just...left them to it. I watched every one of my brother soldiers die, and I did nothing."

CHAPTER 29

There you have it," Hawley said after a long silence. He rubbed a hand over his lined face. "Over two hundred were slain. I rode back to Fangmoor in disgrace, the only survivor of a botched mission. To this day, the locals call that square *Waelbeorg*—'Slaughter Hill.' The guildmasters who survived made a play for power. They paid off a few witnesses to put all the blame on a 'rogue soldier of the Third Company.' They complained to Fangmoor; to the king himself. Said it was all the fault of the Third, that I'd conspired with the outlaws, then riled up the crowd by killing a prisoner to cover up my treachery. It was my fault that the 'great and noble' Baron Rolston had met his end. They even used my meeting with Jon against me, even though I'd gone under orders. Now I was a traitor as well as a murderer. The black mark stuck, and most of the men blamed me for bringing the Third into disrepute.

"I...I've never told anyone all this before. I don't know why I told you now...It's not a story of heroism. Those men *did* die because of me, and some say I should have hanged for it. By the law of the land, they'd be right."

"But what you did was for the right reasons," Iveta said.

"Depends on your point of view. Maybe Commander Morgard thought so. I never knew for sure, but I think he...he struck a deal with Hobb. Give up control of the Third and leave Fort Fangmoor in exchange for my life. That's why I escaped the gallows and got a flogging instead. But Hobb never let go of his grudge against me...In his eyes, the only right is the king's law. He never compromises—ever. He thinks I should've died that day, and he'll not rest until he's righted that wrong, as he'd put it."

"He'd have the finest soldiers in the land put down our own people," Iveta said, with no small disgust. "Hobb is the one who should be ashamed, Hawley, not you! You never forgot where you came from. You stuck to your principles. That's something to be proud of."

Hawley shrugged. "The riots were put down anyway. I only postponed the inevitable. I didn't make a difference."

"But you *have* made a difference. Every time you make a stand, you make a difference. You don't have to save the world. That's a burden too big for anyone's shoulders. Look: that charm you wear around your neck. I asked Vigilant Drake about it. She said a poor woman of Rowen gave it to you, because you promised to find her missing daughter."

"A foolish promise," Hawley said. "Enelda was right—we might never find that girl, not alive. Then what?"

"Then at least you brought hope to that woman for a time. A man of the High Companies, taking interest in the affairs of the poor and forgotten? Offering simple kindness? It's worth more than you think. I imagine her lord has not done as much for her. I imagine she's never even seen the lord of her own manor—the man who owns her property, her very flesh, for as long as she might live. Take my uncle, for example. As far as he's concerned, if a serf can't pay their way, then death is preferable to the dishonour of destitution. Dishonour! For a state of being that they can no sooner avoid than the place of their birth. What kind of laws visit such cruelty on the poorest of us? What kind of man rules so cruelly over his subjects?"

"He...he's your uncle," Hawley said. She was right. Of course she was right. But Hawley was shocked to hear a young lady speak so of her own flesh and blood.

"I love him, I suppose. But he is no saint. Perhaps he hopes he one day shall be. He turns to piety while his people die of simple malnourishment. He hunts boar and deer in his own private forests in order to hold great feasts for his courtiers—feasts with enough food to feed a village like Halham for a month. And Halham isn't alone. Since my uncle saw the light of St. Baerloc, he has turned away from many of his duties. He gives the Vigilants greater control than ever before, and hears not the protestations of his subjects. Tymon was the one who heard the plaintiffs, but had not the power to help them. Now he's gone. My uncle was never a kind man, but he was always a dutiful one. These days he cares not for the serfs who look to him to uphold their basic rights. It's as though..." She stopped short, and poked her spoon around her bowl.

"As though what?"

She took a deep breath. "It's as though he thinks it does not matter. That *they* don't matter. It frightens me how changed he is. Tell me, Sargent...do you know of the Prophecy of Baerloc?"

Hawley shook his head.

"They say when the Living Saint returns, his Holy Fire will scour the sinners from the land and begin a new order from the faithful. That means the lives of unbelievers are of no consequence. My life, your life...Unless we embrace Baerloc before he rises, we'll all be turned to so much ash."

"A cheerful creed, and no mistake," Hawley said. "Your uncle believes this?"

"Abbot Meriet has inducted him into the mysteries of Baerloc on account of his faith. It might account for his change of disposition of late. Perhaps he believes the day of reckoning is sooner than we thought."

"Why've I never heard of this prophecy before?"

"Because you haven't read the secret scrolls carelessly left in my uncle's private study."

"Ah. Like you saw the Book of Vigils in an archive forbidden to women?"

"Precisely. Ignorance is no excuse when the end comes. If knowledge is denied us, we owe it to ourselves to seek it out."

"Well said, dear." Enelda shuffled nearer the fire, the Book of Vigils in hand, opened at some page of illuminated script that Hawley could not make out. She closed it with a loud thud. "Better finish your food and get some rest. Three hours' sleep, no more, then we must away."

"You found something," Iveta said, eyes wide with expectation.

"Perhaps. Too soon to say."

"You should rest fully," Hawley suggested. "I can take double watch."

"No," Enelda said firmly. "We must reach Wyverne early tomorrow, and then press on."

"To where?"

"The Silver River. We're going to take this boy back to where he died. Then we'll have our answers."

*　　*　　*

The Marches were, largely, neutral ground. Wyverne was ostensibly a neutral settlement, insofar as it belonged to no manor, although the archduke offered it patronage for reasons that had never seemed clear to Hawley. Hawley could barely keep his eyes open as the dark outlines of pitched roofs and crooked chimneys appeared up ahead.

There were no tofts, but a loose brotherhood of stone-built houses, all in varying states of disrepair. It would have taken wealth to build them, but that wealth had clearly left Wyverne some time ago. The houses spread outwards in uneven rings, surrounding—and facing, Hawley noted—a domed temple, which looked more like a burial mound than a place of worship. Only a statue above the dark rectangle of a door identified it as a temple at all. A ragged figure carved from dark wood, standing upon a plinth of white stone fashioned into the semblance of the faithful. The ragged man had a skeletal face and exposed ribs, and carried in one hand a sword and in the other a pair of scales.

The wagon rumbled up a steady incline towards the temple. The first ring of tumbledown buildings was spread thin; a trading post, sawmill, bunkhouse, a squat tavern and empty stable with half its roof missing, a few animal pens, a signal beacon, and,

Hawley noted grimly, a tall gallows with three empty nooses. The second ring was more closely packed with humble dwellings with peculiar pointed roofs, all leaning on each other for support like drunken companions after an evening in their cups.

Hawley felt the hairs prickle at the back of his neck. He looked over his shoulder at the grey stone houses. Silent grey figures peered from dark windows, gazing with suspicious eyes at the strangers in their village.

"Keep driving," Enelda whispered.

The third and final ring of houses seemed to part before the approaching cart. The road widened into a circle, the ground covered with white gravel that flickered like fire as the yellow light of the rising sun insinuated itself. Chippings of silver alabaster, the by-product of an industry long abandoned, which had once brought prosperity to Wyverne before the Sylven Empire had fallen.

Hawley stepped down from the cart and hitched the horses beside a water pump. When he looked up, the villagers were no longer skulking behind windows, but stood outside their doors like statues, clothed in stone grey, their sallow faces watching impassively. Mostly women, Hawley noted, and none of them young. Even when he glared at the watchers, challenging their rudeness, flicking his cloak aside to reveal his uniform, none of them batted an eyelid. Disconcerted, Hawley tried to push aside thoughts of the "Witches of Wyverne" as mere superstition.

Hawley assisted Enelda from the wagon. Iveta, now awake and looking warily about at the strange villagers, attempted to alight, but Hawley motioned her to stay where she was. He was surprised that she obeyed, speaking more to the peculiar atmosphere of their surroundings than to any authority Hawley might wield.

"Welcome, strangers."

A priest stood at the door of the temple. A gaunt man, dressed in tattered robes of mustard yellow. He leaned on a gnarled staff, gripping it tightly with both hands, fingernails long and jagged. Despite appearances, his voice was surprisingly youthful and soft. "Is that a High Companies soldier I see? And...a Vigilant? A blessed day for Wyverne!"

He held up a thin hand. At this gesture, the mysterious watchers turned around, one by one, the crunch of their feet on gravel the only sound in the village, and they shuffled into their homes.

"Come," the priest said. "The hour is yet early, but the temple is open to all." He went back inside the ominous barrow mouth, beckoning them to follow.

*   *   *

The temple was cold. Its walls were of rough-hewn stone, and the air was thick with pine smoke from the smouldering firepit in the chamber's centre, which did not escape rapidly enough through the circular opening in the domed roof above, and so drifted about, heavy like incense. The priest led the way to the altar at the far end of the chamber, and bade the visitors follow, offering them seats upon a row of benches carved from natural rock. The benches put Hawley uncomfortably in mind of funerary slabs. He unpinned his cloak and laid it on the rock so the ladies might sit in some small comfort. Hawley sat at the end nearest the aisle, positioning himself between his charges and the door.

Father Llewelyn, as he'd introduced himself, was not so terribly old as he'd first appeared, though his cheeks were sunken, his skin jaundiced as his mustard robe, and his pale eyes were set deep into purple sockets. His hair was stubbled and greying, but mercifully not tonsured. Hawley had had enough of monks to last a lifetime.

Llewelyn took up a taper and set about lighting several dozen candles that sat in mounds of old wax before an altar bearing a small black statue.

"When the village wakes," Llewelyn said, his voice like a chant, "you will see us in a better light, I hope. There are good people here, though suspicious of outsiders. I suppose we all are, in our way."

"Place could do with some labourers to mend its walls and thatch its roofs," Hawley said. "Them cottages might fall down if the wind gusts hard enough."

Llewelyn lit the last of the candles, the light now gleaming off the outer edges of the strange black idol upon the altar, creating an effect not unlike burning coals. "Alas, we here at Wyverne are victims of politics. Because of a treaty signed many years ago, we are freemen, but in name only. The villagers are too poor to leave or to take up any business beyond scraping a living from the land. The Marches are not truly neutral: The Border Companies uphold the laws of Aelderland and prevent the encroachment of Sylven interests. They offer protection against bandits from both sides of the Silver River, but in return we pay a tithe for the upkeep of their forces. Thankfully, we possess property and livestock in abundance, and we are able to escape harsh taxation by offering shelter and...hospitality...to the border patrols now and then."

"Didn't see many men out there," Hawley said. "Bet that hasn't escaped the Borderers' attention."

"An unfortunate product of circumstance. We were singularly lucky in escaping the ravages of the Winnowing, but few male children have been born in Wyverne since. Few children at all, in fact. But our lot is not truly a bad one, despite the odd...sacrifice. We soldier on thanks to charitable donations, not least of which comes from Leoric of Scarfell—a regular pilgrim to our meagre temple."

"I am told four successive lords of Scarfell have paid state visits to Wyverne," Enelda said. "Unusual, is it not, for lords of such repute to visit the Marches."

"We have been lucky," said Llewelyn, with a papery smile. "It would have been so easy to forget a place like this."

That was true, Hawley mused. What had Redbaer called it? A pimple on the arse of nowhere?

"Thankfully, the lords of Scarfell see things differently," Llewelyn said, as if in answer to Hawley's thoughts.

"And the temple to St. Baerloc?" Enelda said. "This is the influence of Archduke Leoric?"

"He has...given generously. It was once a crypt of sorts. The people of this region clung to an old tradition of holding the bodies of their dead in a place of mourning for seven days and nights, only taking them away to the pyre when all had paid their last respects."

Hawley looked down at the slab on which he sat, and suppressed a shudder.

"Such practices are forbidden now, and rightly so, but they only became outlawed after the Winnowing, when contact with the dead was recognised as spreading contagion."

Hawley gritted his teeth, remembering how he had touched the corpse in the ice house.

"Interestingly," the priest went on, "the last body to be held here in such a manner was that of Lady Aenya."

A sharp gasp from Iveta.

The priest inclined his head. "Yes, dear girl?" he said. "You have some interest in the Warrior Maid?"

"I—I..." Iveta stammered.

"I have been teaching her some history," Enelda intervened. "Too few girls understand how and why the king's laws came to pass, and why they are necessary. Don't you agree, Father Llewelyn?"

"I do not speculate on the whys and wherefores. Only on the spiritual nourishment of my flock."

"You were telling us about Lady Aenya."

"Was I? Oh, yes. It was after the unfortunate business at the Silver Bridge, when the great warrior, now in the autumn of her life, was brought low by brigands. Her body was laid here so mourners could pay homage to the great hero of the war. Shortly afterwards, Wyverne was visited by holy brothers of the Flaescine order, who argued strongly for Lady Aenya's beatification. Her young successor, Wulfsige, however, thought such glorification was... inappropriate, given how she had fallen out of favour at court. And so he denied their claims and ordered his grandmother buried, not far from here, in secret."

"Not cremated?"

"No. He gave strict instructions, or so my illustrious predecessor told me. Some say it was because, although he thought it politic to distance himself from her waning reputation, Wulfsige secretly held her in great esteem for her past deeds. The continued visitations of the lords of Scarfell would certainly support that view. But"—he spread his hands innocently—"I am but a humble servant, and as I said, I do not speculate on the whys and wherefores."

"Where is her grave?" Enelda asked.

"Very few know the location of her last resting place, and Archduke Leoric has ordered it should stay that way."

"But you know," Enelda stated.

Llewelyn shuffled about to face Enelda. "I am one of a handful of trustees with that knowledge."

"Good. I would like you to show us where it is."

"Oh, that is quite impossible. What do we have, after all, if not our word?"

"Father Llewelyn, you recognised the trappings of my order right away," Enelda said. "You know who I am. *What* I am. I'm not one of those trumped-up sheriffs who like to fill the gallows with the heads of your flock."

Llewelyn nodded. "I am afraid it is of little consequence. In law, and in creed, the time of the Vigilant passed even before Lady Aenya."

"Ah, but I do not issue any demand of you that your own duty does not dictate." Enelda stood, bones clicking into place as they so often did.

Hawley stood, too, drawing up to his full height. Some considered it bad luck to threaten a priest—Hawley figured his luck couldn't get any worse.

Enelda pulled a surprised Iveta to her feet. "Do you know who this is?" Enelda asked the priest.

"Should I?" Llewelyn replied guardedly.

"This is Lady Iveta of Scarfell, travelling with me on a secret pilgrimage to the grave of Lady Aenya."

"That is well and good, but I still don't see—"

"Don't you?" Enelda said with a cunning smile. "Then you should look more closely."

The priest leaned forward, squinting in the candlelight. His eyes widened; his thin lips parted in surprise.

"But Lord Scarsdale did not—"

"Lord Scarsdale told us to come here, but to keep Lady Iveta's true identity a secret," Enelda lied, so earnestly that Hawley wondered how he could ever believe a word she said again. "The grave appears on no map, and the archduke's state of health is not what it was, and so he bade us seek out the priest of Wyverne, who would lead us the rest of the way. I hope the archduke recovers, naturally. But should he not... You know what this would mean for your temple, and your congregation."

The priest shut his mouth lest he might catch flies in it. His sunken eyes were narrowed by purplish, vertiginous lids. Finally, the priest's inner turmoil resolved itself, and he bowed. "It would be my sincere pleasure to escort you to your place of pilgrimage. But... perhaps not a word to the archduke when he recovers?"

"You shall find us the very pillars of discretion," said Enelda. "Shall we go?"

"Right away?"

"I'm not getting any younger."

*   *   *

They picked their way between treacherous mounds of shale, down a sloping track that had once wound its way through the outer extremities of an enormous quarry. Hawley took each step carefully, Enelda leaning on his left arm, Iveta on his right. Father Llewelyn needed no such aid; he wended his way surefootedly down the treacherous defile, sometimes using his staff to test the ground, but more often tiptoeing his way nimbly without support. The derelict remnants of workers' shacks jutted from piles of displaced earth and scree hills like loose teeth in a prizefighter's mouth. Here and there, the ground twinkled like stars as fragments of silver alabaster, unearthed by decades of exposure to the elements, reflected the milky morning sunlight, too little too late to save the fortunes of what was once a prosperous region.

Father Llewelyn led them off through rough scrub, and then

into a sparse forest of spindly pines, eerily silent save for the occasional mournful creak and a breathy rustle of canopies, like the trees themselves discussed the arrival of newcomers to their havens.

It was past midday when they entered the clearing. The instant Hawley stepped across the boundary of tall dark grasses into the pale circle of scrub, he felt a weight lift from his shoulders; a tension he hadn't realised was there unwound. Where the forest had been dark and silent, now birdsong filled the air, along with the distant drumming of woodpeckers and the incessant trilling of crickets.

Iveta felt something, too. She turned her face to the sun and spun around giddily, delighting in the uplift of mood that this strange place impelled.

At the centre of the clearing was a low, undulating mound of earth, overgrown with bramble and hawthorn, and scattered about with great fallen boughs and jagged shards of alabaster. At first sight it would be overlooked, but Llewelyn picked his way carefully through the tangle, taking a spiral path that slowly revealed the secrets of the clearing. A hidden path descended into the mound, terminating at a natural chamber covered by a canopy of thorny branches: a crypt of briars. The centre of the chamber was dominated by a large, rough-hewn slab of silver alabaster, cracked and unpolished. Not quite the austere grave that Lord Scarsdale had alluded to, but certainly well hidden and unmarked. Only a posy of dead flowers and a trio of burnt-out candles beside the slab indicated its purpose.

Llewelyn said nothing. He stepped as far back from the slab as he could, and stood with his head bowed, thin hands folded neatly in front of him.

Iveta walked slowly to the grave, reaching out with trembling hands. Her blue eyes glistened as tears welled in them.

"Father Llewelyn," Enelda said quietly, "would you give us some time alone?"

"I..." He hesitated.

"Lady Iveta has prepared for this day for some time."

"Of course," he relented. "I shall wait in the clearing."

When he was gone, Iveta sank to her knees and placed her hands on the slab, closing her eyes as if in meditation.

"It's really her..." she said.

"Yes, child," Enelda replied. "This is the final resting place of Lady Aenya, the Warrior Maid. Your great-great-grandmother."

Iveta's eyes opened at once, and she turned in surprise. "No, you have it wrong," she said. "My father was Sir Anselm—he was stepbrother to my uncle. I am no blood kin to Lady Aenya."

"No, child. I am afraid Sir Anselm was made cuckold, for before him, your mother loved another. Leoric is your father."

"What?" Iveta gasped. "Impossible..."

"Plain as the nose on your face, dear," said Enelda, with not enough empathy for Hawley's liking. "Nose, and eyes too. The resemblance is obvious...if one looks for it. Father Llewelyn saw it. Why do you think he agreed to bring us here so readily?"

"L-loyalty, to Scarfell." Tears welled in her eyes.

"Leoric as good as admitted it to me. He said there was too much of Aenya in you. A slip of the tongue that betrayed the truth."

"But why?" Iveta said, now weeping such that Hawley wanted nothing more than to put an arm around her to console her, were it not for propriety. "Why would he treat me as he did if he...if he is my...father?"

"Shame. He did it for shame, because you were a reminder of his infidelity to the wife he lost. More than that, you were a reminder of the woman whose legacy he had striven to bury, as his father had before him. That is why I brought you here. Lady Aenya was the last of the great women who rose to power in Aelderland—power enough to rival the throne, some said. Her blood courses through your veins. With you as Lady of Scarfell, there may be hope yet for the future."

Iveta stood, and wiped her tears away on her sleeve. "Even if what you say is true, it is a fool's hope. Women cannot inherit land and title in Aelderland. Even if they could, my uncle...whatever he is...has never recognised me as anything other than his ward. Ermina is his heir, and I have no intention of challenging her for even that slender honour."

"A noble stance, Lady Iveta, but if the archduke were to recognise you as his daughter...if he were to make amends...it strikes me that someone like you could make a difference indeed to this mearca. You have broken the rules all your life...What's one more?"

"I'd rather be a Vigilant than a warrior," Iveta said. "A True Vigilant, like you."

"The world needs principled leaders, not wizened inquisitors. The world needs a new lady of Scarfell."

"Then it shall have Ermina," Iveta said firmly. There was such strength in her—strength enough to disobey a High Lord, and even stand up to Enelda. Hawley admired that.

"Very well," Enelda said. "Let's just hope Lady Ermina shows the same spirit. Now we shall leave you to pay your respects to your ancestor. Take all the time you need, dear. Come along, Hawley."

Enelda shuffled out of the strange chamber without another word. Hawley followed mutely, offering a consolatory nod to Iveta as he passed, but receiving only a look of cool determination in return.

Outside, Llewelyn loitered at the edge of the clearing, while Enelda poked about outside the mound with her staff, like a bored child.

"Was that necessary?" Hawley asked.

"Yes."

"You going to tell me why?"

"No."

Hawley flapped his arms and marched off to join Llewelyn. He was used to being left out of Enelda's plans, but that didn't mean he had to like it.

*　　*　　*

It was late afternoon when the wagon rumbled on its way, and Hawley for one was not sorry when the tall chimneys and pointed roofs of Wyverne were at last out of sight. Iveta had spoken hardly a word since leaving the strange clearing, and seemed much preoccupied by her own thoughts.

They left the hills behind them, descended slowly down the gentle slope of a vast, sparsely wooded valley, which would eventually bring them to the Silver River. Hawley stayed away from the Gold Road, with its merchant traffic and regular patrols, instead keeping to hunting trails and the ill-used backroads.

Hawley steered as best he could through the uncertain terrain, thankful when the road ahead began to open out a little—he could ill afford a repeat of the debacle in the north, with only Enelda and Iveta to help him out of a ditch rather than a troop of soldiers. He glanced over his shoulder, checking on the position of the sun for direction—as much as he could, given the ominous clouds that masked out most of the daylight.

There were three black specks on the horizon, brought into stark silhouette by the pale grey vacancy of sky. Men on horseback. Hawley said nothing, but steered the wagon on. Ten minutes later, once clear of another straggly copse, Hawley checked back again. Four riders now, but no closer.

"We're being followed," Hawley said quietly, hoping not to alarm Iveta.

"They've been with us since Wyverne," Enelda replied.

She'd already seen them and said nothing, as was her way. Hawley bit his tongue. "Not Borderers and not High Companies, or they wouldn't bother hanging back. Clemence's men?"

"Perhaps," Enelda replied.

Hawley took one more look. "Five riders."

"Six. The other split off to the southwest about an hour ago."

"Why didn't you ... ?" Hawley spluttered, then decided it was pointless. "What if he's trying to flank us?"

"Of course he's trying to flank us. I'm relying on it. Presumably they plan to ambush us by the river. That's why the sixth man took the west fork and why the others are riding so slow. They don't mean to catch us yet."

"Why? They've got the advantage."

Enelda shrugged. "Either they're acting on orders not yet known to us, or they're wary."

"Of what?"

Enelda gave Hawley a wink. "One High Companies soldier is worth five lesser men, remember."

Hawley afforded himself a smile. "Even so, I don't want to ride into a trap. Not with Lady Iveta to worry about."

"Don't worry about me!" Iveta interrupted, poking her head between Hawley and Enelda. "I can look after myself."

"Good girl," Enelda said. "But we're not riding into their trap, Hawley. They're riding into ours. See that ruin up ahead, beside that grove? We camp there."

"Camp?"

"Trust me," she said with a sly smile. "And Hawley..."

"Yes?"

"Every time I've seen you get into bother, you've managed to fumble it."

"That's hardly fair! If you'd actually let me use a sword, I—"

"Which is precisely what I'm saying. The path of the Vigilant is one of guile, of cunning... of careful observation and record-keeping. But every so often, violence threatens—there's no avoiding it. Back in the old days, we would call upon the Baeldorn as enforcers, and woe betide anyone who stood in their way. Now... I have no Baeldorn to protect me, but I have you. A soldier of the High Companies, the best of the best, I'm told. I give you my permission to fight as you were trained to fight. Kill, as you were trained to kill. Do you understand me?"

"Oh, that I *do* understand," Hawley said.

"I can perhaps shorten the odds, but the knife-work is yours. It would be advantageous if you could take at least one of them alive for questioning, but your first duty is to protect us. If you fall, myself and Lady Iveta will be at their mercy... Let's hope you're as good as your reputation."

Hawley flicked the reins. He needed no more encouragement. The thought of anyone harming Iveta—and yes, Enelda too—quickened his pulse and set fire to his blood. He could smell a fight on the air.

At last. A gods' honest fight.

CHAPTER 30

The birch grove stood silent, ghost-silver. Hawley crouched in the undergrowth, leather gauntlets creaking as he adjusted his grip on the thick rope in his hands, feet sunk in forest loam from the weight of his armour.

It was the first time he had donned full armour since departing Fangmoor some three weeks hence. Mail hauberk; the thick pauldron, gardbrace, and rerebrace that covered the left arm, complete with interlocking shield-plates; leather poleynes strapped to his thighs. He wore his helmet, with its flat steel cap or "pot," open-faced save for the nose guard, with an aventail of steel links to protect his neck. A lesser man might have struggled even to stand in such adornment, but Hawley had trained in it for years. He could march for eight hours in it, fight in it, kill in it. To that end, he'd strapped his regulation shortsword to his side and stuffed a dagger in the sheath at his left boot. Godspeaker was already unsheathed to save precious seconds, stuck in the earth beside him.

Through a small gap in the trees ahead, he had a limited view of the dirt road, then the tumbledown drystone wall overgrown with hawthorn that bounded the foot of a low slope, strewn with debris, rocks, and long-dead tree stumps from years-old industry. The wagon had been pulled off the lane, as far up the slope as they could take it without getting stuck. Iveta was hiding in the back, only under the greatest protest. Atop the hill, Enelda was waiting in the ruin of a stone-built farmstead, now only four stout corners and a chimney breast. Enelda's keen eyes had found as good a site for an ambush as any he could have reconnoitered.

He flexed the muscles in his legs, which were again going to sleep. He was glad Iveta had finally relented to hiding; he could not defend her and Enelda both. He would have to spring his trap, deal with the men on the road, and get to Enelda before the remaining riders. A tall order. But what worried him most was Enelda's instruction to Iveta—if the fight went badly, she was to flee with the Book of Vigils and take it to Erecgham Abbey. Even now, Enelda placed her faith in Meriet.

Hoofbeats interrupted his thoughts. It had occurred to Hawley that, should an innocent party come riding by at this inopportune moment, there'd be no time to let them pass without incident. It had also occurred to him that the mysterious riders may not even harbour ill intent. But if that were the case, they should have made their true intentions plain. Hawley couldn't allow doubt to cloud his mind. Hesitation could cost him his life or, worse, the lives of those he protected. He would do what must be done, and ask questions later.

The hoofbeats grew louder; the rope in Hawley's hands vibrated softly at the approach. At least two horsemen, at a gallop. Their shadow blinked across Hawley's line of sight.

He threw his weight backwards. The rope tightened. Chest high to the average rider. Neck high if Hawley was lucky.

The rope strained briefly against Hawley's grip, ripped forward, scorching his gauntlets. The sudden jerk almost pulled him over. There was a cry, a crash, a whinny. Other voices rang out in alarm. That'd do.

Hawley released the rope and rushed forward, pulling his sword out of the ground as he ran. He burst from the undergrowth with a roar that would have given an army pause. There was a black horse in front of him, wheeling around, panicked, the rider confused. Another behind it reared, its rider struggling to control it. A third man lay in the dirt, his horse already galloping away in fright.

All this Hawley assessed in a split second. He threw himself at the horse in front of him, grabbed at the rider's belt. The horse shied away, and the rider fell sideways from the saddle, hitting the ground with a sickening thud. Panicked eyes stared up at Hawley through a black cowl. Hawley thrust his sword down, into the rider's throat. That had been his duty in the battle-line—a grim, efficient executioner. Take each enemy in turn, and remove them from the fight as quickly as possible.

He withdrew the blade and wheeled around as the other rider came on, low in the saddle, longsword arcing towards Hawley's neck. Hawley ducked, barely keeping his footing in the rough ditch beside the lane, and the blade sang as it parted the air above his head. The horse came to a stop, the backstroke of the sword sweeping at Hawley predictably. Hawley swung Godspeaker upwards with both hands, parrying the rider's blow. The man had no room to turn—the other horse stamped and snorted beside him. Hawley took one step back, raised his sword, and slashed his enemy's horse across the hindquarters. The beast, already skittish, gave a shrill cry, reared, and threw its rider. Both horses bolted.

The rider recovered quickly, parrying Hawley's first blow more through luck than skill. Only now did Hawley see clearly what he was dealing with. All the riders wore unliveried black tunics over scraps of mail and leather armour—tunics tied at the waist with knotted cords...cinctures? They wore simple domed helmets over masked faces. Their swords were light, thin-bladed, all identical. They hid their faces like bandits, but were equipped like an organised militia.

Hawley switched the grip on his Felder blade to a single hand, and took a broad outward sweep, powerful enough to take a man's head clean off. The black rider staggered miraculously out of reach again, and immediately countered, dashing low inside Hawley's reach. He thrust his blade at Hawley's gut. Hawley twisted, grabbing the man's sword-arm, drawing him close. He delivered a crunching headbutt to his foe, the steel of Hawley's helmet hitting the exposed nose of the enemy. The man in black grunted, his face spattered with blood. Hawley thrust the bastard sword. The honed Felder steel punched through the man's armour, into his stomach and out of his back. Hawley withdrew the blade, slick with gore, and his enemy crumpled to the dirt.

Hawley could hear nothing but his own breath. He tore off his helmet and wiped stinging sweat from his eyes. Through blurred vision, he saw the first rider stagger to his feet, sword in hand. The trap hadn't killed him. Then Hawley saw the others. Two men in black, creeping up the slope towards the ruin. Towards Enelda.

Hawley fixed the hobbling rider with a murderous glare. There was no time to waste.

Hawley abandoned his helmet in the mud and rushed forward. The rider raced to meet him, shaking off his limp, boots splattering in the sodden earth. Hawley checked, inviting the rider to swing first. A ferocious blow, but clumsy. Hawley skidded to a stop, crooked his left arm, transforming the crescent plates of his pauldron into a shield. The rider's sword struck it with a bell-like chime, the force of the blow bending the thin blade. Hawley dismantled his arm-shield with a click. He sidestepped the rider, jerked the Felder blade behind him, tearing the man's hamstring and putting him to his knees at once. Hawley spun around, striking down at the man's sword-arm. His aim was true, and his blade sharp; the man's arm came away at the elbow.

The rider issued a piercing scream as his blood sprayed across the furrowed track. He collapsed face-first into the mud, whimpering.

"Don't die!" Hawley commanded. He'd promised to leave one alive. This one might do.

He turned to see where the others had gone. They were almost at the ruin, but they'd turned to see the source of the scream. Now they gawped at Hawley and looked at one another uncertainly.

"You're next, you bastards," Hawley growled.

Hawley heard the whistling sound before the flight of the arrow sliced his cheek. He spun about in confusion, half expecting another shot. Behind him, a fourth rider staggered backwards into the undergrowth, clutching his shoulder, where an arrow protruded. This one had a shield, strapped to his injured arm. His sword now lay on the ground.

Hawley's mind raced to catch up with events. This had to be the man who'd separated from the others—he'd travelled ahead, realised Hawley and Enelda weren't coming, and so must have circled back, sneaking up on Hawley through the copse. Hawley looked around again, and now he saw: Iveta stood by the wagon, bow in hand. Gods, but the girl was a good shot.

One of the men on the hill had seen her, too. He split from his friend, moving quickly towards the wagon, crouched low, keeping to cover.

Hawley cursed. He leapt at the newcomer, who managed to jerk up the shield in time to block Hawley's blow. Wood splintered. The man grunted. He fumbled at his belt for a dagger. Hawley locked his pauldron and barged forward with all his strength. He lifted the man up and backwards on his shield, crumpling him into a tree trunk.

The rider looked dazed. Hawley took up his sword in both hands, and thrust. The blade pierced the man's throat and kept going, deep into the aged wood. The rider was pinned upright, gurgling his last, blood oozing from his mouth and throat. Hawley tried to pull the blade free, but it was stuck fast. He tried again, as the rider's glazed eyes fixed on him, their light fading; the sword didn't budge. For once, Hawley cursed the Felder steel.

"Hawley!"

The cry was faint. Iveta.

Hawley abandoned Godspeaker and ran towards the wagon. He could barely see where he was going. He jerked his shortsword from its scabbard, vaulted over the wall. His feet pummelled the sodden ground. Iveta swung the bow at her assailant; the rider tore it from her grasp and yanked her to the ground by her hair.

Hawley hit the man like a wild-eyed bull. The air left the rider's lungs in a heavy wheeze; they both crashed to the ground, Hawley on top. He pushed the man's face into the mud, and as he spluttered, Hawley stabbed him in the ribs with the shortsword.

Rapid, short thrusts, again and again, until the man stopped moving and they were both soaked in blood.

Hawley roared; he could barely formulate a coherent thought, let alone words. The bestial growl surprised even himself. He was tired. His very breaths hurt. Old wounds and new enraged him equally. But by the gods, he felt alive.

He staggered to his feet, his eyes meeting Iveta's. She stood wide-eyed, trembling. She was afraid of him, afraid of the red-masked killer before her. Afraid of the Butcher of Slaughter Hill.

Dumbly, she pointed up the rise, then immediately snapped to her senses and began scrabbling around for her bow.

"Stay there," Hawley managed. He couldn't keep the accusatory tone from his command. Iveta might well have saved his life, but she'd split the enemy. Hawley knew he couldn't reach Enelda before the last rider.

His legs almost refused the climb, making heavy weather of the sodden slope, so carefully chosen to slow down the enemy. In full armour, infantry of the High Companies were meant to hold the line of battle, not run headlong across the field like berserkers.

Loose stones slipped beneath Hawley's mail-shod boots as he crested the hill. He scrambled over the sundered wall of the old ruin, sword readied. And there he stopped.

Enelda stood against a crumbling wall, long white hair tumbling about her shoulders, looking golden in the dancing firelight. At just arm's length from her was a black rider, sword raised. But he'd stopped in his tracks, blinking in confusion. Enelda's right hand was closeted in a leather glove, held to her mouth, palm up. A cloud of dark particles, like coal dust, even now dissipated around the rider's head and shoulders, where Enelda had blown it.

The rider rubbed at his face and squinted his watering eyes. He stepped back, almost falling into the fire, then slashing his sword at the flames as though it had intentionally attacked him. He shook his head furiously, swatting at thin air with his free hand as though beset by a swarm of wasps.

Hawley pulled Enelda to his side. The rider became increasingly panicked, gibbering and wheeling about, the steel of his longsword flashing in the firelight. Hawley withdrew as far as he could from the man; he knew what that dust was. He knew why Enelda was wearing gloves. He didn't want to close with his enemy while the blackrock was in the air.

The rider had other ideas. In his panic, he lashed out in all directions. He whirled and stumbled, first away, then closer. Hawley readied his sword.

The rider stopped.

He blinked thrice, eyes red and sore. He peered curiously at Hawley; his sore eyes widened. He screamed. Whatever he was seeing, it was not Hawley.

"It can't be..." the man muttered. Then his mouth contorted again, and in a cry of both fear and fury, he roared, "I was promised. I was *promised*!"

With this last declaration, he leapt forward, face twisted into a murderous snarl, half-mad with terror, sword arcing through the air towards Hawley.

Hawley batted the sword away with his armoured pauldron, and thrust his shortsword up into the man's ribcage.

The rider locked eyes with Hawley, and even as the life drained from him, he whimpered like a madman, "Not this...please no. Gods save me."

And Hawley saw the rider no longer. He saw Ianto, as he had been in his final moments. And he knew that the rider was seeing not a High Companies soldier, but a creature of shadow, with yellow eyes. A creature that had taken his life, and would likely drag his soul screaming into the Rift.

*   *   *

When they reached the lane, the one-armed man was crawling slowly southwards.

"Told you I'd left one alive," Hawley said.

"But not in one piece," Enelda said.

"You didn't say nothin' about pieces."

Enelda tutted. Iveta stayed very quiet.

Hawley marched over to the man and turned him onto his

back with the toe of his boot. The man had torn off his cowl so he could gasp for air.

"That's far enough, friend," Hawley said. He nodded in Enelda's direction. "This here's a Vigilant. A True Vigilant. But I s'pose you already know that. She's going to ask you some questions, and if you answer honestly, she'll save your life before you bleed to death. If you don't answer, then I'll just have to pull your lungs out through your nose."

"N-no..." the man stammered. He looked half-dead already.

"That's just the way it is," Hawley said. "Imagine I'm a fox and you're a hare."

The man held up his one good hand weakly. Hawley was about to beckon Enelda over, when he noticed the man's hand wasn't held open, beseechingly. It was a fist.

"Stop him, Hawley!" Enelda cried.

Before Hawley could react, the man had brought his hand to his lips, tipping the contents of a tiny glass phial into his mouth.

Hawley spun the man over, slapped him hard on the back, and shook him furiously. It was to no avail. He stopped breathing even as the foam poured from his mouth. Hawley dropped him in disgust. "By the gods..."

"Careless," Enelda said.

"How could I have known?"

"If you hadn't killed the one in the ruin, it would not have mattered."

"He would've killed you!"

"Perhaps. We shall never know." Enelda waddled over to the corpse, now face down in a mud-filled furrow. She poked around the man's tunic with her staff, then stooped, and rolled back his sleeve. His wrist bore a strange tattoo—a swirling sigil that Hawley felt sure he'd seen before. "Most interesting..." Enelda muttered.

"I noticed the cincture," Hawley interrupted.

"Did you? So you also noticed it is not a Flaescine cincture?"

"Eh?"

"The width of the cord, and the number of knots—do you

remember nothing I've taught you?" Enelda stooped with no small trouble, retrieving the phial from the mud. She sniffed it and made a face of disgust. Then she removed the man's bowl-shaped helmet, revealing a head shaved clean—and recently, given the cuts and scratches across the scalp.

"And I suppose this is a coincidence, too?" Hawley said. "A shaven head to remove a tonsure, no doubt. I expect the others are the same."

"And if they are? There is only one order I can think of who shave their heads clean, dress all in black, and wear a cincture precisely five linies thick, knotted five times. They are not monks, and as far as anyone knows they do not even exist any more."

"Who?" Hawley demanded.

"By the gods..." Iveta had been standing quietly behind them, and her interruption caused Drake and Hawley to turn around sharply. Iveta was by the side of the road, staring down at a dead rider. She held the man's cowl in her hand. Except the shaven-headed rider was no man.

"A woman," Hawley muttered. "I killed a woman."

Enelda shuffled over to Iveta's side. "There's no shame in it, Hawley," she said. "The warrior nuns of this order are no shrinking violets."

"Warrior...nuns?" Hawley's head was swimming.

"They're the Sisters of Oak," Iveta said almost reverently. "Lady Aenya's order."

CHAPTER 31

They travelled through the night, the better to avoid Borderer patrols. Enelda took a turn in the back of the wagon, snoring softly. Iveta sat beside Hawley on the driver's board, bundled up against the cold, nose and cheeks ruddy, breath steaming on the night air.

Hawley steered the wagon on. His bones ached, and he could feel the sag of his eyes. As they could ill afford to stop, he drove steadily to spare the horses, and took no turn to rest. They'd at least found one of the horses belonging to the black riders, and it was now tethered behind them, following obediently.

"It's so cold," Iveta said. They were the first words either of them had uttered for hours. "Hard to believe it's almost spring."

Hawley's knuckles had seized up from gripping the reins too tight. He was still angry; angry at everything and everyone. And the more he thought about the many things that angered him, the angrier he became. He'd sat and brooded for hours. Things had gone unsaid long enough. He flexed his aching fingers.

"You shouldn't have left the wagon," he said bluntly.

"What?"

"At the ruin. It was a foolish thing you did."

Iveta sniffed. "You're welcome."

"For what?"

"Saving your life."

Hawley kept his eyes on the road, squeezing the reins until his palms hurt. "I seem to recall repaying you already. And as a result we almost lost her." He jerked his head back, towards the sound of the snoring.

"If I'd been with her from the start, like I asked, perhaps we'd all have been better off. Or perhaps that nun would have stabbed you in the back and put an end to you. Perhaps Vigilant Drake would have used her blackrock magic to drive all of them off. Who can tell what the gods had planned for us? We'll never know."

"No. We won't." It was the cleverest reply he could think of, which in itself made him feel very stupid. Now Iveta had made him think of the nun. Was it bad luck to kill a nun? He still felt bad enough for killing a woman. So much for turning over a new leaf.

"Do you think they followed us from Wyverne?" Iveta said. "Perhaps they are sworn to watch over Lady Aenya's grave. She was one of the holy sisters, after all. Women are forbidden from bearing arms these days, so perhaps that's why most of them were men."

Hawley snorted.

"All right. Where do *you* think the riders came from?" Iveta asked.

"You know what I think. But who cares about that? It's what she thinks that matters, as always." Hawley cursed himself inwardly. He didn't want to pick a fight, and certainly not with Iveta, but the words came of their own volition. He knew this was why he had a reputation for being ill-tempered; he just couldn't help himself once he was riled.

Another, longer, pause.

"You really think Abbot Meriet is behind all this?"

"I'd stake my oath on it."

"But Vigilant Drake..." Iveta lowered her voice almost to a whisper. "Vigilant Drake trusts him. Is that not enough?"

"No. She's a rare one and no mistake, but there are some things she's very wrong about."

"Such as?"

"People. She's spent her life avoiding folk, and for good reason,

I'll grant you. She clings to a belief that people are not capable of wickedness unless they are driven to it by evil influences. You know...*Riftborn*." Hawley almost made the sign of the Saint's Sword, but stopped himself. He spat over the side of the wagon instead. "But I've looked into the eyes of many a wicked man— and woman, too, come to that—and I tell you they weren't controlled by any demon. They were just plain bad."

"You think the abbot is...plain bad?"

Hawley glanced over his shoulder again. Enelda was still sleeping. "I do. She's looking for signs of a demon, and she's found none. I think she's underestimating just how bad a man can be when he wants power, or money."

"You're thinking of your baron. What was his name? Rolston?"

"What?"

"A wicked man. You could have stopped him, but you didn't. Now you think you see the same wickedness in Abbot Meriet, and seek to atone."

"If you say so," Hawley growled.

"What if I told you I overheard the abbot defending you to Clemence?"

"He...Really?"

"I think if Meriet hadn't stayed Clemence's wrath, you may have been arrested immediately, and we'd never have escaped the castle. What say you to that?"

"I...think..." Hawley spluttered. He was out of his depth now. Again, he'd taken a dislike to a man on instinct, and he had no facts to back up his assumptions. He felt sure he was right, and now his frustrations bloomed into pettiness. "He were probably just plotting something. Men like him always are."

"You really are stubborn! I've known Abbot Meriet all my life. He's never seemed to crave either power or money. He may be a pious man, but he seems quite decent to me."

"With all due respect, m'lady, perhaps you haven't met many wicked men."

"You think me a poor judge of character?"

Hawley wasn't sure how to answer that, and fumbled. "Scarfell has thick walls, and the ward of its lord has protections that the less fortunate do not."

"And in spite of those protections, a boy I loved as my own brother was stolen away in the night, perhaps murdered. And you would have me believe my uncle's advisor—a man whom I have known since childhood—is behind it? *And* in spite of everything, you still think me a spoiled rich girl without a thought in my head for others?"

"I..." Hawley's anger was already subsiding. The shame replacing it felt even worse. He searched for the right words, but they couldn't come fast enough.

"You're right, Sargent Hawley," she said icily. "I think I must be a poor judge of character. After all, I'd come to believe *you* were decent."

Hawley pulled his cloak around his shoulders a little tighter, and flicked the reins. He had a feeling this would be a long night.

*　*　*

Some said the Silver River was so named because of how the sun glittered from its vast, shifting surface during bright spring days. In truth, it was merely a bastardisation of "Sylverain." It formed a border so vast and treacherous that it might as well have been an ocean. Hawley had heard the Sylvens called it the *Riviére Peticheuns*, or "River of Small Dogs"—based on a pejorative name for Aelders, who the Sylvens believed were like ill-tempered little dogs, always trying to fight the world to compensate for their stature. Hawley secretly liked that analogy. In his experience, small dogs were the most likely to bite, and the least likely to flee.

The river was just over a league across at its widest point, and barely one-third that at its most narrow, where Dawn Crag stood sentinel to deter any attempt by unauthorised vessels to cross. The Sylven Marches extended along the north bank, terminating in the east at the vast swamps of Maserfelth, where none but the mad would risk landfall, and at the mountains of

Hintervael to the west, where Aelderland and Tördengard met at an oft-contested border, rife with rich mines. There was but one officially sanctioned crossing point: the Silver Bridge, the longest bridge in all Erevale, erected by the Sylvens at the height of their empire to foster trade between their capital and their vassal states to the north. The Gold Road began at the Sylverain capital at Tor'laguille, crossed the Silver Bridge, and extended all the way to Helmspire. Tollhouses and guard posts had transformed the Silver Bridge from a busy thoroughfare bustling with merchants and market stalls to a glorified castle wall, patrolled by the Borderers on the Aelderland side and the Sylven levy on the south.

The trail before them swept downwards to a gravel beach of sorts, nestled between two large promontories of jutting slate. A single dead tree stood atop the right-hand outcrop, its branches worn from years of gallows-rope, from which Sylven spies and Aelder traitors had many times swung.

Hawley carried the boy's corpse down to this beach, where, as near as he could tell from Redbaer's description, the lad had met his end. Hawley had been careful to wrap the body fully this time—he did not wish to touch the dead flesh again, nor see that cold, white hand flop out of the bindings, pointing accusingly at him. A boy of Aelderland, slain by a soldier of Aelderland, at the behest of a lord sworn to protect those less fortunate than himself.

"Hawley!"

At the sudden shriek, Hawley jumped away from the corpse, hand instinctively reaching to his scabbard. A hard tapping sound drew his attention upwards, to the hanging tree. There, a large raven cleaned its hooked beak against the dead wood.

The bird looked Hawley in the eye for just a moment, then swooped past him. Hawley watched dumbfounded as Barty alighted on Enelda's outstretched arm.

"Good boy, Bartholomew," Enelda cooed. "How did you get on? I trust there was no trouble."

The bird cocked its head and darted a sharp look back at Hawley, which made him feel like an eavesdropper. Enelda followed suit. Hawley swallowed nervously.

"How . . . ?" Hawley asked.

Enelda said nothing.

"So you're having conversations with him now?"

"He's the only one who talks any sense," Enelda said. And with that she turned about and walked off, muttering conspiratorially to the bird as she went.

He hadn't really believed it before, but now Hawley recalled Clemence's accusations against Enelda, and what he'd called the raven.

Familiar.

*   *   *

"I've remembered where I saw that tattoo," Hawley declared.

Enelda had been quieter than usual as he'd busied himself setting up camp. Iveta had returned from a shallow spot upriver, where she'd caught a good-sized carp—it seemed there was no end to her talents.

"Tattoo?" Enelda asked.

"On the black rider's wrist. Thought I'd seen it before. It was on Agnead. I mean . . . it's the symbol Ianto carved into the girl."

Enelda didn't reply. Just continued staring into the middle distance. She did now purse her wrinkled lips in thought. Hawley had told her about Agnead before, and Enelda hadn't seemed interested. "Idle threats," she'd said. "He was just trying to scare the girl."

"I've had a lot of time to think," Hawley said, when no reply was forthcoming.

"Do enlighten us," Enelda said. She still sounded distant, her mind elsewhere.

"I still believe Meriet is guilty as sin," Hawley said. "What's more, I think he's not the only man in Scarfell caught up in this black affair."

"Who else?" Enelda asked.

"Redbaer."

"Away with you!" Iveta gasped. "A more honourable man could not be found. And has he not been a friend to you these past days?"

"I wouldn't go that far. He behaves oddly. He alone knows the movements of every guard in Scarfell. He had a hand in the death of that boy we're carting. A boy, I should point out, strangled with a cincture like those worn by the black riders. Where'd Redbaer come by that? It's too much of a coincidence. I think Meriet sent the riders after us, so it stands to reason he and Redbaer are in league together."

"Then your powers of reason must be severely wanting," Iveta snapped.

"Now, now," said Enelda. "Hawley has pieced together the evidence and has made his deductions. We should commend his efforts."

"You...you think he's right?" Iveta asked in disbelief.

"Really?" Hawley asked, even more dumbfounded than Iveta.

"No, of course not," Enelda scoffed. "He has examined the evidence and, on the face of it, has made some rational connections, but as usual has come up short."

Hawley felt his colour rise. "Then set me right!" he spluttered. "You're always so quick to defend the bloody abbot, yet you offer no alternative."

Enelda sighed heavily. "How many times have I told you, Hawley, that we must examine the evidence carefully before jumping to conclusions? And we do not yet have all the evidence. Some of it, I imagine, died with the chamberlain." She paused, her eyes briefly expressing pain at the memory. Did she blame herself for Tymon's death? She composed herself. "We certainly don't have sufficient evidence to accuse any member of the archduke's council—nor indeed his captain of the guard. There are pieces of the puzzle missing, and too many men who would seek to obfuscate the truth and keep those pieces hidden. Now that I have been cast out of the castle like a common outlaw, there is only one course of action remaining to me. A dangerous course, which I would rather not take were there any other choice."

"The Eternal Night..." Iveta gasped.

Enelda said nothing. If anything, she looked afraid.

Hawley coughed nervously. "It's true? You really are a necromancer?"

"It is not necromancy. That's simply what we tell the incredulous so they keep their noses out of our affairs. I don't know how to explain it in a way you would understand."

"The Eternal Night is the space between worlds," Iveta interrupted, breathless with excitement and wonder. "Between the living and the dead, the Rift and the heavens. A space between all things, where echoes of all worlds exist, waiting to travel onwards to the place they belong. And sometimes, when a person meets their end in a tragic or violent way, the echoes they leave behind are very clear. And if someone were to concentrate hard enough, they could use those echoes to enter the Eternal Night and see the past through the dead person's eyes." She beamed, and looked to Enelda for encouragement.

Enelda smiled. "Close enough. Someone has stolen a look at the Book of Vigils more than once, I wager."

"You speak of the spirit world...of Æblácia," Hawley said, "between the Garden of the Aelders and the pits of Uffærn. How can anyone living enter such a place?"

"Oh, they don't go physically," Iveta said before Enelda could reply. "You know how Vigilant Drake concentrates all the time, noticing every little thing—things that you and I would overlook? Well, you more than me...It is said that a Vigilant can concentrate so hard that they can actually see the veil between worlds, and send their spirit into it. They go into a sort of trance, during which their mortal body is vulnerable to attack, and their soul is unguarded in the Eternal Night, where all sorts of evil things lie in wait. Riftborn, you see—they can go into the Eternal Night, too, and when they sense a Vigilant, they're drawn to it like—"

"A moth to a candle flame," Hawley muttered.

"Exactly! That's why it's so dangerous. If the body is slain back in our world, the spirit has no place to return. If the spirit is devoured in the Eternal Night, the body stays here forever, soulless. Or...so the book says." Iveta stopped herself, and suddenly looked embarrassed by her giddy excitement.

"And...you've done this before?" Hawley asked Enelda.

Enelda's wrinkled lips were pursed tight, and her eyes flickered with doubt. "Once. A long time ago." She gazed distractedly into the middle distance. At last she said, "I must prepare myself. I will go to the riverside with the boy. I will call when I need you."

* * *

Hawley busied himself around the camp, but as the hours passed and Enelda showed no sign of having completed her "preparations"—which seemed to involve mostly gazing idly across the river—even Hawley's practical mind ran out of jobs for him to do.

"I'm sorry," Hawley said, after the silence had become unbearable.

Iveta arched an eyebrow in a manner disconcertingly similar to Enelda. "For what?"

"For what I said last night, on the road."

"Which part?"

Hawley sighed. She wasn't going to make it easy. "You'd have me say it?"

"It's hardly an apology otherwise."

He fought his natural inclination to wave her away and march off. Instead, he tried to remember that she was a lady of the realm, and he was a soldier. With no small difficulty, he bowed and said, "My lady, I apologise for both my words and manner last night...They were unbecoming. I'm...grateful you intervened—indeed, you're a finer archer than I'll ever be. And I didn't mean to suggest you were selfish, or spoiled, or...Look, I used to think so, I can't deny it. But no longer. I know you helped the people of Halham when their lord ignored them. I know you wouldn't be here if you didn't care about Anton. I just..."

"Go on."

Hawley straightened, and looked directly into her bright blue eyes. "You shouldn't have to fight. You shouldn't have to live with...the things I do. I don't want you to get hurt. I don't want you to fall foul of dark powers. I'm afraid I won't be able to protect you. At the ruin, I almost lost you, then I almost lost her, and what a fine soldier that would've made me."

"You didn't lose either of us, nor us you. You fought well. You fought more...fiercely...than I could have imagined."

There was sadness in her eyes and in her voice. Something else. Hawley had seen it before, the previous day. "You need never be afraid of me, m'lady."

"I'm not afraid *of* you," Iveta said. "I'm afraid *for* you. You saved my life, and believe me when I say I'm thankful. But...in that moment, in your eyes, I saw it. You enjoyed it."

Hawley hung his head. He didn't know what to say or to feel. When he looked up, it was with sadness in his heart—though sadness for his actions or for the simple fact of Iveta's disapproval of him, he didn't know. "I don't enjoy killing," he said contritely. "I enjoy being good for something. Good *at* something. And by the gods, I kill well. Better than anyone."

Iveta nodded, eyes moist with tears. "And does it matter who you kill?"

"It hasn't always...And maybe the gods won't forgive me for all the souls I've sent their way. But it matters now. You matter. She matters." He nodded towards Enelda, who sat staring out across the river.

"She's a True Vigilant. She can see into the hearts of men, can't she?"

"I think not, else she'd have seen my sins, and we wouldn't be here."

Iveta stepped so close Hawley could smell her woodruff-oil scent. Head bowed, not looking directly at him; tentatively, she reached a hand to Hawley's cheek, tracing the scarred lines of his face. She pulled away. "I think she can. And I think she sees you are good for something, after all."

Without another word, she walked down to the riverside.

Hawley saw belatedly why. Enelda had stood at last, beckoning them. Hawley paused, watching Iveta for a moment. He touched his fingertips to his face, where Iveta's had been. Only then did he follow.

* * *

"What I'm about to do has rarely been witnessed by those outside the order," Enelda said. "Like as not, you will experience nothing untoward during my journey to the Eternal Night, but if you do, you must have no fret. Anything you see here shall be naught but echoes, and echoes can harm none. None but me."

Hawley cast a nervous glance at Iveta. She appeared more excited than worried.

"It is best that I return to you of my own accord, and even if it looks as though I am in distress, you must not attempt to wake me unless you fear my life is in peril. Wake me too early, and I might leave some of my faculties behind in that place, and I have few enough of those to spare these days."

"How long...?" Hawley ventured.

"How long will my journey last? Who can say? Minutes... hours. Time moves differently in the Eternal Night. I might see a lifetime unfold before my eyes while only seconds pass for you. Or I might become lost in a single moment while you count the hours to dawn. But the longer I spend there, the closer it will come. The *Other*."

Hawley shivered, feeling the cold evening air in his very marrow.

The sky darkened with each passing moment, the constellations revealing themselves as the pink haze of day was chased beyond the horizon. Enelda unwrapped the rest of the boy's linens, revealing the pale arms and shoulders, the scarred neck and wrists, the blue lips. She took the lad's cold, dead hand in hers.

"It is time," Enelda said.

As Hawley watched, Enelda's pupils, rather than dilate as night drew in, shrank suddenly, making her eyes look pale and deathly. Her skin seemed almost to grey, as though the life had left her, and Hawley would indeed have thought her dead had her breathing not become deeper and slower. The air around her seemed to shimmer, then coil like smoke—surely a trick of the light.

"She's gone," Iveta whispered.

And Hawley knew it was so.

CHAPTER 32

I t had been a long time. Not long enough.

The river slowed, then stopped flowing altogether. The shadows thickened, their tendrils enveloping her, until the Silver River and the powder of stars above were almost lost to darkness.

When Enelda stood, her limbs were light—her whole body lacked substance, like she might get caught on the wind and blow away.

She concentrated, until she saw through the shadow, into its constituent parts, the shifting fabric of unreality. And onto that she latched herself, her incorporeal form now a part of that unreality. She was given weight at last, or the illusion of it, and with a deep breath she stood at the bank of the river once more, only not in her own world.

Here, all was silent. All was dark. The only colour in the Eternal Night came from the red streaks that pulsed overhead like arteries, flowing with some unfathomable energy. Enelda held out a hand, pale and grey but for the same red pulses that flowed through her own veins beneath translucent flesh. The energy of life in a place where life did not belong. Sustenance for the things that dwelt here.

At Enelda's feet lay the boy, but he was no longer wrapped in swaddling linens. He was naked, his flesh unmarked by Enelda's surgery. Motes of tiny, shining particles drifted idly around him. The light connected all things living and dead, all things in time and space that the boy had ever touched or sensed. A trail, waiting to be followed by those with eyes to see.

She reached out, cupping her hand gently around one of the pinpricks of light. She looked closer; images flickered within the light, drawing her in. A face, no longer just within the dust-like particle, but near to her, above her. A sense of anger, of desolation, of death.

Enelda felt her throat tighten. She was on the ground, wet-ness at her back. She struggled for breath that would not come. A face... Sir Redbaer, eyes full of pity and remorse. Enelda tried to speak, but words would not come. And then Redbaer turned away, and Enelda knew the hands at her throat were not his. With a great concentration of will, she turned her head, and stared into pale, blue eyes, full of piety and zeal. Lord Scarsdale squeezed her neck tighter.

No, not hers.

She was a young boy, terrified, waking from slumber to the pain of his own murder. Weak as he was, he resisted. He pushed at the archduke's face with a limp hand. He grabbed at Leoric's collar. Worn, broken fingernails dug into flesh, raking bloody slashes down his attacker's throat. Leoric grunted, but did not stop. Instead, he held the boy down with one hand and untied the rope at the waist of his tunic. No... a cincture. He wrapped the cord around the boy's neck, pulled him upwards. Held him there. Hanged him. The boy now pulled feebly at the cincture as the life was choked from him.

This is the darkness that confronts us. Even if it means you fear for your very soul, do not shrink from your duty, for St. Baerloc watches over us in this, our darkest hour, and he demands sacrifices of us all.

The archduke's words were felt, not heard. Nothing could be truly heard in this place.

Enelda felt the knots dig into her neck—no, the boy's neck—one by one. With a last nauseous wheeze, the boy ceased his struggle.

All was black. The boy was gone. Lord Scarsdale was gone. Enelda stood alone. She clutched at her throat, gasping for breath, but there was no air to breathe. She concentrated, stilling her senses so all she saw was the sparkling motes of dust once more. Again she watched them swirl in the eddies of time, coalescing into a strand of coiling lights. At the end of the strand, a dim grey figure walked away from her. Redbaer? She was seeing through the boy's eyes, but from a time before. Another echo from the past. She followed.

There was a sound behind her. Unusual. There should be no sound. Breathing—slow and heavy. Then a gravelly exhalation like ecstasy, terminating in a deep, rumbling chortle. Enelda fancied there was a cold breath at the back of her neck, making the hairs stand on end.

Impossible.

Enelda didn't look back. She fixed her sights on Redbaer, and hurried into the dark.

The shadows parted like great black curtains. Reality itself warped and bent; vast pillars of darkness bowed as Enelda passed between them, then fragmented, hardened, taking on a rough and jagged form. Trees, bare and twisted. Enelda's feet found purchase in soft ground, sinking in cold, wet loam and squelching mud. A horse whickered quietly. Enelda's breath steamed in front of her face.

"It has to end here." A man's voice—Leoric's voice.

Enelda was kneeling now. Her hands were bound tight.

Redbaer was nowhere to be seen. Lord Scarsdale instead was speaking to two men in hooded robes.

"A greater price may yet be demanded," one said.

"No," Lord Scarsdale snapped. "A sacrifice was demanded, and a sacrifice shall be given. Tonight."

One of the faceless men laughed, a rattling, phlegmy whisper of a laugh. "*This* is no sacrifice. It is parsimonious at best. When you offer tribute freely, and give of yourself that which you cannot afford to lose, *then* a sacrifice shall be counted."

The archduke jabbed the hooded man in the chest with his index finger. "It is not for you to say! *I* was chosen. *I* made the pact."

Twigs snapped in the forest; night birds fluttered upwards to higher branches. Someone approached. The archduke and the riders all turned in the direction of the sound. Then, wraith-like, the hooded men slipped away, leaving but a whisper on the night air:

"We shall see..."

Still here, little one?

A familiar voice grated in Enelda's head, once comforting, now mocking. Something noxious assailed her nostrils. Sulphurous smoke and fish guts. She had the strongest sense that there was someone—some*thing*—leering just over her shoulder. And it was not part of the vision. It was here and now.

"Master...?" Enelda said. Or thought she'd said. The Eternal Night was silent as ever, all perception just a theatre of Enelda's mind, honed for decades to translate the energy of the twilight realm into a comprehensible form.

I am here. Always shall I be here. Right where you left me.

"What? I...No..." Enelda's pulse quickened. Those vast red veins above her flashed brighter, pulsing in anticipation of her concentration waning. She couldn't help it. The accusation in that voice made her heart ache. It was Cerwyn Thawn.

Yes... You left me in a squalid souk, remember? The back room of a butcher's shop, where old men smoked themselves insensible on kif, *while dogs sniffed around for scraps of rancid meat. There I tried to teach you. And there you failed.*

"Master...No. I never meant..." Enelda felt the shadows shifting all around her. The forest was gone, the archduke was gone. She was losing her grip on this strand. The boy's memories were slipping from her grasp as the voice of her old master whispered in her ear.

Left me to die.

"No. Your heart. You were too sick. Too—"

Too old? Like you, Enelda Drake? You haven't been back since, have you? You haven't dared. And I have waited so long.

The voice began to change. Subtly at first. It sounded like many voices all speaking at once, all fighting to be heard. And amongst them, something hissing, slithering into Enelda's thoughts.

Enelda stilled herself. Though the voice distracted her with words she did not want to hear, in truth she had expected it. This was what they did. They had assumed the voice of Cerwyn Thawn. But it was not her master's imitator she needed right now, it was his training: A face as of stone. A heart as of oak...

"You are not Cerwyn Thawn," she said. Thought.

Are we not? Is he not here, in the dark with ussss? Ah, to feassst on his sssspirit. That was a good day! And to feassst on yoursss...That will come sssoon. But firssst...Your friends. Will they leave your frail old body, like you left his? Or will we sssuck on their marrow and snip-crack their bonesss?

"Begone, demon."

Filthy little blood-sssack. You're in our world now. And when we find you...

"Begone!"

The blackness was gone in a heartbeat. Enelda was in a smoky room, the heat stifling. There was a ramshackle door in front of her. Sunlight streamed through the cracks. Rasping, giddy laughter rang in her ears. She turned, slowly, surveying the familiar stucco walls hung with moth-eaten rugs. Tall, conical pots bubbled away over stove fires. An ancient-looking man with brown, leathery skin and a missing eye cackled incoherently, pausing only to draw on the long pipe of his *sebsi*. Enelda turned a little more, unable to help herself.

There was her master, Cerwyn Thawn. Dead. He sat upright, eyes closed, one hand outstretched towards Enelda, finger pointed at her accusingly. His skin was grey, eye sockets dark and sunken, white beard crusted with sand. His Vigilant robe was tattered and stained, his last days lived like a beggar. The last lesson he had to teach never completed.

Even as his eyelids flicked open to reveal glassy black orbs, Enelda was turning to run. She threw open the door as the cackling of the old addict grew louder, the noonday Sil-Maqash sun blinding her. She stumbled from the souk, spots before her eyes.

Not spots. Motes of ghostlight, drifting serenely through cold darkness. She stood ankle-deep in mud. Four farmhands beside her stopped their toil as a cart approached.

Focus, Enelda...focus.

Over the brow of distant hills peeked two tall, narrow spires. Erecgham Abbey? She noted the position and height of the sun, the length of shadows. The abbey lay northwest. There were sparse woods to the east. Smoke from the village just a stone's throw away.

Raecswold. But *when*?

Words were exchanged, indistinct. The labourers shared a joke with the men on the cart. Monks.

"And what's your name, lad?" one of the monks was asking, in a drawling Maserfelth accent. No vow of silence for him.

"Hodge, sir," Enelda replied. The voice came from her without hesitation. She was the boy again.

"No need to call me sir," the monk said. "We're brothers all."

He pulled back his hood, to reveal his Flaescine tonsure and a thin, drawn face, with a smile that looked as much mocking as friendly.

"I am Brother Ianto," he said.

A jolt. Enelda felt she might fall, and put out a hand to steady herself. She touched rough stone.

Ahead of her, Ianto the monk hurried along a narrow passage, holding a lantern before him. Scarfell. Iveta's secret tunnel.

Enelda followed. This wasn't possible. She was no longer the boy—Hodge?—so how could she see this?

Ianto reached the secret door to the Green Tower. He paused, listened, then opened the door and stepped through. Enelda hurried to reach the door, but too late. Ianto closed it behind him, and the door was gone. And with it, all the light from the world.

All alone, little bloodsack?

Enelda ran. But she now felt every bit her old age, no longer weightless or formless. She stumbled. Behind her, something sharp scraped and scratched on stone—no, it scratched in her mind.

We hunger, little Vigilant. We long to feassst on your soul.

To snip-crack your bones and bite-suck the marrow. But per-hapsss there is a better use for you. Perhaps you will fall. Like he did...

"Liar!" Enelda cried into the void. For forty years she had wondered what had become of Thawn's soul. For forty years she had looked for signs and found none. He could not have fallen, not even in his final moments. Not even while lost in this place.

You believe that? The Other read her thoughts. *You think he was stronger than* us? *You think* you *might be strong enough?*

It laughed. It was a sound like the death throes of a beast. It invaded Enelda's mind, sharp fingernails picking at the inside of her skull.

She ran as fast as her aged legs would carry her. Behind her, something heavy vibrated the very fabric of the Eternal Night. Great footfalls thudding, drawing closer. The Other was coming.

She concentrated hard, desperate to block out the approaching enemy. She focused on the pitch blackness, scanning for any sign of the swirling ghostlights that would lead her back to the boy, or to Ianto—anywhere but here. There was one, then another, and soon the swirling threads stretched out before her, growing brighter as she ran faster and faster. She reached something solid. A black door in the heart of nothingness. She flung it open and almost fell through it.

The air was thick with incense. Lord Scarsdale's chapel was lit only by ten candles.

Ten candles. Ten years. Why that number?

Before the statue of St. Baerloc knelt a small figure. A girl. Lady Ermina. Her father stood nearby, and at his instruction the little girl prayed for salvation, fervently and sincerely. The archduke prompted her when she forgot her words. Candlelight shone from the tears in his eyes.

He walked slowly to the corner of the room. As Ermina prayed, the archduke opened the glass case containing Lady Aenya's relics. He removed the cincture and returned stealthily to the altar.

"No!" Enelda shouted. But he could not hear her. She wasn't there. She didn't even know when this was—none of it was possible. Had it even happened yet? No Vigilant had ever seen the future through the Eternal Night, despite what the commoners used to believe.

The archduke wrapped the ends of the cincture about his knuckles. He stood behind his daughter, her golden hair shining in the half-light.

Forgive me.

Even as Lord Scarsdale stooped over Ermina, Enelda knew they were not alone in the chapel. Somewhere to her left was a dark figure, its presence felt rather than seen.

It appeared before her. Eyes of yellow flame shone from beneath a benighted cowl. Great wings of shadow unfurled from the figure's back. It leapt towards Enelda, and roared.

Foul breath blasted Enelda's hair out behind her. She fell backwards in shock, through the chapel door, hands clutching in vain at the doorframe. There was nothing behind her but thin air. Nothing in front of her but the burning eyes of a monster. And no sound to be heard but her own screams as she fell...fell...

* * *

"Wake up!" Hawley yelled, trying to make himself heard over Enelda's screams. He shook her as hard as he dared.

Enelda's whole body was bunched up tight, fists clenched, eyes squeezed shut.

Iveta had retreated from the unending screams, knees drawn up to her chest, hands covering her ears.

In desperation, Hawley wrenched Enelda away from the boy, and plunged her into the cold, dark river.

"Wake up!" he roared. He pushed her head under the water for just a second, then hauled her out.

The screaming stopped. Enelda gasped and spluttered, spitting out river water, blinking confusedly.

"Light of Litha!" she cried. "Are you trying to drown me?"

"Thank the gods..." Hawley muttered. He scooped her up into his arms. For all her resistance before, she submitted to his embrace. She weighed next to nothing, even soaked through.

Enelda complained all the way back to the campfire, but Hawley said nothing. At least she was alive.

*   *   *

"I do not...I *cannot* believe it." Tears welled in Iveta's eyes.

Enelda sat shivering, shawl pulled tight around her. She said quietly, "There is no doubt. Archduke Leoric killed this boy. I suspected it, but could not be certain. Redbaer took the blame to protect his master. He is a man of conspicuous loyalty."

"What aren't you telling us?" Iveta asked, angrily.

Enelda's mask of vulnerability slipped, as Hawley had seen it do so often before. Her face hardened, her eyes flashed. "Do not question me. If I had something to tell you, I'd tell it."

Iveta straightened, and stepped back. Her lips pursed; for a moment, Hawley thought she might retaliate. Then she bobbed an awkward curtsey. "Forgive me, Vigilant Drake. I did not mean any offence."

Hawley could not help but be disconcerted himself. He felt Iveta was right. Enelda had seen more than she was saying.

Apparently satisfied, Enelda turned to the fire and warmed her trembling hands.

"What now?" Hawley asked. "We'll have to take the body to Raecswold, I s'pose. It's on the way to the abbey...If you ask me, we march in there and drag a confession out of Meriet."

Enelda sank her head into her hands. "For pity's sake, Hawley."

"You saw Ianto in your vision."

"Not a vision..." Enelda said.

"What's it matter? He was in Raecswold, he knew the boy. Thought you didn't believe in coincidence?"

"I don't. I think Ianto was involved in something most sinister, which we are yet to understand. The person best placed to help us understand is the very person you would accuse."

"Meriet?" Hawley gasped. "You'd seek his counsel?"

"It's not Abbot Meriet who is neck-deep in this mire, but Lord Scarsdale. We know he killed this boy with Lady Aenya's own cincture. We have been attacked by mysterious riders wearing those same cinctures. Lord Scarsdale has a familial tie to the Sisters of Oak. He has influence enough to gain even the ear of a High Companies commander. You think Ianto was a Flaescine monk acting under the abbot's instruction? I ask, what if he were part of a more sinister order, who infiltrated the monastery as easily as he infiltrated your company?"

Hawley bristled. He hated to admit it, but Enelda's theory sounded plausible. "Even if it were so," Hawley half conceded, "how could Meriet help us?"

"He can provide sanctuary within the abbey walls. His monks can go unnoticed across the mearca—even within Scarfell. They could find the boy."

"The boy's surely dead," Hawley snapped.

"No!" Iveta cried. "Don't say that."

Enelda prised herself feebly to her feet with her staff. "Anton is worth nothing dead," she said, breaths ragged. "Whoever has him will keep him alive...for now."

Hawley spat into the fire. "You're saying Lord Scarsdale is holding him somewhere? How could he keep it a secret for so long?"

"Think, Hawley!" Enelda rubbed at her head. She rocked unsteadily on her feet, the ordeal of the Eternal Night still plain to see. "Earlier you accused Sir Redbaer."

"You said it yourself, he only lied out of loyalty to his lord."

"Then why could he not have taken the boy under his lord's orders?"

Hawley had no answer. He saw what she was doing. Hawley had come to trust Redbaer, just as Enelda trusted Meriet.

"The Vigilants, then," Enelda pressed. "Lestyn and his...men have the means, the motive...*and* the opportunity." The words were a struggle. Enelda gripped her staff more tightly.

"Now *that* I could believe," Hawley conceded. "But why would Clemence want a war?"

"Clemence has...already made gains in Scarfell—the chamberlain's death was much to his advantage. His allegiance with

Commander Hobb will…cement his power in the mearca, and both men know that a successful campaign will secure the king's favour."

Hawley frowned. That rang true.

"Vigilant Drake." Iveta took Enelda's arm. "You look unwell. Please, sit."

Enelda shook away from Iveta, eyes still fixed on Hawley. "There you have a real possibility. They would profit from war. What would the abbot gain?"

"I don't bloody know," Hawley snapped. "His day of reckoning, maybe."

"We must…go to the abbey…" Enelda struggled to speak.

"I'm not going to Erecgham," Hawley spat. "And that's final."

"Holt Hawley, you are the most pig-headed, bad-tempered, foolhardy man I've—" Enelda's legs buckled. The staff clattered to the rocks, and Enelda followed it.

Hawley reached her first. She was alive, trembling, muttering insensibly. Hawley carried her to a bedroll and covered her with blankets.

"What's wrong with her?" asked Iveta.

"I don't know," Hawley said.

"What should we do?" Iveta asked.

"Wait 'til she recovers, I s'pose."

"What if she doesn't?"

"We'll cross that bridge when we come to it."

*　*　*

Iveta sat atop an outcrop, bundled up against the cold breeze that blew across the river. Hawley had chosen the vantage point for its unparalleled views of the north trails. Comfort had not been in his thoughts.

Now Hawley slept, and Iveta took her turn on watch. The clouds were patchy, the moon slender. How long now before General Tarasq brought her forces across the Silver River? Iveta wondered if the Borderers would oppose them, or whether the Sylvens would be left unchecked until the High Companies rode out. How many farms and villages would burn before Tarasq was stopped? If she could be stopped at all.

A noise startled her, a loud tap, a scuff on stone. Iveta jumped up. Enelda stood beside her. "Vigilant Drake! You should be—"

Enelda put a finger to her lips and looked out across the hills. "The weather has turned," she murmured at last. "It will serve you well for the journey ahead."

"Journey?"

"My dear, you and I have much to discuss. But I'm afraid time is against us."

* * *

Hawley woke to dawn's light. He'd slept too long.

He sprang to his feet, grabbed his sword. Iveta hadn't woken him to take watch.

Then he saw Enelda sitting by a crackling fire, poking at the logs.

"You're up?" he said.

She didn't reply, so Hawley went to the fire. "Don't tell me you took a turn on watch. You should be resting."

"Oh, I was not perhaps as ill as I appeared."

Hawley frowned. Had she been pretending? "Where's Iveta?"

"Long gone."

"Gone?" Hawley looked around frantically. He ran to the trees where the horses were tethered. Only one horse was there now—Baelsine, nibbling dozily on tough grass. From here, Hawley could see the outcrop they'd used to keep watch. Iveta wasn't there.

He ran to the cart and pulled out a saddle for Baelsine.

"You won't find her." Enelda stood behind him now.

"Where is she?"

"On her way to Scarfell."

Hawley gaped. "Why?"

"Because she was right. I did see something in the Eternal Night. As much as Lady Iveta's presence would be useful to us in what is to come, I could keep it from her no longer. She has to go back. She has to see for herself."

"See what?" Hawley said quietly. He knew something was very wrong.

"Ermina is dead."

Ermina. The inquisitive girl with her blonde curls. Hawley reeled. He dropped the saddle on the ground and spun away from Enelda. He touched a hand to his collar, feeling Mildreth's talisman beneath his tunic. Another innocent gone. "Lord Scarsdale?"

"Yes."

"Then Iveta rides into danger." He fixed Enelda with a daggered glare. "I'll go after her."

"If you set foot in that castle, Clemence will arrest you."

"He can try."

"You are not an army, Hawley. Besides, Iveta is in no danger."

"How can you know that?"

"Because Leoric is finished. He is a broken man. It falls to Iveta to pick up the pieces."

Hawley took a deep breath. "Then it's over? Leoric was our man all along?"

"Leoric is a pawn in a greater game."

"Whose game? Not Meriet?"

"No, but with the abbot's help I can—"

"Hang the abbot!" Hawley felt his colour rise again. "You still think Erecgham is safe? You've been blinded by Meriet from the moment he spun that yarn about your master."

"Did you listen to nothing I said yesterday?"

"Aye, I listened. And you're wrong. You were wrong about Leoric. You were wrong about Tymon. You're wrong about Meriet. Ermina is dead…Do you understand that? How many more have to die before you face the truth?"

"After everything I've said, everything I tried to teach you, you still cling to prejudice. Your problem, Hawley, is that you never use your head." Enelda shook, small fists clenched, face pinched and hot with anger. "I must go to Erecgham, and if your oath means anything, you'll set aside your feelings about the abbot. We still have the boy to find—that is our duty now."

"Duty? I have no duty. Iveta said it herself. I'm no soldier any more. I'm an outlaw. I've lost everything because I swore an oath to you—an oath that's brought nothing but trouble. We're no closer to finding the boy. You haven't given a thought to the other bairns... to Mildrith, to this lad, Hodge, 'cept to use him in a bloody ritual. Gods! Everything they said about you is true. Messing about with blackrock, talking to the dead—"

"You think Lord Clemence was right?" Enelda snapped. "You think I'm a witch?"

Hawley bit his lip. "'Awearg,' they always called me. Ill luck, ill-omened. Meet, then, that I wound up with you."

Enelda glared across the flickering flames. "Your ignorance knows no bounds, it seems. I doubt you've ever met a problem you couldn't solve with your sword or your fists."

"You'd be dead if it weren't for my sword," Hawley growled.

"Must I remind you how we met?"

"Well, then... I s'pose we're even."

"You really are a pig-headed, ignorant man," Enelda snapped.

"And you're an old fool playing at being wise."

"*Wise!*" echoed Barty.

"Is that really what you think?"

The anger washed over Hawley now like waves over rocks. "Was it wise to send Iveta into danger, where I can't protect her? Was it wise to abandon Ermina to her fate? And for what? Out of loyalty to the bloody abbot? No, you're too busy tryin' to look clever to actually *be* clever. Making us all dance to your tune... Well, no more. I'm not bloody having it!"

"Then I suppose there is nothing more to say," Enelda said quietly, utterly cold. "I really thought you'd be useful, Hawley, but your usefulness has expired. I release you from your oath. Leave me. Go wherever your conscience takes you."

Hawley marched up the bank and gathered up his bedroll. "I'll take a few days' provisions," he called back. "And Baelsine comes with me."

"I don't need the horse," Enelda said. "Barty will take word to Erecgham. The Flaescines will protect me now."

Hawley spat into the fire on his way back. He couldn't even look at Enelda.

"*Fine*. I'll barter with the Mountain Guard, and be at the Tördengard border in a week."

"Take him with you," Enelda said.

Hawley frowned. Enelda was pointing at the bundled corpse.

"I'm going nowhere near Raecswold."

"Then bury him here, or leave him for the crows. I have no time for missions of mercy when there is a living child to save. And as you said, I care nothing for him, or the others."

Hawley looked to the heavens and swore. "You really are cold-hearted, aren't you? Fine. I'll ride to Raecswold." He marched down the bank again, gritting his teeth before touching the shrouded corpse. He slung the stiff, cold bundle over his shoulder. "I curse the day I met you."

Enelda only nodded.

Walking away was more difficult than he'd thought. But Hawley was tired. Tired of being made to feel like an idiot. Most of all, he was tired of obligation. He'd spent his life in service, and now he was a wanted man, hunted by his former masters. By turning his back on the Third, he'd abandoned the very sense of duty that had bound him his entire life. If he could do that, what then did he owe Enelda Drake? He'd known her barely three weeks.

An hour later, Hawley rode the winding river road, eventually taking the north fork. He'd avoid Wyverne, that much was certain. He'd deliver the boy to the arms of his grieving parents. But what then?

Baelsine crested a hill, and a vast expanse of rolling hills churned northwards for leagues until it met an endless grey sky. Enormous dark clouds rolled in from the east. Hawley felt like an insignificant speck on the wild vastness of the Marches.

It occurred to Hawley that, for all the hardships he'd endured, for all the enemies he'd made and quarrels he'd picked, from the orphanage to Fort Fangmoor, he'd never in his life been truly alone.

Until now.

CHAPTER 33

Wealsdaeg, 12th Day of Nystamand

The rain had started again a few miles from Raecswold. Baelsine plodded wearily, overburdened with armour, supplies, and a dead boy. Hawley huddled low to the horse's neck. The beast's every laboured step made his bones ache; the pain in his ribs had returned, as though in protest at being so far from Enelda's doctoring. He pulled his hood as far over his head as he could, until he could barely see the trail for the drips.

The downpour was heavier still by the time Raecswold's cloistered hovels appeared as smudges on the edge of vision; Baelsine's hooves sloshed through deep, rain-filled furrows. Hawley could barely keep his eyes open. He now leaned so far forward in the saddle he was virtually asleep at the reins. He couldn't even discern the surly villagers who came to greet him, taking his reins and stilling the grateful horse.

"Long way from home, soldier," one of them said.

Hawley blinked away rain. "The boy," he said, struggling to force coherent words from chapped and chilled lips. "Back of the horse. Dead. Name's Hodge...one of yours."

An exchange between the figures, then a reply, "Ours? I don't think so."

There was something about the tone. Something mocking, menacing. Familiar.

Hawley pushed himself upright, wiped the rain away from his face, squinted through the deluge.

From beneath the brim of a large hat, Swire's lips twisted into an ugly grin. "Awearg."

Hawley snatched at the reins. Strong hands grabbed him, pulled him half out of the saddle. He tried to heave himself upright again, but a sharp pain cracked at the back of his skull, and the ground rose up to meet him.

*   *   *

When Hawley came to, his head felt like his brain had been removed and replaced with dung. He gingerly prised open one eyelid at a time, and even the meagre light of whatever foul chamber he was in jabbed at his eyes like hot needles. He tried to stand. A deep, unwholesome ache seeped across his ribcage, up and down his spine, permeating his bones from skull to ankles. Chains rattled.

Hawley shook his manacles. He was slumped on a mildewed floor, slick from something he didn't want to think about, but which his nose reluctantly identified. The cell was squalid; there were bars on three sides, and a stone wall behind, set with a tiny window—more of a chute—through which sunlight begrudgingly filtered.

Only then did Hawley hear the whispers. There were other cells beside his own. To his right, a giant of a man dressed in rags slept like a baby. To his left, hazy light gleamed from the wary eyes of frightened strangers, huddled in the shadows.

A key turned in a lock. Bolts were withdrawn.

Hawley would not be seen as weak before his captors. As a heavy door groaned open, throwing light into the blackness of the jail, Hawley crawled to the cell door and pulled himself up against the bars.

A lantern threw its glow into the foul-smelling pit. Hawley caught an impression of his fellow prisoners in the next cell—a man and a scrawny youth, then another cell farther back where a haggard woman reached imploringly towards the figures who entered.

A man approached Hawley's cell, the corner of his cloak pulled across his face against the stench.

"A fine mess you're in now, Hawley."

Hawley laughed in spite of himself, causing the pain in his skull to stab a little harder. "Redbaer. Of all the people to find in this shithole."

Redbaer drew close to the bars, lowering the cloak. Hawley noted the man with the lantern was clad in green. A Scarfell guard.

"Why did you come here? Where is Lady Iveta? Where is Drake?"

"No idea," Hawley grunted. A pang of worry beset him at the thought Iveta may be lost, but he betrayed nothing to Redbaer.

"But Lady Iveta is ... safe?"

"Safer than she'd be with you. Or should I say, your master?"

"What do you mean by that?"

"The game's up, Redbaer. We know about the boy, and we know who he is. That's why I'm here."

Redbaer paled. "Wh-who is he?"

"Some farm lad named Hodge. Trust me, I'd rather be any-where else. I just wanted to bring the lad's body home. One last good deed ... and look where it's bloody landed me."

Redbaer glanced nervously to his soldier, who made a show of not paying attention. Redbaer drew nearer to the bars.

"Listen to me, Hawley," he hissed. "Lestyn is here, and he wants you dead. That's why I came—I knew if Lestyn's men found you first, they'd kill you. But now he has to play by the rules. Now he has to wait for Hobb's word before he can execute you. There isn't much time."

"Why're you telling me this? You going to set me free?" Haw-ley scoffed.

Redbaer pushed something through the bars. A small knife.

Hawley didn't take it. "What am I s'posed to do with that?"

"Do what you must. There's little more I can do for you, but damn it, you don't deserve to hang."

Hawley pondered this, then took the knife. A little thing, with a handle of carved horn. Next to useless.

Redbaer sighed with relief all the same.

Hawley leaned in close and whispered, "You knew about the boy. You knew about Lord Scarsdale. You said nothing. So maybe you know who really kidnapped Anton Tarasq."

"I don't..." Redbaer spluttered.

"Who's the one in charge?" Hawley growled. "Scarsdale...or Meriet?"

"No...That is...I don't know. Meriet and the archduke keep close counsel. I always thought the abbot kept my lord in check, but...maybe..."

"Maybe what?" Hawley snapped, a little too angrily, causing the man with the lantern to reach for his sword.

Redbaer waved at him to stand down.

"Maybe you're right about Meriet," Redbaer said. "He appears to have advised my lord Scarsdale against fighting Clemence. I never thought I'd see the archduke capitulate so readily to such a blowhard. Meriet holds great influence over the archduke, but that's not proof of anything...is it? Beyond that, I swear I don't know any more than I've already told you."

"Sir..." the guard said nervously. "Someone's coming."

"Hide the knife," Redbaer said.

Hawley stepped back into the shadows.

The door swung open again. More lights were carried into the jail; footsteps approached.

"Redbaer?" Lestyn's high, caustic tone was unmistakable. "I gave no leave to interrogate the prisoner."

Hawley slumped to the floor of his cell, stuffing the knife into his boot.

"Forgive me, Vigilant Lestyn," Redbaer said, with unusual deference. "I was merely anxious for news of Lady Iveta."

"And?"

"He doesn't know where she is."

Lestyn glared down at Hawley. "You should know by now lies come as easy as breathing for this one. He shall tell us all we need to know before the end."

Hawley looked up. "You mean to execute me, then?"

"Once your commander arrives."

"Hobb's coming here?"

Lestyn smiled wickedly. "He barracks at Erecgham Abbey. Word has already been sent. Does that trouble you?"

"No more than your ugly face," Hawley said.

Lestyn's smile flickered into a snarl. "Hanging is too good for you. I'll be sure to recommend something more fitting."

"I'll wait for you in Uffærn. I'll have a warm welcome for you."

"Silence, dog!" Swire stepped into the light, face twisted with contempt, spittle flecking his blubbery lips.

Hawley forced his most wolfish grin, and stared threateningly into the stout soldier's eyes. Swire, momentarily unsure of himself, looked away, much to Hawley's satisfaction.

"Let us in there, sir, just for a minute," Swire said. "We should work on this one, in case he gets any ideas."

"Now, now, Swire," Lestyn said, "that won't be necessary. Not yet. Sir Redbaer, you were saying about Lady Iveta? I really do feel you should be out looking for her. We have things in hand."

"What are the charges?" Hawley interrupted.

Swire and Lestyn looked at him in surprise, like he was a talking animal.

"What are the charges against me?" Hawley demanded again.

"Theft," Lestyn said. "Of horses, wagon, and supplies. The assault of my guards. Kidnap."

"Kidnap?" Hawley spat.

"Aye, of Lady Iveta Snowsill of Scarfell. Cavorting with a suspected necromancer..."

"Prove it. Any of it."

"The defiled corpse you brought with you is proof of your mistress's dark arts."

"Defiled? Your own master was present, you worm. You can't hold me. You've no authority."

"Why?" Lestyn sneered. "You are no longer of the High Companies. Commander Hobb says you're a deserter. That, Holt Hawley, is a charge I *can* prove, for I have Hobb's written word that you had no leave to be at Scarfell. You know the sentence for desertion?"

Hawley nodded. Neither of them needed to say it was death by hanging.

"That will do for now," Lestyn said. "When I return, it shall be with questions. And if you desire a quick death, be prepared to answer them truthfully."

With that, he ushered Redbaer and the soldiers out. He presented a rictus grin to Hawley before following the others.

Hawley cursed.

"*Psst.* You...Hawley? That your name?"

Hawley squinted into the inky darkness, eyes still spotted with residual torchlight.

"Who wants to know?" he growled.

"My name's Amos...just a farmer."

"All right, Amos 'just a farmer.' Seems you're just a prisoner, like me." Hawley was in no mood for idle chatter, especially not with those condemned to the dark for who knew what crimes.

"Please...You mentioned Hodge. A boy called Hodge."

"What of it?"

"My nephew is Hodge. He's been lost this past month...My sister is beside herself with worry. You have news?"

Hawley rubbed at his face and mouthed another curse. These were hardly the ideal circumstances. But at least the boy's mother wasn't present to hear what Hawley had to say.

"Aye," Hawley said. "He's dead."

A gasp.

"I'm sorry," Hawley added as an afterthought.

A choked sob from the dark. Then, "The man next to you... his name's Bened. A simpleton. He's been arrested for Hodge's kidnap, and others."

"Then he's innocent," Hawley sighed. He pinched the bridge of his nose between finger and thumb. His head hurt. He'd come here on a mission of mercy, again led by the sense of duty that always seemed to land him in trouble. But now he was here, he just needed time to think.

"You must tell them," Amos said. "Bened never harmed any-one. He doesn't understand what's happening to him."

"Not my problem, friend," Hawley snapped. "They won't lis-ten to anything I've got to say about this Bened, or Hodge, or anything else. They're going to hang me...if I'm lucky."

There was silence for a while. Then the man spoke again.

"Do you...know how it happened? How Hodge died?"

Hawley hoisted himself to his feet again and checked the strength of his manacles half-heartedly. "Aye," he said. "Lord Scarsdale strangled him."

A chorus of gasps now. A muttered prayer in the dark.

"A cruel jest. A foolish one," Amos said.

"If you knew me, friend, you'd know I don't jest. And foolish? Ha! What more can they do to me? They'll execute me without trial. Might as well speak the truth in the time I've got left. I'm done serving these bastards. I'm done serving anyone."

"So you are the one they spoke of. The deserter. High Companies."

Hawley shot a glare into the shadows. "What've you heard?"

"They were talking about you. They thought you might be bound for the abbey."

"Erecgham? Why would they think I was going there?"

"You mentioned Abbot Meriet before—it was one of his monks, came by yesterday. Said his master was worried—you'd taken a dislike to him, and were wont to murder him."

Hawley snorted a rueful laugh. "He's not wrong."

"Don't take the abbot's name in vain here. He's been a friend to this village. I doubt we'd have made it through the winter were it not for the reverend father."

Hawley shook his head. It seemed everyone was taken in by the Flaescines. "What else did the monk say?"

"That a rider had been sent along the east road to look for Commander Hobb. That the men of the Third Company were on their way to protect the abbot."

Curious, Hawley thought. Enelda had openly protested the abbot's innocence. So what had gotten Meriet so scared? And why would Hobb answer Meriet's call? Surely he had more important things to do.

Hawley's thoughts were rudely disturbed. The snoring to his right stopped with an abrupt, porcine snort. Then came the rattling of chains, frantic, as the man flailed about. Finally, a scream— more a bellow, the roar of an angry bull. Hawley saw only a massive, dark shape leap upwards in the cramped cell beside him, and rush first to the door, then to the bars that separated them. A pair of enormous, hairy-knuckled hands wrapped around the iron bars, and powerful arms shook them so the whole cell rattled.

Hawley pressed his back against cold iron, as far away from the bellowing as possible. Hawley's head told him it was this Bened fellow. But in his mind he pictured only a huge black shadow with yellow eyes and sharp teeth.

The bellow became a howl, which tailed off into a sob. The man slunk to his knees, hands still gripping the bars tightly. Then he sobbed.

"There, there, Bened." Amos's voice again. "You're with friends. Remember? Don't be afraid."

"Don't like the dark!" Bened wailed.

"What did we say about the dark?" Amos said, his tone singsong, like he was telling a story to a child. "The dark is just...?"

Bened sniffed loudly and phlegmily, and mumbled, "Places where the gods aren't looking."

"That's right. And when the sun comes up, the gods will look again."

Hawley puffed out his cheeks and blew out a protracted sigh. The last thing he needed was to be stuck in the middle of... whatever this was. "What's wrong with him?"

"Nothing," Amos replied guardedly. "He's just scared, is all. He's no more than a child himself."

Hawley looked warily at the hulking figure in the next cell. "Some child..." he muttered. Then, louder, "You say he's charged with kidnapping?"

"I never!" Bened shouted, tugging on the bars so hard Hawley truly thought they might bend. "Bened is a good boy!"

"All right, Bened," Hawley said, the same way he'd talk to a skittish horse. "I believe you. Settle down."

"That's why they arrested him, true enough," Amos said. "Because he's friends with the children. On account of his mind being—well...you can see."

"Aye."

"That was enough for the Vigilant to arrest him. Says he must be behind all the disappearances hereabout, stretching back years."

It made no sense, naturally. How could peasants—strangers to each other, in far-flung settlements—be responsible for the mysterious disappearances of so many children? And what about Anton Tarasq? Lestyn was vile, but he was no fool. He knew what he did was wrong, but he did it anyway.

Bened started to cry.

"Quiet, Bened!" Hawley snapped, his head still throbbing. "They won't hang you. Even Lestyn needs evidence."

"Not if he has a confession," Amos said. "Bened didn't last a day. Confessed to abduction, witchcraft...Murder. Now he can barely talk."

Hawley winced. He reminded himself that not so long ago he'd have dragged the man to the gallows himself without question, if orders dictated. And when he asked himself why he wouldn't do it now, his only answer was:

Enelda Drake.

"How many children we talking about?" Hawley asked. He pushed thoughts of Enelda aside.

"Two this year," Amos answered. "First Aggie. Then poor Hodge..." The man cleared his throat, but his grief was palpable. "Four last year: Effery, Anna, Ysmine, and Kol. Three the year before that...There's others. It's been hard, with so few bairns. This village is dying."

"How long's this been going on for?" Hawley asked.

"I remember when it started—a black day indeed. Ten years ago, almost to the day."

"When Lord Scarsdale's daughter was abducted by her own wet nurse," Hawley said.

"You know about that? Well, aye, it's true. She was taken in here by Mother Florell, an elder. Poor old cow was hanged for her part in it, but how could she have known? She thought she was sheltering a poor woman and her babe from a storm."

"Do you know anything about the nurse? Why she came here?"

"Only what I was told. Said she'd come seeking the blessing of St. Baerloc for the babe. But she never made it to Erecgham. She was sick, see. She ran off into the Northwood with the child, gave us all a scare. Then the soldiers came, an' that was that."

"And I suppose the Vigilants have paid close attention to Raecswold since?" Hawley asked.

"You'd think so, but no; we barely saw a Vigilant 'til last year. That's when they built this jail and started sending militia through now and then. But things have only gotten worse since then. Vigilant Lestyn is more like to confiscate our grain and levy extra taxes than he is to find them bairns. Earl Wynchell is our lord, but he cares not for the likes of us. So mostly we go to the abbey just over yon, and petition the abbot. He's taken up our plight with Lord Scarsdale directly, so he says. And true enough, the archduke has been to the abbey many times, and even come here once or twice, which was unheard of years ago. But still nothing has been done."

"Aside from building this jail," Hawley mused.

"Aye, aside from that. A jail that holds our own villagers more often than not, and most of them arrested go to hang."

"Or burn." Hawley let the word hang in the air.

Silence. Then, "What do you know of that?"

"They say the Witches of Wyverne came here before they were executed for their black arts."

"No!" Bened cried out, rattling the bars in agitation. "*No-no-no-no!*"

"Enough, Bened!" Amos snapped, his gentle patience worn thin.

"He knew the Thrussels, I take it?" Hawley pressed.

Stony silence now. Hawley fancied he'd struck a nerve.

"Why'd they come here? The witches," Hawley asked.

"I...wouldn't know."

"Visiting the abbey, I s'pose?"

"No. They were wicked people," Amos said. "Comin' here during a holy festival...The Thrussels brought a curse upon this place. I doubt they'd have dared stand in the presence of Abbot Meriet."

"So they came here and practised their dark arts. And you allowed it?"

"We did not!" Amos gasped. "Indeed not. The Thrussels spent most of their time in the Northwood. No one goes to the Northwood."

"Except witches and child-snatchers?"

Another long silence. The garrulous farmer had lost his tongue.

"So tell me, Amos," Hawley said, "in this village of sin, what're you in here for?"

"*Pah.* Not the black arts, that's for sure. Simple disobedience, s'all. Vigilant Lestyn demanded food from our stores to feed his men. We told him we had little to spare but would share what we could. That wasn't good enough, so he took one of my brother's bulls and slaughtered it. That bull was our best stud—we'll have no calves come spring now. My brother is a meek man, so I spoke up for him. For that, Lestyn took three of my goats and had his men feast on them, too. I stood in their way when they came back for more. Told him I'd take the cost of the goats from the annual tithe. That was that—he threw me in this cell, on a charge of agitation and refusal to pay my due. Can't afford to hang me, or there'll be few enough left in Raecswold who can work. He'll flog me 'til my bones show. Gods know what my wife'll do while I'm laid low. Who'll run the farm? How will we survive?"

Hawley had stopped listening, though the criss-crossed scars across his own back began to itch in sympathy. Hawley was holding his talisman, rolling the woven stalks between his rough fingers. How many more would suffer before the truth came out? How many innocent men arrested, and children abducted for some sinister purpose? And should Hawley die here, what then? He no longer thought Enelda capable of serving justice. Who here cared about these children?

Through the small window, the weak light was already reddening. Hawley had wasted a whole day in his cell, each passing moment bringing him closer to a reunion with Commander Hobb.

He patted the knife in his boot. That's what he was keeping it for. It was a fool's fancy to dream of escape. He was no hero of the people: He would no more honour his promise to find Mildrith than he would find Anton Tarasq. Hawley had an appointment with the gallows; there was no avoiding it. But if he had a chance—the smallest chance—he'd take Hobb with him. Hobb was the architect of Hawley's misfortunes, and by the gods he would have at least that small revenge before his time was done.

"Hawley," Amos whispered urgently. "What are you going to do?"

Hawley rubbed his hand across his face and said, "Sleep. I suggest you do the same."

With that, he slumped down to the cold floor of his cell and did his best to fall asleep, with Bened's soft sobs echoing around the stones.

CHAPTER 34

Hawley dreamed not, for once, of ravening shadows in distant forests, but of Fort Fangmoor.

He knelt on hard flagstones, in a narrow courtyard bounded on all sides by high grey walls. Around him stood several ranks of straight-backed soldiers, his brothers in arms, ceremonial spears at their sides.

Hawley stretched out his neck, heavy wooden stocks rubbing his skin raw. On the balcony above, Commander Morgard's lined face looked more dour than ever.

Captain Hobb paced the courtyard, the heels of his polished boots rapping the stones. He was delivering a speech about honour, duty, betrayal. How the Third were destined for a great fate in the annals of history, and how each failure diminished their glory.

Hawley had heard it all before. Hobb's words were a drone, the buzz of flies around a stable. Around a corpse. He hadn't noticed when Hobb stopped proselytising. Now the captain glared down at Hawley, who could barely raise his head in defiance. Behind Hobb, Morgard nodded.

Crack!

The pain was like fire, licking across Hawley's back. He didn't cry out. His teeth clamped on the leather bit. The whip cracked loud, the only sound in the courtyard. Hawley's brothers watched with mistrust in their eyes. Holt Hawley had seen his troop slaughtered at Herigsburg. Holt Hawley had not followed orders, and his brothers had died as a result. He had brought shame on the Third.

Crack!

Blood oozed down Hawley's back. He bit down so hard he thought his jaw might break.

Crack!

Hawley hadn't expected it to hurt so much. His vision filled with a thousand pinpricks of blinding light. When lesser soldiers were flogged, they were tied to a whipping post, and the punishment continued even if they fell unconscious. When a High Companies soldier was flogged, they had to carry their own stocks and stay upright under their own strength. If they passed out, they would be revived, and the punishment would start over. It had been known to take all day and night.

Crack! Crack! Crack!

Hawley lost count of the lashes. The bit fell from his mouth, but by then he didn't need it. He was barely conscious. His head sagged. Time and again he slumped, almost unconscious, but each time he forced himself awake. Each time he defied Hobb. He would not fall.

He only knew it was over when water was thrown over his back, and he watched his own blood wash between the cracks in the stones.

Every soldier thudded the base of their spears on the ground in unison.

"*Ra-Hoo! Ra-Hoo!*" they shouted, the chorus deafening.

Hobb knelt, pulled back Hawley's head by a handful of hair. Hawley looked upon that thin, bloodless face, grey eyes expressionless; more statue than man, a product of generations within "the Blood," where children were born soldiers, every ounce of compassion drummed out of them before they came of age.

"You are a blight on this company," he snarled. "'Awearg,' they call you. Tainted blood. Ill-omened. If I had my way, you'd be dancing a jig from the end of a rope, but the old man has other ideas. Just remember this, *Sargent*: Morgard is old. He won't be around forever. When he's gone, I'll see justice is done."

Hawley hacked up what little phlegm he could muster, and spat it onto the flagstones between Hobb's shiny boots.

Hobb drew back in disgust. He stood, and turned to Morgard, who only nodded again.

The soldiers thudded their spears thrice more. *"Ra-Hoo! Ra-Hoo!..."*

* * *

"...Ra-Hoo!"

Hawley jolted awake. The spears thudded too loud, the guttural refrain accompanying them too real. He looked around in confusion. Cold, grey eyes met his.

Hobb was crouched low on the other side of the bars, a wicked smile on his lips. His face gleamed in the early morning light like smooth alabaster; he'd always looked younger than his years, like the corpse of a young man preserved by unnatural means.

Three High Companies men stood behind him, fully armoured. Their helms hid their faces.

"Sleep well?" Hobb asked.

Hawley clambered to his feet slowly, fighting against stiff joints and aching muscles as though he'd aged thirty years overnight.

Hobb rose to meet him. He ran a gloved hand through his hair. "No salute for your commander?" he said.

"Lestyn tells me I'm not a soldier any more," Hawley growled. "So you're not my commander."

"Your crimes were committed as a soldier, so you'll be tried as one."

"Crimes?" Hawley half stifled a bitter laugh. "What about yours? You tried to have me killed."

"You have evidence to support this claim?"

"The only witnesses were the assassins," Hawley said.

"Assassins indeed? You mean the men under your command? Tell me, Hawley, where are they now?"

Hawley said nothing, but stared unflinchingly into Hobb's eyes, with all the menace he could muster. Hobb didn't look at all flustered. He was a man apart—quite different from a jumped-up bully like Lestyn. For all Hobb's moral failings, his pettiness, his grating sense of superiority, he was still not a man with whom to trifle.

"Let me answer for you," Hobb said. "They're dead. Men of the High Companies deserve better than to be butchered in some northern wilderness by a turncoat."

Hobb held out his hand to one of the men behind him. The soldier passed him a heavy Felder bastard sword, scabbarded in leather. Godspeaker.

"Butchered," Hobb went on, "with this very blade. A symbol of our great company, defiled by a traitor. A deserter. A *murderer*."

Hawley threw himself at the cell door. He reached through the bars as far as his manacles would allow. Hobb took a half step back. Two soldiers came forward, crossing spears in front of their commander. Clockwork soldiers, drilled and efficient. Men Hawley had fought with, supped with. Men who doubtless hated him just as much as Beacher had.

Hawley withdrew. The spears parted.

Hobb's lips twisted upwards a little more at the corners. "What of the recruit?" he asked. "Ianto. Why would he wish you harm? He barely knew you."

"You know damn well why. Why was Ianto even inducted into the Third? He was no soldier, he was a monk. One of Meriet's saint-worshippers. So, 'commander': Where'd you barrack last night? How much of Meriet's silver lines your purse?"

Hobb tutted and wagged a finger. "Well, well...It seems you really have been taken in by that old crone. Convinced you she was a True Vigilant, did she?"

"As it happens, she thinks the sun shines out of Meriet's arse. But I see through him like I see through you." Hawley felt liberated for the first time in his life. More free within this cell than at any time marching to the drum of his commanders.

Hobb's eyes narrowed, his mouth tightened. Finally, a reaction.

"And to think I came here to let you atone. To perhaps avoid the gallows."

"No you didn't," Hawley said. "You came to gloat. 'Cause you're a petty shade of a soldier, not fit to lick the boots of the man you replaced."

"A pox on you, Hawley," Hobb spat. The sudden outburst, its viciousness, caused the men at his back to flinch. "You always were Morgard's lapdog. I admired the old man as much as any. But when he put his stock in mongrels; when he failed to see *you* for what you truly were...when he gave you *this*..." He held up the sword. "That was when I realised he was no more fit for command. I saw it. The men saw it. 'Awearg,' they call you, and awearg you are! Bad luck follows you like flies around the dead. When at last you swing from the gibbet, a shadow will lift from our company. The Third shall once more march to glory."

"March? You expecting a war?"

Hobb stopped. He stroked his long face and smoothed his hair, setting his features firm once more.

"The next time our company sees war," Hobb said, quietly and calmly, "you shall not be around to bring us misfortune. Your name shall be struck from the record. No man shall ever speak of you. It will be as though Holt Hawley had never existed."

Hawley shrugged. "I came from nothing. I'll go out that way. Least I can say I tried."

Hobb scoffed. "Well, you won't have to try much longer. You hang at noon."

Hobb turned on his heels, and the men with him. They'd barely taken three strides when Hawley called to Hobb. The commander paused.

"They confessed everything," Hawley said. "Beacher, Tarbert, Nedley...spilled their guts. They took a blood oath to kill me, on your order. You think I'd come back to Fangmoor knowing that?"

The soldiers' eyes twitched. Perhaps this was news to them. Perhaps they were just surprised Hawley knew.

"I care not what they said. I care not what you say." Hobb sniffed.

"Couldn't bring yourself to sully your lily-white hands, could you?" Hawley leaned forward on the bars of his cell door. "Just so you know, they died like dogs, but not on my sword. It was Riftborn that did 'em. If I really am awearg, maybe they came at my bidding. Maybe they'll come for you, too." He forced a wolfish grin. Hobb was no longer looking at him, but the soldiers were. Superstitious bastards, like most of the men at Fangmoor. He could see the uncertainty in their eyes.

Hobb tarried no longer. He strode to the door, snapping his fingers so the soldiers followed in his wake. A moment later, the heavy door slammed shut behind him, and the jail was quiet once more.

*　　*　　*

The first time Swire had come, it was just to get even. It took two of them to hold Hawley down while Swire beat him. When Hawley had woken up face down in the dirt, he was so sore he couldn't tell where one injury ended and the other began.

The next time he came, it was with Lestyn. Hawley hadn't the strength to resist as Swire and his men strung him up by his manacled wrists so that he dangled from the ceiling like a fresh carcass in a slaughterhouse.

Then the questions began. The same three questions, over and over.

"Where is Lady Iveta?"

"How should I know?"

Thump. A cudgel to his cracked rib, making sure it was broken.

"Where is Anton Tarasq?"

"Shit on you."

Crack. A cat-o'-nine-tails sliced open Hawley's back. He grimaced. He would not cry out.

"Is Enelda Drake in league with the Riftborn?"

Hawley had accused her of as much himself, but hearing it from Lestyn's lips sounded ridiculous. He laughed at his torturers, like a maniac. Lestyn asked the question again. Hawley kept laughing as fists and cudgels pummelled him, and his blood flowed to the cell floor in rivulets. When Lestyn came forward to gloat, Hawley spat blood in his doughy face.

For that, they'd cut Hawley down, and Swire grinned as he kicked him unconscious.

At least it put an end to the questioning.

Hawley woke with one eye fully closed by swelling. With his good eye, he counted the hours watching the small square of sunlight from the window slide up the wall. Outside, the hammering was incessant. Soldiers, erecting the gallows.

Occasionally, Hawley would hear Amos whispering. Sometimes Bened would stop sniffling, and instead babble to himself, before jumping up and rattling the bars. He'd always tire himself out eventually and slump back to the floor with a whimper.

As noon approached, the hammering finally stopped. All fell silent.

Hawley thought he'd be thankful for the peace, but he wasn't. All he could think about was his failure, his broken promises, his bitter parting from Enelda. He wondered what had become of Iveta, and resolved to tell Redbaer where she'd headed, if he saw the knight again before the end.

The jail door swung open. The Vigilant Guard marched in, single file. They went past Hawley's cell, one by one. Swire was the last of them, and he spat at Hawley from the door. Hawley hadn't the energy to stand.

They opened Bened's cell. Two soldiers went in, kicked the big man awake.

Bened curled into a ball and squealed like an injured child. It took both soldiers to drag him into the passage, and a third to finally hoist Bened to his feet. The man's rubbery features quivered with terror.

Swire grinned at Hawley. "Testing the gallows with this one... make sure it's ready for you."

"I thought he was for questioning," Hawley said.

"He confessed. We'll put him out of his misery, then we'll come back for you."

They hauled Bened along the passage. Amos and a couple of others pawed at him as he passed. Then they were gone, and the door was closed again.

The faint sound of Lestyn's voice drifted into the jail, rising and falling in pitch as he read some proclamation of trumped-up charges.

Bened wailed like a banshee. A drummer struck up a sombre beat to drown him out.

Hawley closed his good eye. The drums stopped, and the trap-door thudded.

Amos cried out in anguish. It was done.

Another prolonged silence. Hawley guessed they were clearing away Bened's body. Another innocent tossed as fuel to the pyre. More evidence lost.

Hawley waited for the soldiers to come. Instead, he felt only a low tremble of the ground, and slowly the sound of hoofbeats grew louder, reverberating through the mossy flagstones of the jail.

A large number of horsemen drew to a halt outside. Hawley heard shouts of alarm, then of anger. Orders were barked. Mail-shod boots pounded stony ground.

There was a fight brewing.

Hawley clambered to his feet. He tried to jump up to the window, but not only was it too high, the effort caused pain to shoot from his ribs to his cracked head. So he leaned against the wall and listened.

More muffled voices. Hawley was sure he heard Hobb, but couldn't tell what he was saying.

The jail door flew open abruptly, banging loudly in its frame. Two of the High Companies men marched in, and Hobb followed, face like thunder. A moment later, the soldiers were in Hawley's cell. They grabbed him roughly by the arms.

"For a cursed man you have uncommon luck, Sarge," one of them whispered.

Hawley examined the man's eyes through the slit of his helmet. He did know him.

"Sherrat?" he asked. Armsman Sherrat was a decent man. One of the few who'd break bread with Hawley.

"Silence!" Hobb snapped. "Bring the prisoner. Let's get this over with." He made a face as though his words were hornets in his mouth.

"What's happening?" Hawley asked. Sherrat averted his eyes, disheartened by Hobb's reprimand.

They half dragged Hawley from the jail. The light stung his eyes. He took a grateful gulp of cleaner air and looked warily at the gallows, the trapdoor still hanging loose from Bened's drop. Soldiers flanked the gibbet, some in Scarfell green, some in Vigilant black. They faced not Hawley, but away, towards a row of formidable-looking horsemen, spears aloft, pennants fluttering.

Blue pennants, adorned with silver towers. Sylven pennants.

Hawley craned his neck to see over the heads of the soldiers.

In the centre of the horsemen was a small cabal—commanders, singular in their appearance: A man in black, cloaked, with a wide-brimmed hat pulled low over his eyes against the sun. Beside him, a young ensign carrying a white flag of parley. Next to the youth, on a sturdy warhorse too big for her, was an old woman dressed in grey, white hair tumbling rebelliously about her shoulders, a knotted staff held up like a royal standard.

That she was here with Sylven soldiers, itself an act of war, barely mattered. What was one more rule broken, as she'd said?

A hand shoved Hawley forward. Soldiers parted for him. Hobb grabbed Hawley's collar and dragged him forth himself.

"Here he is," Hobb shouted. "But by the gods you will not have him. He is sentenced to death."

"On what charge?" the man in black called out, in heavily accented Aeldritch.

"Dereliction of duty, murder, desertion, and treason."

"No, Commander Hobb. I hear this man was sent to find a True Vigilant, perhaps the last Vigilant in all the world. She tells me his own men tried to kill him, and if they had succeeded, she would still be lost to us. If this Hawley had reason to fear for his life, it excuses his actions, no?"

"Fearing justice, you mean," Hobb snapped. "You've made a mistake bringing soldiers here, Sauveur."

"You would threaten me under a flag of parley?"

"I threaten foreign soldiers on Aelder soil in contravention of the Accords."

Sauveur shrugged. "You don't have enough men to kill us. If you did, it would be done already. Besides, when the truth comes out, I doubt even your boy king will see it your way."

"What truth?" Hobb's grip tightened on Hawley's collar.

Hawley knew Hobb was weighing up the numbers. There were eight of the Vigilant Guard, Redbaer and five castle guards, and, crucially, five soldiers of the Third. Hawley counted fifteen riders, and an unknown number of men on foot behind them. And women, too, he noted. The Sylvens, much like the Felders, had no rules forbidding women service to their king as long as they could swing a sword.

The odds were bad for Hobb, but not insurmountable.

Sauveur spoke again, confident in his own strength. "Vigilant Drake has shown me compelling evidence that your land is plagued by evil, and it is not of our doing. I have heard stories of witchcraft. I have heard tell that Anton Tarasq was stolen away by us—his own people! I am here to set right such scurrilous rumours. I am here to help Vigilant Drake find my general's son and bring justice to this cursed land."

"We do not recognise this woman as a Vigilant!" a shrill voice cried. Lestyn pushed his way forward. His men crowded around him protectively. "I am justiciar here, not you, Sauveur."

"Be silent, you odious little man!" Enelda Drake finally spoke. Lestyn's mouth dropped open. "Commander Hobb, see reason. There's no need for a fight today. Let Hawley go, and come with us. I will show you the evidence you need. There is still time to do the right thing."

Hobb's eyes narrowed. "The right thing..." he muttered. And to Hawley's dismay, Hobb drew his sword and shouted, "Men of the Third, to arms!"

Hobb yanked hard on Hawley's collar. Hawley doubled over. The two soldiers who had held Hawley's arms released him, stepping forward, thick armour plates facing the enemy, swords readied. The others followed suit with a cry of "Ra-Hoo!" Then the Vigilant Guard presented spears, and the castle guard with them.

The Sylven cavalry line thinned. A dozen soldiers rushed forward to fill the gaps, crossbows ready.

Everyone paused, waiting to see who'd strike first, each expecting the other to back down. Enelda Drake shook her head wearily.

Along the line, Redbaer looked back, his eyes meeting Hawley's for just a moment. And something in the look he gave mirrored Hawley's own thoughts.

From his prostrate position, Hawley was almost able to reach his boot. He stretched, fingertips feeling for the knife.

Hobb raised his sword. "This is your last chance, Sauveur. Think carefully—the last act of your miserable life will be to reignite war between—"

Hawley pushed upwards, breaking Hobb's grasp. He wrapped his manacles around Hobb's neck, and pressed the small blade to his throat. "That's enough," Hawley growled.

The men turned their swords on Hawley.

"Tell them to stand down, or I'll slit your throat."

"You wouldn't dare. If I die, you follow. You know they won't hesitate."

"Think I'm afraid to die? This was always the plan. I was going to kill you before I swung from the noose. I'd be doing the Third one last service."

Hobb grunted as the chains bit into his throat. He held up a hand to stay the swords of his men. "You...you'll kill me anyway."

"Order the Third to surrender, and I'll spare you. Denying my revenge is a small price to pay for maintaining the long peace." Hawley pricked the flesh of Hobb's neck with the point of the knife.

Hobb hesitated. He was not a good man, but he was no coward. To Hawley's relief, he relented. Hobb threw his sword to the ground.

"Sheathe your swords," he said. The soldiers did not comply at once, and Hobb grunted, "That's an order!"

Sherrat was first to obey. At his gesture, the others complied as one, sheathing their swords, taking one step back. The Vigilant Guard looked around, confused.

"No!" Lestyn shrieked. He stepped into the no-man's-land between the two forces. He pointed a bony finger at Hawley. "Kill that man! Kill him, and fight! Fight for your king!"

"Sir Redbaer," Enelda called. "If you do not trust Monsieur Sauveur, then trust me. Do your duty to your household, to your mearca. Arrest Vigilant Lestyn."

"On what charge?" Redbaer called back.

"Corruption. Embezzlement. Racketeering. That will do for now."

Redbaer took a deep breath and gave the order. His men turned on the Vigilant Guard. Swire and his fellows closed ranks around Lestyn, prompting the Sylven crossbows to take aim. The black-uniformed guards' resolve drained away in an instant. The castle guard pushed them aside with little resistance.

Redbaer grabbed Lestyn by the throat. "I've waited a long time for this," he said. Then to his soldiers, "I want these men in irons."

Soon, Amos and the other prisoners were led from the jail, blinking astonishedly. At sword point, Swire and the Vigilant Guard were encouraged inside to take their places.

"Let him go, Hawley." Redbaer nodded to Hobb. "Commander Hobb, do I have your word as an officer that you and your men will stand aside?"

"You'll hang with Hawley," Hobb snarled.

Hawley gave a pull on the manacles, drawing a yelp from his old commander. The High Companies soldiers tensed; Hawley didn't want to push things much further. They might easily choose to fight after all, for the honour of the Third, numbers be damned.

"You have my word," Hobb said at last, through teeth gritted both with discomfort and ignominy.

Hawley sent Hobb into the arms of his men with a shove.

Hobb wheeled around angrily.

Redbaer stepped between them. "You gave your word, Hobb. Don't take up arms, or you'll be sharing a cell with Lestyn."

Hobb rubbed at his neck, now raw and red. "Once a Borderer, always a Borderer! This is treason."

"Not for you to decide. Not today. I intend to hear what the Vigilant has to say. If she's right, we'll all stand to learn a thing or two. If she's wrong...well then, I suppose your hangman will have me and Hawley both."

"I'll have these manacles off," Hawley said.

Redbaer waved over a young soldier, took a key from him, and unlocked the iron cuffs.

Hawley rubbed at his wrists gratefully. He looked to Hobb once more and growled, "And my sword."

"Property of the Third," Hobb said.

"It was given to me."

"You were its custodian. You are its custodian no longer."

Redbaer shrugged at Hawley. "I wouldn't push your luck, Sarg—*Master* Hawley."

Master. Even that hurt. What was Hawley now? A freeman? No, not until he'd cleared his name. So he couldn't be called Master Hawley at all, except as a courtesy. He was nothing but an outlaw, with no guarantee he'd amount to anything more before his time was up.

Hoofbeats thudded across the no-man's-land. Sauveur pulled up, his ensign with him, the white flag aloft. He touched the brim of his hat in salute.

"Thank you, Sir Redbaer, for your good sense. And to you, Commander Hobb...I hope it will not be war between our people, truly I do. But if it comes to it, we will be ready."

"As will we," Hobb replied.

"Come, Hawley," Sauveur said. "Much has been risked here today, and some of it for you. Be grateful you have a friend in Vigilant Drake. Now leave here peaceably, and give thanks for your good fortune."

Hawley took one last look at Hobb, who gave him a mocking smile.

Hawley clenched his fists.

"Go with Sauveur," Redbaer said, placing a hand on Hawley's shoulder.

Sauveur turned his horse and trotted back to the line of

Sylvens, where Enelda waited. Something in her eyes encouraged Hawley to push aside his bitterness. Redbaer slapped him on the arm, and they walked together in Sauveur's wake.

"Coward," Hobb called out.

"Ignore him," Redbaer said quietly.

Hawley took another step, trying his best to rise above it.

"Traitor. Coward," Hobb persisted. "You have sullied the name of the Third. You have brought a curse upon us that will not be lifted until you're dead. And worse, you've blackened the good name of Commander Morgard. Ever will he be known as the man who recruited Holt Hawley, the traitor."

Hawley stopped. He took a deep breath.

"I'll see to it that Morgard's name is never uttered again. I swear by all the gods, when we return to Fangmoor I'll have this butcher's blade melted down. It's cursed, like you. Like Morgard."

Hawley spun around and fixed Hobb with a murderous glare. Redbaer swore.

Hobb smiled. "You want the sword, Hawley? Fight me for it."

"Hawley, don't..." Redbaer cautioned.

"Fight me," Hobb repeated. "Sauveur, Redbaer, you are my witnesses! Hawley has evaded punishment, and so I offer trial by combat, as is my ancient right. A Sylven tradition, but one we gladly keep alive. Do you hear me? I challenge you, Holt Hawley, under the eyes of the gods. By Sygel and Vanya; by Haelstor and Feorngyr; by Nysta and Litha; by the Three and all the saints, I challenge you."

Hawley felt anger swell in his breast. He knew it was folly—knew it right through his bones—but his eyes blurred with rage and hatred for this man he'd once saluted. He was vaguely aware of more than one voice imploring him to resist.

"To the death?" Hawley shouted back.

"To the death," Hobb confirmed.

"Fine by me."

CHAPTER 35

Hawley sat on the stump of an old ironwood, glaring down the hill at the jail, where Hobb and his men waited, under the watchful eye of the Sylvens.

"All you had to do was walk away," Enelda said.

"That's the one thing I couldn't do," Hawley said.

"You men and your pride... You owe them nothing. You could come away now and forget about the duel."

"How? I accepted."

"*Pish!* Hobb has made you an outlaw, and what is the word of an outlaw worth? So a few men think less of you. They might even call you a coward. But what of it? Does their opinion matter to you?"

"No. But my own does. If I leave now, it *would* be cowardly, and how could I live with that? I got myself into this, and I'll get myself out of it."

"You'll get yourself killed. Look down there. You know Hobb. Does he strike you as someone who would pick a fight he couldn't win? He's a swordsman, Hawley. He was eyeing you up like a cut of meat. He's a cold-blooded killer."

"And I'm not?"

"No. You keep saying it to punish yourself, but you're no killer. You are a soldier, a fighter. But it's battle lust and desperation and sheer bloody-mindedness that drive you in battle. You are no murderer. But Hobb... He'll take you apart piece by piece, and he'll rely on your rage to blind you."

"I can't stop being angry. Not at him."

Enelda sighed. "I know. And that's why you'll lose."

Hawley felt a lump in his throat. "You believe that?"

Enelda nodded. "I saw you fight those riders, and it was a thing to behold. But you can't beat Hobb with brute strength. Even if you could, by some miracle, what then? You won't win your freedom, whatever Hobb says. You'll be hunted to the end of your days. You must walk away."

This wasn't the reunion Hawley had hoped for. It wasn't what he needed to hear. "I can't," he answered.

"Then either use your head and prove me wrong, or die swiftly. I could not bear to see you suffer."

*　*　*

The soldiers of every stripe had formed a large circle near the jail—fittingly, in the shadow of the gibbet. Tradition dictated the circle be twenty paces across, and any combatant seeking to leave it would be pushed back into the fight by soldiers bearing shields. That, or forfeit the challenge, and their life.

Hawley tested the ground with a stamp. It was still muddy from yesterday's rain, uneven and pockmarked with deep brown puddles where the Sylven riders and marching militia had churned it up. The footing would be treacherous. Poor conditions for a duel.

Across the circle, Hobb took a few experimental swings with his sword. A fine weapon—a Third Company cavalry sword. The blade was a handspan longer than an infantry shortsword, and almost an inch narrower. It was finely balanced, polished and honed, chased with bronze filigree. Hobb's armour was of similar quality. On his left arm he wore the pauldron, gardbrace, and rerebrace of all his company, but Hobb's was finer, lighter, and more ornate than any armsman's. His officer's helmet was open-faced save for the noseguard, and bore a tall horsehair plume dyed crimson. Despite the muddy ground, there wasn't a speck of dirt on him. Shit never stuck to Hobb.

Hawley, on the other hand, had been denied his shortsword

and armour: the tools of a loyal soldier, he'd been reminded, not a deserter. Instead, he wore an uncomfortable dark leather jerkin requisitioned from Swire—the only man whose armour was broad enough to fit—and an ugly Sylven helmet with a flat top and eye slits that allowed only a narrow field of vision to his front. But he did have the sword.

Hobb had thrown the Felder sword to the ground with contempt. "It's cursed, like you," he'd sneered. "Use it one last time."

Hawley was thankful for it, perhaps more than Hobb realised. It meant he couldn't use a shield and wield the large sword effectively, as Hobb had doubtless planned. Instead, he'd accepted the loan of a steel buckler from a Sylven crossbowman. It felt like a tin plate on the back of Hawley's left hand, but it was better than nothing. For the first time, the reality of his situation hit home. He felt naked without his High Companies armour. And worse, he felt dispossessed of all he'd ever earned, all he'd ever aspired to.

"End it quickly, Hawley." Redbaer stood at Hawley's shoulder, forming part of the ring of shields. "You're in no shape for a prolonged fight, and every swing of that ridiculous sword will sap your strength. The longer it goes on, the more it favours Hobb."

"I've been swinging this sword for many a year," Hawley growled. Redbaer was stating the obvious, but Hawley wasn't yet ready to acknowledge it.

"Not against Hobb."

"I know Hobb better than you." What Hawley didn't say was that most of the stories were true. Hobb was formidable. He'd rarely seen real combat, and had graced the training grounds of Fangmoor in rarer circumstances still. But when he had, he'd fought unlike any other brother of the Third. Whether in the wall of steel, or with two swords, or spear, or even polearm, Hobb was as skillful as any man alive. Some said he was even better than Morgard had been in his prime. But without a war—a real war—to test him, how could anyone know for sure?

"Any last words of advice?" Hawley asked of Redbaer.

"Don't get killed."

"Thanks." Hawley looked about the circle. Sauveur waited in the centre, having agreed to officiate—it was, after all, a Sylven tradition that they now honoured. There was no sign of Enelda. Hawley didn't really blame her for not wanting to watch him get killed.

A drummer struck up a slow, monotonous beat. It grew faster, became a roll, and stopped. The whole village fell silent.

Hobb stepped up, swinging his sword. It sliced the air with a whistle.

Hawley went to meet his foe.

"This challenge has been called in the presence of all the gods of this land," Sauveur announced. "It is under their gaze that you must fight. I need not tell you this is a matter of honour, and so you should refrain from any action that might call into question that honour. Do you understand?"

Both men nodded.

"And you submit to the judgement of the gods?"

"Aye," Hawley said. Hobb simply nodded again.

Sauveur took five long paces back. He held a black cloth aloft.

Hobb stared coolly into Hawley's eyes.

Hawley tightened his grip on Godspeaker's hilt. The leather creaked.

Sauveur dropped the cloth.

At that signal, Hawley launched forward, his first swing double-handed, striking the air as Hobb jumped backwards. The second was a backswing, one-handed. Hobb barely parried it in time. A third, a fourth, all of Hawley's strength behind them. Hobb seemed ill-prepared for the raw fury of the assault. He moved backwards quickly, sure-footedly at first, then slipping and sliding in the churned earth. Another blow glanced from Hobb's vambrace. The commander tried to counter-thrust, but not even the cavalry blade could compensate for Hawley's reach. Godspeaker arced down with visceral force. Hobb's arm-shield clicked into place; Hawley's blade rang off it. The force of the blow jarred Hawley's arm and dented Hobb's armour, but still the commander stood.

Hawley roared, and battered at Hobb again and again. No man had ever stood before such an onslaught. No man had met Hawley's full wrath and lived. Yet Hobb skipped away with feline grace, until finally, as Hawley had planned, the commander had nowhere to go.

Hobb met the wall of shields behind him. His face sank.

Hawley brought down the bastard sword with all his strength. Somehow, Hobb brought up his own blade to meet it. He turned Hawley's blow, but the force still took him off-balance. Hobb's trailing foot slipped in a mud-filled furrow. He fell to one knee.

Hawley adjusted his grip, not wanting to swing his sword in such proximity to the circle of soldiers, who were only doing their sworn duty. A sly smile crossed Hobb's lips. He hadn't slipped at all.

Hobb thrust clinically. Hawley barely had time or room to twist aside, and he felt steel slice beneath his ribs. He roared as Hobb withdrew the cavalry blade. Hawley's blood spilled onto sodden ground.

In rage and agony, Hawley spun, sweeping Godspeaker in a wide arc that this time did have the soldiers breaking ranks.

Hobb was already gone. He danced around Hawley with palpable confidence. The damned Sylven helmet made Hawley half-blind. Hobb came unexpectedly from the right, jabbing his armoured sleeve hard into Hawley's cracked rib.

Hawley staggered away in agony, reaching out towards the wall of soldiers to get his bearings, fingertips touching shields. He was painfully aware of the blood seeping from his wound. He heard Hobb's step in the mud, light, regular. He was toying with him, stalking his prey.

"What were you expecting?" Hobb said. "Your world is out there, on the battlefield, butchering. This is *my* world. Here, the gods favour me."

Hawley couldn't even see his enemy. He tried to get away, but the footsteps came first from his left, then his right. In desperation, Hawley pulled off the helm.

Hobb pounced. Hawley leapt backwards, almost tripping over his own feet. He met the wall of shields, felt them push at his back, towards Hobb's waiting blade. Hawley used the momentum, added it to his swing. He switched hands, brought the sword up with his left with all the strength he could muster. The wound beneath his ribs tore with the exertion. No one would have expected it. It was folly. It was *rash*.

With no time to parry, Hobb turned his body, clicked his shield into place.

Hawley's mighty uppercut clanged against the steel, glanced over it, deflected off Hobb's pauldron, and bashed into his helmet.

Hobb's head jerked back. The helmet whipped from his head and flew into the mud. The onlookers gasped. For an instant they thought Hobb's head was still inside.

But Hobb staggered away, clutching his ear. Blood poured down his sculptured face, staining his polished armour red.

Hawley was slow to press the advantage. The pain was getting worse. The blood loss sapped his strength. He wondered if the wound might yet kill him.

He hacked clumsily. Hobb parried Hawley's blade expertly, so the strike sliced the ground, spattering both men with mud.

Hawley felt the bite of steel through the leather strapping at his left thigh. He roared again, tore himself away. His vision blurred. On instinct, Hawley struck at the shadow of his tormentor with the flat of his buckler. By some miracle, he felt Hobb's cheek slap against the cold iron. Hobb backed off. Gripped by battle madness, Hawley rushed forward, thrusting the Felder blade at full stretch, towards Hobb's throat.

Hobb clicked his shield-armour closed, but not fast enough. Almost half Hawley's blade scraped through the crescent-shaped protrusions before the shield was formed. Then it stopped, trapped.

In his bloodlust, Hawley forgot his training. He struggled to withdraw the sword from the jawlike grip of Hobb's armour. His vision cleared, he saw Hobb's smirk. Hawley knew he'd made a terrible mistake.

Hobb pivoted on his front foot, using Hawley's own strength to flex the unforgiving Felder steel.

The bastard sword shattered fully in half. The hilt end tore violently from Hawley's hand, landing in a radial splash of dirt at the feet of the watching High Companies soldiers. Soldiers of the Third who had thought that blade a symbol of their company's honour. The shards fell around Hobb like silver rain. Hawley had heard of the technique many times, but he'd never seen it done. He'd never have believed Felder steel could be overcome by a duellist's trick.

He stood dumbstruck for a moment too long.

Hobb raked his blade down Hawley's face. Hawley's vision turned red. He didn't know if his eye was gone. All he knew was that he could barely see, and the pain threatened to overwhelm him.

"The old man should have spent less time granting you favours and more time training you," Hobb sneered. "The curse ends here."

Hobb drew back the cavalry sword, readying the killing strike with parade-ground proficiency.

Hawley lurched wildly into Hobb's guard, seizing the commander's sword-arm before he could strike. Hobb punched his armoured gauntlet into Hawley's ribs. Blood misted from the wound. With a roar like an enraged ox, Hawley went low, grabbed Hobb's leg with his other arm, and hoisted him clean off his feet.

Hobb shrieked. Hawley staggered just a few steps with the struggling man on his shoulders. It was all he could bear. He shrugged Hobb off him, headfirst into the circle of shields. Men fell to the ground under Hobb's weight.

Hawley limped to the centre of the circle, to the broken shard of the Felder blade. It'd have to do.

Footsteps splashed heavily and rapidly in the mud. Someone cried out, "Behind you!"

Hawley somehow deflected Hobb's charge, but the commander adjusted quickly, slashing, driving Hawley back until there was almost nowhere to go.

"Sarge!"

Hawley heard a splash beside him. The scuff of a boot. A

sword slid across the ground, and Hawley swiped it up. A High Companies shortsword.

Sherrat gave him a nod; one last favour from armsman to sargent, for old times' sake.

Hobb's next strike was met by a regulation blade. The commander screeched a curse, all composure lost.

Hawley dashed low, snatched up the shard of the Felder blade, now little more than a parrying dagger. But he had two weapons. Hawley saw uncertainty on the commander's face, and forced a grin loaded with the promise of violence.

"You cannot win," Hobb said. Another testing thrust. "You know why I became the best swordsman in the company? To impress Morgard. A fool I was! The old man put all his stock in you. To rid myself of Morgard's ghost, all I must do is kill his champion."

"Good luck with that." Hawley slashed twice, clumsily. Hobb dodged easily.

"You'll bleed out before I kill you. When you reach Uffærn, give Morgard my regards."

Hawley voiced a vicious curse, made a weak thrust, overextending. He grunted as his wound tore further.

Hobb's eyes lit up. He met Hawley's blade, flicked his wrist. Hawley fell forward, his sword flew from his hand. A disarming manoeuvre, straight from the practice ground.

Precisely what Hawley had counted on.

As Hobb smiled with the joy of inevitable triumph, Hawley powered through his guard and delivered a headbutt to the bridge of Hobb's nose so hard his grandchildren would see stars.

Hawley grabbed Hobb's sword-arm. He pulled the commander to him, finding the weak point beneath Hobb's pauldron with the jagged, broken blade. He pushed the shard into Hobb's shoulder with all the strength he could muster. To his credit, Hobb didn't cry out; he only grunted through gritted teeth. Hawley let go of the hilt, punched Hobb hard in the gut, doubling him over, then delivered a crunching knee to his face. The commander dropped his sword and crumpled to the ground.

Complete silence descended on the village.

Hawley retrieved his sword. He limped back to Hobb, then dropped to his knees, straddling Hobb's chest.

Hobb grasped around for his sword, found it, brought it up weakly. Still fight in him.

Hawley snaked his muscular arm around Hobb's sword-arm and pulled.

Hobb's arm snapped. Now he cried out—a wail that echoed around the hovels of Raecswold.

Hawley readied his sword to strike one last time.

"Do it...you...whoring *coward*!" Hobb spluttered. Blood bubbled onto his chin.

Hawley wavered, sword hovering over Hobb's throat. Hawley didn't see Hobb at all. He saw Jon Gale, breathing his last. Jon hadn't deserved death at Hawley's hand, but by the gods, Hobb certainly did. Hawley wanted to end it, and if he did, he'd be a free man at last. But what then?

He glanced upwards, almost for the first time remembering there were others watching, their eyes burning into him, anticipating.

When he saw Enelda, just briefly, amidst the ring of soldiers, something changed within him. He could have this moment of vengeance, but it would define his future. His freedom would be bathed in blood, just as his servitude had been. And for the first time in his life, Holt Hawley asked himself: *What kind of man do I want to be?*

Hawley struggled to his feet. He looked down at Hobb. The commander couldn't move. His breaths rattled in his chest.

"Ill luck, you called me," Hawley said, voice ragged. "All you speak of is luck, and destiny, and the will of the gods. And that's why you'll never know greatness, *Commander*. You wait for the hand of fate to bring you glory. I don't believe in fate. I don't believe in curses. I just fight. You need worry about me no longer. You need never see me again. You'll have to find someone else to blame for your troubles from now on. When next you fail, it'll be all your own work."

Hobb couldn't muster the venom to reply. His head lolled to one side; his blood spilled into the mud.

At last Sauveur proclaimed, "The contest is to the death, Master Hawley."

In reply, Hawley threw his sword into the mud. He glared at Sauveur.

Sauveur locked eyes with Hawley. Then the Sylven announced, "The victor is Holt Hawley. He has chosen the path of mercy."

Hawley staggered to the edge of the circle on leaden legs. He wiped blood from his eye, wincing at the touch. Gods knew what he must look like.

Soldiers, stunned into reverent silence, parted before Hawley. He limped towards the jail, to the High Companies wagon, feeling many pairs of eyes staring at his back. There, Hawley searched wearily through the supplies, dragging from the wagon sacks, bedrolls, lockboxes, until finally he found what he was looking for. His own equipment, confiscated by Lestyn and returned to Hobb.

He wiped his eye once more, then stared down at his armour and uniform. One last look. Hawley pushed them aside ruefully, reaching only for his own shortsword and scabbard. He turned defiantly to the assembled soldiers—to the High Companies men in particular. His former brothers. He held up the sword.

"I'm keeping this," he declared, hoarsely. Nobody argued, so he strapped the sword to his side.

Through the bloody haze of his vision, Hawley became dimly aware of figures approaching him.

Redbaer offered Hawley a shoulder to lean on. Instead, Hawley collapsed into Redbaer's arms.

*   *   *

"Damnedest thing I ever saw..." Redbaer muttered.

Enelda handed Redbaer a long strip of linen. "Tie this around his thigh before he bleeds to death; tight as you can."

"Clean water," Enelda called. "And cloths." A village girl bowed and ran from the pavilion to fetch them.

Sauveur entered, removing his hat courteously.

"Madame." He bowed to Enelda. Then to Hawley, he said, "Sir, you fight with the strength of one of your saints. I fear you will regret sparing Commander Hobb's life, no?"

Hawley couldn't muster the energy to reply.

Sauveur shrugged. "If you are lucky, he will acknowledge your victory and thank his gods you were merciful. But I sense you are not a lucky man, and Hobb is not the forgiving type."

"Hobb called upon the old traditions," Enelda said. "If he has any honour, he will accept your verdict."

Sauveur bowed. "A man like Hobb, he will find some other way to take his revenge, no?"

"We will see."

"Vigilant Drake, we will leave soon on this mission of so great import, yes?"

"Yes, once I've seen to Hawley."

"Of course. But we do not have much time."

"I understand."

Enelda took a wodge of linen strips and pressed them to the great gouge above Hawley's eye, eliciting a sharp hiss from her patient.

"Hold it there," she instructed. "Tip your head back."

"How bad is it?"

"You still have your eye. That's the best I can say."

The girl returned with water. Enelda set about bathing Hawley's wounds. The water quickly turned red. When Enelda was finished, she reached into a bag and produced several jars and pouches.

"Don't spare me," Hawley sulked. "Sear the wound with a hot blade. Quicker the better."

"He's right," Redbaer agreed.

"Barbaric!" Enelda said. Instead, she took a small root from one of the pouches, gnarled and black and smelling of cinders, and pushed it into Hawley's mouth.

"Chew."

Hawley obeyed. He bit hard on the foul-tasting root as the thread pulled through the skin. Five stitches in his forehead, another in the fleshy mound beneath his left eye, and four more in his cheek.

When she was done, Enelda opened a jar and daubed a thick unguent over the stitched wound.

Hawley winced. "Smells like cat's piss."

"Cow piss," Enelda corrected, still dabbing. "Among other things."

Hawley recoiled.

"Don't be a baby. Let me work, or the wound will fill with pus, and you may yet lose your eye."

That seemed the greater of the evils on offer, and so Hawley sat forward again and gritted his teeth as Enelda worked.

"You did well, Hawley," she said kindly. "And you did something I hadn't thought possible."

"Oh?"

"You surprised me." She stood back and wiped her hands on a cloth. "There. In a few days it will scab, and you will heal. I'm afraid the scar will stay with you as a reminder of your folly."

"I'll add it to my collection."

From outside, a warning cry, followed by the blare of a trumpet. Beyond the opening of the pavilion, the Sylvens were rushing to arms. Then came the pounding of hooves along the south road.

"What now?" Hawley groaned.

"A complication," Enelda said. "But not an unforeseen one. Can you stand?"

"Maybe. But don't ask me to fight."

"You won't need to. With a face like yours, you'll scare off any foe. Sir Redbaer? With me, if you please."

Enelda took up her staff and waddled from the tent, Redbaer in tow. Sauveur strode to Enelda's side, his soldiers taking up positions ahead of him. By the time Hawley had limped outside, the horsemen had gathered.

There were thirty at least, black cloaks over dark green tunics, longbows on their backs and longswords at their sides. Some carried tall spears, green pennants dancing on the breeze, giving sinuous movement to the gold dragon of Aelderland upon them.

"Borderers," Hawley muttered. He spat onto the ground.

The leader of the band cantered forward, bringing his horse contemptuously close to the line of Sylven crossbows. He was a man of considerable heft, weather-beaten and trail-worn, a fair beard and ruddy complexion shadowed beneath his hooded cloak.

"You stand on Aelder soil," he shouted, "in clear breach of the Accords. By order of the King, I command you—"

"Raelph! Ho there!" Redbaer pushed to the front, hand raised in friendship.

The Borderer reined in, confused. "Redbaer? What transpires here?"

"A bad business, Sargent," Redbaer explained. "But not what you think. Viscount Sauveur here is known to you, yes? He came to parley, by invitation."

"Whose invitation?"

"Mine." Enelda stepped forward.

The burly sargent was about to challenge the strange old woman before him, but thought better of it. He looked her up and down, eyes eventually fixing on the amulet of Litha about her neck.

As if on cue, a black shadow swept overhead, causing the Borderer to duck, and his horse to swing out. Barty circled once, then alighted gracefully on Enelda's shoulder.

"By the gods, then it's true," Raelph said. "A Vigilant. A real bloody Vigilant."

"Aye," Redbaer said. "And if we need a real bloody Vigilant, then you know these are exceptional times. Will you parley and let me explain?"

Sargent Raelph weighed up his options. Finally, he signalled his men to lower their weapons. Sauveur did the same.

Hawley puffed out his cheeks and blew. If he'd had to stand much longer, he'd have collapsed.

CHAPTER 36

The Northwood groaned in protest at the intrusion.

Hawley leaned heavily on a makeshift crutch. Redbaer and Raelph stood in awed silence, shoulder to shoulder with Sauveur, a man who by rights should be their enemy.

Raelph hadn't taken much persuading to join the expedition to the Northwood. He seemed overjoyed to serve Redbaer again, and showed the knight of Scarfell such deference he may as well have been his captain. That, and Raelph's evident glee at hearing of Hobb's defeat, had convinced him to throw in his lot with the renegades.

Redbaer had wanted to ride to Scarfell after Iveta. Enelda had told him she'd sent Iveta away for her own safety—that Redbaer must stay for the good of the realm. She said nothing of Lady Ermina, and Hawley let the truth go unspoken. Enelda manipulated Redbaer as she had manipulated Hawley. If the ends didn't justify the means, there'd yet be a reckoning for that.

As one, the strange companions stared down the slope of a vast, blasted crater. Whatever trees had once stood here had been torn asunder, the violated stumps splintered, blackened from fire. The rocks, too, were scorched, and the sandy ground glittered where intense heat had fused it to tiny shards of glass. Far below, in the centre of the enormous circle of desolation, the earth was churned up, and scattered with broken rocks. Not a single plant grew; nature had not yet reclaimed this place. Evidence lay all around that men had toiled here, long ago—wooden scaffolds, half-rotted, still clung here and there to the slopes, amidst piles of rocks and blasted earth.

"What is this place?" Sauveur asked.

"The birthplace of a saint," Enelda replied. "This is where St. Baerloc fell from the heavens, entombed within a comet—a great lump of rock sent from the heavens. It crashed here, tearing a rent into the earth, killing everything around it, and setting a fire so intense it burned for forty days, so they say. With it came the Winnowing, the great sickness that claimed so many lives. Until, that is, St. Baerloc strode from the dead and blackened forest almost five moons later, his body charred and cadaverous, and healed the sick with his touch. Shortly before dropping dead."

"Dead?" Sauveur frowned. "But they call him the Living Saint, no?"

"Yes. They say his spirit never left his body, and even now he works to heal himself, over the course of many long years. That's why the Flaescines rededicated the abbey—they needed somewhere close to this holy site to entomb the remains of their saint, and watch over them until they were ready."

"Ready for what?"

"To usher in a new age for the faithful."

"And what happens to the rest of us?" Hawley asked.

"That depends on whether you think the Winnowing was an accident, or design."

"Designed by who? St. Baerloc?"

Enelda nodded. "Look around you. The earth is barren, and not because of a fire that raged years ago. No, it is barren because of what came here with the saint. Those scaffolds were erected by the Flaescine monks after Baerloc rose from the ashes. Why? What do you suppose was so important in this crater?"

"*Roched'ebén*," Sauveur said, barely in a murmur. "What you call the blackrock. Yes, even now I feel it. We Sylven know all about it. Our wise women make it into powder, our alchemists distil it for all manner of purposes. Anyone with good sense stays well away from it. That is one thing on which your king and I, we agree."

"What you have never encountered," Enelda said, "is a concentration of blackrock, ignited by the power of an angel. That is what the saints truly are—it is what the Vigilants have always known, but many in the clergy still deny. 'Baerloc' is not the true name of this creature—it is a mortal name, given by superstitious men. From fragments I read in the archive at Scarfell, I have my suspicions of who—or rather, *what*—we are dealing with. If I'm right, then this angel…this Majestic…fell from the heavens, and the resulting explosion of power unleashed fire and plague both. It is why the stigmata caused by the use of blackrock are so similar to the welts caused by the Winnowing—they come from the same source. The Winnowing was unleashed to rid the land of the weak. 'Baerloc' wants only the strong in his new world."

"The boy…" Redbaer muttered.

"The boy indeed," Sauveur said. "Who your lord would have used to turn the blame on my people, no? I saw for myself the stigmata on his body, and now we know he hails from this very place."

Enelda nodded. "Everything points to this place as the origin of the evil we must now face."

"You said the Flaescines gathered the blackrock," Redbaer said. "To what end?"

"To hasten their lord's return. The Majestic was born from it, feeds upon it. But I gather they exhausted their supplies long ago."

"Why do you say that?"

Enelda rummaged in her bag of tricks and brought out a small box, covered in rough-beaten lead. Very carefully, she opened the box. It made Hawley's head throb. Everyone else took a pace back.

Enelda closed the box hastily. Sauveur breathed a sigh of relief.

"The merchant I took this from," Enelda said, "sold his cargo to the monastery. I imagine he is not the first."

"How do you know this? How did you even know about this place?" It was Redbaer who posed the question.

"I rather kept you in the dark. I kept everyone in the dark…"

She looked uncertainly at Hawley. "Believe me when I say I had my reasons. I only knew for certain after our visit to Wyverne—that's when all the other clues became clear. Why did the Witches of Wyverne come here? Why was Ermina's wet nurse found here? It is all connected. The people of Wyverne are not what they seem. They are loyal to an old order—the Sisters of Oak—who still exist in some form today, though they are no longer nuns. Not all of them."

"The riders who attacked us on the road," Hawley said.

"Yes. And Father Llewelyn, too—all part of the same creed, no longer just warrior maids, because the king's law made it impossible. But all faithful to St. Baerloc. Or the Majestic who claims to be St. Baerloc. It is my belief that Lady Aenya was once host to that Majestic, and her deeds on the field of valour brought great renown to the Sisters of Oak. At the behest of King Ealwarth, the sister superior exorcised Lady Aenya. But the king reneged on whatever promise he made—the Sisters of Oak were dissolved, their convent destroyed, and the sister superior regretted her actions. The descendants of her order would see honour restored. But they cannot do this while their blessed saint is a pile of bones in Erecgham Abbey. Three times now they have tried to bring the Majestic back into their fold, and three times they have failed. The first were the Witches of Wyverne. They came here as pilgrims, to visit the site of their saint's return. They had with them a wunscæd—their intent must have been to banish the Majestic from the corpse in the abbey, and bind it instead to one of them."

"The blade can do that?" Hawley asked.

"So it is said. My master wrote of the rituals many moons ago, though I have never seen it done. The Thrussels risked madness or death, but they must have believed it necessary. Of course, they never made it as far as the abbey. Someone reported them to the Vigilants, and they were executed.

"Next, then, a simple-minded wet nurse stole Lady Ermina from her crib and brought her here, of all places. At first this seemed like an attempt at sacrifice—one more child snatched for some dark ritual, just as many others were taken across the mearca. But I believe that nurse was in the pay of the Sisters of Oak. They feared for the life of Lady Ermina, because someone had chosen her for sacrifice. They had other plans. With a true descendant of Lady Aenya in their ranks, they believed they could persuade St. Baerloc to inhabit one of their own once more. They wanted the Majestic to take the infant Ermina as a host."

"Sacrifice..." Redbaer gasped.

"And I know this, because ten years ago, Lady Iveta was selected as a sacrifice. But Lord Scarsdale refused, because she was not his ward, as he would have everyone believe, but his daughter. His refusal cost him everything—his wife, his power, his sanity. He has been paying for that decision ever since, and he pushed Iveta away as a result."

"Iveta is...Leoric's daughter?" Redbaer was dumbfounded.

"Days ago, a true descendant of Lady Aenya wandered into Wyverne of her own free will. Lady Iveta, at my side. It was their reaction that confirmed my suspicions. The faithful of Wyverne saw another opportunity. Here was a young woman of uncommon strength, who might yet allow them to realise their ambition. They attacked us later, on the road, in a bid to kidnap Iveta. Oh, they would have killed Hawley and me just to ensure there were no witnesses. But they wanted Iveta alive—a host, not a sacrifice."

"Again you say 'sacrifice'..." Redbaer said. "Who wants these sacrifices? Why?"

Enelda stared at her own feet and took a deep breath. "Abbot Meriet."

Redbaer stood open-mouthed.

"I bloody knew it!" Hawley shouted. He kicked a rock petulantly, sending it skittering and clacking down the slope, then pulled up immediately as his wounded leg protested.

"Indeed. But again, I had my reasons for misleading you. When this is over, I shall explain everything."

Hawley shook his head. He paced around in a wide circle, trying his best to shake off his anger.

"St. Baerloc needs more than just blackrock," Enelda said. "He requires the very essence of life, from sacrifices of a certain age. Children, in their tenth year—a number whose significance I have not yet discerned. It is why, once Leoric had protected Iveta for a whole year, he feared for her no longer. She was too old for the ritual, and so she was left to her own devices while he turned all his attention to Ermina's safety. He forgot, of course, about Anton. Perhaps he didn't think Meriet so rash as to start a war over his beliefs. Or...perhaps it was precisely what they both wanted."

"You're suggesting Lord Scarsdale knew about this all along?" Redbaer's confusion was evident. Here was a man who had served his lord faithfully, above and beyond the call of duty. And for what? Hawley knew something of that, too.

"He resisted for the longest time—this I can assure you. But only recently he was inducted fully into the mysteries of Baerloc, into the inner circle. You have seen the change in him for yourself. His fits of melancholy and rage have nothing to do with the toils of leadership. I would wager anything that he has the stigmata now. If you need evidence of his crimes, ask why he keeps rubbing at his neck. Under his collar are scratches—deep and infected—inflicted by a young boy in his final moments. A young boy named Hodge of Raecswold, murdered by Lord Scarsdale on the shore of the Silver River. A boy whose vital organs were charred on the inside, for he had already been slowly feasted upon by a Majestic—a creature of fire.

"I think for his betrayal, Leoric was sworn to a pact with the Flaescines. He had denied them Iveta's life—her very soul. Now Ermina has come of age, another girl from Aenya's line. And so, ten years later, it is Ermina they want."

"And Anton?" Sauveur interjected.

"It is possible they took Anton Tarasq as a sacrifice. If that's true, and the boy is dead, I am sure his mother will tear the world asunder in a new war. But I do not think it's true—not yet. I think they wanted Leoric to give up Ermina willingly, as proof of his devotion. But with the hour of the sacrifice fast approaching, they took Anton as a bargaining chip, to ensure Lord Scarsdale did as he promised."

"He would never harm Ermina!" Redbaer said. His face was flushed white, his lips bloodless and purpled.

Enelda's whole body seemed to sink; she gave a sigh redolent with regret. "I hope you're right."

"I will have Leoric's head for this!" Sauveur seethed.

"I doubt you will get the chance, once the truth is out," Enelda said. "Sir Redbaer, when our fight is done, it will be your duty to protect Lady Iveta. She will be Lady of Scarfell; let none doubt it."

"Fight?" Redbaer said. "Is that what comes next?"

"We must gather our forces from Raecswold, and go to Erec-gham at once."

"Madam, I've known you for only a few hours," Raelph said, "and you're asking me to march upon a holy abbey, at the side of a foreign militia?"

"If what I have said here has convinced you of the truth, then yes, Sargent. That is precisely what I'm asking. I would still hope to avoid battle, but fear it may be too late for that."

Raelph looked to Redbaer, who gathered himself enough to nod assent. Raelph slapped his arms to his side resignedly.

"Viscount Sauveur," Enelda said. "If Anton Tarasq is alive, he is at the abbey."

"Then I go to this abbey," Sauveur said, "with or without their help."

Raelph rolled his eyes. "Very well. I'll come, if only to keep an eye on the foreigners."

"Then let us waste no more time," Enelda said.

CHAPTER 37

Scarfell
Sygesdaeg, 13th Day of Nystamand

Iveta pounded once more on the chapel door, her fists now red and sore.

"It will do you no good!"

Iveta turned. Clemence bustled along the family corridor, breathless, red in the face. He had two guards with him. Iveta had three of Redbaer's men with her. On her way into Scarfell, she'd taken the liberty of visiting the barracks, where she knew she could always find friends.

"Lord Clemence," Iveta said, eyes narrowing. A few days in Enelda Drake's company had lowered her opinion of Clemence's order considerably, and it hadn't been set high to begin with. "Be so good as to unlock this door."

"Do not presume to command me, child!" Clemence snapped. He came to a halt, belly and chins wobbling with their own inertia. "Do you think I haven't tried? Your uncle has barred the door."

"Lady Ermina is with him?"

"Presumably."

"You don't know?"

"The archduke has not been seen for two days, and I don't concern myself with the whereabouts of children."

Iveta only glared at him.

"Besides," the High Vigilant went on, "if some ill fate has befallen the archduke, it is thanks to you. Yesterday he was shouting through the door, asking for you. And where were you? Gallivanting around the countryside with a necromancer and a traitor."

Iveta didn't say any of the things she wanted to say. "He asked for me?"

"Yes."

"Break down the door."

Clemence's face tightened. "I have told you already, my lady, I do not take orders from—"

"Lord Clemence!" Iveta snapped. "You reside in *my* home only at the sufferance of *my* uncle."

"I speak for the king!"

"But you are *not* the king. If you won't help me, then get out of my way. Or we'll see what happens when your men and mine have a disagreement."

"*Your* men?" Clemence looked left and right at the guards flanking Iveta. He saw their grips tighten on their halberds. He touched his fingers hesitantly to his great chin as he considered this unfortunate turn of events.

Finally, he turned to his guard. "Fetch something to break down this door."

And Iveta breathed a little sigh of relief.

*   *   *

With a crack, the great oak door, carved centuries ago by Sylven craftsmen, buckled and split. The lock tore away, the door swung open awkwardly. Censer smoke drifted into the passage. A few candles reflected eerily from the blood-red walls of Leoric's chapel.

No one dared enter, and so Iveta went first.

The smoke stung her eyes. She picked her way through the darkness, towards the altar where surely Leoric would be. She stubbed her toe on some solid object, almost tripping. From the floor, a silver skull grinned at her, set in a cowl of carved ebony. St. Baerloc, toppled from his dais.

"He promised so much." Leoric's voice was weak.

Iveta squinted, her eyes settling at last on a shadow, huddled beneath the stained-glass window.

"So much... He would remake the world. And I would rule at his side. But... the cost was too great. When I saw it, I knew..."

"What?" Iveta asked, picking her way through debris. A smashed idol, broken bottles, sundered furniture. "What did you know?"

"That the sacrifice would not be a noble one... That the price of my ascension would be her damnation. I had to, you see? I had to save her soul."

Now Iveta reached the alcove by the window, where the smoke was thinned by cold draughts filtering between the facets of coloured glass.

Leoric sat on the floor, fur-lined cloak bundled over his shoulders. From beneath the cloak, from his cradling arms, Ermina's hair tumbled to the floor like spun gold.

"Ermina..." Iveta started forward.

Leoric drew back, holding Ermina closer, protectively. The folds of the cloak fell away. Ermina's head lolled back. Lifeless eyes stared up at Iveta from a pale face.

Iveta reeled. The room spun around her. She steadied herself upon a great glass-fronted cabinet. She saw her own face reflected in the glass, hovering ghostly over a mail coif and tattered habit, as though she herself was the Warrior Maid. She tore her eyes away, and saw in Leoric's hand a knotted cincture. He held it out beseechingly, then dropped it on the floor.

"I had no choice." Leoric stared blankly into the shadows. His voice was weak, childlike. "I sacrificed a poor boy to save the kingdom, but it was not enough. They wanted Ermina, as they had wanted you. And now... by my own hand she goes to the Garden of the Aelders. Baerloc will not have her soul."

Iveta screamed. She lunged at the huddled form of Leoric. He barely raised a hand to stop her as she clawed at his face.

Someone grabbed her. She wrenched away once, twice, snatching at Leoric's collar, screaming in his face with all the rage and hate and grief within her. He did not resist, even when her nails drew blood and her slaps reddened his otherwise bloodless pallor.

Now the guards succeeded, yanking her from Leoric as she fought wildly. She snatched at him once more as she went, tearing his tunic. Exposing his throat, revealing long, black welts running in furrows down his neck. Once the mere scratches of a dying boy, now infected with something dark, something unnatural. The stigmata of Baerloc were upon the archduke.

She wrestled against the guards, tears streaking her face.

And now Leoric stood. Slowly, on shaky legs, still cradling Ermina to his breast. And with all his strength he roared, "Unhand my daughter!"

Everyone stopped. Clemence had entered the chapel, too afraid to approach Leoric himself. The steward had come, too, and was gawping in stunned silence at what had become of his master.

"You admit it?" Iveta croaked. "You would call me daughter?"

"It should have been you..." Leoric said. "Ten years old you came back to me. And ten is the number. It was too perfect... It was fate. But for sentimentality, I robbed the Blessed Saint of his due. And ten years later it has come back to haunt me."

Clemence gasped. "Are you saying... that Iveta Snowsill is your true daughter? Of your own blood?"

"Aye. And I should have said it sooner. All of you are witnesses. Do you hear?" He looked at Iveta, his eyes appearing lucid at last, if only for an instant. "Forgive me."

Iveta could say nothing. Forgiveness was the one thing she couldn't grant.

Leoric held out Ermina's body with weak, trembling arms. "Someone... take her. I have but one daughter now. Serve her well."

The steward dashed forward, taking Ermina before the archduke dropped her.

Leoric stumbled away. There was a flash of steel. Leoric plunged the dagger into his heart, and fell.

He didn't even cry out as life left him.

CHAPTER 38

The unlikely allies marched towards Erecgham under a sky the colour of fire. For the first time in weeks, it seemed, the clouds were sparse—just a few gilded claw-marks raking at the sunset.

Hawley winced as Baelsine jolted him again. Much as he'd missed the brute, he was in no condition for riding.

Enelda rode beside Hawley on a borrowed pony, plodding only at the speed of the foot soldiers' march.

"What you said about men being led astray by Riftborn..." Hawley ventured. "It wasn't true?"

"Who says it wasn't?" Enelda asked.

"But Meriet—he's in league with angels, not devils."

"I told you, Majestics can be just as bad. They're just harder to spot because their wiles are more subtle."

"What I mean is," Hawley persisted, "that some men are just wicked. Of their own free will, like. 'Cause before, you said—"

"I know what I said. It wasn't a lie. More a... simplification."

Hawley frowned, deep in thought. He wondered about all the wickedness he'd ever seen, and who or what had been responsible. He thought about Baron Rolston, how easy it'd be to explain that bastard as being possessed. But Hawley's views on the capacity men had for evil had not changed. "Take Hobb, for instance," he said.

"What about him?"

"I hate him—aye, I know, hate can let the Riftborn in. But

that's not the point—it's just that…I don't think him 'evil.' Not exactly. He said something back in the jail that made me understand. It was about Morgard—how the old man had lost his edge and put his trust in the wrong people. People like me. So that made me think Hobb started down a dark path 'cause of jealousy. It's a good old-fashioned reason, isn't it, jealousy?"

"Another good way to let the Riftborn in."

"I s'pose. But then he started going on about the glory of the Third. About how he'd never be rid of Morgard's legacy until he led the company to victory in war. He was looking forward to it, like he'd be happy to die for it. And that made me think it's more than jealousy with Hobb…it's pride. He knows he'll never be spoken of in the same breath as Morgard until he's proven in war."

Enelda no longer had her eyes on the road, but was looking at Hawley intently, face heavily lined with worry. "He said that? He said it was war he wanted?"

"S'good as."

"This is the first time you recall him saying so?"

"Aye…Is it important?"

"Perhaps." Enelda's brows knitted in concentration. Presently she looked ahead and said, "We're almost there."

Sauveur spurred his horse and came alongside Enelda. "I hope you are certain about this, Vigilant Drake. We Sylvens don't worship the saints, but we are wise enough not to make enemies of them. It must be bad luck to kill one."

"Oh, you cannot kill them," Enelda said. "You may be able to banish them for a time, but only if you know their true name."

Sauveur looked wary. "And you know it?"

"Have no fret, I'm working on it."

"With respect, Madame, you should work faster." Sauveur kicked his heels and spun his horse around, signalling his militia to form ranks.

The abbey hove into view, all brown brick and pointed steeples, blooded by the portentous, lingering rays of dusk. Brought to ruin during the war, Erecgham Abbey had been half rebuilt by

Sygellites, left abandoned during the Winnowing, and now for the most part restored by the wealth of Archduke Leoric and the sheer righteous endeavour of the Flaescines. Or so the story went.

A dozen or so holy brothers worked the land just beyond the walls, toiling in silence, coppicing hazel trees, and pulling stubborn weeds from furrows.

"Bit late for gardening..." Hawley said.

Redbaer shrugged. "Flaescines. As long as there's light, they work."

"They do not seem concerned to see us," Sauveur said.

Only one of the monks so much as looked up. He stared impassively, raising a hand in greeting only when the soldiers drew closer.

"They all part of Meriet's plan?" Hawley asked. "Or is it just the abbot?"

Enelda didn't reply. She had that look about her, of staring into the distance, her lips flexing about as though she were ruminating on some puzzle. Her fingers tapped against her thumb, one at a time. Hawley rarely asked her what she was thinking about. Or, rather, what she might be thinking so hard *for*.

"They know me well enough," Redbaer said. "Let me speak with them."

Sauveur signalled the column to a halt as Redbaer approached the monks. One pulled back his hood, revealing grey hair and a ruddy face, well-lined. The conversation was one-sided, as could be expected from brothers under a vow of silence. But eventually the monk bowed, then walked to the gates, beckoning Redbaer on.

"Follow me," Redbaer called back.

The company advanced, passing through the large gates into a rain-slick courtyard of cobbled stone, reflecting the blood-red rays of the sun's last rind.

Two of the monks lit torches and waved the company into the courtyard. The crossbows entered furtively, keeping close to the outer wall. Then the footmen, in loose formation. Raelph and a few of his Borderers entered the courtyard on horseback, ducking beneath the gate arch and forming up behind Redbaer. Hawley and Enelda followed, then Sauveur.

"Where's everyone else?" Hawley said. "Too bloody quiet."

"They're hiding," Raelph said. "They're monks, not soldiers."

"I knew at least one who was a soldier."

"Pah! Maybe the odd fighting man who's taken his vows. If the Sygellites were still in charge here, I'd think twice, but Flaescines are timid lambs in comparison."

"Tell the abbot we're here to see him," Redbaer commanded. "Tell him Vigilant Drake and Viscount Sauveur are with me."

The gates creaked shut.

Hawley swung his horse around. A monk stood just a few yards away, torch in hand. The horse turned again, nostrils flaring in anticipation of danger. Hawley saw five monks now, all with torches raised. And as one, they dropped them to the ground.

"Trap!" Raelph shouted.

The ground was not slick with rain at all, but with oil. Flames licked upwards around the monks. They stood silently as they were engulfed, immolated in sacrifice. The ground lit up.

Horses shied. Three riders were thrown. Footmen recoiled from the spreading fire. One man ran blindly into the centre of the courtyard, patting flames from his sleeves. An arrow took him in the throat.

Archers stepped from behind shadowed pillars. Others fired in indirect volleys over the inner walls from a hidden courtyard beyond.

"Ride!" Hawley shouted. His horse bucked beneath him, making his ribs rattle. He slapped Enelda's pony on the rear, sending it off towards the nearest cloister, and spurred Baelsine after her.

Redbaer followed, a couple of men at his back. Hawley could see nothing else. Smoke filled the courtyard. The shouts of soldiers rang in his ears.

Hawley got clear of the flames. He clambered from the saddle, letting Baelsine run free across the courtyard. He helped Enelda down.

There were shouts now of anger as well as pain; of sworn oaths and battle cries.

A monk rushed at them from a shadowed alcove, swinging a mace with grim purpose. Hawley pushed Enelda behind him, barely dodging the attacker in time. He broke his crutch across the monk's back, sending the man into the path of a galloping Borderer, where he was lost in the thick smoke.

Enelda stumbled, dazed. She let Hawley lead her towards the cloister by her arm. Another monk charged, this one with an ancient-looking axe. Hawley barely had time to draw his shortsword, but he managed to thrust in the nick of time, and the charging monk ran onto the blade. The monk died without a sound, holding his vows until the end.

Finally, they made it to the cloister wall, their eyes stinging, throats clagged with smoke. Hawley sat Enelda on the lip of a stone fountain. Battle was joined in the courtyard—those men and women of Sylverain who had braved the flames fought half-blind against silent attackers.

"Why didn't you see it?" he asked Enelda, more in wonderment than annoyance. "You see everything."

"I...I can't," she murmured, still staring into nothingness. "I have to keep him out."

The smoke parted, and Redbaer appeared, his horse spinning nervously, hooves clattering on stone. "They're mad!" he shouted. "The monks are bloody mad!"

"Where's Sauveur?" Hawley called.

"He got out." Redbaer turned his horse and cut down a monk who'd tried to rush past him. "He's no fighter. But these monks... Kill one, and two more take their place. Vigilant Drake, if you've a plan, now would be the time to reveal it."

Enelda just stared, numbly.

Hawley rounded on her in exasperation. "Snap out of it! Where's Meriet?"

"Meriet..." she mouthed. Then abruptly, she stood, blinked away her confusion, and pointed to a door halfway along the wall of the west cloister. "There," she said. "They wait for us."

"Let's have at them, then!" Redbaer roared.

As if in answer, a pair of heavy gates opened nearby. Beyond was another courtyard, and from it poured a good thirty men. More monks, this time clad in scraps of armour over their habits, and bearing shields as well as their motley collection of antiquated weapons. They flooded across the courtyard like dark crashing waves, the sheer ferocity of the attack driving men back into the smoke.

Redbaer's horse reared, almost throwing him. He fought to bring it under control, slashing at monks left and right with his sword.

"Go!" he cried. "I'm right behind you." He shouted for the Borderers, and Raelph answered the call, forming up between Enelda and the oncoming threat.

Hawley pulled Enelda close, and half carried her towards the ominous door.

* * *

The stairs circled downwards seemingly forever. With each step, the air grew thicker with smoke, and the heat intensified. Many times, Hawley faltered, head swimming. He leaned upon the soot-covered wall, gasping for breath. His addled mind convinced him the walls were soft, spongy. Alive.

Redbaer looked just as reluctant to descend. His eyes were wild, nostrils flaring like a spooked beast. Duty pushed him on, beyond the point of reason. Hawley understood. For him, only the resolute advance of Enelda Drake impelled him onwards. She'd released him from his oath, but he wasn't ready to renege on it yet.

When they reached the foot of the stair, Hawley stopped, wheezing, and looked back whence they'd come. It was a normal stairway, nothing more. Perhaps thirty steps, curving up to the courtyard from where the sounds of battle still echoed.

Clutching his ribs, Hawley limped after Enelda. They advanced through a long, dark chamber lined with tombs, to a heavy door once shut fast with many locks, but which now lay open. Enelda did not pause.

For Hawley, one step over the threshold conjured in him a feeling of such dread he almost left Enelda to her own devices. He drew his sword and cursed himself for a coward. He stepped into the dark, guts clenching a warning that he had not the sense to heed.

"It was so very clever of you to get this far." Meriet's disembodied voice resounded from the ancient stones of the vaulted chamber. "But you must know this is the end."

Hawley gripped the hilt of his sword a little tighter. He squinted against the flickering shadows.

Enelda moved cautiously on, and Hawley followed. From the darkness loomed a large, black shape, a sharp-edged slab of smooth stone. Something about it made the hairs on Hawley's neck prickle.

"Go on." Meriet's voice seemingly came from every direction. "See that even a Vigilant of old can be wrong. See just how wrong you were."

Enelda didn't stop. Slowly, she approached the edifice. A sarcophagus.

Hawley and Redbaer followed hesitantly. The temperature in the chamber rose with every step. Hawley tugged at his collar as hot air filled his lungs. Sweat dripped from his brow, stinging the ugly, stitched wound on his face. Something deep within him, some part of his soul, screamed at him to go no closer to the sarcophagus. But he went on regardless.

The sarcophagus was open. From the dark void within, tendrils of black smoke drifted gently upwards into the shadows, accompanied by a low hiss, like a fire extinguished by water. Hawley wrinkled his face as an odour like rotten eggs reached his nostrils.

Enelda reached the lip of the sarcophagus. She gasped, stepped back, hand over her mouth. Hawley steadied her.

Redbaer refused to take another step.

Curiosity overcame the prickling fear in Hawley's mind. He leaned forward to peer inside.

Enelda croaked "Don't," but it was too late.

Hawley recoiled as though struck. He fell to his knees. His

sword clattered to the ground. The images flashed before his eyes even after he'd torn himself away, seared into his mind. He felt the thing in the sarcophagus scratching inside his skull as he tried desperately to block it from memory. Blackened flesh; exposed bones—too long, too numerous, too unlike any creature in the world. Long limbs; a purple heart within a sundered cage of jagged ribs. Still beating. And those eyes...

It was the Living Saint. The Burnt Man.

But whatever lay in that box was no man.

"Now you see your error." The shadows parted. By dancing firelight, Abbot Meriet strode across the chamber. He reached out a hand idly, gently brushing the rim of the black sarcophagus with his fingertips.

Even this act seemed like madness. Hawley wanted to cry out, "No!" at the very thought of touching that thing, but the words didn't come. He looked around desperately for the fallen sword.

"St. Baerloc is no mortal vessel," Enelda said, sounding very weak and distant in this place, with its thrumming stones and cloying shadows.

"Indeed," Meriet said. "When our Blessed Saint fell from the heavens, he revealed to his followers the true form of the angels themselves. How could any look upon this messenger of the gods and not be awed?"

Enelda straightened, leaning heavily on her staff. "Indeed. Even a Vigilant might abandon their oaths for the merest glimpse of such power. If they had not already abandoned them."

Meriet smiled wickedly. "I underestimated you, Enelda Drake. I thought you a mere novice, dogmatically following the strictures of a dead order. But I see now Cerwyn Thawn taught you well. You completed your training."

"Long ago," Enelda said.

"And you tricked me. I did not think such a thing possible. It would appear your mastery over the Eternal Night rivals even my own."

"It is how I know what you are. A Fallen Vigilant—an affront to our order."

"Affront?" Meriet chuckled. "Oh, my dear lady, I have not been a Vigilant for a very long time. I am so much...*more*."

"I see that. You are older than me, though you don't look it. The Fallen are traditionally struck from the Great Roster—an act that did you a favour, for it concealed your identity. You will not tell me your name?"

"Who I was is of no import. That name is no longer...*us*."

"Tell me then, 'Abbot,' what about the name of the Majestic? What puppet master pulls your strings?"

Anger wrinkled across Meriet's face.

Hawley tried his best to shake away thoughts of the burnt thing in the sarcophagus. While Meriet was distracted, Hawley slowly felt across the warm stones, until his fingers found the hilt of his sword.

"The relationship is a harmonious one," Meriet said. "As you could discover for yourself. Come, Enelda Drake—do you not long for more strength in those tired old limbs? Do you not wish you had more time?"

"Time for what? To steal children from their beds? To sacrifice them to...*this*?" Enelda waved a hand contemptuously at the sarcophagus.

"Regrettable—but necessary," Meriet said, shaking his grey head sadly.

"Necessary? How can it be necessary to torture mere children by burning their insides?"

"Not torture. A blessing! The stigmata of the Living Saint take many forms. In some of the devout, their organs blacken, just as St. Baerloc's did on the fateful day when he came unto us and tasted mortal air for the first time."

"Air that his kind were never meant to taste."

Meriet ignored her. "Some bear black marks across their bodies—blessed reminders of a close brush with divinity."

"Or blackrock poisoning," Enelda said flatly, drawing a shrug from Meriet. "This sarcophagus is made from blackrock pulled from the ground in the Northwood. But even that was not enough, was it? Your monks are spread far and wide across

Wulfshael, trading illicitly for more blackrock. That merchant I helped in the Elderwood... Your people did not chance upon him at the market in Eastmere. He brought the blackrock right to your gates, bought and paid for. And when he told you, a trusted abbot, about his brush with death and the strange ring he'd found... Well, that was when you formed your plan. I imagine he was killed to assure his silence?"

"Very good!" Meriet said. "An opportunity almost too good to be true. Our sort should never overlook fate when it stares us so plainly in the face."

"*Our* sort, indeed..." Enelda snorted, indignantly. "And your monk—Ianto—a man with military experience before joining your order. You persuaded, or perhaps bribed, Commander Hobb to take him in, but to keep his true identity a secret. Feeding Hobb's fantasy of a coming war would have won him over readily, I think. You doubtless told Hobb that a mission to the Elderwood was a fool's errand, but one that would win much favour with the archduke. And so he used that fool's errand for a mission of his own."

"To destroy Sargent Hawley. And what might have transpired had Hobb succeeded? We shall never know." Meriet clapped his hands together. "Gods, it has been too long since I have bandied wits with a worthy adversary."

"Enough of this!" Redbaer barked. He stepped into the torchlight, sword pointed at Meriet.

"Found your courage at last, Sir Redbaer?" Meriet said.

"Where is Anton?" Redbaer demanded.

"What a failure you are. What a weak fool! A man who'd do anything for his master, no matter the price. Do you know where your master is now?"

"Ignore him, Redbaer," Enelda said. "His words are venom. He seeks only to mislead."

Meriet laughed. "You'd know all about that, Enelda Drake. You didn't tell him, then?"

"Tell me what?" Redbaer asked. He looked uncertainly from Meriet to Enelda.

"Your master is dead," Meriet said.

"Lies!" Redbaer snarled. He stepped another pace forward, sword almost at Meriet's breast.

"By his own hand, just hours ago. Look at Vigilant Drake—look into her eyes. They betray the truth. She *knew*, and she did not tell you. Had you not left the castle in search of these two, you could have saved him. And the girl."

"That's enough!" Enelda snapped, but her words drew only a venomous smile from the old monk.

"Girl..." Redbaer croaked. "Iveta?"

"Ermina," Meriet purred. "Destined for greatness, yet murdered by her own father. Such a tragedy."

Redbaer trembled. His sword wavered. He looked to Enelda, and whatever he saw seemed only to confirm his fears. His face fell. Then his eyes narrowed, and with a snarl of rage he lunged at Meriet, grabbing the abbot by his robe.

"This is your doing!" he roared. "I'll have your head!"

Lightly, innocuously, Meriet touched a hand to Redbaer's arm.

Redbaer screamed. His sword fell to the floor. He released Meriet and wheeled away, clutching at his left arm, which visibly shrank, blackening, withering. Black smoke drifted from his flesh with a hiss. His hand became a skeletal claw draped in dry, grey skin.

Redbaer's eyes widened with terror, then he fell to the flagstones, unconscious.

"Gods..." Hawley muttered.

Enelda rapped her staff hard on the stones, the sound unnaturally loud. She held aloft the sigil of Litha and stepped towards Meriet. The monk recoiled a pace.

"One more crime for you to answer for," Enelda said. "It ends here."

"It does, but not in the way you would hope. Do you not see it has all led to this? You are here because I willed it so. I would rather you were here as a friend than at the head of a war band, but the result will be the same. I engineered all of this, just to find *you*. Because you are the key to changing the world. You are the key to ending the sacrifices."

"Oh, I intend to end the sacrifices, Abbot Meriet. You can count on that."

Meriet laughed. "Defiant to the end. Denying your very destiny even when face to face with a Majestic. There is only one way to stop the sacrifices, Enelda Drake. I have tried for years to revive the Living Saint, but it is a slow process. Yet now, here you are. You have proven yourself a strong and worthy opponent. More than that: You have proven yourself a worthy *vessel*. The last True Vigilant in all the world—only you have the strength to coexist with a Majestic, as I do. Side by side we could create something new from the dying embers of the old ways."

"Your ways have brought only death, Meriet. Your creed is built on lies. Your followers are ignorant of the truth. They do not even know your name."

"Do *you* know it? I think not." The smile grew more sly.

Enelda smiled. "No. But I know *his*." She reached to her belt, beneath her cloak, and withdrew a dagger. The blade of covenant once wielded by Ianto.

Meriet's eyes narrowed. "You know nothing!" he sneered.

"Really? I know that any who spend too long in the presence of this monster turn their thoughts to violence. To war. Even Commander Hobb was led to dreams of glory in battle, and I think it not entirely his own ambition. The Witches of Wyverne came to Raecswold with a dagger much like this—though not the same. There was a drawing of their dagger in an old book in Scarfell, and it bore a particular sigil I did not immediately recognise. Not until I was in Lord Scarsdale's chapel did I see it again, engraved in the broken blade of Lady Aenya's sword. Hawley saw it again, carved into a poor girl's flesh by *your* careless servant. The Sisters of Oak bear this mark, because the saint they hold dear, once known as Lady Aenya, is the very same creature that now lies in that coffin."

"Are you so sure?"

"Sure enough. The creature led Lady Aenya to war. It lent strength to her arm. After the war was over, it used her to create discord between the mearcas, until finally she did what few have ever been able to do—she cast the Majestic out and reclaimed her life. Much weakened, she became old and frail, and died in ignominy. But it was not bandits who slew her, but her own sisters. The Sisters of Oak sought the favour of this Majestic, to invite the creature back into their ranks and restore the order to glory. But it did not accept their offer, for they had no worthy vessel. They have tried several times since, but their prayers have gone unanswered. And all this time, the Majestic has watched and waited for an opportunity."

While Enelda spoke, Hawley clambered to his feet. He felt nauseous. His head swam. Was it a trick of the light, or was the smoke from the sarcophagus growing thicker?

"When it returned," Enelda went on, "it set about sowing the seeds for another war. Now, with the abduction of Anton Tarasq, it seems it might get its wish."

"Yet still you do not speak his name." Meriet smirked. "This ruse grows tiresome."

"Ruse? Oh no... The *Books of the Majestic* are quite clear on this matter, and the *Canticle of St. Baerloc* only confirmed his identity. That blackened creature is *Tezryan*, Bringer of Fire—an avatar of war. His birth into the world requires a mortal vessel, who must give themselves willingly unto the sacred flame, which burns for forty days and nights. It is said that Tezryan is armoured in the souls of innocents and armed with the screams of the martyred. His sacred number is ten—a tenyear is the ideal age of his sacrifices, and ten moons is the darkness that heralds his coming. His strength grows as the weak are culled. Or *winnowed*."

A low hiss from the sarcophagus. The torches around the chamber seemed to crackle all in unison, throwing up hot sparks that drifted unnaturally towards the black edifice.

Hawley crept closer to Meriet, circling in the shifting shadows.

"He hungers for endless war," Enelda continued. "To war, the Riftborn are drawn—the oldest enemy, with whom Tezryan loves to battle. He cares not how many mortals are slain in the name of this pursuit. Once his rebirth is complete, he would remake the world in fire and blood to achieve his ends."

"You really are too clever for your own good, Enelda Drake," Meriet said. "And all this you concealed from me? The strength of your mind is quite extraordinary. You will make a formidable ally."

"We cannot be allies, you and I. When I am done with your master, I shall drive out the creature that resides in you. I do not know its true name, but it will tell me. *You* will tell me...before the end."

Meriet stepped aside and held an open hand towards the sarcophagus. "Be my guest, Vigilant Drake," he said mockingly. "Plunge the wunscæd into the heart of the Majestic, and say the words of banishment. Free us all from this terrible curse."

"Watch him, Hawley," Enelda said.

Hawley blinked hard to clear his vision. Yet still the air seemed thick, distorted. He stepped towards Meriet warily, sword held firm. Meriet merely smiled at him, benignly. Fatherly.

Enelda shuffled towards the sarcophagus, staff rapping on flagstones with each step.

Hawley's eyelids felt heavier as his limbs grew lighter. The shadows around him contorted; ancient Sygellite tombs twisted. Those scattered sparks cast up by the torches still swirled all around, growing in number and brightness, like fireflies.

A vision flashed into his mind, visceral, violent—the entire monastery in flames. Something black and skeletal strode through an inferno, and in its clawed hand it held a dead, charred figure, whose long, white hair fizzed as the flames caught...

Hawley reached towards Enelda. "Wait!" he warned.

With a sound like crashing waves, a torrent of thick smoke erupted from the sarcophagus, spiralling up to the vaulted ceiling, where it became one with the shadows. Black dust blasted through the chamber. Hawley dropped to one knee, shielding his face, suddenly terrified that the air was filled with blackrock.

Perhaps it was. When Hawley dared look, he saw Enelda for an instant, grey robes almost glowing in the darkness, then she was consumed by the swirling smoke. And for an instant, the billowing smoke formed a gigantic, hideous face, horned and bestial, mouth gaping in a hateful moan, eyes glowing like hot coals. The face evaporated, smashing into Enelda, *through* her. Some faint, glowing essence, like a ghost, was pulled through with it, before both vanished into shadow.

Enelda's body crumpled lifelessly to the floor. The smoke was gone. The torches flickered in their sconces, then brightened. There was a moment of silence.

"Perhaps *he* will be more persuasive than I..." Meriet said.

"What've you done?" Hawley cried.

"Me? Why, nothing. She is a sister of the Vigilant Order. I wish her no harm. But she is in the Eternal Night now, and the rules there are... different."

Hawley stood. He pointed his sword at Meriet. "Bring her back."

"Quite impossible. Tezryan has her now. He will either persuade her to our cause, or destroy her. I would have advised him against such forthright action, but he is quite impulsive. There really is no reasoning with him."

Hawley took a knee at Enelda's side. She was breathing. Her eyelids twitched rapidly. Hawley had seen this before, and he'd only brought her back by dragging her into the Silver River. He looked guardedly at Meriet, who stared down benignly, as though he really were a holy man.

"Stay back," Hawley growled. He pointed his sword in Meriet's direction again.

"My dear boy, what do you expect to do with that?"

"If she doesn't come back, you'll see," Hawley said.

Meriet chuckled. "If she doesn't come back, nothing will ever be the same again... It all rests with *her*."

CHAPTER 39

Enelda's feet kicked infinite emptiness. Her hands reached out desperately, towards the swirling motes of ghostlight far above, towards the red, pulsing arteries of the Eternal Night, which grew smaller and fainter, plummeting away from her.

So violently had she been torn from her body—so powerfully, by a force unlike any she had ever experienced—that she'd almost forgotten her training. But now, as it flooded back, in infinitesimal detail, her descent slowed.

"Tezryan!" The word issued strongly from incorporeal lips and airless lungs. The red veins of the Eternal Night pulsed brighter. Enelda's feet touched solid ground—or at least her mind created the semblance of reality around her. It mattered not which. She had always thought reality was simply what one made of it. Were it not for the soft thrumming of those hideous arteries far, far above her, she would have had no concept of up or down.

Ahead now came a flickering orange light, illuminating vast, cavernous walls in brief flashes, veined and pitted with branch-like seams of black. Now came the booming resonance of great footfalls; cloven hooves pounding in Enelda's mind, followed by long talons scratching insidiously at her thoughts.

I am coming, it seemed to say. *Run, little bloodsack.*

This was not the Other. This was Tezryan, intruding upon the Other's domain just as she was, only without the good grace to be discreet about it.

Enelda focused as hard as she could. A dim grey mist appeared in front of her, growing brighter, longer, more solid, until a shaft of silver light formed itself in her hands. A staff. A weapon.

RUN!

The voice roared in her ears. Behind her.

Enelda spun around in terror, clutching the staff of light, illuminating a great, blackened face with bestial eyes that gleamed like stars. She stumbled. She fell. And she didn't stop.

* * *

Enelda's body convulsed. Spittle foamed from her mouth. She croaked something, quiet, indiscernible.

Meriet circled them slowly.

"What's happening to her?" Hawley snarled.

"She is ... *conversing* ... with the Blessed Saint. They will reach an agreement, or she will die."

"Bring her back. Now!"

Meriet chuckled. "Always so impatient. It is no wonder the Living Saint likes you. I think if he were mortal, you would be two peas from the same pod."

Hawley's head still swam in the hot frowst of the smoky chamber.

Enelda murmured fitfully again. Another convulsion. Hawley barely had time to slip his hand beneath her head lest she crack it on the flagstones.

In that instant, Meriet came a pace closer. Hawley pointed his sword at Meriet again, cursing his lapse of concentration. But the sword felt uncommonly heavy in Hawley's hand. The blade now trembled. Meriet's face began to blur as though viewed through tears.

"Aren't you getting tired, Holt Hawley?" Meriet purred. "Aren't you weary of all this fighting? Wouldn't you like to rest until all this is over?"

Hawley swayed like he was aboard a boat on a swelling tide. With every breath, smoke entered his lungs, forcing a hacking cough.

"Remember Herigsburg?" Meriet went on. "When you sat on the battlements, the signal fire warming your back, the fight unfolding without you? Wasn't it so...freeing? You have all the time in the world to rest now. Just rest."

Hawley's eyelids grew heavy. He felt like a raw recruit on a picket, too weary from the march and too far from home. Worse, he remembered that day of Slaughter Hill. The sounds of battle a distant echo, the fire hot all around him, the smoke thick on the air.

As his eyes drooped, and his body tilted forward, he saw the knife held loosely in Enelda's hand. The sigils seemed to glow with inner light. Hawley thought he heard a distant whisper— Enelda's voice.

Hawley let go of Enelda, snatched up the blade of covenant, and rose resolutely to his feet. Pain be damned. He glared at Meriet with murderous intent.

Meriet stepped back. Whatever was left of the mortal he once was shrank from the soldier before him.

"Whatever you are," Hawley snarled, "I warn you: If any harm comes to Enelda Drake, you die."

Meriet clapped his wizened hands together with delight. "And how do you propose to do that?"

"I've killed every manner of creature that walks under the gaze of the gods," Hawley said. "I'll happily add a Majestic to the list."

Meriet tutted loudly. "Sargent Hawley, please..."

"Don't call me that. I'm a sargent no more."

"Oh, but you are *my* sargent always." There was something different about Meriet. Something uncannily familiar about his eyes. And that voice...

"You remember the day you returned from Herigsburg?" Meriet began to circle again, never taking his eyes off Hawley's. "Hobb wanted your head immediately. But he did not know the truth, did he?"

"What're you talking about?" Hawley said. But his heart thumped a little harder in his chest. His insides swilled about like ice-cold waves in a black cove.

"Your commander could have pardoned you. Exonerated you of all charges. But the two of you agreed on the more difficult path. You took the lashes—you *chose* them—so that the men would come to respect you, and perhaps Hobb would leave you be."

"Tricks... You're guessing," Hawley said with growing uncertainty.

"Morgard told you to spy on your brother soldiers, and if necessary prevent them from turning a peaceful protest into an uprising. What was it he said? *By any means necessary?*"

The smoke seemed to thicken. The heat grew unbearable. Hawley thought only of Herigsburg. He felt the flames of the beacon fire. He remembered what he'd done—the things he'd never even told Iveta. His head felt so light he thought it might drift away from his body. Through gritted teeth, he said, "Get out of my head."

"There is no one in your head, Sargent Hawley," Meriet said, gently now. "You are a man of great honour. Even after your commander's death, you kept the secret. Commander Morgard ordered you to root out evil from your own company. He gave you permission to see those men dead. Cut the diseased boughs from the tree. It would have destroyed his good name had the truth come out... and so you took the whole burden on your shoulders. And yet you omit that part from the story even to this day."

"I... I've told the story only once..." It was a feeble retort. Hawley felt his arm relax, the sword now pointed to the floor. And then, there was Meriet, a wrinkled hand on Hawley's shoulder, grey head shaking sadly from side to side, tutting softly in sympathy.

"Not the whole story," Meriet said. "You didn't tell the girl how Carrow caught up with you on the walls. How he threatened to have you hanged. You didn't tell her what happened next."

Hawley almost choked. He was back there now, on the walls. Carrow was lunging at him. Hawley parried, drove his sword into Carrow's gut. Watched the life drain from the captain's eyes. Then he'd thrown him onto the beacon fire and let the evidence turn to ash.

"No one could blame you, Sargent. You were acting under orders, after all."

"I..." Hawley couldn't think. He could barely move. Worse, the cloying smoke filled his nostrils, and with it came the unmistakable smell of roasting flesh.

Meriet smiled benignly. *"When I'm gone, I need you to lead. Not as an officer, but as a man of principle."*

Hawley stared in disbelief. Grief welled up inside him, threatening to overwhelm him. How long ago it all seemed since Morgard had spoken those very words to him. How was it possible that Meriet knew them? Unless...

"And did it work, Hawley?" Meriet asked. "Did the men respect you thereafter? I think not. Morgard was a great man, but not the man he once was."

Hawley felt his resilience drain away. In spite of everything, he wanted to embrace the abbot, let despair wash over him. Most of all, he wanted to rest.

"That's it, Sargent. There, give that to me. Unburden yourself at long last." Meriet took the blade of covenant from Hawley's hand.

Hawley pressed his back against a stone pillar. His eyelids drooped until the flickering torches became indistinct smudges. He leaned heavily against the warm stone. His legs wobbled. What if he just slept? Perhaps he was already asleep. Perhaps this was a dream.

When his eyes at last closed, he heard a strange sound. Distant, indistinct. The mewling of a cat, or the shrill bark of a fox at midnight perhaps. And in his mind's eye, those sounds sparked a memory. An image formed in his mind. A crude stick figure like those drawn by a child. A corn dolly, the braids entwined around a strip of leather, from which hung wooden beads and a single white feather...

* * *

Again, through an endless void Enelda tumbled, tossed about like a seed on the wind.

A vast shape, indiscernible against sheer blackness, swept past her as she fell, a falcon circling a tiring old goose.

Something tore at her. A gleaming talon from the darkness, ripping across the soft flesh of her belly. She felt... pain. *Impossible.*

"No," she said. "There is no flesh here. I cannot be harmed."

For the first time, perhaps, she was not so certain of that.

Ringing, mocking laughter reached her ears. A horrible sound, like the grunting of a thousand swine. Then the flashing claw again, and her back exploded with pain.

As the darkness rushed by, with neither end nor beginning, Enelda screamed.

* * *

Hawley opened his eyes. His left hand was tracing the talisman at his throat. His right hand, thankfully, still gripped his sword. Some instinct drilled into him after years of soldiering had at least ensured he was not unarmed, even if momentarily unmanned. He struggled to focus. The cry came again—a child. Distant, echoing, little more than a whimper. And not just one voice, but several, crying out for help.

Enelda convulsed violently. Meriet knelt beside her, chanting something in a tongue Hawley couldn't understand. All Hawley knew was that Meriet held the blade of covenant over Enelda's heart, and the old woman's pale robe was streaked with dark red blood.

With a roar, Hawley threw himself forward. He clattered into Meriet, flung him across the chamber floor, then marched menacingly towards him.

"Sorcerer!" he hissed.

Meriet stood, one hand held outwards. "Sargent, there is no need for such outbursts. Remember what—"

Hawley delivered a punishing blow to Meriet's midriff, doubling the monk over. "No more tricks," he growled.

Meriet's lips curled upwards in a sinister smile, more wolfish and dangerous than any Hawley had ever mustered. Hunched over in the guttering torchlight, Meriet looked less than human.

"Have it your way," Meriet snarled.

With speed belying his age, Meriet struck outwards with the palm of his hand. The force of the blow sent Hawley flailing backwards.

He crashed into a pillar, the air leaving his lungs. Meriet stalked rapidly towards him. In that moment, Hawley swore it was not Meriet at all, but a black shadow—some amorphous mass of pure malevolence.

Something gleamed in the torchlight, small and sharp, arcing through the smoky air. Hawley squeezed away from his attacker on instinct alone. A blade nicked his arm. He slashed with his sword where he thought his assailant should be. The blade met nothing but shadow.

Now Meriet was in front of him, face contorted with spite, blade of covenant held in his hand, dripping beads of Hawley's blood onto the stone floor.

But Hawley had drawn blood, too. An ugly slash ran across Meriet's stomach, staining his robes.

"You'll have to do better than that, my boy," Meriet said with a grin. "I have lived for so, so long, and suffered much worse."

The monk lunged. His eyes flared with a hellish yellow light.

Hawley turned aside as the monk extended his lunge. This was his training, a muscle memory. He thrust clinically. The shortsword slid between the abbot's ribs, out through his back. Air escaped Meriet's punctured lung with a hiss. The blade of covenant clattered to the floor.

Hawley withdrew his sword and pushed Meriet away with contempt.

Meriet spat blood, bubbling up from a punctured lung. He made a wet, gargled grunt, growing steadily louder into throaty, mocking laughter.

Hawley's jaw dropped.

"You cannot kill me," Meriet spluttered. "Your story will end here. But I...I will endure!"

Hawley's eyes narrowed. He spat on the cursed ground. Something moved in the shadows behind Meriet. A dark shape crawling fitfully across the flagstones, now rising.

Redbaer. Weak, trembling. In his one good hand, he held the wunscæd.

Hawley thrust with his sword.

Meriet slapped Hawley's blade away with the palm of his hand effortlessly.

Then his eyes widened. He staggered backwards.

Redbaer slumped back to the floor, bloodied knife in his good hand. The monk groped around at his back, shock etched on his wizened features. The blade had hurt him.

Hawley took a swing. The monk reached out to stop the blow, and his hand fell to the stones, severed at the wrist.

Now he cried out. Not a human cry, but satisfying nonetheless.

Hawley spun about full circle, whipping the sword outwards at the last moment. Meriet's head departed his shoulders. It hit the floor with a wet thud and rolled into the shadows.

The body, to Hawley's horror, remained standing. Staring right at him, if headless bodies could be said to stare. Black smoke and dust swirled around Meriet's decapitated form. Wind blew through the chamber, guttering the torches in their sconces. Hawley shielded his eyes from ash and dirt, braced himself against the force of an unnatural gale that tore at his clothes and whipped his hair from his face.

Then came the howl, like a wolf pack mourning the loss of a matriarch. Myriad inhuman voices bayed in agony, rage, and despair all at once. Hawley chanced a look at Meriet's body, half expecting to see it reform before his eyes and attack once more. But what he saw instead, just for a fleeting second, was a great black shadow with formless limbs, yellow eyes, and long, sharp teeth. No sooner had Hawley seen it than it was gone, blasted apart in a great torrent that covered every surface in a film of grey ash. Meriet's body slumped to the floor with a dull thud, spilling ichor from the stump of its neck.

The chamber was silent; a little brighter, perhaps, as the shadows appeared to retreat, and the torches stopped their infernal guttering and burned more steadily.

Hawley spat ash from his mouth, wiping it from his face in disgust.

And Enelda wailed.

*   *   *

Do you feel it? The booming voice rang in Enelda's head. *Do you feel just a fraction of the power that could be yours? I do not seek to destroy you. I seek to give you a mighty gift!*

"You would make a puppet of me, like Meriet. Who inhabits the Fallen Vigilant? Which Majestic has enslaved him?"

Laughter. A sound like worlds colliding. It grated through Enelda like the roar of an avalanche. She felt her ethereal form flicker.

Meriet is no puppet, and neither shall you be. We shall be one, you and I. Accept my gift, and your aged limbs will feel strength like never before. Your withered flesh shall never corrupt. You will be born anew!

"At what cost? A war to end all wars? The destruction of civilisation?"

Civilisation? Everything these filthy bloodsacks have was built upon lies. These creatures called Men are corrupted vessels for the whispers of the Rift. They would stab their brothers in the back for far less than the prize I offer you. They will jump at the chance of war, and in doing so they will help me cleanse their world of corruption. Imagine it! The world can start anew—it can rise from the ashes as I did. And you, Enelda Drake, can help me rebuild. Together... think what we could achieve.

The fire in Tezryan's eyes grew a little dimmer. The baleful voice softened.

"But what then for Tezryan?" Enelda asked. "What is an avatar of war when there is no war?"

Perhaps the time has come to eradicate the Riftborn forever. Would that not be a worthy destiny for Enelda Drake?

"You know as well as I that the Riftborn can never be defeated, for they are born of the darkness within every soul. Men hold within them both good and evil, and the balance makes them what they are. To attempt the eradication of the Riftborn—of the dark half of all men's hearts—is nothing more than a declaration of war for all eternity. There could be no end until every living thing is dead."

Think very carefully, Vigilant, before rejecting my offer.

Enelda smiled with incorporeal lips. "Oh, I have spent my whole life thinking about it. You must know that I have already considered every conceivable offer you could make me. Nothing you can say could change my mind, and surely you know why."

Say it.

"I am a servant of the light. I am the blessed of Litha. We are both servants of the gods... but you make the mistake of believing you *are* one."

SAY IT! The fire blazed bright once more.

Enelda hissed, "I reject your offer."

The Majestic howled, until the void itself shook.

Enelda shouted as loud as she could, barely audible over the raging lament. "Tezryan, I banish thee!" She held up the blade of covenant.

Laughter again, so loud Enelda feared her astral body would be torn asunder. She gripped her staff of light more tightly.

You are powerless here, Enelda Drake, the creature mocked. It leered forward, so large now, the eye a polished mirror of yellow gold. Enelda saw herself reflected in it, not as her own self, but as a warrior, with shining armour over her robes, a sword in her hand instead of her staff, white hair trailing in plaits to her waist. She had never looked so strong.

In a heartbeat the image was gone, replaced by a withered ruin of a woman, weak and small, clinging for dear life to her staff. Her eyes were sunken pits, and her leathery skin was scored with manifold wrinkles.

What you could have been, and what you will be, Tezryan boomed. *You know this pathetic country is but a shade of its former self. A boy sits on the throne, a weakling king who rules because his mother murdered his even weaker father. The people suffer at the hands of petty nobles. You could have had the power to end it all. To bring castles toppling down about the ears of kings. Instead, you reject this mighty gift. Instead, you choose to be food for the worms.*

"You forget yourself, Tezryan," Enelda said, her words belying the fear that gnawed at her heart. "Your mortal form is still but a shrivelled husk. How long will it take for you to realise your plans? Another ten years? Ten years after that? And your secret is out now. If I don't banish you, another will."

If it takes a thousand mewling souls to restore me, the ones you call Meriet shall see it done. They owe me that much! Even now your allies lose ground. My acolytes lay down their lives for me willingly, and when they are done, no one will remember the words of Vigilant Dra—

Tezryan stopped. The great eye shimmered, becoming momentarily translucent. At once the gigantic form retreated, growing smaller, more distant. The creature muttered in some garbled, alien tongue—a stream of rapid, glottal utterances both curse and ritual.

Enelda concentrated as hard as she could. She reached out with her consciousness. She focused on her own body, back in that baking-hot chamber. She searched for something to latch on to, and for the briefest moment she found Hawley. And through his eyes she saw blood and shadow. She saw death.

Yes—one could always rely on Holt Hawley to do something rash.

"Something the matter?" Enelda asked innocently.

Tezryan roared. The great form of gold and ebony rushed forward with the force of a hurricane.

Enelda raised her staff and brought it down. This time, it struck solid ground, with a chime like the clearest temple bell. The sound pulsed forth in all directions, an echoing wave of clarity in a place of hopeless murk.

What are you—?

A clarion call, reverberating in the darkness. The pinpricks of light, so distant, began to come nearer, swirling in clouds. Spirits gathering around a new presence. A powerful presence, a hunter in the dark, attracted by Enelda's call like a wolf scenting blood.

The Other had come.

Tezryan turned to the gloom, which now shifted and warped maddeningly. Smoke snorted from the Majestic's nostrils; fire licked around his great maw. Silver talons clacked in anticipation of battle.

Enelda felt a thousand screams tear through her mind. A ravening horde of incorporeal demons swarmed through void-like blackness, forms shifting in size and shape in the blink of an eye, at once distant and near, gargantuan and tiny. And at their heart a presence of uncommon power, a mind like a queen ant, controlling a swarm of soldiers, thirsting for souls.

Enelda almost lost her nerve. But at the last, when the horde was so close she feared she would go mad, she stilled her mind and said, "I'll leave you two to get acquainted."

Tezryan roared.

Enelda struck her staff once more, and the vibration thrummed all around her.

In its wake, everything changed. The darkness was rebuilt into more familiar territory. Stone walls with ivy gripping the mortar, shelves lined with fat old books, comfortable rugs in front of a crackling fire.

Enelda took a seat in her favourite armchair by the fire, pulled well away from the draughts and the drips from the roof. And she waited.

*   *   *

"Gods..." Hawley muttered.

Enelda had become very still. Her lips had curled upwards, almost content. Her skin took on a pale, bluish hue.

She looked dead.

*   *   *

Tezryan wheeled around in confusion at finding himself in Enelda's tower. The Majestic was no longer a fearsome celestial, but instead a tall, skeletal man with blackened flesh, dressed in tattered rags. He was St. Baerloc now, because Enelda willed it so.

He gasped fitfully. He had battled the Other, and now, weakened and wounded, he was summoned like a familiar, into a place conjured by a Vigilant's will.

Enelda focused. The Eternal Night was not the Majestics' domain, as Tezryan had claimed. In this place of emptiness, this spirit realm,

Enelda could make equals of gods and mortals both. She solidified every detail of the home she'd inhabited for forty years, until it was indistinguishable from reality. Every bump and groove of the walls, the striations of the flagstones beneath her feet, the patterns in the floor made by rainwater leaking through the ancient roof, the worn lettering on the spines of her books, the tiny holes in her favourite rug made by the spitting fire. Mundanity, minutiae—the elements that made the Vigilants' minds impenetrable, memorised, compart-mentalised, until they became a prison fit even for an angel.

With a great effort, the Majestic roared, attempting to assume a more imposing form. But his body only flickered like firelight, providing the merest glimmer of his true form, before returning to the ragged man, exposed heart pumping behind charred ribs.

Enelda held the wunscæd out once more, and now it felt much more solid. Much more dangerous. She smiled.

"Tezryan," she said. "I banish thee."

The ragged saint crouched, beast-like, hissing like a wildcat.

Enelda stepped towards it, into the light. "Tezryan," she said again, voice growing stronger with every syllable, "I banish thee!"

With a howl, Tezryan pounced. Enelda had expected it, but even so, the ferocity and raw power flung her backwards against the unyielding stone of her own creation. St. Baerloc pinned her arm against the wall, squeezing her wrist until the blade fell from her hand. He had no face. Beneath his cowl was the endless void, which stared into Enelda's very soul.

Enelda's tower shook. Dust and debris fell from above. Cracks formed in the walls, through which the shadows of the cold dark hissed.

Tezryan laughed.

You think you can control me? I am no Riftborn to be pushed aside by charms and symbols. I am the conqueror. I am the reckoning. You worm!

Tezryan's black fingers grew longer, talons of silver forming at their tips. He curled his hand about Enelda's shoulder, and the talons bit deep. Five spears of ice dug into Enelda's flesh, pricking at the bones.

Enelda struggled to maintain the illusion, but already it began to crack. She was not Cerwyn Thawn. How could she have been so stupid?

"No!" she cried. She pushed aside the doubts—doubts driven into her mind by the Majestic. "Tezryan, I banish thee! I banish...Tezryan, I...banish thee..."

But the words trailed into a ragged whisper.

They ended with Tezryan's laughter.

* * *

Blood spotted at Enelda's right shoulder; neat, round puncture marks seeping through Enelda's robe. Her lips moved rapidly, she flailed left and right, fists pounding at the stone floor.

Hawley tried to hold her still. He remembered how she'd been at the Silver River—how he'd feared for her soul. This was worse. Something assailed her in the Eternal Night, and by the looks of things, her physical body wouldn't survive.

Redbaer dragged himself to Enelda's side. His left arm was a ruin. He held the dagger in his good hand, gripping it like a talisman. He stared vacantly, like a man who had seen true horror in battle—horrors he would never forget.

Hawley tried his best to stop Enelda's head hitting the floor again. He grabbed her hand.

"If you're going to do something, do it quickly," he urged.

Enelda's hand tensed, squeezing Hawley's, her ring jabbing into his fingers painfully.

Hawley gritted his teeth. When he saw the ring, the Vigilant sigil, the Eye of Litha, he cast his eyes upwards and muttered, "Litha, Lady of Light. I've been remiss in my prayers, but Enelda Drake has not. I wouldn't expect you to help me, but surely *she's* worthy. If ever she needed you, it's now."

From the corner of his eye, Hawley saw movement. A shadow, coalescing above the sarcophagus. He didn't dare look.

Enelda's fevered muttering grew louder. Hawley leaned closer, and could almost make something out. Something repeated over and over.

"Tezryan. I. Banish. Thee."

He frowned. Then Enelda's hand wrenched free of his. Fit-fully, blindly, she groped around the floor. Her fingertips found Redbaer's hand.

"The blade..." Redbaer muttered.

Again, Enelda mouthed the words, "Tezryan, I banish thee!" over and over.

She wasn't delirious. She was sending a message. A message from the Eternal Night.

She convulsed once more, back arching. Her eyes opened wide in abject horror, mouth contorted. She screamed.

"Take it," Redbaer said. He held the knife out to Hawley. He looked more like his old self, though his eyes spoke of a cowed spirit. "You must...do it. I...cannot." He looked away, ashamed.

Hawley wrenched himself away and took the knife from Red-baer. He approached the sarcophagus, shielding his eyes from whirling smoke. Sharp fragments of stone spat at Hawley in a thick torrent. They sliced at his skin, plucked at his clothes. The unnatural wind buffeted Hawley like a ship in a storm, but still he pushed on. Enelda fought within the Eternal Night, and that being so, perhaps this so-called angel could not bring its full power to bear against him.

"I've killed every manner of creature that walks under the gaze of the gods," Hawley growled. He'd said it to Meriet, and now he said it to himself—a mantra over the din of the howling wind. "What's one more Majestic?"

He reached the black sarcophagus at last. The gruesome form within almost sapped the last of his courage. He couldn't look straight at it. Those maddening limbs covered in black flesh that now bubbled and popped, steam rising up with a serpentine hiss.

Hawley gripped the dagger tight, held it over the misshapen ribs and that still-beating heart, as Meriet had done to Enelda. His hand shook as though some terrible, invisible force resisted him.

A pair of eyelids, black and crisp, opened with a horrible crack. Yellow eyes beheld him.

Hawley lost all sense of himself. He felt a tear run down his cheek. He felt the scratching in the back of his mind return, like a thousand sharp fingernails picking at the insides of his skull. He heard himself scream before he even knew he was doing it.

He could no longer see those hideous eyes and that charred flesh. He saw only a shaft of light in the darkness before him. In that light, he saw a single white feather.

The scream died on his lips. A feeling of tranquillity washed over him. The tears still fell, but they were no longer tears of terror and madness, but of sadness. Sadness for the lost children taken by a monster never meant for this world.

Hawley plunged the blade of covenant into the purple heart of the Living Saint.

"Tezryan," he growled, "I banish thee."

Hawley felt himself go weightless. The stones of the vaulted ceiling spun above him, then the walls, then the floor. Round and round they spiralled. There was a noise, too. A bestial roar, distant, a drone in Hawley's mind. It was as though all time had slowed to a crawl as Hawley tumbled through empty space.

When he found solid ground, it was with a force that pushed all the air from his lungs. The dream state left him rudely, and Hawley woke to pain.

The smoke was gone. The sound of mail-shod boots scraped on the stone stairs of the vault. Someone shouted, "Sir Redbaer! Madam Drake! Are you down there?"

Hawley sat up in a stupor. He was twenty yards from the sarcophagus. He blinked away his confusion.

Enelda Drake looked down at him, shaking her head with more than a little disapproval.

Hawley laughed.

CHAPTER 40

G ods," gasped Raelph. "You killed the abbot."
       "And with it our chance of ending this menace for all
       time." Enelda was cross.

"Thought you'd be pleased!" Hawley growled. He pushed himself upright against the wall. Even that small effort felt like a monumental task.

"Oh, Hawley...A mortal does not simply best a Majestic in battle. If you slew him, it was because he willed it so. Don't you see? He realised I would not submit to Tezryan, and his chance of victory was slipping away with each passing moment. He knew he could goad you into destroying his mortal form before the proper rite was performed. That leaves the Majestic free to return to its own realm and plan its return to our world. Even now, it is looking for another body to inhabit, and it will begin its plan all over again, however long it takes."

"What plan?"

"We don't know that either, do we?" Enelda snapped. "Because we never learned its true name. For now, its machinations are hidden from us."

"Least you're alive," Hawley pointed out, angrily. "You'll get another chance to find this Majestic."

Enelda looked as though she were about to make another sharp remark, but thought better of it. Instead, she placed her small, wrinkled hand on Hawley's arm. "You're right. You did well. Today you have vanquished one Majestic and dented the plans of another. And...you saved an old woman's life in the bargain. I could ask no more of you than that."

Sauveur cursed. While Hawley and Enelda had bickered, the Sylven had quietly inspected the scene of the fight, and had at last come to the sarcophagus.

Enelda rounded on him. "Do not touch that!"

"Madame, I would not touch this...abomination...for all the riches of the Old Empire."

Raelph peered over Sauveur's shoulder, then wheeled away and was violently sick.

"A Majestic..." Sauveur muttered, awestruck. "You have slain a Majestic..." He rolled his shoulders, visibly gathering his wits and courage. "The sarcophagus...it is blackrock?"

"Aye," Enelda said.

"So you were right. Dark magic was at work here."

There came a faint, mewling cry in the distance.

Hawley jolted, as though waking from a dream. It was the same sound he had heard earlier, though he had thought it a hallucination. "Gods!" he said. "The children. They're here."

* * *

They descended again, more steps, spiralling downwards through rough-hewn rock, emerging at last in a cramped, mossy chamber. Water trickled down ancient walls. Now and then, they would find bones, both human and animal, crammed tightly into niches. Sometimes there were skulls, carved with Sygellite runes, empty eye sockets staring at the intruders in their twilight domain. The walls thrummed with energy, drawing arcane power from the bowels of the world. This was an old place, its purpose as mysterious as the shrouded history of the First Aelders.

Hawley covered his nose and mouth as the stench hit him; rotten food, mould, sweat, and piss.

Raelph retched, shook his head, and retreated a few paces back up the steps.

"We've looped back on ourselves," Enelda said. She pointed upwards, and the three men held aloft their torches. The ceiling looked like a natural cavern, save for a large rectangular opening carved into the ancient rock. "We're directly beneath the sarcophagus."

They reached an iron grille, bolted, covering a dark opening from which came not only the foul stench, but the soft cries of children.

Hawley slid back the bolt and threw open the grate. A steep slope led to a sharp drop. There were no hand- or footholds, and no ladder or rope he could see. He held out a hand to Sauveur, who in turn beckoned Raelph to come down and help. Raelph looked uneasy about the whole affair, but nonetheless came down to use his considerable weight as an anchor.

With a torch in one hand, and two men to bear his weight, Hawley took a tentative step into the darkness.

The slope was so slick with green slime, he struggled for purchase. Raelph and Sauveur lowered Hawley as far as they could, and Hawley thrust the torch into the darkness.

Eyes shone back at him. Dull, skeletal faces. Pallid flesh; thin, small limbs.

"Drop me," Hawley said.

He splashed into filth and mulch, into a narrow space little more than a culvert. Five children, half-naked and emaciated, leaned upon each other for support. Their thin wrists were tethered to iron ring-plates; they could not sit or lie down. They must have slept standing up, eaten whatever they could catch that was thrown down to them. And in the sludge beneath them, Hawley saw the corpses. Fresh ones on top, flesh sloughed from wasted wrists finally free of their bonds. Beneath them, blackened and charred bodies. Small bodies, almost numberless, buried in the composting remains of Wulfshael's waifs and strays.

"My god..." Sauveur muttered, as the light of Hawley's torch revealed the true horror below.

Hawley wedged the torch into a gap between two stones. One by one, he cut loose the children, five in all—four boys and one girl. He could not tell their ages. They were malnourished, weightless. None of them said a word. He passed them up to Raelph and Sauveur, the boys first in line. The fourth had dark hair, eyes ringed red and sore. Brown eyes, flecked with amber. When Sauveur hoisted the boy out, he said something in his own tongue, and Hawley knew he'd found Anton Tarasq.

The fifth child reached up to him, and he took her arms.

"Mildrith?" he asked.

She shook her head.

"Do you know a girl called Mildrith? She had a charm, like this." He held up the corn dolly, with its single white feather.

The girl pointed back along the culvert, into the dark...into the pile of bodies.

Hawley faltered. He had come so far. His fists clenched.

"Hawley," Raelph hissed. "Pass her up, man. Let's get out of this gods-forsaken place."

Hawley cursed himself. He held the girl close, told her everything would be all right now, even though it could not possibly be so, and passed her up. Then he took up his torch and stepped into the gloom.

He heard the faint cry again, the cat-like mewling. This time, he was almost certain, it was in his head. Perhaps it always had been.

Hawley waded knee-deep through the filth, pushing through the decaying bodies of the charnel pit. He thought he had seen every atrocity the world had to offer, but he had been sorely mistaken. Behind him, Raelph called for his return, but he pushed on. The sludge grew deeper, the tangle of bodies thicker. He stooped low as the ceiling sloped downwards acutely, and he held the torch as far out as he could, for the walls grew narrower. Square stones gave way to bare rock and moist clay. By firelight, Hawley fancied he saw worn patterns, drawn by men long ago. Paintings, carvings, depicting long-extinct creatures driven out before raging fires, personified as grotesque demons.

The torchlight danced erratically, the temperature rose. Noxious vapours assailed his senses. His head swam. Maybe he imagined it.

From the murky, viscous water ahead came a shimmering light. It was not from the torch; it was purest white. A small, shining object beneath the dark liquid. It called to Hawley. It wanted to be found.

Hawley had not the will to resist the lure. He reached into the sludge, fumbling around, cringing at the touch of solid objects float-ing by, imagining bones and sloughed flesh and far worse besides. His fingers at last curled around something of familiar shape. He pulled from the water a charm—a necklace—and with it came a body.

In a fog of sadness and anger, stupefied by the horror of the place, dazed by all he'd endured, Hawley picked up the remains of the little girl. One half of the body was blackened, burned brit-tle like charcoal. The other was wasted and rubbery, skin translu-cent after too long in the water. Hawley couldn't look at the face, little more now than a skull. He could only see the few remaining locks of fair hair, and the beaded charm hanging about her neck. A corn dolly, its single feather, once white, now black.

There is no promise so hollow as one that cannot be kept.

* * *

They sat on a hilltop and watched thick smoke billow across the paling sky, blotting out the moon and stars. Behind them, Bael-sine grazed as though none the worse for his ordeal. The horse had been the devil to catch, but in truth Hawley wouldn't now be without him.

The flames had begun to die down. Half the spires had col-lapsed, leaving a few skeletal frames and obstinate buttresses to tell future generations what had once stood here.

It had been Enelda's idea, in a way, though she looked less than pleased about it now. No one had known what to do once the children had been recovered, the bodies dredged up, the monks slain or subdued. The unlikely allies had scoured the abbey for what scant evidence they could find, and then argued amongst themselves for a time, until Hawley had asked of Enelda, "What would you have done, in the old days?" And quietly she'd replied, "I'd have burned this place to the ground, salted the earth, and hanged every monk along the road a mile hence, as a warning to others not to court the darkness."

"Then that's what we'll do," Hawley had said. He held no rank, but he'd made the decision. It had seemed simple, obvious. He'd wanted blood and fire and retribution. He still did.

Sauveur had offered a half-hearted protest when the oil had been fetched, concerned as he was about preserving the evidence. Enelda had assured him that her word, and Redbaer's, and his own, would be enough. "Besides," she'd said, "some secrets are better left undiscovered."

"You knew what was going on long before the rest of us, didn't you?" Hawley asked.

Enelda looked across at the drifting smoke. "That is the burden of the Vigilant," she said.

"When did you know? About Meriet?"

"I knew from the first time he and I met," Enelda confessed.

"You—?" Hawley stopped himself. There was little point in recriminations, given everything that had happened. "How?" he asked instead.

"Let me first tell you something of our ways," she replied. "Of the Vigilants' ways. When we use the Eternal Night, the most skilled of us can see through the eyes of the dead at points in their past. There are some with such command of the Eternal Night that they can spy upon the thoughts of the living—upon their very memories. Imagine what a power that is. To see the innermost secrets and fears of an enemy, the misdeeds of the wicked. But it is not easy. In fact, it is downright dangerous. But because we know it can be done, we learn to safeguard against such intrusion. First, we learn to mask our thoughts, like an impregnable castle wall, or a gate barred and bolted. But we are none of us infallible, and so we devised methods to confuse potential enemies even when our guard is lowered. Through concentration, and meditation, and many, many years of practice, we can create false memories, which to an intruder might appear as real as the day is long. Most Vigilants managed to make one such memory— a moment in history, changed forever when perceived through the Eternal Night. A skilled opponent could see through it easily enough. Some few Vigilants managed to make two—some very rare individuals managed to create three. The more you create within the deepest pockets of your mind, the harder the illusion is to maintain. Any who manage to delve deeper than three such memories would be certain indeed that they had finally hit upon the truth, for surely no Vigilant could uphold so many false narratives within their mind at a single time."

"But... you did?"

"I spent over forty years in that tower, Hawley. I did not keep the Riftborn at bay by counting the holes in my rugs. Powers of observation are the first weapon in the Vigilants' arsenal, but by no means the last. I meditated, focused, trained—in case one day the powers of evil tracked me down. And at last, they did."

Hawley considered how someone could spend forty years in a ruined tower training their mind against a thing that *may* happen, while never embracing the present. What a life wasted. He didn't say this. Instead, he said, "So what gave Meriet away?"

"When Meriet and I first met at Scarfell, do you recall what he said to me?"

"Something about seeing you before, when he was a boy."

"At the High Temple at Shaelcrest, yes. And that night in my bed, I thought back to that memory, retrieved it from my mind as one might retrieve a book from the archive. In the memory, I stood beside Cerwyn Thawn as he spoke to the priest about the mysterious incident of the Vanishing Martyr. Behind the priest was a gilded mirror, and I focused my attention upon it, for in the mirror was reflected the chancel, and behind the chancel, a small figure. A boy, awestruck at the presence of the Vigilants, spying on what transpired. That boy was Meriet. There he was, in my memory. But there was one problem..."

"The memory wasn't real," Hawley said with some wonderment. He knew Enelda would not call this "magic," but to Hawley it sounded no different.

Enelda smiled. "I was never at Shaelcrest. I was a hundred leagues away when my master visited that temple, and only learned what transpired there later. I created the scene from a dozen other memories. Meriet even recited back my master's own words to me—'My duty is not to the throne, but only to the truth...'— but he could not finish them, because that was where the invented memory ended. And so he paused, letting me end the sentence, which I did only to humour him. 'And ere my duty is done, I shall answer no summons but the call against the dark.' I confess I was so shocked to learn I was standing before a Fallen Vigilant, I must have seemed very shaken, and that played to my advantage, for Meriet seemed to think the memory of my master had upset me. You see, Meriet had been spying on me through the Eternal Night. He had found that memory amongst many others, and thought it real. He had used his considerable powers to implant himself within it, not knowing that very act would give him away."

"But...how had he been spying on you? How could he have known who you were, or where, before he met you that night?"

"Through your friend Ianto. Meriet must have been searching for me from the day my ring was found. It was so careless of me to lose it. He had scant time to prepare, and so he paid Hobb to take on a new recruit—oh, I'm sure he came up with some story to sate Hobb's sense of propriety, but ultimately the commander must have known it was wrong to accept Ianto into the ranks. You can never underestimate the persuasive power of a Majestic. When Hobb sent a party north to seek me out, Meriet ensured his own man went with you. When you found me, Ianto used the blade of covenant to conduct a binding ritual, allowing the essence of the Majestic into his mind, sharing it with Meriet. Through his eyes, Meriet saw me, and that was all he needed. You may not have known I was the Vigilant, but Meriet knew it at once."

"So why kill Ianto?"

"To tidy up loose ends. Meriet needed me at Scarfell, and not Fort Fangmoor. Therefore he needed at least one of you to make it out of the woods alive—but it couldn't be Ianto. That man had been sloppy. He'd abused his position, breaking his vow of silence in Raecswold and making a black name for himself amongst the servants of Scarfell. If he returned to the castle in the regalia of the High Companies, he'd have been recognised. But I think Meriet's hand was forced when your men tried to assassinate you. It threw Ianto's own mission into uncertainty, and Meriet acted rashly to correct the unexpected error. When you emerged from those woods alone, carrying the blade of covenant, you provided me with a clue. And I had to try very hard to conceal what I knew from that point on.

"I am afraid many times you guessed correctly Meriet's intent, and many times I had to throw you from the scent. I am sorry about that, Hawley, truly—but we had to tread carefully, for his power and influence were too great. I very loudly decried your theories about him. I told you falsehoods—that story about Meriet's wedding band? A lie. The marks on his finger were from the cutting away of the Vigilant's ring, an act of desecration unthinkable to our order."

"But you wear the ring on your forefinger," Hawley said.

"Aye, because it is not my ring. No more were made after the Dissolution, and so I never received my own. This one belonged to my master and was always too big for me."

"Why make up the story?"

"Because I suspected Meriet had eyes and ears everywhere, so I let him believe I was mistaken about him. The lie was for his benefit. All of my suspicions were later confirmed. The last time I spoke with Meriet at the castle, I mentioned my master had died in Sil-Maqash. When I entered the Eternal Night, sure enough—I saw a vision of my master, dead in a souk in that far-off land. The circumstances were...similar...and I regret them every day, but my *real* memories of Sil-Maqash, the city of Heaven's Gate, are mostly happy ones. Cerwyn Thawn died in similar circumstances, and the pain is still too real, but it was far from that sun-baked land."

"You set a trap."

"Indeed I did. It was not the Other who created that vision, or who taunted me within the Eternal Night. It was Meriet's Majestic, whoever it may be. When Meriet pitted his mind against mine, we were linked just for a moment, and I was able to see through *his* eyes, just as he'd seen me through Ianto's. Meriet was in the Eternal Night, whispering promises and threats into the mind of Lord Scarsdale—threats that drove the archduke at last into madness. In the vision, I saw the creature not as Meriet, but in its true form. There was no doubting it then."

"That's when you saw Ermina...You should've told Iveta."

"What good would it have done? We were too late to save the girl, and I had to see my plan through to get Redbaer and Sauveur on our side. Only by having the two of them unite could I stop the war. Any misstep would have set our two nations on an irreconcilable path. Killing Meriet after that would have achieved nothing. Tezryan would have won."

The two of them sat in silence for what seemed the longest time, staring out across the dark hills as the horizon began to pale and distant birds began to strike up their chorus.

"Will he really be back?" Hawley asked eventually. "Meriet?"

"You said I may yet get another chance to find Meriet's Majestic, and perhaps you were right. Remember the sigil on the Thrussels' blade of covenant? The one Ianto cut into that poor girl? That's what helped me identify Tezryan. Perhaps, with study, the sigils on Ianto's blade will help me find the thing that possessed Meriet... or whoever he was."

"Could... could Meriet have used his powers on me?" Hawley asked.

No answer came. The old Vigilant simply stared, shivering a little from the cold.

"Before the end, he said something," Hawley persisted. "Something nobody could've known. Words once spoken to me in private, by Commander Morgard. Did Meriet read my thoughts? Or was he once...?"

Hawley couldn't finish. The idea that the creature who had controlled Meriet to such a dark end may once have inhabited the Silver Lion was abhorrent. Besides, he didn't even think Enelda was listening any longer.

But after a time, her wrinkled lips turned up into a thin smile, and she said softly, "It's funny."

"Funny? How?" Hawley frowned.

"What was it you said to Hobb, at the end? That you didn't believe in fate." She turned to him, with such an unfathomable, knowing look in her eyes, she could as well have been the goddess Litha as the Crone, come to impart some dark knowledge to a naive mortal. "It seems fate believes in you, Holt Hawley."

CHAPTER 41

Raecswold
Haelsdaeg, 16th Day of Nystamand

They'd taken Redbaer's arm at the elbow, and thanked the gods Enelda was there to do it. He hadn't protested—the ruin of his left arm was a grotesque, blackened thing, fit only for a bonfire. They gave him only two days and nights to recover from his ordeal, and could spare no longer. They needed Redbaer for what was to come.

In those two days, one of the boys had died. The girl was sure to follow. They never even learned her name. All the children were sick. Enelda surmised that they had been burned, from the inside out, just like Hodge. Tezryan consumed his sacrifices with fire, body and soul. It was only expedience that had spared Anton Tarasq, but even he had been injured as the Majestic's hunger increased. The boy had spoken not a single word, nor barely slept. In Enelda's opinion, it was unlikely he would ever speak again.

Sauveur had mainly kept his own counsel. Only Enelda had managed to appeal to him, persuading him to send word to General Tarasq that her son was found. Persuading him, also, to omit the worst details for now.

Messages were exchanged with Scarfell. Iveta named Redbaer Lord Protector, and bade him return as soon as possible to oppose Clemence's claims on Scarfell.

Redbaer had come to terms with the loss of his arm with

uncommon bravery. He'd appointed one of his guardsmen as an aide, and refused to stay abed. He looked a pale shadow of his former self. His eyes were ringed red, his golden hair had silvered at the temples almost overnight. The stump of his left arm was hidden under his tunic, the sleeve pinned up at the shoulder.

They assembled once more, for what they expected would be the last time, in the black pavilion at Raecswold.

"When we return to Sylverain," Sauveur said, "there is still much to be answered. That Anton is so tragically struck mute by his ordeal . . . may work in our favour."

Everyone stared at Sauveur in confusion.

"When I tell General Tarasq what has happened, she will be furious. That Abbot Meriet was to blame, and that he is dead, *might* be sufficient to stay her hand. But if she learns Lord Scarsdale was complicit . . . *no!* Her wrath will be savage and righteous both. She will petition our king, and there will yet be war, mark my words."

"But . . . justice has been served," Redbaer said. "They're both dead!"

"Justice? That the lord of an entire mearca—the guardian of the general's own son—allowed the boy to be thrown into a charnel pit, facing a slow and painful death? No, good sir knight, she will not be as reasonable as you imagine. She will want answers. She will want to know who else was involved. She will march on Helmspire if need be, and extract those answers from King Eadred."

"Sylverain is not quite so powerful as all that," Raelph said. "Do you really want to test our armies?"

Sauveur shook his head solemnly. "No, I do not. I think we are powerful enough to burn half this country, and many lives will be lost . . . on both sides. And I think then your forces will seek retribution, and the cycle of violence will weaken us both so that our mutual enemies will strike at us from all sides, like crows upon a carcass. Set aside your bravado. You know what will happen if we go to war. Forget the Felders and the Garders. Forget the Northmen. It is we two—the oldest foes—who decide the fate of all Erevale. This war, over the treatment of one child, would destroy the lives of generations."

8

486

Mark A. Latham

Silence.

"What do you have in mind?" Enelda said at last.

"The truth—the whole truth—need never be known. For the good of all, I will see to it General Tarasq never learns of Lord Scarsdale's involvement. Or at least make it look as though he was just an unwitting pawn."

"She won't believe it."

Sauveur shrugged. "She will if we can present her with a guilty party."

Again, everyone gaped at Sauveur. All except Enelda, whose thin smile belied her discomfort.

"A scapegoat," Enelda said.

"Ah, yes, that is how you say it. A *scapegoat*." He folded his accent around the word. "Someone in a position of authority, perhaps even complicit in part of the affair. Enough so that any accusation will seem reasonable to your king as well as my own."

Redbaer stood on unsteady legs. "I suppose you have someone in mind?"

"I am a stranger to this land. Although...it has occurred to me that we have a number of men in that jail down the hill. Men of dubious honour, not loved by any of you." He shrugged again, spreading his palms innocently. "Unless there is a better suggestion."

"Much as I dislike him," Raelph said, "I hope you aren't suggesting Hobb."

Sauveur smiled. "I would wager Master Hawley feels differently."

Hawley stiffened as all eyes turned to him. He imagined turning Commander Hobb over to the Sylvens. An ignominious end for one of the High Companies. It would certainly make life simpler.

"Hawley gets no say in the matter," Redbaer interjected. "No offence, Hawley. In fact, I'm not entirely sure any of us have a say."

"*You* do," Enelda said. "Lord Scarsdale is gone. Tymon and Meriet are gone. Clemence may cling to power, but the truth of the Vigilants' corruption will soon come out. He's a spent force. I'd say yours is the final word in this mearca, until such time as a High Lord is appointed."

Redbaer pressed his fist into the table. "But...it's not honourable."

"Ah," Sauveur said, "but is it not *noble*? Now you have a chance to save many thousands of lives by sacrificing one. Is that not the choice all great leaders must make? Now you see, Sir Redbaer, the burden of rulership."

"The Vigilant creed would say otherwise," Enelda said.

"Your creed is responsible for many deaths," Sauveur said. "As is mine."

"Only the guilty, never the innocent."

"Are you so sure?" Sauveur said. "We all make mistakes."

"Not when lives hang in the balance."

"Lestyn," Hawley said. He'd been thinking about Hobb, and he couldn't reconcile having the commander executed, no matter how much he hated him. But Lestyn, on the other hand...

"Hawley, not now," Enelda said.

"No, he's right," Raelph spoke up. "I've heard tales about Lestyn that'd make your toes curl. He's hardly an innocent."

"Then he should be tried for the crimes he *has* committed," Enelda said, "not for ones he has not."

"That's just it," Redbaer said quietly. "In the eyes of the law, he's committed no crimes that we can prove. He speaks for Clemence, and Clemence speaks for the king. He is above the law."

Hawley stood. "But we all know what he is. What he's done. Stealing from his lordship's coffers is one thing. Falsely accusing poor folk of witchcraft is another. I shared a cell with an innocent man—a true innocent, with the mind of a child. Bened was his name, and now he's dead, 'cause of Lestyn. Think of all the innocents Lestyn executed *instead* of finding the guilty party. As if he was drawing attention away from his own crimes. He hanged them. He drowned them. He bloody *burned* them. And that's evidence enough, isn't it? We saw those bairns. They were burned. Mutilated. Takes a sadistic bastard to do something like that, and we've got a sadistic bastard in a cell down there, and a line of witnesses from here to bloody Helmspire who'll testify to it."

A stunned silence now. Hawley had surprised himself with the strength of his hatred. Maybe it wasn't just for Lestyn. Maybe it was for all Lestyn represented.

"Hawley," Enelda said quietly, "it is wrong. He is not—"

"Don't tell me he's not guilty," Hawley growled, shaking with anger. "You saw him at Rowen. You know what he did. That little girl—Mildrith—I fished her out of the pit. Her mother asked Lestyn for help, and what did he do? Had her sister put to death and left the girl to rot. I swore I'd save Mildrith, and I was too late…" He wiped his hand across his face in anticipation of tears that didn't come. He couldn't hold his voice steady. He was too angry to feel embarrassed. "But I can see justice brought upon that bastard. And I can let Mildrith's family see it, too, and all the other families. And maybe it'll bring 'em some peace; maybe it won't. You promised them people justice. I promised to save the girl. Maybe we'll both be damned for promises made in Rowen. I tell you this—nay, I *swear* it—if he isn't put on trial for all the wrong he's done, I'll cut his whoring head off myself and carry it to Rowen."

Redbaer gaped at Hawley.

Enelda didn't reply. She didn't look reproachful; only sad.

Sauveur rapped his hand on the table by way of applause. "There we have it! After all I have seen, if Master Hawley swears to kill a man, I do not doubt him. So this Lestyn is virtually a condemned man, and is as good as complicit in the crime. I propose we make a formal accusation and send messages to Helmspire and Tor'laguille to that effect. When his head rolls, peaceful relations between our great nations can resume. All those in favour?"

Sauveur raised his hand. Hawley was next. Then Raelph.

Enelda shook her head. "It would make life much simpler, I concur. But for the good name of my order, I cannot agree to this."

"Put your hand down, Hawley," Redbaer said. "I already told you, you don't get a say."

Hawley glared at Redbaer, but reluctantly complied.

"It falls on your shoulders then," said Sauveur. "*Lord Protector.*"

Redbaer looked down at the table, as though searching for the secrets to life itself. Then finally, he nodded. "Scarfell will see it done."

"I suppose there must be some physical evidence," Sauveur said, "should our word be questioned."

Hawley placed the blade of covenant on the table. All but Enelda inched their chairs away.

"This was used by one of Meriet's men," Hawley said. "It's evidence of witchcraft...among other things. I don't bloody want it."

"We can link it to Lestyn?" Sauveur asked, eyeing the dagger warily.

"Aye. Lestyn conducted a famous trial, condemning the 'Witches of Wyverne' to death. Drawings of a knife very much like this appear in the archive at Scarfell, rendered in Lestyn's own hand."

"This precise knife, or one like it?"

Hawley shrugged. "What does it matter? It'd take a True Vigilant to know the difference."

"Then it is settled," Sauveur said. There was a wicked gleam in his eye—Hawley wondered how many men Sauveur had sent to their deaths. In this company he seemed agreeable enough, but a man didn't earn a reputation like Sauveur's without cause.

There was little more to be said. Plans were made to free Hobb, and the Sylvens were ordered to leave before that happened, with an escort of Borderers. Lestyn and his guards were to remain imprisoned until the trial could be arranged. Before departing, Sauveur extended an invitation to Enelda, should she ever find herself in Sylverain.

"I tire of this country," Sauveur had said. "It is cold and wet always. The sky is grey and the wine tastes of mud."

Their time over at Raecswold, Drake and Hawley hitched a cart and made their own preparations. They rode as far as the crossroads with Sir Redbaer, in silence, until the time came for them to part company.

"After all we've been through," Redbaer said, "I'd like to invite you back to Scarfell. But..."

"We understand," Enelda said.

"I also wish I could give you leave to go home, but I think

you'll be needed when Lestyn goes to trial. I expect the king himself will need to hear your testimony."

"We'll find an inn at Eastmere," Hawley said decisively. "There's somewhere I need to visit on the way."

Enelda didn't argue. Hawley remembered how she'd refused to stay at Eastmere when they'd first set out, for fear of encountering corruption in every dark corner of the little town. He wondered if she'd learned to tolerate people more readily, or if she'd simply been proven right. That'd been less than three weeks ago; it seemed a lifetime.

"I'll send for you," Redbaer said.

Hawley nodded.

"Sir Redbaer," Enelda said. "Now that we're alone, I must tell you something of great import."

"Go on." He looked wary of her. Hawley didn't blame him.

"Lady Iveta is the true daughter of Leoric. His only living heir. And yet her home is under threat. Clemence will already have his claws in her."

"Don't worry about that," Redbaer said. He looked ruefully at his folded sleeve, perhaps wondering if he'd ever fight again. "My men are loyal to me. We'll see Iveta treated fairly."

"That's just it. Under the king's law she *cannot* be treated fairly. Unless..."

"Unless what?"

"In the archive you will find a writ, signed by King Ealwarth himself, relating to the affairs of Lady Aenya. It will be under lock and key—Tymon valued it highly. Find it, and keep it safe. I imagine Iveta will be in no state to consider its implications, but I know you, Sir Redbaer. You will do your duty."

"My duty...?"

"Lady Iveta is the last of her line. She is your mistress now, and she will have no one else on whom to depend."

Redbaer swallowed hard. His eyes moistened. He looked almost relieved.

Hawley wondered if Redbaer had been afraid of life without purpose. If ever a man needed a duty to perform, it was him. Enelda had given him that duty, and Hawley envied him for it.

"Lady Iveta can always count on me," Redbaer said. "Now… I should bid you farewell."

"Redbaer?" Hawley said. "I know I can't really ask a favour… not another. But…"

"Go on."

"Don't tell Hobb where we are. He'll catch up with me soon enough, but by the gods I'd like to get some rest first."

"You have my word."

"Look after that arm like I taught you," Enelda said. "It'll take weeks to heal. Don't overdo it."

Redbaer nodded sorrowfully. "Vigilant Drake; Hawley… Look after yourselves."

With that, he wheeled his horse, looking awkward in the saddle with only one hand to steady the reins. An aide led Redbaer to the rest of the waiting soldiers. It would be some time before the knight could ride unassisted, but he was too proud to be carried.

"Eastmere, then," Enelda said after a while.

"As good a place as any. At least the rain has stopped."

"Haven't you noticed? Sauveur was wrong—the sky is blue. The bees are returning. The farmers are out planting. Spring is almost here."

He hadn't noticed. But something about the bright afternoon sun and the pale blue sky lifted even his damp spirits. With the thinnest smile, Hawley flicked the reins and turned north.

* * *

Six days later, Hawley travelled to the city of Ravenswyck for Lestyn's execution. Enelda had refused to go. Hawley instead travelled with Master Rolfe and his wife. They were thankful to the point of distraction that Hawley had brought their daughter's killer to justice. Hawley felt sick at the deception.

By all accounts, Lestyn had protested his innocence longer than any had expected, even under torture. But he caved in the end. They always did.

It was the day after Nystede, the spring equinox, blessed day of the goddess Nysta. It was unlucky to take any life at such an auspicious time, so the executioner had waited for his due.

Hawley stood in the crowd as the charges were read out by a stony-faced Lord Clemence, under the watchful eye of Iveta. Many in the crowd had come not for the execution, but for a glimpse of the Lady of Scarfell, whose legal challenge to rule the mearca seemed almost certain to succeed. Hawley had heard more than one man whisper the name of Lady Aenya, as though Iveta was the Warrior Maid reborn.

Beside Iveta stood the twelve lords of Wulfshael. Those same lords had, on their own initiative, sanctioned a cruel and unusual form for the execution, such was the severity of the crime. Impalement—a punishment traditionally reserved for child-killers. And thus, before the baying crowd, five iron spikes—one for each child retrieved from the charnel pit—were plunged through Lestyn's body. Then, before he was dead, the headsman decapitated Lestyn with a sword even broader than Hawley's much-missed Felder blade. The head would hang over the gates of Ravenswyck, as a warning to all who would consider a like crime.

Above it all, a foreign woman looked on, standing apart from the others in stony silence. Uncommonly tall, commanding, dark; armour like polished glass, carved with twin unicorns flanking a castellated tower. General Tarasq herself, granted royal dispensation to see the execution of the man who'd tortured her son.

Hawley made no attempt to contact Iveta. He didn't know what he'd say. Instead, when it was over, he returned to Eastmere, still in possession of the corn dolly charm, which Mildrith's parents had tearfully insisted he keep.

He was grateful when Enelda didn't question him about the day's events. He felt like a fraud.

That feeling had only worsened the next day, when the king's herald arrived.

CHAPTER 42

The herald was a foppish sort, and far too haughty for his own good in Hawley's opinion. Here was one of the highest-ranked servants in Aelderland, second only perhaps to the king's own steward back at Helmspire, and he'd been sure to have himself announced with all due pomp and ceremony. And so sat before them "Sir Ricard Caelvedon, Earl Marshal of Aeldenhelm, Herald Pre-eminent of His Majesty King Eadred II," rosy-cheeked face framed by a mop of golden curls. His livery of red, green, and gold was immaculately clean, considering his weeks on the road, and he looked with distaste around the humble coaching house in which Enelda and Hawley roomed. Save for a single scribe, Sir Ricard left his attendants outside, much to the relief of the innkeeper—the sight of an entire entourage of king's men, from soldiers to minstrels, had instilled within the man a great sense of inadequacy.

Hawley had not considered that he would be called upon to sign statements, writs, warrants, and decrees, but Sir Ricard insisted that he and Enelda would have to bear witness to it all, and that was that. After the first hour, Hawley regretted the ale he'd consumed that afternoon. After the second, he wished he'd drunk more.

Most of the business involved Enelda's testimony regarding the investigation at Scarfell, the death of Lord Tymon, Lestyn's guilt, and the razing of the abbey. Ricard made a play of not questioning their accounts of the first two matters, but the truth of what Abbot Meriet had been up to at Erecgham—and what was rumoured to have resided in the crypt there—had not escaped the king's ear.

The true version of events would become a state secret, and Drake and Hawley were bidden to sign several documents to that effect.

"And what of Scarfell?" Hawley asked, as much to stop his eyes glazing over as anything. "Who rules Wulfshael now?"

"Ah." Ricard paused, a twinkle in his eye. "You've doubtless heard that Lord Clemence's interim governance of the mearca is set to come to an end."

Hawley had heard rumours. He'd also heard Redbaer had made Clemence's brief flirtation with power unbearable.

"The king pondered this matter most carefully. There are many lords in Wulfshael who would make fine successors to the troubled Archduke Leoric. After all, he left no male heir. But there is the small matter of a daughter, already of age. It may surprise you to learn that King Eadred was petitioned by the Sylverain delegation, not to mention Sir Redbaer, to allow Lady Iveta to rule Scarfell. As you can imagine, there was considerable opposition—the manor of Scarsdale is of singular strategic importance, and no woman has been permitted to rule it since the fabled Aenya herself. I think that ancestry is the reason why His Majesty the King saw fit not to change the law, but to make an exemption on Lady Iveta's part. She will indeed be permitted to rule Scarfell as High Lord of Wulfshael, at least until such time as she takes a husband."

Hawley smirked at the idea of any man trying to tame that one and take away her hold.

"Sir Redbaer will stay on as Lord Protector of the manor and Lady Iveta's chief advisor. Lord Clemence, who I believe you know, shall serve as her sheriff."

"Sheriff?" Enelda spoke up.

"Ah, yes. You see, another thing has come about as a result of your...adventures. In the king's view, his Vigilants had become prideful, their powers too extensive. By the very act of retaining the title of Vigilant, they developed an ill-judged sense of their own authority, acting in the *name* of their king, without truly *consulting* with their king, you see. So much was their position abused, that some even dared to speak as kings themselves, issuing commands to soldiers of the High Companies, whose solemn oath is to the throne. With a heavy heart, the king removed the title of Vigilant from his justiciars. From now on, the senior law-keeper in each mearca will go by the old title of 'sheriff,' and be not answerable to the king, but to the lord of his mearca."

"That...won't go down well," Hawley said.

"Indeed not! And such a lack of humility rather proves His Majesty's point, don't you think?"

"And the other Vigilants?" Enelda asked. "The likes of Les-tyn, and all his men?"

"Those lower-ranked Vigilants deemed...trustworthy enough... will become constables. The Vigilant Guard will be dissolved: Places will be found for them in the local militias; otherwise they shall have to find trades in one of the manors. We can't have mere constables roaming the land with personal retainers—what would the world come to? No, should a constable find evidence of a crime, he shall have to appeal to the manor's lord to help him prosecute the guilty. There shall be no more hangings and what have you without proper authority."

Enelda sighed.

It was obvious even to Hawley that these reforms wouldn't have helped one jot in finding Anton Tarasq. Still, in Wulfshael at least, the sheriff would have to serve Iveta, so perhaps there was a glimmer of hope.

"The king insists *your* title be restored as a point of honour, my lady. It seems there is only one Vigilant in Aelderland now," the herald said, and smiled.

"Not necessary," Enelda said, fidgeting in her seat.

"Oh, it is a fitting reward. You now answer only to the king. He may have certain...official requests of you from time to time, but in all other respects you may be considered a free woman, equal in rank to a knight. May none hinder you in the pursuit of your lawful duties, and so on and so forth. I have the writ here somewhere..." He rummaged in his bag and produced a scroll. "A-ha! Oh, and you are to present yourself for a private audience with His Majesty at your earliest opportunity."

Enelda put her hand on Hawley's arm. The thought of visiting

Helmspire, largest city in Erevale, was of obvious concern. "I think not," she said. "I just want this over and done with so I can go home."

The herald smirked infuriatingly. "You mean…surely you can't mean…Not to the Elderwood? To that ramshackle tower?"

"It is not much, but it has been my home for so long, I know nothing more. I need nothing more."

"Then my heart is heavy, my lady, for it is quite impossible. The last I heard, pilgrims from across the kingdom were already travelling to the fabled tower in the woods, eager to see for themselves the refuge of the last Vigilant. The king dispatched guards to protect your belongings from the…overzealousness…of the faithful, but you know how it is." The herald shrugged, as though the desecration of Enelda's private possessions was just one of those things. An act of the gods. "Whatever was recovered is already on its way back to Helmspire."

"*Back* to Helmspire? It doesn't belong in Helmspire!" Enelda shook, her distress evident. It was Hawley's turn to place a hand on her arm, to calm her as she so often did him.

"Would it surprise you to learn that a fine house has already been selected for you in the temple quarter? It is yours whenever you wish to claim it. The king knows you like your privacy, so in his wisdom he chose a house with a walled garden—a beautiful one, at that—and only a modest complement of servants, paid for from his own coffers. What say you to that?" The herald beamed.

Enelda diminished before Hawley's eyes, shrinking away as she calculated what all this meant. She no longer needed to seclude herself away. She had her freedom, but she didn't know what to do with it.

"Vigilant Drake is…most grateful," Hawley said on her behalf.

"Excellent. However, that does lead me to broach the subject of one final…problem. It concerns the wrongful imprisonment of Commander Hobb, at the village of Raecswold."

"A necessary evil," Enelda said. "We had not the time to persuade Hobb to our cause, and he was quite ready to fight on behalf of Vigilant Lestyn, who we now know was a practitioner of the blackest arts."

Sir Ricard pulled his cloak around his shoulders at the mention of witchcraft. "Quite...I'm sure His Majesty understands. On the matter of Commander Hobb, however, there is a complication regarding the status of 'Master' Hawley..."

Hawley fixed the fop with his steeliest stare, which had no obvious effect. Hawley worried he was losing his edge.

"Hawley is a freeman now," Enelda answered on Hawley's behalf.

"Perhaps not. Holt Hawley stands accused of some rather serious crimes. Desertion, assaulting an officer of the High Companies...even murder."

"Murder! I—" Hawley half stood, but Enelda stopped him instantly and he sank back to his seat.

"The ancient tradition of trial by combat is not recognised by the Crown. It is at the complainant's discretion whether transgressions are absolved by the result of a duel, and I'm afraid Commander Hobb has chosen not to abide by the custom."

"Sounds about right," Hawley grumbled.

"However, given Master Hawley's part in averting a great disaster for our nation, the king deems it unfit he should face the gallows. Under the law, Commander Hobb still has maintenance over him..."

Hawley shifted, part in discomfit at the thought of being Hobb's property still, and part in annoyance at being spoken about like he wasn't there.

"Would Holt Hawley return to duty in the Third, should the king require it?" Finally, he looked Hawley directly in the eye.

"If...the king wills it." The words almost stuck in Hawley's throat.

"But the king bade me ask a question, and in this matter use my own judgement. If you were pardoned—for argument's sake—and were free to choose your own path, what would it be?"

Hawley narrowed his eyes, expecting a trap. At last he said, "I...would not be free, even then."

"How so?"

Hawley looked to Enelda, then to the herald. "I swore an

oath to protect Vigilant Drake." It was a small lie, perhaps, as Enelda had technically released him. But he still considered Enelda's words at the Silver River part of a ruse, and therefore his duty unfulfilled. "Vigilant Drake can release me with a word. But until then...I must honour that oath."

"Spoken almost like a knight of the realm," said the herald, a thoughtful expression crossing his smooth face. "But the king, appointed by the gods, could release you from that oath, could he not? So, I pose the question again. If you were free—of *all* obligation—what would *you* choose? Where would you go? The truth now—the king demands an honest answer."

Hawley squirmed a little. He knew Enelda was staring at him, but he couldn't meet her eyes. He thought hard, took a deep breath, and said, "I would serve Vigilant Drake willingly, oath or no."

"Ha! Here is a man to whom an oath means something! A rare thing in these benighted times." The herald again reached into his bag, and eventually produced another parchment. "The king bade me give you this, should I feel you deserve it. It is a pardon, Master Hawley. You are a soldier no more, nor servant, neither! You may take whatever path you wish, but as long as you serve Vigilant Drake, maintenance of your person will be borne by the king himself. You will receive the freedom of the city...right to bear arms in service to your king...let no man hinder you... blah, blah, blah. It's all written down there. Do you accept?"

Hawley somehow stopped gawping. Finally, he managed, "I do."

"Splendid! I'll have the scribe draw up any remaining papers. Now, as I said, Vigilant Drake, you are to present yourself to the king at your earliest opportunity—within one moon, if you would. Master Hawley, I trust you'll see to it that Vigilant Drake arrives safely."

Hawley nodded.

"Good, good. You can make arrangements with my man there. Now, just a few more things to sign and we can all be on our way. How you stand it out here amongst all this mud really is beyond me."

The remaining formalities were completed after what seemed

an eternity, and at last the herald and his entourage left Eastmere, seeming rather pleased to be doing so.

For the longest time, Drake and Hawley could only sit at the table in the little coaching inn and stare at the parchments before them in silence.

*　　*　　*

Vansdaeg, 11th Day of Rennemand

As a sargent of the High Companies, Hawley had travelled the length and breadth of Aelderland, and sometimes beyond. Only once before had he been to Helmspire, and even then he had only seen the great palace from afar. Now he approached it in a covered carriage adorned with the royal crest, driven by a liveried coachman.

Hawley looked down at his borrowed tunic, not for the first time, and found himself wishing he could still lay claim to his old uniform. He felt entirely unsuited to meet the king.

Enelda had clung to Hawley ever since they had passed the final watchtower on the approach to the city. Occasionally, when they passed by one of the numerous groups of fellow travellers, he saw her fingers tapping rhythmically as she concentrated, filling her mind to guard against corruption and darkness.

The air began to change; the salt tang of a fresh sea breeze blew in from the east. Gulls circled overhead, crying like bairns.

The carriage crested the last great rise, and Hawley's eyes took a moment to adjust to the sudden glare of the morning sun gleaming off the sea below. Enelda's fingers tightened around his arm. The sight took his breath away.

Helmspire was built around a vast port, but had sprawled inland for centuries, becoming so large that every mearca sent tithes of produce monthly to feed the city's enormous populace. From here, the tall ships and swollen galleys looked tiny, black specks swaying slowly in and out of the glittering bay, bringing untold wealth in trade. Yet the more impressive sight was the palace itself, clearly visible upon a massive crag—an unassailable natural fortress that towered over crashing waves, reachable only via a wide bridge of pristine white stone. The palace was one of only two great buildings in all Aelderland to retain its old Sylven architecture in its entirety, the other being the Temple of the Trysglerimon on the other side of the city. It was a storied huddle of enormous stone towers, each tapering to a needle point, giving the city its name. From lofty heights, thousands of statues, carved in the likenesses of dragons, boars, wolves, hawks, and bears, stared down impassively at visitors to the ancient seat of kings, visitors who shuffled like pilgrims to pay homage to their Boy King. It was the twin of the Silver Palace at Tor'laguille, built by the master masons of old Sylverain, whose knowledge was fabled to have come from a long-dead race of elves, and was now lost to time.

Enelda scoffed at Hawley when he'd mooted the legend of elf-craft, but Hawley found it easy to believe as he gazed out at those dizzying spires, adorned with pillars of marble and gold, dragon pennants flicking like serpentine tongues towards the clouds.

"Hawley," Enelda whispered. "I've changed my mind. Let's go back."

She had spoken barely a word over the last few miles. Hawley couldn't imagine how she must feel. Her world had been turned upside down in the space of a month.

"There's nowhere to go," he said. He glared at the watching page, who quickly averted his eyes. More gently, Hawley said, "Come on...Was it not the duty of the Vigilants to report to their king in such times?"

Enelda looked distantly through the carriage window. "Yes," she said. "And it always led to more trouble."

"You've already come so far. I suppose...this is your home now."

"*Our* home," Enelda corrected.

"I'm just a servant, remember?"

"And a finer servant I am sure I could not find."

"I know you only offered the post to save me from Hobb's wrath," Hawley said. "After all, you've coped well enough alone all these years."

"I don't need a servant, stupid boy," Enelda said sharply. Then her eyes twinkled, her lips turned upwards to a smile. "I need a Baeldorn."

Hawley stopped. "What? Why?" He couldn't form a sentence.

"Because the Boy King has forced my hand. He wants to collect me. To keep me as his very own pet Vigilant, a 'living legend' to show off to his courtiers. So...I have decided to keep him happy by coming out of retirement."

Hawley's mouth dropped open.

"How many times must I tell you: Don't gawp." Enelda smiled. "I've had a lot of time to think, and...you were right all along. I have the power to help people. No matter how difficult it is, or what dangers I may face, it is wrong of me to deny those in need. But I do not have my order to call upon, and so I need help. In the old days I would have taken an apprentice, but we're both too old for that. Besides, the world is much changed—these days a good sword-arm is better surety against evil than a stern glare from an old woman, more's the pity. That said...you'll need training. But Baeldorn you will be, if it suits."

There was a lump in Hawley's throat. Had he not joined the militia in his youth to find some useful purpose in life? Had he not joined the High Companies for the same reason? Both times he had been found wanting, and of late he had felt...lost. Enelda didn't offer him a post. She offered him what he'd searched for all his life: a calling.

"Aye," Hawley managed. "It suits."

"Then I have arrived safe and well, and your oath is fulfilled." Enelda looped her arm in his. "Today we meet the king. Tomorrow, our work begins."

The two unlikely companions sat in silence as the carriage rocked and bumped its way towards the vast city gates. Just weeks ago, neither of them would have ever imagined coming to Helmspire. It was a place of wonder, of vibrancy, teeming with life of every stripe. But it was also a place of hardship, of intrigue and danger. To Enelda Drake and Holt Hawley it was now far more than that.

Now it was home.

The story continues in . . .

KINGDOM OF OAK AND STEEL: BOOK 2

Keep reading for a sneak peek!

ACKNOWLEDGMENTS

The Last Vigilant was not an easy book, but here at its publication I can safely say that it's the most rewarding of my work to date.

Maybe it's because this book contains the most intensely personal characters I've ever written. Hawley, Enelda, and Iveta come from some deep wellspring within, often hidden; and many times they had to be coaxed, cajoled, or wrestled onto the page, such was their reluctance to lay themselves bare. Hawley—predictable, rash but straightforward Hawley—put up the biggest fight, as one might expect, and the result is all the more brutal and pleasing for it.

Maybe, though, it was the sheer difficulty of hammering the mystery into shape. At times the intricacies of the plot threatened to drive me more than a little mad, so that by the end, I fully understood why Enelda spends so much time chuntering to a raven. My dog was most bemused throughout the process and probably wondered if it'd ever end, given that the book took three times longer to finish than my previous longest effort.

Through this, it was the encouragement, advice, moral support, and invaluable feedback of some wonderful people that got the book over the finish line.

First, my wife, Alison, who's not only my trusted alpha reader but who greeted the time I spent obsessing over yet another draft of the book with "Do what you have to do." Without her support I really wouldn't have been able to.

Next, Nick Cristofoli, whose extensive knowledge of classic mysteries led to numerous productive (and a few not-so-productive) literary (and some not-so-literary) discussions in the local pub. Likewise, Pete Borlace—always a steadfast supporter of my work—was an integral sounding board. His innate knowledge of worldbuilding (not to mention unarmed combat) proved more useful than he might have guessed. It also helped that we did most of our talking about *The Last Vigilant* while walking the rugged hills and forests of North Wales, which ended up forming the basis of many of my depictions of Aelderland's wilderness. This trio is rounded out by George Mann, whose encouragement, advice, and *belief* in this book got me through more than one tough spot.

The Last Vigilant had probably the most brutally honest (and therefore most helpful!) beta read from Lisa Ward, who challenged all my preconceptions and triggered a fair bit of soul-searching as well as word-wrangling.

A particularly huge thank-you goes to Lisa's other half: my friend and fellow Orbit author Matthew Ward, who always has an uncanny knack of knowing how to help me through the trickiest problems—whether it means offering his expertise at story structure or just letting me talk while he gets the drinks in. In any case, there's no way this book would be finished even now without his support.

Skipping ahead, I of course must thank my agent, Jennie Goloboy, of the Donald Maass Literary Agency. It was *The Last Vigilant* that I used as a springboard to find new representation, at a particularly turbulent time in the industry. Jennie not only shared in my vision for the book but gave me plenty of sage advice that ultimately led to it finding a great home at Orbit. I've never had a publisher roll out the welcome wagon quite like the wonderful people at Orbit US, and I'm thrilled to be part of the family. My editor, Bradley Englert, has turned out to be one in a million, and his input along with that of Nick Burnham helped shape the novel you hold in your hands. (It's a rare and wonderful thing to find editors willing to give one the freedom to make an already lengthy book *longer*, but that's what we had, and I'm thankful for it.) If you're reading this in the UK, which is where this book was birthed, then you have James Long to thank for its final form, and I'm very grateful to have such a fine fellow pick up the book on home turf.

Last but not least (and at the risk of being a cliché of a writer), a shout-out must go to the guys at my favourite local café bar, notably Caleb, Réka, Jemima, Keeley, and Hilary. There were times when only a change of scenery got me through some difficult mental blocks, and these lovely people provided me with a workspace away from the office, not to mention excellent coffee (okay, and *maybe* the odd cocktail) and friendly banter when I needed it most. Cheers!

APPENDIX

DRAMATIS PERSONAE

Agatha: A woman of Rowen, drowned as a witch.

Agnead: Servant of Scarfell.

Amos: A farmer.

Bartholomew: A raven.

Beacher: A soldier.

Bened: A man of Raecswold.

Clemence, Lord: High Vigilant of Wulfshael.

Drake, Enelda: Former Vigilant of the old order.

Ermina, Lady: Daughter of Archduke Leoric.

Everett: Steward of Scarfell.

Fyrne: Tithing man of Rowen.

Gereth: A freeman of Godsrest.

Hawley, Holt: Sargent of the Third High Company.

Hobb, Commander: Commanding officer of the Third High Company.

Ianto: A soldier.

Jens: A man of Halham.

Leoric, Archduke: Lord Scarsdale; High Lord of Wulfshael.

Lestyn: A Vigilant.

Llewelyn: A priest of Wyverne.

Malbuth: A cofferer of Scarfell.

Meriet, Galdwin: Lord Abbot of Erecgham.

Mildreth: A girl, kidnapped.

Morgard: Former commander of the Third High Company; the Silver Lion.

Nedley: A soldier.

Parnella: Nurse.

Raelph, Sargent: A soldier of the Border Company.

Redbaer, Sir: Knight of the realm, captain of the Scarfell Guard.

Ricard, Sir: Earl Marshal of Aeldenhelm; the king's herald.

Rolfe, Mistress: A woman of Rowen.

Rolfe: A man of Rowen.

Sauveur, Viscount Phillippe: An agent of Sylverain.

Sherrat: A soldier.

Snowsill, Lady Iveta: Ward of Archduke Leoric.

Swire, Sargent: A Vigilant Guard.

Tarasq, Anton: Boy of Sylverain, hostage of Scarfell.

Tarasq, General: Commander of Sylverain's northern army; mother of Anton.

Tarbert: A soldier.

Tymon, Lord: Chamberlain of Scarfell.

AELDERLAND AND ITS MEARCAS

Aelderland is but one nation of Erevale, the great continent that was once the seat of power of the Sylven Empire. This empire dominated almost a third of the world (called Valdymion by the most learned scholars). The other two major continents of Valdymion are Cravania and distant Skarnoth.

The seven great regions of Aelderland are called *mearcas*, each ruled over by an ancestral "High Lord" (at least a baron in rank) and divided into a number of manors (as few as twelve in Iniswaed and as many as thirty-nine in Wulfshael). Each mearca is possessed of its own unique character and customs based on geographical and cultural peculiarities.

- **Aeldenhelm:** Seat of kings, the wealthiest mearca. The capital city, Helmspire, is located here, near the shoreline at the mouth of the River Avonmyr. Aelderland's second city, Randburg, is located close to the border with Reikenfeld, and its incredible fortifications have earned it the moniker "The Shield of the North." Aeldenhelm's towns and cities are home to the most temples in the realm, as well as its famous universities and libraries. Knowledge is said to be guarded jealously in Aelderland, with only wealthy scholars permitted to study at these fine institutions.
- **Iniswaed:** The king's larder. The smallest mearca, but one made up of the most fertile land in the kingdom. Its hills are populated by sheep, its farmland is incredibly productive, and its sheltered location inland means it also has passable vineyards. Given its fairly low population, it has few lords to rule it, and only a small number of manors. Much of the harvest thus relies on itinerant workers from neighbouring mearcas.

- **Strenshael**: Far-flung and strange in its customs, Strenshael is home primarily to fishermen and seafarers. This province provides experienced sailors for Aelderland's navy and trade fleets, but it is also a holy place, where priests of the old ways still worship at stone circles. Just off the coast, the Isle of Shaelcrest houses a vast fortified temple, where priests of the Trysglerimon—the Blessed Three—are trained before setting forth to serve communities across Aelderland.

- **Wulfshael**: Once a wilderness covered almost entirely in forest, this unclaimed land derived its name from the hundreds of outlaws—or "wolf's heads"—who migrated there after falling foul of their lords' justice. Now it is one of the largest and most prosperous mearcas. The forests are mostly cleared, revealing vast tracts of fertile land. The region boasts two heavily fortified cities, Ravenswyck and Wulfsreach, as well as the stronghold of Scarfell, which boasts its own walled town. The **Gold Road**—the main thoroughfare between the capitals of Aelderland and Sylverain—runs for more than half its length through Wulfshael and is guarded by the eight border forts, home to Aelderland's best standing army and each a manor in its own right. The southern portion of Wulfshael comprises the Sylven Marches, a buffer zone between Aelderland and Sylverain. By treaty, only one company of soldiers is permitted to encamp there—elite rangers dubbed simply "the Border Company"—and the entire region is placed under the protection of the manor of Scarfell, currently ruled by Archduke Leoric.

- **Maserfelth**: The poorest mearca, Maserfelth is a mist-wreathed land riven with many leagues of fens, lakes, and swamps. Its people scrape a living from the mud and waterways, and are often derided by the folk of other mearcas due to their peculiar dialect and slow pace of living. The portion of Maserfelth that borders the Silver River is poorly protected against invasion, because the environment itself is anathema to invading armies—woe betide anyone who tries to ride heavy horses across the fens.

- **Hintervael**: This mountainous region extends almost the full length of the western border with Tördengard and, as a result, has seen more than its fair share of fighting against the unpredictable Garders. Raiders from the far north often make ingress via Hintervael after negotiating passage through Garder lands. This mearca is the heart of Aelderland's mining industry, providing enormous amounts of copper, iron, and silver for domestic purposes and trade. Some whisper that, at the king's behest, black-rock is still mined in Hintervael, and exported to Sylverain and Reikenfeld in secret consignments for high prices.

- **Aeldervael**: Some treat Aeldervael as part of Hintervael, and there is much dispute over its borders. This tiny province in the extreme southwest of the country is separated from the main region by inhospitable hill country. It is a poor land, but proud, and its people are some of the stoutest in Aelderland. Scholars believe the first Aelders arose in this region, a theory supported by the strange dialect the Vaelmen speak that has more in common with Old Aeldritch than the common tongue. These days, the Vaelmen believe themselves to be independent, having more common lineage with Tördengard than other Aelderlanders yet feeling they belong to neither kingdom.

MEASURING THE YEARS

The Aelderland calendar comprises twelve months, each of thirty days. Four extra days occur after the spring equinox, sometimes erroneously referred to as the "month" of Setenstede. This is a time of celebration and reflection. One extra day is added to the month of Winterlith after the winter solstice—a day of prayer (Symbeldaen) to send unsettled souls back to rest.

1. **Endelfrost**. "Eternal frost." Aelderland is a place of deep winters and mild summers, and this name signifies the feeling that winter might never end.

2. **Sollomand**. "Month of mud." Not just a description of the land, accurate though it is in this time of thawing, but also descriptive of cake mixture and dough, because this is a month when bread and cakes are baked in celebration of winter's end—some are offered up as sacrifices to ensure a good crop later.

3. **Nystamand**. "Nystia's month," in honour of the goddess of fertility. Spring begins at the equinox, dubbed **Nystede**.

• **Setenstede**. A four-day festival of cultivation and planting. These make up their own short "month."

4. **Rennemand**. "Rain month," when half the country suffers a deluge and the other half scattered showers for almost a whole month. On the second Nysdaeg after Setenstede, most villagers are given the morning off from their labours to go out and "beat the bounds" of the manor with switches of willow and rowan. This reinforces the ancient boundaries and blesses the crops and animals.

5. **Trismilce**. "Three milkings," when livestock are so well-fed on spring grass that they can supposedly be milked three times a day.

6. **Sygaerra**. "Before the sun." The first month of summer.

7. **Sumersmand**. "Month of summer," really the height of summer.

8. **Weodermand**. "Month of plants," when the fields are burgeoning and the forests are lush.

9. **Holigmand**. "Holy month," when thanks are given to the gods for a fruitful harvest—or sacrifices made to ensure a better one next year if it was not so good. On the fourth day of this month, **Arborstede** is celebrated, ostensibly commemorating the end of the great war and the signing of the accords. In the capital, the king walks from the palace to the city square, where he ties a ribbon on a branch of the ancient oak. All over the country, peasants go to the

edges of forests and do likewise, making wishes as they tie the knots. It is a ceremony marking the end of Sylven customs and a return to the "old ways."

10. **Winterlith.** "Winter's moon," the month sacred to Litha. The first full moon of winter falls in this month, marking a day of sombre reverence. There are thirty-one days in this month, with **Symbeldaen,** a day of prayer, directly following **Feorstede,** the festival of souls held at the winter solstice.

11. **Blotisstede.** "Festival of Blood." Though the practice is now less popular, this is a time when sacrifices of livestock were traditionally made to the gods to see people through the winter.

12. **Lonnichstede.** "Festival of the Long Night." In this month, the nights are darker for longer, and several fire festivals are held so that Sygel, the sun god, does not forget the people of Aelderland during his long hiatus. Also contains the festival of **Modrastede,** "Night of Mothers," when Nysta is called upon to bless new mothers and babies during the winter.

COUNTING THE DAYS

The seven days of each week are named as follows:

1. **Lithadaeg.** Named for Litha, goddess of the moon.
2. **Feorndaeg.** Named for Feorngyr, god of the hunt.
3. **Haelsdaeg.** Named for Haelstor, god of darkness and of spirits.
4. **Vansdaeg.** Named for Vanya, goddess of storms, sky, and sea.
5. **Nysdaeg.** Named for Nysta, goddess of fertility and the harvest.
6. **Wealsdaeg.** The only day not named for any god. Loosely translated as "water day," the traditional day of rest for workers, where they would bathe in lakes and streams.
7. **Sygesdaeg.** Named for Sygel, god of the sun.

WEIGHTS AND MEASURES

The following system is used by Aelderland and its close neighbours, Reikenfeld and Tördengard. Sylverain has its own system
that was once imposed across its empire, since rejected by most of
the realms after the War of Silver and Gold.

Weight

- **Dram** (dr): ¹⁄₁₆ of an ounce. Based on the amount of silver
  legally required in the minting of a king's shilling (or stan-
  dard "coin of the realm"). Not to be confused with the
  volume measurement of the same name.
- **Ounce** (oz): 16 drams.
- **Pound** (lb): 16 ounces.
- **Stone** (st): 14 pounds.
- **Hundredweight**: 8 stone, or 112 pounds.
- **Ton**: 20 hundredweights.

Measurement

- **Linie**: ¼ of a barleycorn (¹⁄₁₂ of an inch)
- **Barleycorn**: ⅓ of an inch. The "base unit" in agricultural
  trade.
- **Finger/Fingerwidth**: ⅞ of an inch.
- **Inch** ("): Based on the length of a man's thumb, from tip of
  the digit to the first knuckle.
- **Handspan/Span**: About 6½ inches.
- **Foot**: About 12 inches.
- **Yard**: 3 feet (36 inches). Base unit for most distances.
- **Fathom**: 6 feet (2 yards).
- **Pole/Rod**: About 5½ yards. This is an administrative
  measurement used to mark off areas of agricultural land.
- **Furlong**: 600 feet (200 yards). Roughly the distance a
  plough team can work without rest.

- **Acre:** Area measurement. The boundary of a single field that can be worked by a farmer, for tax purposes. It is five rods in width by one furlong in length.
- **Mile:** Thought of by most folk as 1000 paces. Technically 5280 feet (1760 yards).
- **League:** Commonly understood as 3 miles (the distance a person could walk in an hour). A military league is longer (4–5 miles), calculated by the distance a soldier can march in an hour.

Volume (Liquid)

- **Dram:** ⅛ of a fluid ounce. Also colloquially used as any small measure (about two fingers) of strong distilled liquor.
- **Fluid ounce:** ¹⁄₄₀ of a quart, or ¹⁄₂₀ of a pint.
- **Pint:** ½ of a quart, or 20 fluid ounces.
- **Quart:** 40 fluid ounces, or 2 pints.
- **Gallon:** 4 quarts, or 8 pints.
- **Firkin:** 9 gallons.
- **Hogshead:** 54 gallons.

THE PANTHEON

Most people of the settled lands concur that there are two strata of deities. The most enduring creation myth is the tale of the Blessed Three, also called the Trysglerimon, who once held dominion over the world. These three siblings were born of the sun, the moon, and the space between. All life stems from them, and all cultures have some theory as to where They themselves came from. It is said that the Three could not agree how best to rule the land over which they held dominion. Thus they waged a bitter feud, splitting the land into three vast continents from which they cast spells, directed spies, and created armies to attack their rivals.

The Trysglerimon, the creators of all things, are known by

varying names. The people of Aelderland tend to use some varia-
tion of the following:

- **Erieste the Wise,** fairest of the Three, creator of Erevale
  and of the first Fair Folk. She was first to return to heaven,
  leaving her land in the hands of her creations and her
  brothers to squabble among themselves.
- **Skar'gol, the Destroyer,** creator of Skarnoth, the Dark-
  lands. It was he who inadvertently created the first Rift,
  bringing forth creatures from a realm unseen.
- **Vanalith, the Trickster,** creator of Cravania and of Men.
  Vanalith imbued his creations with the capacity for good
  and evil and every stripe between. Though at first enslaved
  by Skar'gol's creatures, they soon cast aside their shackles
  and spread to every corner of the world, conquering all, until
  the elder races became little more than half-remembered
  legends, and only Men endured.

When their own war ended, the Trysglerimon ascended to the
heavens once more, turning their attentions elsewhere. United at
last, they made a race of celestial beings, the Majestics, to serve
them and to act as a bridge between themselves and their mortal creations. But the Majestics soon found the lure of earthly
delights too strong to resist, and often stole away to Valdymion
to revel in the power they could exert over lesser folk.

The trinity tend to be worshipped only on the major feast days,
particularly at the solstice or, in Aelderland, during *Holigmond.*

Each culture or even nation then worships their own bespoke
pantheon day-to-day. In Sylverain, for example, only one god is
recognised, but her many aspects are often personified as ethereal spirits that must be honoured and appeased. In Tördengard, the gods are a race of powerful warriors, who live in great
halls where the mightiest heroes can join them in the afterlife. In
Aelderland, they are nature deities linked to the harvest cycle, to
the forest and streams, and their signs can often be seen in the
behaviour of animals or the sound of wind through the trees. In

some instances, when the gods truly do walk amongst men, it is perhaps the Majestics merely posing as gods for their own inscrutable ends.

The Principal Gods of Aelderland (the Six Elders)

- **Nysta** (f) (fertility, harvest)
- **Feorngyr** (m) (hunting, forest and heath)
- **Haelstor** (m) (darkness, the spirit world, cunning)
- **Vanya** (f) (storms, sky, the sea)
- **Sygel** (m) (the sun, fire, courage)
- **Litha** (f) (the moon, love, healing)

These gods look down on their people from the Garden of the Aelders, where the folk of Aelderland believe their spirits will go upon their death—should they be deemed worthy. In addition, there are two otherworldly realms often referenced in Aelder scripture: Uffærn, or the Rift, from whence evil spills; and Æblácia, the spirit world, sometimes called the Pale or, by the Vigilants, the Eternal Night.

Lesser Deities

Many gods are worshiped in Aelderland, and some are entirely regional—there might be a god of particular river or lake, or a harvest god invoked only in a particular region. Superstitious peasants believe these gods are present in one form or another—they walk among mortals, disguised as humans or animals, or they take abstract spirit-forms and sweep through woods and across streams. Many professions also invoke their "patron gods."

Majestics are often confused with lesser gods by the ignorant, making their influence all the more dangerous.

Saints are those pious mortals whose devotion to one or more gods made them a vessel for divine powers during their mortal lives, allowing them to perform miracles and incredible feats. It is widely believed that prayers to specific saints are as effective as those to the gods—sometimes more so, as the saints remember their mortal kin and look down from the heavens with fondness.

In truth, many revered saints were nothing more than charlatans, or powerful nobles beatified after death by their followers for political ends. Some were in fact Majestics, "riding" mortals for some unknown purpose. Irrespective of this, temples and monasteries dedicated to certain saints pop up all over Aelderland, and travellers give what donations they can to secure blessings.

MONASTIC ORDERS

The most widespread denominations of Aelderland are:

- **Aelderites:** The oldest order in Aelderland, who reverently mark every holy day of all the traditional gods of Aelderland regardless of their place in the pantheon. Most everyday worship ultimately stems from scripture first recorded by these monks.
- **Eriestenes:** Argue that there is only one god—Erieste the Wise—and all other gods are merely aspects of her. This idea is a foreign "import" from Sylverain.
- **Flaescines:** Believe the saints and Majestics are literal deities, and often devote their lives to just one or a handful of them.
- **Haelstenes:** Chosen of Haelstor. Deny themselves most earthly pleasures, believing that only in darkness can light be found.
- **Sygellites:** Chosen of Sygel, the sun god—a warrior order, known for their fire rituals.
- **Trysglerites:** Believe only in the Three, and that all other gods are merely aspects thereof.

extras

orbit

meet the author

Sandi Macleod Photography

MARK A. LATHAM is a writer, editor, history nerd, frustrated grunge singer, and amateur baker from Staffordshire, UK. An immigrant to rural Nottinghamshire, he lives with his wife and dog in a very old house (sadly not haunted) and is still regarded in the village as a foreigner.

Formerly the editor of Games Workshop's *White Dwarf* magazine, Mark writes for tabletop and video games and is an author of strange, fantastical, and macabre tales.

Find out more about Mark A. Latham and other Orbit authors by registering for the free monthly newsletter at orbitbooks.net.

if you enjoyed
THE LAST VIGILANT
look out for

KINGDOM OF OAK AND STEEL: BOOK 2

by

MARK A. LATHAM

Look out for Book Two of the Kingdom of Oak and Steel.

Chapter 1

Helmspire
Wealsdaeg, 27th Day of Sumersmand
190th Year of Redemption

The man in black was an easy mark. A big fellow, but nothing the gang couldn't handle. He'd strutted through the marketplace like a peacock, too pleased with his own wealth to have come from money, and Wuldric would be only too happy to relieve the man of his purse, returning him to his roots.

Wuldric nodded to Bernhardt and Aethelwyse. At this silent command, the two thieves slipped through the bustling noonday crowd like ghosts, fanning out wide, well out of sight. They didn't need eyes on the man in black—only on Wuldric. He had the keenest eye, the lightest tread, and the sharpest blade.

Truth be told, they didn't need another score today. But gods, this big oaf made it too easy, too tempting. Wuldric patted the long dagger at his side—a Sylven poniard lifted from a pompous merchant last winter. It had seen plenty of service since that day, because Wuldric liked it when his marks put up a struggle. Thieving was business; a spot of knifework was a pleasure.

They tracked the man in black down Potter's Row, where the heat from the kilns warmed their backs and thrower's mates called out special orders for the day's trade. The wealthiest patrons always sent servants to do their buying, with notes of credit instead of coin. They'd learned long ago that market days were dangerous places for foppish nobles with gold in their scrips, more's the pity. As pickings became slimmer, and the city watch more vigilant, the gang had grown more vicious by degree. They guarded their patch fiercely, and were free with their blades when relieving targets of their gold—that way, the sheep learned not to resist, and the wolves knew not to stray onto the wrong turf.

The man in black stopped to talk to a potter, not even bothering to haggle over the price of a garishly painted chamber pot. The big lump paid in silver, and rather than arrange delivery, he hoisted the pot under his arm and went on his way, a whistle on his lips. That confirmed it for Wuldric. The man had come into money, but had not yet acquired servants. And he certainly couldn't have lived long in Helmspire, or he'd have at least learned to never pay the marked prices in the trade district.

Wuldric signalled to Bernhardt to go wider, and for Aethelwyse to drop back a little.

The mark didn't continue down Tanner Street as expected. Instead, he turned into an alley that wound downhill towards the docks. Maybe he was a sailor on shore leave, perhaps a foreigner, which would explain his naivety. It was too perfect—the alleyway branched into a network of snickles and narrow gulleys, shadowed by windowless storehouses. A few workshops backed onto the alley, but nobody but apprentices and gossiping goodwives would be out there at this time of day, and they'd turn a blind eye to trouble if they knew what was good for them.

Wuldric held up three fingers, and Bernhardt scurried down the next street to get ahead of the prey. Now Aethelwyse drew to Wuldric's side, and the two of them followed the tall man, blending into the shadows, their practised steps silent as alley cats. They tailed the man in black past the first two junctions, and sure enough he stayed true to the predicted route. The third junction wound through the tannery yards, and that was where Bernhardt would be waiting. When the man in black was less than twenty strides from the junction, Wuldric nodded, and the two thieves quickened their pace, preparing to strike.

* * *

Holt Hawley heard the scuff of a boot on the cobbles behind him and smiled to himself.

"How do you want to do this?" he said, loudly. The footsteps stopped. "One at a time, or all together?"

Hawley rounded on his pursuers: a stout youth with straw-coloured stubble covering an angular, Felder jaw; beside him a wiry, dangerous-looking man with a thin moustache, a broad-brimmed hat shadowing his eyes. That was Wuldric, better known as Shambles the Knife—a petty thief who'd lately graduated to murder.

Wuldric lifted his head deliberately enough to reveal the intent in his eyes. That was the look of a killer. Hawley had seen it often enough; time was, he'd see it when he looked into the mirror.

"Hand over your gold, stranger," Wuldric said, "and nobody has to get hurt."

Hawley responded by shifting his stance, straightening up. His muscles thanked him by popping back into place. All morning he'd wandered the market in the way Enelda Drake had taught him, slouching his posture to appear a little smaller, a little lazier, adopting a gait befitting a happy-go-lucky guildsman. Now he was no longer a mark. Now he was a threat. Six feet of solid muscle, with the bearing of a battle-hardened veteran, dark eyes appraising the two thieves coolly.

Wuldric took half a step back.

Hawley flashed a wolfish grin.

"We both know you like 'em to put up a fight... Shambles," he said. "And I'm happy to oblige."

"Bold words for a man carrying a chamber pot," Wuldric snarled, but the edge to his tone was purely for show. He wasn't so sure of himself any more. Not quite afraid—not yet—but he soon would be.

"If a man's going to get robbed," Hawley said, "he should at least make sure he's got a pot left to piss in."

"Not something you'll need to worry about where you're going."

Finally, the third man arrived, quiet as a temple mouse. Hawley might not have heard the rogue, but the Felder, trying far too hard not to give anything away, allowed himself the most minute glance over Hawley's shoulder.

Now they could begin.

"Can we get this over with?" Hawley said. "I'm a busy man."

"You're a dead man."

Hawley took a breath, stilled his mind. He absorbed every detail of the alley in the blink of an eye, and everything he couldn't see, he calculated. Every bead of sweat on a man's brow, the tensing of their muscles, the way they held their daggers, the position of their feet; every change in breeze, every shifting shadow—they all told a story. Hawley surveyed the scene as if from above, like a bard plotting the details of his play. Somehow—and he didn't fully understand it himself—Enelda had taught him to pre-empt his opponents with cool logic rather than animal instinct. He knew precisely how many paces behind him the third man now stood. He knew exactly how and when each man would strike. And in the heartbeat it took him to surmise these things, he strategized.

extras

Step.
Turn.
Trip.
Pot.
Knife.
Break.
Pot.

Wuldric sprang to Hawley's left, crossing behind the Felder who darted right with surprising speed, but no real intent. A feint, nothing more.

Hawley stepped between the pair of them, turning quickly as Wuldric's blade thrust harmlessly past his ribs. He stuck a foot out, and the Felder went over it, hitting the hard ground face-first.

Barely a shaft of midday sun shone into the alley, but in the narrow golden sliver Hawley saw the shadow behind him; an arm swinging, weapon in hand. He swung the chamber-pot backwards in a wide arc, connecting with the third man's temple. A dark-haired man with an unkempt beard. He flew into the east wall, head cracking on stone. The pot remained unbroken. Hawley made a mental note to buy his pots from that trader in the future—quality merchandise was hard to find on a bodyguard's wage.

Wuldric had waited for an opening, and believed he'd found it. He crouched, looking for a way past Hawley's defence. Now he lunged, dagger aimed at Hawley's ribs.

Hawley moved barely an inch—it almost wasn't enough, and he cursed his miscalculation. The knife blade scraped on the leather armour beneath his tunic.

He let Wuldric extend his reach fully, off-balance, twisting to compensate. Hawley grabbed Wuldric's head in the crook of his arm, swung the smaller man around like a rag doll, felt the neck break.

The others were petty thieves. They were barely worth Hawley's consideration, and the reward for their capture was a pittance. Wuldric, however, was a murderer, plain and simple. The cruelest. A mad dog, addicted to the kill.

Hawley dumped the man's body on the ground with contempt. *Step. Turn. Trip. Pot. Knife. Break.* Not bad, he thought.

"Where do you think you're going?" Hawley growled.

He turned to face the fourth thief—the one nobody had seen coming, not even the rest of the gang. The best of them all—the leader. The one he'd come to find.

The woman was dressed all in black, face covered by a scarf so only the eyes were visible—keen eyes that saw the gang defeated. She'd been close, and quickly thought better of it when Wuldric died.

"Sylaene, I presume?" Hawley said. "There's a big reward for you."

"Aye," said the woman. "But you aren't quick enough to claim it."

With that, she spun on her heels, and took off like all the devils of the Rift were at her back.

Hawley sized up the target, diminishing rapidly along the alley. With some regret, he flung the chamber-pot in her direction. It arced in the half-light. For a moment, he wondered if he'd got the angle wrong—the woman was a mote faster than he'd expected.

He needn't have worried. With a dull thud, the pot struck the woman on her crown. She fell to the ground with the barely a sound. The chamber-pot hit a rock upon landing, finally yielding to the battle, and cracking into two neat halves.

The Felder was getting to his hands and knees. Hawley gave him a brisk kick for his trouble, and the youth rolled onto the ground, making a show of staying down.

Hawley patted the man's tunic, and relieved him of a purse of coins, then did the same for the scruffy man, who was still unconscious, and then likewise for Wuldric's corpse. A good haul, by all accounts—five purses in all, laden with gold and silver, a fine necklace, two gold bracelets, a cloak pin with a coral head, and a pouch of good quality pipeweed—Tareshi, by the smell. Hawley pocketed that. He wasn't much of a smoker, but he wouldn't pass up on the good stuff.

Then he went to the woman, Sylaene. Out cold, but alive. Blood trickled from beneath her headscarf. Hawley took off his cloak and bundled the woman into it, trying his best to disguise her. He grimaced at the thought of getting blood on his best cloak—it had once been part of his High Companies dress uniform, and though he held no fondness for those bastards, it was a good cloak, expensive to clean. Needs must. The last thing he wanted was for someone to think he was a kidnapper, or carrying off a dead body. Satisfied, he hoisted the woman over his shoulder, and made his way southwards, downhill. It meant taking the long way round, but he'd be far less likely to draw attention at the docks. Folk down there knew to turn a blind eye, whether to kidnappers, or murderers.

Hawley reached the bustling street, where the smell of salt air, fresh fish, and cheap ale always felt so strangely comforting. He adjusted his grip on the valuable bundle on his shoulder, and wound his way through streets loud with industry and entertainment, stopping only once to deposit five heavy purses in the collection bowl of a blind monk, who could barely utter his surprise before Holt Hawley was gone.

if you enjoyed
THE LAST VIGILANT
look out for

THE OUTCAST MAGE
The Shattered Lands:
Book One

by

Annabel Campbell

A mage bereft of her powers must find out if she is destined to save the world or destroy it, in this glittering debut fantasy perfect for fans of Andrea Stewart, James Islington, and Samantha Shannon.

In the glass city of Amoria, magic is everything. And Naila, a student at the city's legendary academy, is running out of time to prove she can control hers. If she fails, she'll be forced into exile, relegated to a life of persecution with the other magicless hollows— or worse, be consumed by her own power.

When a tragic incident further threatens her place at the academy, Naila is saved by Haelius Akana, the most powerful living mage. Finding in Naila a kindred spirit, Haelius stakes his position at the

*academy on teaching her to harness her abilities. But Haelius has
many enemies, and they would love nothing more than to see Naila
fail. Trapped in the deadly schemes of Amoria's elite, Naila must dig
deep to discover the truth of her powers or watch the city she loves
descend into civil war.*

*For there is violence brewing on the wind, and greater powers are
at work. Ones who could use her powers for good . . . or destroy
everything she's ever known.*

1

NAILA

It felt wrong to be sneaking out in the bright light of afternoon.

Dusk would have been better; there would have been shadows
for Naila to slip into, her dark robes and pitch-black hair blending
into indigo twilight. As it was, she emerged into a bustling Amorian afternoon, robed strangers hurrying past her, shafts of purple
light scattering through the glass dome high above their heads. She
paused at the edge of the surging river of people, expecting someone
to point out that she wasn't supposed to be here, but no one even
glanced her way. They ignored her just as a real river would have,
while she faltered at the edge of it, unsure of how or where to cross.

She slipped in at the periphery, her head bent, her bag clutched
to her chest so she would look less like a student. She could feel her
heartbeat through her tightly folded arms. It was ridiculous to be
this nervous; pupils in the Southern Quarter ditched their lessons
all the time. The difference being, of course, that Naila wasn't a
normal student: she was a prospective mage, training at the magical Academy of Amoria.

Still, unless she was recognised, no one would suspect her truancy. Her robes were edged with a stitched-in ribbon of white, marking her as a mita – the lowest rank of mage – but she was old enough to simply be an untalented or unconnected graduate. No one else knew that the class she was missing, Introduction to Elemental Magic, was just another in a long list of classes she was failing year-on-year.

The crowds carried her away from the Academy, past the pastel-painted shophouses which skirted the edge of the Market District, and the open fronts of teahouses with benches that spilled onto the wide avenues. Ahead of her were the narrower streets and crooked buildings of the Mita's District, paint peeling despite being sheltered within Amoria's glass. Naila's room was only a few streets away, in one of the old Academy dormitories that now stood mostly empty. She'd thought being close to home might calm her nerves, but it only made it worse. A low and menacing heartbeat pulsed beneath the normal murmur of the crowd.

She'd been hearing rumours of the march all day: the great Oriven was coming to speak to the people, descending from Amoria's lofty towers to the streets of the Central Dome. Mages were gathering from all over the city to hear him speak, and he could have found a crowd anywhere: the sparkling avenue of Artisan's Row or one of the wine bars in the Sunset District. But he had chosen to come to the Mita's District, to the poorest mage homes, to meet them on their own terms.

It didn't seem to matter that he was a lieno, the highest rank of mage, his robes edged in gold thread that cost more than most mages would earn in a month, or that he lived high above them in luxurious apartments framed in Amoria's violet glass. Never mind that he was a member of the Lieno Council, who ruled over all of them, and whose decisions made Amoria every inch of what it was today; the lower ranks of Amorian mages still clamoured for him, greeted him like one of their own.

Naila knew she should be going in the opposite direction. She was close enough now that the uneasy heartbeat was resolving itself into the shouts and chants of a restless crowd. The sound built like a roar in her ears. The streets near her home were almost unrecognisable, packed shoulder-to-shoulder, anticipation rolling off them in waves. Even if she wanted to leave, she was now caught by the current of people, dragged beneath its surface. Battered between shoulders and elbows, Naila clung to her bag, the buckles digging painfully into her arms.

But there was still that stubborn curiosity lodged in Naila's gut, the burning desire to see this Lieno Oriven for herself. Too many of her own classmates had whispered eagerly at the prospect, and Naila needed to understand why. Surrounding her were mages who not only looked down on people without magic, but who actively *hated* them, attending the rally of a man who had coaxed this hate from a flicker to a blaze. *Hollows* they called the magicless population of Amoria; empty inside.

In front of her, someone shot a spell into the air; a lurch of power, followed by a sharp crack which ricocheted off the inside of Naila's skull. Her heart seized and she stumbled backwards, her mouth filling with the hot, metallic taste of magic. Her foot glanced off someone else's and a man shoved hard into her back.

"Hey! Get off!"

Stumbling, Naila half turned to apologise and instead locked eyes with the mage behind her. His expression slipped from directionless anger to malignant interest, his gaze tracing over the raven sheen of her hair and the unusual black of her eyes. For an awful moment, Naila thought she'd been recognised.

She didn't wait to find out if it was true. She ducked further into the crowd, no longer caring if she was shoved sideways or took an elbow to the ribs. It was too late to fight her way back to the Academy, so she pressed onwards, using her long limbs and narrow frame to force her way to the edge of the crowd. She slipped under arms, pressed between shoulders, and dived for the briefest gap in the throng.

Breaking free into the alleyway felt like surfacing from underwater, a stumbling, breathless release. She pressed a hand against the cold wall of the neighbouring shophouse and bent forward, swallowing huge gulps of air into her lungs. Even here it felt like the crowd was pressing in on her from all sides, their magic and their intent thickening the air, making it heavy and harder to breathe.

She shouldered her bag, searching the smooth shophouse wall for likely handholds. There: a window ledge and the rusted bracket of the store's sign. It had been many years since she'd been a child scrambling over the rooftops of the Southern Quarter, but her body hadn't forgotten the way. There was one gut-lurching moment where her foot slipped against the smooth facing, her slipper hanging from the very tip of her toes. But she already had her arm over the lip of the shophouse's flat roof and she managed to wrench herself up in one final burst of effort.

She sagged onto her arms, her lungs heaving, but with the sweet taste of success on her tongue. She was so caught up in her accomplishment that for a second she didn't realise she wasn't alone.

Of course she wasn't. Mages had magic, and they had used that power to lift themselves up and out of the crowd. There were fewer people up here than in the street below, most of them with robes edged in gold or silver; levitation magic was no easy feat, and so those who had used it were from the upper classes of mage. But where lieno and trianne lined the other rooftops, there was only one mage on Naila's, a conspicuous circle of empty space around him. It was as if everyone else was keeping a wary distance, and in an icy moment of realisation Naila understood why.

This mage's robes were edged in the gold of a lieno, but alongside the gold stitching was a braided cord of vivid scarlet. A wizard.

There were only eight of them in all Amoria, mages with the power to level mountains and shape the world as they saw fit. A single wizard had more magic at their command than half the population of Amoria put together. They were the heads of Amoria's Academy, and even other mages eyed them with a mixture of awe and apprehension.

Worst of all, he'd know exactly who Naila was. There wasn't a mage in the Academy who hadn't heard of the *hollow mage*.

Naila found herself paralysed by fear. She was still crouching at the edge of the roof, her heart pumping ice water through her veins instead of blood. She couldn't even make herself look at him, her eyes instead fixed on the hem of his robes, her gaze level with his boots. The wizard himself made no move to acknowledge her, his thick coat perfectly still, his body angled towards the crowd. She could feel the enormity of his power, though, as if the whole world was bending down towards him.

Hardly daring to breathe, Naila dragged her gaze away, making herself stand and cross to the edge of the roof facing the street. She had to pass in front of him to do it, and she could feel his attention switch to her like a shadow falling across her back. She was trapped now, between the mob and this powerful stranger.

Below her, the crowd surged against a makeshift stage, individuals lost within a single, heaving entity.

And there he was, the origin of this commotion, like a stone thrown in water: Lieno Allyn Oriven.

He moved along the edge of the crowd, impossible to miss even among the clamouring throng of people. He bowed and waved, taking people's hands as he passed. The hem of his robes was so heavily embroidered with gold that he was dazzling to look at, the sun catching golden threads when he moved. The sinuous form of a dragon was stitched along one of his sleeves, the mythical ancestors of the mages, a badge of power. He looked like the perfect Amorian, composed and powerful, and Naila hated everything about him.

Oriven mounted the stage with one arm raised, his smile bright against the black of his beard. "My fellow mages!" he announced, his voice warm with a touch of amplifying magic. "I am so heartened to see so many of you with us, so pleased to be among our great people."

Another thundering cheer. Each of these mages possessed a thread of power, and they tugged at the magic around them, in the stone, in the air, in the glass walls of Amoria herself. To Naila, they felt like eddies on the surface of a lake – and no pull was greater than that from the wizard behind her.

But Naila found herself searching instead for the points of still-ness in the crowd. She could just sense them, hanging back in doorways, pinched faces peering out of windows: the non-mages of Amoria. The hollows. It was their stillness and their fear that Naila could feel winding itself around her heart.

"Our momentum is growing. Soon the Lieno Council will be forced to listen to our – to *your* – demands!" Lieno Oriven opened his arms, embracing the crowd with his words. "Our fair city is in decline – we've all seen the signs. The Southern Quarter is so dangerous the Surveyors won't even patrol those streets any more, and the Mita's District is not far behind. We're overcrowded, our resources stretched: we must act!"

Oriven would never actually say that non-mages were to blame. He didn't have to. All he did was point to what was wrong with Amoria. It was true: the city was overstretched; the streets of the Central Dome were crumbling and crowded with people – but not with mages. As Amoria's magic-users dwindled, the number of non-mages only grew, and it was all too easy to infer the source of Amoria's apparent decline.

The rest of it seemed to happen on its own. Oriven had the mages in his feverish grip, his words creeping insidiously into their minds and falling back out of their mouths. They leaned into his speeches like starving flowers towards the sun, these people who didn't wear the gold of the lieno, but the bronze and white of the lowest ranks of mages. Their lives were as far from Oriven's as they could get while still having magic, and yet still they drank in his words.

Naila couldn't see the non-mages any more – the crowd had swallowed them up. Tension was building, thick and stifling. It was the same dragging sensation she'd felt in the crowd, as if all of them were being pulled down towards some inescapable con-clusion – a long inhalation before the slow, inevitable unfolding of disaster.

The man who stumbled and fell was unremarkable. A non-mage, from the cut of his tunic and the absence of colour on the hem. He caught himself on his hands and knees, oblivious to the circle of attention growing around him – and of the mage who was sprawled at his side.

"He pushed her!"

Naila couldn't see who had spoken, but the words spread like fire through the crowd.

"The hollow attacked her!"

The mage drew back into the body of the crowd, but the man was still penned in. Naila saw his fear and confusion as he tried to push free, but he was met with a wall of bodies and shoved back into empty space. The first spell flew with a sharp crack, and threads of gold magic choked his arms and legs. He collapsed hard on the ground, mages closing in around him.

There were answering shouts of surprise and outrage. Non-mages tried to break through to reach the man, but their way was blocked by people wielding a power they could not hope to match. Naila looked with desperation at the stage – surely even Oriven didn't want *this*. He had to summon the Surveyors; *someone* had to.

But Oriven was already gone, the stage damningly empty.

No one was stopping them. *Naila* wasn't stopping them. Her heart was pounding, caught impossibly between helplessness and a burning desire to act. She was already edging forward, her toes over the seething crowd below. If she didn't do something, no one would. If she didn't act, she was no better than the other mages who were backing away.

Naila drew a sharp breath and—

A thin hand closed on her shoulder.

"Don't." It was the wizard who shared her rooftop, his voice hard and cold.

The buzz of magic was right against her now, a hot breath against her skin. The very air trembled with his anger.

"Why isn't anyone stopping them?" she whispered, her voice cracking. "I have to—"

"Go *now*." There was no spell or incantation, but the last word seemed to ring in Naila's mind like a word of power.

She was on her feet, stumbling towards the edge of the roof. Ahead of her was the path home, the path to safety, while behind her was the howl of the crowd and a city she didn't recognise any more. For a moment she hesitated, her heart aching to turn back, to do something to stop those awful cries. But what could she do in the face of such power?

Naila scrambled down the side of the shophouse and ran.

2

LARINNE

Larinne was unusually withdrawn when they left the council chamber. Her sister was doing what Larinne should be doing: greeting other senators, grasping the hand of an ally or offering a curt nod to her opponents. Dailem was born to this life: resplendent in butterfly-light robes, teal edged in gold, her dark hair curling over one shoulder. Despite being five years Larinne's senior, Dailem's tawny brown skin was flawless, her face rounder and softer than Larinne's. There was an ease and confidence to her, unruffled by the events of the council meeting, while Larinne could feel herself drawing inwards, becoming sharper and less approachable.

She had already seen a few weighted glances, could read the mood of her fellow senators like magic on the air; she needed to smile, reassure, pull others into her confidence, but she couldn't make herself do it. They shouldn't feel reassured, and there was certainly nothing to smile about.

The wide stairway was crowded with Amoria's political elite, lingering outside the council chamber like children after the school bell. There were too few of them, in truth. Every lieno in the city was invited to attend the Lieno Council, to understand the workings of their city, but around her Larinne could only see familiar faces. Like Larinne, they were the senators, the politicians and the heads of committia – the lieno responsible for running the city. The growing disinterest from the rest of Amoria only left more room for people like Allyn Oriven to thrive, unfettered and unobserved, his influence creeping through the Senate like a shadow growing in the dark.

There was a slight commotion by the arch of the chamber doors, and a small knot of people emerged: the representatives of the Shiura Assembly, the only non-mages invited to attend the Lieno Council meetings. They moved as a unit, a defensive formation if Larinne had ever seen one, their strides perfectly matched.

As the Consul of Commerce, Larinne worked closer with the Shiura Assembly than anyone else on the Senate. The members of the Shiura managed more of Amoria's exports than Larinne did; they were the ones with connections in the caravans and their representatives in Jasser. The non-mages of the isolated city wielded their own kind of power. She knew she ought to stop them, say something – but what would she say? *Oriven doesn't represent all of us, the council will protect you, we won't let him get his "Justice".* But how much of that was true?

She took half a step towards them, forcing a smile onto her thin lips, and tried to catch their attention.

"Honoured members of the Shiura," she started.

Only one of them heard her and looked up, his eyes narrowed in suspicion. He inclined his head exactly enough to be polite and then continued onwards, not even breaking his stride. Larinne was possessed by the certainty that she had failed a critical test.

"Your face is showing," Dailem said close to her ear, and Larinne bristled at the admonishment.

It was something their mother had always said to them: the council sees your position, not your face. Anything you gave of yourself was a weapon to be used against you.

With a deep breath, Larinne composed herself. "And you're not shaken by this at all?"

"Oriven preaching about the *hollow threat* isn't exactly new."

Larinne flinched at her sister's casual use of the word hollow. "Dailem!"

"What?" Dailem smiled coolly to a passing senator who had clearly wronged her in some way. "They're his words, not mine. Hollow is a meaningless term."

Anger flushed through Larinne's veins, but in the Tallace family tradition she kept it from her face. "You know it isn't. Haelius—"

"Haelius needs to watch himself now. That business with Oriven's rally . . ."

Larinne grimaced, an uneasy feeling twisting in the pit of her stomach. There wasn't a single person, mage or otherwise, who hadn't heard about the violence at the rally in the Mita's District. When Larinne found out that a wizard had stepped in, using magic to restrain the crowd and extract the unfortunate non-mage, Larinne had known immediately that it had to be Haelius. At first, she'd been relieved he'd been there to help, but the more she heard, the more it sounded like an innocent mage had been attacked and the wizard had only added to the violence.

Whatever happened, it was clear that Haelius was less popular than ever with Oriven and his allies.

"He's never made peace with the council," Dailem added, reading Larinne's hesitation. "Be careful with that one."

Larinne failed to suppress a scowl. "It's Oriven we should be careful of. He's using what happened as an excuse to push through this new 'army' of his. What if he succeeds?"

For the first time, there was the smallest wrinkle between her sister's eyebrows. "Even more reason to be careful."

"You think this motion will pass?"

The Justice, Oriven had called it, a special force of mages dedicated to the protection of Amoria. A magical army by another name. The Surveyors had always been the law enforcement; a constantly rotating group of lieno who anonymously patrolled the city. This would be different – a group of mages dedicated to combat and defence, and who answered expressly to Oriven. There had never been such a thing in Amoria, not even when they were still on the brink of war with Ellath.

"Dailem," Larinne urged at her sister's silence. "You can't think he'll get this?"

"Won't he?" Dailem asked quietly, and Larinne was surprised by the bitterness in her sister's voice. "I think this offers the Senate everything they want. They've been drawing lines in the sand for years; might as well get themselves an army to stand behind it."

"But the Assembly—"

"What are they going to do about it, except make their own army in response? This is the beginning of something, Larinne. If Oriven gets this, it will set us on a path we can't easily come back from. I've never seen an army without a war to fight."

Another council member bowed as they passed, and a warm smile spread across Dailem's face. "Ah, Lieno Gadrian, I was hoping to catch you – I hear we have an Ellathian visitor. A *priest*, no less."

Dailem was walking away, her hand on the lieno's arm, a brief glance at Larinne her only farewell. But her words lingered behind her, settling on Larinne's shoulders like a physical weight.

A war to fight. Surely such a thing was impossible. The Amorian mages and non-mages had lived peacefully alongside each other for hundreds of years. There'd always been some tension between them, rivalry even, but outright conflict? That would serve no one.

And if lines truly were drawn between the two halves of the city, on which side would Larinne stand? More to the point, on which side would *Haelius* stand?

Dailem's words continued to weigh on Larinne as she descended the Central Tower, making her way slowly back towards her own offices. The council chambers were situated at the top of the city's tallest tower, a true linchpin of Amoria. Up here, she was above even the glass dome of the lower city. It sloped away from the Central Tower like an enormous canopy, enveloping Amoria in a protective bubble of amethyst glass. Far below, she could just make out the wide streets and colourful shophouses of the Market District, and beyond that the glittering curve of the Aurelia, a circular canal which separated the city into two great concentric rings. The dome itself was so vast, Larinne could barely see the edge of it.

Amoria was the stuff of legends: a magnificent glass edifice, raised from desert sand and dust in a feat of magic that few now could even imagine, let alone understand. It towered above the Great Lake, delicate spires piercing the dome with bridges strung like ribbons between them. Here, Larinne could just make out the luminescent stone of the White Bridge, connecting Amoria to the mainland: a bright artery of life and trade. From this height, it looked like little more than a thread stretching out towards the distant shore, fragile enough that a sudden storm could sweep it all away.

These days, that felt all too true.

"Larinne!"

The call startled Larinne from her thoughts, but when she turned she found a familiar, old mage hurrying down towards her, one laborious step at a time.

When he reached her, Larinne bent to kiss him at the top of his forehead, the skin beneath her lips as thin as paper. "All right, slow down. You caught me."

"Good. Hmph, no, none of that." Reyan waved Larinne away as she offered him her arm. "I'm not *that* old."

Instead of answering, Larinne pressed her lips together and slowed her pace to walk alongside him.

"I sent a communication to your office today," he said with a thin note of reprimand; Lieno Reyan Favius was an old friend of her mother's, and he was the only mage in all Amoria who would still talk to her as if she was a child.

"Did you? Well, I'm afraid I haven't received it."

"That assistant of yours not doing her job, eh? I could find you a better one from among my people. A senator of your prominence ought to have no one less than a trianne working for her."

"My assistant is excellent and not *less than* anyone," Larinne snapped back; Larinne's assistant was a non-mage, a point on which he frequently voiced his disapproval. "She's worth ten of your witless new trianne. If you had any sense, you'd be trying to steal her for *your* office."

Reyan's eyes were pale grey and watery with age, but they'd lost none of their fire as he glared at her out of the corner of his eye. "Yes, yes, all right. I'm sure she's very good, if she's managed to earn *your* approval."

Somehow, Larinne knew this wasn't meant as a compliment.

"Still, didn't give you my message, did she? I suppose I'll have to get to the bottom of these missing documents on my own."

"What missing documents? And what does that have to do with me? Communications are *your* area, not mine."

"Clearly! If you'd got my *communication*, then you'd know." That imperious tone had entered his voice again, but he glanced over his shoulder, a touch of anxiety in his expression. "Best not to discuss it here. Get your 'excellent assistant' to put your poor Uncle Reyan into your busy schedule."

Larinne tolerated the rebuke with only a small twitch of her eyebrows.

"This business with Oriven . . ." she started.

"Yes, well, best to stay out of these things."

Larinne blinked, not expecting the suddenness with which he'd shut down the conversation. Eyeing him shuffling down the stairs beside her, Larinne couldn't quite tell whether his silence meant he was for or against Oriven's proposals, but then Reyan was as hard to read as her sister.

They walked the rest of the way in silence. When they reached the arched bridge that led across to Larinne's offices, Reyan stopped and looked up at her, deep wrinkles carving worry into the lines of his face.

"You need to meet with me, Lieno Tallace," he said gravely, startling Larinne with the use of her title. "This is important."

Larinne's mouth lifted in the edge of a smile. "I know, Uncle. It's always important."

"Hmph. You wouldn't think it, with the way you children ignore me. Give my regards to your sister. She's even worse than you — always rushing off somewhere."

"I've never seen you stand still for even half a minute."

"Yes, well, at my age you have to move twice as much to get half as far." He narrowed his eyes at her, unusually serious. "Stay out of trouble. Your mother asked me to keep an eye out for you both, and I intend to."

"When am I ever in trouble?"

Reyan dismissed her with a wave of his hand.

Larinne stood for a moment with her arms folded, watching him continue down the stairs, her fingers tapping an uneasy rhythm against the tops of her arms. When he'd vanished around the bend in the stairway, Larinne let out all of her breath at once. She straightened her shoulders, set the face of Lieno Tallace back into place and then turned to head back to work.

orbit

Follow us:

/orbitbooksUS

/orbitbooks

/orbitbooks

Join our mailing list
to receive alerts on our
latest releases and deals.

orbitbooks.net

Enter our monthly
giveaway for the chance
to win some epic prizes.

orbitloot.com